THE
NEW
EARTH

THE
NEW
EARTH

A Novel

JESS ROW

ecco

An Imprint of HarperCollins*Publishers*

THE NEW EARTH. Copyright © 2023 by Jess Row. All rights reserved. Printed in the United States of America. No part of this book may be used or reproduced in any manner whatsoever without written permission except in the case of brief quotations embodied in critical articles and reviews. For information, address Harper-Collins Publishers, 195 Broadway, New York, NY 10007.

HarperCollins books may be purchased for educational, business, or sales promotional use. For information, please email the Special Markets Department at SPsales@harpercollins.com.

Ecco® and HarperCollins® are trademarks of HarperCollins Publishers.

FIRST EDITION

Designed by Angie Boutin

Title page illustration © korkeng/shutterstock.com

Library of Congress Cataloging-in-Publication Data has been applied for.

ISBN 978-0-06-240063-5

23 24 25 26 27 LBC 5 4 3 2 1

This book is for the dreamers: the activists, academics, researchers, lawyers, journalists, artists, and ordinary civilians around the world who work every day, against the world's cynicism, against seemingly impossible odds, for a just, free, and peaceful future for Palestine and Israel.

When the storm dispersed them, the present was shouting at the past: "It's your fault." And the past was transforming its crime into a law. As for the future, it was a neutral observer.

Mahmoud Darwish

The postscript, being rebellious, has taken by storm the place of the prologue. Everyone knows that postscripts go at the end of letters and not at the beginning of books, but here, in the mountains of southeastern Mexico, we have a "new kind" of discipline, that is, that everyone does what they want. The dead, for example, never stay still.

Subcomandante Marcos

Who shall have rest and who shall never be still,
Who shall be serene and who torn apart,
Who shall be at ease and who afflicted.

Unetanah Tokef

Contents

/2

THE
NEW
EARTH

/1

THE UPPER WEST SIDE
BOOK OF THE DEAD

Recovered from: Drafts Folder (Unsent Message)

From: "Bering Wilcox" <carebear@hotmail.com>
Last saved: March 12, 2003 at 9:13:44 PM EST
To: "Patrick Hakuin Wilcox" <dharmaboy@yahoo.com>
Subject: The Upper West Side Book of the Dead
Wadi Aboud, March 12

When the journey of my life has reached its end,
and since no relatives go with me from this world,
not even Great-Aunt Estie, who survived the Shoah,
two husbands, one in semiprecious stones,
one in schmattes—who always patted the couch
and said, "sit next to me, you make me feel younger,"
while she told the filthiest jokes—
when the journey of my life has reached its end,
in other words, may the peaceful and wrathful buddhas

send out the power of their compassion
and clear away the darkness of ignorance.

When parted from beloved friends, wandering alone—
as if I got up out of my sleeping bag, in Palestine,
and decided to walk home, as if there were
no barricades, no barbed wire, no blast walls,
and return to my childhood bedroom, on 79th
and Broadway—and when the terrors of the bardo appear
on that journey, the worst things I've ever done,
may the peaceful and wrathful ones, who know
all my secrets, sweeten my tongue with halvah,
chocolate-covered if possible, shoplifted
from the Zabar's checkout counter.

When I suffer through the power of my karma,
heaped up in this strange place, birthplace
I never chose, from the grand precipices of CPW,
the Dakota, the El Dorado, the stately brownstones,
that Nora Ephron domesticated New York,
lox-and-herring-and-Sunday-Times New York,
to the projects, the mamas smoking in pink
velour outside the McDonald's on 91st and Columbus,
smacking their kids, barking *no me diga,*
may the peaceful and wrathful buddhas remove
my impacted feelings like a bad molar
and give me new eyes, fresh eyes, to
forgive everyone their hypocrisies.

When I see my future parents in union,
may I see the peaceful and wrathful buddhas
with their consorts, with power to choose
my birthplace, for the good of others, may I do

more than just laugh and say, "well, it couldn't
get much worse"—because first I have to turn
and forgive them, my current parents, yes you,
Mommy, and remember you made me a birthday cake
once, from scratch, green frosting—
We ate it together at the dining table,
and then the lock turned and Trick rushed in,
cake!—dug his finger in, no hesitation—
And Daddy standing there, shrugging,
in the hallway: *Easy, tiger.* There's still
the dent in the plaster from where
the Pyrex hit the wall. It's not easy,
throwing a full baking dish across a
prewar dining room. If Trick hadn't ducked
he might not have his front teeth now.

We sat there eating frosting off the wall,
frosting mixed with paint chips, eating
the building, as you two screamed in the kitchen.
When it was clear no one was making dinner,
Winter emptied her piggy bank,
and we went downstairs to La Caridad,
twelve, ten, and nine, ordered black bean chicken
and rice and beans to share three ways.

My point is: remember the cake, too. Sweeten
my tongue with that cake. When I am truly
lost, peaceful and wrathful buddhas, remind
me I am forgivable, they are forgivable,
none of us are only one thing, we have past
and future selves. You could say: I came here
to know Israel and Palestine, two implacable
parents at war (Yoron told me, the first

day of nonviolence training, *you look like*
someone who's used to arguing) only to realize
the abject stupidity of this rhetoric of bodies.
Terrorism of postures, terrorism of the present.

I came here to learn what peace actually means.
It means implacable patience. It means having
a better memory than those around you.
But most of all: sweeten your tongue.
When Heba saw me leave yesterday morning with
my Day-Glo vest and International Monitor helmet
she brought me a last cup of tea,
I taste it now, like a mint gumdrop, and
said, *la hawla wala quwwata illa billah,*
which means, roughly, when you follow your karma
and accept the consequences, without refuge,
may the peaceful and wrathful buddhas be your refuge.

My point is this. I didn't mean to write it
as a poem. A letter would have sufficed.
But that's just it. We Wilcoxes have never known
what would have sufficed. We wanted too much
and got nothing. I declare, game over. For the
time being. For this lifetime. This marriage of
five unhappy minds, this purgatory between park
and river, I hereby suspend on behalf
of the world's suffering. My attention
is required elsewhere. I step out of your karma
and take up my own.

And when I see my future parents in union,
may I see the peaceful and wrathful buddhas
with their consorts, with power to choose

my birthplace, for the good of others,
may I receive a perfect body adorned
with auspicious signs, whatever they are.
Wherever I am born, at that very place
(somewhere other than upper Manhattan,
if at all possible), may I attain the power
of non-forgetfulness and remembrance of past lives.
Wherever I am born, may that land be blessed,
so that all sentient beings may be happy.
Samantabhadra Allah Adonai, Great-Aunt Estie,
Tupac and Biggie, O peaceful and wrathful ones,
infinite compassion, power of truth in the pure
dharmata and on the 1 train downtown,
and residents of rent-controlled apartments everywhere,
may their blessings fulfill this inspiration-prayer.

THE APTHORP

"Ruth," he starts again, "I'm going to say something, and if you can, do me a favor and save your questions for the end. Hear me out and then you can reject my advice and we'll move on. But I just have to say this, because I look at you and I recognize you. You understand what I mean?"

She gives him a shrewd squint, lifts and drops her shoulders with a sigh.

"We're the same age," she says. "Roughly. I suppose."

"We're the same demographic," he says. "And I'm not saying this because I knew Stan a little. I can tell just looking at you. In ten minutes we could probably name ten friends in common. We're Upper West Siders. We have fantastic apartments we'd never be able to afford today. We remember what it was like when you couldn't walk on Amsterdam. Crack vials crunching underfoot. That's how we raised our kids, in a different city. When everything wasn't so *easy*. Those organizations they have today, we started those. NPR. Mostly Mozart. Shakespeare in the Park. Writers in the Schools."

This time she actually rolls her eyes, visibly, up to the ceiling tiles. A deeper sigh. Joni, his assistant, stares over her monitor at something invisible in the hallway.

"Am I wrong?"

"No. You're not *wrong*. Irrelevant to my case, maybe. But not wrong."

"Then stay with me here. You want me to cut to the chase, but I'm not cutting to the chase. Sometimes time is not of the essence. You have to let a thought expand. What else does it mean, getting old, if you haven't learned that? Anyway, I'm only asking for a few minutes. Before you cut us a retainer bigger than your annual rent."

"All right, all right," she says. "I'm all ears."

Ruth Liebler. Second viola, Met Opera Orchestra. Stan Liebler's widow. Stan was a graduate of some Ithaca commune who'd returned to the family fold and become a costume jeweler specializing in low-end silver, the kind you find at head shops and Renaissance fairs—pentagram rings, spiky skulls, Celtic crosses, Iron Crosses, Om Mani Padme Hum bracelets. He was party to a patent-infringement suit that went on for nearly a decade, and a major fixture at Fein Lewin in the old days. Many lunches billed for no conceivable reason. Lewin was lead counsel, but he'd always get dragged in because Stan liked him. A fellow traveler. You should meet Ruth, Stan would say, my classier half, and here she is, in a long brown dress with a scarf cinched too tight around her wattling neck. She has the pinched look of the perennially aggrieved. Orchestras, as he understands it, are like colleges—they have tenure, they have committees, every tiny incremental shift arbitrated by amateurs full of sedimented rage. So Ruth was capo di tutti capi of the something something committee, had been for twenty years, and a group of younger players hatched a scheme, probably for reasonable reasons, and voted her out. Will Diamond, his best associate, already told her that you can't file for wrongful termination if you weren't actually *getting paid*. But she doesn't want to hear it. She wants to sue.

At this age you can't say a single thing without feeling the weight of worlds around it. He senses that. Why begin here, in this conversation, of all places? Because the novel holds us all in place. He, who is speaking; I, writing; you, reading. The novel does our thinking for us. At the beginning it holds us around the legs. Walk out into the waves and you can feel the tides move. The trillion trillion gallons.

"So let's go back a few. I grew up in Davenport, Iowa. How about you, Ruth?"

"Fall River," she says, "Fall River, Massachusetts."

"Two not-dissimilar towns. Same size. Working-class. The Mississippi, the Atlantic. The working river, the working ocean. Barges, freighters. Coal and steel. Corn and wheat. Industries mostly gutted, now, of course. Outsourced. Trump Country. In our time, already teetering into decline. That sound about right? Not that we noticed. We had decent schools. Cyclone fences. Neat little gardens. Little tufty, scabby lawns. Stable families, tight neighborhoods. Big Fourth of July parades. Lots of Catholics. Lots of vets. Big union halls, American Legions. Kids started going to Vietnam early. Like '65, '66 early."

"And coming back in coffins early. My best girlfriend's older brother. Norman Feldkrantz. Killed in March of 1967."

"I mean, what is there to say anymore about the sixties? Turn on PBS these days and it's the deadly nostalgia channel. Peter, Paul and Mary, still in the same turtlenecks. *Embalmed.* But what are we supposed to do? It's us. It's the weight of something dreadful called, I don't know, *experience.*"

"Except for Mary. She's actually dead now."

"I would never get into it, except for one thing: we can't avoid it. It's material evidence of who we are, our ridiculous expectations, our sensitivity about failure. Et cetera. I *told* myself to avoid it, for years. I felt like a survivor, which is ridiculous. Here I am, a white guy, and I never got drafted—too young, by a hair—never got gassed. Kent State happened while I was at Oberlin; we drove there that same night, stood outside holding candles. That's the closest I came to any physical danger. That and organizing out in Chico, in '76. Nearly run over by a pickup truck in a field of celery. But my point is—and I think you know what I'm talking about—1980."

"Don't even mention that cursed year."

"It was like a door closed, and I told myself I was living a new life, for better or worse. Morning in America. I had a job, all of a sudden. A real job. I had kids, soon enough. In my case, like in your case, we were a two-income family. Everything was sink or swim. Nobody was marching for anything. Lennon died, and the lights went out. Like the song said, remember? *This is not my beautiful house! This is not my beautiful wife!* More clichés, I know. I'm helpless with them."

She inspects her hands.

"I was in the car," she says, "in my little Beetle, on I-95, on the way back from my great-aunt Sylvie's funeral. On election day. I was planning to drive straight back to New York that night. I was pregnant, five months pregnant, with Andrew. I had my viola in the car with me, because Sylvie had asked that I play something at the memorial. Some Yiddish song she loved. 'Oyfn Pripetshik.' Anyway, by around New Haven I was starving and so I pulled over at a diner, a truck stop. I remember it was a truck stop, because it had pay phones right there on the tables, one at every booth. So I was sitting there with the case between my knees, I was too scared to even leave it on the seat next to me, and I decided I would call Stan and just let him know I'd be home really late, past midnight. And when he picked up, he said, 'Thank god you called. I just got off the phone with James Levine. You passed the audition. You got the job. Also, Reagan won.' And do you know what I remember thinking?"

"No, what?"

"'Life is very long.'"

They laughed together.

"Because I'd already had what I thought of as a full life. A *whole* life."

"Tell me about it."

"We'd put our skin and blood, what's the expression? Blood, sweat, and tears, into that farm. New Morning Farm. For six years, before it collapsed. We all got hepatitis. Stan probably never told you the story."

"He alluded to it."

"In any case. The details aren't important." She seems childlike, he thinks, seized with eagerness. It makes him recoil. "When Reagan came to power, to us it was like the end of Weimar. Jimmy Carter was a Weimar president. Massive inflation. Social chaos and disorder. Metal machine music."

Now she licks her lips. Actually licks them.

Because he gets so many of the off clients, the *characters*, Mark calls them, the firm has configured his office so he can see straight over the client's shoulder through a window to Joni's desk, and Joni, whoever she is at the moment, can look up, periodically, and if he raises an eyebrow, rescue him. *Ethan needs to ask you a question.* Also he leaves the door open an inch or two, in violation of every American Bar Association guideline. Because sometimes it's all in the intonation. Joni gives him a questioning look. He smiles and shakes his head.

"You know, we were going on with our lives, just as you said. Raising Andrew and Sarah. Making actual money. And for me, of course, playing extraordinary music, night after night. I'm not talking about the repertoire. I'm talking about *Koyaanisqatsi. The Death of Klinghoffer.* And all the time, I was expecting that Reagan was preparing for the end, for the *next* Holocaust. God, you know, that was the eighties. People actually ate caviar, you remember? They served it, at parties. Ordinary people. And the whole time, because of course I was doing it too, I was eating caviar and waiting for the sirens that would tell us the coup had started. I don't think I had a single good night's sleep until the wall came down in '89. And by then the kids were almost teenagers."

This conversation is losing its usefulness, he thinks. Its direction. A wayward paper boat of a conversation on tidal swells of historical anger.

"You know what happened to me recently?" he says. "I went to my doctor, after the election, because I was having heart pain. Seriously. Not the crushing heart-attack kind. And not heartburn. Heart *pain.*

It was hard to look at things, hard to see things and feel alive. I felt crushed."

"Well join the goddamned club."

"I mean outside of the mishegas in Washington. I'm talking about everyday misery, people yelling at their kids on the street. Homeless people. Syria. Not to mention kids in cages in Texas. It all whips together with your memories, the things you've seen, the people you've *been,* right? That pain," he said, "is congestion. Congestion of emotions. A calcification of feelings. Too much feeling over too much time. And I said to the doctor, what do I do about it? *Do?* he said. Feel lucky. Be grateful you still have the capacity."

She's looking at her hands again.

"I remember," she says, "and forgive me for mentioning it, but back when your daughter passed . . ."

(She didn't pass. She never passed.)

". . . and Stan said, that guy works at Fein Lewin, I *know* him, I've seen pictures of that poor girl on his desk. I remember that. Watching the news about it, and thinking, that could have been so many of us. Our kids. Whatever else you want to say, she was an idealist. There aren't many of them left. That's what I appreciate. Even if she was, I don't know, *misled.* And there was so much hate being expressed about her. I don't have to tell you that. Our supposedly liberal friends, Stan always said. It was sickening, to me. I was almost physically ill. I just have to say that. Never having met you."

This is my meeting, he wants to say. I called this consultation, and you can go now. And then: oh go ahead and sell her, sell your dead child. As if it's never happened before. It's a relationship business. Sympathy drives relationships. In the short term. It works only as a clincher, when the rational faculties are spent. Someone could write a book about it. *Personal Tragedy: The Art of the Deal.*

"Well, thanks, Ruth. Thanks for those kind words. I appreciate it."

"There was a saying we had," she says. "At the farm. *Justice has to come from everywhere or it exists nowhere.* We really believed that. Looking back, it seems like a nightmarish thing to imagine, in a way. The either/ or part, I mean. But that's where we were at in those days. And when I heard about Bering, I felt like, that girl was one of us, so to speak."

Now he has to imagine sleeping with her. It worked, once upon a time. It got him through interviews, back when they were still giving interviews. Never, though, with a woman quite this far along. Not so much in years, or in gravitational compromises, as in sheer compactness of spirit. You see these women all over the neighborhood now. How would you go about seducing such a person? What would be your point of entry, physically, literally? Would you take her hand? Find a particularly appealing fold in her elbow crease?

Naomi isn't like that. There's still give.

"Thank you," he says. Without knowing why. "I appreciate that. I really do." More filler. "But you want to know why I'm bringing this up, Ruth? Because, as far as I can tell, you've lived a good life, a well-intentioned life."

"Psssht."

"And yet. And yet. The world goes the way it goes. There are unintended consequences."

"That's the understatement of the millennium."

"And thus the congestion. It hurts, but feel glad that it hurts. Getting wrapped up in a lawsuit is going to rob you of that capacity. You'll be a little twig flushed over a waterfall. Your savings, your health, whatever hard-won emotional stability you have—it all goes. Take it from someone who's barely escaped this profession with his mind intact. There's *nothing* the law can't take from you. So what I'm asking you to do is, don't take the bait. Look at yourself. You've already given so much. You have! *We've* given so much. It's true that not everything worked out the way we wanted. By a long shot. But you have to step back and reassess who you're really doing it for. The kids are grown and gone. Your protégés, your students, whoever, if you were lucky to have any—you taught them what you knew. You made an impact. I promise you that. But it's time for people like us to start taking care of ourselves. The world has used us up and frankly we've used up our share of the world."

"I was cc'd on an email," she says, "and this is just one tiny example, believe me, but I was mistakenly cc'd on an email in which the first chair said, 'She's had that stick up her ass so long, if you took it out she'd have to have reconstructive surgery.'"

"Yes, you were insulted. I'm sorry. Yes, the process was abused. Your colleagues treated you badly and should apologize. But I'm telling you that you have to stop trying to be the arbiter of everything. I know the last thing you ever expected was for someone to tell you to take a load off and not take everything so seriously. That's why it has to come from a fellow traveler like me. Stop ignoring your grandkids. Before you know it they'll be grown and gone, too, and you'll be moldering alone. Cultivate those *ties.* What do you want, at your time of life, at *our* time of life, with a lawsuit? Not that you can't afford it. I'm casting no aspersions. And believe me, there's lawyers in this town, in this *building,* on this *floor,* who will take your money. But you don't need it. *We* don't need it, any of us."

Deep breath.

"What we should be talking about, if you want my opinion, is estate planning. If you're like me, your files are a mess and your kids are always after you about it. Not this minute. But not *not* this minute, okay? Let's make an appointment for three months."

He's had people in tears at the end of the speech. He's been embraced by women wearing supportive garments not visible through their loose drapey dresses. Lots of nodding and reaching for the Kleenex. One poor guy even applauded. But Ruth Liebler sits alone and stoic. Unmoved. She writes him a check on the spot, shakes his hand. *Thank you for your time.* Maybe she's Congregationalist on her father's side. Her eyes saying, You are a hypocrite, a calumnist, a failure, and a sellout. And his eyes saying, back to her, he hopes, why stop there?

My last client, he's thinking. She senses something. Later she'll say, there was something off about him, but I couldn't put my finger on it.

"It's funny," she says on her way out the door. "Stan always said, 'the thing about him is he's actually not Jewish.'"

"I'm not," he says. "Like I was saying. Davenport, Iowa. United Church of Christ. My dad, rumor has it, once went to divinity school. Naomi's Jewish. My kids are Jewish. We were members of Beth Shalom for thirty years. I read Hebrew. I fast on Yom Kippur. My firm is Jewish. Ninety-five percent of my friends are Jewish. My shrink was Jewish. Should I go on?"

"You never converted."

"No, the technical term for me is *stranger in the camp*. In the old days my rabbi used to call me a righteous gentile. You'd have to ask him if it still applies. At shul, once, a guy came up and said to me, 'people like you don't really exist.'"

"Of course you do. Here you are."

"That," he says, "is no evidence of anything."

/

As he exits the elevator Jean-Louis, the security guard, catches his eye over a corner of the *Daily News* and waves. He waves back.

One twelve in the post-meridian, Wednesday, April 11, 2018. Fifteen years and twenty-nine days of the New Life.

Imagine him as he is, the novel asks us. Imagine me, he says to no one in particular, go ahead. Imagine me, on this, my last day on earth.

He's out on the ground, on the street, Fifty-Sixth between Fifth and Park, jingling the keys in his vest pocket, the sun dry and blinding, an unfeeling forty-eight degrees in the shade. This in the middle of April, some spring we're having. He's left work early. The prerogative of the senior partner. Joni, he said, a first and last lie slipping from his lips, my urologist had to reschedule. If you need anything, I'll be on my phone.

April 11: Primo Levi Day. His private holiday.

Circa 2010, he sat for a week on the porch in Blue Hill and read all of Levi's later books—*The Periodic Table, The Drowned and the Saved*—and then two of the biographies, one by Thomson and one by Angier. To make sure he had the facts straight. On April 11, 1987, at 10:20 A.M., Levi jumped from his third-floor apartment into the interior courtyard of his building in Torino. He was sixty-seven. *No immediate cause for the suicide was identified,* one article said, as if suicide, presumptively, has an immediate cause? Some investigators believed he might have fallen by accident, due to dizziness from a prostate medication; this theory was considered and rejected. Levi had collected his mail from the building's concierge only a few minutes earlier: he appeared perfectly healthy. It was an ordinary spring morning. Nothing had changed. His mother and mother-in-law, in their nineties, suffering from dementia, were in another wing of the apartment with their live-in nurse; no one else was home. Life was going on. He stepped out of it.

Cynthia Ozick described Levi's suicide as the final proof that his rage over the Holocaust had no end: "The rage of resentment," she wrote, "is somehow linked to self-destruction."

Elie Wiesel said, "The Holocaust killed Primo Levi forty years later."

In 2003 a *Haaretz* columnist wrote: "If the Holocaust created the state of Israel, then the Holocaust is responsible for all the deaths of Palestinians over the occupation, and by proxy, Bering Wilcox, too, a Jewish American, is a victim of the Holocaust who died defending other victims—"

That's all as may be, he says out loud, enjoying the looseness of the phrase on his tongue. A Davenport phrase, something Mother used to say. But the truth is: life is very long.

Primo Levi Day: the day of the perfect death. The golden ratio for a man. A swift removal from life, no announcement, no explanation. Elected and autonomous. An end that speaks for itself. He named the impulse in 2010, but when in his adult life, his post-Vermont life, has he not promised himself some version of it? In, say, 1987? 1989? 1993?

To say nothing of the later and more obvious dates? But he had to reach *this* moment to be ready. Choosing to die, he's thinking, as if delivering a lecture, step by step down the sidewalk, amounts to a statement about the nature of time: time flows only in one direction, it's all chronology, in the end, chronology is order and necessity, the order of moments, no matter what, and there's a moment when one has collected oneself from all the disturbances, reassembled a shattered life, put one's affairs in order, faced the clock, and put a finger on a number. Chosen a day. Call it the beauty of the refusal, the beauty of saying *no more. Naomi and I have decided to withdraw from the arena,* he emailed the reporters in May 2003. He knows it by heart, every white-knuckled word. *Not to continue the appeals, not to establish a foundation in Bering's name, though we've been asked to by generous friends, and not to grant any more interviews to the press. Because nothing we can do will change the events of March 13, and for the health of our family we need to mourn and recover in private—*

And who's to say, he asks the air along Fifty-Sixth Street, facing west, grinning into the midday sun, that Levi never recovered, that he was not, in the end, perfectly composed? Nothing so extraordinary as life glimpsed through a closing window. He has an hour left, at most. Life palpates everywhere around him. A woman in a herringbone suit, shielding her eyes, digging in her purse for her sunglasses. A garbage truck pulls around the corner, huffing and clanking; a little girl cranes her neck around her stroller to watch. Perfect. Perfect. Perfect. The small consolations of the everyday, right up to the end.

His eyeballs flicker around the edges with blue fire.

Upward is where this goes. Away.

Dearest Marie, Heinrich von Kleist wrote to his sister in 1811, moments before he shot his lover Henriette Vogel and then himself, *If you knew how death and life take turns to garland these last moments of my life with the flowers of heaven and of earth, surely you would be content.*

His phone buzzes in his pocket; he should have known better than to leave so abruptly after lunch. "Sorry to bother you," Joni says. "But someone named June called? From your dry cleaners? You have clothes that have been ready to pick up for almost two weeks. Should I send a messenger?"

"To pick up my dry cleaning?"

"That's exactly what Joanne said you would say."

"I'll pick it up this afternoon. They can wait two more hours."

"Are you sure? Because I can just book it right now."

A stippling in his pulse. As if he's anxious about being found out.

"I have time. Tell Joanne people are abusing the messenger account."

"She told me to tell you to let her do her job and you do yours."

"Got it. Over and out."

/

I, I, I, he's thinking, on the way to the subway, ducking under the vast Moorish bulk of Carnegie Hall to get out of the glare, have lived enough moments, which is not to say wasted them; he refuses to put it that way. I have exhausted them. I have put the first-person singular at the beginning of enough sentences. He narrates his life, for the most part, in individual lines. Not paragraphs. The novel arranges them into paragraphs for ease of access, with added commentary. This is called *free indirect discourse*. Why not walk all the way home, as he used to do in warm weather, pretending it was exercise? Or take a car? It was the bane of his existence, back when he still used that phrase, having to walk three and a half long blocks to the 1 at Columbus Circle, in the snow, in the subzero winds. He refused to take a cab. Never. Not as a matter of habit. Twelve dollars each way, five days a week? He wouldn't have it. He hated his commute, could never reconcile himself to it, short and unremarkable as it was. Sensei used to say, Your problem is you do everything too fast, and he would say, I hate being in the middle of things. I'm impatient, so shoot me. I hate inefficiency. I hate feeling surrounded and nebulous. I hate repetition.

You have to discover the secret of what is *inside* repetition, Sensei said, and now he has. The secret to repetition is choosing when and how it ends.

A shot of pure joy; as if his heart jumped, or something did, his gullet, Adam's apple, esophagus. Something jammed in his throat. To have gotten it right for once. The day is a window I can close. See everything now, one last time, without trying to grasp it. See it and let it go.

A pigeon flutters in a shaft of light in the stairwell. Fifty-Seventh Street. The screech of a train rises up, and a gust of subway-station air, which always smells and tastes the same. Machine oil. Straining brakes. Rainwater pooling on the tracks. He drinks it in.

Alexander Wilcox, Lawyer in Holocaust Art Fraud

When did he write that? Two or three months into the grief group; that would put it in 2005 or 2006, the middle Bush years, when he billed nearly nothing but pro bono hours reviewing pointless appeals from Clare Hynes at the NYCLU. Six or eight hours a day looking at photographs of torture victims, and then two hours of grief group, three nights a week, Monday Wednesday Thursday. He wasn't drinking then. He was done with drinking. Naomi was drinking. *He* was going to grief group, and when Dr. Simmons-Cheng said, bear with me on this, it sounds insane, writing your own obituary, but we all do it on the inside anyway, and that's what group is about, it's about bringing out *everything*, no filters, no boundaries, he went home and filed five hundred words in crisp Times copy. It took fifteen minutes.

Alexander Wilcox, Lawyer in Holocaust Art Fraud

Alexander Wilcox, a lawyer who exposed his own client as the perpetrator of the largest known fraudulent claim on art seized during the Holocaust, died on _____ of _____. He was _____ years old and lived in Manhattan.

Wilcox, who was known as Sandy, was a young partner at Fein Lewin *in 1992 when he was contacted by Irwin Klaufelt, a wealthy Cleveland industrialist. Klaufelt claimed he was grandson and heir to Jonas Klaufelt, a garment manufacturer and then art dealer in Bavaria who before World War II owned one of the world's largest private collections of Netherlandish art, including a Rembrandt etching of one of his own ancestors, the rabbi Manasseh ben Israel. Wilcox aided Klaufelt in recovering a related set of Rembrandt etchings, with an estimated worth of at least $1 million, from a Swiss art dealer in 1996.*

In 2000, Wilcox was contacted by distant relatives of Jonas Klaufelt, living in Israel, who suggested that Irwin Klaufelt was an impostor. After conducting his own investigation, Wilcox negotiated with the Manhattan district attorney's office and was able to protect Fein Lewin from a criminal indictment for malpractice. Irwin Klaufelt was later convicted of two counts of wire fraud. He suffered a stroke and died before his sentencing hearing in March 2001.

Wilcox returned to the public eye briefly in 2003 when his daughter Bering, 21, a peace activist, was killed by an Israel Defense Forces sniper during a protest in the West Bank village of Wadi Aboud. Following an international outcry, the Wilcoxes were asked to file charges in Israeli criminal court but declined.

Wilcox was married for _____ years to Naomi Schifrin Wilcox, the climate scientist and author of the bestseller The Shiva Hypothesis, *who survives him, as do his daughter Winter and son, Patrick.*

And now the beautiful revision:

Alexander Wilcox, a lawyer who exposed his own client as the perpetrator of the largest known fraudulent claim on art seized during the Holocaust, died Wednesday after falling from a window into the interior courtyard of his Upper West Side apartment building. Police said no foul play was suspected. He was 66.

So many satisfactions to be had in the brief obituary, the column stub, the quick take. No mention of Davenport, for instance. None of the nubby words that make up his version of the 1970s, like *Oberlin* or *Zen master* or *Vermont*. A slightly longer version would have to take in some of those uncomfortable lacunae. *Decades of psychotherapy and a few years of outright analysis.* Too predictable. *Survived by his wife, Naomi, fellow-sufferer in a disastrous marriage.* Too gloomy; too much like a Puritan epitaph. Where's the spanner to throw in the works?

Naomi Schifrin Wilcox, whose biological father was the African American physicist John Downs, a fact she only confessed to her children in December 2001, in a Chinese restaurant on Sixty-Ninth Street—

No. Too much of a tangent.

Saved an unhappy marriage through decades of masturbation.

Too general; too pathetic; needs nuance.

Benefited from his sole experience with hallucinogens.

In San Francisco, in 1976, they had a friend named Dallas Good-year. It's a good story to think about now, traveling in the bardo of the subway, the birth or death canal, the liminal zone. Dallas was the first Black philosophy professor hired at Berkeley, also the first in non-Western philosophy, which meant he was responsible for everything from Avicenna to Zoroaster, though his own field was comparative shamanism. He'd done fieldwork in Korea and Peru. You met these people in the seventies: actual ostensible Americans who seemed like emissaries from a different planet. A few years later Dallas's appointment was moved to Ethnic Studies and he quit in protest and moved to Chicago to teach at UIC, but for that year he was still an actual Berkeley professor: a tiny impish man, his hair bound up in a single long braid down his back, who wore only white clothes and no shoes. Sometimes the three of them drove out to the valley on weekends, canvassing farmworkers; Dallas spoke beautiful Spanish but could also get by in Mam and K'iche' and several other Indigenous languages. Dallas playing with six kids in the wretched thin shade outside a tar-paper shack on an unnamed dirt road ten miles east of Fresno, across from twenty acres of lettuce, the irrigation sprinklers pumping chemicals in a fine rainbow mist every fifteen minutes. Learning all the kids' names, tickling them, singing them folk songs from Puebla. Then climbing back into the cab of the United Farm Workers pickup and taking out a stack of papers on Descartes to grade.

Did he and Naomi have any idea, even then, how bad, how shameful, how *isolated*, things would get in their world, racially speaking? He loved Dallas. And was in awe of him. There's no right order for those sentences: each precedes the other. He had never had a Black man as a personal friend, an intimate friend. And—this is the horror of it—never would again. The ghost of a father-in-law didn't count. In the great racial retrenchment of the early eighties they lost touch with everyone: Shirl Watson, Naomi's classmate at Berkeley, who dropped out before finishing her research to teach high school in Oakland. Damon and Charles from Boalt. Fred Paul, who played the clarinet at their wedding. The Apthorp, when they moved in, had a grand total of three Black families. By 1990 it was down to one. After the Central Park Five were convicted—those nightmarish years, the absolute nadir, Howard Beach Tawana Brawley Crown Heights—Bering looked across the dinner table at them and said accusingly, You guys have no Black friends at all.

What was he supposed to say? *There's always your grandfather? We are our own Black friends?*

Having that thought makes his skin flex and contract, an unwatered cactus.

Dallas liked to laugh and slap him on the thigh. There was one Spanish radio station in the valley, KLT or KLP, and he played it loud, with the windows open, putting his arm around Sandy's shoulders and insisting that they sing along. You want to know people, you have to get to know their songs, he said. Dallas's hot meaty breath in his ear, as they rolled under that flat summer sky the color of jaundice. Everything felt necessary and significant under Dallas's eye. That was the thing. He felt, maybe for the first and last time, *seen*.

And Dallas operated as a shaman himself, though he never used the word. It was under his guidance, as part of a study, that he and Naomi took psilocybin—just that one time. In the darkened living room of their apartment in North Beach, in January, on a cold night, an electric army heater wheezing in one corner. Candles everywhere. Lying next to each other on the kilim, covered in some kind of grass blanket Dallas had carried up six flights of stairs. He remembers the little dry knob dropped on his tongue, the sensation of Dallas's fingers, a taste of dirt and sawdust. He was mortally afraid of choking on his own vomit and had carved a special foam prop to keep himself from rolling over onto his back.

There was a sensation of flying, which was also floating; he was aware of his limbs swimming around in a medium that wasn't air or water, but some third thing. He had gills running up and down the sides of his body. He was a fetus, rotating in oil: it smelled and felt like oil, now, very clearly black petroleum. Now his ribs couldn't take the pressure, and the bubble of breathable air around his head became an oval, squeezed smaller and smaller. The oil was suffocating him. He started singing "After the Gold Rush," at the top of his lungs. That was hilarious. He was drinking the oil now; it flushed through him, it was poisoning him, but he remained alive, somehow, only covered in gray moss. He was weak and soft to the touch. He was spongy. He thought, *I will come back here, to the place where I've swallowed all the poisons and survived*.

He came to and Naomi was lying with her head in Dallas's lap, silently weeping. As it turned out he hadn't vomited at all. He drank some elderflower tea and sat cross-legged at Dallas's feet, or as close as he could get, and told him what he'd seen. God, it was the seventies. He'd drooled into his beard; he desperately wanted a shower.

Dallas said, "You've received an unambiguous message."

"It feels pretty damn ambiguous to me."

"You've put yourself on a path of liberation," Dallas said. "A new path. A dangerous path. You're not the person your parents ever imagined you would be."

"Get to the point."

"That is the point. You may not get much farther than where you are right now. And that's all right. One life isn't very much time."

"But I'm only twenty-four!"

"You could die right now, and it would still be meaningful."

Naomi reached out and took his hand. "My soul is trapped and may never emerge," she said. "That's what Dallas says. And it's true."

It was all true. Never was anything in their lives more true. His quest for liberation peaked at age twenty-four, and Naomi remained a trapped soul, unable (as of about 1982) even to call herself a soul. Forty-two years later, and it's all the same. He wants to laugh. Cut through the weight of their circumstances, their possessions, their accumulated griefs, as if you're slicing a cross-section through a mountain of guano, and there you have it: Sandy and Naomi in profile. In utero. In shit instead of amber. They tried so hard to free themselves, and for what?

He should have written to Dallas, should have found a way to reach him, to find out the conclusions of his study. If it was ever completed.

/

It's the weather, the dry wind sweeping across West Seventy-Eighth from Hackensack. The land wind, the continental drift. Climbing the last few stairs out of the subway, back into the light, he feels his corneas begin to water. Eyes always leaking now that he's cleared sixty-five. Am I moved, he asks himself, am I still congested? He should be arguing with himself now; it should be a contest, a debate, with citations on both sides. He read the halakhic literature on suicide long ago, in connection with a bizarre case involving a Lubavitcher family, a tennis academy in Rockland County, and a diamond merchant from Scotts-dale; he knows the arguments around the divine spark and the offense of presumption of G-d's will. It all melts away. He craves something else, immutable and immovable, not open to dispute.

I'm getting bitter, he's thinking, bitter and maudlin, exactly how I promised myself I wouldn't be. Losing my resolve. Not on Primo Levi Day. The fear of being lugubrious and maudlin. I should have a band behind me. "Swing Low, Sweet Chariot." I want to hear music. The impulse glows and fades. It's not a day for celebration, exactly. It's the quiet after the party is over.

/

Because he found family life unbearable and life without a family un-bearable.

Because he tried, for fifteen years, which is long enough.

Because, biblically, his children abandoned him, and his wife aban-doned him.

Because the world's vital signs are at an ebb. Because the body politic he clings to has been rolled, set upon, kicked into a corner, and offered only the faintest, saddest semblance of resistance. Perpetually indignant, shamed by its hypocrisies, tripped by its compromises, ad-dicted to throat-clearing on the op-ed pages of the *New York Times*, above all made complacent by the easy life. The life of constant small adjustments and upgrades. And he's no different. Fallen into his life, recessed, barely able to read the paper, and now, for these brief few weeks, obsessed only with planning and curating his exit.

Not just *no different*. When we came back from Vermont, he re-members telling Brisman, more than once, in eighteen years of sessions, I was convinced we could still have an enlightened existence, here in the city, detached and engaged all at once, compassionate and purpose-ful. I mean we were senior meditators, for Christ's sake, I thought, You can't just wipe away the sheer depth of perception you gain from thousands of hours of zazen. And yet it was wiped away, in a heartbeat, I mean for a few years we were carried along in the torrent of child-raising, once Bering was born, especially, the sheer stress of the three of them howling like little jackals—we woke up sometime around 1989, after Naomi's tenure case was finally settled, and realized we were no more than the sum of our resentments, we were caught in the obverse of Indra's net, the narcissistic prism of so much seriously unfinished business, the price any couple pays for getting married at twenty-two, only slightly exaggerated by certain karmic residues—

What Sensei always said. When the great truth is forgotten, only the great lie remains.

White, he said to Louis once, is something no one can actually be. Except maybe Swedes and Norwegians. No American can *be* white, in the simple declarative sense. They have to say it defensively, antagonistically. *I'm white and it's not my fault.* And Louis said, actually putting a hand on his shoulder—they were sitting on a bench near the Great Lawn, waiting out one of Patrick and Jacob's interminable baseball games—It's all right, man, it's going to be all right. Someday she'll be ready. Give her time.

The kids will be fucking traumatized, he said, when she finally gets around to telling them it's not just that they *tan easily.*

The wind crosses him again as he crosses Broadway for the last time, so that he has to lean into it, so that it holds him up like a scarecrow. Women flattening skirts, newspapers whirling. The land wind. I'm sick of walking, he hums to himself. I'm done with walking. He thinks of the Audi, nestled in the dark, three inches to spare on all sides, the battery probably on its last legs. When was the last time it was inspected? Before Naomi left they'd been meaning to sell it, then he insisted on keeping it. We've had two cars all these years, he said, now you're saying we should go down to zero? Plus, I might want to come visit you.

Yeah—she said. *Yeah* with a high intonation, as if with another unvoiced word attached. *Yeah, right. Yeah, you bet. Yeah, that's likely.*

This was last July, when she was packing, when he still thought a one-year fellowship was a one-year fellowship, and then noticed a slab of boxes in the little study, tied up like a gift with plastic cord, delivered neat from the movers. There were movers? Look, she said, I bought a house there. Might as well put some stuff in it. We're bursting at the seams. I'm going to get some of Winter's college paintings framed. I want it to feel like a home.

Which was an odd phrasing, he thought at the time. Not *my* home or *our* home. What it did mean, absolutely, was what Naomi said when she'd packed the Subaru, filling every inch of the back with plants— most of the surviving plants from the front windowsill, in fact, some of which had been there for thirty years, growing rust rings around their bases, living on milky, striated apartment light, waves of radiator heat, and a baseline ambient degree of human pain. They'd probably had a slight anesthetic quality, these plants, the way the Northeastern US forests absorb carbon—not enough to make a difference, but a gesture, nonetheless.

Naomi said, "You know I'm not going to be back for a while."

"Yeah," he said, "I can tell."

"Simon's already circulating a rumor that Columbia's going to try to fire me. For moving the lab."

"Columbia can't fire you."

"I'm not saying they *can*," she said, "I'm saying they can see which way the wind is blowing, which for geophysicists is saying a lot."

And with that she gave him a good, substantial kiss, a schmack; passed a hand over his chest, patted him, as if to reassure herself that he still existed; and hopped into the driver's seat.

"Call me when you pass Hartford," he said.

"I'm not planning to stop," she said. Gripping the steering wheel with both hands now, staring straight ahead. "I'll call you when I get there."

/

Still alive, he returns to his apartment.

There were times in the early years, coming home from work, when he would stop on the street and stare up at it with a flutter of disbelief. Of course it helped that Naomi would be upstairs with Bering draped over one shoulder, Winter howling with wet undies in the bathroom, Patrick poised for a flying leap off the couch. Anyone would hesitate and take a breath. When William Waldorf Astor visited New York in 1905 and handed prints of the Pitti Palace to Clinton and Russell and said, make it something of that kind, he intended the passerby to stare. A three-story arch. Cobblestones around the fountain, just visible from the street. Putti under the eaves. Laurels. Gilded antelope heads. A fucking loggia on the roof. And yet somehow it's neither a folly nor a Gilded Age birthday cake. It stands up straight. Massive. At the time of construction it was the largest apartment building in the world. Made for people to live in, though not, perhaps, in Astor's imagination, shrinks, dentists, oboists, and CUNY professors. Certainly not Jews in such profusion. To think of Astor wandering the halls, circa 1986, say, on the first night of Hanukkah, the smell of frying latkes seeping into his ghostly pores!

How many are left? In 2008, when the condo conversion finally happened, there were 79 stabilized and 17 rent-controlled out of 163 total units, with 27 vacant. Ninety-five layabouts and leeches on the new management's good graces, which meant, according to Anglo Irish Bank logic, that there would have to be about sixty upstanding billionaires willing to pay $3,000 a square foot for a building with no pool, no gym, no view of the park or the river. Just Gilded Age street cred. No wonder it's been a roiling sea of litigation ever since. Twice teetering on the very brink of default. Three of the light fixtures on his floor are still busted. Last he heard they were slashing prices so hard it might almost be worth inquiring about an insider deal. But for what? So he could own a slice of some Massapequa slimeball's private equity wet dream?

All those years he spent hating the tenant life. Kissing Reynaldo's ass so he'd come up in the middle of the night when the Fitkowskis' pipes broke and water was running down the walls. All that regulation paint going from white to gray and then flaking off and then having to threaten to call in Housing Court before they repainted. Begging Naomi to look at the Real Estate section. When duplexes on West End and town houses by the park were going for a song. All that animosity, all those poisoned Sundays—

Your body is a rental car, Sensei used to say. In this city, this life, this Earth.

He stands in the entryway, surveying the scene. The battered Shaker bureau. The antique mirror he inherited from Uncle Philip, growing a little smokier at the edges year by year. The double rows of coat hooks along the opposite wall, now empty except for his winter overcoat and rain parka, and at the other end, a long burgundy robe. Patrick left it the last time he was back from Nepal, thirteen years ago. A newly minted home-leaver, returning home for some rugelach and an infusion of cash, and in all other ways so like his former self that despite carrying almost nothing—robes, sandals, backpack, laptop—he managed to leave his spare robe behind for someone else to worry about.

There were entire years—forget it, the better part of two decades—when it was physically impossible to keep the entire apartment clean all at once. You could sponge the counters and mop the kitchen, but then someone would have left the toilet in the rear bathroom wadded and overflowing. This was a given. Then in 2005 they decided, without quite discussing it, to remove every last encrustation of their child-rearing years. He hired an interior designer and an architect to repaint every surface, redid the floors, new cabinets, new appliances. He'd thought Naomi would love it. When she came back from teaching summer lab in Boulder and stood in the entryway—right where he's standing now—she merely shrugged. "It looks like the inside of a catalog," she said.

"Is that good or bad?"

"Is it what you wanted?"

"More or less."

"Well then I guess the joke's on me."

It was the last conversation they had about décor of any kind, except the couches: she could never stand the couches. Despised them. Too low. Too flat. Too *shiny*. They were Roche Bobois; they cost fifteen thousand dollars each. Finally he caved; it was the night of Obama's first victory, the first time they'd actually sat next to each other on the couch watching TV in years, eating popcorn, talking with Winter on the speakerphone, and he said, when it was all over, you know, Naomi, get the couches you want. Just do it. Life is short. And a week later some Albanians in an unmarked truck delivered these swollen brown leather things, whalelike, sofas you'd buy to match the chairs at the Harvard Club. Hate couches. That's how he thinks of them. And then, a few years later, the hate TV. That thing belongs in a frat house, he said to Naomi when it was delivered. She'd already turned on Charlie Rose, her feet perched on the coffee table. The guy at Best Buy said it was the right size for our space, she said. Cracking sunflower seeds and spitting the shells in a coffee cup. We can get it mounted on the wall. A TV *mounted on the wall*.

What do you do with a person who has no sense of space, no feeling for the tone of a room?

Say, with a shrug, we got married in a field in Ohio in 1974, no one told us we'd have to worry about sconces.

/

There are stages to suicide, the experts say, and the critical one, the turning point, is making a plan. Millions of people are latently, slowly suicidal their whole lives, without formulating a way to act; they find other ways to harm themselves, as he has; they kill themselves slowly, which is to say they align themselves with the body's natural tendency to degrade and make it morbid and socially grotesque. After years of exercising—he saw a trainer twice a week for years—he stopped showing up one September and never went back. Eventually even canceled his membership. He redeveloped a passion for the Zabar's takeout line, after years of no nitrates, no saturated fats. You're getting *heavy*, Naomi said once, in February of 2014, when she came back from her paperback book tour, not even bothering to hide the disgust. I never thought I'd see the day. It wasn't true: metabolically, he'd never get fat, he wasn't built that way, but he had extra poundage along the belt line and went up a waist size.

He meandered along that way for years, from 2012 to 2016. Work was work, intermittently stimulating; Naomi retreated back into the lab, refused to say anything more about *The Shiva Hypothesis,* tried to rebuild her reputation, with little success, as far as he could tell; Patrick had moved to Berlin and apparently stopped being a monk, for reasons he refused to explain to anyone; Winter moved Zeno into her house in Providence. Life went on. Things happened. He turned sixty and refused to celebrate, not that Naomi tried hard to convince him.

Then on the night of the election they were at Judy's—Louis and Judy had always hosted election parties, Oscars parties, Super Bowl Sundays, the secular nonessentials, Louis called them, and Judy had decided to soldier on alone. This one last time, at least, she said. To elect a woman president. Louis would want me to. It was a crowd of people he'd known mostly for thirty years. The Alcoffs. Bill and Diane Westbrook. Sunita and Pyush. The Rosens. Irene Chow. Mark Filstein, who'd just retired, that very week, as head of ophthalmology at Mount Sinai. Portly men in sweaters and their compact wives, in silk drapes, with practical hairstyles, chunky earrings, splashes of violet and rose. He was terrified by their hands, jutting out over the hors d'oeuvres. They had claws like dowager countesses, his woman friends, his contemporaries. Judy had bought a new TV for the occasion that she'd pushed up against Louis's floor-to-ceiling shelves; Wolf Blitzer appeared almost life-size. There was something wrong with it all, he realized, very early in the evening. Too much hilarity, the glasses of wine a finger too full. He felt himself taking short breaths and went into the bathroom and checked his pulse. Someone in the hall was babbling about Nate Silver's pessimism and the Milwaukee suburbs. "I've got to go home," he said to Naomi, and she stopped in midsentence and stared at him full in the face.

"You shouldn't have eaten that chicken," she said. "It was in the fridge for a week."

"Maybe that's it."

"This is a huge night."

"But maybe not in the way we want."

"I would appreciate it if you stayed. I might be walking home very late."

"Then take a cab."

"A cab, from Louis and Judy's? Three blocks?"

"We're senior citizens now. We can take cabs three blocks."

He remembers it now, the way she was looking at him: the last time she exhibited what he would call, what anyone would call, *tenderness*. Of course what it was was surprise, salted with the tiniest accent of contempt.

"He's going to win," she said. "That's what it is. You always know these things."

"I just can't be around these people," he said. "I can't watch. I have to go." He picked up his coat and gave Judy a wordless squeeze; she stared at him, amazed. That was the kind of night it was. Not a soul moved on Seventy-Eighth Street. A few cabs inching warily down Broadway. Every few seconds his phone vibrated in his coat pocket and he had to tell himself again not to reach for it.

Now, the thought came to him, now they'll know what it feels like, they'll all know. The thought smelled like burning hair.

He walked through the apartment without taking off his shoes, he walked straight through the living room and unlatched the French doors, it took a little extra twisting to undo them, Francine only ever opened them for cleaning, once every few months. The air smelled like the river; it streamed past his face into the dark room. Brisman, he was thinking, I should never have quit you. He pressed himself against the railing. All it would need would be a pivot at the waist. When the kids were little, they'd kept the doors closed with a padlock. On September 11, kneeling there, you could smell the smoke, weeping. His thoughts were disordered; he tried to settle them. The five heaps arrange themselves in order to disperse. He crossed his wrists over his chest. He put them together in gassho.

Maybe you had to run, to gain momentum, to propel yourself across.

This is the way to do it, he breathed, but not the moment. To tie your death forever to that heaping steaming shitpile of a Roy Cohn acolyte and wannabe Capone, that blond pompadour with the bloated cheeks, pinched squinty eyes, who was a New York joke thirty years ago, going from bankruptcy to bankruptcy with nothing but a gold-plated name stamped on everything within reach? "Fuck you, Donald," he said, trying to snap himself out of it. But in the open air the possibility seemed too delicious to let go. You could just *do* it. When was the last time he had felt such an impulse? Or, for that matter, *any* impulse?

His phone rang.

It was still in his pocket.

"You were right," Naomi said. "He won. It's over."

"Come home," he said. How strange, to have something comforting to say! "It's not over," he said. "I'm here. Come home."

/

He unlocks the doors now, again, and steps back, the familiar ambient city noise flooding in, the coolness that actually smells like something, like spring. There are still things to do. He isn't ready yet.

I will come back here, to the place where I've swallowed all the poisons and survived.

He opens his laptop, opens YouTube, and clicks on the first playlist in his account: *Japanese Temple Chants*.

In the bathroom, with the door open, the drone of the Heart Sutra filling the dark apartment, he ducks his head over the sink and turns on the clippers. Hanks of silver and pewter and gunmetal-gray hair, piling up in the sink: he flushes them away, and uses one of Naomi's hot-pink disposable razors to finish the job.

I look like Mr. Clean, he thinks, allowing himself one glimpse in the mirror, or Yul Brynner, though he can't remember either face in great detail.

He fills a bowl with arborio rice—the only kind left in the cabinet—and shakes a dusty stick of incense from a dusty incense box abandoned in Patrick's room ages ago. An old matchbook from Café La Fortuna, marooned in the bottom of the silverware drawer.

The sulfur pops; the tendril of smoke rises and wavers away from the window, from the city air.

Everything is coming together.

He changes the music. Arvo Pärt, *Tabula Rasa*. Bows fluttering over the violin strings like wings beating. He draws out the half-sized bottle of Mumm from the refrigerator door—someone handed it to Naomi at the party on election night, 2016, she stuffed it in her bag and absentmindedly brought it home. Cold foam runs over his hand when he pops the cork. He pours himself half a flute; his hand doesn't even tremble. "L'chaim," he says, to the empty apartment, and smashes the glass on the kitchen tile.

He practiced tying his robe and rakusu three times that morning, so his hands wouldn't shake. Who knew it would stay preserved so well, after thirty-eight years, wrapped in paper and jammed into the bottom of a cedar chest with Naomi's wedding dress, Bering's tallis, the few scraps of fabric they couldn't throw away? Unfurled, the sleeves flapping under his wrists, the robe breathes out a last sigh. Sweat and something else: the ashes in the incense burner at the temple, which he once, long ago, poured over his head, sitting on his knees in front of the altar. The robe remembers. He balled it up and thrust it into a tattered suitcase at the last minute, when they left Vermont in '80: never had it dry-cleaned, never gave it a moment's thought.

Now comes the hard part.

He faces the open doors, his cheeks against the faint breeze, and cracks the old paperback open, ruining the spine for good. He's sweating. He didn't realize he'd be sweating, that the mercifully cool air would reach out for him, and his body would do its one last job.

"When the journey of my life has reached its end," he reads, though he knows it by heart, "and since no relatives go with me from this world—"

When he's finished with the first four stanzas he steps over the rail. One leg lifted, pulling up the long hem of the robe. Gratitude for every inch of his height. An awkward pivot, then the other leg, and he's over, he's there.

The air is everywhere around him; the Apthorp has almost let him go. Its mass is no longer his mass. He doesn't look down. He knows everything there is to see. Taxis honking, jostling, as the light changes out on Broadway. A car door slams outside the building entrance. The ivy and the pin oaks and the freesia all reeking with spring. He hasn't thought about where he will land; he won't be conscious of landing; his consciousness will have already taken flight.

"Namo amida butsu," he says out loud, as he always knew he would do. May I be reborn in the Pure Land. There was a samurai movie, one of the early Kurosawa movies, he saw at Oberlin, where the shogun's first wife shouted out the nembutsu before leaping off a sinking ship.

Grateful now, grateful for these observances, this weird assemblage, for knowing how to die.

Now he will step into the flood of life, the rushing stream. It only takes one foot, one small movement. His hands go up to gassho, to the position of prayer; he's balanced on four inches of stone ledge, the air already tugging at the hems of his robe.

Someone knocks loudly at the apartment door.

It's like something out of a dream: the vertigo, the very edge of the building's lip under your toes, the voice or sudden noise that jerks you back to life.

The knock comes again, loud, insistent. Then: the heel of a palm thumping against the paint, loud enough to wake the neighbors.

Why should he, in his present state, have to answer the door?

No one would knock that way unless they had to.

A fist slams down, once, twice, three times.

"*Fuck*," he says out loud, and in that instant becomes himself again. He grasps the rail across his body and rolls over it back into the apartment, crashing down to the floor, tangled in his own folds. Something gives in his shoulder. "Fuck fuck fuck!" He's up and limping across the floor, ripping the robe from his shoulders, who needs it now. "Coming! *Coming!*"

Throws open the door. No one.

No one, up and down the hall.

Barefoot on the tile, he reaches out at the last minute, instinctively, to stop the door from slamming, to keep himself from being locked out: a self-protective instinct he recognizes, too late, for what it is.

He remains firmly shelled.

The novel has called him back to life. The story is not over. He senses it: he knows it for what it is, a force outside himself, a prolongation, an irruption, a change in plans. He feels it embrace him, one animal embracing another; it smells like wet fur. The novel is another form of life outside life. He feels himself giving in to it. It holds him when there is nothing else to hold. His feet growing cold now, on the tile, he goes back inside to the flickering candlelight and the monks' chanting, and takes up the stump of the stick of incense, no longer than a roach, flicks the ember and presses it against the skin at the crook of the elbow, as monks do. Moxibustion: the burn that seals one life from another. I'm yours now, he tells the novel. I'm yours now, he says to you. Where are my car keys. I'm leaving.

What does it mean, to still have a body?

Driving suspends the question. In the driver's seat, you're no longer a body, you're an *operating principle;* you serve the machine. The machine wants to go. It cups you, cradles you, hides you. It's a, what's the phrase, the hideous sixties phrase? *An extension of man.* This car is so quiet, the salesman told him, it's technically noise-canceling, some people find it a little weird. Like it's a sensory-deprivation tank, ever heard of those? But then you turn the music on, and you go, *oh, I get it now.* It's a me car, the salesman said, twentysomething Paul at Mamaroneck Audi, razor bumps on his milky neck. A guy like you, you've probably had the kids car, right? A minivan, a station wagon? And now you're ready for a car that's all about you, not about compromises.

My sleek missile, my escape pod.

His shoulder hurts. A crick in his neck when he rotates to the left.

The body and its disappointments. He carries no medications with him. Zantac—you can get that anywhere. Wellbutrin. He went off it in October, leaving a six-month supply. Xanax. Occasional use. Dr. Sharf is script-happy; his motto as a GP is *Try anything once.*

Coffee. They have it in Vermont. He'll have to buy something, a French press, a Chemex.

The body and all its disappointments. Having failed to dislodge them.

He knows where he's going. To get there, you ride I-91 up its long valley, the Connecticut River upstream; turn left at White River Junction; follow ridge over ridge into the middle of the Green Mountains; turn right at Montpelier, left at Hardwick, right on Craftsbury Road, by the state plowing yard. Eight hours with no traffic.

Eight hours plus thirty-eight years.

The house as he last saw it, when it was still a temple, still Mujo-ji: a yellow farmhouse with a gray barn rising behind and to one side, on a sloping hillside, falling away from the road, pastures down to a line of trees, disappearing out of sight, the mountains rising behind. Not peaks but nubs, white until July. A Japanese gate over the path from the driveway to the house, a hand-painted sign hanging from a chain. *Craftsbury Zen Buddhist Temple.* All gone now. Eaten by termites, cut up for firewood, tossed by the side of the road? He's only seen the pictures; Airbnb required him to approve them. Can you really own a house and not see it, for a lifetime, leave it in the care of overseers, never touch it, never feel its presence, in what sense is that *ownership* or possession, shouldn't it have devolved by now to some obscure clause of abandonment or neglect-in-practice? For thirty-eight years he's received a tax bill from the town of Craftsbury Common and paid it, promptly. Printed on the same blue paper.

You don't stop owning things just because you've forgotten them.

Late capitalism and its disused objects.

Out of habit, in the garage, still in a daze and wondering if he was capable of driving, he clamped his phone into its cradle on the dashboard and plugged it in. Occasionally it buzzes with a news alert or a text. He would have to squint to read them, so he doesn't: he drives.

But driving is boring.

After attempting suicide, he wants to say, suddenly an authority on the subject, after giving up that enterprise, you have to change your entire relationship to time. Having more of it, suddenly. Having all of it. Having no longer assigned an end. No, I'm not comfortable saying that. The urge might return. Will almost certainly return.

I can no longer lead a dissipated life, a one-day-at-a-time life, occasionally overwhelmed by my own hideousness, and nearly always bored. I have been bored continually for a decade. I have embraced futility, now I have to un-embrace it. That's the only point. I have to make goals, I have to have *intentions*. A focus. A period.

I have to tell someone.

Thinking this way, he sits up straight. He aligns himself and wishes he had something bracing. A triple flat white. A shot of wheatgrass. There was a summer intern at Fein Lewin who used to bring them around on a tray.

What is a detail?

My next of kin.

"I'm just home from the lab," Naomi says instantly, almost as soon as he dials, over the speaker. "What is it? Something wrong?"

"And hello to you too."

When he hasn't spoken to her for a while—in this case almost two weeks—he still notices, the way he noticed forty-odd years ago, her Bronx-by-way-of-Armonk inflections. *Something wroong?* She falls back into them when she's out of breath. "Well, what is it?" she says. "You scared me. You freaked me out."

"Nothing. I'm just taking a little unplanned vacation."

"You what?"

"I'm going up north."

"What north?"

"Are you going to use more than two words?"

"Are you going to tell me what's actually happening?"

"Nothing's *happening*," he says, "I just need a little space, and I've got nothing to do at the office that the associates can't do without me for the time being, so I'm taking a trip. Just FYI."

"You told Winter, right?"

"Why should I tell Winter?"

"Why should you—because she's *Winter,* Sandy. She worries about you. You're going to be in cell phone range the whole time?"

A Lincoln Navigator—a glorified taxi!—sneaks up in the left lane behind him and flicks on its bright headlights, as if that's supposed to send him quailing off. He stays exactly where he is, the cruise control set at seventy-seven. Another wink of the lights. He's tempted to roll down his window and give them the finger.

"You're going to get there in the dark, you know."

"I brought a flashlight."

"Remember we talked with Eiger about putting it on the market? We've just let it sit there, a dead asset, all these years."

More often than not in their conversations, after the first two or three minutes, he feels overwhelmed by the futility of responding. When dialogue, discourse, seems a purely abstract principle, like higher calculus. Noble silence. It was one of those terms people threw around in the seventies, and everyone assumed everyone else knew what it meant.

"You're forgetting the end of that conversation," he says finally. "There's a tax abatement for unused property."

"Still, it's ridiculous to hold on to it forever. Maybe you can put out some feelers while you're there. Go down to Montpelier and talk to some agents. The second-home market's coming back, they say. Woods Hole prices are up fifteen percent."

"Anyway," he says, "that's assuming we want to sell. I was kind of thinking the opposite."

"The opposite of what?"

"I was thinking," he says, taking a slow breath, "of going up there again. Reclaiming it. Taking the time. What's the word? *Transitioning.* Partner emeritus. Or maybe just partner exitus."

"Starting when?"

"Well? For example? Starting now."

He sees a sign—*I-91 Left Exit 2 mi*—and momentarily panics, forgetting where he is. Featureless Connecticut, no markers at all. He changes lanes without signaling, and a green Jetta honks irritably behind him.

"You're not going to say anything?"

"Sandy, what am I supposed to say? You're telling me you're retiring and moving to Vermont, is that what you're telling me? As a fait fucking accompli?"

"Well, you could say that we've finally done it, that we've become the cultural and generational cliché we've always aspired to be."

"No, that's what *you* would say."

"Are you actually dumbstruck? Or just stalling?"

"Actually," she says, "not that it matters, or that you care, but this is some very strange timing. I was meaning to call you, because I found something of yours. It was in storage. Remember, from the first time I had an office in Woods Hole? In, what was it, 1988? I thought I was coming back the next year and left a box of papers and books. Arpana Gopal found it in the basement and dropped it off in my office yesterday."

"You have to be careful with those things. Lab closets. You heard about how they found smallpox from 1954 down at NIH? Next thing you know they'll be letting out swarms of tsetse flies. Bubonic rats."

"Let me just find the passage."

"What, it's something I wrote? A text? A Valentine's card?" Though that would be silly, he thinks. By 1988 he'd long since given up writing Valentine's cards.

"Here it is. You ready? 'A monk asked, I hear you have a saying, that the whole world in ten directions is one bright jewel—how can a student understand this? And the master said, The whole world in ten directions is one bright jewel—what does that have to do with understanding? The next day, the master asked the same monk, The whole world in ten directions is one bright jewel—do you understand? The monk said, What does it have to do with understanding? And the master said, I knew you were making a living in a ghost cave in the mountain of darkness.'"

"Sounds vaguely Hasidic."

"Don't be a moron, Sandy. It's Dogen. *You* gave it to me. You *typed* it, for god's sake. In San Francisco. It was stuck in my atmospheric sciences textbook. That was your typewriter, the one with the funny E. I borrowed it to write my dissertation, remember?"

"I was a mystic in my youth."

The Navigator pulls around him to the right. In fifth gear its engine has the subtlety of an oil drill battering through layers of shale. As it passes him the driver rolls down her window—*her* window! A girl Winter's age, if that, in a lime tank top, the straps of her pink bra exposed, her face contorted in rage, mouthing, *Learn to drive, asshole!*

"No," Naomi's saying, "I just—I just—I can't believe how much time and effort we invested in those things. Once upon a time."

"In what things?"

"Enlightenment. Sensei. Et cetera. Jesus, I forgot that's what it was called. The cintamani jewel. The wish-fulfilling jewel. God, remember, I used to give lectures on that stuff? When Sensei didn't feel like delivering teisho. I spoke without notes."

"As I recall," he says, "when we moved back to New York—remember, when we moved into the apartment?—*you* were the one with the little Buddha statue in the kitchen, burning incense and doing the rice offering every day. *You* went out and bought those lumpy meditation cushions in Chinatown."

"I should have invested in more comfortable cushions."

"Nay, what the hell is this? A little walk down memory lane? Are you actually trying to get at something?"

In his rearview mirror, by some accident of geography and astrophysics, the sun has aligned itself precisely in the wedge of sky visible as the highway recedes. In front of the car is its perversely elongated shadow. That was a koan, too. Something about how can you walk without stepping on your shadow. Which, come to think of it, isn't such a bad question.

"Just explain one thing to me," she says. "I get the bit about the jewel and the teacher and the student. Anyone who's been on a dissertation committee understands that part. But what the hell is the ghost cave in the mountain of darkness?"

The laugh, when it comes, feels as if it's been stuffed in his throat for weeks.

"That," he says, wiping away a tear, "is when a student reaches a certain level of insight, attainment, whatever, but doesn't quite get all the way, and misunderstands some crucial bit of whatever it is, but *thinks* he knows what he's doing, with complete certainty, and then gets completely, totally, ineffably stuck. Stuck for a lifetime."

"And this is funny because . . . ?"

"Because," he says, "I mean, what else have we been doing for the last thirty-odd years? I mean, what other kind of living have we been making?"

"So this is it, then?"

"This is what?"

Before she answers the question, he hears, distinctly—the wonders of cellular telephony, and a quiet car, a massive suspension, a recently paved stretch of interstate—three distinct actions. A kettle whistles. A mug clanks on the counter. A chair squeaks across a polished floor. And feels nothing. No longing. Nothing missing. This is it, this is the point: I have always occupied a material space, he says to himself, a material existence, I have needed that, I have enjoyed it.

"You're leaving me. Yes, Sandy? This is what you're saying? Finally, after all this—I mean, what am I supposed to say? Is there a word for it? The super-empty-nesters? The forty-four-year itch?"

"Leaving what?"

"Don't play games with me."

"No, I'm serious. Nay, what exactly is there to leave? I mean, I wasn't going to bring this up, but you didn't even call me. It was the fifteenth anniversary, and you didn't even *call*. I talked to Winter. I talked to a reporter from Al Jazeera and one from *Haaretz*. Plus a whole stack of emails I never got around to answering. *CounterPunch*. *Peace News*. Electronic Intifada. Everyone wanting a statement from Bering Wilcox's *parents*, not *parent*. I told them you were away. In Antarctica."

"That's low. That's extremely low, Sandy."

"Why?"

"Tell me that you would have wanted to get a call from me that day. Tell me how you would have loved to have that conversation."

"A voicemail, then."

"As if that makes a difference? As if otherwise, what, it indicates that I *forgot* the anniversary of my own daughter's death?"

"There are certain gestures. We have a fundamental disagreement about gestures. About the symbolic weight of common human, what's the word, *expressions*. Which leads to a very basic question, Nay. Is there anything left that we do agree on?"

"I thought we agreed on the value of making plans and not acting completely at random. Or so I thought. I'm racking my brains here trying to think of a single reason you would choose this moment to exit your entire life."

"Because it beats dying."

"It sounds a little like dying to me."

"I should know," he says, feeling his throat constricting, "I should know the difference, because I came very close to killing myself this afternoon. At about three forty-five."

A moment passes. He hears something, possibly, like a gulp, or a flinch.

"So what happened?"

"'So what happened?'"

"Well, what am I supposed to say? Isn't that the operative question?"

"I'm taking a vow of silence," he says. "That's what I called to say, really. Just letting you know where I'll be for the next three months. *In silence.* I'll be in touch on July eleventh."

"You can't take a vow by yourself," she says. "Someone has to administer it. You vow *to* someone. Is that what you're saying, Sandy? You're becoming a monk again? Two monks in the family? You're going to find a new teacher and start over, thirty-five years behind—"

He pulls the earbuds from his ears; he reaches over and throws the phone away, over his shoulder, but it hits some padded surface, some part of this richly carpeted interior, and vanishes, the buds and their cord still attached, so he won't hear it ring, or, hopefully, even buzz; as if he threw it off a cliff at night, or down a mineshaft, into a place where voices disappear because the dark has eaten them.

WOODS HOLE

When the phone rang she had been hunched over the dining table reading the latest *Harper's* and bobbing the tea bag up and down in her mug, though it had long since released the last of its tea-ness, its oils and tannins and antioxidants and catechins and caffeine. That was what she was doing, ostensibly. What she was actually doing was watching the road outside, through the picture window she'd paid to have cut through the cedar paneling, waiting for Wilson Thorpe to come home from work, leave his Forester idling, half out in the road, and roll his garbage cans up the driveway and safely into the lee of his house. Then, and only then, would she go out for a walk. She was dressed, stretched; she had even put on her shoes, though she never wore shoes in the house. Putting on your walking shoes, without walking in them: like holding a cigarette between your lips without lighting it. Which she had also been in the habit of doing, once upon a time.

This is ridiculous, she had been telling herself, five minutes before the phone rang, you could always turn *left*, for god's sake. But then, if Wilson wasn't coming home directly from the lab, if he'd driven up into Falmouth, to the Wine Outpost or ShopRite or whatever other asinine thing he might think of doing on a Wednesday afternoon after knocking off early, he could just as easily be approaching from the left. He could be approaching from any side. She could not, it seemed, go for a walk in Woods Hole, a *power* walk, a walk for exercise, a low-impact, cardiovascularly correct, precisely computed exercise routine, without that honk, without the tires' crunching in the gravel, and the sound of her name, which she could not ignore. She couldn't not hear her own name. In New York, city of a thousand distractions, there are ways to anonymize yourself, there are doorways, restaurants, subway stairs, there are *other people,* you can always say, *the delivery van got in the way and I didn't notice you there. I had my earbuds in, didn't you see?* By comparison in Woods Hole you and your pursuer might be the only two people alive within a square mile.

You'd think he was your boss, Tilda would say. And she would say, had said: He might as well be my boss. Being, to put it precisely, the friendly ex-husband of the director of the Woods Hole Oceanographic Institution, where *friendly* means *having access to her account on the server.* Where it means *vetting all grant applications.* Sitting in on all Faculty Advisory Council meetings, too, though he aged off the FAC years ago, the limit being four consecutive terms.

The cardinal rule of real estate in Woods Hole, someone remarked to her at a summer cocktail party, is to choose your neighbors carefully. Not that it even would have mattered, because how was she supposed to know he was on the prowl? He seemed, like every other late-middle-aged male scientist she knew, cheerfully neutered. Like he'd be really happy to mow your lawn if you were away. She did not imagine his eyes raking over her, what do you call it, "figure"? As she goose-stepped down Ransom Road? And that was only what she could see when he was looking at her *from the front.*

You should be proud, Tilda said once, you still have an ass that can stop traffic. Maybe it's not something wrong with *him.* Maybe it's something different about *you.*

Walking, now, is what she's doing. No Wilson in sight. No more timetables, no more waiting. She left her phone hot on the table in the kitchen, practically smoking, not wanting the follow-up call, not that Sandy is in the habit of following up. And that sheet of paper, with the Zen quotation typed? That relic of their sainthood, in a past life, with bits of ancient Scotch tape still clinging to it, from where she'd attached it to the wall next to her bed, she remembers it now, in the summer of 1976. When she would get home from twelve hours of correcting Krieger's math, with Wite-Out, in page after Selectric page of lab notes, and then sit zazen until two in the morning? She whirled around with it like a fucking dervish. A thirty-six-year-old piece of typewriter bond, brown at the edges, held stiff in the 1974 edition of Paulson's *Introduction to Oceanography*. She couldn't recycle it. Couldn't tear it to shreds. She didn't have it in her. Palmed it against the refrigerator door and dropped a *Town of Falmouth 2017–18 Municipal Recycling* magnet to keep it in place. Things that can't go in a landfill. Rare earths. Cadmium, lithium. One bright jewel.

Walking. Treads in the gravel. Elbows out for a count of five. Arms spread for a count of five. Arms straight up. Diver's pose. It's all on a website: Walking Yoga. Tilda set it as the start page on her browser and she has, now, in effect, learned it through Internet osmosis. Hands outstretched and pointed in front: dolphin pose.

She thinks, I am a free woman.

She thinks, freedom's just another word for—

And giggles.

She thinks, I should call Tilda and tell her that one.

/

Ahead of her, as she walks, in the full range of her vision, as Ransom Road curves to the left, an unremarkable spread of Cape Cod woods: pitch pine and scrub oak, red cedar and common juniper. Trees thin as pencils, clustered too tight to be stately, or sylvan, to have that foresty feeling. It's actually a conservation easement, donated to Falmouth back in the fifties, a nesting ground for Henslow's sparrow, rarest of all the

Cape songbirds; there's a trail that comes in from the other side, Barnstable Road, where the birders cluster in the spring and summer, their Subarus and Volvos neatly lined up on the shoulder, with matching Audubon Society decals. They pull all the way off the road, mulching over the ferns and marsh grass, because no one's told them that the easement also protects a specific subspecies of the adder's-tongue fern. Which grows nowhere else on earth. At least the sparrow would have a fighting chance if you stuck it in an aviary, she should tell them, pulling up her own Forester alongside, one of these Saturdays, but that *fern,* for Christ's sake, the fern you just crushed with your fat all-wheel treads, only lives here, in these sandy soils, this particular pH balance, the dissolved magnesium from the thin, nitrogen-poor leaf layer. We're talking about a plant that survives on a very particular kind of deprivation. And thence derives its superiority, its moral high ground. It's the pinot grape of Northeast woodland ferns. You should be familiar with the type. So park your car in traffic, nitwit, take a chance with your left-hand mirror for once, if you want to traipse around in here alarming those poor extremely sensitive birds you're so intent on *bagging* with that five-thousand-dollar substitute phallus around your neck.

So relaxing, these mental rants, these prosthetic rages. Better than yoga. She's almost reached the corner of Ransom and Sippewissett, she's broken into a fresh sweat, rimmed all over with her own toxic brine, heart rate kicking up into the 130s, and no sign of Wilson Thorpe anywhere. Relaxing and reaffirming when you rage on foot. In her current state of mind, purged, flushed, *cleansed,* she could walk right into Falmouth, run three discrete, unrelated errands. She could buy three obscenely priced bottles of wine at Fitzroy's. *Three!* And irises for Tilda at Swan's. And ibuprofen, at Parker Drugs! Normally she would never set foot in the place. It smells like Armonk smelled in 1955. Like pot roast and Lysol and cigarettes and the gluey side of the stamp. She could glide right through town, wishing they would tear the rotten charming brick piles down and put up one of those town/malls in its place, with a Starbucks and a Panera and a California Pizza Kitchen.

If she'd brought her phone, which she would have, in any other circumstance, she'd be plugged in and listening to her Ravel string quartets right now, maybe waiting for Tilda to call. Usually they check in during the evening hour, the turn of the working day. Tilda spends nine-to-fives in the lab, no matter what, which makes her guilty, because she doesn't, anymore. It's a habit she got out of while writing *The Shiva Hypothesis*. In the beginning she wrote only in her office, which was the lab, effectively, Columbia quarters being what they are; she wrote on her dinky laptop while her grad students and postdocs labored next door on gigantic monitors, top-of-the-line supercomputer networks, running the equations she'd taught them to run, the staggeringly complex models that were the only way ever to understand anything about temperature in the ocean. They were working in and as *her* earnestness, her proxy, her grant dollars, while she was hacking away at the whole edifice with one whimsical paragraph after another. And after a while, after the book deal, she decided she didn't have to do it anymore. She had Sawyer, the best postdoc a jaded soon-to-be-ex-scientist could ever hope for, and Sawyer ran the lab as if it were his own, with a kind of inflexible male arrogance that reminded her of the monsters of Columbia's past, the monsters she'd had to sue to keep her job, of course, she kept having to remind herself of that, lest things get out of hand.

"The upshot being," she thinks out loud, actually speaking, for a change, "I don't write at the lab anymore, not even correspondence or grants; ergo, I don't spend enough time at the lab anymore at all; ergo, I've become some kind of weird paper-pushing exile even in my own place of exile; ergo, if people were most honest about it, this is the state of science itself. A lab proprietor, a head scientist, a primary author, is ninety-nine percent an administrator; even if I *were* to be more active, more scientifically ambitious, trying to kick out a paper a year, I'd be writing grants, shuttling back and forth to Logan, one conference to another, panels, presentations, PowerPoints, sucking dick at NOAA and NSF, not to mention whatever billionaire ding-dong is getting his fingers into the climate-change pie these days—and Tilda would *still* be running things."

Which is like the reasons people always give for not getting divorced. Judy always used to say, meet Louis, my first husband. If questioned, she would say, I'll never get divorced, because I'll just wind up with another version of the same guy. Most likely an inferior one. I know my type. God, she thinks, for years we lived under the umbrella of that Judean logic. We were the unshakable ones. The unicorns. The families who made it through. And how is Judy, now? She called once, around New Year's; that was the first time they'd spoken since September. How are you, Judy? Still in the office four days a week. Shrinks never retire; they just recede. Doing a lot of yoga. Pilates. No more marathons now, since the knee replacement, but a lot of vehement bicycling in the park. Found a boyfriend, Judy? More than three dates? How does it feel, three years in, how does it feel, that groove that one man carved and recarved into your face for four decades, that watercourse shelving one side and eroding the other? Is it like scar tissue? Any feeling coming back?

Past the last house, Sippewissett descends at an easy grade toward the water; she's walking faster, almost stumbling, gravitationally inclined. Should hang a left and then another left and be home in ten minutes.

Something momentous has happened, after all.

Tilda would say, this is a sign of what you're not willing to admit to yourself, that your feelings actually matter.

My husband has left me.

It's an awesome phrase. In the traditional, non-colloquial sense of the word. It makes her think of glaciers, of course. Ice sheets, cracking. She thinks—she quotes, from herself, an annoying habit, but write a book and it will happen to you too—*I am one of relatively few people on earth who has not only seen an ice sheet cracking but calculated and anticipated it in advance, and if that doesn't give me a certain moral authority, a kind of gravitas, what does?* The problem with *The Shiva Hypothesis* is it was just too much fun to write. She took too much pleasure in it. Not acquiring moral authority but shedding it. When you spend so much of your life entertaining yourself with ridicule and private jokes, and someone says, here's money, and a laptop, give me eighty thousand words—why shouldn't it be fun? As the reviewer in the *Wall Street Journal* said: "Wilcox shreds the earth-worshipping pieties of the climate change movement with caustic glee."

This, on the other hand, isn't fun.

My husband left me isn't fun.

It makes *me* the tear-soaked rag, to be wrung out, for Christ's sake! Dried-up divorcée, menopausal *hag*! When it should have been the other way around, when I should have hired a fucking plane to sky-write it above Seventy-Ninth Street, if it weren't a matter of feeding Nora Ephron enough clichés for three more movies, *I AM LEAVING YOU FOR A QUAKER WOMAN WITH A FAT ASS WHO GIVES ME BETTER ORGASMS THAN YOU CAN POSSIBLY IMAGINE.*

She does not turn left.

She is still headed, it appears, toward the harbor, toward the village, the docks, where she hardly ever goes. The picturesque. The old encampment of her tribe. Just for wine. Libations. Her cupboard, on that score, is dry. It embarrasses her to buy wine by the case, the way other people do, returning from Trader Joe's in Boston with a trunk full of $2.99 specials. Just because it's as cheap as water—on the other hand, the alternative is this constant enervation, leaving hot food on the stove and battling your way through podunk-town rush hour at six P.M., risking a ticket, paying $25 for an off-year Pouilly-Fuissé just because it's what's left in the back of the cooler.

At least this time she's on foot, and has no plans. No promises.

Which is to say that she should already have called Tilda, texted, left a message, whatever, and said, the way they've practiced, *I need your support, I need you to be here for me.*

This is a landscape you're not supposed to pay attention to; she looks down the slope, to where Ransom turns into Sippewissett, rather abruptly, through a pair of stone pillars, now almost hidden by vineage.

Just more scrubby woodland, an even gray-green. A deciduous kind of neutral. A smudge. Away from the water, if you ignore the tang of salt in the air, you can almost forget you're not inland; you could be anyone's wife power-walking in any other respectable, handsome, leafy, dappled Northeastern suburb, anywhere from Bethesda to Andover. Not standing on this decorative fringe, this afterthought, thrust out into the North Atlantic.

That's the thing about the East Coast: it's a nice place to rest your eyes when real life is going on somewhere else.

And then Wilson's Forester appears, as she knew it must, coming toward her, but from just far enough away that conceivably she could bolt, pretend to be jogging, hang a left on Barnstable and then go up into the reserve and out of sight, but she does not. She changes her mind, the way a free woman can. Today is a day, for once, to lean into the world's sheer perversity and tell at least one man exactly what she thinks of him. She stops and raises a hand. Like her mother hailing a taxi. Not hailing. Beckoning.

/

Txting you from Wilson Thorpe's phone. Don't ask.

This had better be good

It is. Promise. Meet me at home in half hr?

Have library committee mtng

It's an emergency

???

I need your support. I need you to be here for me.

Coming now, where are you

Fitzroy's

K. See you in 15 mins

"The truth is," Wilson says as he makes a one-handed U-turn out of his parking space into the facing lane of traffic on Church Street, causing a green WHOI pickup to pull up short and honk, "there are times when I just tell myself, *I don't believe in his research,* which is not to say, *I don't believe the data,* of course, I just don't think that *conceptually* he's doing anything more than repeating what Lofgren did thirty years ago. I know that the grant money is there, but we still have to sign off on it, and look, the technology for dissolved oxygen is still at an infant stage, and I don't know exactly how he finds the justification for all this new hardware . . ."

She can smell him.

Driving, he's wearing khakis, of course, a green-and-blue checked plaid oxford, of course, a blue fleece WHOI vest, of course. Those funny shoes that are halfway between sneakers and hiking boots. Gold wire-rimmed glasses that have survived since the high Robert Redford era. She smells, incredibly, Ivory soap. It may be that in this prison camp for the biological sciences, where people wash up one decade and never leave, there are grown men who use the same soap their mothers bathed them with in 1957. But that's just the superficial layer. Underneath is the tangy sweat of earnestness, of belief in the data, of the data itself.

He keeps glancing over at her while he's talking, because he just can't stop talking but still wants to appear as if he's having a conversation. It's not just his natural obnoxiousness. He's nervous. She waved him down—who does that? In running clothes, and then to say, *I'm so sorry, Wilson, this sounds very odd, but I'm wondering if you could help me run a quick errand and then take me home.* It's not right. He senses her perversity. Protocols, like ice sheets, are shattering.

It's warming up in the car, because the weak spring sunlight, circulating in a small space, is creating what is known as, god help us, a greenhouse effect. It falls on her legs, snug in their Lycra, and makes them chafe. A deep chafe. A working-on. A working-up.

What would he do, she wonders idly, if I said, find a place to pull over where we won't be seen.

It's natural. It's the body's response. A jolt of, what is it, pseudo-endorphins, female desire, corrective desire. It's natural, yes, that I want a man's body. One last fucking hurrah. Here he is chattering away, he's moved on to someone named Bridget she's never heard of, a kelp forest researcher, and what's wrong about the tone of her emails—don't you understand, Wilson Thorpe, that I want to suck your cock right now, you witless drone, you pitiless braincase, maybe you'd like a day off from masturbating into a Kleenex, looking at pictures of fifteen-year-old cheerleaders—I could be the last blow job you ever receive, the last one to ram her mouth up against your salt-and-pepper pubes, to taste your thin, flavorless, vasectomized come—

She reaches down into the Fitzroy's bag and takes out the coldest of the five bottles, a Pinot Gris, a screw-top, and cracks it open, as if it's a bottle of Poland Spring, and takes a good swig.

"Wilson, you want some?"

He nearly swerves off the road.

"Oh! Jesus. You surprised me there, Naomi. Nope. Not while I'm driving. No thanks."

"Driving? This isn't driving. We might as well be in a golf cart."

You know what I've got between these legs, she wants to tell him, I've got a ghost cave in the mountain of darkness.

"You know, we talked about that, actually," he says. "Buying a fleet of golf carts. So people could stop using their cars in the warmer months. This was years ago. Before hybrids came on the market. Before the faculty started moving en masse out to East Falmouth and Mashpee. The funny thing was, it wasn't the expense, or even the maintenance, it was the liability. Owning a fleet of company cars, effectively—and you'd be amazed at how dangerous golf carts are."

"Do you ever think," she says, "these days, Wilson, that you could die at any moment? Statistically speaking. Do you ever imagine that you could, say, *pop an aneurysm,* and the last thing you were talking about was some hypothetical fiscal priority decision from seven years ago? I do. It happens to me all the time. Don't you feel, at times, overwhelmed by the triviality of it all? And even the triviality of saying *triviality.*"

"Actually, Naomi—"

"No, forget it. I'm sorry. I know you don't. What I meant to say is, I envy you, Wilson. Because you get up in the morning and you're actually genuinely excited about giving your life to the work of this absolutely and unquestionably worthwhile institution, and *honored,* to feel that you're part of all this *groundbreaking research,* and that's not just an empty corporate phrase to you, either, is it? And I, I have never once had that feeling."

"Clearly," he says with a dry cough, "you've never had to read a WHOI annual funding audit."

"It may be because I had to sue my way to tenure. That puts a damper on the warm, prickly institutional belonging-feeling. Sure you don't want any of this?"

"We're almost there," he says. "You just sit tight." His voice sounds swollen, gummy, and vacant. His hands fast on the wheel. I've upset him, she's thinking. This perfectly nice man. When I should be sucking his balls, his leached, purposeless balls, and sticking my finger up his ass to massage his prostate.

The bottle is half-empty.

"You know," she says, staring straight out her window, "there's never been any reason people shouldn't masturbate as much as they want. Keep that in mind, Wilson. It's only a problem if you think it's a problem."

"Honestly, I have no thoughts about the matter one way or the other."

"Well, that's nice of you to say."

/

Resting her head on the dining table seems to have some small effect. And keeping her eyes closed. Move an inch in any direction, and the curdled bilious soup inside her sloshes thisaway and that. Tilda is making dinner, chopping something, carrots or apples or, who knows, being Tilda, jicama, parsnips, rutabaga, daikon. The warty stepchildren of the vegetable kingdom cluster in her crispers. Nearly every time they become things that are infallibly, improbably delicious. Living alone, Tilda says, you learn to entertain yourself with cooking. It's that, Lean Cuisine, or suicide.

"This is *All Things Considered*," the radio says. "I'm Robert Siegel." "And I'm Michele Norris. Coming up later in the program, we're going to be talking with Secretary Pompeo about the status of the ongoing nuclear negotiations with Iran. But first, a report from scientists at the University of British Columbia—"

"We observe the sacraments in this household," she announces, to no one in particular. "White wine and NPR at five P.M."

"Drink that coffee."

"If I do, I'll hurl for sure."

"You'll *hurl*? Who are you, Molly Ringwald?"

"I'm Molly Ringwald's alcoholic mom."

"That's funny. I like that."

"Seriously, though, isn't there something I'm supposed to be doing?"

"Other than sobering up? And writing a very, very humble email of apology?"

Still she can't stop thinking about Wilson Thorpe's balls. That's all there is in life, sometimes, is balls. Loose testes, hanging askew, as they always seem to, fringed with gray-gold hair. This must be what it's like to be a man, she thinks, and to be surrounded by breasts, which to them are objects of fascination, held up nearly at eye level.

"No," she says, "I mean, now that my husband's announced he's leaving me. Aren't I supposed to lawyer up, get a separation agreement, pay a retainer, consolidate my assets? You were divorced. Counsel me."

"I was divorced when I was twenty-five," Tilda says, "and our assets were a rusted-out Toyota pickup and ten acres of shitty farmland in Duckfield. We paid five hundred dollars to a guy in Northampton and did the whole thing in an hour. I got the truck; Bill got the farm. Does that help?"

She clanks the lids on some pots and comes sweeping into the room. A skirt rustles, Birkenstocks tsking across the new floors. Sits a little farther down the bench, within easy reach. A heavy woman. There's no other way to say it. The wood flexes beneath her. When she topples into bed it's a minor seismic event. An easy guess would be one eighty. Though Tilda never weighs herself. Scales, she says, are bad for the soul. It doesn't matter. It's never mattered. When you see her naked, every bit of it makes sense.

"How are you feeling now?"

"I haven't made your job harder in some way I didn't anticipate, have I?"

"*My* job? Of course not. Though I don't know about *your* job."

"What's he going to do, file a harassment complaint?"

"You sat in his car, plied him with alcohol, and talked about masturbation."

"I didn't *ply* him. I made a sociable offer."

"When you say things like that, you sound like a character in a Wendy Wasserstein play."

"I'm a Baby Boomer Jew from the Upper West Side. Just imagine me as a character in a Wendy Wasserstein play, adapted by Beckett. Just a, like a, *skein* of shabby old neuroses. Okay, in my case, yes, dyed a particularly dark, even tragic shade, you might say. But still."

"Hold on. I have to check on the risotto."

She gets up, still a little wobbly, clasping the mug of black coffee she isn't going to drink, and follows Tilda into the kitchen. A pile of skinny asparagus on one counter, a mound of delicately minced garlic. A brick of Parmesan, flaking off at one end. Health aside, you'll never know Tilda to stint on the cheese. One-fifth of her weight is cheese.

They were at a party, she would say, if anyone asked. At the golf

club. A WHOI party, of course, an official thing. Rodney Phelps's retirement party, it was when I was up here the first time, just for the
summer, the year Winter graduated from law school. She, you, Tilda,
was wearing a long batik dress with a plunge neckline and drinking
a glass of sangria, using her fingers to pluck the fruit out of the glass.
Whose drunk wife is that, she wondered out loud. No, someone said,
that's Tilda, you must have met Tilda, she's a lab tech, mostly IT
stuff, she's been around WHOI forever and a day. Since the nineties,
at least.

She would say, if anyone asked.

No one has yet asked. She hasn't given them the opportunity. The
official story is: Tilda had to move out of her apartment, Naomi had an
extra room, and it just made too much sense, ecologically and logisti-
cally, not to try being roommates. They maintain a three-foot distance
at work. If there's gossip to the contrary, she hasn't heard it.

"You know," she says, "the worst part about this whole business is
that once it's over they'll like you a lot more than they like me."

"Who will?"

"Winter, of course. And Zeno. And Patrick. Probably even Sandy.
In five years, three years, once all the hurt feelings have dissipated—"

"So you're planning to tell them?"

"Of course I'm planning to tell them."

"Thanks for letting me know."

"I just realized it myself."

Tilda turns around, brushes a few strays off her forehead, and leans
against the counter, her arms crossed lightly. "Tell me more." Training
those hazel eyes on her.

"This isn't my strong point. Big speeches."

"Oh, go on. Stretch yourself."

"Well, to begin with. Sandy and I were finished, actually *finished*,
a long time ago. Emotionally. Sexually. I'm talking years. I'm talking,
say, the Obama election. If I remember correctly, that night was actually the last time we ever had any kind of memorable sex."

They had been at a party at Louis and Judy's, predictably. It seemed impossible that anyone would ever gather in that way, with that kind of naïve national optimism, after the events of the last eight years. 9/11, Abu Ghraib. Bush v. Gore, Bering. Netanyahu, Wolfowitz. The full catastrophe. Louis and Judy's apartment looked just the same as it had in the eighties, she remembered noticing that, the sagging shelves, the knickknacks, everything needing a dusting and a new coat of paint, and she looked around it and thought, *we have officially become old.* But then, on the other hand, there was Obama and his forehead. She loved his forehead, the clean razored line of the hair above it. It made him look Roman, maybe that was it. Imperial. She loved, just for that moment, the spectacle of American victory, the clanging on CNN, the TV bursting with strange, giddy voices, and the First Family coming out onstage in Chicago at midnight. Who wouldn't have believed, at that moment, in some kind of new beginning? People at the party, responsible adults of the left, people with advanced degrees in labor studies and phenomenology, were saying *God bless America,* spraying bad champagne all over the leather couches and the kilims. So yes, she let Sandy ravish her when they got home. My god, he put his hand up her dress in the elevator. The election of a Black president, for him, was some kind of mind-blowing aphrodisiac. And then that was all. Some kind of argument, the next day, a real shouting match, and it was back to life as normal—

"Go on," Tilda says. "I'm listening."

"But that's not even the half of it. I'm talking about recovering aspects of myself that have *always* been hidden. I'm not talking about being a lesbian."

"I know."

"I'm talking about *wanting to be loved.*"

"Yes."

"I'm saying, my life has largely been a mistake."

"Okay."

"*Okay?* That's all you have to say to that? *Okay?*"

"I want you to speak your truth," Tilda says. "Get everything out. I'm not afraid of anything you have to say."

"Oh god," she says. The dizziness has returned. She lurches toward the fridge, hangs off the door handle, opens the freezer, palms a Ziploc of brussels sprouts. She presses it to the back of her neck. "I'm sorry. I don't know if I can do this."

"Do what?"

"Be with a person who says things like *speak your truth*. Even my shrink didn't talk that way. Pritchard used to say people who insist on telling you the truth about themselves are almost always lying."

"And I," says Tilda, and her sweet, blossoming smile, "I don't know if I can be with a person who seems to want to worship and degrade me. Simultaneously. Who has lived an unbelievably privileged, fortunate life—"

"Oh, stop."

"—who has never had to worry about paying a single bill, so far as I can tell, who *did* have a life partner, for forty-four years, who raised three children and all that entails, yet doesn't know how to clean grout or change a tire, who's never done the steps, who was in psychoanalysis for seventeen years—"

"Sixteen."

"—but you can't really tell, who seems never to have known a single lesbian before me, who is a work addict of the first order—"

"Enough, already!"

"—who is *my supervisor,* who fills out my performance review, who worries about my being part of *her* family, but has never once so much as asked about *my* family."

"Your brother lives in Colorado and thinks the Rothschilds run the UN. It's not the basis for a close lifelong relationship."

Their faces, now, within breathing distance, within catching-a-cold distance, Tilda having sidled forward, hands on her hips. She can smell garlic on her hands. She thinks, this is a moment of life in high definition. The data capture level is extremely elevated. The pixelation. But also the variation, the probability, within loose parameters, of know-able outcomes. What a *yes* or a *no* could mean. She thinks, honestly, of terabytes of memory, and the grant money that will pay for them.

The problem with men is that a penis has no weather. It simply ex-trudes into the given world. It has no seasons. It is up or down. Women, she thinks, unforgivably, are climatologists by nature, because we have weather within us.

"Well go on, then."

"I don't feel like it."

"Neither do I."

"Neither do you what?"

"We should be celebrating. *I* should be celebrating."

"I think you've done enough celebrating."

/

The dream, or daydream, the one she still falls into at times, putting gas in the car, or chopping endive, or marking RDPs: the One Inter-view. It takes her back to 2013, that vale of sorrows, the year *The Shiva Hypothesis* was published. The year of interviews. The year of Lindsay the Publicist. Lindsay, who was all of twenty-eight, a Smith grad and American Ballet Theater reject with painfully erect posture and skin like Oil of Olay. Lindsay booked her on everything. She received ten Lindsay emails an hour and sometimes twenty or thirty overnight. They Skyped at seven A.M. at the breakfast table to review their daily sched-ule on her new iPad. Like most twentysomethings Lindsay seemed ex-quisitely fragile, her quivering antennae tuned as if from birth to the circuit boards of power. You didn't want to disappoint her.

And so she said, once and then always, okay, Linds. Put me in. I'll do it. Every author falls in love with her publicist a little. She wasn't ashamed to admit it. How she quivered when Lindsay brushed her cheek with a kiss. It was always yes, and now here she was, in the chair, in the greenroom. The makeup was making her forehead itch. They troweled it on; it was the consistency of hummus. She had visions of herself on television with a Dead Sea mud mask. Not a bad idea, either, necessarily. It would make the trigger-finger channel surfers pause for another fifteen seconds. If it didn't crust around the mouth and keep her from talking at all.

When she imagines her One Interview, it's not Colbert or Charlie Rose, Linda Wertheimer or Gwen Ifill, god rest her soul, or Bill Maher. It's one faceless older man, not like, but not unlike, Pritchard. Unsurprising that all those years of therapy were practice for self-presentation to the media. Invisible microphones, cameras out of her field of vision. The pancake makeup is gone. One interviewer, and Lindsay waiting in the greenroom to give her a fingertip hug and tell her what the best part was.

—This was in a snowstorm, she's saying. I was five or six. The power went out, and all we had, in our big suburban house, was a box of Shabbat candles. No wood for the fireplace. We piled up all the blankets on my parents' bed. For Westchester, this was a serious storm. In the single digits. We all slept there together, my two parents, me, and my brother. They had just bought a single bed, a queen-sized bed, for the first time. Thank god. And I remember sticking my arm out of the covers in the middle of the night and feeling something that told me, death is close. Put that arm back in.

—And your response was to get angry. Whereas most of us would say there's nothing more pointless than getting angry at the weather. You write, *As a child my fascination with the weather began when I realized it was capable of killing me.*

—I was *interested.* But yes, you could say that not long after that I became aware of something within me that refused to accept the power, the aggression, the *hostility,* of nature. That was what made me a scientist.

—You felt like you were studying the enemy.

—Remember what the fifties were like. There was the assumption, everywhere around me, that somehow nature was already tamed. We assumed that in our adult lives we would be living on colonies on Mars. It was already Tomorrowland. That, I didn't buy.

—You write, *Somehow in my very orderly, almost hermetically sealed-off childhood I developed what we would now call an ecological conscious-ness, by which I mean a feeling of intense foreboding and helplessness.*

—What I really mean to say is that I had that feeling and then forgot it. I went to Oberlin, in the early seventies, and believe me, I fell hard for the environmental movement as we defined it at the time. I sewed my own clothes. I made tofu. I lived in a Zen temple that was more or less a commune. Virtually everything I ate, at one point, con-tained wheat germ. And at the same time I was a graduate student in geophysics, then oceanography, specifically, thinking there was some way we could harness the energy of the oceans. Which led me into studying ocean temperature, which led me, in a circuitous route, to climate change.

—And eventually to *The Shiva Hypothesis*. Which is not, as you say, strictly speaking, a scientific argument.

—Of course. I want to make that very clear. This book is a specula-tion, not an outcome of my own research.

—And then where did it come from, exactly? After all these years of precise and limited research, why the impulse to write such a far-reaching book?

—I began to feel actual despair. It's difficult for a scientist to be capable of despair. It's not in our training.

—Tell me more about that.

—I was at a conference—hosting a conference—at Columbia. All the bigwigs in the field were there. I mean what I do, future sea-level projections. The impossible field. For once, at least for the first time in a decade, we were all in one room, a seminar room. No cameras, no reporters allowed. None of the funders. None of the stakehold-ers. *Just* scientists. You have no idea how hard that is to pull off. So someone brings up the first slide, and for the first time, I could just see it, right there. We were all looking at it, doing the math in our heads, and there was no other way around it. This was a sketch, in layman's terms, of the best-case scenario. And the best-case scenario, if you don't know it, is still totally catastrophic. Now, today, it's even worse. We know more about glacial melting and freshwater displacement. Anyway, late that night, there was a dinner after the meeting, and I was walking down Broadway, going home, thinking about the policy side of things. Which I never, ever think about. I just can't. It's too insane. I've been spared attacks by the deniers, myself, I assume because my work is just too hard to follow. But virtually everyone I know has had at least one. And so we don't do much actual advocacy, unless we're called to testify before Congress. We keep a low profile. It's a survival strategy.

—It sounds as if you've been coping with despair, in that realm, for years.

—No, no. Cynicism and despair are different. Here's what happened that night, that particular night, in 2009, just as I was passing Harry's Shoes on Eighty-Third Street. You know all the running shoes now come in neon colors? I stopped and just stared at those shoes. The amount of detail. The unbelievably *bright* colors, the riot of colors. Thirty years ago it was only the kids who wore these things; now we're all supposed to. And why the hell not? This is the fun of being human. It's refusing the *drab*. It's saying, to hell with the mud and the snow, and the smell of shit, and the wet wood that smolders but doesn't burn. Who cares if all that red dye poisons the Bay of Bengal? *The point of that red is to be poisonous.* And it came to me that climate change isn't just real. It's *intentional*. It is a willed thing, an intentional human response to nature. Not a byproduct but a goal. We are destroying the ecosystem because we want to destroy it.

—The Shiva hypothesis being the inverse of Lovelock's Gaia hypothesis, that the Earth is a single self-sufficient organism.

—I read *Gaia* in college, of course. Everybody did. It didn't matter that it was ludicrous from an empirical perspective. It was pure genius, just to be able to conceive of the planet as one unified system. It was the best kind of science fiction. Without Lovelock, this book never could have happened.

—Though Lovelock has denounced you, on his website, calling your book *fashionable eco-pessimistic rubbish.*

—Well, what did you think he was going to say? *I'm happy to be disproven?*

—You sound a little defensive. Understandably so. The critiques have been quite personal.

—Oh, I have the world's best publicist. I wouldn't be able to do any of this without her. She filters out the trolls and gives me the headlines. Pull quotes. It's like being president for a month. But seriously, listen, I'm drawing on a large body of research that demonstrates that *all* indigenous societies internalize the threat of an aggressive environment as a basic continuity of existence. If you've ever spent time among indigenous peoples, as I did, many years ago, in Alaska, you'll know that their lives are by and large extremely harsh. These are people who know what it means to die of exposure. This is outside of any belief system or concept of harmony with natural deities. I'm talking about what Spinoza calls the *conatus,* the fundamental life force, which calls us to resist what will otherwise kill us. This is disharmonious. We tend not to assign powerful negative emotions to indigenous groups, out of our own condescension. But why not call it like it is? Why not say that there is a natural place for rage, perhaps even for so-called irrational destruction, in their world, just as there is, so obviously, in Judeo-Christian theology, in Indian religions, in shamanism, even in Confucius?

—Does it surprise you to get such sharply negative reactions from religious groups, from Hindus in particular?

—Of course not. This is not a book designed to make anyone happy.

—And you're aware that an Orthodox rabbi, Meir Kalman, has attempted to connect the book directly to your daughter Bering's death at the hands of the Israeli army in 2003, saying that this is a purposeful sacrilege, an attack on the basic premise of the Torah, intended for a Jewish audience?

She wants to reach out and touch his rubbery face, to pinch it, to see if it slaps back into shape when you stretch it. I asked for this, she's thinking, I thrust myself into the glare. And no wonder we use that word, *thrust*. What could be more phallic than this theater of opinions? *I am somebody.* It's just the homoerotic/homohysterical narcissism of publishing. This is a theory she's developing on the spot. You imagine yourself to be in the phallic position, thrusting your thought-penis into the public's willing wet orifice, when really you're bending over and allowing, *inviting*, the public and its proxies, the reviewers, the bloggers, the pundits, the Amazon two-star clickers, to fuck you dry and raw. I abandoned penetrative sex to write a penetrative book, she thinks. I've got to tell Pritchard about this. This is fucking brilliant. I should talk about it right now, in this interview, on TV. It's the insight of a lifetime.

—Maybe I'm misreading you, but it seems to me that you're saying, or *suggesting*, pre-arguing, whatever you like to call it, that human beings actually, intrinsically, hate nature.

—I'm asking why it is that we're so uncomfortable with the *idea* that humans are hostile toward nature. Why we should want to maintain a natural order that is hostile toward us. Rather than destroy it, even possibly remake it. Considering that for most of human history, in most places, modification, destruction, was the only acceptable position.

—For most of human history, we didn't have anything like the climate science we have today. We didn't know what *ecology* was.

—On the other hand, many so-called primitive cultures, Stone Age cultures, have a much more robust sense of local ecology, of observed cause and effect, as well as, of course, a much more pronounced sense of vulnerability and fragility.

—And none of them, according to you, developed a theory of interdependence. Furthermore you say it's a myth that Native Americans live, or lived, in harmony with nature. Not surprisingly, that particular claim is making a lot of people angry. There have been calls for your resignation at Columbia.

—Again, everything I say is well supported. It's just not polite.

—Some commentators have expressed sympathy for your argument but have been, well, almost scandalized by your language, calling it violent and sexualized, even pornographic.

—Put it this way: I'm sick of realism. And I'm sick of being reasonable. Scientists go on TV and Big Carbon stomps on them like grapes. We live in a cartoonish universe. We live in an action movie.

We forget that fear of the elements was the defining feature of life for premodern societies, particularly those who lived outside the tropics. The defining condition of life. The human "conquest" of nature that began in the industrial revolution has alienated us from our own species-memory of the constant threat of death by natural fiat—death from freezing; from famine; from infectious diseases; from predators; from drowning; from fire; from poisonous insects, reptiles, or plants; from landslides, floods, volcanic eruptions; or (as was so often the case) from some cause that could not be predicted or understood. Today when human deaths occur as a result of "natural disaster," for example the Indian Ocean tsunami of 2004, we have a sense of collective outrage, as if every possible phenomenon should already have been predicted and prepared for by science and public policy. We no longer find the smallest amount of natural contingency acceptable. One could theorize that human rage against nature still exists in a conscious way through the public demand for further conquests over the least understood, least regulable natural processes left—the climate, for one, but also earthquakes (still after more than a century of research unpredictable) and cancer (which is usually thought of as a "disease" but in fact is nothing more than a disordered version of life itself, with as much possible variation as the life it feeds on).

The argument of this book in a nutshell is that human rage against nature is nature. Virtually all cultural historians, and many educated people, understand that the idea that human beings should "love the earth" or "live in harmony with nature" is a product of European Romanticism that arose with (and in reaction to) the industrial revolution. It is an idea we superimpose on other cultures—Native American belief systems, or Taoism, for instance—not one that springs from them. It runs counter to the Adamic covenant in Genesis, to Pauline Christianity, to Islam, to the Vedas and the whole Brahmanical tradition in India. Environmentalists and in particular the "deep ecologists" have had to reach back to a putative pagan or matriarchal tradition in the Bronze Age to find any evidence for a generalized human worship of nature.

Or, to state the question more directly: who among us has never thought of nature as a cruel, unforgiving tyrant, a capricious and sadistic overlord? Forget earthquakes and tsunamis and landslides; I'm talking about the everyday indignities of the weather, the ones we're told never to complain about. Consider the thousands of little degradations we suffer every day. If you live in the Northeast of the continental United States, as I do, you experience, every year, three months of intense cold weather, dipping down to zero or even subzero temperatures, and three months of miserable, swamplike summer heat. Take an even more extreme example: the Upper Midwest, Minnesota and Wisconsin, where winter temperatures can reach minus-fifty Fahrenheit and summer temperatures one hundred and five Fahrenheit. These are places where, if I can use myself as evidence, a sensitive human being experiences the weather as simple violence, as a force hostile to human existence. Indeed, unless we are unlucky enough to live in an abusive home, as children the first aggressive violence we experience toward ourselves is the weather. Winter is the worst thing that has ever happened to us. In Indian Buddhism the primary metaphor for samsara, the cycle of wretchedness that defines sentient existence, is the turning of the seasons. If you have visited southern Nepal and east-central India, where the Buddha spent his life, as I have, it's not hard to understand why: Bihar, the Indian state where the site of Buddha's enlightenment still stands, is known for its hellish, withering heat and catastrophic monsoons. If I hadn't been able to afford an air-conditioned hotel and an air-conditioned tour bus to and from an air-conditioned plane, I think I would have lost my mind.

Far be it from my intention to say that we need to "own" or "get in

*touch with" our indigenous human rage against nature. If we look hard
at our own actions, we will see that rage is not far from the surface in any
case, not as far as we might think. Rather I would suggest that we need to
stop deceiving ourselves about the world we actually live in. Anthropogenic
climate change (even with its most catastrophic consequences) is not a result
of ignorance, short-term thinking, selfishness, capitalism, lack of will, or
geopolitical inertia: it is a natural event, a predictable event, an act of human will.*

The one time she ever tried to watch herself being interviewed on
TV—on the couch at home, the lights off, Sandy away at a deposition
in Cleveland—she closed her eyes after a few moments, then opened
them and muted the sound, then turned it off. Why didn't anyone tell
me not to do this, she said aloud, in a cold fury. Why didn't anyone tell
me I look so *decayed.* The concealer across her frown lines just made
them worse. That purplish-blue blazer, like the front row at a Westchester funeral. Her hectoring, strident, braying voice, so very Jewish. So
very Bronx Jewish. "I didn't do anything you said," she said to Lindsay,
who picked up on the first ring, though it was after midnight. "I didn't
maintain eye contact. I didn't smile once. I didn't even say *I'm pleased
to be here.*"

"You were nervous. It'll be better the next time."

"There's no way I can do this again. It's a farce."

"The head producer said you were their best guest in months. Just
relax and own it a little more. Act like you have a right to be there,
because you do."

"That is an abject lie."

But she couldn't bear even a flash of disappointment on that
eggshell face. You're young enough to be my youngest daughter, she
wanted to say to Lindsay, over and over, in fact you are very nearly the
same age as _____. You share the same tendency, to mold the world
to your furious demands. So the interviews went on. Seven or eight of
them, she lost count. It got easier, knowing she didn't have to watch;
all it was was saying words into dead air. She digressed, she changed

course midway through an answer. It got to be almost fun. The hate mail increased; they delisted their address, unplugged the home phone, she had to stop checking email entirely. After Lou Dobbs said something about her—or was it Glenn Beck?—Columbia posted a security guard outside her department. Like 2003 all over again. Worse. It hurt. She misses it. The secret delight of using words that way, burning and being burned.

/

Current time in Berlin: GMT+1:00 (EST+6:00) 8:42 A.M.

Tilda has gone to bed, apparently. The kitchen light off, the dishwasher making its soft heaving sounds. She's moved to the plank table in her study with her laptop and her fifth cup of tea for the day. A sixtysomething woman, alone, in a darkened room, still in her walking clothes, her face lit up by the blue glow of a laptop screen. Edward Hopper could have painted this picture. Rounding off the nose a little, shaving off the lips. Hopper didn't paint Jews. A Jewish face, in repose, to Wasps like him, was an impossible thing. Jews were always thinking about something, their low brows furrowed. Like world domination. To have the proper forlorn beauty, the absence of emotion, you had to come from Iowa. Like Sandy. Sandy has the high forehead, the jaw. It was Leon Lewin who said, the first time she had them over for dinner, you know we hired Sandy because he looks a little like Gregory Peck. There are still some judges in New York where you want the guy who looks like he just stepped off his sailboat in Nantucket. To us it's affirmative action.

Patrick Wilcox . . . connecting . . . , Skype still says. White dots bouncing across the screen toward the black box where his photo should be. He won't be there, of course. Though his laptop is online. Everyone is always online. And not.

And then, with a whoosh, he's there.

"What's up, Mom?"

He's gained a little weight since last time. Not quite so skull-like. A few days of stubble shadowing his cheeks, though his head, as always, is neatly shaved, almost gleaming. A blank office wall behind him, a slice of blue sky.

"Is this a bad time?"

"Not at all," he says, still looking to his left. "I just got to work. No one's yelled at me yet."

"People often yell at you at work?"

"Never. It was a joke. They ask insistently, and in German, that's all you need."

"I got a call from Dad." Her voice echoes, as if she's shouting into a bathroom stall. "He's taking early retirement. This is what he told me. From the road. Done deal. Fait accompli. From Connecticut. He's moving back up to the temple. The house, I mean. And here's the crazy part. He said he's taking a three-month vow of silence."

"I don't get it. This is all out of the blue?"

"*I* didn't see any warning signs."

"How often do you guys usually talk these days?"

"Once a week. I mean, briefly. Maybe less."

"Then what do you think this is, a late-life crisis? You think he's really going to follow through? Leave Fein Lewin behind, after thirty years, on a whim?"

"I have no idea. *I'm thinking about relocating.* He says, *I'm thinking about early retirement.* And you know him. The man has no thoughts. *No thoughts.* Until he does. And then, whatever it is, it's done. So that's that, then."

Someone is moving around in Trick's background; he looks behind him, murmurs something, a door clicks closed. "Sorry, Mom," he says. Hard to tell through the screen; it could be a cloud shadow, or his face turning red. "Give me a minute. I have to drink this."

"What is that, chocolate milk?"

"It's a protein shake. You know that. I'm on a schedule."

Not often, but every once in a while, someone asks her what her children do for a living. It comes up. It's a habit, in the achieving classes, it's the only yardstick people at Woods Hole potlucks use for measuring success: they can't exactly compare cars, or golf games, or breast implants. Winter is a lawyer in Providence and Patrick is a, a what. A what in Berlin. A computer scientist. A software engineer. No and no. If I told you what quantum computing really is, she always wants to say, you couldn't handle it. These things, these phones, laptops, apps, Xboxes, you have no idea how they work or what they do, let alone what they *could* do. They are not for sharing videos of cats. Turing, Einstein, Heisenberg, never dreamed of where we would be right now. But that's not even it, of course, that's just the prideful, digestible version. He was a monk in India, he blew up his mind, tantra, philosophies of extreme negation—again, things you really can't explain at cocktail parties—and nearly killed himself with dysentery, as one does. Fell in love with a Danish nun (Katrinka? Katherina?), moved to Berlin, as one does, still physically at death's door, somehow stumbled into a highly lucrative job in the Western equivalent of tantra, quantum mechanics as software. The power of uncertainty, neither-one-thing-nor-another, in which the universe actually resides. Now she sounds like Bill Moyers. He broke up with the ex-nun, as she understands it, though they work at the same company. Lost about thirty pounds, seemingly for good, and he was thin to begin with. She and Sandy visited him once in Berlin five years ago, out of sheer parental concern. He galloped them energetically around the sights—the terrifying maze of the Holocaust memorial, Checkpoint Charlie, the Reichstag, the Jewish museum, each with a gift shop!—and wouldn't eat a thing. He sat with them politely in restaurants, drinking tea and joking with the waiters. A hunger artist in Hitler's ruins. He refused to introduce them to the nun. We're lucky he's still alive, Sandy kept saying, and she did her best to modulate her horror, except for the one time when they had a blowup argument over quantum computing as a weapon of war. He was fatalistic, he shrugged, he told them he got calls from DARPA and the NSA all the time. All we can do at Avansys is refuse to collaborate, he kept saying.

I have one dead child, one good-cause-nonprofit child, and one child who blows up the universe, theoretically, as a career, would be the best way to sum it up.

"So, Mom," he says. "It sounds like what you're trying to say, or what he's trying to say, is he's leaving you."

"You know what he said? When I asked him that question? He said, 'Leaving *what*?'"

"Well, you have to admit he has a point."

"Because I left first."

"I didn't say that."

"Because, as a logical outcome of clear and defined events outside of my control, I had to relocate my work—"

"That's one way of looking at it."

"Because I bought a house, using my own assets, instead of throwing away rent, year after year? Because, by some arbitrary measure, what's the legal term, *all mutual affection had ceased*?"

"Are you asking for my opinion?"

"Not really."

"Good." His voice has a way of flexing up, more nasal, informative, when he feels in control of the conversation. "You know I'm not going to take sides, don't you?" he says. "If you two really are splitting up. I'm not here to endorse your opinions of each other. Though I'm happy to listen. I have to reserve my own judgment. I'm not going to arbitrate anything. Neither will Winter. You're not going to put us in that position."

"Winter would have to be speaking to me first," she says, "to be put in any position at all."

"Is that how it is, between you two? Seriously?"

"In the sense that I haven't heard from her in months, and she lives an hour away. We had a huge fight, as you probably know. Over nothing. Zilch. Something I said that she took the wrong way."

"Try apologizing, then."

"It's a slippery slope, with you kids. Apologize once, it's like opening a vein. It never stops."

"That's not a very healthy attitude."

"Don't pretend to be above it. As if you don't have your own storehouse of blame and hurt feelings and, what shall I say, *recriminations*, or condemnations, whatever word you want to use. Your own karmic bank account."

"That's not what karma is," he says. "You know better, Mom. It's not a place to store grudges and resentments. It's about what you *do*, not what you think—"

"Don't be pedantic. You know what I mean."

"A storehouse of blame and hurt feelings? Of course. I have that. But that's my problem, and my business. What am I supposed to say, Mom, *you deserve to suffer*? No. I love you, and I'm sorry."

They should leave it at that. Isn't that a nice, mature, grown-up way of putting it? Lo and behold, an act of—what was the name of that terrible book, the book everyone was going around recommending to everyone else, about 1998?—emotional intelligence. There are so many things worse in this world than having your thirty-eight-year-old son tell you he loves you, in an unforced way. Why can't she be happy and hang up, tell him she'll keep him updated? Let him have this one. Concede that, yes, it may be that Buddhism has actually made him better.

No. The problem is, she knows him too well. Every time she speaks to him—this has been going on for years—he sounds like he's recovered his ability to speak after a stroke. Of the four of them, he is the most damaged. And why should that be? He and Bering were extremely close, she became quite dependent on him, idealized him, in the years before he left for college—as far as she can remember, acknowledging how little attention she paid to either of them, any of them, at the time—but afterward they hardly seemed to speak at all. Maybe Bering wrote him letters while he was at Harvard. She's never asked. This is what she does every time, speaking to her living children: dives down a well of questions, groping in that black water for the bottom.

"Well," she says, "well, I—"

"Hold on. Just one second. I have to ask Nazim something." He stalks across the office and out of sight, leaving her staring at a closed door.

"Tilda," she calls out. "You in bed yet?"

She appears in the doorway, in her long gauzy nightgown, barefoot. Reading glasses, a copy of *The Spiral Dance* tucked under her elbow.

"How much longer are you going to be?"

"Not long."

"Well, don't rush things on my account."

Everybody's being so nice to me, she wants to say, and it hits her again: Because I am the abandoned one. I am the woman in rags. I should rise up like some terrifying goddess. Like Kali, with a necklace of heads. Tilda can help with the details. There could be ceremonies. Rituals. I'm ready, she thinks, I should just tell her now. So ready.

In Berlin, Patrick's face reappears.

"I'm back," he says. "Were you talking to someone?"

"Of course not. Who would I be talking to?"

Rangy, healthy. Lean. Blowing across his mug. She could touch him. Touch his biceps. What would that do, exactly? It would reclaim him. Remand him to the world of the living. Talk faster, she wants to beg him, sometimes, the way you used to, like a New Yorker. Make fun of me. Make jokes at my expense. Without inserting a rest between sentences to acknowledge the unsaid.

"I have to go in a second, but, Mom, tell me, please, is there anything I can do? Like right now? Should I call him? Should I call Winter? I'm at a bit of a loss."

"Nothing," she says, and blows out air, sweet futility. "Just do me a favor and think about one thing. The apartment is vacant. If no one's there, we'll lose it. You know that much. They pay the doormen, they hire detectives, they use hidden cameras. Kicking kids off the leases left and right."

"But you technically, I mean, you still—you're a *professor at Columbia*. You live in New York. Dad *lives in New York*. When we were growing up half the goddamned building was on tour with their orchestra or dance theater or mime troupe half the time."

"Times have changed."

"Not that you asked, but my thinking is, Dad's had some kind of a breakdown. Someone should go find out if he's really okay. Whether or not he wants that. This doesn't have the hallmarks of a rational decision."

"You should have heard him on the phone. He sounded perfectly reasonable. Happy, actually. You know how he is, when he's made up his mind about something without telling anyone."

"A person can sound totally reasonable while they're getting ready to jump off a cliff."

"Well, at this point, if that's what's going on, I have to respect his wishes. He spelled it out to me categorically. I'm not going up there to ask him to reconsider."

"Well, so what is your point, then?"

"It's our home," she says. So weepy, so contemptible. The way the word sticks in her throat. "It is what it is. Yes, true, nobody seems to be able to stay there for long these days. But can you imagine losing it? Can you imagine us, *us,* not having a foothold, a home, in New York? I don't want to be the only one thinking these thoughts. Making provisions. It's not my strong suit. I want you to be involved. You're the inheritors. You and Winter. I went through that. Now it's your turn. And I thought you said you could do your work from anywhere, you're not tied to Berlin, it's just a stopping point."

"That was years ago," he says. "I'm not moving, not anytime soon. I like it here. And never, ever, to New York. I apologize if I ever gave you that idea. Not the U.S. at all, almost certainly, but never to New York, certainly. But that's just not the point, Mom. I don't want to have a conversation in euphemisms. I want to be there for you. But nothing about this changes the shape of things, the way we are. Whether you and Dad are ostensibly together or apart."

"What the hell does that mean?"

"It means," he says, a vein seeming to twitch on his temple, "I've organized my life a certain way, I finally have some stability, my condition is under control, my feelings are under control, not that you'd ever ask. That's it, really. I finally have some equanimity. I think Winter feels the same. You and Dad haven't really given us much in the way of support, per se, in the last fifteen years—"

"A debt-free life, college, law school, the down payment on Winter's house—"

"Apart from material conditions, and note that I've never asked for anything. We're fine. After a long time, we're fine. So I think we'll adjust, if you do split up. It isn't as if it'll be a shock. More like a profound historical irony. If the apartment goes, it goes. If Dad wants to live in Vermont, or Spain, or Zimbabwe, fine. You should learn to mourn and move on, for once in your life. Actually acknowledge what it is you've done."

"What *I've* done?"

"The role you played, yes. You decided you wanted to have a separate life from Dad. Now he's agreed with you. If you want him back, you'll have to work together, come to some new understanding."

"You're so sanguine and impartial," she says, "because your life is so perfect, you've learned from our mistakes."

"Nothing in that sentence is true. Honestly, Mom, you know very little about my life."

"And you want to keep it that way, apparently."

"I've said I want to support you and Dad—"

"That isn't the same thing."

He looks away, he gazes off into the middle distance. Probably, given that he works for a software company, another monitor. None of us know what we want, she wants to say for him. If she could touch his biceps, then what? If you can render your adult son material, instead of six thousand miles away, then what? He's alive; he has animal warmth. If he were there in person, she would feel better, because humans are animals. How has she known and not known this all her life? Families are supposed to live close together. How did an entire substratum of the species, the most supposedly intelligent, self-aware, self-analytic, miss this basic point?

You stopped speaking to *us*, she wants to insist, for three strategic years, the years after Bering's death, on retreat in Nepal. To make up for it—although the connection may well only be in her mind—ever since he moved to Berlin, he's sent them expensive, thoughtless Hanukkah gifts. A wine-of-the-month membership. A set of hand-painted ceramic goblets. A Tibetan rug, woven by former victims of torture or burn victims or something ghastly, she doesn't remember the details. It's all so horrible and messy and awkward, but what if the original mistake is so much farther back? We should have bought a brownstone in the West Nineties, like the Furmans and Peter Lowenthal and Judy and Shep Rosen, with apartments set aside for the kids, the fucking mishpocheh. We should have told them we wanted them to stay in New York, that we would babysit the grandkids, et cetera. You have to affirm the needs of the species if you want to be happy. It's a little late now.

"You know," she starts, "it was the fifteenth anniversary—"

"Yes, I'm aware."

"Well, did anyone reach out to you? I didn't hear a word. Dad said he had media requests, but I didn't get any."

"Do you check your Columbia email?"

"Of course."

"Well I guess they think of Dad as the contact person."

"I mean, not that it matters, no one's saying anything."

"We could have had a phone call, at least."

"We should have. I should have thought of that."

It's time to leave him alone, exhausted. All avenues exhausted, all topics covered. They haven't had a conversation this long in years, and now what. I love you and I'm sorry, he said. What more does a mother want. Share my outrage, share my pain. It's all triangulation, in the end. She's angry at Winter for not knowing; angry at Judy, who's having a hip replacement tomorrow and promised she'd call back at the end of the week; angry at Tilda for not understanding people she's never met. This day has been so absurdly long and yet she can hardly stay seated, let alone sleep. She could go for another walk in the blessed, Wilson Thorpe–free dark.

"I still think someone should talk to Dad."

"I assure you he's fine. Let him have his moment. Maybe it'll be a shock, being up there all alone."

"A shock, and then what?"

"I guess we'll have to see."

"And if he wants to come back, will you take him back?"

The door to her study is open, Tilda left it open, which means she wanted to hear the sound of her voice, not sleep in peace. She will still be awake, reading, her glasses pushed down on her nose. This is a matter of craving, she can't say where in the body it starts. As always, in the wrong order, at the wrong time. Intuition, not order, leads her, as an animal, where it will.

"Of course," she says. "Of course I will."

/

"The Earth spins on an axis at an angle to the sun," she said. "Like any rotating body, its relationship with gravity is complicated. Even a spinning top, a gyroscope, a dreidel, is complicated—and that's a rigid body within a single gravitational field. Let me put this as simply as I can. Any three-dimensional object that rotates around an axis has to be described using three angles, representing its three coordinates, x, y, and z. These are its Euler angles. When you measure the Earth's Euler angles, you see that the moon's gravity and the sun's gravity actually move the angle of its axis around slightly, over a period of years. By as

much as seventeen degrees longitude. That's called an ordinary nuta-
tion. It's been understood for centuries."

"I get it," Patrick said.

He was nineteen. In Maine, in Blue Hill, in August, two weeks before he was due back in Cambridge. On the deck at the inn, of course.
She was drinking a gin and tonic. It was 1998. She was wearing a blue
sundress and had her legs up on a chair. Why not just come out and
say it? She was basking in his glow. You can do that, with a son going
to Harvard.

"Okay. But do the math, and you'll see that there's *another* set of
nutations that also affect the angle of the axis. Nutations not accounted
for by any extraterrestrial body. Free nutations, they're called, and the
primary one, the biggest one, is called the Chandler wobble."

"That's really what it's called?"

She took a long swallow.

"The Chandler wobble," she said, "meaning the Earth wobbles very
slightly, of its own accord, on its axis of rotation, and until about ten
years ago, no one knew why. Of course, we all know the Earth is not a
perfect sphere and is not rigid. There's no set of stable calculations for
any of the nutations, no matter how well understood. People thought it
could have something to do with magma inelasticity. The core-magma
boundary. The thing is, the physical properties of liquids, *all* liquids,
just don't make a lot of sense to us, mathematically. That goes for ocean
currents, for lava, for highly unstable liquids, like nitrogen. We just
don't get it, somehow. And yet the Earth is largely made of liquids. It
is a liquid sphere."

"And so . . ."

"And so, you know, I was up in Alaska, when you were a baby, doing all that work on bathythermographs, on measuring deep-sea ocean
temperatures, temperature calibrated in terms of pressure. Well, it was
only a few years after I came back from Alaska and had just started
at Columbia that I met this guy at a dinner party, some boring thing
organized by the dean of something or other. He was seated next to me

at this long awful table. Richard Grasso, who worked at the JPL, who told me he was doing research on the Chandler wobble. He was one of those guys who just doesn't stop once you get him going. No social graces whatsoever. Anyway, he took out a napkin and drew me a little graph of how the Chandler wobble varies over ten-year intervals, and I said, that's funny, because it's the exact same shape as my benthic pressure readings over a decade. And he said, that's not an accident. It can't be an accident. And, as it turns out, it wasn't. Once we got together and got an NSF grant and a supercomputer and ran the numbers, it was plain as day. The largest factor in the Chandler wobble is fluctuations in the pressure of the benthic boundary layer."

"In other words," Patrick said, "what you're saying is, the way the ocean shifts, these deep-water ocean shifts, actually changes the position of the Earth in space. It moves the Earth around in space."

"Yes."

He leaned back in his chair until it tipped against the deck railing, and she suppressed the urge to tell him to sit up straight. There was a long sheaf of damp hair hanging over his eyes; he'd been studiously growing it all summer, and now he reached up carefully, a practiced move, and flipped it over. Only then did she notice that the front-desk girl, the Ukrainian girl, had come out onto the deck and was rearranging the cushions on the lounge chairs, trying not to look at him. How do you account for this feeling, she wondered, that in the aristocracy of the senses, your own son is about five ranks above you? In high school he would never have given her a second look.

"I feel like I should make a speech right now," he said.

"What do you mean?"

"Not a speech. A monologue, I mean. I feel like, like, you've given me the perfect metaphor for our family, and I'm supposed to explain it to the audience. *The Chandler Wobble.* I should write a book now. A family romance. Don't worry. I'm not actually going to do it. But if I was going to, I guess I would say, the pressure within the deepest layer—"

"Oh, stop it."

"You don't want to hear my interpretation?"

"You're not qualified to interpret anything. You're nineteen years old. Anyway, I wasn't finished."

He made a grand, expansive gesture, a sitting bow. She wished there was something wrong with him. She wished he would develop *acne*. "Go on," he said. "I'm sorry, Mom. Seriously."

"It was all an accident," she says. "That's the way science works. Not metaphors. It's not logical. And it's not fair. It just so happens that Rich and I got this grant, and co-wrote this paper, and that's what got us the computer time, the access, and because of that, purely as a byproduct, I developed the coefficient, the first way of calculating the pressure-temperature matrix, which also happened to be the best way of predicting global sea-level rise."

"The Wilcox coefficient."

"That's what they call it."

"Dad showed it to me, in middle school. It was in some journal you left sitting around in the kitchen. He took my highlighter and circled it. *Mom did that,* he said."

"Well," she said, testing, "just because they put my name on it doesn't mean much of anything. It's a tool. One small tool."

"It's not a metaphor."

"It doesn't have anything to do with me. Or *us*. Your father doesn't understand it. Your sisters don't understand it. *You* don't really understand it, either, though you took AP physics and calc, so I can give you the basic idea, at least. And that's okay. To me that's a relief. Because then I can focus on what really matters, which is the data, and trying to drill down and get the most data we can while there's still time, and get it to the only people who can do anything about it."

"I thought the whole idea was that *we* are the only people who can do anything about it."

He looked earnest, and she laughed at him.

"Are you talking about *think globally, act locally*?" she said. "You know how hard it is to think globally? I've been trying to do it my entire life. When people say that, what the hell do they mean? I've never really understood it. Like, buying recycled toilet paper? That's not thinking globally. Thinking globally means using Liouville's equation and the Gaussian curvature K. It means literally trying to understand what it means to live on a sphere. I used to spend a lot of sleepless nights thinking that we're doomed as a species because our theory of isothermal coordinates doesn't work well enough."

"And now?"

"Now I've accepted that, in fact, we have bigger problems."

She was ruining it; she knew that. He was trying to tell her he was proud of her, or something, and she was running off at the mouth, telling him she didn't care.

"It's okay, anyway," he said, "because the novel is dead." He shifted his leg, and she saw that in his lap were two books, the top one with a white cover and a clumsy line drawing of two fingers pointing at each other. Milan Kundera, *The Art of the Novel.*

"You're telling me that book is called *The Art of the Novel* and it's actually about the death of the novel?"

"Sort of. More or less."

"I should write a book like that," she said. "*The Art of Living on a Dying Planet.*"

This was the point where they stopped listening to one another. Their last real conversation. She can see it in his face: he knows, and yet he goes on speaking, not because he doesn't care, he desperately cares, but he can't admit to himself how desperately he cares. These children, Patrick and Winter, they're so desperate to be affirmed by her as the geniuses they already are. Why don't they turn to Sandy for affirmation? Why do they trust him, trust his belief in them, trust his unconditionality?

She's drifting now. Patrick drones on, with the seagulls. That Ukrainian girl is still there, pretending to read. She itches for him. And why not? Probably she comes from some village of arms traffickers and underage prostitutes, their babies swollen and drooling. Fetal alcohol syndrome. This may be the best job she will ever have. Attached to his prospects, she could change the course of history. A Ukrainian peasant and—cut his hair, make him stoop, grow out some payes, give him some round wire glasses, a gabardine overcoat—a passable shtetl Jew. The nightmare of rabbis and priests everywhere made flesh. Probably in a loft in Tribeca. She'll bring the borscht. Everyone agrees on borscht.

Drifting, again.

This is the end of it.

Because the last of the wine is finished.

Just as Bering appears, coming up barefoot from the beach. Brown as only she could be in August. Brown enough to be someone else's child. Carrying a pearl, an oyster's pearl, cupped in her hand. This scene is fading away. This scene cannot be told. She will not speak to her. She is sixteen years old.

/

We are deep in the first night of this novel.

She thinks.

Sandy has by now arrived. He is there. His car, his expensive car, the Audi, whose tires have never known the bite and slosh of a gravel road. He is standing in the driveway, the temple driveway, in the slush, or maybe even the snow. Early spring in the Northeast Kingdom, a certain softness in the permafrost. He looks up at the old farmhouse, built in 1879. As if all the secrets of our lives are kept there. The ancestral wound. Call it a house, or call it a temple? The house we brought Patrick to as a newborn. The temple where I got fucked. Literally and otherwise. That chasm in the world. Where the seventies ended. Where Reagan got elected and we put away childish things.

For at least five minutes she's been lying with her head tipped over the edge of the bed, chin pointing at the ceiling. Now she pulls herself up and tumbles over onto the disorderly hump of pillows Tilda uses to get comfortable during sex. Tilda who has changed back into her nightgown, made another cup of tea. It's three hours after her normal bedtime.

"You were asking me," she says, "why I didn't call Winter first."

"It's fine, you don't need to explain yourself."

"Winter is angry because we disagree about racism. I mean recently angry. We had a fight about it. Because of me, I mean, because of who my real father was. Because of John Downs. And who that makes me. I mean *what* that makes me. I'm no good at the terms, you see. That's always been a problem."

"Go ahead, tell me what you actually said. Don't summarize."

"We were talking about some kind of training she was doing for law students at the clinic, about their intake interviews for new clients, and she was saying something about how she teaches them not to assume anything about the clients' ethnic backgrounds, and she said, for example, no one here would assume I'm actually multiracial, and I said, Winter, that's because you're *not* actually multiracial. And she said, oh yes I am, my grandfather was Black and my mother is biracial. And I said, I'm not biracial. Not really. And she said, that's ridiculous, of course you are. And I said, don't I get any say in the matter? And she said, you may not self-identify as Black, but the fact is that you *are,* your biological father is who he is, or was who he was, and so you are biologically biracial, and I can call you biracial and identify as multiracial, and I do.

"And I said, you were raised by two white parents, with two white siblings, in a city where Black people and Puerto Ricans and Chinese and Koreans and Africans and whateverthefuck are not theoretical, not *identified,* but actually there in front of you, they are *different* from you, and yes, I withheld the truth about your grandfather until I thought you were old enough to handle it, a decision I still question, by the way, but I certainly didn't tell you about John Downs to give you some kind of racial complex. I told you because what happened with my mother and John Downs was a terrible, ugly historical event, it deserves its place in the record of the family, and also, of course, it demonstrates the *idiocy* of racism, the *idiocy* of racial categories. But the fact is that I was raised by Phyllis and Herman Schifrin, Herman Schifrin was my father, we were a nuclear family, a classically neurotic one, yes, and not only did my father never let on that I was adopted, but I honestly believe that after a certain point he *forgot* I was adopted. He was an accountant and an Eisenhower Republican. He couldn't tolerate much cognitive dissonance. When my mother told me the truth, in 1969, this country was on fire. Whiteness and Blackness were not negotiable. I wasn't about to *go in search* of something. And yes, later I tried to find John Downs, spent a lot of money to find him, to learn about him, to contact him, and I'm glad I did, and of course I wish I'd gotten to meet him. It was a menopausal thing. A hormonal thing. And because I thought that's what my mother would have wanted."

"That's ridiculous," Tilda says.

"What's ridiculous?"

"Your whole series of rationalizations. Your fatuous logic."

"Wow. Tell me how you really feel."

"I am completely serious," Tilda says, coiling a body pillow and shoving it behind her. "Sometimes with women your age I get the feeling your political consciousness stopped at *The Female Eunuch*. Do you get, can you grasp, how seriously fucked up it is that you can deny your racial origins, that you have that option? That's what Winter is trying to say to you. In a nutshell. Of course you identify as white. Your parents didn't give you any other choice. That doesn't mean they weren't *lying*. Why try to obfuscate that? You were deceived. Your actual origins, your parentage, your heritage."

"My heritage is that I am a human animal," she says.

"But only whiteness lets you say that."

"So white people, according to your logic, have some kind of lock on objectivity? The scientific method, empirical validation, that's all some kind of racially demarcated *preserve*?"

"If you want to put it that way, yes."

"You might as well say it only belongs to men."

"It does. Because it's a fantasy, and you know it. Objectivity is a fiction, an instrument of control."

"When I hear people say things like that, I can never decide whether I want to shoot myself, vomit, or strangle them first, and so I never do anything, which is so unsatisfying."

"So say it your own way."

"Objectivity is relational," she says, "and a matter of survival. If you are adrift on a lifeboat and your water supply runs out, you will have to drink your own urine. It doesn't matter if you're Sri Lankan or Chilean or Eritrean or from Duluth, Minnesota. You need to find a way to capture and consume your urine. There's something about this in Peirce, you know, Charles Sanders Peirce. About how reality is that which is independent of what anyone thinks about it. I think, honestly, at the baseline, that's what all scientists agree on. They *have* to. Don't call it objectivity, if that word gives you hives. Call it *data necessary to sustain life*. I don't know."

"So you're okay with racism as a scientific invention, with the Milgram experiments, with Mengele, with Tuskegee?"

"Listen. I'm still explaining this in my own way. When I first found out who I really was, I had a full-on identity crisis. Of course. This was in 1969, right before I went to Oberlin. I mean, it was *1969,* for god's sake. MLK had just died. There were riots everywhere. And I had not, to be honest, been especially engaged in it all. Obviously, I was against the war. I was a good liberal child of good liberal parents. But I had no Black people in my life, and I mean none. Our maid was Maud Flynn from Tipperary by way of Yonkers. I never went into the city. I was studious and I was a goody two-shoes, never-been-kissed type, extremely earnest, and really I would say I was folded in on myself. Still a chrysalis. You know how some teenagers can be. Asexual. Not that I didn't have friends or do high school things. But my friends were all like me, more or less, they reinforced my limitations."

". . ."

"So when Mom had a crisis of conscience and dropped this in my lap, I took it up to my room, my little room over the garage, and I sat on it, I cried, I dreamed it, I dwelled on it all alone. Didn't tell a soul. You wouldn't do that, in Armonk, even in 1969, and even if she hadn't sworn me to the utmost secrecy. What was I supposed to do? I was a Black woman. For a second there, I actually believed in the one-drop rule. Not an unusually olivey olive-skinned Jew with unusually, though not unmistakably, black kinky hair. I was a Black woman with a schnoz. This is not a story I tell very often. In fact, ever."

"I'm not surprised."

"Does this happen to everyone, when they get divorced? This time-travel?"

"Nothing happens to everyone."

"I am so ashamed of what I'm about to say. I put on what I thought was my sexiest dress. A minidress. Say halfway up the thighs. I went down and stole a pair of gold lamé heels from Mom's closet. I pinned up my hair. I think I was trying to look like Nina Simone. I put on an Aretha record, that was the best I could do, and I danced. I tried to dance. I stuck my ass out and waved my hips around. Imitating, I don't know, *American Bandstand*? I had some concept in mind. Staring, staring at myself in the mirror the whole time. I mean, I *tried*. I was sweating it up. I was testing myself."

Tilda rolls over and palms her forehead, as if checking herself for a fever. "I think we're past the point, culturally," she says, "of having to apologize for things we did in 1969."

"You know what I saw? The whole sad pretense of having a body. Any body. I decided, I guess you could say, that I didn't have to inhabit my skin. That sounds worse than it is. I wasn't *rejecting* my Blackness. What I saw was something unrecognizable trying to get out. At that moment I decided I needed to be freed from thinking of myself as anything at all. And mark my words: I didn't choose to be in that position. It was done *to* me. By my mother. By John Downs. I take no credit for this discovery, none whatsoever. This is what he wrote me, back in 2001: he said, *Your mother and I created you but couldn't protect you. You had to learn to BE all by yourself.* Capital B, capital E. *You discovered that to be alive is the main thing. That's enough of a miracle by itself.*"

"Spoken like a true microbiologist."

"So this is how I've lived my life, dear. Now I've laid it all out. Tell me why it's all wrong."

"May I remind you," Tilda says, "the issue here isn't you. You need Winter, she isn't there for you, she can't be, because you fucked this part up. You didn't respect her autonomy. She too is responding to a given set of facts. It's nothing a simple apology can't address. You don't need to be stubborn about it."

"You say this as if there's no such thing as an irreparable breach— I was about to say in the body politic."

"The family body politic."

"The political family body."

"No, I like mine better."

"As if there was such a thing as a *simple apology!*" She sheds the bed, again, Tilda collapsing backward with a groan. "I can't sleep," she says. Shuffling into her slippers. "It's not my fault. I have to go outside. I need air."

She sweeps aside the curtains and tears the plastic film insulation away with her pinky nail. French doors onto the deck, never used. Unlocked, they won't budge. It's like an air lock, this house. Pounds with the heel of her palm. Leans in with a shoulder. "Fucking Christ," she says. "Help me get this open, will you?"

"You're on your own, bug."

She stands back and delivers a front kick, a totally satisfying move, until the ball of her foot shatters the pane of glass nearest the doorknob. At the sound of the crack, practically before the shards fall tinkling out onto the planking, Tilda springs out of bed, seizes her foot, and holds it in place. "Don't move!" she barks. "Otherwise we'll be in the ER till morning. Point your toe like a ballet dancer and lean back."

"OK. OK."

She lets herself go, still stunned, and Tilda holds her ankle, eases her down gently to the floor.

"Told you you should help me open the door."

"It's like everything you do is a cry for help today. You could have severed a tendon."

"I wonder why," she says, and is surprised at the wetness in her eyes. "I find myself overcome," she says, still lying on the floor. I *find* myself. Who invented that expression? Oh wait, I remember. Dante did. *Nel mezzo del cammin di nostra vita, mi ritrovai per una selva oscura, ché la diritta via era smarrita.* I found myself in a dark wood. *Mi ritrovai.* It sounds better in Italian. What does that verb mean, *ritrovai*? To return, probably. I returned. I came to my senses. A *ritrovai*-ness. A retrovirus.

Tilda has returned with a piece of cardboard and a roll of masking tape.

"Make love to me again," she says, not yet getting up.

"Nah. Not feeling it."

"Then I'll be able to sleep. Please."

"There was a missed call on your phone. I heard the beep."

"I'll look at it in the morning."

"You sure you want to wait?"

"I'm not beholden to anyone," she says. "Except maybe you. If you'll let me be."

"I have no idea what that means."

"We should get married. Since it's legal. We should do all the legal things, just to say we did. We should make plans for retirement."

"I can't afford to retire."

"Yet. *We*, on the other hand, can, could, afford for you to retire."

"This isn't the time. Go to sleep. You're exhausted."

"Help me up, then."

"You can help yourself up."

"Oh, so now it's tough love?"

"The first step is admitting you have a problem."

"My name is Naomi, and I'm addicted to gravity. I'm a gravity-holic."

"Hi, Naomi." She turns out the light. "That's enough for one day."

THE VASTNESS OF THE WORLD

October 9, 2002

Dear Naomi,

Thank you for that last letter.

It seems to me you've gotten a measure of clarity about what you want from this correspondence.

I apologize for the delay in responding, too. I have been going to the eye doctor almost weekly and it looks like I may be developing a macula condition, macular degeneration. I assume you're familiar with the dilation procedure that makes it difficult to read or type. Of course that's nothing compared to the long-term effects. Eventually I'll have to give up driving, for example. It's just time, the body's parts wearing out. I try not to dwell on it too much.

You asked if I could help you by remembering more about what happened ~~that summer~~ the summer of 1951, between your mother and myself.

When I try to come up with an answer I feel like I'm being

squeezed. Like the proverbial elephant is sitting on my chest. I wish you knew me. Not in the sense that I wish you could have been my child, my actual child (I don't), but in the sense that we are both scientists; we could by rights have been colleagues and I could be explaining this to you ~~rationally~~ as a colleague, someone I've known for twenty years, not as a ~~strange white woman~~ stranger from across the country. I wish I could trust you, enthusiastically, with the information you're asking for.

The problem is, you're arriving too late. It makes me skeptical. The question feels too abrupt. I don't know if, as the kids say, I am willing to "go there." In other words, I have to ask you to understand my position before I can even attempt to help you understand why you exist. That's the cost of your curiosity.

There was a woman I worked with for years—Joyce. Our department secretary. When I was acting director of my institute, she was my assistant. She must have been about ten years older than I, born in the early 1920s. She lived somewhere in Ventura County, a very long commute, but she was always in the office before I arrived, the lights on, the coffee perking. A ~~consummate~~ professional. She wore her hair in one of those up-dos that were popular in the sixties and never changed it, never dyed it, until it became a kind of frosted beehive, and the younger people called her the Bride, a.k.a. the Bride of Frankenstein. We respected each other and even liked each other, I would say. She appreciated how neat and orderly I was. Always have been. Nat Hechinger and Patrick Leary, the two other senior biophysicists in the lab, were slobs, who thought nothing of abandoning a coffee cup on a shelf until it grew a thick green skin, who never washed their lab coats, whose idea of office attire was blue jeans and flannel shirts. ~~"They think I'm their servant"~~ "They think I'm their mother," she often said. She had a master's herself, in engineering. She'd wanted to work for Boeing, but got pregnant too young (she told me that, openly), and then her husband was killed in a car accident, so she moved in with her parents and took a secretarial job just as a way to survive. But she was a master proofreader and had an excellent grasp of chemistry. Like a lot of women of her generation her mind and skills largely went to waste. And she was extremely kind, in her way. When my father, your grandfather, died suddenly in 1971, she bought the plane tickets and drove me to the airport herself. At the funeral home, when I arrived, she'd already sent a huge wreath of white lilies.

And then there was the time, not long afterward, when Leonora brought Vi to the office without telling me first—this almost never happened—and I was sitting at my desk, I heard a child's skipping feet (Vi was six or seven), and her voice, calling, "Daddy! Daddy!" and she came rocketing in at full speed, and Joyce was standing in the doorway, as if to try to stop her, with a look of appalled horror and disgust such as I've rarely seen on anyone's face. She'd forgotten for a moment that this Black girl, with her bouncing braids and long swinging arms, must belong to me. Vi didn't see it and Leonora didn't see it, though she could tell, from looking at my face, that something was up. Joyce turned back and sat down heavily in her chair, as if she'd just had the shock of her life. And in a way she had. She'd just seen, for the first time, a Black child who expected to be loved and admired, who hadn't learned (because we deliberately hadn't taught her) to be wary of and deferential to and shamefaced around white people.

I had to work with Joyce for another ~~nineteen~~ seventeen years. We remained cordial. Leonora wanted to know why when I asked her not to bring the children to the office. I said the other scientists found it disruptive. That was my cowardice. I didn't want to admit to her that I couldn't fire Joyce (probably

I could have, if I'd tried hard enough, but it would have been a scandal, and all sorts of ~~other prurient~~ guesses would have been made about my real motivations) but I also didn't want to. Maybe, I told myself, she just didn't like children. Which was nonsense. She cooed over Nat's babies when Sheila brought them by. I sacrificed my dignity and Vi's dignity. All I could do, all I did do, was become cold and withdrawn. Not just to Joyce—to everyone I worked with, by degrees.

This is to say that in my early working life I became quite hardened. I learned to wear the mask. Hard, severe, demanding, austere. For a long time I carried around the consciousness of having been betrayed time and time again and for a long time I was an angry and closed man. I was a sort of legend at Salk for being such a hard-ass. At my retirement party people drank too much and smiled and laughed when they thought I wasn't looking, out of relief.

Ten years ago, right after I retired, I ~~went cold sober~~ quit drinking. I started going to AA meetings, here in Pasadena, and it turned out my only possible sponsor, the only one available, by happenstance, was a guy named Anton Czernowicz. It's a very long story. I won't bore you with all the details. I'll just say this: Anton was a Polish immigrant, and he was gay. In the late 1970s he was expelled from Poland, disowned by his family, excommunicated by the Church, of course. And so he wound up living alone in a tiny apartment in South Pasadena, working as a carpenter, and sometimes as an escort, and also sometimes as a low-level dealer. When I met him he had been sober for five years and had turned his life around, he had his own cabinet business, two people working for him, a van, a little house with a pool. But he also had rapidly progressing HIV. He was diagnosed right around the time I met him.

We argued constantly about racism. Like a lot of Europeans

he thought Americans were obsessed with race, used it as an all-purpose excuse and explanation. I told him I knew (as he knew) exactly how it felt to have the state and the majority of the population want to kill you. I said I knew what it meant to be marked as subhuman, and that infuriated him. He said that he could never have been as successful in Poland as I was in America, and I told him that he could have if he had hidden it better. He could have been a priest, for example. He had to admit I was right on that score. But he was right about something else: he said, over and over, "You have to confront your anger, your anger is your rigidity, and your rigidity is an addiction, you depend on it absolutely." He got in my face about it. I would never have let a white American say the things he said to me. Or a man who wasn't a gay man. And he knew that. He said, "You're not threatened by me, because I was never taught to hate you." Which wasn't exactly true. But essentially correct in the way that counted at that moment.

The whole time I was working the steps with him I was also desperately trying to get him into treatment, into the AZT trials, all the different cocktails they were trying in those days. I called every specialist in Southern California. Nothing doing. I wasn't a doctor, just a researcher who knew a lot of doctors, and I didn't really have anything to offer in return.

It turned out that all I could do was be an empathic friend. I could drive him to appointments, help him shop for groceries, clean his house. He was getting sicker and sicker, precipitously. Finally he had to give up working. His last boyfriend, Bill, hung on with him to the bitter end, and Bill and I together moved Anton down to an AIDS hospice in Venice Beach. He only lasted a week. All the windows were open, so he could breathe the sea air, the day he died. He looked at me, very close to the end, when he had a breathing tube in and could hardly speak, and said, "It's good, I finally know you love me."

Is this making any sense to you? It did to me, but only for the remainder of that day. I couldn't explain it to Leonora. Maybe I didn't need to explain it to her. It was a transcendent feeling. I'll put it this way: I felt the ~~platform~~ clay container that had held me up all these years was cracked all over. Imagine that. Cracked, but not in such a way that it would fall to the floor. Not a chrysalis you break and get out of. That's not the way it happens with old men, I don't believe. It became, and maybe this image doesn't work—it became like a set of moving pieces, almost like a suit of armor, with chinks and joints and exposed places all over. I could never regain my stride, the back-ramrod-straight cadence I had all those years. I almost felt like I needed a cane.

(I didn't, though. Fortunately, though my spiritual life may have been changed, I kept the same routine of calisthenics I've had ever since my father taught it to me at age nine. He learned it in the army, at Fort Dix, in 1917.)

I don't expect you've ever heard of the stone churches of Lalibela. They were tunneled and carved out of a rock formation in the twelfth century, so that when you come upon them from the top, you see the roofs level with the ground— the churches themselves go down five or six stories into the earth. They're comparable to any church in Europe, any great cathedral—and I've seen most of the great cathedrals. A remnant of a great unknown civilization, to us, of course, not to Ethiopians, the one unconquered nation of Africa. Ethiopians to me have always resembled the actual people of the Bible, with their slender features and high cheekbones and enormous-seeming eyes. They are so regal and haunting. They serve coffee as a sacrament.

Three years, this past August. I traveled there for an entire month, by myself. As a late retirement present. Just me, the Lonely Planet guide, an Amharic phrasebook, and a Visa card.

I'd been promising myself that trip since I was seven years old and read about Haile Selassie in the *Afro-American*.

It was there, at Lalibela, so far from anything else in my life, in my world—I just had this feeling of the vastness of the world. ~~It was the one time I've ever had the impulse to make something, a piece of art—a film, a novel.~~ I wanted to say something about the vastness and interrelatedness I experienced at that moment. And when I say vastness I mean something very particular, which is not emptiness, but rather the mutual interdependence of seen and unseen patterns. I felt in that moment that the universe's basic attitude to life is, "Yes, that too." That was precisely what I wanted to express by way of a story, although I have no idea what kind of a story it would be. Or if it could be. I had this feeling that the universe is always making room for new things, and the things we think have disappeared haven't actually disappeared; they just no longer stand out in the pattern. It all came to me with this rush of expectation, though for what, I have no idea. Traveling is like that.

You who are reading this want something particular from me. Whoever is reading this wants one story from me. I want it too. I want a digestible, reconcilable version, the one I can tell as a confession, because I believe in confession, whether or not my church does! But not all of us have our wishes answered. In fact millions of us will never have our wishes answered. Not only am I not obligated to answer your question; I'm almost obligated to deny it to you, and, in a way, to myself.

The cruel and austere way to phrase this would be, Why should I show mercy? When have I been shown mercy? Why is it even a question of mercy? You chose to live your life as if I didn't exist.

But the loving version, which I think I am capable of aspiring to, is: I don't believe you're ready. From the tone of your letter. From the very lateness and anxiousness of your desire to make contact. I came across a very interesting article you wrote, a very short piece, the sidebar to the paper on Antarctic core samples and the salinity gradient in *Nature*. You wrote, "This evidence is concerning. It tells us how much we don't yet know about salinity and thermal coequivalents, but it also suggests we may have very little time left to acquire these reference points before dramatic and unstoppable change in polar temperatures occurs. Scientists are always supposed to be the ones saying 'don't panic,' but I sometimes wonder if all climate researchers feel as panicked as I do, writing this in the year 2000."

This suggests to me that you have something of an ulterior motive. You seem to be feeling your own mortality through what I might describe (though I'm not an expert) as an exaggeration or worst-case-scenario version of the current science. (Would it shock you to know that I'm a moderate Republican? I am indeed, and I suppose you could call me something of an enviro-skeptic as well, though by no means a denier of the data on global warming or anything else; just an instinctive disbeliever of anything Greenpeace promotes in its sanctimonious way. Vi despises me for voting for Reagan, as I did, twice, and I suppose, in this way, you and she would be in perfect agreement.)

I have a bit of perverse, but heartfelt, advice for you: your life will be improved immeasurably when you have grandchildren. Things will fall back into place. I've been spending a lot of time with Tonya. You remember from the last letter: she's three and a half now. I pick her up from daycare on Wednesdays and Fridays, and she sleeps at our house Friday nights, to give them a break. Her name for me is Papa John. Everybody laughs when she calls me that, and she gets the joke, she shouts, "Like the pizza!" I don't know what it means to be a grandparent. I

hardly knew mine at all. My mother's parents lived in North
Carolina, and never traveled, so I saw them only three or four
times in my childhood, when we had the money to go down in
the summer. My father's parents died very young, before I was
born. We were very much a closed family, a nuclear family, if
that word had existed.

(You should know this much about them, at least: their
names were Verna and Thomas Downs, your paternal
grandparents, and our address was 465 V Street SE,
Washington, District of Columbia. The house still stands,
but it's abandoned and boarded up; the people I sold it to left
sometime in the 1980s. I took a taxi to see it the last time I was
in the District and couldn't even bear to get out of the car.)

I'm not used to Tonya and her exuberance of love. She finds
my clothes hilarious. I still wear a tie most days, a shirt and tie
underneath a V-neck sweater, the same clothes I've worn all my
life, and I find no reason to stop now; but she's unused to it, no
adult in her life wears a tie. Jayson might put one on on a very
special occasion, but he's a California Casual surgeon: most of
the time when she sees him he's leaving for work in scrubs, or
coming back from the gym in workout clothes. I don't know
why I'm telling you these things, why you would be interested,
except that you want to know everything, you seem hungry for
details of all kinds.

I'll say this much: it's in the back of my mind, all the
time, the question of what it would have been like to have a
white-appearing child, or what it would be like to meet my
apparently-white biological grandchildren, with their strange
and austere names, Winter, Bering, Patrick. It's hurtful. I feel
the anger coming back. I've felt so angry at myself, for that one
half-hour of weakness, and so ashamed, and angry at you for
bringing all this up again, though I tell you at the same time
that I respect you as a scientist, I respect your allegiance to the

facts, if not your "right" to them. And I extend a kind of love to you, which itself probably feels quite austere, but I assure you it is love. These are three separate responses, and not one of them, at this moment, takes precedence over the others. That doesn't count as much of a response, or perhaps it does.

Yours, John

FEELING TIME

"Si sospechas algo," Winter had been saying to Yunque Ruíz, the phone pinched between her temple and right shoulder, "si sospechas *alguna* acción illegal, lo mas importante es tener la prueba. Proof. Con la ley lo que es necesario es proof, no sospechar. ¿Entiendes, Yunque?" Her desk was wobbling, as it always seemed to in the mornings, and she was down on her knees trying to fix it, in jeans, her blouse riding up, her ass crack visible for anyone to see through the open door, when she heard the low, otherworldly ring of a rotary phone. It was Skype, it was Patrick calling from Berlin. "Sí," Yunque was saying, "es exactamente lo que yo digo, pero—" "Perdón," she had to say, "Yunque, te llamo más tarde, OK?" She banged her head against the edge of the desk but still hauled herself into the chair, blew out a breath, clicked *Accept*.

"What's up?"

"What's *up*?"

It was as if he were in the next room. Or the same room. One office to another. Her big brother, in his corporate-drone disguise, a navy button-down and steel-rimmed glasses. She couldn't help thinking everything he wore was a costume, sported ironically, any more than she could help wanting to say *you're getting older*. Which he was: almost forty. Silver tints in his stubble; deeper dents in the crow's feet. Still thin, nearly skeletal, but in a way that was maybe less immediately alarming. Or maybe she was finally getting used to it. It was sunny in Berlin; she could see half a window's worth of blue sky.

"So I got this call from Mom saying *Dad's on his way to Vermont and he's not coming back*. What the hell's going on, Win?"

"Sorry. Say that again."

She closed her eyes, just then feeling the head rush. Avoid swift movements, she'd read somewhere. As the baby grows, your inner ear is constantly realigning your center of gravity.

"Which part, the part about Dad leaving Mom for good?"

"I'm sorry," she said, "I was just on a call. My mind is in two places at once. I'm having trouble taking this in. Tell me exactly what Mom said Dad said?"

He explained. She tilted her head back and closed her eyes again, surely annoying him, though he kept going without saying anything.

Just that morning she'd been thinking, randomly, about a tiny detail in *The Shiva Hypothesis:* the feeling-time paradox, Naomi called it. Humans understand time intellectually but can't actually feel it passing in the body. As opposed to other organisms—bats intuit the speed of sound, that's how echolocation works, also some single-celled organisms, primitive ones, who are aware of both their environment in the present and a few seconds before. Even whales, hearing calls from miles away, can feel how long the sound has traveled. For humans, apparently, this is a critically lost aptitude. *On a moment-to-moment level*—that was the tone of the whole book, that popular-science certainty—*humans think they're immortal; the only exception might be when a woman knows she's pregnant.* She was thinking about that line while grabbing the headboard to steady herself; she gets head rushes all the time now, but especially first thing in the morning. How it feels to finally be the exception. The expectant one, who sees time as a curve sickeningly turning back upon itself. As the novel itself curves, the double curve, around her belly and what it holds. From within you can't see a novel's future any more or less than a baby's future, or, for that matter, the curvature of the Earth.

"Hello? I can't see you. Are you there, Win?"

"I have no idea what's going on with Mom and Dad," she said. "You know more than I do. I haven't heard from either one of them in—well, I don't even remember when. Weeks."

"Well—now you know."

A ping on her desktop, another unfamiliar sound: it was a new computer, the office had just gotten a grant, and she hadn't had time to configure it the way she liked. *Your Inbox Is Over Quota.* Three hundred forty-two new messages.

"The last time I saw Mom," she said, "I told her that I had to draw the line somewhere with her, that I didn't have to listen to her telling me one more time that I was wasting my life."

"She doesn't believe in racial justice," he said. "She's an apocalypticist. It's like she's a Jehovah's Witness, only with a PhD and a sense of irony."

"I know that. I'm just explaining why she didn't call me first. We're not on speaking terms at the moment, I guess, officially."

"I asked her if she wanted me to come home, like right now, and she acted as if that was an insane suggestion. Instead she started talking about how the apartment is unoccupied and if I don't move back from Berlin we're going to lose it."

"You can't expect her to say anything coherent about her own emotional needs. That's not who she is."

"Of course. Obviously. But I still feel like we have to do something, right? At least make sure Dad is okay. We can't let this pass without, without—I don't know. At least hearing from both of them."

It was so like him, she wanted to say, to express interest and then stop speaking in midsentence. A person of obscure motives, maybe even to himself. Frantically needing to get in touch, then not calling for weeks, months. A post-genius condition, was the phrase she often used, mentally, as a place marker. Of course he still *was* a genius; only his arrogance had been shattered, and replaced with, well, whatever this was. Tiptoeing between interest and neutrality.

All the time, in life, she wants someone to hear her observing these things, a third party. Her third party has disappeared. Hence, the novel, absorber of inner monologues. The novel listens when no one else will.

"I'm sorry, Trick," she said, "I have so much to say on this subject, you have no idea, but I also have a client who needs me right now. Like, *now* is too late. She's suing ICE for assault, rather her husband is, he's at urgent care with two broken fingers."

"Jesus Christ. Then go. It's two in the morning here; I've got all night."

It was beginning to come to her: time is different now. This is the time of my parents' separating. I'm allowed to be melodramatic, the way he's being, and fall out of my life. *Allowed by whom,* though, was an excellent question, a question she wished the novel would answer.

"No, fuck it," she said. "I keep meaning to call you, and call them, too, I actually have important things to discuss, preceding this, believe it or not, and I can't keep putting it off. It's not as if this is going away. I have to operate in multiple, overlapping, absurd time frames, like everyone else caught up in this shitstorm of a state of emergency."

"That's what you're calling it?"

"We're too busy to come up with an official term. All I know is I've got fifty-two cases on my desk right now. That's a figure of speech. The number changes every day and I'd need a desk the size of a basketball court."

"Last time you said that the media stuff was overblown, and it's hardly worse than Obama, from where you sit."

"Trick, that was nine months ago, when they were just getting started. The new rule is zero tolerance at the border, plus incentives to agents for literally hunting people down. I've never seen anything like it. And when you hear an immigration attorney say *I've never seen anything like it,* pay attention. It's all about heads in beds. They're running up the numbers any way they can. Shock and awe. That's an ICE agent talking, not me. He said that to my client's face, two weeks ago."

"Does it affect Zeno?"

"Of course it affects him. He's undocumented like anyone else."

"I just thought, as a lawyer, I mean you obviously have used his case to his best advantage—"

"That mattered under Obama. It doesn't now. It's the fucking Wild West. They're committed to getting rid of all the brown people, basically, it's no more nuanced than that, and they'll detain anyone who fits the profile—don't get me started. I feel like I'll choke if I talk about it too long. It's the air I breathe, but I don't have to *talk* about it all the time. How's your health these days, Trick, anyway?"

"Fine. Better. My weight's stable; I've got protein shakes I can stand, for once. No issues."

"Well thank god for that."

She let her eyes travel away from the screen, angled her face a half turn, so she could take in the bulletin board with its manila pockets for every hearing scheduled in the next month. Thirty days, sixty-two hearings. Cortez/Wong. Achitwonsaree/Singh. Hernandez/Rodriguez. Akbar/Park.

"You know, I'm glad Dad left," she said.

"Don't say that."

"The healthy choice," she said, "the only healthy alternative, when you're married to a fucking *banshee,* somebody you've spent your entire adult life compensating for, not to mention constructing a huge anthill of codependency, when your entire body is just layers of scar tissue that shred and shear off so much you're like a leper, maybe still you can wake up one day, something can hit you, and you realize that you've still got a decade or so of reasonably healthy joints, but only that, and so you're off. It could actually be that simple, Trick. I know that nothing else about our family has ever been simple. And we wear that as a point of pride. So? Dad's the only one left at home. And that is a sucky place to be. He doesn't want to be the custodian of our old sorrows. For god's sake, let him go."

"That's giving him a lot of credit."

"I'm not interested in giving anyone credit. I'm just saying we, or rather they, should drop the pretense and move on. Without getting into the thorny question of whether they ever loved one another. Something had to happen, Trick, for god's sake, we've all become so ossified. He deserves happiness on his own terms, god knows, whatever they are."

"And Mom's happiness?"

"If you ask me, she sounds like she's living her best life. Happy as a clam on Cape Cod. Her resentments keep her company."

"That's not at all the way she sounded."

"I'll call her. I have to call her. Whatever, I'll try to be a good listening ear and sort this out. Don't buy a plane ticket yet."

"Good. That's all anyone expects of you."

"You're not letting me finish," she said. The novel gives her a breath, a semicolon; it fills a space on the page with air. "Circumstances have changed, dear brother. And, though it's so like them to take up all the oxygen in the room, I have to share it with you, anyway. I'm pregnant."

"No you're not."

"I so fucking am. I have been hurling like you wouldn't believe."

"Now I'm the one having a hard time taking it in."

"You mean you thought the world had ended and that meant no one was having babies anymore, that we were all committed to ending the horror of the bourgeois family reduplicating itself, the sheer banality of procreation. It may be hard for you to believe, but people stopped buying that line about ten years ago. Parenting is cool again."

"Do you even have any idea what you're saying right now?"

"I'll just say it in my own words, Trick: there's nothing wrong, politically, with being happy. Quite the opposite. That may not be very intellectual of me, or very Buddhist, although somehow they manage to reproduce, too, when no one's looking. Having a baby with Zeno may be the most meaningful thing I ever do. It's quite likely, actually."

"You haven't even paused to let me say congratulations."

"Is that what you wanted to say?"

"I think it's possible to have serious reservations," he said, "even fatal reservations, about the nuclear family, and still want children. And be happy when other people have them. It's one of the strange paradoxes of our age."

"*I* believe in families," she said, "in the sense that I don't believe in keeping children from knowing their relatives, their points of origin, so to speak, as unfortunate and fucked up as they undoubtedly are, it's bigger than me or me and you, and we've seen the consequences of secrecy and outright lying and denial in that regard, and I'm not repeating it. And therefore we have to reconstitute ourselves, somehow. We have to be in the same room. I can't believe I'm saying this, and saying it *now,* one second after Dad administers the coup de grâce, but Zeno and I are getting married, and all three of you need to be there."

"When?"

"*When?*" She was shocked, momentarily, by the banality of the question. When does one have a wedding? "August," she said.

"In Providence?"

"Eghh. No. No one wants to be in Providence in August. In Blue Hill."

"You're getting married in Maine, in Blue Hill, *this August,* that is, four months from now. And I'm supposed to come? I can't, anyway. We have a major project due in August, and quarterlies."

"That's the dumbest excuse I've ever heard. It doesn't even demand a response, that's how dumb it is."

"I'll cut to the chase, then. Winter, babe, it's the thing itself. Marriage, I can't support it."

"You have got to be fucking kidding me."

"I can *live* with it. I will love my niece. Or nephew. You know I love Zeno. But I can't stand up there and uphold it. I can't stand to watch you break that glass in the napkin and have someone give the little speech about the tiny splinters of light and tikkun olam and l'dor va'dor and all that supreme bullshit, how it all goes on, handed down generation to generation, that sanctimonious murderous lie."

What if we wanted a Catholic wedding, she wanted to say. Her eyes were wet, not surprisingly; she wiped them with a Kleenex from the client box, wondering why it took this long. Would that be better. A liberation theology wedding, a Zapatista wedding. Probably that could be arranged. Would that be acceptable, would it be actually kind of cool and exotic. If familiarity is the problem, if the concern is repeating the past, carrying the Wilcox stain, the family curses, forward another generation, which god knows is also my concern. Why couldn't she just tell him that. We don't disagree. Which is not the same thing as agreeing.

"I'm not going to cry on the phone with you," she said. "But I have to say, after everything, Trick, why do I have to be disappointed in *you*? Again? Answer me that."

"I hate to put it this way," he said, "but I forgot to tell you the kicker. There's no way you're planning a wedding this summer. Dad claims he's taken a three-month vow of silence."

"What the fuck does that mean?"

"Just what I said. He said he'll talk to her on July eleventh."

"Like hell he gets to pack his things, leave the city, leave Mom, and take a vow of silence. That's a vow of *you can't hold me accountable*. I'm going to find him and make him talk to me, even if I have to drive all the way up to Craftsbury myself."

"Good. I'm glad to hear you say that."

"And if I can convince the parents, will you come then?"

"The two things aren't connected."

She wasn't even angry. At moments of great stress, anger leaves her. That makes her a lawyer. One kind of lawyer, anyway. She becomes slow and effortful. An amorphous, surrounding thing. A middle child. Soft at the center.

"You realize you're making a terrible mistake," she said. "A, a *rupture*."

"A small one, probably, in the greater scheme of things. You just said yourself that you believe in families, didn't you? We have to reconstitute ourselves. So we will, eventually. Once the dust has settled. You get married, Mom and Dad get divorced, things sort themselves out, I try to get a little healthier, a little stronger, then in two or three years I'll come for a low-stakes visit. I promise."

"In other words, the Wilcoxes keep hobbling along, pretending to have meaningful relationships, as pissed-off as ever, never actually speaking face-to-face, until we're all dead. The only rupture is death. Death is the only way to end this argument."

"I guess that's the glass-half-empty way of putting it."

"People who die alone are miserable, Trick. That's a bit of conventional wisdom I believe is borne out in fact."

"That's what you're predicting for me, then? That's what you worry about."

"Isn't it what everyone worries about?"

"You know, probably, or you *knew*, because I explained it to you, that I have a lot of training in thinking about death. Three years of it. We spend time anticipating it. Rehearsing it. It's a core practice for Gelug monks. The Six Yogas of Naropa."

"That doesn't really mean anything to me."

"Because you're not an internally directed person. A meditator, a yogi. And that's fine. No one expects you to be. But I am. Or at least I was. And the thing is, for me, death is an interior event. We can't control the outer circumstances. I'm not really focused on the *manner* of my death, like whether I'm ninety-three and surrounded by my children and grandchildren in some nice hospice place on East Ninety-Third with flowers and a harpist. Because I've actually already experienced death many times. I've practiced it. I'm comfortable with it. Why are you crying?"

"I don't suppose you can imagine why I'd be crying, contemplating the death of one of my siblings, the day my parents announce they're getting divorced."

"What I'm telling you is, don't worry about me. Psychologically. Be angry with me, sure, but don't think I'll wind up in a room somewhere gumming TV dinners and watching *Judge Judy*. It sounds weird, but I have death under control."

"Now that's an image I have to scrub out of my mind."

"You know what you should do," he said, as if the thought had just occurred to him, "you and Zeno should move to Mexico. We have a software developer from Mexico City, Simón, he says it's great. Not nearly as dangerous as the media makes it out to be. Incredible architecture, food. Insanely cheap, by your standards. I mean Mexico City, I don't know about the rest of the country. Presumably you wouldn't want to move back to Chiapas."

"*This* is how you change the subject?"

"You and Zeno have never talked about it?"

"Yes, you inscrutable, affectless shit, we have talked about it. In fact we kind of have a plan in place."

"Obviously, with what Zeno does for a living—"

"The thing is, yes, and yes, we could both find jobs, of a sort, it's not as if there isn't work for U.S. immigration lawyers in Mexico. It's always in the back of our minds. He could get picked up tomorrow, the way things are with ICE right now. He has a DUI from 2011, not even a conviction, but it doesn't matter. But he loves it here. Actually loves it, I mean Providence, specifically. New England. It speaks to his soul. I'm not joking. He's an immigrant, not a migrant. That isn't true of everyone and it shouldn't have to be. But Zeno is the real thing. He has American feelings. Seriously, it's scary at times."

"That is scary."

"Right now he's reading *Moby-Dick*. Listening to it, I mean. He finds the English a little hard to follow on the page but on tape he loves it."

"And shouldn't that be enough? You, Zeno, and the white whale? You're about to have a baby, you're starting over. Why stage a wedding, a big heternormative performance, when you already have everything you want? You don't need our affirmation, and you're not going to get it, so why bother? Why do the rest of us even matter?"

She had to turn away from the screen and take a breath. I have never won an argument with you, not once in my life, she wanted to say. But this time I have the authority. I am bearing a child. Shut up and respect me. You can hate people and still need them. The proof is that I'm here talking to you.

"The thing is," she said, "death is not actually an interior event. No matter what you say, Trick, in your yogic wisdom. Not in this family. Death is not private, and neither is life. How you live and die matters to me, and apart from all your bullshit, vice versa. It also matters in the world. Take it from someone who's waiting, literally, *waiting*, for her husband to be imprisoned, brutalized, and deported. It's odd, frankly, as a Buddhist, that you can't grasp how these things are connected. I'm not leaving you alone on this. Mom and Dad can get divorced if they want. It's probably healthy. But you are not dead to me. Don't insult me by saying you're comfortable with dying and I shouldn't worry about it. Don't insult Bering's memory. Showing up for my wedding is the least you can do."

He sipped something out of a bottle, nonchalant. Showing off his bone structure, the cut of his jaw, his objectively beautiful—one could even say chiseled—face. On which all emotions were visible. And therefore, since boyhood, he had practiced being impassive, even slack, looking into space, betraying nothing. I have gotten to you, ha ha, she wanted to say. I've cornered you. I finally win. Only big brothers never lose, they just invalidate the game.

"Call me if you find someone who *actually* wants to be there," he said. "I can't be the first."

/

Because she needs to get up and walk every fifteen minutes or so, because she can somehow feel the baby's tiny weight already bearing down on the base of her spine, because, talking to Patrick, her feet have fallen asleep, as if all her extremities would rather withdraw from her body, she takes long, deliberate strides down the carpeted hall, hands on her hips, carefully avoiding the waiting room. Every phone, it seems to her, is ringing. Everyone else in today—six attorneys, three staff—is either with a client or on the phone.

In the waiting room, through the doors at the other end of the hall—her office is near the front—at least fifteen people sit for their turn. Every chair is taken. Leona and Jill, their front-desk assistants, keep count; at the most crowded they've seen nearly fifty people in the waiting room and waiting in a line or in groups outside. Though no one, these days, would wait outside. ICE patrols the streets around the clinic, the rumors go, and could swoop in at any moment. Inside the building, inside a lawyer's office, everyone is protected. This is only approximately true, but no one wants to test the theory.

Which is an indication of just how fast the rule of law has evaporated, she's thinking, at the same time feeling exquisitely guilty for getting up from her desk in the first place. She doesn't have another client in the waiting room at the moment; instead she has about ten hours of paperwork to do in four hours, before the federal filing deadline at three. On top of which she's supposed to be standing in for Louis Chen, who's down at the city courthouse waiting for three clergy, arrested on Monday, to be released. A pastor, a reverend, and Sister Frances, who spent thirty nights in city jail last year, a new record. Louis's clients have been notified, but sometimes calls, emails, and texts don't reach them; there could always be a floater, an anxious client who shows up anyway, just to have a safe place to be.

The waiting room.

A Bengali grandmother, her sari wrapped over her head, and her H-1B son, his spouse-visa wife, their U.S.-born four-year-old twins, pounding on matching iPads. Three sisters from Oaxaca, housecleaners, one with a green card, two sin papeles, seven children between them. A Sudanese man who can find no suit to fit him at TJ Maxx, so he keeps fingering the hems of his pants, wishing they were longer. Haitians and Croatians, Eritreans and Bhutanese Nepalis. Ten years as an immigration lawyer and she's met people of every nationality on Earth, even ones she couldn't place on the map immediately: Guinea-Bissau, Ladakh, Suriname. Northern Europeans only rarely make it to New Americans of Rhode Island, but they do come, too, often attached to someone more predictably a client: a Swiss man married to a Sri Lankan, a Norwegian senior at Brown who's fallen in love with her Ugandan roommate.

She can't face them. She enters the office by the back door, ostensibly closer to her parking space, which irritates Leona and Jill to no end; they never know when she's at her desk, so she texts Leona every morning: *I'm here.* I want so badly to help them, she told Lourdes, the last time they talked, but there are so many of them now and I'm still the same person. Actually less the same person, since the baby eats 6 percent of your brain.

Because there are only so many ways I can say *I don't know.*

We have to wait and see.

It depends on what happens at the hearing.

It depends on where you fall in line.

It depends on how high they set the bail.

This is the way the law works, she wishes she could tell them, this is its structure, it decrees that each individual, each case, is its own particular well of despair, oppressed by circumstances that seem explicable to no one, not even lawyers, who handle cases like it every day. She regularly meets families who've lived their whole lives in soul-corroding limbo, convinced they're the only ones. Every one with a different status. Dad is sin papeles, Mom has a green card, one kid U.S.-born, one a Dreamer, one a Dreamer in the Marines. *Depende.* This is a whole lifetime, a skein, of *depende.* Each one, each person, marked by the will of the state, a change in the national mood. A lottery, an amnesty. A need. A fit of anger. You could say that the system exists to create a contingent and precarious labor force with few or no legal protections, that its absurdities are all by design, that it's analogous, yes, to chattel slavery and the breaking apart of families in the slave trade, that capitalism depends on *sub jura* populations to exploit, that's what Zeno believes. Or that's what Zeno believes his mother would have believed. How a Zapatista would describe Trump: just the least imaginative American politician ever, he said, the one who's too lazy to think up excuses, euphemisms, and metaphors, so he just tells the truth.

She can't go there. She doesn't believe in world-harnessing theories. Too much has changed, she says, the system is too porous, too haphazard. Follow the profits, he says. Then why are you here, she wants to know.

I followed them and found you, he says, I was ensnared, which is of course also by design. When you think it's just human messiness, look at where the profits are going.

Yolanda, like her, is standing up, shoes off, doing lunges with her phone headset loose around her neck. "Winter," she calls out, "c'mere, I need some moral support."

"Only if you have chocolate."

"It's in the top left drawer. Listen, our Mailchimp account is frozen again. I've got a major funders email ready to go and it keeps saying 'server not found.'"

"Restart the browser. Restart the router."

"That's what they teach you at Yale Law?"

"*This* is what you have? Kit Kats? Snack-size Milky Ways?"

"I stole them from Perry's goodie bags. He had three birthday parties last weekend. A four-year-old shouldn't eat that much sugar in a month."

She collapses onto the love seat—Yolanda, the director, the only one with an office big enough for actual furniture—and says, before she can stop herself, "So, my parents are separating."

"Shut up."

"And Zeno and I are getting married. I decided that, five minutes ago. Come on, tell me something, distract me."

"We've got a hundred protestors from Sanctuary due at the federal building at six and we need someone to get on the mic. Other than me."

"Keep going."

"Heads up on a raid at the Ruby Tuesday at the Kingston Service Plaza, but it may just be a rumor. The bail fund's down to our last five thousand and we have thirty-nine requests. Tricia called me and said Furstein is on the bench Friday through Wednesday."

"Fuck. She's so slow."

"She's slow, and her interpreter is a nightmare. You know, the guy from Madrid who claims he can't understand Central American Spanish."

"I thought we filed a complaint on that guy."

"She won't touch him."

"And we need someone to do accompaniment trainings on Monday and Tuesday night at the Unitarian Church."

"This isn't helping."

"You need a hug."

"I need one, but I can't stand up."

Yolanda doesn't sit; she swoops, folds her head against her capable, CrossFit-toned shoulders, half smothering, half arousing. "Poor baby," she says, "my god, I mean that's the thing, we're in a state of fucking emergency here, and yet life goes on, doesn't it. Babies still get born. People fall in love and split up and all that shit. You're just dealing with life on every level. You can't have any more or less life, right?"

"This is why you're good at giving speeches."

"Don't try to get out of it. You're my mascot. My pregnant mama lawyer who's going to say *families belong together*. You just need to work on sticking the belly out a little more. I need a good picture for the Facebook page."

"I'm really bad at public appearances."

"You're an immigration lawyer and this is fucking D-Day, pobrecita, I know you feel like shit and this isn't exactly what you signed up for, but it's all hands on deck. Don't tell me your dad is trying to screw your mom out of all his assets or whatever."

"No," she says. "It's not like that. She's fine. She's better than fine. Financially. Just alienating as all hell, is all. This has been in the works for, like, forty—"

And there they are, the tears.

"I'm sorry," she says, after Yolanda has handed her a second box of tissues.

"This is why we buy them at Costco."

"I'm a mess. I'm a puddle."

"I would say take the day, but that's not an option. Take lunch. Seriously. Go home now and come back by two. You're lucky, you live close. Call Zeno. He should be with you at a time like this."

"He's not driving anymore."

"Then go pick him up."

"No," she says, despairing of explaining anything, "he's *at* home, he's insulating the attic. If he had his way he'd wrap the whole house in plastic. Says he's going to cut our gas bill by two-thirds."

"Good man. He's nesting."

"When he should be packing."

"Jesus Christ, don't say things like that, you'll bring the evil eye."

/

Ronaldo Quiñones was in a traffic accident, T-boned by a limo full of drunk bachelorettes on the way to Newport, absolutely not his fault in any way, but he slugged the driver, who called him a wetback, and accordingly is being held at Wyatt with a very fragile hold on immediate deportation to Paraguay. He's not actually Paraguayan; he's a Paraguayan national because his drunken, abusive sailor father was. He grew up in Sonora. Three kids, and Juana is expecting number four. Also under order of eviction.

Green Clean Makeup Cleansing Balm, 1.7 ounces for $23.99. She's used it before; she slips it into her tote bag without reading the label. Burt's Bees men's deodorant; Zeno likes it, though he'd never pay for it, at $8.99 for one stick. Three of them, into the bag.

It's appallingly easy, if you're wearing business clothes, if you're a thirtyish white-appearing lady stopped at Rite Aid, clearly in a hurry, with a reusable shopping bag: the mark of the righteous. No one checks. You simply forget to place every single item on the counter. Your attention is elsewhere. Your phone is buzzing. There are security cameras and theft-detection devices in these stores, but something even more powerful than technology is at work, she's thinking, which is the vital power of not giving a shit. The girl at checkout is no more than seventeen, with a grown-out purple dye job, heavy eye makeup, and wobbly lips, probably because she needs dental work. She makes eleven dollars an hour, tops. Alone, stranded, in the front, with a manager stocking Doritos and two pharmacists in the back. You can't bully a worker like that into taking an interest in the marginal losses from theft. Suburban drugstores don't have security guards.

Revlon Volume + Length Mascara, excellent for court dates.

Tom's of Maine toothpaste, peppermint gel. That she'll pay for. She supports Tom's of Maine.

Ronaldo's case rests on an evidentiary hearing about the traffic accident. The key is to petition for a stay on deportation based on his necessity as a witness, though immigration judges very rarely give a shit about principal criminal cases once deportation orders are in effect.

The one to get is obviously Gupta, though she's been sick for a month, and every immigration lawyer in Providence is terrified she'll retire or die before Trump leaves office.

I'm getting married, is a thought she could be having. I've chosen my wedding day.

My parents, married since 1974, are divorcing.

Why divorcing and not getting divorced? She prefers the single active verb. A divorce is a legal decree, yes, but that's secondary; what matters, according to her, suddenly an expert, is the emotional gesture or movement of divorcing, putting distance between.

This is a day I'm not allowed to forget, would be one way of putting it.

She remembers, strangely, randomly, going with Patrick and Bering to the Duane Reade on the corner of Seventy-Seventh—farther than they were allowed to go by themselves, technically, two whole blocks, but they didn't have to cross Broadway and Dad knew the manager. While Patrick stood up front choosing candy, trying to stretch his two or three dollars as far as they would go, she took Bering by the hand to the cosmetics aisle. They walked very seriously past the mascara and lipstick and blush, making their choices. Why has she never brought back this particular scene before? They never contemplated stealing makeup—they had no real interest in makeup, not at that age—only in studying the mechanics of adulthood. Just old enough to read the labels.

It does happen, after fifteen years: she forgets Bering's face at certain ages, the timbre of her voice, the warmth of her small hand. Mostly the voice, which was once her voice. They were so close in age, their sounds were indistinguishable in the dark. A game they played: pretending to be each other when Bubbe and Zayde called. These are the kinds of things you would tell a therapist about, only she doesn't have one. The last therapist she saw was in New Haven, in law school; through some loophole Sandy got his insurance to cover it. They talked about this exact thing: the problem of time. How she would get old, and it would be fifty years since Bering died. More likely than not, she would be alive for that anniversary. Those multiple additional lifetimes. At that point what is your dead sister but a blur in an old photograph, she belongs to history.

A baby makes time circular, like a novel does. It has its own implications, she might say. Certain things become vivid, vibrant. The novel wants that. It bends the image forward.

"And a pack of American Spirits," she tells the girl behind the counter, pointing at the yellow pack she means. "And a lighter." Dangling the bag at waist level on two fingers, with $50 in unbought merchandise, just out of sight.

At the last minute, she adds a king-size Twix. Zeno loves them.

Juana, Ronaldo's wife, needs a stay of eviction, which Trevor, her intern, should have filed and copied her on. She hasn't seen it. It may have landed in her Junk folder.

"Twenty-one seventy-five," the girl says, expressionless, and she slides her card automatically into the slot, scoops up her purchases, and drops them into the bag. You have to be careful if you're stealing pills or tablets, anything that rattles; but in this case it's the smoothest sailing. Units arrive and leave. What does anything actually *cost*, when you're talking about Unilever or Luxe Brands?

"You know, you remind me of someone," the girl says now, suddenly. "You're not, like, *famous*, are you?"

"Me?"

"You were on TV."

"Oh! Yes. I was. I'm an immigration lawyer."

"My boyfriend posted it. He's a total kook for that stuff."

Her phone buzzes in her open purse, and she glances down: a message from Patrick.

Don't forget to call Mom, at least.

"Sorry," she says, distracted into politeness. "What stuff?"

"Oh, you know. Breitbart. The Daily Caller. Stormfront. Infowars."

Amanda, says her name tag. Underneath her uniform blouse the sleeves of her T-shirt read *Woonsocket UFD*. She's like Shelley Duvall in *The Shining*, wide-eyed, all hips and elbows. Who modeled her performance, it's said, on Squeaky Fromme, the girl from the Manson Family.

"And what about you?"

The girl looks from side to side and shrugs. "I'm down, I guess."

"Down with what?"

"*You* know." At her side, at hip level, the girl makes a circle with her thumb and forefinger, fans out the other three. "White pride."

Two minutes later she's escaped to the parking lot, the bag banging her knee, and a sound detonating inside her—or the absence of a sound, a concussion, she can almost feel it making her ears pop. For a moment she rests, propping herself against her car door. Holds her phone lightly, thumbing its impossible glass. "It's too much," she announces, hoarsely, to the assembled cars, a Civic, a Volvo, a Porsche Cayenne, a battered Saab.

Marriage, divorce, and Nazis.

Cracks the pack and slips a cigarette between her lips without lighting it, as if that ever helps.

Mom, she thinks, I could really use one. I could use a parent right now.

She balls and unballs her fists, tastes salt at the rear of her throat, and sweats in unexpected places. The backs of her knees. Not her palms but the webbing between her fingers. The crack of the ass.

"Incident report," she says to Yolanda's voicemail, once she's inside the car with the door closed. "I ID'd myself at the Rite Aid on Pemiwasset Spring Ave and the cashier told me, 'White pride.' And flashed her little gang sign."

It's reminding her of something, but she can't quite say what.

Now you'll know how Israelis feel.

She heard that saying the first time, probably every other New Yorker did, after 9/11. It was in the air. Spoken not by actual Israelis—she didn't, at that moment in her life, know any Israelis—but by other American Jews, those who'd been or had cousins or were for whatever reason on the Zionish side of the spectrum. People given to vicarious imaginings of themselves, however plural *themselves, ourselves, us,* under attack. Given to using, without attribution, the word *them.*

I need to turn these thoughts around to Ronaldo Quiñones, she's thinking, Ronaldo Quiñones, Ronaldo Quiñones, Ronaldo Quiñones.

It was true that she'd gotten death threats. Not as many as her parents, who had to alert the post office and the police, who had their landline disconnected for three months. Her yale.edu inbox was full of them; that's when she switched over to Yahoo. One or two came to her box at the law school. They all seemed inconsequential. They had nothing to do with actual death.

Also, she could have said, I don't care about dying. She well and truly didn't. Not during that first year. She walked across Elm Street in traffic. She veered across lanes on I-95. It was a symptom, someone told her, that indifference. She never used a condom—not with Aaron, or Colin, or Dave, or Murray. They never complained. The pill took care of babies. She got chlamydia twice. The nurses at Student Health talked to her sternly.

Just met an actual nazi at Rite Aid, she texts Lourdes. Tell me what to do.

I want to know what you mean when you say you've experienced death many times, she texts Patrick.

No one writes back. No one is there, in what used to be called, quaintly, cyberspace. The car is getting cold; she turns on the engine, adjusts the heat, makes sure the doors are locked.

If she calls, Zeno will come get her. He'll take a cab, because he can't drive. He'll drive her home, if circumstances absolutely dictate. He understands fascists, he understands Nazis. But he doesn't understand this. You don't see, or can't embrace, the worst horror of someone else's idiom, though it could kill you. He understands being excluded but not being included. She can't explain it. She can't explain why she can't explain it. Does this always happen, she wants to know, do we always want to protect the people we love from the truth about our shitty families. Which is the wrong way of putting it.

There was that one time in Jerusalem—they were being escorted out of the municipal court, there was a metal barricade and at least a hundred protestors behind it, and a man's arm shot out, she couldn't see his face, just the hairy hand, grasping at her, and Naomi, behind her, took the hand and twisted it. Like turning a key. The way in judo you learn to break someone's wrist. A policewoman pushed them away and shouted something in Naomi's face. They never talked about it afterward. It was immaterial. In a different story, in a different life, she's thinking, Naomi would have made an excellent soldier. Quick and matter-of-fact. No hesitation about inflicting pain.

She has *Mom* on the screen, under her thumb.

I can't bear for it to go on, this life, she wants to tell someone, this circle of pain and miserable excuses. These courtrooms, stations of the cross or circles of hell. I am not raising a child in this nightmare of a country.

The number rings and goes to voicemail. She holds the phone away from her ear, so as not to have to hear the message, and waits for the beep.

"Hi, Mom. Patrick told me what happened. Maybe you were planning to call tomorrow or something. I don't know. It would be pretty sad if you felt you couldn't call me at all. But maybe that *is* how you feel. In any case, I tried Dad's cell, but it just went to voicemail. I'm guessing there's no signal in Craftsbury. I can't quite wrap my mind around it."

The voicemail beeps. Filled up.

"What I meant to say was," she says, next voicemail, "we have let ourselves get so fucked up as a family. We are not even, recognizably, a family.

"And you know it's not about Bering and it's not *not* about Bering. We are so chronically inflamed. I know you hate hearing these diagnoses. Whatever. I don't care."

"What I'm calling to say is," she says, next voicemail, "I'm pregnant. Only eleven weeks. Anything could happen. But you're allowed to tell your mother.

"Also, Zeno and I are getting married. In Blue Hill. In August. You're expected there. So is Patrick. So is Dad. Zeno's dad is coming, all the way from Chiapas.

"But that's not the really important thing. To hear the really important thing, you have to call me. I'm not saying it on a recording."

Now she can drive. She is driving. She is moving, the novel is moving. It is unrelenting. The next moment is always required. I am thirty-seven years old, she says to no one, making a left on Parker and a quick right on Wilmot to avoid the long line of cars already outside the elementary school. I'm thirty-seven years old with an Ivy League law degree. My husband-to-be is skilled in a dozen building trades and could build a house from scratch. We will have a healthy, beautiful baby.

And, she's thinking, I have money. Not much, in the greater scheme of things, but also a staggering amount, in the greater scheme of things. Money to buy a house or an apartment in another country. Transition money. Expatriation money. Money that makes options, money with options attached.

Which is something they never talk about. Their financial lives have very little overlap. Only when she saw how much cash he was keeping in the house—bundles of twenties, thick as books!—she bought him a safe at Home Depot. His transfers home are a complicated arrangement he's worked out with Nestor. His phone is prepaid. He uses transferable debit cards. He's never bought anything online. No social media, just WhatsApp, which is how they text and call one another, mostly. Nothing in America has changed him.

America, the one thing I can't give him, the one thing that can't be bought.

/

From: "Naomi Schifrin Wilcox" < nwilcox4@columbia.edu>Date: April 15, 2018 at 11:48:35 AM EST

To: "Winter Wilcox" <wwilcox@newamericansRI.org>

Subject: your message

Winter, I rec'd your phone message. Thank you for calling.

I have no further information about your father's whereabouts. I suggest you ask him, though he told me he is taking a "vow of silence," terms not defined, therefore he may not answer his phone. The number at the temple in Craftsbury is (was?) 784–3812. Area code 802.

If you would like to meet, I suggest we choose a mutually convenient location. Halfway between Providence and Woods Hole gets us to approximately Fall River. Why don't you choose a coffee shop or someplace equivalent and let me know. I can meet you most days in the midafternoons around three or four. Suggest a day and I will get back to you.

Mom

THE WEATHER

He works in attics and basements, on long ladders, the occasional roof-top. Weatherizing, energy efficiency, retrofitting, and solar panels. Better than hauling timbers or welding girders, let alone wheelbarrows of sod or cement, all of which he has done. Nothing heavier than a new set of windows. It appeals to his cast of mind. The laws of thermodynamics in action, for one thing. The conservation of matter. Providence with its bottomless supply of leaky wood-frame houses, brittle as dry bones, to be stuffed and sealed and caulked and reinforced, cutting a heating bill by two-thirds, paid for in tax rebates over fifteen years. Wilbur does the sales patter, in the kitchen, while he and Jorge take the measurements. Wilbur takes the checks, and of course, pays them in cash. Sixteen an hour. It used to be twelve; then Wilbur ran into him with Winter, randomly, crossing a parking lot on Watkins Glen between the Bowl-a-Rama and Pho 909, and Zeno said, Hey, Wilbur, this is my girlfriend, and Wilbur said, Pleased to meet you, I didn't think you lived around here, Zeno, and Winter said, Oh no, I work there, and pointed across the road to the New Americans clinic with its sign, *Ayuda Gratis por Inmigrantes*.

And the next week he and Jorge got a raise.

Their house, Winter's house, at the top of Smith Hill, had single-pane windows from 1954 when she bought it; he found a bill of sale under a moldy valise in the basement. Window-unit air conditioners kept in place with wadded paper cups, folded newspapers wrapped in masking tape. Mouse nests in the ducts and a cheap no-name insulation job in the attic, eighteen-inch layers when it should have been twenty-four. You've got thirty thousand dollars of work to do here, he said, and she wailed, *They said it was move-in condition, so I moved in.* Now it's nearly done. New windows, samples he begged from the Andersen sales guy. Central air humming on its gravel pad next to the compost bin. A new furnace, a new boiler: Wilbur put dibs on them when his cousin sold out of the HVAC business. Energy Star rated, best in class. Wilbur's other cousin Bill does solar, and could get him an enormous discount, plus free labor: Jorge's brothers Luís and Felipe work for him. But the Historic District won't allow panels on the roof and the backyard is 80 percent shade.

There are houses in Germany and Sweden with two-foot walls, triple-insulated windows, air locks, geothermal wells, that require no energy whatsoever. Even the ventilation is passive. Add solar to that and you have a house that sustains itself, that exists out of time, let alone the fluctuations of the energy market. Wilbur's office gets a pile of magazines every month, for the waiting room he doesn't have: *Popular Mechanics, Environmental Engineer, Glass Monthly,* and weirdly, *Utne Reader, Mother Earth News.* Take all that shit, Wilbur says, and he does, he takes them and fans them out on their glass coffee table, a Pottery Barn closeout for $50. In Chiapas, he told her once, you could build a house with reclaimed wood, insulate it with compressed biomass—banana leaves, palm fronds—power it with solar, use the solar to run an evaporator plus a rainwater collector, build a composting toilet, and you'd have a place that would run forever for $10,000.

And she said, "You sound like one of my interns."

"What does that mean?"

"Better living through innovation. You should write up a grant proposal and get someone to fund it. People would be all over it. You should write a book."

"I don't want to write a book. I want to build a house."

"You could build a thousand houses. Why do it just once and not tell anyone?"

"Because I don't have the money."

"It's not about money. I mean, yes, it is about money, but I'm not saying you should be a property developer, I'm saying you should start a nonprofit, an aid project, a development project. I'm saying you could be a *social entrepreneur*."

"My mother was a Maoist, remember?"

"Okay, but are *you* a Maoist?"

"He lifted a lot of people out of poverty. He emancipated half a billion women."

"We're seriously having an argument about the pros and cons of Mao? That's what you want to talk about?"

"In Chiapas people take Mao pretty seriously, you know."

"Yes. I know."

"And they're not big on international aid projects, because that's neo-imperialism."

("Where did you learn to speak English like that?" She'd heard him talking to Wilbur on the phone, in the doorway of her office: it was a lunchtime appointment, he had to take the call, in case Jorge was sick again. He saw the remains of a chocolate cupcake in a crumpled napkin on the desk and a smear of frosting across the tip of her nose. Instead of answering the question, he levered himself across the desk and flicked it away. "Sorry," he said, and then, for no reason at all, "You have a really pretty nose.")

/

Zeno, Jorge says, the problem is, you have too many things you *don't* believe in. This is true. This has always been true. Tortuguita, his father used to say, when he crossed his arms, drew up his knees, and refused to move, tortuguita, sal de tu caparazón, and knock hard with his knuckles on his head. Respeta mi autonomía! he would shout back, a word Mama taught him. Child of a communist and a literary critic— his father raised his eyes to heaven—the worst of every possible world. Nothing can ever be *simple*. He says to Jorge, I'm not really an immigrant, I'm a transient. *Immigration* is old-fashioned. I could wind up anywhere.

He hasn't wanted to admit it to Jorge, to anyone—with Winter nearly in her third month—that he was right all along. The three-legged stool, Jorge says. Papers. Money. Kids. It doesn't really matter what order they come in. But you have to have all three. That's the future, that's the goal.

Jorge is from Sinaloa and very philosophical, and also has a weak heart, an aortal valve prolapse, and is also a master whistler, a virtuoso of whistling. He can whistle the Bell Song from *The Marriage of Figaro*; he does "Cucurrucucú Paloma." All day, working side by side: he never repeats himself. Banda, norteño, old ballads, Taylor Swift. Whatever Lisa is listening to, he says, talking about Lisabeta, his oldest, I hear it once and whistle it back. Drives her crazy. It's all just melodies, he says, except for that garbage, rap and reggaetón, I tell her to turn that off if she wants to stay in my house.

He says, the way you speak English, you should already be running a business, not listening to old books on tape. As if you need to improve when you're already fluent. *I* should be listening to the books, not letting Lisa translate for me everywhere, here I am thirteen years in the U.S. and I'm still too shy to order a pizza.

And he says, Jorge, look, I'm still paperless just like you, just like everyone else.

Not for long you're not.

She's not a miracle worker.

Her dad's a big-time lawyer in New York, you told me, right? A Jew.

What does that have to do with it.

Jews have connections. They're the ones who actually run stuff. Half the guys on the Supreme Court. Bloomberg. Spitzer. They're all Jews, and the ones who aren't are married to Jews, like Clinton and Trump.

I've never even met her parents.

Soon enough, loco. They're going to love you. Liberals are going to go crazy for you. You'll be in Congress one day, or mayor or something. You've got a big future.

You're the one with the kids, the family, the house. What have I got? Twelve years here, and I could get kicked out tomorrow, and no one would even know.

There's nothing keeping you from getting married. Nothing *I* can see. Your eccentricities are your business.

It won't help. It could make things worse.

Este pinche güero will be out of office one day, Jorge says. Don't let him get in your system. We're going to outlast him, like cockroaches. This country belongs to us too. Half of it was stolen from Mexico in the first place. Deport all the paperless and no one's going to get a manicure in this town again. Or a dry-cleaned shirt.

Or an oil change.

Or a Chinese meal.

Look, Jorge says, the way I see it, I'll be dead soon anyway. Let them send me back. Rita's got the green card. The kids are pure Americans, thoroughbreds, they shit Twinkies and piss Coca-Cola. Lisa got all As last year. Our kids are our revenge. You should be working on that. Forget marriage. Plant the seed. Write the check and hope it doesn't bounce.

He wants to tell Jorge but won't. It's bad luck.

/

"Zeno," she says, tromping up the stairs. She's supposed to call him when he's working in the attic or on the roof, but her phone's out of battery again; six months old and it hardly holds a charge. *"Zeno."* Takes a broom out of the hall closet and taps the handle against the ceiling. "Hey there! Queequeg! You're needed belowdecks." She bangs the trapdoor ladder.

"Cuidado," he says, looking down at her. Still in her work clothes, her clinic clothes, that is. Jeans, flats, a DKNY blouse he told her to buy at Marshalls, the same fraying suit jacket she wears everywhere in warm weather, even to court. Bun askew, sunglasses at the tip of her nose. Her makeup has all been removed; her face looks pink and scraped. She's been crying, and recovered herself, washed herself, to face him; he feels a little disappointed. "You left the front door open," he says. "Your keys are in the lock. Que pasó?"

"Y como sabes?"

"I'm telepathic," he says. "Que pasó, querida?"

"Come down, please. We have to talk."

At the kitchen table, her chin resting on her hands; on the couch, head in his lap; stalking in front of the TV; in the bedroom, furiously folding laundry, she tells him. Between bursts of tears. Let it out, he says. Let it out all at once. I have to go back to work in ten minutes, she keeps saying. He takes her phone and puts it in his back pocket. It buzzes every thirty seconds. Let it all out, he keeps saying, just say whatever you think.

"I really do have to go back to work," Winter says. "I feel like shit. I feel feverish."

"Don't go back to work. Stay here, drink some tea, I'll be finished in an hour and make you dinner."

"I forgot to tell you the other part."

"There's another part?"

"I told Patrick we were getting married."

"We are?"

"I mean, I was very specific. I said we're getting married, in August, in Blue Hill. I basically set a date."

"But we are? I mean, that's what you want?"

"Haven't we talked about it enough?"

"It's not practical," he says. "It's romantic. If you want to get married, we should do it now, here, in Providence, not wait five months and plan something."

"Something that may not happen?"

"Yes."

"So you're admitting it now."

"I suppose, yes."

"Zeno Cuauhtémoc, master of disguises, worker of systems, trickster de todos, you too are mortal, you are deportable."

"You think this is funny."

"I think this is what I do ten hours a day. So if I say we're planning a wedding, trust me that I've considered all the alternatives."

"Okay."

"I'm not afraid," she says, and her voice wavers, because she really means it. Because Freud says men marry their mothers no matter what. Kali, he wants to say, like his father said, looking at her, Kali, with your eight arms and your necklace of heads, you have grown twelve feet tall. "We've thought of all the contingencies. If it has to be Mexico, it'll be Mexico. You have your business plan, I'll figure out something to do, we'll make a life there. *If* you're deported. *If* it gets too unsafe. It happened with your great-grandparents fleeing Franco, y es lo mismo con Trump."

"If, if, if, is no way to live."

"You're telling me. But seriously, I have to go back to work." She launches herself off the bed, where she's been sitting too long, clearly; she grimaces and grabs his shoulder for support. "I feel like my spine's fusing," she says. "And this is nothing. Imagine what it's going to be like when there's an actual baby in there." He watches her limp down the hall to the bathroom. Is she thicker now in the rear? Her breasts have grown a cup size, not that that's saying much. The queasiness was bad in the beginning, has ebbed for the moment. It's like she's swollen with undisclosed information. Her closest friends and his closest friends know. Lourdes, Priyanka, Sarah, Bill, José, Nyele. The clinic knows. Patrick knows, now. But a fetus isn't fully implanted in the mind, somehow, doesn't have psychological validity, until it's announced to, heralded by, every living parent.

"Who's coming to this wedding, anyway?"

"That's a good question," she says, still on the toilet, her voice reverberating off the tile. "The thing is, I want everybody there."

"Everybody? Which everybody?"

"All three of our parents, both of our siblings. Toda la familia. It shouldn't be so hard. There's so few of them."

"What did Patrick say?"

"He won't come unless my mom and dad say they're coming."

He's leaning against the banister, testing its weight, speaking to the door, which needs repainting.

"You know my father hasn't been to the U.S. since 1979."

"Even though he *can* come anytime, with an EU passport."

"Nestor will come, though. If he can get a visa."

"It's good to know someone wants to."

"I didn't say my father won't *want* to come. I'll ask. I guess. It's going to be a very strange conversation."

"Speaking of which," she says, "I'm going to have coffee with my mom. In Fall River."

"Why Fall River?"

"It's halfway between Providence and Woods Hole. It was her idea."

"So you're going to tell her all of this at once, you're going to put it in her lap. You're pregnant. You're getting married. You're maybe moving to Mexico."

"*We're* going to tell her. I need you there for moral support."

(At the same moment, because a novel can do this, Naomi turns to Tilda and says, "I need you there for moral support.")

"I'll do it," he says, "even though it's a mistake, because I love you. But that's the last *yes* you get out of me today."

THE QUESTION OF HAPPINESS

A deep male voice is reading.

"At the same foam-fountain," it reads, "Queequeg seemed to drink and reel with me. His dusky nostrils swelled apart; he showed his filed and pointed teeth."

He bones the chicken breasts, pounds them flat with the back of a cast iron skillet, and drops them, skin-side down, in the Dutch oven.

"On, on we flew; and our offing gained, the Moss did homage to the blast; ducked and dived her bows as a slave before the Sultan. Sideways leaning, we sideways darted; every ropeyarn tingling like a wire; the two tall masts buckling like Indian canes in land tornadoes."

Rings of leeks and shallots, flecks of garlic, slowly caramelizing before he adds the wine and the roux.

A character is a person, some novels say, who appears on the page fully formed, and it's up to us, readers, to understand that person, all his hidden depths and oblique references. A character is a sign, a device, the noise of a name, the shape a word makes in ink on dried and flattened pulp, a marker, a gesture, an instance of wishful thinking. The novel says, I wish I could understand human beings fully, but I can't, so I will create this semblance of a being and make him do things that appear credible and consistent, I will create a trick of the light, a summoning, by saying, for example: Zeno. There can be no other one like him. I can do this by fiat, the novel says, that is my power. I call on Zeno to appear. Zeno who is sliding the seared chicken breasts into a sauce of leeks and white wine, on April 18, 2018. The novel says: register the moment. Imagine this life, imagine this life matters. Look at the frame, look at what the frame contains. Look at the drawing, look at the pencil. This is a way for the novel to say, I wanted to create the image of another human being, but I could only create the image of an image of another human being. What does that mean. What does the image of an image mean. What does the wanting mean.

The novel curls around the baby the way it curls around all fragile things: indifferently. This is what Zeno would say, if he needed to say it. The novel doesn't want what humans want. That would be a category mistake. The novel is not there, Zeno would say, for my protection. To be inside it is not to be contained by it. As much as any of us might want to be contained.

/

Winter went back to the office, after taking two Advil and a half-hour nap; there's just too much to do, she said, when he begged her to stay home the rest of the day. I wasted forty-five minutes arguing with Patrick. Her voice sounded foggy; that wasn't like her. But she promised she'd be home by eight, they'll eat by nine, on the couch, watching one of those British mystery shows he can never tell apart, the ones where cheerful, raw-faced old women in raincoats always wind up dead.

Ordinarily she's the one who gets home early enough to cook on weeknights, and he cooks on Sundays, and they always go out on Saturdays; though lately, spending these afternoons at home working on the attic, he's been able to take over weeknights too. When she cooks it's vegetarian; he braises pork shoulders, makes pots of chili, sears duck breasts, steams whole fish with coconut milk and limes. They have a shopping-list app and alternate weeks at the supermarket. They could go a week without having a single conversation, literally a line, about food, other than *that smells good*. He does the dishes when she cooks and vice versa. She does the laundry and he folds it. Saturday mornings they do their budgeting, review the credit cards, go jogging along the river, have sex in the shower before lunch. They do not argue. They do not. They get annoyed and swat each other. They curse in Spanish and do math in English.

They do not argue. They do not.

That's the main thing. Coming from families who argued habitually, in different registers, depending on the time of day, the weather. Children never knowing when the clouds would roll in. She said to him, the third or fourth time they talked about children, I will only consider having a baby with you, Zeno, if you swear to god we are not going to re-create our childhood houses. It took him a second to understand what she was getting at: the sound of a house where parents are always arguing.

And then he said, miranos, nos dos, look at what we've made for ourselves already.

It all has to do with the question of happiness. This came up so early, on their second date. He took her to a sushi restaurant downtown where his friend Pedro worked, tending bar, to make absolutely sure they would have a quiet booth, way in the back. That was the evening they told each other their stories. Really just the outlines of their stories. Which alone took hours. They finished a bottle of sake and weren't nearly done, so Pedro brought them green tea, for stamina. It was the longest conversation he'd had since arriving in the U.S., or since college. Maybe ever. Finally they closed the place down, Pedro unlocked the front door and walked out into the rain—October in Providence, always raining—and she said, what we are, you and me, Zeno, we're the uncommitted ones, the only un-obsessed ones in our obsessed and overcommitted families, we're the ones not driven crazy, you know, animated by rage or justice or mystic order or whatever. So what does that make us? And he said, it makes us able to chill out, just be happy. That was when she stopped and kissed him, clamping her cold hands over his ears.

So they have a philosophy of happiness, that's a necessity, because it doesn't come naturally. Not coming from families like theirs, not coming out of layers and layers of loss. He thinks of it as *insist on the ordinary*. That was something Papi used to say derisively all the time, why do you have to insist on being so ordinary, Zeno. As if he couldn't answer his own question if he thought about it for a minute, or listened to the echo of his voice in the house. In response he would say things like, someone has to do the dishes, Papi, I thought leftists believed in the dignity of all work.

We are making a new kind of ordinary, normal family, they say, to one another, and in different voices, to themselves. They've been saying it for years. Since peak Obama. You guys *are* peak Obama, Yolanda said once. All hybrid glamour. You're so *sleek*. And optimistic. You give me hope, you really do. Your kids are going to be something else. At the time he had no idea what any of that meant, but now he recognizes it: it's a kind of ironic doublespeak Winter's friends use constantly. No sincere opinions, just a fog of jokes. They all work for NGOs, or tiny legal clinics, or law firms that do nothing but sue the government, but they're not ideological. They don't know anyone who was a member of the Party, not even in their parents' or grandparents' generation. They're unprincipled, undisciplined. Not that it matters to him personally; it's just odd. What *does* matter is this: when they get together they drink white wine and make salads.

That's the difference, he's thinking, knowing the ridiculousness of the metaphor. He keeps meaning to plant a garden in order to grow his own salads. Not that he knows anything about gardening. But he'll figure it out, once the baby comes. A hydroponic garden, a roof garden. Vertical planters, a greenhouse. There should always be salad. It's an indication of the delicacy of life. The foods he ate as a child were delicious but heavy. Pozol, huaraches. Menudo. Tamal. Designed to be filling and immediate, eaten standing up. When Doña Martinez from across the street came to cook for them, which was often, he and Nestor were allowed to eat in the kitchen, in the glow of the oven. Before charging back out to the street, or down to the plaza, wherever the game was. His father sometimes made omelets with salads, of course there were greens for sale in every market, but he didn't wash the lettuce correctly and it was always gritty. Not until he visited Nestor for the first time in Mexico City, not until he was an adult, that is, did he encounter a proper salad, tender, delicate, with frisée, dressed correctly.

I believe in gardens and not war. Which is ridiculous, in the voice of my ancestors who grew gardens *and* went to war. It's a bourgeois affectation, would be the easy way to put it. But that's a special kind of idiocy, fetishizing the food of poverty; he remembers his mother going nuts about it when he and Nestor spent handfuls of tiny coins on chips and candy, this is the food the multinationals are going to kill us with, making us addicts for their preservatives, MSG, industrial sugar and salt. She believed in health. She always intended to quit smoking. But in any case, he wants to say, impatient with his own reverie, it isn't about the ideologics of the 1930s, what matters is the 2030s, when my children will come of age. What will life be like for them? There are certain eventualities you can take for granted. Resource wars, drought. The U.S. will be majority Latin. New York, not Tegucigalpa, will be the largest Honduran city. That isn't the question. The question is, from what vantage point do they begin? Where is the struggle? The struggle to live, to live in a way that makes sense.

People are going to have to learn to grow their own food.

Not only that. People are going to have to build greenhouses, manage water supplies, fix their own solar panels. This is what he worries about. The collapse of technical knowledge. They say no one person understands all the hardware and software in a laptop computer made today. Forget that. How many people know how to grow protein-bearing crops. How many people know how to grow and process their own corn.

Whatever kind of garden he grows has to have corn.

The thing about Winter and me, he said to Nestor once, it's not just that we had *sad childhoods,* of course that's true, it's that we've been exposed to the same kind of intensity, we have been hit so hard, and we were not protected. And that's exactly what's not going to happen, when we make a family, even now, because we're already a family, the two of us. A family is supposed to be a zone of protection, of safety.

Hence the need for a garden.

"So full of this reeling scene were we, as we stood by the plunging bowsprit, that for some time we did not notice the jeering glances of the passengers, a lubber-like assembly—"

He presses pause; he's not really listening. Lulled into the cadence of the sentences that turn into his own thoughts.

Even the matted leaves in the gutter and the cold, the bricks, and the arching trees, I love a steam boiler and a properly insulated roof, the heaps of snow, even the severe and ridiculous statues, all those pointed chins and Roman noses, Protestant capitalist santos. Libraries where books rest on the shelves and never grow mold, protected in stone buildings like castles.

I want to bring you here, he says, only now realizing he's speaking to his father. Because you would love the libraries, and you would find people to talk to. It's that simple. It could be post-ideological. A hemispheric retirement. You who have already read Melville and Hawthorne and Longfellow, and dozens of Zane Grey novels, the ones you kept in the plastic Fanta crates under the bed. You already know all the critiques. There are worse places for an old man with a homeless mind to try to let go of some bitterness. Maybe the cold will freeze your bitterness and snap it off, like doctors do with certain types of wart. Or maybe the rest of you will snap off and only the wart will remain. Maybe that's the risk you don't want to take, though, for everyone's sake, you should.

Also because children should know their grandfather.

Winter's calling; he wipes his hands and presses the speaker button.

"I'm between meetings," she says. "Yunque's husband got out of urgent care, he's going to be fine, it only took a couple of stitches. I put her in touch with Lee Patterson, he's going to help her with the brutality complaint."

"That's good news."

"Well, probably not, but it could have been worse. I have three more clients, then I'm leaving."

"Cómo te sientes?"

"Lo mismo que antes."

"I think you're too tired to drive. Call an Uber."

"Don't be silly, then my car will be here."

"Yolanda will pick you up tomorrow."

"I'm not doing that to her. That's twenty minutes earlier she has to leave home."

"You know she'll do it. Or you can just call another Uber."

"Oh! Porqué somos tan ricos?"

"People who've had so much money all their lives, they really lack a sense of proportion."

"Ouch. I didn't need that."

"I think maybe you do need to hear it. Think of the baby."

"Trust me, I never think about anything else."

THE QUESTION OF MELODRAMA

"She was named Bering after the Bering Sea, obviously," Winter says. "Where Mom was doing research at the time, that whole winter of 1982. Running a lab out of the back of a pickup truck, with Dad and Patrick and me marooned in some yahoo suburb of Anchorage a hundred miles away. That was the research that led to the big paper, the sea-level paper, the Wilcox equation, the one that got her tenure, finally. I mean, she had to sue them first."

When Winter drives long distances she always puts on the same playlist, her Classic Post-Punk mix. The Smiths, Joy Division, Echo and the Bunnymen, the Jam, Siouxsie and the Banshees. He knows the songs too: Nestor learned them all, plunking them out on his guitar, the summer they lived in Mexico City. Nestor's girlfriend, Coraline, drove them all to the beach one weekend: Nestor with his feet on the dashboard, playing song after song, the headstock of the guitar sticking out the window. Lips like sugar, sugar kisses.

"What is the equation, actually?"

"It has to do with calculating how the density of water in the oceans changes with even very slight temperature variations. Obviously that's the key to understanding sea-level rise, because it's not just about volume of water, it's about density, especially in the benthic layer. I know that much. I took atmospheric science in college and got a C+. I couldn't really do the math, and I didn't want to ask her for help. It almost kept me out of law school."

"Take it easy when you switch lanes."

"Anyway," she says, "Bering was always a handful, always intense. I'm sure I've told you some of this. Even as a baby, she was very very focused on learning things and doing things. We were only thirteen months apart, that's practically twins, and we sort of shared two halves of one personality, especially when we were little. She desperately felt she had to keep up. Mom and Dad always used to tell the story of how she decided to potty-train when she saw me doing it."

"Potty-train?"

"Ir al baño."

"Oh."

"She was really terrified when Mom and Dad fought. And she couldn't stand it when we fought back, when we argued with them. You know, the three of us, we all had our own roles. Patrick was the instigator, I was the mediator, and Bering was just the opposite, like, I don't know, the conscientious objector, the Greek chorus saying *stop*, *stop*, all the time. She just couldn't take it."

Two snare beats: it's the beginning of "Kiss Off." She fumbles with the phone and skips to the next song: "The Queen Is Dead."

"Let me deal with the phone. You focus on driving."

She rolls down her window for no particular reason, other than it's spring and the air from the vents smells like a broom closet. Her pulse is tremulous. I am going to see my mother, a newly single woman. A free woman. What does that mean? Since when was Naomi Wilcox not free to be exactly herself, would be the real question to ask. Since when has she not flown through the world in her own pressurized cockpit. *Alone*, what would that mean to someone who has never not felt alone.

This is what the novel has done: altered the very air, for its own purposes, its own shape and trajectory. This is not a good feeling. It makes her extremely nervous, as it should. So she talks about Bering instead, about the part of the story that's ostensibly over.

"She was darker than the rest of us. Notably darker. Even a little darker than Mom. Occasionally, not often, but occasionally, people would ask if the three of us were related. She was mistaken for Dominican, or Greek, or Israeli. You would look at me or Patrick and think there's no way we could have a Black grandfather. But with Bering, like Mom, you could imagine it. Just. If we had grown up knowing, that would have been one thing. Just one fact among many. We could have even turned it into a joke."

"In Mexico," he says, "finding out that your grandfather was this or that, secretly, or not secret but unmentioned, it's very common, actually, and it wouldn't be a big deal. Of course, if you had a family that was obsessed with racial purity, that would be different. But maintaining racial purity, white purity, in Mexico, that's an achievement. Here it's just ordinary, it's not even obsession, just logic. You *have* to know exactly who you are."

"You do, yes, but it's not as if we didn't grow up around lots of mixed families. We had plenty of friends who were biracial, or a quarter this and quarter that—it wouldn't have been remarkable at all, and honestly we would have embraced it. That's what made the lie so painful, honestly, it was that she robbed us of this aspect of who we were, because *she* was ashamed of it, and then that transferred the shame onto us."

"I get that."

"And Bering was the youngest, the most vulnerable—anyway that was her personality, she was never what you'd call stable—and it affected her the most."

"It radicalized her, it made her committed, that's what you're saying."

"It exposed something she found unbearable, something very specific. For those of us who grew up there in the seventies and eighties, the Upper West Side was *Sesame Street,* the TV show. Like it literally was. It was the model for the show, down to the stoops and the garbage cans. Maria and Mr. Hooper, the actual actors, lived near us; we used to see Maria walking her dog on my way to dance class almost every Saturday."

"And why is that a problem?"

"Well, just think about it. Think about that era when everybody was obsessed with *The Truman Show* and *The Matrix*. Real life is a simulation, we live in a bubble, everything is pre-scripted. Well, we did that. We lived in a simulation. In those days the Upper West Side was the kind of neighborhood where you knew the old German lady who ran the bakery and the waiters at Empire Szechuan and the guy who sold you candy at the drugstore. We thought the whole world was like that and always would be. This was a world where we actually believed adults were benevolent and got along and *children came first,* and every little crowd of us was multicolored like sprinkles on a Mister Softee cone. Chinese and Puerto Rican and Black and white."

"Sounds nice to me."

"It was fantastic. A dream, literally a dream. We were the Potemkin Village of racial harmony. And that is the heartbreaking truth of our lives, that some people, like Bering, having lived in a utopian village or commune, even if it's based on a lie, will never be satisfied, will never stop looking for that kind of perfection, while the rest of us go on living compromised lives."

"That part I know about. It's something my dad always says about my mother: after she went into the mountains for the first time, to the Zapatista villages, she never was happy anywhere else."

"And here's the most perverse part. In all those years, it never occurred to my mother that she could stop being ashamed of who she really was. It would have been perfectly all right for her to acknowledge having a Black father. In fact it was a unique window of time where it would have been *ideal* to talk about it. But she went the other way: she never, ever, wanted to talk about race when we were little. It made her itchy, impatient. Humans are humans, she said, a million times. Science teaches us humans are humans. But eventually that Sesame Street bubble burst and we were living in the world of Dinkins and the Central Park Five and Howard Beach and Amadou Diallo, and 'humans are humans' didn't cut it. Racism was just as alive in our time as it was when her mother slept with a Black man and couldn't tell anyone. In her mind, she had moved beyond it. But that didn't work for anyone but her."

"I think you're saying that you had to feel Black, somehow, whether you liked it or not. After your mother told you the truth."

"I didn't, but Bering did. It's the sixty-four-thousand-dollar question, what would she have done if she lived and came back to the U.S. Would she have said, I'm a Black woman. Maybe she went to Palestine to avoid that question, or work it out in her own mind, or, I don't know, maybe she was actually sufficiently radicalized that she would never have come back at all. I'll tell you something I don't think I've ever told anyone: before she left, I wondered if maybe she would become a suicide bomber."

"You didn't really think that."

"It was the Second Intifada, there were bombings happening every week. It was right after 9/11. Yes, obviously, it was stupid. But that's how devastated Bering was, after Mom told her: she was like a different person. When she came back from Evergreen that May, May of 2002, you couldn't be in the room with her without feeling like she was accusing you of something. She'd already done a semester of intensive Arabic, she was wearing a kaffiyeh everywhere. She knew she was going to Palestine. The one time I tried to talk to her she just said—I'll never forget—*this proves it was never about me*."

"What does that mean?"

"I'm still not sure, exactly. Patrick could explain it better. He was much closer to Bering when we were teenagers; it was like they had a secret language. He could always tell what she was thinking. Whereas I always feel like I'm translating, when I talk about her motives. Trying to make it rational or linear, or something. It wasn't."

"I know that feeling."

"Of course you do. Effectively, if I had to try, she was saying her whole life was a lie, it had no pretext, no basis, no side. Of course she was right. And when you start interpreting the world that way, nothing is safe. We were used to pretending we had no particular power or influence; we weren't at the center of anything. We had ideals, principles, not, you know, *assets*. Or *power*. Bering looked at all of it and named it for what it was: one gigantic fucking fraud. This dreamland of moral superiority. Classic liberal American bad faith, I mean, you feel vaguely bad all the time about how your country is ruining the world, but what's to be done, have another Chablis. I think she wrote, in one of her letters, *the only two things that will break the inertia of the bourgeois family are absolutism and death*."

"That's a pretty impressive conclusion for someone of her background."

"Do me a favor, will you? Talk about your mother, instead. This is helping me, this conversation."

"You mean not talking about *your* mother."

"Yes. It's taking some of the pressure away."

The tag on his collar has come loose; it's itching the back of his neck. A new dress shirt, still with its creases from the original packaging. Everything else in his closet seemed old and dusty; he hasn't worn anything other than a T-shirt and Carhartt sweatshirt in weeks, since their last date, in fact.

The song now is one he doesn't know, it's a woman's very high, very English voice. *It's a little souvenir of a terrible year.*

Melodrama, a story with music. A story is characters forced into a defile, a slot, they can't escape. He never wants to accept that. This makes him a less-than-ideal character. He's too relaxed. His thoughts aren't scaling the future like it's an invisible wall. Tortuga, his father says again. Or was it Mama? Ayotl, she would say, prodding his back with her slipper when he was crouched on the kitchen floor, playing marbles.

Is melodrama the same as propaganda, was a question he always wanted to ask. But didn't know whom to ask. Maybe one of his literature professors in Tuxtla could have helped. Does melodrama require one set of enemies and one set of victims. For example: is political radicalism, among hopelessly naïve privileged people, always a performance, is it always done as a kind of entertainment. Or: when a marriage ends, is there ever one wronged party. They are driving toward this question, literally driving into it, following the novel's dictates, he sees that now, like the clauses of this sentence, a helpless spiral.

"She wasn't an easy person to know," he says. "For one thing, she hated making conversation. Like really, really avoided any kind of small talk. I was never sure if it was more her personality or if it was cultural, because I didn't know her family very well—we only visited them twice, in Veracruz, the whole time I was growing up."

"I didn't even know that's where she was from."

"And she avoided speaking Spanish if at all possible. Outside of teaching. Of course she spoke it to my dad, because he really never learned Nahuatl, but otherwise, with us, Nahuatl, and with her comrades, Tzotzil. She refused to publish in Spanish. She refused even to have anything she wrote *translated* into Spanish. It was perverse, but she was absolutely the stubbornest person, the purest indigenous Marxist, you can imagine."

"If she were alive today, what would she think about me?"

"You know the answer to that."

"She wouldn't even acknowledge my existence."

"Maybe she would have mellowed out. Like you said, that's the big question. The one question."

"You try to imagine them in this world, but if they were here, it wouldn't be this world, would it. Even saying *this world* makes a mockery of it."

"My dad," he says, picking up a thought in midstream, "really had a hopeless love for her. He didn't approve of her politics, not at the end. Or better to say he didn't participate in them. Though in a way he loved her for being a guerrilla. It gave him a perverse pleasure, having her guns in the house."

"She kept guns in the house?"

"Of course she did. Hidden. Not actually in the house, in the well. We had a dry well, a fake well, with guns at the bottom. At midnight, she took them out, pulled them up on the rope, and cleaned them."

"Did she ever kill anyone?"

"I never asked her that."

"But she was shot, in the end."

"She was robbed. I told you the story. Betrayed. By fakers, fake rebels. Just hooligans, really. Marauders. It could have happened to anyone, anyone walking on that road that particular night."

"But she had her rifle."

"They shot her in the back, from a truck. I told you."

"It makes it easier, hearing you talk about it. Because you're comfortable saying the words. I still sometimes want to say, *she died in an accident.*"

"It wasn't an accident."

"Of course it wasn't."

"She died in a war of liberation, a liberation struggle. You know that's not even a little bit unusual. Think of the people disappeared in Argentina, in Ireland, in Syria, in Tibet, in Peru, in Bolivia."

"But that's not what I want to say either."

"It doesn't give you even a little bit of comfort, knowing that she died for a reason, in a collective struggle?"

"Does it comfort *you?*"

"My mother died doing what she wanted to do, what she felt she was born to do."

"That doesn't answer the question."

"It doesn't have a single answer."

"Well, there you have it," she says. "Let me put it this way. I don't want my politics to be defined by acts of murder. I don't want to live in a world circumscribed by my losses. And I don't believe in revenge."

"Justice is not revenge."

"Precisely. So I don't want justice for Bering, I want it for the Palestinians *and* the Israelis, on behalf of all the murdered activists and also the ordinary uncommitted people, who just want to raise their children, do laundry, have sex, eat hummus."

"You know what people say in Chiapas, los Yanquís solamente quieren comprar Coca-Cola para todo el mundo."

"That's mean. True, maybe, but you could think twice about saying it just now."

"It's a joke."

"You know," she says, "sometimes I forget why you came here in the first place."

"Here where?"

"Here to the U.S., dummy. Considering you're not exactly a fan of los Yanquís."

"Because I'm a poor Mexican, why else?"

"You had options, resources, an education. You could have been a teacher, an engineer, a professor. You could have gone to the city, or, I don't know, someplace better. Argentina. Spain. You didn't have to take all these stupid risks."

"Maybe this is where the real struggle is."

"I have no idea what that means."

"I don't either. It just occurred to me."

"Be serious, for once."

"Okay," he says, "on a pure economic level, como sabes, my education in Chiapas was pretty meaningless. I had no serious job prospects. Engineering in Mexico, if you want to really do it, you have to have contacts, you have to have a degree from UNAM or from an overseas university. That's what I thought I would do, most likely, when I got the visa to study at URI. Get my master's, if I could manage to stay in school, and go back and try my best. But the chances were never good."

"And what about Nestor?"

"Nestor is a DJ who has a new girlfriend every other month and somehow they keep paying his bills. He doesn't exactly make long-term plans. But if you're asking does he think I should stay here, hell no. He's anti-imperialist. He's always telling me to come back, saying Mom would be ashamed of me. I just tell him Mom would be even more ashamed of him. It's a stalemate."

"But what do you think? I mean, what do *you* want?"

"I want to stay here," he says. "I like it here. I like the cold. You know that. I like New England, it's so mysterious and dark. Full of ghosts. I like the silence. I want to go to Nantucket, visit the whalers' graveyard."

"You're crazy."

"But whatever, mostly I just don't want to die, or get thrown in prison, I mean, I have to protect you and the baby, I'm a father now."

"Now look who wants to buy the world a Coke."

"And I love you too."

"No, but I want to say *why* I love you," she says. "Because no one ever told me that people like you existed."

"I'm not sure I want to hear you explain that."

"Also, I love your work clothes. I love smelling them, even in the laundry."

"Claro, estás fetichizado a la clase trabajadora. Anyway, you're about to miss the exit. Watch out, that's the last thing we need."

/

Let me drive, Tilda said, you're too stressed to drive, but Naomi insisted. This is my errand, she said, my doing, my progeny, my fault. They left the house without her phone, then without her wallet. This is not like me, she said. That's why I should be driving, Tilda said. She entered the directions for the bakery in Fall River Winter had named and then turned them off because she couldn't stand the phone talking to her and telling her obvious things in that bright cheery way, that singsong rhythm. TAKE the EX-it. It reminded her of the Oompa-

Loompas, she said. They missed the turn on the roundabout for 95. Fucking Christ, she said, no one told me that parenting leads to early onset Alzheimer's. I feel the plaques setting in.

"I'm still not really used to hybrid cars," she announced when they were finally on the highway. "After all this time. They're too quiet. I forget I'm driving. You know my last car before this one was the last of our Volvos, and toward the end it sounded like it didn't even use its muffler."

"Mmm."

"I read an article saying that gangbangers were using Priuses for drive-by shootings. That's what got me interested, actually. An environmental technology that was really having an impact on the world."

"For the record," Tilda said, "I don't think there's any doubt about what you should say. You're taking me to meet the family. It's a big moment."

"I'm not going to make a speech about it or anything. The focus needs to remain on Winter and *her* problems."

Tilda rolled her head in a slow half circle, rubbed her temple, the bridge of her nose. Long, streaming breaths. How amazing it is, Naomi wanted to say, to meet someone who still believes their body matters, their body can change things. As opposed to just being there for incoherent relief. I, she's thinking, I haven't arranged my body into a coherent posture since 1981.

"I didn't realize you were so stressed. Maybe you shouldn't have come, after all."

"Just admit to Winter that you got a little weepy the other night. You felt excited. You said, 'I'm going to be a *grandmother*,' like that was a good thing. Open yourself to, I don't know, sharing happiness? Like, 'I'm so happy that you told me X. And I'm also happy to tell you X.' Start from there. It's not that complicated."

She wanted to laugh, it was such an absurd thing to say, flying down the interstate. Uncomplicated things can be addressed in a phone call; they don't require driving at insane, maniacal speeds toward bakeries in unfamiliar towns. The whole thing, she wanted to tell Tilda, is such complicated, slow-motion blackmail, every bit of affection and support counted out and paid for. She could already imagine not being allowed to ask any relevant questions. Why have a child whose father might disappear one day, any day. Wouldn't that be like having a child with a felon. Is it a plan, a strategy, an anchor baby. Isn't any baby, on the other hand, an anchor baby. Wasn't Patrick an anchor baby. Anchoring who or what.

This is exactly what happens when you say, yes, let's meet, let's get together. Your mind begins to improvise, melodramatically. As if everything you ever wanted to say has to be said at once. Someone is going to start crying, though probably not me. And why do I never keep tissues in my purse. Am I the only woman alive who has never had tissues in her purse. Surely Tilda has some.

"I just keep thinking of that email I have to send to Jerry Mizaki," she said instead. "And the NSF report. And the broken printer. Seriously, the timing couldn't be worse. Two weeks left of funding, and we have to waste a whole day."

"One whole day, yes."

"I have a life, a new life, I want Winter to appreciate that. Especially now. I can't just be, *available*. I mean, it's not like I've retired."

"You can't act as if it's already happened, as if people already knew something you've just told them. I've noticed this about you. You expect people to have already processed what they don't yet know. I've never known anyone who does that."

"That's just being a snappy New York Jew, love. Also it's quantums 101. Patrick could explain it to you."

"I wasn't asking for an explanation. I was asking you not to act that way. Because it just isn't true, and you know it isn't true. It is actually not easy for you to process anything. You'd have a better life if it was."

"Winter has never processed anything with me," she said. "That isn't our relationship. She's always had her friends for that, or Patrick.

Or Zeno. I have no access to her in that way. And vice versa. We respect one another's autonomy. And I know what you're going to say."

"You're expecting her to be angry, but I don't think she wants to be angry. Or shocked. Or whatever. I actually think she wants the exact thing you want, to be recognized."

"We recognize each other from afar."

"Ha ha, that's hilarious."

"No," she said. "I mean it. This is important." But how can she mean it, is the question, how can you explain something so basic, so imprinted? Sometimes with Tilda she runs straight off the cliff of time. "I can choose who I'm available to," she said, stumbling over the obviousness of the words, "to be close to, be loved by. So can she. That's my point."

"For Christ's sake," Tilda said, "don't have a point. Have a day. One fucking *day*."

/

"Mira," Zeno says, pointing. "Look at that car sideways in the intersection. What the hell happened?"

/

"Go inside," Tilda says to her. "*Inside*. You look like you're about to have a heart attack. Go get some tea or something. It's just a fender-bender."

"I swear to god I was looking right at him."

"We both know that's not true."

"I have to talk to the police."

"I'll get you when they get here."

The other driver, of the white Corolla with the *Murray's Dry Cleaning* decals, is rummaging in the glove box, trying to find the registration and insurance, talking loudly on his phone in Vietnamese. The cars haven't moved. It would be hard to move them, the way the Prius's nose has nestled itself in the passenger-side door, the side that was mercifully unoccupied. The Corolla's frame, Tilda's thinking, is clearly a total loss. You can't unbend those supports. Plus the door and the glass, and the rust, and the two-tone paint job, and about 200K miles from the looks of things, and you have a car destined for the junkyard.

"Hey," this thirtysomething girl says to her, coming up out of nowhere, in the hoodie over the print dress with clogs. Such a recognizable New England outfit, she wonders if she knows her from somewhere. A little like Chloë Sevigny, if she lost a decade and dyed her hair. "I'm sorry, I thought this was my mom's car. Is everything okay?"

"Are you Winter? Then this *is* your mom's car."

"Where is she?"

"In the bakery. She was looking really stressed, so I told her to go sit down. She's fine, though. No one was hurt. Air bags deployed, the whole deal. Police are on their way."

As Tilda is saying this Winter watches Zeno get out of the car and walk quickly, purposefully, toward the door of Fall River Roasters, and then sees Naomi sitting in the window, staring in the other direction. She and Zeno are a couple. They have deployed, automatically, in helpful positions.

"I'm sorry," she says, holding out her hand. "You know my name, but I don't know you."

"Tilda. Very nice to finally meet you."

"And you're—"

"For the moment, we're both in some kind of bad movie," she says with a sideways grin, "because I'm your mom's girlfriend, which she was planning to tell you, that is, she was planning to introduce us, before she drove into this poor guy's car."

Suddenly, the novel wants to say. Suddenly something happened. The novel opens its hand. Let me shock you, let me embarrass you. Cover your eyes, cover your mouth. Turn the music up.

Tilda, by her estimation, is about fifty, about fifty pounds over-weight, in cargo pants, a navy polo with a WHOI logo, running shoes, her white-streaked straw hair in two long braids over her shoulders. She is unquestionably a lesbian, and what is it that tells her that? The effortless taking-charge, the directness, the unapologetic self-control. That's not fair. The blocky muscular formation of her mouth. This too is where the novel resides. She looks too long at her mouth, for lack of anything to say, as if it too is a circle, a spiral, a recursive object, and then puts her hand protectively on her stomach. This swelling thing.

"You don't have to say anything," Tilda says. "Maybe you should go inside, too."

"Well, someone has to wait for the police, and the tow truck. I'll keep you company."

"Okay. Whatever you want to do."

The tall Vietnamese man has stopped speaking on the phone, stopped scrabbling in the glove compartment. "Look," he says to them over the Corolla's hood. "I can't stay. Can't stay here."

"You have to stay," they say at the same time. "This car's not driv-able," Tilda says. "We need a tow truck. Just wait a second, okay? The police will be here. They'll tell you what to do."

"No, no," he says. "*I* can't stay." He opens his wallet. "I have one hundred eighty," he says, and hands Tilda the wad of twenties.

"They'll have your license number," Winter says, digging into her purse for her card. "You'll be traced. Leaving the scene of an accident is a class-one misdemeanor. Believe me, I'm a lawyer. You could go to jail. You have options, just stay here and let me talk you through it." But when she looks up he's running already, the deliveryman, in his white clothes, from his white car, dodging across the intersection with his phone in one hand and wallet in the other, disappearing down the hill, toward the water, and Winter says, helplessly, "He should have known Fall River won't check his immigration status, it's a city statute, I could have told him that."

"Look," Tilda says, "the backseat is full of clothes. Piles of clothes. We need to call the dry cleaners and tell them to come get the car."

Finally, sirens.

/

"In construction," Zeno says, wadding up his napkin and palming it, not sure what else to do with it, "they say you can sense it on the day someone has an accident, you can taste it. Some people say it actually tastes like blood, you know, that sour taste if you bite your lip."

"The coppery, metallic taste, that's all the iron."

"Anyway, the important thing is that you're okay, and the other guy is okay."

"Where is he, anyway?"

"I don't know."

"That officer is taking his sweet time. I should go out there and talk to him."

"No, I think they have it under control."

"Why 'they'? You think Winter is actually getting involved, what, she's acting as my lawyer now?"

"She's talking to the cop, anyway, probably she's being very helpful."

She puts her head flat on the table and fences her fingers together over it. "This is a fucking disaster," she growls, "who knows how long it's going to take the car to get towed back to Falmouth, or wherever, and then the insurance claims, the estimates, probably it all has to be done at a dealer because it's such a *special* car, not just any grease monkey can handle this one, and I've got to talk to Sandy about it all, the GEICO paperwork is all in the apartment."

"It looks to me like it's actually not so bad, all front-end damage. It could have been much worse."

"I'll be stuck getting rides with Tilda. Or maybe I can lease a car. You haven't asked who Tilda is."

"She's your friend, who drove with you here."

"No she's not," Naomi says, "she's my, my—shit, I don't know the word. Girlfriend. Lover. Adulterous lover."

"I thought you and Mr. Wilcox were separated."

"As of a week ago we are."

"Yes. But living apart longer."

"You're ruining a big moment here. I'm supposed to be telling Winter, or someone who cares, evidently."

"Mrs. Wilcox—"

"Call me Naomi, please, or I'm going to bean you over the head with this coffee mug. Has Winter told you that my father, my biological father, was a Black man, a scientist in California I never knew?"

"Yes."

"Has she told you that Sandy nearly went to prison for legal fraud?"

"No. Not that I remember."

"Has she told you about Patrick?"

"I've met Patrick. On Skype. Three times."

"Has she told you about Bering?"

"Of course she has, she's been very open about that."

"Well congratulations to her. I wonder if there's a bar on this block."

"Do you often drink at eleven in the morning?"

She stares at him wildly, her hair askew, startled out of sleep, with a tiny pit of a mouth.

"I can't place your sense of humor," she says finally. "That bothers me. I can't help but think you're laughing at me, that this is all a big joke to you. It's because your English is too good, too composed. You exemplify some kind of heroic, noble ideal of the New American that seems right out of central casting to me. I just don't buy your character, is what I'm saying. Did you accidentally go to Harvard in your spare time or something? Were you actually born here and raised by eccentric linguists?"

"I was raised by eccentric linguists, I guess you could say that."

He looks down at his phone.

I'm sorry to leave you there with her
My mother is a lesbian, apparently
Her name is Tilda

"Look," he says, "the wrecker is here. You know, I think they probably take cars to Falmouth all the time."

"Why do they call it a wrecker?"

"A wrecker is a flatbed truck you use for taking a damaged car a
long distance, in this case because of the bridge, I'm guessing."

"How do you know that and I don't?"

"Because you're a scientist who works in a lab, and I work in construction, which I think is sort of like being a grease monkey."

"There's that sense of humor again."

"No, I was trying to be funny that time."

/

"Summer is coming," Tilda is saying, "and we are totally going to have
you guys up to Woods Hole, very soon. I'm buying your mom a grill
for her deck. She's already committed to patio furniture. It's criminal
to have a deck like that and not use it."

Winter is trying not to be a person who avoids interactions by staring at her phone. That is the height of rudeness, that defensive curl, the
ducked head, the *sorry did you say something* glance to the side; I'm not
really here, it says, here doesn't matter. On the other hand, in this case,
here is wrong, *here* is accidental, it wasn't supposed to happen this way,
you don't meet your parent's lover unannounced, openly, alone. Under
the pretense of searching for a towing company, she scrolls through her
New Americans emails, making note of the new client registrations:
six yesterday, four the day before. Chang and Xie. O'Leary. Silwan.
Beaujardins, a Haitian national, two drug convictions in the nineties,

one a felony, served three and five on probation. Her eyelids are leaden. This will not do. Tilda is patiently standing there, waiting to be acknowledged, and I, she thinks, am not and have never been as cold as my family reputation warrants, just searching for the mean, or the average, the balance, the measured response. The half. Among a family who never does things by halves.

"Tilda, what do you do?"

"I work for your mom. In her lab."

"You're a postdoc? A grad student?"

"That's very flattering, no, I'm just a lab tech. I've been at WHOI for fifteen years."

"Oh. That makes sense."

The sun is beginning to crack the day's ordinary Atlantic cloud cover, just overhead, making the world suddenly high-contrast, wet at the edges. Even the metaphors feel off. There is such a thing as a melodramatic sun, even if it rarely appears over New England. Now she has to shield her eyes to look at Tilda, and pretend what she's just said does, in fact, make sense, when it manifestly does not, or that *sense* is the guiding principle of this outing.

"I'm sorry you feel ambushed," Tilda says. "If you want, you and Zeno can leave, we'll do this another time."

"People keep saying that to me, but I don't have another time. My clock is ticking. Whatever this is, it needs to happen now. Welcome to the family, I guess, is what I'm trying to say. This is as good a way to meet the Wilcoxes as any."

"Do you need some water? Do you need to sit down?"

"Because I'm pregnant? No. I'm fine, I'm running on adrenaline. God, you don't have kids, do you?"

"No kids. I had a cat, but he died a few years ago, before your mom and I moved in together."

"Good, she's deathly allergic."

"So I've heard. Lesbians without cats, what will they say."

Love, is the terrible fucking song at the heart of the cloud, your mother has found love, and now the cracked cloud spills out like the carcinogenic center of a Cadbury Creme Egg all over Fall River, Massachusetts. The Wilcox family history reduced to a sick transaction. The novel pulls them apart and shoves them together, damp pieces of meat at the butcher's.

"I'm sorry to be so direct, Tilda, but what you're saying, I don't know, your being here in the first place—you act as if you're actually in love with her."

"I am in love with her."

"Well, this also bears saying and repeating: you are out of your fucking mind."

/

Rest. The opposite of melodrama: bodies not moving, bodies suspended. Winter is driving. The situation has been resolved. It's no big deal. The wrecker is taking Naomi's car back to a body shop in Falmouth. It took twenty minutes to arrange. At first Naomi refused to sit in the passenger seat; then Winter said, Mom. We were supposed to talk. This is how we get to talk. The initial result: five, six minutes of silence. The outskirts and tendrils of Fall River, nail salons, Discount Tire, Papa John's, the smooth tongue of the on-ramp, the cushiony hum of 95.

Winter wants to say: Just the other day, Mom, I was thinking of your book. It seems the kind of thing any author would want to hear. Something you wrote stayed with me. It turns out the body, as you observed, cannot sense time, except in the case of pregnancy, as you also observed—Mom, she wants to say, you have indirectly passed a bit of human wisdom my way, unintentionally, like a kidney stone. But when you have a writer in the family, does any of this need to be said. Here we are, pretending not to experience time together. Unable to voice or value it.

From the backseat, out of nowhere, Zeno says, "Winter, I forgot you and your mom have the same car."

"Everyone should have the same car," Naomi says. "Everyone should drive *this* car. Once you've driven a Prius, you realize all other cars are ridiculous, that the internal combustion engine is about as relevant as the typewriter and the telegraph."

"I went back and checked the safety records," Zeno says gamely. "Once Winter got pregnant. They're excellent. As you saw. Here you are, walking away, no problem at all."

"Of *course*." Naomi's voice squeaks a little, like a toy accordion; she claps her hands and turns to face Winter with an off-kilter, palsied smile, like she's halfway to a stroke. "I knew there was something I was forgetting. I haven't even gotten to say congratulations."

"Is that your way of saying it now?" Winter says.

"How does it feel? Physically, I mean. What does the doctor say?"

"Midwife, and she says everything is normal so far, but it's early stages."

"You're not using a doctor."

"There's an OB in the practice, yes."

"But you're not consulting with him."

"Her, yes, we've met with her, and she *also* says everything is normal."

"It's good to have choices, right?" Naomi says. She crosses her legs and inspects the bottom of one shoe; her voice changes, becomes more throaty, more herself, the way only she can curdle the air. "You can declare that Western medicine is just a social construct, and use healers now, and shamans, and you're probably planning to give birth at home, and burn sage, and play pan flutes, but you always have a hospital and a doctor, that is, empirical evidence and actual treatment options, as backup."

"Zeno's grandfather was a healer," Winter says with gritted teeth.

"Zeno, is that true?"

"Yes," he says. Winter looks in the mirror and sees him wrinkling his brow, as if there's an intense pain in the middle of his forehead. "In a manner of speaking. I only met him a few times, when I went home to Veracruz with my mother."

"Culture," Naomi says, "is the whole assemblage of things we take for granted and never have to think about. That's what my anthropology professor used to say. Speaking of which, you're getting married, is that right?"

Winter starts to laugh; she tries to cover her mouth, which doesn't stop it; puts her palm to her chest; coughs a few times; rests her elbow on the door, adjusts her visor, anything to distract herself. "I'm sorry," she says finally, "but, Mom, you've lost the art of the segue. You have to give us a little more time to warm up. It's not an interrogation."

"I think what Naomi means to say," Tilda pipes up, "is we're just genuinely curious about it. I mean I am, anyway. What kind of ceremony. What you're thinking about. No judgment intended. Just genuine interest."

"We genuinely haven't given it much thought," Winter says. "It depends on who's coming. I think Zeno prefers it to be straightforward, a civil wedding. A secular wedding. Whereas I'm a little more ambivalent. I had a bat mitzvah, after all. I'm Jewish for all intents and purposes. My children will be Jewish. I don't have a rabbi, so to speak, but we do. Did. Our family did. We were very close, at one time. This is a sensitive subject, as you can probably gather, Tilda. Right now is the part where Naomi says Rabbi Art is going to marry us over her dead body."

"If you're expecting me to perform," Naomi says, "like a cartoon version of myself from 2003, Winter, think again."

It's a shift, a tilt, in the car's tightly packed energies: Winter, Naomi is saying, are we going to do this the way we've always done it, pretending these new people aren't here? Or are we going to perform our family history for them, the new arrivals, like shadow puppeteers, each one with a grimacing mask? In other words: for whose satisfaction is the melodrama performed? Winter feels her body gathered up and wrung out. Naomi says, I was dried out, desiccated, you crumbled me to dust. The novel hates metaphors; it just holds them. Turns them the way the car is going, toward the future.

"What I meant to say is," Winter says, "I think if we're doing any kind of religious ceremony at all, or anything personal, really, we need to acknowledge Zeno's heritage, *I* think, anyway, and we're very much hoping his father will come, though the chances aren't good."

"How anyone could come from Mexico to the U.S. in this climate, at this moment," Naomi says, "I can't even imagine. He could be detained. He could be killed."

"He has a Spanish passport, as a matter of fact," Zeno says. "He's an EU citizen. His parents, my grandparents, were born in Spain. Under Franco. They came to Mexico as exiles."

"Which means he doesn't even need a visa," Winter adds. "He just needs to update his passport. And no, in case you're wondering, Zeno can't become a Spanish citizen. I mean, he could. There's a law that specifically allows it, the Law of Historical Memory, but you have to provide documentation, your grandparents' birth certificates, their passports, and so on."

"My grandparents died in an apartment fire, you see," Zeno says. "After the Mexico City earthquake. Some wiring was dislodged in the walls of the building, but no one knew, and so about a month later there was a huge fire with no warning. Twenty-five people died. It destroyed an entire block of Roma Norte."

"And therefore," Tilda says, "you're an undocumented Mexican citizen, instead of a legal Spaniard with a green card. For purely accidental reasons."

"Everything about the immigration system is accidental," Winter says. "The accident of birth, the accident of time. Anyway, Zeno overstayed a student visa. You can get deported for that no matter where you're from. Getting a student visa from Mexico in the first place was a small miracle. Anyway, we're straying from the point. We're having a wedding. Everything about it is open-ended except the fact that it's happening. And you're invited. Maybe that's too neutral. You're expected. You're, um, *assumed*."

"I just don't know what any of this is going to look like by August," Naomi says. "You want my honest answer? That's my honest answer. I try to see the landscape of our family standing there by the chuppah, in *Blue Hill,* of all places, the last place we were all together before you-know-what happened, our own personal Custer's Last Stand of togetherness, and what am I supposed to be picturing? I'm standing there in some kind of matching outfit with Tilda. Will it be a dress and then Tilda wearing a suit? Or will we both be wearing suits? Or both dresses? If there's some kind of lesbian code for these things, Tilda hasn't explained it to me yet."

"There's no—"

"Sweetie, let me finish. Then I'm picturing your dad, all alone. For some reason I'm seeing him with a beard and twigs sticking out of his beard. Of course, that's unfair. Or dressed as a monk again. Or with some twentysomething, rosy-cheeked farm lass he picked up at the Feed and Supply in Hardwick. And then Patrick, who might be in his robes, or maybe not, but in any case looks like he just walked out of Theresienstadt, because apparently he's transcended food, or whatever his condition is."

"You know very well what his condition is."

"And then you, my dear stable child, my gainfully employed daughter with the house and the car and the yard and the sweet, sweet man, this painfully nice person—and I'm sorry to refer to you in the third person, Zeno, but please give me the benefit of the doubt—and you are a pregnant bride, and what I see, when I project into the future, is the storm troopers kicking down the door, the ICE agents, whatever you call them, and dragging my grandchild's father off never to be seen again, and what with everything, and then everything else, it's a lot of violent iconography, a lot of militaristic symbolism, it seems somehow that we, the Wilcoxes, have taken the basic business of biological coupling, mating, preening, nesting, and through our own efforts, our own *internationalism,* so to speak, we've basically made ourselves into enemies of the state, or something."

Tilda has begun to laugh. "I'm sorry," she says, almost panting.

"I know it's not funny. None of it's funny. But don't you ever have to laugh, when she gets like this? It's kind of beautiful, in its own way."

"I was trying to talk about my feelings, that's all. I was trying to express concern and love."

"Love," Winter says, feeling entirely not herself, so much so that her ears begin to pop, as if the car has suddenly risen to ten thousand feet above sea level, "in this case is like the difference between a jar of honey, which you can unscrew and dip your pinky into, or your tongue, and just *taste,* and an entire rotted hollow tree full of honeycomb, an active hive, most of the honey already dark and rancid, where you have to suit up with protective netting and one of those smoke canisters, and stick your hand up there and probe around, with bees stinging you all over, hoping a bear doesn't come up and maul you for taking her stash."

"I know what that is," Zeno says. "That's an epic simile."

"So, Mom, what you're saying in a nutshell is that your children care too much about *other* people, with an emphasis on the other," Winter says. "And it would have been so much easier if we'd just dated *within our own circles,* limited ourselves to the square mile between Ninety-Sixth and Sixty-Third—"

"Don't be ridiculous. Harlem, the Village, brownstone Brooklyn? You had so many options."

"You whose career has literally been about the substance, the material, of the entire Earth, how one part is indivisible from another."

"If you're trying to call me a hypocrite, you're doing a bad job," Naomi says. "That isn't how science works. That isn't how metaphors work. Anyway, it's utterly beside the point, because what you're avoiding, the part I really don't get, is why you *want* any of this. Why it's necessary for you to keep, or should I say *force,* the family together."

"I don't believe in lies and I don't believe in secrets," Winter says. She can barely hold the steering wheel, the atmospheric pressure is so intense; her eyes are being squeezed. Giving the same speech a second time, it turns out, doesn't make it easier. "We have an obligation, in the face of everything trying to separate us—yes, including each other—to, I don't know, *face* one another, for fuck's sake. For once. It may be the only time, ever, that these people appear in the same photograph. I want to be able to show that to my kid. Let the record show, we were a family. We existed. Say it's to honor Bering's memory, if that makes you happier."

"Well. It had to come down to that."

"Nobody is making this a tribunal. No one gets to call anyone to account, if that's what you're afraid of. You're welcome to be a silent participant. I mean it. No speeches, no part in the ceremony. Just purely a witness."

"Hold on," Zeno says. "I have an idea. I've been listening to this, but now I want to say something."

Naomi swivels, suddenly, so much so that Winter's hands jerk on the wheel and the car swerves and recorrects. "*Wait your turn,*" she says. "I was asking my daughter something. Not you."

"Don't fucking talk to him that way," Winter says. "Or you can get out and walk. I am not kidding. Watch yourself, Mom."

"I don't need a man with a bad case of machismo speaking for my daughter."

"I swear to god, I'm going to pull over right here."

"Listen, listen," Zeno says. "All I wanted to say is this. *This* is a family, in this car. It's already happened. These five people. It just, it just occurred to me to say it. That terrible thing you're so afraid of, it's already happened."

THE FUTURE

Recovered from: Drafts Folder (Unsent Message)

From: "Bering Wilcox" <carebear@hotmail.com>
Last saved: February 12, 2003 at 9:13:44 PM EST
To: "Naomi Schifrin Wilcox" <nwilcox4@columbia.edu>
Subject: in Jerusalem

I was thinking about this story you told me once—about how when you lived with dad at the commune (sorry, temple) you took advantage of any excuse to go into Montpelier so you could go to the public library and sit in front of the air conditioner. You said you felt guilty and I never really understood why.

So here I am at the Mamilla Hotel on the seventeenth floor, wiggling my toes between the white sheets as I write this with my hair up in a towel and the a/c on full blast. Yes I used the Mastercard so you will see this on the statement, or at least dad will. I intend to order a bloody steak from room service and a caesar salad if they have that and a bottle of red wine. I'm grossing myself out but I think I will eat it regardless. West Jerusalem is so sad and timid and I can't bestir myself to walk half an hour up to Damascus Gate and get some decent food.

I wasn't supposed to leave Wadi Aboud this soon (protocol is you stay on-site for a month before your first rotation out) but fuck Soldiers for Peace and Yaron and Jerome and all their stupid rules. I made up a lame excuse about having to get a ride to Yatta for feminine products and then took a serveece from there. It's only about two hours with checkpoints. This weekend there's a cease-fire in Hebron so I figured it would be a good time to go. At the border they took us all out and searched us and when the young girl soldier got to me (she was Ethiopian and so beautiful, my heart ached for her) she said, Yehudi, why are you on this sherut (in Hebrew of course), and I asked the woman beside me to tell her, I belong here, and then she said in English, any of them could kill you, and I said, any of you could kill me.

I'm sorry this is so disconnected. I should try to explain things in order. But I'm on kind of a high wire here emotionally so let me just get one more thing off my chest. I'm making this trip just to tell Jerome fuck off in my own mind because it's exactly what he wanted to do, what he kept saying, I want to spend some time with you, we can't do anything here, when he'd already insisted on dragging our sleeping bags out into the wadi so we could fuck bare-assed in the soft night air. Am I shocking you?

Okay, now let me start from the beginning.

If you look at a West Bank map (and you have to get the right one, the UNRWA map or the one published by B'Tselem) you can find Wadi Aboud southeast of Hebron, north of Susya. *Wadi* means valley or properly a desert wash or ravine, and that's where we are, on a hillside above a stream that only runs seasonally. The village is about fifty houses, which makes it reasonably big for the South Hebron Hills. This is dry and unforgiving land and always has been, since the days

of Abraham and long before him, too. And of course Abraham was
here. This was exactly where he lived. As I understand it, the farmers
and herdsmen of Wadi Aboud, the fellaheen, are basically the same
people, I think anthropologically speaking, genetically speaking, as they
were then. At least that's one theory. They were Canaanites; they were
Israelites; they were Philistines; subjects of the Babylonians, the late
pharaohs, the Roman Empire, the caliphs, the Crusaders, the Ottomans,
the British, the Jordanians—and basically all this time they've been
harvesting olives and thyme and wheat and sumac and pomegranates
and grapes, milking and shearing and slaughtering sheep and goats,
praying for enough rain and not too much rain. *Fellaheen* means "those
who work the land."

I'm not saying this romantically or anything. Qasim, for example,
who's our landlord (our little SFP hovel is the first floor, really the
basement, of his house), is a jerk who wears Adidas tracksuits, drives
a souped-up Camry with stick-on tinted windows, and treats Heba, his
very young wife, i.e. basically my age, like a dog. He wants to start a
mobile phone business, not maintain the farmland and the grazing rights
passed down from his father and probably from a hundred generations
before his father. He's been shot at and nearly run over and beaten up
by settlers all his life, and it doesn't faze him, but he's not the least bit
political, either, other than to complain about the PA.

So let me say a little about the settlers.

Wadi Aboud has existed as a village for maybe a thousand years. (I
asked Abu Salim, the oldest person here, how old the village is, and he
said, "American girl, when was the first pomegranate tree planted? Maybe
a little later than that.") There were IDF military bases nearby after the
Six-Day War—we're not far from the Negev and the Israeli nuclear base,
among other things—but the settlements began in earnest in the 1980s.
This part of the West Bank is so far from Jerusalem and Beersheeba,
really from any major Israeli city or town, that the settlers who came here
in the beginning were the true fanatics, the back-to-the-land movement,

which as Yonatan explained to me is only one tiny offshoot of Gush
Emunim. There are three outposts on the high ridges around Wadi
Aboud, each belonging to an individual settler. Yakob, Yoel, and Zev.
Yakob is a farmer who took over several acres of Qasim's uncle's
land about ten years ago, installed barbed wire around it, and built a
greenhouse, growing lettuce and tomatoes and such. Yoel and Zev
do nothing, as far as the village can tell, but start fights. They're both
relatively old now, in their sixties, but they have sons and grandsons,
who patrol the high slopes, often taking potshots at sheep or goats or
shepherds. One of Qasim's cousins is in prison in Israel for killing one of
Zev's sons in 1996. He beat him to death with his shepherd's staff, after
the son shot three of his sheep. That was called, in the Israeli media,
"terrorism."

And then there's Gilal, which is much newer—it was begun about
ten years ago, right before the Sharon-Arafat handshake—and it's
a real settlement, which means it looks like a gated development in
San Diego, with red tile roofs and plane trees and stucco walls. Like
all settlements it has water piped in from Israel. Inside, people tell
me, there are green lawns, and in the middle of the houses there's
a communal swimming pool. It hovers up there above the wadi like a
mirage. I'm told it's rare to run into settlers from Gilal, because they
live entirely within those high walls, surrounded by a perimeter fence
at 25 yards, and then a dirt track constantly patrolled by IDF jeeps and
APCs. There's a gas station and convenience store just outside the
settlement, on the road to Hebron. Aboudis wouldn't use it even if
they were allowed to, but Yonatan and I stopped there because he
was running out of gas and I desperately had to pee. Inside it was air-
conditioned, of course, and the teenager behind the counter, who was
very dark, wearing a knitted kippah and an L.A. Lakers jersey, didn't give
us a second look. There were two soldiers standing at a counter eating
popsicles, their M16s with grenade launchers slung over their backs. I
bought some large bottles of Perrier and some Snickers bars. (You can
never have too many Snickers bars—they're the world's best emergency

food.) As always the kid at the counter spoke to me in Hebrew and I answered in Hebrew, in this case, just "Toda." I could have been some other person on some other journey in some other life. Of course you know I have friends (like Rebecca Easter from Hebrew school, remember her?) who have stayed or lived in settlements. Sam Rainof's father grew up on a settlement, one of the ultra-orthodox ones north of Jerusalem.

I am in every way much more of the settlers' world than the world of Wadi Aboud. I don't just mean because I'm Jewish; I mean because I come from the class of people who run things and control things, The People In Charge. We still think of the Apthorp as a shabby rent-controlled relic but it's not, not anymore. It's a fancy doorman building. I don't think you appreciate what it was like to grow up in Giuliani's New York; you weren't paying attention. (For all I know you voted for him, like Louis and Judy.) Giuliani and his cops are no different from settlers; they'll go out of their way to let you know who's in charge. Look at what happened to Abner Louima. When I'm out on Broadway with you and dad and we see a homeless guy staggering across the sidewalk or two or three black kids coming out of Foot Locker talking loud—I can feel, I can sense, how you draw up into your whiteness, your rigidity. Because you know the police are paid to protect people who look like you. And of course me too.

Now, of course, I could change. (For that matter, you could change too! But you never will.) I could tease my hair into locs and get some hoop earrings and a kente headband and pass for Lauryn Hill's lighter-skinned cousin. I could disaffiliate with the way you raised me—that is to say, with the lie you raised me to participate in. And maybe I will. But not in New York. Never in New York. How could I be so fraudulent as to do that? I'd run the risk of getting killed. You know I'm used to arguing with cops; I'd do something crazy, like stepping in when I see the cops beating some kid on the subway. Thinking I was still one of the People in Charge. In other words: I can't unlearn being a white New Yorker. I'd have to learn to be an adult black woman in, I don't know, Cleveland.

New Orleans. Oakland. Paris. Johannesburg. I don't know. It would just be a different pretense wherever I went.

So you see why I feel homeless. I have no way of living anywhere without pretense, without feeling dispossessed or fraudulent. And here I am fighting for these people to keep their homes as an expression of that, a diaspora Jew fighting to keep Palestinians from becoming stateless. I'm sure people here recognize the irony in that. Or maybe they're just too overwhelmed by the larger irony of the settlers—*other* diaspora Jews—coming here to do unto others exactly what was done to them. Which is another way of asking the eternal unanswerable question: is it whiteness, blackness, or Jewishness that brought me here? Is this identity-schizophrenia something you burdened me with fourteen months ago, with your Great Confession, or is it something passed down in the womb? Or should I stop looking for it on that scale at all and say this is the essence of bourgeois self-consciousness and the real disaffiliation is to become a revolutionary, an undifferentiated foot soldier?

A FORCIBLE SWITCHING OF TOPICS:

Because I'm avoiding it, obviously. Jerome is from Durham, North Carolina, his parents are Duke professors, but when people say where are you from he says, "Berkeley." He went to college there. He was radicalized, supposedly. He has the biggest adams apple of any man I've ever met, and I've seen some big ones, also big knobby wrists and knees. I've given away the key thing already, which is we're sleeping together, in violation of the rules and common sense and the customs of our hosts, to put it mildly. I have his kaffiyeh here in my bag—which is a singularly bad idea in a fancy Jerusalem hotel—because it smells like him.

The first time we met, which is to say my first night in Wadi Aboud, we had a huge fight, in his bedroom, which isn't even really part of the three rooms we rent in Qasim's house—it's basically a crawl space, or a cellar, with a crude wooden door that leads into our kitchen. With no

windows and no direct access to the outside, it's also a darkroom and
a bomb shelter and a storage locker. It stinks of his cheap hand-rolled
cigarettes. We were arguing about—I'm not even sure where we started
but it was about U.S. Black antisemitism, about Farrakhan and Malcolm
and Amiri Baraka and Public Enemy, and I was clear that I consider
myself black and Jewish, which made him only more insistent that
black antisemitism doesn't actually exist, it's only a form of divergent
nationalism, and something from Jameson about how conspiracy
theories are the politics of the poor.

I should say that Jerome is white, in a U.S. context, actually
Armenian—his full name is Jerome Hagop Sarkissian—but numbers
himself generically among the oppressed. He THINKS he speaks
Arabic, which is hilarious, and Aboudis generally try to get along and
guess what he's trying to say, which is not easy. He's so cosmically
threatened by the fact that I can actually hold a conversation without a
lot of wild gesticulating, which means I, the newbie, wind up translating
for HIM.

I'm circulating around the fact that he's absolutely charming, in his
greasy, pungent way. The Aboudis love him, all the kids want to play
with him—he's excellent at soccer. It's just that he has a militant reason
for everything he does. Try to talk to him about soccer, and he'll start
quoting Vo Nguyen Giap and acting like SFP is the Vietcong.

We can't work together without fighting, which is what made me
originally want to write this letter (surprise! I have a topic after all!).
We fight over who forgot to plug in the camera battery and who was
supposed to make the daily check-in call to the SFP office. Why he
gets a room to himself and why he won't wash the dishes, even his own
dishes when no one else has been eating. But the important thing is, I
can't help it: fighting with Jerome makes me think about you and dad.
Not so much now, or even in my lifetime, as who you were before. For
the first time I have an intense curiosity about that. I've just now come
to accept that whatever you were doing in Vermont was actually legit,

not just some kind of hippie summer camp. You were embracing total commitment to a path, which is what I'm doing here, I guess. There's the same rush of feeling, WHAT I AM DOING IS RIGHT, WHERE I AM IS WHERE I'M SUPPOSED TO BE, and then at the same time WHY CAN'T I STOP BEING SO PETTY AND SO WRAPPED UP IN THIS OTHER PROBLEMATIC PERSON.

(I wonder if you and dad will ever realize, if there's any way I can make you realize, how terrifying you were to me. I remember the first time I went to the African wing in the Met and looked at the masks: you must have taken me, or dad, and I couldn't have been more than five or six. Do you remember when I looked at those faces, the scowls, the protruding teeth, the slit-eyes—not all of the masks, of course, I mean only the ones meant to be the most terrifying—and I said, "it looks like you"? What I meant was your angry faces appeared in my nightmares. How else am I supposed to say this? Your face, balled up in disgust, shouting over your shoulder as you were giving me a bath.)

When I get sick of Jerome, and sick of myself, which is often, I go upstairs—that is, into Heba and Qasim's house proper, where I'm welcome as long as Qasim isn't home. Heba is 24 and has three kids, a boy and twin girls: Mustafa, Leila, Soraya. Nobody actually calls her Heba; her name in practice is Umm Mustafa, and Qasim is Abu Mustafa (Mustafa is also Qasim's father's name, that's the custom; also Heba and Qasim are cousins, though I'm not sure how closely related— another custom, don't ask me how it all works.) The twins are almost three and Mustafa is five. Mustafa will, now after several months, trust me enough to sit next to me on the couch and listen to me read a book. (I can read the few children's books in Arabic they own, which gives me much joy.) But the girls are still shy. When I'm in Heba's house I pull my scarf over my head, a kind of makeshift hijab, out of respect, but of course they see me down in the courtyard washing dishes in my army surplus pants, and when I'm hot and no one seems to be around I've been known to shuck my overshirt and wear a tank top, and once or twice I've seen Qasim and the girls staring down at me. They're so tiny and adorable, and always in Heba's way, and I wish they would let me watch them to give her some peace.

Whenever Heba lets me, I help her in the kitchen. This is the highlight of my journey, maybe the highlight of my life. I really feel like everything worthwhile on earth starts in the kitchen—not exactly a feeling I learned at home, frankly I don't know where I learned it. Yesterday we were making maklouba, which is an upside-down baked rice dish, sort of like arroz con pollo. Our neighbor, whose name I can never quite get—Maryam or Marya—brought Heba the chicken, her largest hen, killed by a roving dog but still fresh. I helped her scald it and pick out the feathers. She showed me how to cut off a chicken's head and feet with her heaviest cleaver. This you'll never learn to do in New York, she said. Our hands and arms were covered in blood. Oh, the tangy, coppery smell of blood! How do you have a relationship with meat, how do you know what you're really eating, without it?

Who is Heba? She grew up in Yatta and married Qasim when she was only nineteen. She's not an Aboudi and didn't sign up for this life, on the front lines, but I don't think she minds. I can't tell how she feels about it, actually. We don't talk about politics, not directly, because there's no reason to, if you live here. Kibush is the constant, not the distinctive thing. She has never seen the Mediterranean. We talk about that. She would like to go to the beach, in Yafo. Even in Gaza. Just to see the water, she says. She can't swim. She's never been to the Dead Sea either, but that's not within the realm of possibility; she has no travel documents for Jordan. She wants to take Mustafa, Leila, and Soraya away from Wadi Aboud; she wants to go on vacation. I have digital photos saved on my laptop and once I brought them up to show her and the kids. Cairo, New York, Maine. And of course lots of photos of Olympia and the peninsula and the coast. Mustafa is very solemn and knows his world map but the girls just point to everything and say, Filistin, and I say no, THIS is Palestine. They already know that Palestine is away, is where they are not. And I don't know what to say except to want to hug them and have them sit in my lap, and they just lose interest and flit away.

I look at Heba and she looks at me and she sees that I want what she has, which is in a way incredible, but also so basic: it just means I want kids, I want to be a mother, I want to feel grounded and rooted in time and space with an inarguable ROLE, which is not to say the fifties domestic role at all of course but the universal righteousness of all mothers who defend and fight for what is best for their children, who have "common sense," which also means a sense of the common. I look forward to that. I can't imagine where it will be. No, that's not true. I do imagine it. And I can say one thing: not in New York. Not even, in my mind's eye, in the U.S. I imagine myself, say, in Costa Rica. How amazing it would be to live in a country without an army! Or Mexico, or Brazil. I don't know why, my Spanish isn't that great, and I know only a handful of words of Portuguese. Or maybe Morocco or Tunisia, where I can go on speaking Arabic and my kids will grow up speaking it, Arabic and French. Someplace with a lot of sun and climbing flowering vines, maybe even a grape arbor. I have an image of myself playing with a baby in a courtyard in the sun, surrounded by the smell of jasmine or hibiscus or sumac.

The funny thing is, of course, I have no image of who I will love, who will be my partner, which is another way of saying maybe I won't have a partner, just kids. In this dream life I think I would feel comfortable sleeping with a man in one place and then writing him from another place and saying, I'm pregnant, my IUD didn't work after all, you don't have to get involved. Or maybe not saying anything. Is that terrible? When I look at all that Heba does, basically without a lick of assistance from Qasim, I think I would be solid as a single mom. Maybe the business of child-raising is intrinsically distinct from loving someone else, and it's just part of Western familial ideology that the two are conflated. I love sex, I love having sex, I love the idea of motherhood, but do I love "love," per se? No. You of all people should be able to imagine why. And I say that not to be spiteful.

I feel guilty sometimes for thinking about the future, because obviously that's a way of wishing myself out of here. Do you remember the one time I tried doing a Buddhist retreat, at the IMS temple in Seattle? I tried to tell you and Dad about it afterward but we got caught up in other things. The whole time I was obsessing about how much I was obsessing about the end of the retreat. I found myself constantly thinking about what I would do when I no longer HAD to be sitting and eating two meals a day and keeping Noble Silence and all the rest, and then constantly getting angry with myself for thinking about it, and debating whether or not it was all part of the process or the proof that I wasn't supposed to be doing it at all, etc. So look, while I'm here I've resolved I'm not going to feel guilty for feeling however I feel. I AM thinking about the future, but when I imagine a future (at least this is what I tell myself) it's also Mustafa, Leila, and Soraya's future. How can that be? People have asked me if I would ever consider settling in Israel and becoming a full-time activist, because I could, of course, and I always say no, not Israel as an occupying nation, but in a future Israel, after the occupation is over, maybe. Which is bullshit and waffling. If I wanted to leverage my Jewishness, the answer is obvious: I should make aliyah and commit to being an activist on the ground, live in Jerusalem, learn Hebrew and Arabic, be a refusenik, go to jail if necessary. I could make that commitment here and now. But I don't know if I can or if it would help or if I can mentally stand being X of this particular X/Y binary my entire life.

I get to the end of these thoughts and then still realize I'm an emotional/imaginative perfectionist, I never want to give up hope that the future can never happen until the world is at least a LITTLE more resolved than it is now, that my responsibility is to grow it into being, which is part of why I want children, but of course you would say and Dad would say that people turn to raising children after they've realized that the world is not what they want it to be, that children are an expression of disappointment.

On that subject, I wonder how it makes you feel to hear me say

I identify as black and Jewish. This is a question I would like to hear answered, though I can't imagine asking it to you in real life. I'm sure it makes you furious. But that isn't the point. I refuse, in my own mind, to let you stop there. When I first told Jerome the story, he asked (of course), how can you consider yourself black when you didn't grow up that way, when you only learned the truth so recently. He said, you have all the habits and assumptions of white privilege, and you know perfectly well you could go on living that way if you wanted to. To you it is truly optional. And for once he wasn't trying to one-up me or prove a point, he was just confirming my own thoughts on the matter. I am sure you are so disappointed, I am sure it confirms your own certainty that you never should have had children (and don't ask me how I'm so certain of that; I grew up with you, I saw that look on your face nearly every day), but I want to tell you, at this moment, lying on this bed, I actually feel weirdly optimistic. I'm young. Time is on my side. To say "I identify as black and Jewish" at least throws the conversation forward to a different life; it forces me to acknowledge I'm in the right place, and frankly wherever I go next will be the right place, because it isn't the Apthorp and it isn't New York.

I think that this relationship to time is the essence of the conflict, it's the basis of kibush, because the enemy is just over the hill waiting for the right time to swoop in and take these last remnants of Palestine. And the right time is when the world stops paying attention, when the media is distracted by whatever Bush and Cheney and Wolfowitz do next. Israel thinks it's going to win the waiting game. Which is why our bodies have to be here, obviously. THEY'RE not the ones in crisis, do you see what I mean? But Heba says, and she's right, of course, the truth is sumud: that is, by refusing to leave, by staying on the land and multiplying, the Palestinians will win in the end. Which is what Israelis call the "demographic threat." I hate that idea, I want to say that the solution can't be to just have more children, where are the Palestinian feminists, etc. etc. Why should she have to use her uterus as a weapon? Why is having more children, on this godforsaken planet, a solution to anything? It feels to me like the enemy has already won.

Heba has never taken a vacation in her life. If I could, I would bring her here—not here, Jerusalem, but here, a five-star hotel, somewhere in the world. Paris, Tokyo, L.A. I would get her a room by herself and tell her to order anything. I would buy her a massage, send her for a facial. The strategic politics of luxury, or something. I want her to feel like a free woman for once. To draw a bath for herself and sit there as long as she wants. I wonder if she ever learned to masturbate. (Is it possible NOT to learn to masturbate?) I wonder if she's ever had an orgasm. And then I tell myself not to pity her, ever. And think about all the things she knows that I'll never know.

I keep waiting for these thoughts to turn into something meaningful, to turn into art, but they just sit here, limply, awkwardly, on the page. I'm going back to Wadi Aboud. I wanted to know that I don't have to. It's pitiful, isn't it, how anxious we are for our little individual lives, our precious freedom? Having freed myself from the story, I'm going back to the story. It can't happen any other way.

NOTES TO INSERT OR NOT:

I know that I've recovered, I'm happy that I've recovered

Palestine is part of my recovery

But that's part of the problem, thinking I've borrowed Palestine for my own therapeutic purposes

I shouldn't have had to go to Palestine to discover how to have sex without feeling guilty, without being transported back to my childhood room

Insert ref to "early trauma, you don't need to know all the details"

I was so depressed after you told me about John Downs, but not for the reasons I said, it wasn't JUST the racial politics, I could handle that, it was the secret sex

I felt like I couldn't escape it

Like the whole world is just one gigantic act of concealment

"I can't say I had sex with _____, therefore we must go to war"
How many children raped in closets
Or sisters sleeping happily with their brothers
I have, I have raised myself out of this spiral
I have found something in this world that doesn't care about me

THE NEW EARTH

VoiceMemo002.20180123.m4a

Sometimes I think I have only one story left to tell, and no one to tell it to.

So I'm telling it to you, in this ridiculous way, on this bit of glass I'm supposed to work with my thumbs. Probably I will use the app incorrectly, and the file won't even be saved, and it will be for nothing, though Nestor said it's idiot-proof. And then, even then, even though you promise you listen to my recordings faithfully—

Well, maybe Nestor will listen to it, if you won't.

Nestor also told me something else, which I find fascinating. This phone, this glass shard, because it's hooked up to something called "the cloud," has essentially endless storage capability. I could speak into it all day, every day, for the rest of my natural life, which God knows won't be all that long anyway, and it would all be there, captured by Voice Memos.

I'm sure this is a terrifying prospect for you, as it would be, reasonably, for anybody. I don't even have to send the files

to you over email or text—they exist in "the cloud," he told
me, in a shared Mail Box, which you and I and he can all
download, which is the right word for once. Son, take down
my load. No. It sounds better, in this case, in Spanish. Hijo,
quitame esta carga pesada, de mis hombros. De mi espalda.
My father, who probably said these words to me a thousand
times, being in the newspaper business (which occasionally
also meant the newspaper delivery business), would lapse into
Galician when he wasn't paying attention, and say: Levame esta
pesada carga dos meus ombros, agora, agora!

I won't go on like this. I promise. The prospect of having
to listen to one's father's voice on a never-ending recording is
a horror not even Kafka conceived of, especially a father who
is a college professor and used to droning on, without notes,
without anybody listening.

VoiceMemo002.20180126.m4a
I am thinking of you right now, doing your house-repairing
job, your job in energy efficiency, which makes it sound so
noble, this cutting and measuring rolls of fiberglass that will
probably kill you before you turn fifty, installing windows
on second and third floors with no safety equipment, even in
the sickening cold of the North American winters. I know all
about those white clapboard houses and the small yards and
the sandy soil of those New England seaside towns, which
Melville described so beautifully.

It must be that in some perverse way I prepared you for this,
that I wanted this all along. Nestor says I have to learn to forgive
myself, not because he agrees with me, but because that's just it, I
have to learn to live with my disappointments too.

When we first came to San Cristóbal de las Casas, when we
bought the blue house on calle Flavio A. Paniagua, I wanted
to make it like my parents' house, since by then my father

had already died, my mother had sold the house and moved
in with my sister, leaving me with a truckload of carpets, wall
hangings, framed paintings and prints, silver and china—all
the things they'd accumulated since 1939 to replace the world
they'd lost in Madrid. But your mother said no, absolutely not.
We battled over this for weeks, and she finally relented and said
I could decorate my study however I wanted, which is where
I'm sitting now, of course, this odd room under the eaves with
only a skylight I paid to cut out myself.

I saw no reason for a house to have tile floors so cold in
the winter they burn your feet, and stucco walls that could
be matchboarded and painted, or wallpapered. It wasn't that
I wanted to re-create my childhood home; I was in argument
with everything about this provincial town, all the things
the tourists love so much about it, the narrow streets and
cobblestones, the colonial architecture, the houses and shops
all crowded together in a shallow dish between mountains,
even the symmetry of the place annoyed me, the streets leading
straight from the plaza to the Church of the Virgin Guadalupe.
What good is a city where it's impossible to get lost? I had a
horror of a place without neighborhoods, without ambiance,
without parks, only untamed Nature on every side. So I built
my inner sanctum, which you and your brother loved so much
when you were small. My father's 1902 globe on its mahogany
stand; his old maps of Zaragoza and Toledo and Venice; his
Escher and Holbein engravings; and all those leather-bound
books with their unmistakable smell. For my part I added
a great bookcase of paperbacks from my college days, most
of which I haven't read in thirty years, and my one great
investment, a Thorens turntable and stereo I bought in Munich
and shipped home in a packing case stuffed with all my
clothes, the leather overcoat and heavy Irish sweaters I thought
I'd never use. Until I came here. Now my electric heater is

plugged in nearly every day of the year; Nestor replaced it last fall, though I saw no reason to.

It pleases me to do this inventory, and to think of you when you were about seven, when you would come inside out of the blazing light of a summer day and very carefully, as I taught you, select a record out of its sleeve—I remember you loved Aaron Copland's *Fanfare for the Common Man,* also one of your mother's favorites, one of her few concessions to American culture—and lie on your back on the carpet with your knees up, the music bursting from the speakers. You loved tearing the edges from the dot-matrix printer paper. Occasionally you would let me read you an article from the *International Herald Tribune,* which I received from Mexico City a week late.

I'll admit it: I was afraid, for both of you, that you would become chiapanecos. Of course you already were chiapanecos; I didn't want you to be simple provincials, is what I mean, of course, interested only in football and chasing girls, drinking pox under a guttering streetlight outside the stadium in Tuxtla . . . and now, I'll admit, I crowded your lives a little, with Enid Blyton and Roald Dahl and *The Last of the Mohicans* and *Peter and the Wolf* and *A Young Person's Guide to the Orchestra,* whereas Mama would only respond if you spoke proper Nahuatl, and plied you with those pre-Columbian history comic books published by UNAM in the early eighties.

Like so many children of mixed marriages—which sounds like I'm being ironic, since in what sense is any proper Mexican marriage anything other than mestizo?—you were brought up in a petri dish, a guinea pig's cage, and I can't admit to being overjoyed at the result any more than you must be. I never imagined that *neither* of you would become an intellectual, a scholar, since you both showed such great aptitude and sensitivity at a young age. I must have slowly pressed the desire and interest out of you, slowly suffocated you, I acknowledge that I feared that would come to pass.

Since your mother's death, as you well know, my belongings and my way of living, my *lifestyle,* have crept out of my study and gradually overtaken the rest of the house, so that we now have carpets almost everywhere, and Silvia is always reminding people to take off their shoes at the bottom of the stairs. I still spend most of my time in here. It's still the only room I can keep consistently warm. If you were here, you would find a way to insulate the house so that it would finally, perhaps unlike any other house in San Cristóbal, be adapted to its climate, still cool under our unforgiving dome of sunlight, still warm at two in the morning, so you don't wake to go to the bathroom as I often do, an old man with a hardly functioning prostate, and see your breath.

VoiceMemo002.20180203.m4a

Of course it's the story of a lost book. What other story would I have to tell?

Or, to be perfectly accurate, two lost books. One of which was mine.

Hold on. Someone's calling.

VoiceMemo002.20180208.m4a

I've decided I should improve these recordings by really treating them like letters.

So here goes:

Querido Zeno. I can't say your name without telling its story.

When you were a baby, and I was still traveling, I used to meet people at parties who understood the reference immediately. "Cool," they would say. "How clever, why has no one ever thought of that before." There were always people at those parties, in Madrid, in Barcelona, in Mexico, in London, who knew Svevo's work, people for whom the reference went without saying.

It's been years since I've met anyone like that. My copy of *La consciencia de Zeno* may be the only one in all of Chiapas. Of course I say that and it's only my arrogance, as if we didn't have, here in San Cristóbal and down the mountain in Tuxtla, full-fledged universities and colleges now.

When your mother was alive here and the house was full of comrades they would all assume it was a reference to Zeno the philosopher, Zeno's paradox. And they would look at me askance. They knew I reeked of bourgeois irony and individualism and the pessimism of the intelligentsia. It upset them when I occasionally spoke to your mother in Nahuatl. They accused us of being Aztec colonialists, if you can believe that. They accused her of being an academicist, whatever that meant. Even some of the other professors accused her of that, which was beyond the point of hilarity, but really it was all because at that time hardly anyone else at the university had a European degree, or a completed doctorate at all.

VoiceMemo002.20180213.m4a

You know that I went to Madrid in 1978 to begin graduate school, and that only about eighteen months later I met your mother. That much you know. But I've never told you about what it was like at first—that first year, in so many ways the most important of my life.

I had a great-aunt still living in Madrid, a very old woman I'd only met once, when she came to Mexico carrying my grandparents' ashes—my grandparents had sworn not to be buried in Spain if Franco was still in power. Tía Hilda was her name. She owned a block of three apartments in a building around the corner from the Círculo de Bellas Artes. She let me have the smallest one, which had long ago been servants' quarters; it was just one room with a kitchen at one end, and at the other a tiled three-quarters bathroom with a toilet and a rubber shower hose behind a curtain. But it had a balcony overlooking the street, and the previous tenant had filled the balcony with potted trees, a dwarf avocado and a Chinese orange and another that produced tiny limones, I mean limes, with blood-red flesh. I've never seen any fruit like that again. Sometimes I think I imagined it.

At the beginning I didn't know anyone in Madrid, of course, and I was fabulously lucky to have an apartment of my own, for next to nothing—Tía Hilda refused to take my money but I left a hundred pesos in an unmarked envelope in her mailbox every month, because I knew she desperately needed the income. The other students in my classes were all Spaniards, and they looked at me very strangely when I spoke, and I realized it wasn't just that I was Mexican; I was trying to speak Castilian Spanish the way my parents and Tía Hilda spoke it, formally, with Galician inflections and idioms that were now thirty years old.

I was so lonely, and I thought, What better time to write a novel. I should write a novel. Before I became so thoroughly ensnared in philology, before I had a hundred people peering over my shoulder, so to speak.

I tried writing in notebooks. I tried writing on my typewriter, the old manual, my father's second-favorite, which he'd loaned me until I could get a better one. I had probably already read a thousand novels by that point, more or less, in English and Spanish—especially if you count all the Enid Blyton and Zane Grey and Agatha Christie paperbacks that my English teacher, Mr. Connelly, loaned me from his classroom shelves—as well as a few each in French and German.

I had had an excellent literary education, in high school, while desperately trying and failing to lose my virginity.

Of course I had brought very few books with me from home, but that wasn't the problem. The problem was jealousy.

Oh, if only I could tell you how intense and how poisonous is artistic jealousy when you're young! Remember it was the late seventies, and Latin American novelists were still glamorous— García Márquez, of course, and Vargas Llosa, Fuentes, they were young and strong, the bookstores were full of new titles every week, it seemed to me. I was so grouchy and stiff and arrogant. I had nothing to say about the campesinos, about towns in remote mountains where the dead ruled the living, or women who waved their menstrual garments around like flags. I had no organic metaphors. My parents were Spanish (although actually Galician) Republican exiles and my teachers were Italian and German and French and Irish Jesuits. To say that my education was *Eurocentric* discredits the very idea of a circle: my education was Europe, full stop. If I was going to write a novel I wanted it to be alienated and febrile and lyric and desperate, in the first person but not autobiography, like Rilke's *Notebooks of Malte Laurids Brigge,* which I had already read in the original.

It was just at this moment, after a few weeks in Madrid, that I stumbled on my first copy of *La consciencia de Zeno* in a bookstore just around the corner from my apartment, a place I often wandered into when I couldn't bear to go upstairs and stare at my typewriter anymore. At first I read only the translator's introduction, which said that Svevo, who came from a mercantile family, spoke only the Triestine dialect of Italian but had to write in the Florentine, *good* Italian, in order to make himself understood. He never quite managed it, as a result of which, in the original, his language seems quite awkward and unlyrical.

And then I got home, made myself a cup of very strong coffee, lit a cigarette, and started to read.

It took only a few moments before I recognized I was defeated. The novel I wanted to write had already been written.

Let me try to put it this way: I was thrown back on my own particularity, on my Mexican-ness, which I had never wanted to acknowledge or indeed thought much about. By virtue of having nothing else that was actually my own. Mexico, of course, was my Trieste. This is nothing more than a litany of clichés, of course. I lacked the brilliance of voicing it in any original way, like Svevo, or Paz, or Galeano, or Borges, in "The Argentine Writer and Tradition," or, for that matter, Deleuze and Guattari, in their book on Kafka.

And here's another cliché: every philologist is a defeated poet. It was only by failing to write a novel that I actually gave myself permission to continue with my studies.

I knew I would name my son Zeno, if I had a son, as an acknowledgment and an act of self-protest, if that makes any sense.

So that's the story of your name, and also the story of the first lost novel, the one I had to lose in order to get on with my life.

VoiceMemo002.20180213.m4a

I had a friend from high school, Tomás; people used to call us dos sombras, because we were inseparable, for a time, or los dos poetas retrasados, because we would walk down the hall reading or arguing and run straight into a door opening, or slip on a puddle on the sidewalk. Now Tomás works in the Ministry of Education and has a Mercedes and a driver, and an enormous gut, and lives in a penthouse in Polanco with a separate apartment just to house his wine cellar, but forget about that for now. This is a story about 1978. We traveled

abroad to go to university the same year, not surprisingly; we
even took the same flight to Paris, convincing our parents that
it was cheaper to fly to France and then take the train to our
final destinations. It wasn't.

Not long after that, during my first vacation from school,
I visited him in Bologna. He was very eager to introduce me
to one of his professors, who was originally from Uruguay,
on the faculty of Hispanophone letters. Philomena Gonzalo
de Torres Palayo was her name, one of the very few female
professors of that generation. She had had a very promising
start to her career as an Italian translator of certain early
Argentinean and Chilean and Uruguayan female writers,
sentimental novelists, who mostly circulated their work in
manuscript, all but unknown outside their very tiny literary
circles, but then later on, during the seventies, she had gotten
bogged down in a project that seemed to have no beginning or
end. She was urged from all sides to publish some extracts of
this new translation, Tomás told me, but she refused, saying
that it all had to emerge as one, and then later she claimed,
apparently not without some merit, that her translated
manuscripts had been stolen from her office by agents of
some national intelligence organization. I know it sounds
incredible, and it sounded incredible to me, but sitting there in
her office I succeeded in not allowing my incredulity to appear
on my face, which encouraged her to go on and tell me the
entire story.

Apparently she had stumbled across a manuscript in the
uncataloged archives of the Papal States, which are housed
at Bologna. It was a manuscript from the early eighteenth
century, in good Spanish but with many phrases from
indigenous languages left intact, which was why my friend
wanted me to meet this woman in the first place. She had
realized quickly that although it was not at all her speciality,

translating this kind of document, her experience with
texts that emphasized local color in Uruguay, for example,
made her one of few people in the world who would have
the patience to wade through this mess of a document.
There was no indication of authorship. It appeared to be a
travelogue, perhaps even a fictional one, although when she
verified the dates and locations later they all matched existing
historical records of the British Caribbean islands, Barbados
and Jamaica especially. Because although the language used
in this text was Spanish, it became clear that the author had
been a mariner for many years aboard British vessels, in
the period which was the height of the trade for sugar and
slaves. When I say a mariner I mean actually a navigator, a
professional skilled in the use of the astrolabe and the compass
and the depth-sounding instruments and the primitive
charts available at the time. Which forms a vital part of the
story, as it turns out. Because the text, as a whole, was the
account of a massive slave rebellion, a rebellion of staggering
dimensions, highly organized, which began on Barbados in
1719, spread to Jamaica, and then resulted in the organization
of a transatlantic armed fleet, a convoy of thousands of
mutineers, freed Caribbean slaves, privateers, and indeed
newly enslaved Africans who were liberated on board the
very slave ships bringing them from Senegal and Togo and
Ghana, given arms, and turned around toward England, and
that this convoy of at least a hundred ships evaded British
naval defenses and actually attacked the British mainland at
Gravesend in June 1720, resulting in a fire that decimated
the town and killed several thousand residents, before being
entirely wiped out in a battle that cost hundreds more British
soldiers their lives.

The author of the document claimed to have survived the
battle and then languished in a British prison for a decade

afterward, before it was shown that he was a captive with no role in the rebellion, after which he was returned to South America, deposited at Porto Alegre, at which point the tale ends.

At no point is it explained why or how this event could have been covered up, left completely out of all historical records, simply erased from the minds of the tens of thousands of people who must have witnessed it or heard about it. Of course, the natural conjecture is that the text is an early novel not at all unlike *Robinson Crusoe,* which indeed appeared in England within the same period, and this Professor de Torres Palayo confessed that she had labored under that assumption for years while in the throes of the translation. But then the original manuscript simply disappeared from her office one day. And she was told that the chair of her department had received visitors of uncertain nationality who had insisted on meeting with him behind a locked door. When she inquired he grew pale and said that he had been forbidden to say anything more, that it was an issue of state security. Of course he had a key to all the offices in the building. She had not, up till that time, kept her project a secret, though to be honest few of her colleagues ever really inquired about the details, other than to encourage her to publish something, anything. But there were one or two people who knew the whole story and could have circulated it.

Her conclusion was that there actually had been such a rebellion in 1719, not just a rebellion but a full-scale anticolonial war at the height of the Age of Empire, a war deliberately intended to bring the consequences of the slave trade home to its point of origin, and that somehow the nations of Europe had successfully conspired to eliminate every trace of the story, for obvious reasons, up to the present day. This was a story that would have made the Haitian Revolution look

like a prelude. It would change our entire understanding of the
Middle Passage.

What were Tomás and I supposed to do with this
knowledge? We looked at each other, two nineteen-year-olds,
rawboned, enormous brains on terrifyingly skinny bodies,
Mexicans, who of course had a stake in this story, a claim, but
an ambiguous one at best. It was as if we had been inserted in
a kind of Schrödinger's cat–type experiment. Visit the office
of an old scholar, who will tell you the most incredible story,
concerning a lost document for which there is no evidence,
no proof, other than the testimony of the scholar herself. You
are in the presence of something that, if true, has enormous
potential consequences, but with no empirical evidence,
regresses, so to speak, into a thought experiment. It could or
could not be true. If it were a thriller, if I were Umberto Eco,
or the other one, Dan Brown, we would have gone chasing
through the underground passages of the Vatican—but no.

I wish I had the temperament for paranoia and conspiracy
theories. There's so much money in them; but more than
money, there's that other thing we all live for, don't we.
Tension. Or just call it desire. Which is all a secret is, as Barthes
says in *S/Z,* it's a strand, a cord, a string, that pulls us forward
through a story, promising we are going somewhere. Toward a
revelation.

I am a modernist who has never pretended to be anything
else, an adherent of what Auden once said, that the only
hierarchy that matters is the hierarchy of consciousness, and
I don't believe in paranoia, mysteries, or the fetishizing of
hiddenness, or opacity, or secret occult explanations. I believe
art is the revelation or laying-open of consciousness and plot
is something the novel should apologize for, as Forster put it
in *Aspects of the Novel.* When Tomás and I left the professor's
office, we went across the street to a café that was popular with

students and ate a very large meal in silence, as if we hadn't
eaten in days. I remember there was a *zuppa* with tiny tortellini
in it, handmade, of course, that almost brought me to tears.
It was such a relief to be back in the material world. I finally
said to Tomás, "I don't know how to feel." "Everyone says she's
a little mad," he replied. We looked at each other again. Of
course, we felt the weight of a certain historical responsibility.
"Even if it were only fiction," Tomás said, as if reading my
thoughts, "it could be the greatest novel of its era, a second
Quijote, a monument of—" "I wouldn't bet my life on its
existence," I said. "If you want it to exist, I think you should
write it yourself."

He laughed at me, and we said nothing else.

VoiceMemo002.20180213.m4a

How did it happen? A sentimentalist would say: love is like
that, it attracts opposites, it requires sacrifice, et cetera, it
creates its own aura of impossibility. I refuse to see it in those
terms. For me, this is always the story of not one event but
three: my failure to become a novelist; my encounter with
the story of a lost novel (or historical account); my falling
desperately in love with a communist who, brilliant as she
was, was infuriatingly concrete and could never encounter an
idea without testing its application to the struggle. A life of
the mind was never meant to be just a life of the mind, in my
case. Improbably, or maybe not. It was just the first few years
after Franco, and Madrid was seething with new life, positions,
arguments. I wanted to stay in my room, but something
dragged me into the streets. What was it? How was the proud,
grouchy shell of my younger self shattered?

I had a horror of politics. In some ways I still do. Of
course, when I was in secondary school, at the Colegio de
San Ignacio de Loyola Vizcaínas, there were teachers who

were involved, as we said in those years, we had several prominent experts in liberation theology on the faculty, and there were maybe a dozen students every year who simply left, sometimes in the middle of the year, to go into the countryside, to go to Guatemala or El Salvador or Colombia or wherever. We weren't a militant school, of course, quite the opposite, but it was the 1970s, and anyone who wanted to could become a revolutionary overnight. I walled myself away from all of that, I sneered at it, even, but I was also absolutely forbidden by my parents to have anything to do with radical groups.

More than anything, like many philologists (and of course, ironically, most modernists), I hated the present. Not surprising, maybe, being the son of a newspaper publisher. I hated the urgency of journalism and the smell of newsprint, which seemed to be everywhere in our house. I loved the smell of old books bound in leather. I loved the mustiness of libraries. I listened obsessively to seventeenth- and sixteenth-century music, "early music," they call it now, to Palestrina and Dowland and Bach, Bach above all, of course. I also listened to the solo piano recordings of Thelonious Monk, which remind me so much of Bach.

One of the first times your mother stayed overnight in my room, I remember, I woke up very early, somehow sensing she was no longer in bed with me. She was sitting in a chair by the window, running the thin rayon fabric of the curtains through her fingers, and gazing at the street. "I can't be with someone who's such a shameless elitist," she said, "who is so unapologetically bourgeois and apolitical. If you want to be with me," she said, using a vulgar expression in Nahuatl I didn't understand at the time, and which would shock you, even now, "you'll have to become a Marxist literary critic." I laughed, which was the wrong response. "I've already read too

many books to be a Marxist anything," I said. She wept. Her
whole body shook with weeping.

"Tell your comrades that I have my own philosophy," I
said. "Tell them I'm an ascetic anarchist, that I've sworn to
withdraw from the struggle but will do nothing to hinder their
efforts."

"That's the dumbest idea I've ever heard," she said, very
reasonably.

"That's why it will work," I said, and dredged up a little
Latin. "Tell them my motto is *Non serviam, quia non ad
tempus,* that my politics are withdrawn until a future moment
in the struggle yet to be revealed."

And it worked. I don't know exactly how or why. I wasn't
there for the conversations she had with her comrades. Or,
more important, whatever conversations she had with herself.
In a second, half-awake, when I was a scrawny teenager,
thinking, to be frank, mostly with the lower half of my
body, hoping to get her to come back to bed, I invented the
rationalization that has dictated the rest of my life. Not a
coherent philosophy, just a sloppy remark.

She didn't come back to bed, she wordlessly got up and
got dressed, but then she gave me a long, undeniably romantic
kiss, and I lay there, still in bed, and lit a cigarette, feeling
ridiculously pleased with myself.

Professor de Palayo's story dislodged something in me. It's
the only explanation, poor and incoherent as it is. Call it "the
novelization of life." I've often thought of this but have never
managed to put it into the proper language: Once a person is
offered a glimpse of the world not as it is, but as it could have
been otherwise, that person's view of what we call "reality"
is never quite the same, if the glimpse happens in the proper
circumstances. You start to become skeptical of the very idea of

chronology, of the idea of time's arrow, of history as a straight line.

VoiceMemo002.20180213.m4a

There was something, a small detail, that came back to me not long ago, when I was standing in front of the photocopier in the office, something Philomena told me long ago, from her stolen manuscript. This is what made me want to explain this all to you and your brother, at long last.

The lead ship in the invasion of England in 1720, the flagship of the slave rebellion, was rechristened *Novae Terrae* by the slaves themselves, that is, the *New Land* or the *New Earth*. Which is not the same as saying the *New World*. They knew what was meant by that phrase. In their minds, the new world was not a lost paradise full of noble savages, not to be the fountain of youth or the City of Gold or the enchanted island of *The Tempest* or Bacon's New Atlantis or Blake's prophetic America; the new world, the world they found, was a purposeless hell of sweat and feces and pain, it was like a gigantic maw, a mouth that fed on the bodies of Africans and Indians, who died shivering in their own shit, or collapsed when their hearts exploded in the cane fields, or were whipped to death in front of European women as entertainment. We know of course about all the forms of resistance Africans and even the surviving Indios evolved, the forms of survival that became our culture, but we know nothing about the anonymous genius of 1719, or perhaps even the collective genius, who first conceived of the most heroic act of resistance, the reversal of the Middle Passage, the invasion of England and the continent of Europe by enslaved Africans and by Indians.

Its purpose was to attack and pacify and colonize the old world, to call it to task, to remake it in its own image, to make

one New Earth. A cosmic settling of the score, you might say
a cosmic rebalancing, in which all the colonized and enslaved
peoples, the fodder for this great world experiment we call the
industrial age, modernity, set sail for Europe itself, not content
merely to have sovereignty over themselves, but to call time
itself to account. A reversal of history itself, a way of saying it
is possible to undo its consequences, if not to actually bring
the dead back to life, to create new life which replaces the old.
What could be more modern than that.

A novel is always a form of prosthetic satisfaction, which
is why it's the noblest art form for old men. This is what I'm
telling myself. Prosthesis as opposed to prophecy. The true
story has never been told, which is why we have to imagine
it—history being as always written by the victors. It could
be that this is your mother's final revenge; this is the way she
defeats me, only without a struggle. I'm going to tell it, if I
ever do tell it, into this tiny glass box that may or may not be
recording. I'm too old to sit at the computer, or, god forbid, my
old Smith-Corona, and pound it out in words.

VoiceMemo002.20180302.m4a

Here's one more thing. Do you remember how we found out
about you and the bees, about your fatal flaw? We were out
in the countryside, in the Blue Mountains, all four of us. You
were so young, only three, I think, so it was 1989 or so. The
villagers had cracked open a whole tree full of honey and were
carrying it around, distributing bits of comb, and of course
they handed you one, and you turned bright red and then
blue and nearly stopped breathing. Thank god a bus happened
to go by, and the driver went straight to Margaritas without
stopping, even though the passengers protested, and we were
able to get to the clinic in time. The doctor said it was a mild
case, in fact, and the next one would be almost certainly fatal.

You were so young, and that was the end of trips into the field for you. Our lives changed so dramatically—more so than we knew at the time, of course!—after that day. In a sense, that was when you became my child more than your mother's. Only then did I start speaking English at home all the time, and only then did I start to think about your education. I hadn't thought an education as such was possible in Chiapas. But what is an education, after all? I have yet to know where it ends. Ask me on my last day and I'll tell you.

A SORT OF HOMECOMING

On the deck of the Blue Hill Inn, in 1998, in August, his obscenely pale legs stretched out in the sun. *The Art of the Novel* on his lap. Naomi has just gone inside, looking for Winter, who's sulking, who doesn't want to be in Maine her last week before college. He hears footsteps in the gravel.

"Trick," Bering says. "Tricky Trick Trick. Check it out. I found a pearl."

"No way."

"I did!" There it is; she's placing the shell, with great care, in his outstretched hand. Her hair like a curtain over the sun. The breeze is picking up; she powders him with sand. A pearl packed in a little nest of sea grape, teardrop shaped: the size of a peppercorn. "It took an hour," she said. "There were these kids doing it, they had an extra knife with them, a shucking knife, and I got, you know, swept up in the excitement."

"Clearly something big is about to happen," he says. "It's a portent. You should buy a lottery ticket."

"Something big *has* already happened."

"Okay, then buy me a lottery ticket."

"It's the randomness that gets me," she says. Behind and all around her, the walls of a palace open, walls of white marble. She sits on the deck chair beside him, but crossways, upright, her feet still on the deck. Where her feet plant themselves, lotuses bloom. "A pearl, you know, it's like a tiny speck of dirt—"

"I know how pearls form, yes."

"Mineralization of a foreign object. Or something. It's essentially a scar formation, a living wound."

"That's very poetic, you get an A."

A car passes with the windows open, the bass throbbing. Summer. "Come along and ride," she sings, sotto voce, "on a fantastic, slide, slide, slippity slide—"

"You should put that away somewhere where you won't lose it."

Bering brushes her hair out of her eyes and leaves her hand loosely, as if stuck, at the nape of her neck. A dakini in a resting posture. She has four additional arms. One holds a bow, one holds a vase of pure nectar, one holds a conch shell.

"At some point, we're going to have to have a conversation," she says.

"About?"

"You know exactly what I'm referring to."

"I exactly do not."

Because her eyes are always shadowed, because she's permanently underslept, or something—will she grow out of it—she can stop a conversation just by looking at you. With all three of her eyes, in this case. Her wisdom eye doesn't blink. It rocks his head back. "Oh," he says. "That."

"We fucked up, Trick. We can't blame them or anyone else. But I keep feeling we have to make amends."

"Don't take this the wrong way," he says, "but I can't tell if you're acting out a scene from Ibsen or what."

In fact she had a secondary role in *Ghosts* that previous spring; everyone had said she'd been the star. She was always just a version of herself, with the intensity dialed down. She'd played Antigone in eighth grade, recruited into the UNIS high school play by an over-zealous drama teacher. Whose name, if he remembers correctly, was actually Mr. Hyde.

"Fuck you," she says. "This isn't easy for me."

"I'm sorry. You actually want to talk about it."

"Sometimes I feel like I'm already ruined for normal life," she says. "A year ago, that might not have mattered to me. Now it does."

"Now, at age sixteen."

"And there you go again."

"You're not *ruined for normal life,* whatever that means," he says. Unable to keep the habitual quotation marks out of his voice, the re-flexive disdain. "Your life has barely even started. We made some to-tally understandable, not-ideal choices. I did. I was the older one. I should have stopped it."

"You know that isn't true," she says in the lowest possible tone above a whisper. "I was fully in control. No one is other than the age they are. Technically, you deflowered me—"

"Eww. That's the word you want to use?"

"It was my first time. I bled, if you don't recall."

There's a disturbance, a flutter. He's lying in bed with his eyes closed, hands folded over his sternum. In 2018. In this position, he's found, space-time flows evenly, back and forth, like waves in a bathtub. He can slow his breathing to match the wave. He's forgotten the word in Tibetan. The something something samadhi.

And now it's not working. A pellet, a grain, falls into the bathtub, sinks to the bottom, refuses to move. There's a disturbance in the Force. When agitated, humans breathe with the top third of the lung, a physi-ological response. The brain senses the decreasing oxygen and focuses on the immediate threat. When no immediate threat is perceived, it keeps refocusing; that's a panic cycle. Stay with the object at hand.

There was blood, not on a sheet, on a She-Ra blanket. A blanket from childhood. He balled it up and took it down the hallway to the trash chute. No one noticed. Francine probably noticed, thought Bering had finally gotten sick of it.

He holds it in mind, the novel holds it in mind. We are held for a moment, he is held. The grain at the bottom of the bathtub, the unbearable object. Is the novel a mirror of the mind. Is the mind a mirror of the mind. Do we want to be held. Does he want to be held. Does the novel want to be held. In the slipstream of time, are we growing cold. He shivers, in his apartment in Berlin with the blanket thrown off, and pulls it back on.

Bering continues. "What I'm saying is, actually, I did it to myself. I *deflowered* myself. Don't take that choice away from me. Wrong and stupid and damaging as it was. Don't pretend we can go back in time and unmake ourselves."

"I don't understand what you're saying."

They've both turned, in their attitudes, angling just enough toward the doors of the hotel to see who's going in and out.

"I'm saying I wish I felt sorrier. I should have a, like, normal reaction. To what we did. To, you know, *incest*."

"Oh Jesus."

"And that very fact is what's so damaging, that I should feel worse and I know I should but I don't."

"You need a therapist, Care Bear. I can't do this for you, for obvious reasons."

"Fuck therapy. Everyone in this family is in therapy and it's a scam, it's a way for bourgeois people to manage their guilt without changing anything."

"That's my line," he said. "You don't get to steal it. That is actually not what therapy is for, and you know it, and you have to be able to separate your fucked-up Upper West Side training from your actual mental needs—"

"I feel like all I really need is for you to say something."

"I don't know what to say other than what I've already said. I mean, I could say something about the history of the taboo and what it means anthropologically, or some bullshit like that. Are you waiting for me to say that it's fucked up my life, too?"

"Maybe."

"It has. It absolutely has. But at this point I have a hard time differentiating it from all the other terrible aspects of our upbringing."

"And you think about it. You think about me."

"Yes, and yes, of course. Mostly I just fucking worry about you all the time, Bear, about how you're going to make it to your twenty-fifth birthday."

"I'll be just fine," she says. Marigold petals rain from the clear sky. She picks one up and eats it. "That's the irony at the heart of all of this. It'll all turn out to be a phase, and I'll wind up, you know, forty and working as, like, an environmental lawyer or something, medium-happily married. People like us are always guilty of excessive self-love. It affects everything about us. God knows it affects our novels. But it turns out all right in the end, nearly always, because we're *good people,* after all."

She looks at him with one of four possible faces. The color differences are slight. You would hardly know, unless you were looking for them, the marks of the Buddha families. You would hardly notice the wrathful head of Amitabha, scowling, yellow, jaundiced, floating above her.

"It wasn't a mistake," he says. "It wasn't *not* a mistake. That's the place we have to get to. It just was, it was something that happened. Feeling what we felt at the time. Knowing as little as we knew. It happened. It started, it ended. It didn't last very long. Four times."

"Five times."

"Five times. It's not uncommon. We're not alone."

"It isn't the sex," she says. "It's keeping the secret. How can you not keep revisiting that thing you can't tell anyone. How can you not see it as a substitute for any other meaning in your life. A substitute, I don't know, soul."

"Incest is not a substitute soul."

"But you get what I'm saying."

"Not exactly."

"I don't like keeping secrets. It's counterproductive. It's baggage, it's mere psychology, quote-unquote trauma, it doesn't help anyone, it's not revolutionary. Sometimes I think, fuck it, I just want to tell everyone, and be completely open, I'm the girl who fucked her brother when she was thirteen, just deal with it. Let's get some perspective. I don't need a support group, I don't need to be an *incest survivor*. But the world doesn't work that way. I don't want to ruin our lives. Therefore it becomes this portal, this, I don't know, splitting, it divides me into what I'm allowed to express or relate and what I'm not. I don't want that. I want to be a free person."

"And I'm telling you you still can be. Just refuse to pass judgment on yourself. That's how we're going to get through this."

"As if it was that easy."

"I'm not saying it's easy."

"'We're going to get through this.' You really mean that."

"You said so yourself. We're good people."

"I was joking."

"We are, though. In the greater scheme of things. We have work to do. We have these tremendous advantages. We have no reason to feel sorry for ourselves, if you want to put it that way."

A screen door rattles open behind him.

"Winter," she calls out over his shoulder. "Come check this out. I found a pearl."

Here is a scene. He opens his eyes in 2018 in Berlin. Which is now. Which is the present. His eyes are open, the novel holds him in its hands. This is us, we are held in its hands. We are living through it, we are getting through it.

Come back to me, he could say. Winter, hold on. He could take her hand and lead her down the road toward the beach, leave Winter for the moment with her Walkman, her Natalie Merchant CD, her terrible taste in music. He could say to Bering, Come on, finish the thought. Come back to me. And she would say, I will come back to you but only in my perfected body, the clear light shining through her. Actually she doesn't need to say anything. Immutable in her perfected body. She doesn't need to say, You already know.

/

http://campfireahy2uf22.onion/chat.php
Accessed April 22, 2018 at 2:21:46 AM MESZ
CAMPFIRE: OPEN FORUM FOR FORMER PERPETRATORS OF INCEST/ SEXUAL ABUSE

WARNING: This forum is intended for ***former*** perpetrators of incest/ abuse who are committed to recovery and healing. Any endorsement of/ networking about/strategizing about abuse will be deleted immediately with the threat of doxxing/report to authorities. We r hackers /// dn fuck with us. Perpetrator/survivors welcome. Survivors not welcome. You have your own (many) resources compared to us. Find them.

apthorp2935c: People are asking me to define entanglement. It's too complicated & OT for this forum but I'll give you the thumbnail version:

Think of two tennis players hitting the ball back and forth.

Every time one player hits the ball the other player instantly reacts (if she's a good tennis player) by getting in position to return it.

You can't measure one player's movements without at the same time measuring the other player's movements. They don't move independently, as long as the ball is in play. If one hits the ball from right to left, the other instantly moves left.

That's quantum entanglement. A subatomic particle, like a photon, is shown to be entangled with another particle so they can't be measured independently of each other, even though they are not physically connected by gravity, space-time, etc. Sometimes particles are entangled *even if they don't exist at the same time* (because photons appear and disappear v. quickly). Einstein called it spukhafte

Fernwirkung, "spooky action at a distance," & refused to believe it exists. But it does, the final proof was in 2015, you can look it up.

It doesn't really matter (unless you care about karma, the nature of time, causality, determinism, etc.) except that you can do stuff with it, esp. stuff with really difficult/long computations, like oh, I don't know, meteorology, the stock market, etc., but that's a subject for—oh never mind.

On another note: I went through a period of being obsessed with *The Blue Lagoon* when I was little, does anyone still remember that horrible movie? The movie that made Brooke Shields famous? It's a, whatdoyoucallit, an antediluvian fantasy, a prelapsarian fantasy, where these two kids are plane-crashed on a desert island and never rescued, and they survive and (of course) discover their own bodies and each other's bodies . . . this is the movie that was famous because BS's long hair was conveniently glued over her nipples, that was the level of weird prudery that constitutes American popular taste.

That movie is a kind of tableau of incest, or what I mean is a template for incest, really both, because, biblically, that's the idea, right? Incest is sex with the only available person/because no one else is present/ because no one else signifies? They're not actually siblings, but if they were, it wouldn't make a difference. There are only two of them. It's the dawn of civilization all over again. In the context of the movie they are *meant* to be together. They discover their bodies through each other. They discover what their bodies are for. It's organically obvious and logical.

I was taught about sex in the way many children of liberal, former-hippie parents were in the middle eighties, which is to say not so much deliberately but through books left around the house where it was easy to find them. There was one for kids, called *Where Did I Come From?*, with horrible, embarrassing cartoons of chubby, hairy, quasi-Jewish thirtysomethings like my friends' parents—I avoided that one like the plague. I read *Our Bodies, Ourselves*. I read *The Joy of Sex*. And the message of *The Joy of Sex* is, basically: do what feels good.

It isn't that literally no one ever told us people aren't allowed to have sex with their brothers and sisters. That circulated in our world like a nursery rhyme, as it probably does for all kids everywhere, the basic sorting-out of the world. That isn't what I'm saying at all. I'm saying it was possible to feel so cosmically alone in that apartment, in that era, even with five people present. There was so much that *wasn't* said. My parents, for example, never talked about the three years they spent on a Buddhist commune in New England, where I was born. Never. (Only many years later, by accident, did I piece together the story: my mother had an affair with the Zen master, the head honcho, and that's what broke the place up, apparently—no other details.) My parents never talked about their work when we were young; how would they have explained it? Their conversations, most of the time, were utterly obscure to me; they were always aggrieved with one another but rarely about the matter at hand. Does that make any sense?

Oh, I'm not doing this right. Apologies to anyone still reading.

What I mean is that they watched me grow up with a certain curiosity and very little overt direction. Me in particular, since I was the oldest and I was a boy. Whatever toys I wanted, within reason, I got. I was the emperor of my room, a fastidious tyrant.

Was it the era? Was it their own disaffection, dissociation, from one another, the bizarre, entropic way they'd stayed married, when they had every reason to split? What I can say is that in all those years no one at home ever asked me how I *felt*. As a family, we filtered all our emotions, including affection, through arguments. Everything was contested. I wasn't private by my own volition or instinct, I was private because no one ever asked me to share anything of myself.

I identified so deeply with that sun-bleached boy, of course without knowing it as such.

The point is we thought we were free people. I don't know who gave us that idea; it would make more sense to say what DIDN'T give us that idea.

/

"It's called simple anorexia, or medical anorexia, as opposed to anorexia nervosa," he says to Joachim, just as they step off the train onto the Jannowitzbrücke platform. "It's a biological condition, the total loss of appetite. Rare, but not unheard of. I just don't ever feel the need to eat. No physical symptoms of hunger at all."

"But you must feel tired, a loss of energy, inability to function."

"Not as quickly as you might think. I can go for days without noticing anything at all."

"Of course, some might say that's a condition of working in the software industry."

"Right. Which is why it took years to get the right diagnosis."

"And you use an app to tell you when to eat."

"Mostly. I drink a lot of protein shakes, whenever I feel thirsty." He holds up his thermos.

"Oh, right. Like a bodybuilder."

"That's me. A regular Schwarzenegger."

Joachim puckers his eyebrows for a moment and laughs.

Berlin, late in the early twenty-first century. Everything is too easy. You look up from the Jannowitzbrücke platform and see the Fernsehturm plainly, from the east, its supercharged onion dome pointing to space, because you're standing in East Berlin. All the records of the Stasi could be saved on a thumb drive. The city swallows its history and exhibits it in vitrines; nothing is disregarded. Nothing is unbearable, as it turns out. No wonder the Earth no longer wants to live beyond its appointed time. He wants to make some observation to Joachim, but you don't talk to Germans about Germany. You just do not. You ask them about their vacations, their fantastic, long, globe-circling vacations. Joachim, for example, spent last August in Tanzania, on a coffee farm. He wanted to see where his caffeine came from.

"How did it happen? Your condition, I mean."

"There were various factors," he says, hoping the English evasiveness won't be mistaken for German precision, "but, to be honest, it was mostly self-inflicted. During my three-year retreat, in Nepal—"

"I always forget that about you, that you were a monk."

"—I got very sick, which is common. Giardiasis. Had to be evacuated all the way to Delhi. Three weeks' recovery. Afterward I was on a very restricted diet for months, and somehow I lost the sensation of hunger, there was a neural shock, as the doctors say. No one quite understands how it works. One of the many failings of Western medicine. Gut bacteria, digestive signaling—it just fell apart, in my case. I tried Ayurvedic medicine, and that made it worse. Acupuncture, too. Nothing helped. Of course, while I was in retreat, people were cooking for us, and it was possible to eat very little and get by. You never have any choice in what you get anyway. But on my own, with no schedule, no support, just a blizzard of bad options everywhere, it turned out to be a nightmare."

They're crossing the actual brücke itself now, zipping their collars against the wind off the Spree. The water rises up, stippling, with that steely gleam city rivers so often have, resentful and guarded. As if water can ever be so carefully managed, so ornamental. I will claim you, it wants to say.

"I remember I heard you saying to Gretchen once that you gave up being a monk because you needed to have a regular job, in an office, with a schedule, in order to stay alive."

"Basically true, yes."

"And when you do eat? What happens then?"

"Everything is as normal. I haven't lost my sense of taste or smell. Just hunger. I tend to eat very little. Mostly I manage my weight through the shakes."

"It's a permanent condition, then."

"Well," he says, "nothing in life is a *permanent* condition."

"You're the calmest person I've ever known," Joachim says. "In a work circumstance, that is. Of course, I have no idea what you're like the rest of the time. It's a very valuable skill, it seems to me."

"It isn't a skill."

"But you know what I mean."

"It's the feeling that everything has already happened," he says. "You could say that. The worst has already happened. So, if we don't get this round of funding, big fucking deal. That kind of thing. An alteration of perspective. Actually," he adds, "I just learned yesterday that my parents are separating. Almost certainly divorcing. After forty-four years."

"That's awful. Christ. I'm very sorry."

Saying it out loud produces a tone vibrating through the air, like an EDM track with the drum machine turned off. A pulse, a throb. People are still dancing, you don't know why. You can't find the downbeat, you can't find the one. In his first few years in Berlin he went to clubs constantly. It was what you did on the weekends, and he was determined to have a normal life, to be ordinary and legible. He barely danced, he didn't know how, but it didn't matter. No one paid attention. His clothes were soaked when he came home at three or four in the morning. He ate scrambled eggs and drank Gatorade, standing up in the kitchen, before going to sleep, to make sure he wouldn't slip into a coma. Katerina was pregnant, not speaking to him outside work. He'd proposed twice and she'd refused twice.

"Thanks, but that's not why I bring it up. It's terrible but understandable. It's not a surprise."

"You're saying they had an unhappy marriage?"

"That's the understatement of the century."

"I think it affects so much of your life, whether your parents were happy. My parents definitely were. It was like a joke, my friends always used to say, Joachims Eltern sind immer noch *verliebt*, like it was something disgusting. It was definitely uncool."

Joachim is—he always forgets—twenty-eight? Twenty-nine? From the Schwartzwald. A town he's never heard of. He was an undergrad at Frankfurt and got his master's in systems analysis at Case Western Reserve. Still a fanatical fan of Cleveland. The Cavaliers. The lake. Ohio. The Rock and Roll Hall of Fame. He collects Stratocasters. Unironically, and without prompting, he will play Stevie Ray Vaughan in mixed company. Even his hair hangs a little long at the back, as if he dreams of a mullet but can't quite bring himself to grow one. He isn't married, and not for lack of trying; he's dated nearly every single woman at Avansys, who all report back (so the office gossip goes) that he's unbelievably thoughtful and respectful, a good cook, sexually willing and cooperative, and totally incapable of laughter or even sarcasm.

"There was a long Twitter thread yesterday about quantums," Joachim says. "You were mentioned."

"Was I."

"You really should check your account more often."

"Every time I tell myself, this funny thing happens. I just go on living my life."

"There's this article, though, on Gizmodo—"

"I'll ask Nazim to write up a summary. That's what assistants are for."

"The point is, you're very good at encapsulating what Avansys does. I think everyone feels that way. Not that you should be in corporate communications or whatever, just that you're extremely good at putting it in ways laypeople can understand. I can't even explain to my parents what it is we do."

"Do they understand how binary code works?"

"Probably, I think so."

"Ask them how hard it would be for a computer to guess their ATM password. There are X number of possible combinations for a four-digit numerical password; how long would it take a regular computer to guess the right one, using binary code? Then tell them how fast a quantum computer could do it. You know, bits versus qubits. That's the best illustration."

"But that's not the cool part, the stuff about how time doesn't really exist."

"Tell them about the tennis players, then. You've heard me give that speech a hundred times."

"I just can't make it sound convincing."

He watches Katerina arrive ahead of them, getting off her bike and folding it neatly, front wheel, back wheel, handlebars. I illustrate it thus, he wants to tell Joachim, pointing at her. You see a perfectly ordinary Berlin office worker, forty-one but still looks like she's in her late thirties, vegan shoes, string grocery bag in her back pocket. I see a nun spattered with mud, head to foot, jumping off the back of a motorbike at the monastery's back gate, on her way to meet Rinpoche, barely giving me a glance. It's 2005. I'm sweeping the steps, wearing snow goggles. The morning light reflected off the snowfields gives me migraines. How can I convince anyone of that. Not how you understand it, how you stand it. Why would anyone want to take one more step.

/

"Patrick," Winter is saying, "Patrick, all you have to do is say a definitive no."

He props his sock feet on his office windowsill, between which he can see down Rungestrasse to the white dome of the power plant and its grassy berm overlooking the Spree. He argued for office space two blocks over, riverfront views, but all the Berliners at Avansys overruled him. It stinks, they said. It turns green in August. He unscrews the top of a second shake—banana-chocolate flavored, unspeakably awful, but Nazim bought a case of them by accident, and to send them back would be insulting and bring about a snarl of paperwork. And he loves Nazim, who always, always, the defining characteristic of a good assistant, closes the door behind him.

"Look," he says, "okay. Imagine I come home this summer. First time back in the U.S. in forever. And it's a great wedding. Of course. It will be. And all your friends will be there. No one's going to miss a Maine wedding in August. You've just secured about a hundred K in revenues for the small businesses of Blue Hill. Think of the sheer volume of crustaceans, the gallons of melted butter, the reams of napkins, the bushels of sweet corn, the cases of local IPAs and summer ales. Imagine the ice, whole trucks full of ice. Imagine the gratuities, scribbled on greasy receipts."

"So?"

"So nothing: it's just that I don't fit into that picture. I'm a buzzkill, I'm a downer. I don't drink, I hardly eat, I'm terrible at small talk. I'm not on Instagram or Twitter. I don't get the references. I'm like the minister with the black veil, just a shadow on your happy day, because, look, I hate to say it, but I actually don't approve."

"You are a self-righteous asshole, and it's almost a relief to me, honestly, to know that will never change. Also, if you're about to say *I love you too much to ruin your wedding,* I'm going to come to Berlin myself and slit my wrists in your bathtub."

"I don't have a bathtub."

"That's going to make your bathroom much more difficult to clean up."

"There are decisions you make in life, commitments, that deserve to be respected, and not casually unmade. For example, I chose to leave the U.S. and never come back. I don't think I've ever put it this way before, exactly, because I didn't want to hurt anyone's feelings unnecessarily, but it's true, by default, *and* by design, that I made this choice as a critique of, as a protest against, the rest of you."

That buys him a heavily padded silence.

"Wow. Wow. I can't believe you're saying this now."

"Please don't cry. Or at least not until I'm done."

"It's my party, and I can cry if I want to."

"I'll just go ahead and say it this way: I went off to Nepal in 2003 because I was absolutely certain that karma had already destroyed our family. I became a home-leaver, you know, that's the technical term, in the truest sense. And I still am. And that doesn't change just because I have a beautiful sister who is marrying a wonderful guy in a fantasy world, a pleasure garden, I no longer believe in."

"You're actually threatened by the idea of coming home," she says. "That's not consistency. That's fragility."

"You're right. I am extremely fragile."

"You're a white-appearing American man, extremely wealthy by global standards, with no major physical ailments—"

"You're a doctor now?"

"You can survive an airplane flight and a few days in a hotel in New England. For Christ's sake, you've got your regimen. Those shakes and whatever."

"You're not an authority on what I can and can't survive, and New England is no small thing, either. Especially that particular patch of it."

"You know what?" Winter says. "I'm sick of this conversation. Let's talk about something else."

"Tell me what you're working on."

"What *I'm* working on? Well, deportation orders, pretty much twenty-four/seven. Repatriation of minors. Custody. Refugee status claims. Tons of those. That, and then supervising forty-odd interns. They're quite fragile, some of them. I keep having to buy more boxes of Kleenex. Some of these kids have really not experienced suffering or abjection, or even really imagined it. And then they get all huffy when someone laughs at their terrible tenth-grade Spanish. But what are *you working* on?"

"Apart from translating quantum gravity into usable computer technologies, harnessing the fundamental properties of the universe to make better Xbox games? No, nothing. I'm planting a flower garden on my balcony. It's good for the bees."

"Are you getting better?"

"You mean the eating thing? No. It's stable. It's managed. I thought you meant something else."

"Okay, then, I'll bite. Are you well? Psychologically? Are you happy?"

"Unquestionably not."

"Are you in therapy?"

"I stopped believing in therapy fifteen years ago. As you know. But I'm working on myself. So to speak. I'm stable. And before you ask any other questions, remember, we've talked about this before. It's the paradox of religious materialism at work."

"Only you would expect anyone to know what that means."

"I sent you the article years ago. We talked about it. The idea is, in a materialist culture no one accepts religious experience as valid, so religious practitioners have to constantly try to make themselves legible in materialist terms, i.e. the health benefits of meditation and mindfulness, but the more legibility, the more you sacrifice to materialist logic, or capitalist logic, if you like, in other words you constantly reduce the non-legible content to make yourself seem valid, but a materialist culture can't accept parallel validities, and anyway the whole point is you're not *trying* to be valid—"

"I remember now."

"You do not."

"I know more than you think I do. I did my reading. Those books you sent me, back in 2011. I read them all."

"I sent you books?"

"There was one called *The Journey Is the Goal.* I liked that one."

"Do you remember what a yidam is? The deity you practice seeing, then becoming?"

"Vaguely."

"And you're genuinely curious."

"For the purposes of this phone call, yes."

"So the deities, the yidams, that I've been practicing seeing, visualizing, for years now? I find they're blending together with visions of you guys. Memories. It's like I'm visualizing my memories, but in this radically different, sacralized form. Including memories of Bering."

"So?"

"Good point. So what? I don't know. I think it means something. I think I'm onto something. It's a major spiritual breakthrough, if it happens."

"I hope it happens. I have no idea what you're talking about, or why it's germane to *this* decision, but great, terrific. I mean, when people ask about you, I say, my brother is a computer scientist and a yogi, and they think I'm being ironic, which of course is the curse of people our age, and then when I say, no, I'm completely serious, they ask if they can buy your book or take your class, and I'm always sorry to disappoint them. So promise me you'll write a book or scribble something on a napkin, at least."

Bliss, joy, arising from the direct perception of reality, the direct perception of emptiness. When you stop applying classic physics to a quantum universe, you get sunyata, the nonaffirming negative, you stop having to uphold any concept in itself and achieve flow from one to another. There's no particular mystique, he wants to say, rolling his neck, flexing his hips, staring straight up, it's not complicated, total absorption in a ritual, the cultivation of sacred space, the sensation of merging and oneness with the deity, which is not a separate being, just a device, an object of mind you merge with. I had that. I worked to achieve it. Nearly a million full prostrations, from upright to facedown. Millions of mantras recited. Morning-to-night language study, memorization. Overachiever, what did I achieve.

"But listen," she says, "as crucial as what you're telling me is, there's something else, too. We have to mark it. Or celebrate it. Or something. Mom has a new, um, *partner.*"

"What the hell are you talking about?"

"She's seeing a woman. Her name is Tilda. Someone she works with, a lab manager. At WHOI. We met, kind of accidentally."

"A woman. She's seeing a woman. Mom is a lesbian."

"I guess you could put it in those terms, yes."

"And she didn't actually tell you this herself, you found out by happenstance."

"I would say she let it happen, passively, she didn't make any effort to stop it from happening."

"Well, that's characteristic, in so many ways."

"It is, but that's not really the point. I just want to give you some time to respond. I should have led with this, but it's a separate issue, or a mostly separate issue, or a nonissue, in any event I can't control it. I said they should both come, and she said she would consider it. And then Tilda texted me—"

"*Tilda* texted you?"

"She said, 'I look forward to seeing you again soon.'"

"So what you're saying is we have an actual new member of the family here, another person to, like, *be in dialogue with,* another point of view to consider, a set of priorities."

"You make it sound like the worst thing that's ever happened."

"Does she know who we *are*? I mean, does she know what she's getting into?"

"As if we're the only family that's ever suffered a catastrophe—"

"As if the event itself was the catastrophe."

"I'm not sure what that means."

"Just this," he says. "Our existence is a catastrophe. I'm trying to get you to see that. It's really quite simple."

/

freanor(-)eepeep: so as I was saying . . . its taken me years to admit to myself that everything we did was, yes, abuse. every time i touched him. it was intentional/sexual in nature.

gangstalean220: and before that? what did u think it was lol

freanor(-)eepeep: well i mean i thought it was voluntary on his part, that's how i justified it to myself, though now i accept he was too young to give consent, obvs at the time i didn't really have that concept in mind . . .

apthorp2935c: For a long time I/we convinced myself/ourselves our case was unique.

freanor(-)eepeep: yes classic "the rules don't apply to us" it's LUUVVV

freanor(-)eepeep: don't mean to diminish it or nothing, just showing solidarity bro hope u understand

apthorp2935c: no worries, I get it.

freanor(-)eepeep: go on, say more

apthorp2935c: Well it's a long sorry tale.

gangstalean220: I'm a security guard, Ive got all night

freanor(-)eepeep: oh shit you're not using a work computer are you

gangstalean220: I'm dumb I'm not that dumb lol, this laptop here is my baby, all VPNs and Tor, no worries

apthorp2935c: No autobios please guyz

gangstalean220: world's full of security guards, I just happen to work at the Burj Khalifa;-) just fwu

apthorp2935c: OK well the basic scenario is it started when I was 16 and she was 13. We were/are a very close family. Before saying any more though I have to clarify: she's no longer living.

freanor(-)eepeep: fuck you have to be more specific bro

apthorp2935c: She died in a completely unrelated way, rather she was murdered, in another country, when she was 21, a long time ago. I can say that much. This is a big part of it for me obvs, she was an "adult" for a very short time and we never had a chance to come to terms with what happened, it was never disclosed to anyone and I'm about 99% sure no one else ever knew, not my parents or sibling. Basically it dies with me. Unless I say something to someone.

gangstalean220: jfc that's a new one, never heard that story

freanor(-)eepeep: well you're telling it to us

apthorp2935c: correction, my therapist knows but that's it. He knows and you know, whoever you are.

freanor(-)eepeep: tricky question obvs but who was the first to initiate

apthorp2935c: she was

freanor(-)eepeep: and how long did it last

apthorp2935c: very sporadically, 2 years 3 months

gangstalean220: what happened exactly. I mean not to be graphic or nothing. how far did u go

apthorp2935c: everything, intercourse

freanor(-)eepeep: I'm so sorry bro. Yeah it's complicated but I just have it in my heart to say that right now. It's so bad.

apthorp2935c: It's terrible, thank you for saying that. It's ruined my life.

freanor(-)eepeep: Most horrible question of all, did you have a sense of how it affected her afterward

apthorp2935c: God don't hold back or anything, that's only the question I've been thinking about every day for _____ years

freanor(-)eepeep: fuck obviously that's why we're all here

freanor(-)eepeep: it's not about us it's about them, it's about guilt and responsibility

apthorp2935c: She was not an average person, ever. She was never going to have an average life. She went to extremes. That was why what happened happened, in a nutshell. She never believed boundaries applied to her. I think none of us did. We were too smart for that or something. She wanted to experience everything. It was like, consume or be consumed.

freanor(-)eepeep: ^^?

apthorp2935c: That was some shit a friend of mine used to say around 2000, like life in late capitalism is this big nebulous blob of signifiers and allegiances and identities, and either you're making your own world or you're an instrument/object in someone else's.

gangstalean220: you're blowing my mind. how old are you that you were saying shit like that in 2000.

freanor(-)eepeep: don't answer that

apthorp2935c: I was in college in 2000, if that helps. An "elite" college. I wouldn't mention that except it matters.

Anyway to get back to your unanswerable question: I was honestly never sure if she was paying attention to her own life, tracking her day-to-day activities, from about the age of 12. She was the youngest of three kids and neither of us, her older sibs, were exactly low-key personalities, so maybe she felt a lot of pressure to stand out, typical birth order family dynamic stuff. She was hanging out with older kids in her middle school, trying stuff—weed, maybe even acid once or twice, definitely smoking, some low grade cutting and self harm. She pierced her bellybutton and got it infected. That kind of thing. My parents were freaking out.

freanor(-)eepeep: I'm dreading where this is going

apthorp2935c: It happened one night when I got home super late and very drunk. She came in and started giving me a back massage. I was all but passed out in bed. No idea what was happening. Actually, I still have no idea what happened that night, exactly. When I woke up she was gone but there was . . . evidence.

gangstalean220: this is such a familiar story, I mean when I was inside, in group everyday, you'd hear a million sick fucks and this was always the way it started

gangstalean220: no offense

apthorp2935c: I think we're beyond apologies here.

apthorp2935c: What are you going to say besides this isn't really happening. I mean we had a private door connecting our bedrooms, it was an old house and they were once part of a connected master suite. My parents never thought twice about it when they moved her in. She was a baby of course. These were our childhood bedrooms. Hers, especially, was like a time capsule. She never bothered to change much. She didn't decorate, she put things on top of other things. I never went in there. Except when she let me hide drugs inside her stuffed animals. That's another story. Those years, my sophomore and junior years of high school. "How are you?" "Oh, I did great on my physics AP and I'm fucking my sister."

freanor(-)eepeep: Concentrate on your own responsibility. I'm not hearing you own your responsibility.

apthorp2935c: I had no concept of it at the time. I'm just trying to explain my mentality.

freanor(-)eepeep: I get that but you have to go farther. You are an offender. Just because you never got caught.

apthorp2935c: Incest is a taboo not a crime.

freanor(-)eepeep: Statutory rape is a crime. If you don't believe that gtfo. You're talking to ex-cons here, years of probation, registries, living-in-grandma's-basement ppl. Fucking admit you're a criminal, bro. You said you took ownership, take it.

apthorp2935c: I should have stopped. I failed her. Do you think I don't know that?

freanor(-)eepeep: Admit you belonged in jail.

apthorp2935c: This is what I'll admit: I went through this phase where all I could listen to was U2. Day in and day out. Also a friend of mine told me I should take Dexatrim, it was like low-grade speed if you took enough of it. So I would pop three or four of those and put on "Gloria" and feel like I was flying. Do you know those songs? Does anyone still listen to U2? I'm hardly ever online, I don't watch TV, I'm not sure Bono is even still alive. How they did what they did is still a mystery to me. Those four-note melodies! There must be terms for what that guitar style does: just notes, almost no chords, and that hollow, echoing sound that makes it sound cathedral-like. It had a strange effect on white teenage boys: it was soul-inflating, virtuous, saintly. Girls loved Bono because he was fucking hot but boys soared with him. Ephedrine, you know that's what Dexatrim was in those days, ephedra and caffeine, and, say, "A Sort of Homecoming." Across the fields to the morning light in the distance.

freanor(-)eepeep: This is . . . I don't even know what this is.

apthorp2935c: It's not complicated, I was trying to purge myself, I was trying to live on a different plane.

Scratch that. It's complicated. Why am I avoiding saying what I'm saying? It was a vision, it was a visualization, a word I only learned to appreciate later; I could explain why, but the explanation would be in Tibetan and wouldn't help anyone. It was my *Catcher in the Rye* fantasy. You know it's time to go, through the fields, the driving snow, across the fields to the morning light in the distance. These aren't the exact words, I know, don't bother to correct me. A flat plane, a desert plain, to the horizon, where the clouds are breaking and the sun is coming up. This is not original, this third-generation warped pseudo-Romantic sublime. It's not interesting. But it's mine. The idea is this, simply: return, return. Return to something you don't recognize but still calls to you. The act of returning without a place to return to.

What was I doing? Jews don't confess. There's no expiation of guilt as such. Also no vision of personal redemption. Later in my studies I thought of the vision of "A Sort of Homecoming" as yearning for the tathagatha-garbha, usually called "Buddha nature" but better translated as "the womb of Buddhas." That's more like it, conceptually, although you don't let go of accumulated karma in the tathagatha-garbha. But maybe letting go is not what I was after.

freanor(-)eepeep: It's not about guilt and it's not about confession. OWN WHAT YOU DID. It's too simple, that's the problem, you act like youre above it & you're not.

apthorp2935c: When I was sick in India—this is a different lifetime ago—I was quite sure I was going to die. If you've had dysentery, giardiasis, cholera, you know what it's like. The shitting diseases. I couldn't stay hydrated, I could never get people to bring me enough of those electrolyte packets. Even in the clinic at Gaggal they never had enough for me. My weight dipped down to 125. I was very close to death, medically. And of course I had accepted I was going to die. I was doing the phowa practices, projecting myself into another body. At that time I often imagined myself walking places without knowing where I was going. I walked through every neighborhood, every wild place, basically everywhere I'd ever known. I walked up Amsterdam and stood in the nave of St John the Divine. I walked up the Hudson River jogging path all the way to the GW Bridge. I walked down Mass Ave from Harvard Square all the way into Boston and back. I climbed Mount Katahdin from memory. Every time, I knew exactly where I was going, although I never saw it. I never saw my apartment, or dorm room, or any place I associated with home or rest or whatever. I had absolute confidence that I was on a necessary journey. Later when I recovered and before I left India I asked my guru about it and he said those were pure experiences of karma being inscribed in your womb consciousness, your storehouse consciousness that continues into future lives, and I said, I don't understand, what was I *doing*. But I knew better than to ask him to answer that question. You can't look directly at karma; it will sear your eyes shut.

Anyway, after all of that, my "personality" never really recovered. That's what I have to admit/own. If you insist on using that stupid word, "own." Part of me died. I am less than I was. It's not the worst possible outcome.

/

Katerina's hands, the large, well-defined knuckles, the palms always blushing, blood racing in them from place to place. Has he ever studied another person's hands in such detail. They sat facing each other once for a week, leading a meditation retreat in Mussoorie. It was a small room; his eyes naturally rested on her lap. That was before they'd slept together, obviously. Monk and nun. Rinpoche laughed at them, three years later, and said, "Evidently I'm a matchmaker."

She pours the tea out of a new teapot, handmade, in the shape of a cat, where the spout is shaped like a paw. "Kurt's new design," she says. "It's very popular, apparently. He sells them to all the cat cafés in Japan and Korea."

"It's hideous."

"That's what I told him. He says sensitivity to trends is how he stays in business. You can't blame him."

"Well, *I* can."

"Don't be juvenile. As if you're here to talk about my relationship problems."

"You have problems?"

Mathias swoops into the kitchen with a Star Destroyer, just missing Katerina's legs as she puts the kettle back on the stove. "Patrick, du musst mein Piratenschiff reparieren," he says gravely, batting hair out of his eyes. In a button-down shirt and V-neck sweater over corduroys, with wire-rimmed round glasses, like a five-year-old eccentric novelist.

"Ich habe meine Reparatursache vergessen," he says, momentarily forgetting the word for *screwdriver*.

"English, please."

"Dein Onkel Patrick klingt wie ein Idiot, wenn er Deutsch spricht," he says, catching the boy around the waist, seating him on his knee, his legs dangling now almost to the floor. *The boy.* "I ordered a new set of DVDs," he says. "*Sesame Street, Dora the Explorer,* all the hits. English, no subtitles. I'll bring them when they come in."

"It's not necessary. They have enough English materials at school."

"Obi-wan Kenobi," he says, taking the Lego figure Mathias hands to him, "you are my only hope. Can you say that?"

"Who are mein honely yope."

"Correct."

Mathias vanishes, skidding across the tile silently in his socks. He stands Obi-wan carefully on the table and sips the tea: chamomile and something else, grassy and vegetal. Probably St. John's wort. He wouldn't put it past Katerina. Medicating him on the down low. She stands on tiptoe, snipping bits of herb from pots dangling from ropes in the window: forty-one years old, her sweater riding up, slender at the waist, broad at the hips, taut in the belly. Hair braided into a coil, as it always is on weekends. Katerina's mother was a well-known Danish feminist; she grew up in the Fristaden Christiania commune in Copenhagen. A self-sufficient and many-skilled person. A manager. A helper. A generation or two ago virtually all her female relatives were nuns.

In Nepal, when they first met, when she was Venerable Khenpo, her eyes shifted continuously when men talked to her, as if searching for a thought or wondering what better use she could be making of her time. Even Rinpoche. It drove people crazy. She was so tall. Not tall for a German, but among Tibetans she stood up like a staff, and her head glowed with ginger stubble. She still teaches, at the FPMT center in Burckhorst. Night meditation classes, twice a week. Lama Katerina Wilgehoff. Her tantric vows, as far as he knows, are intact.

Their dormitory at Dawa Ling was perched on the mountainside above the communal latrines, which meant, with the prevailing winds, that it always smelled sweetly of shit. He didn't know how else to say it. Shit-sweetness. There must have been something in everyone's diet. It was a concrete building where you were always cold unless sitting or standing in the direct blazing sun. That was where he lived for three years. That's how your body learns gratitude. *I feel so comfortable here,* his body wants to say. He stretches out his sock feet on the rug under the table—a Tibetan rug, given to her by the refugee co-op she worked with for years in Dharamsala; she did physical therapy for burn patients and victims of torture. Everything fits and has its place, except him. Or even him, but only as a guest.

"I realized," she says, "in the midst of everything you were saying about your father, and the divorce, that you never told me much of anything about him. In all the years I've known you. I don't think I even know his name."

"Sandy. Alexander. That much you should know. It should be recorded somewhere, in the Wilgehoff family Bible."

"I'll call up my great-grandparents and see if they still have one lying around."

"The one vital piece of information about Sandy Wilcox is that he's a man without a past. A classic American variety. He appeared one day fully formed at Oberlin College in 1970 as a Jewish-Buddhist hippie, a crusading lawyer and deeply insecure and neurotic urban Noo Yawk husband and father-to-be, even though he was actually born a white blue-eyed Protestant, dirt-poor, in middle-of-nowhere Iowa."

"I feel like I should be taking notes."

"He's spent his whole life compensating for things the rest of us don't know about. His father died when he was a baby and his mom died—I don't even know when, exactly. He inherited nothing. No friends, no photos, no high school reunions. But, after a certain point, you have to let go of that theory and say that in fact what happened was he met my mom very very young, and they fell in love, and he warped his life around her."

"That much I remember you telling me about. Your grandfather is Black, African American."

Mathias reappears, holding a spiral notebook and a tin box of colored pencils; he flops down on the floor in the middle of the kitchen, so that any step will be a step over him.

"But of course what matters here," he says, "what you're really asking, is why we haven't been in touch, why we're, so to speak, estranged, or not quite, but extremely distant."

She shrugs. "You've never forgiven him for the way he responded after Bering's death, that's what you told me."

"His refusal to file a lawsuit, to pursue all the available options in Israel, to make it a public case. That was his choice. He was under considerable pressure, although he denies it, to make the whole situation go away for the good of his law firm, his career. But that's making too much and too little out of one chapter of our lives. The real problem with him is he's a shapeless fuck, a hopelessly outclassed intellect who's flailed around in a failed marriage for forty years to a real, certifiable genius, who also happens to be intolerable and borderline psychotic, who never should have had children in the first place."

"You wish you had never been born."

"Don't you, sometimes?"

"Of course not. A human rebirth is infinitely precious."

"But just a little?"

"You need to eat something," she says, looking at her watch and rising. "It's almost two. I have some carrot-ginger soup. I'll make you just a little, a mug of it."

"Ginger gives me heartburn."

"It's just a little. Just a flavoring."

"We once got into a fight," he says. "Me and my dad. An actual fight, a slugfest. He gave me a black eye. I nearly broke his nose."

"Just once?"

"Just once. It was the fall of my senior year of high school. Right around the time I sent off my college applications. At the peak of my teenage arrogance, my dickheadedness. It was mostly my fault—the way it began, that is. I said something insulting to my mother, and he lost it. His detachment broke down all at once."

"I don't need all the details."

"Don't you? Why not?"

"I might meet him someday, and I don't want to have those images in my mind. The outline is plenty. No wonder you're estranged. Or whatever the word is you want to use. There might be other instances, too, that you've repressed. It doesn't matter. The trauma is there."

In the shelf over her bed, the custom-fitted bookcase built by Kurt, painted, unaccountably, purple with turquoise dots, she has a whole set of titles in German by Alice Miller, who wrote *The Drama of the Gifted Child*. He read that one in college—Stephanie, whom he was dating at the time, was taking ed psych. Twenty pages in, he was enraptured; after page 100 he gave up. It's a one-size-fits-all argument, he said to Stephanie, it's so reductive, to think of children as passive recipients, as victims. They are, Steph said, one way or another. All children are victims of their parents' narcissism. But that's not the same thing, he insisted. Anyway you could just as easily say parents are the victims of their children's narcissism. Why was he so invested, at that age, in defending them? And still he has a hard time admitting he was wounded.

As if he weren't a victim of their narcissism, not because of the imprint but because of the lack of one, because of the neglect.

I don't believe in primal scenes, but I'm still governed by them.

"Just to clarify, I'm extremely happy Dad's finally left her," he says, watching her move about again, in her green canvas cargo pants. Does he still find her sexy? "I'm thrilled. I hope it sticks. He deserves to have his own life for once, for the time he has left, on his own terms."

This is an abject lie. I don't feel anything one way or another, would be a more accurate answer. I've lost the ability to feel happy for other people—anyone, even people who actually deserve it. Dark misery spreading everywhere. Why should this be happening now? He needs to change his medication, but the psychiatrist assigned to him by the clinic, Dr. Stadler, is so relentlessly cheerful, so resolutely in favor of exercise and sports—a former tennis champion, who keeps trophies in his office, along with an autographed letter from Monica Seles—that he's avoided him for nearly a year and a half.

"You should tell him that."

"Apparently he's run off and says he doesn't want to speak to anyone."

"Send him a letter, then."

"I've never sent him a letter in my entire life. I wouldn't know how."

"That can't be."

"I mean, I've sent casual emails. When I couldn't call. Businessy emails. I'll be in New York on such-and-such a date, or please transfer more money into account X. I've never written him a meaningful letter, not once. We've never had that kind of a relationship. We have bitter verbal exchanges, where I tell him all the things he's wrong about, and vice versa."

She starts to laugh. "I'm sorry. It's just that I was reading this stupid magazine in the doctor's office the other day, and it said that the most important rule of relationships is, never date a man who hates his father."

"That's excellent advice," he says, "and you've done a good job taking it, in that you're not dating me, and you've ensured that Fabian"—that's their name for Mathias, when they're speaking in his earshot—"doesn't know who I am."

"Fabian is five years old. I haven't kept you away from him either."

"He can always hate you instead. Or in addition. You'd be amazed, in families, at how much hate there is to go around."

"Ah yes," she says, looking at her watch. "How could I forget that the mother is always the real target, always at fault."

"That's not at all what I meant."

"You've made your feelings clear about your mother. I mean, just now. Just in the last five minutes."

She pours the steaming soup into a mug decorated with bats, delicately drawn and then glazed with some kind of knobby black ink, so the porcelain seems to pulse with their shapes. Brimful of Bats, this one was called. Kurt sold them by the thousands. Everyone has to have a life, a principle he still finds it hard to grasp. Some people are whimsical potters. He met Kurt once, at a small Christmas party Katerina threw two years ago. Very tall, with a prominent jaw, a cable-knit sweater that seemed as long as two ordinary sweaters, and a disconcertingly strong grip. And no English. Or at least he refused to speak English. In a circle of Katerina's friends from Avansys, he kept referring to himself as a kleiner Handwerker, "a mere artisan." It wasn't clear if that was supposed to be funny.

"It's amazing to me how some people can manage to keep their lives so tidy," he says.

"You make it sound like an insult."

"Gelwang Rinpoche said, remember, in lamrim class? You have to hate samsara with your whole heart in order to believe you can escape it. *This world is a hellhole,* he kept saying."

"As if that's an excuse to let your laundry pile up in a corner until your cleaning woman arrives."

"I thought we were supposed to despise our bodies and everything that proceeds from them. I thought we were supposed to be destroyed."

"It's funny," she says. "I don't remember reading the part that says a nun is supposed to be destroyed."

"That isn't the word they would use. Or maybe it doesn't apply to nuns."

"Or maybe you're full of shit," she says, taking evident pleasure in pronouncing the word. "If this is another opportunity for you to ask me to help you figure out what to do with your life—"

"Don't kick me out quite yet."

"I've never kicked you out. Never. And in this case, you're going to drink this soup, or I'm not letting you go."

"I'm asking you to help me make a decision."

"Go. Don't go. You're acting as if this one trip is supposed to sew your entire world back together, or not. It won't. People travel places, for god's sake."

"I don't."

"Take your medications, make it a short trip, don't expect anything. You'll feel glad you did afterward. It'll be a step forward. A step in the right direction."

"You enjoy this," he says. "Being brusque with me. Being a problem-solver."

"Not as much as you might imagine."

"I really am in trouble. I don't know what I would do otherwise."

"At least you're able to admit that."

/

apthorp2935c: The problem is that using darkweb for these conversations is too much like the original behavior. I mean those of you who have POs or shrinks, are you out to them that you're using this forum? I'm not.

godsmack8888: i would love to get a therapist where do i get 1, r there even therapists who talk about this ish?

taipeibottom12: apthorp2935c I think about this all the time, I feel so angry that I have to act like I'm a terrorist or sthing to find a support group.

frin8ell4mer8chan: obvs you ppl havent been targeted by the sensitivity police much IRL or youd be used to it by now, freethinkers always live in the margins

campfireMod1: frin8ell4mer8chan you are at risk of being blocked. Abuse/incest is not "free thought." Own your behaviors or get out.

freanor(-)eepeep: lots of signal to noise issues in the group today

campfireMod1: tell me about it

apthorp2935c: I mean look I don't worry myself about being caught or "outed" on here. I assume most of us have the capabilities not to risk that?

taipeibottom12: But you see that's the whole problem risky behavior is addictive and using the DW sets off those same receptors, that's exactly what you're talking about right? So ppl might "want" to get caught, etc, when what we're really here for is healing not triggering, albeit you always take the risk of self-triggering just to get here . . . exhausting

apthorp2935c: Tbh I don't have anyone I can tell the truth about my entire life. Is that common, on here?

campfireMod1: Jesus yes from what I've observed

godsmack8888: yes

spaghettimonster3: yes

pr0crastin8trix: yes

4545jesus4545: yes of course

taipeibottom12: I mean not just this kind of stuff, fuck I'm not even out at work about my nationality, it's complicated but it's like they can assume I'm one thing and not the other bc we speak the same language . . .

freanor(-)eepeep: I feel philosophical about it sometimes bro like who am I to ruin their lives by knowing all of my terrible back story. I mean I'm married and my kids are teenagers. They know some shit, like they know I was in prison, but not the worst of it. I wish someone would know after I'm dead. I mean someone who had a stake in me, an actual friend. I could tell a priest or something.

pr0crastin8trix: You can tell God. I'm not trying to proselytize don't @ me moderator, just saying, I started doing the 12 steps inside and have been doing them for 10 years, and in meetings you hear all kinds of crazy shit, but I can't tell them my shit. No way. I believe secondary trauma is really real. But I know I can tell God. I do, I try to be real specific in my prayers.

godsmack8888: I would do anything to feel less alone

campfireMod1: godsmack8888 I will ask you to contact me privately if you need support/general forum is not for handling acute crisis

/

"I am the father and mother absorbed in union," he says, cross-legged, in the candlelight. He has to keep a window open; otherwise the incense sets off the fire alarm. A car stereo reverberates down the block. A dog whines and skitters across the sidewalk. Berlin, a Saturday afternoon in spring. Couples holding hands. Pizza-delivering motorbikes. A bicycle club clusters on the sidewalk across the street, outside Tattoo Espresso. An aggregation, a miscellany.

"Arriving from the crown of my head to my throat: joy. Arriving from my throat to my heart: supreme joy. Arriving from my heart to my navel: distinguished joy. Arriving from my navel to the tip of my gem, here arises deep awareness of simultaneously arising joy. Whereby both the supporting and supported mandalas take on the essential nature of inseparable blissful awareness and emptiness."

It's Saturday. Once a week, the entire ritual, the long sadhana. Sadhana Shabbat. It takes three hours. Phone off, Wi-Fi off. His own translation, the one he worked on painstakingly with Geshe Jinpa for a year. Once a week, in his full robes, head freshly shaved. He makes the torma himself, out of barley flour he orders over the Internet. Only one concession: olive oil instead of yak butter in the lamps. On the altar, pictures of Rinpoche, Rinpoche's guru, His Holiness, Alan Turing, and Bering, a cheap snapshot she mailed him from Jerusalem.

At Dawa, on retreat, before he got sick, he practiced it six days a week. It was easy. He was never not Heruka. He always felt slightly flushed, even outside in the cold, sweeping the walkways, shoveling coal into the hopper. His joints were soft. It was as easy to sit in full lotus for an hour as it was to stand upright. He could recite the long mantra a hundred times without taking a sip of tea. At the self-generation stage he could smell the ashes and the blood.

A car horn toots twice downstairs. Laughter. A woman's voice shouts Takashi, Wilhelm. A voice full of springtime. Takashi, vergiss deinen badeanzug nicht.

"I take Chakrasamvara Heruka as my yidam and Vajravarahi Dakini as my consort, the father and mother absorbed in union."

Hovering at the edge of the mandala, Naomi's face.

On the opposite side, Sandy's face.

Practice seeing your mother as all mothers, Rinpoche told him, and when he asked for clarification, Rinpoche said, not all mothers smile. Practice seeing her as a life force. Give her Durga's face, give her Kali's face, but still, it's your mother. She gives you life. You and she are inseparable. The visualization won't work otherwise.

He sees Sandy and Naomi on a futon on the floor. It's an old house, the temple in Vermont; they're trying not to make the floor creak. She's on top, pulling a blanket around herself, it's so cold. They look impossibly young. He's seen pictures. His father stretched out naked, skinny, shaggy, with a patchy beard. His mother, working her hips, her eyes closed. Face turned to one side, as if thinking of something else. They don't know what they're doing. Have compassion for them. Turn your face to the side, see them as their perfect selves. When the rage burns away, see them as their perfect selves.

"All twenty-four heroic lady virinis," he says, returning to the text, "have one face, two arms, and three eyes. Embracing their fatherly partner with both arms, their right hand holds a cleaver, while threatening with the threatening mudra all malevolent beings in the ten directions. They are naked, with the bodily form of ferocious women, beautified by having hair hanging loose, they are bedecked with the mudra-seal of the five bone-ornaments and have a crown of five human skulls."

Bering looks at him straight when he closes his eyes, in her full armor, her perfected form. Blood trickles down her cheeks and shoulders. She can still climb astride him. He can still smell her. Her sharp ornaments pressed up against him. Burn me away, he wants to say to her, dissolve me in clear light. Don't make me Heruka. Then who will carry me. No one can carry you.

/

freanor(-)eepeep: I think its just the two of us up this late/early
apthorp2935c: Ok so let me try this one on you again.

freanor(-)eepeep: Hit me with your best shot

apthorp2935c: Imagine there was a school of thought, or better yet, a process, like the twelve steps, that involved going back and facing your negative/abusive urges and emotions directly and purifying them, like, re-experiencing them and then purifying them.

freanor(-)eepeep: Sounds like some kind of fucked up therapy

apthorp2935c: It's not therapy, though. It's a kind of meditation. You have to do it yourself. It takes years of training.

freanor(-)eepeep: OK go on

apthorp2935c: You visualize these . . . beings that are like your avatar or video game character, like a perfected, ideal version of yourself, and you merge with them, and what happens is, in theory, whatever your destructive thing was, it becomes expressive of something beautiful and perfect.

freanor(-)eepeep: Wait what? that sounds like compensatory bullshit to me

apthorp2935c: No not at all. I don't think so at least.

freanor(-)eepeep: Dude this is addictive behavior you can never say you've like "transcended" it

apthorp2935c: Ok but let me try to explain it. Look for me it was one person at one time long ago. I'm not a, like, "pedophile."

freanor(-)eepeep: Do you look at porn?

apthorp2935c: Wtf does that have to do with anything?

freanor(-)eepeep: Because what I'm hearing you say is that you're so convinced this is all in the past and it's about "healing" or "mourning" or "perfecting" and that is all BS. Stop trying to forgive yourself the only way to do that is not to abuse again

apthorp2935c: You're not hearing anything I'm saying. The whole point of this process is that it is the present. It's happening now. That's the whole point of the thing, it's an array, a mandala, where the past present and future are simultaneous.

freanor(-)eepeep: That sounds like self-justifying BS and also it doesn't make any fucking sense apthorp2935c: Put it this way: do you believe your mind can ever change?

freanor(-)eepeep: You still haven't answered my question do you look at porn?

apthorp2935c: I wish I could.

freanor(-)eepeep: wtf does that mean?

apthorp2935c: I miss having a sex life. I had tons of sex. In college, after college. Good/bad/indifferent. I was a fucking hot property if I may say so. I felt extremely human. Once I came out from under the shadow of my family. It was all so beautiful. How would anything in my life have happened without that energy. It was all one thing, undifferentiated. I was a sexy fucking genius. What happened to that person. I live in the ruins of that body.

freanor(-)eepeep: What a fucking pity party give me a break

apthorp2935c: I'm still more alive than you

/

He goes to bed early. Dinner at six, whatever he can force himself to eat, an hour of TV news, an hour of reading, in bed by nine.

It's easy to lose track of time, when you spend so much of it alone, so he makes lists. Endless lists, on yellow legal pads. There's always one by the bed. Weekly, daily. And a paper calendar. He tries not to bring his laptop to bed; otherwise he'd never stop writing into the forum, or working, or switching back and forth.

Sitting up in bed, he puts his book aside—a new translation of Tibetan commentaries on Vasubandhu, too dense and systematic to absorb more than ten pages at a time—and picks up the pad, the calendar.

August, so far, is entirely open. There's a conference in Bucharest the last week of July, and he'd considered stretching it out another week, taking a car and driving down the Croatian coast. Also there's the Tibetan Summer Intensive in Dordogne; they're always asking him to teach, or at least give a lecture.

He has no idea of Katerina's plans for Mathias. Probably they'll spend two weeks in Copenhagen, where he's decidedly *not* invited; on the other hand, they might go to Sardinia, where Katerina's younger sister runs a B & B. He's visited them there before. Jova has three kids with two different fathers, one local, one from Sri Lanka; she's not judgmental.

Which is to say: there's no particular reason, in August, for him to be anywhere, or nowhere.

Across the fields to a light in the distance.

There's a difference, he wanted to say to Winter, between not particularly wanting to live and wanting to die, and that, for me, is the difference between Berlin and New England. It gives him a faint quailing of nausea just thinking about it.

On the other hand.

When you've abandoned the possibility of reconciliation, healing, there's always the possibility of sheer awareness. Moment-to-moment observation of one's mind without clinging.

Not wanting to live, wanting to die, living as if already dead.

Or, to put it another way: not choosing.

Something is happening: the novel is happening. The novel is, he would say, if he knew the words, this third possibility.

I'll have to bring Mathias, Mathias has to meet his grandparents, occurs to him out of nowhere. Mathias will climb Blue Hill, will do one thing in his childhood that I did in mine.

He flips to a new page.

Patrick Wilcox
May 2018

A statement to be released after my death

I had a psychoanalyst once—this was in 2001–2002, when I had moved back to the city after college, my brief and single attempt at living a normal life—who tried his best to convince me that external objects exist. I don't mean that's what he was trying to do explicitly. I mean that he sat there, utterly self-satisfied, homeostatic, among his geometric paintings, jade plants, and excellent midcentury furniture, and waited for me to admit that he was real, the Upper West Side was real, my neurotic responses to my neurotic parents were real. And all the time I was withholding reality from him, I feel almost regretful about it. When I realized the play of withholding was the substance of my therapy, I stopped going.

For a period of sixteen months (give or take) in 1995 and 1996 I had a sexual "relationship" with my sister Bering, when I was sixteen and she was thirteen. This relationship was entirely consensual. It was sporadic. Bering was (in the simplest way I can put it) experiencing extreme depression during this time and initiated the relationship with me because she was struggling to maintain a sense of being alive in her own body. It seemed necessary to do what we did. It seemed pleasurable. I did not experience feelings of guilt or fully comprehend the self-destructive, destabilizing, indeed self-corroding effects of our actions as such until years later.

Bering of course died in 2003 without having told anyone (to my knowledge) other than her therapists, if indeed she told them.

I have been haunted, if that is the word, as the bearer of this secret my whole life. Does that sound like a sentence out of *Wuthering Heights*? How else am I supposed to put it? I bear it like a weight, I bear it like a sentence. Bering once said to me, This is our substitute life. So I have been living like a substitute. You can't understand anything that's happened without understanding this thing only I know. Is the nature of the world like this? No, but also yes.

Properly speaking the nature of the world is only

perceptible through direct yogic insight into emptiness, but so few of us ever experience any such thing for more than a moment at a time, it remains on the periphery of our consciousness, a flutter of black wings in the corner of the eye, reminding us that nothing else we experience is valid. All our grasping, in this sense, is guilt, compensation, and substitution. My whole life with Bering was one long confirmation of that.

Well, so what? I should have died in the hospital at Gaggal, I was already dead. I went on living. I have been living, cheerfully unencumbered with any basis for doing so, ever since. That's what I have to say. You who are reading this, know that I am grateful to have been liberated from delusion by Bering's skillful means, her arrival and departure severed the root of my clinging with Manjusri's diamond sword. I return home, I am coming home.

/1A

A world of evanescent impressions; a world without matter or spirit, neither objective nor subjective; a world without the ideal architecture of space; a world made of time; a tireless labyrinth, a chaos, a dream.

Jorge Luis Borges

SYMPOSIUM ON JORGE LUIS BORGES, "A NEW REFUTATION OF TIME"

Naomi

I was watching her take a bath, so she must have still been quite young. Four. Maybe five. She was playing with Patrick's battleships. He had a whole fleet of them. She separated them into groups. The big battleships took care of the little battleships. They were like ducks. Winter came into the bathroom, already in her footie pajamas, to brush her teeth, and said, You're supposed to divide them into sides, so they can fight a war. She'd taken all her baths with Patrick, obviously. And Bering said, very loudly, "There aren't *sides*."

There, is that what you want? Is that the point of this exercise?

Victor

Borges believed fervently in the mind as a library, cross-referenced, endlessly citational; most readers can see that, but the key point is that in *his* library, chronology is the least important factor. You couldn't find a more anti-Hegelian, anti-Leavis, counterprogressive, antimodern modernist; so much more so than Pound, for example. Berkeley, Leibniz, Sextus Empiricus, and Chuang Tzu matter more to him than, say, Bergson, G. E. Moore, Bertrand Russell, Wittgenstein, or any other thinker of his own era. This is the key point about this weird and self-undermining little essay: it's not philosophy, it's not systemic, but quite the opposite. As Borges admits in the preface, not even the title works, because if a refutation of time is "new," it hasn't refuted time. See?

If you're familiar with post-Cartesian European idealism, the underpinning of his argument is quite obvious: he quotes Berkeley, Hume, Schopenhauer, et al. about the nonexistence of space and matter outside the mind that perceives and structures it, and then goes on to argue that the idealists are naïve in assuming that time is any more real than space. How precisely are we supposed to say that one mental state is any different from a previous or subsequent mental state, even if they're, say, thirty years apart? We know this, he says, through mental experiences of repetition or even déjà vu. As a writer of fiction, Borges knows (in a way that philosophers almost never seem to know) that you have to embody a theory, not just outline it; so he quotes himself, in an earlier essay called "Feeling in Death," describing a walk through the Barracas neighborhood of Buenos Aires, a place remembered vividly from his childhood, and having the sensation not only that nothing had changed, but that he was actually alive, again, in the 1890s:

> I felt dead, I felt as an abstract spectator of the world;
> an indefinite fear imbued with science, which is the best
> clarity of metaphysics. I did not think that I had returned
> upstream on the supposed waters of Time; rather I suspected
> that I was the possessor of a reticent or absent sense of the
> inconceivable word *eternity* . . . That pure representation of
> homogeneous objects—the night in serenity, a limpid little
> wall, the provincial scent of the honeysuckle, the elemental
> earth—is not merely identical to the one present on that

corner so many years ago; it is, without resemblances or
repetitions, the very same.

Patrick

What follows from this way of thinking? Two dilemmas. If all moments are the same, all experiences are equally valid; if all experiences
are equally valid, then, as Borges quotes from the Mishnah: "he who
kills one person destroys the world." Or, from Bernard Shaw: "Neither
poverty nor pain are cumulative." Misunderstood, this way of thinking forms the heart of a painfully familiar kind of bourgeois-liberal,
all-I-need-to-know-I-learned-in-kindergarten ethics, if you grew up on
the Upper West Side, or, say, northwest Washington, or Santa Monica,
or Burlington, Vermont. The absurd moral inflation of small gestures.
Save a tree, save the world, etc.

And the other dilemma, which is, if anything, even worse: if you
view all your experiences simultaneously, you're no longer capable of
recalling the *first time* of anything—that is, no more innocence. "I
deny the successive," Borges writes, "I deny, in an elevated number of
instances, the contemporary as well. The lover who thinks, 'While I
was so happy, thinking of the fidelity of my love, she was deceiving me,'
deceives himself: if every state we experience is absolute, the misfortune
of today is no more real than the happiness of the past."

The Novel

A mission statement, for those who have been patient enough to wait.

A statement in the form of a question in the form of a statement.

Who killed Bering Wilcox.

Was she killed.

Is she alive.

Was she alive.

Was anyone punished.

What does a novel have to do with punishment.

Is punishment the same as justice.

Is a novel the same thing as justice.

Can justice take the form of a novel.

Yoav

You already know the answer to every question you could possibly ask me.

Heba

I wonder if you even know what a ghouleh is. A monster, a black-skinned monster who eats human flesh, who can take on a human appearance. There are male ghouls and female ghoulehs. Is there a word for them in English, I wonder. In school I learned the ghouls are shayatin that once lived in heaven but were cast out by Jesus. That's what the teacher said.

There was a story I always wanted to tell you, my favorite story from all the stories my grandmother told me when I was little. But you would never have understood it, your Arabic wasn't nearly good enough, and there was never anyone around who spoke enough English to translate. I told it to Mustafa, of course, many times and he loved it.

In any case, here is the story. There were two children, a brother and sister, whose mother had died long before, and who were brought up by their father. Then, suddenly, their father died and they were left all alone. They had a chicken coop and survived by eating eggs.

One day, the sister was searching for eggs in the straw, and she found a heavy bag of money. Her father had hidden all his savings there in the chicken coop, and so she knew they were saved. But she didn't tell her brother right away, because she knew he would spend the money; he wasn't mature enough to save it for the future. They survived for years, fending for themselves, until finally he was old enough and she told him. Then they set out to make their fortune in the world.

Who knows what happened next? The story doesn't say, exactly. Only that the brother and sister happened upon a farm where a young woman lived alone. She was very beautiful, and the brother fell in love with her and married her. But she was a ghouleh. After their first child was born, a girl, the ghouleh ate the baby in the middle of the night and smeared the blood on the lips of her sister-in-law. When her husband woke up in the morning, she said, "Your sister is a ghouleh and she ate our baby!" But the sister said, "By Allah, I did no such thing!" He did nothing. He didn't know which one to believe.

But then it happened again: another baby was born, a boy this time, and the ghouleh ate the baby in the middle of the night and smeared the sister's lips with blood. This time her brother realized he had to act. He took her out into the hills, and stopped next to a well, and said, "How could you eat my children?" "By Allah," she said again, "I did not eat them!" But he didn't believe her; maybe his mind was bewitched by the ghouleh's beauty, or maybe he was just crazed with grief. He cut off his sister's hands and feet, there by the well. In return, she cursed him: "In Allah's name," she said, "you will get a thorn in your foot you will never be able to pull out."

And it happened! The brother got the thorn in his foot as he walked home to his wife's house and hobbled the rest of the way. When he was almost there, he saw the strangest sight: a rooster running across the yard, and his wife chasing after it with both hands outstretched, her face red-black, the color of dark blood. And he knew that she was the ghouleh. He turned around and hobbled back into the hills, and lived that way for years, out in the open, sleeping under trees, begging for food from passing caravans on the way to Jerusalem, or stealing fruits and vegetables from farms and orchards he happened to pass by.

What he didn't know is that his sister had been saved, there at the well, by a mysterious female snake. The snake appeared to her and said:

"Hide me under your skirt, a male snake is chasing me." She did so, and when the male snake appeared, the she-snake hissed the word "Explode!" from under the skirt, and he burst like a sack of blood and fell to pieces into the well. In return for saving her, the female snake, who was gifted with very rare magic, rubbed against the bleeding stumps of the sister's hands and feet and they reappeared instantly. The sister went on her way, and in time she found another farmer's family and married one of the sons and had children of her own.

Years later, her brother, who was now a grizzled and sunbaked tramp, limped through the village. She immediately recognized him, though he didn't recognize her. She told her children, "When a man with a limp comes to our door, remind me to tell you the story of the woman whose hands and feet were cut off." And yes, he came to the door and begged for charity, and she showed him inside and washed his foot and took out the thorn with a needle in just a few moments. After he had cleaned himself and she had fed him dinner, her children clamored, "Tell us the story of the woman whose hands and feet were cut off." And she did. As she did, her brother's face turned from confusion to shock to horror to grief. She embraced him and he lived happily in her home for the rest of his life.

There, the story has flown like a bird! That's what my grandmother Umm Tariq always used to say, when we were clustered around her. And then she would say, I leave it in your hands.

I wanted to know what you would make of this story, where the girl is the hero. Not just the hero, the calm and sensible one, the one who knows what to do. Qasim didn't like it that you came into the house; he didn't like it that you spoke Arabic, terrible as your Arabic was. He didn't know what to make of you, wanting to come into the kitchen and help wash the dishes, play with the kids. Of course we expected you would leave any day. But there was something about you that disturbed him, even so, every time you were in his eyesight. Of course he was aroused by you. I think a man can tell, just by the smell, whether a woman is a virgin or not, whether she knows what sex is and wants sex.

Pardon me for speaking this way. But anyone could tell that about you. You carried that musky odor with you everywhere, even I was always aware of it. Maybe you didn't bathe the way we bathe. I don't know. I used to smile to myself and think, *she's my ghouleh, she's the ghouleh in the story, coming to eat my children and smear my lips with blood.*

When I was little I loved most the part about the female snake who yelled "Explode!" We used to say it together with Umm Tariq.

Naomi

The investigation of faults, as in, "it's your fault." Fault-finding, after all, is the most basic form of time travel. Children learn to employ it almost from birth. The most primitive kind of rage is an infant's rage after the object has been denied. This is how we learn to employ the past tense: *you took that away from me. You did it to me.*[*]

"Blame," from the Old French *blasmer,* from the Latin *blasphemare,* from βλασφημέω, "to speak profanely of sacred things," "to speak ill, malign, defame, slander." To blame is blasphemy. To speak accurately is slander. The confusion lies at the root. Powerful people dislike blame; they avoid accountability. Families generally feel the same. This is why blame matters. It's refreshing. It's a splash of cold water across the eyes.

Blame stretches across time and space. It binds together history. Supposedly a form of causal analysis, in that event X had to happen before event Y, it often defies chronology. Children get blamed, rightly,

---

[*] Wilcox, Naomi Schifrin. *The Shiva Hypothesis: Climate Change, Human Rage, and the Future of Planet Earth,* Basic Books, 2011: "The process of child socialization makes us less and less capable of acknowledging our basic (and likely evolutionary) impulse to locate and blame an immediate cause for our distress . . . when I was a young girl, I was often told it was wrong to punch boys on the playground when they pulled up my skirt, yanked my braids, and teased me. I refused to stop. I kept on punching boys until *they* stopped molesting *me.* Over and over my teachers told me, 'They're just going through a phase,' or, 'Boys will be boys.' I told them, not in so many words, that while appreciating boys' development in the abstract was their problem, I had to deal with it in real time; I wasn't interested in understanding them, I was interested in blaming them for their concrete actions, doing something about it, and then getting on with my eight-year-old life. You could say this was my first education in Newton's Third Law: for every action, there is an equal and opposite reaction."

for events that occurred long before they were born. This is the part I appreciate most about "A New Refutation of Time": Borges says, "The lover who thinks, 'While I was so happy, thinking of the fidelity of my love, she was deceiving me' is deceiving himself: if every state we experience is absolute, such happiness was not contemporary to the betrayal." Which means, if I understand it, not only that we should assume that happiness should not be excluded from a feeling of betrayal or disappointment, but that disappointment should not be excluded from the universe of possibilities when one is happy. There is no innocence and no starting over, except in the momentary, incidental sense. I am allowed to state that everything matters. Therefore everyone has to be present. Simultaneity is what I'm after, not plausibility. I am allowed to state that the world is reducible not to irreducible, equally important momentary experiences (as Borges seems to believe) but to a kind of lowest common denominator. As we all know, malignant cancerous cells colonize and overwhelm benign noncancerous cells, not the other way around. Therefore—among other things—the universe is reducible to the blame we all share for the worst of everything.

The Novel

Two words: *novel, story.* A novel is new. *Nouvelles,* the news. A novel perspective. That which has just arrived. A story is a recitation of that which has already happened. Story, history, histoire. A novel tells a story, and renders itself impossible. It has a polar structure, an unresolvable binary structure.

Situated between these two poles is an animal that doesn't like you. You wish it were less indifferent. You wish you could look it in the face but its face is always hidden. You wish its fur didn't smell so bad. On the other hand, it keeps you warm for now. It has limbs, but they hardly ever move. It seems to squat. It has no other purpose than to sit here and not move. It doesn't speak. But you can't unfeel it. You are not numb. Does it have a name, you wonder, knowing already that this is its name. The novel is speaking, that is its name. It doesn't move no matter what you do to it.

Bering

We were awake most of the night in the olive grove.

Naomi

We were happy when we were animals. All three of them were good babies. They slept, they nursed. Of course it was most intense with Patrick—we were alone together, the three of us, that entire winter in Alaska—but the first eighteen months of motherhood with each of them remains quivering in my memory, raw as can be. Being a mammal. A human infant searching for the nipple, no different from a piglet or a puppy. You don't know what it's like, unless you've done it yourself. There's no way to describe being roused out of that state and told to get dressed, you have a class to teach. You have an appointment with the provost. This was the early eighties, you could still walk into a faculty reception at Columbia, stinking of old carpets and sherry, and be the only woman. In the beginning I had one tweed suit and three frilly blouses, all from Alexander's, and I could never get the spit-up stains off the shoulders.

Isn't part of our great disappointment that we are not animals?

Bering

There are stars visible in the desert in Palestine and nowhere else on Earth. That's what the fellaheen say. Wadi Aboud is fifty-four miles south of Bethlehem. We were lying in the fields under the skies that looked down on Joseph and Mary and Abraham and Isaac.

Omar had his CD Walkman, a tinny battery speaker, and a copy of George Michael's greatest hits. Sex is natural, he kept singing, elbowing

Heba as she lay on my sleeping bag, curled up, trying to ignore him. Sex is natural, sex is fun, sex is best when it's one on one.

She kept cursing at him in Arabic and then saying to me, don't ever say that. Just erase it from your vocabulary.

All night there were people coming and going. A delegation from Christian Aid came over from Susya in a van, and for some reason refused to turn their headlights off. I tied a bandanna over my eyes and curled up in a ball. Footsteps in the dirt, murmurs, the chuffing of a backpack dropped carelessly at one's feet. Flashlight beams flickering everywhere. Ringtones of every description. Flaring cigarettes. Comrades, someone called out in English, please silence your phones, we're trying to rest. I looked at my watch then; it was four thirty. The roosters up the hill in the village would be starting at any moment.

Close by, I couldn't hear who it was, not a familiar voice, reciting a poem in Arabic. Not that I can understand poems in Arabic, but this one seemed grammatically simple and obvious. Statements. Kanat tu'sama Filistin.

Sarat tu'sama Filistin. Oh, I know that poem! I almost said. Of course. Darwish. We watched a video of him reciting it in class. She was called Palestine. She will be called Palestine. Omar groaned and rolled over. It's like hearing the national anthem: not how you feel, how you're supposed to feel. The rockets' red glare. I thought, save this thought, make it another essay. Paradoxes of nationalism. The wind rose up; I could hear it sighing in the branches of the tree just above me, and the tamarisks, just twenty feet away, at the edge of the wadi. Omar and Heba and Lucien and Felice were still now, probably asleep. I knew it was too late for me. If I slept now I would be a groggy mess in three hours.

I wished I could steal away up the hill, just now, in the last moments of darkness, and go wash my face, change my clothes. I had four pairs of underwear hanging on a string in the bathroom; they had to be dry by now. I'd given up changing underwear every day, with all the preparations underfoot for the Day of Action; then at the last minute I washed every extra pair I had, so they'd be clean when I got back.

It was easier, now that Jerome was gone. He complained that the bathroom was festooned with drying bras and panties, so that he could hardly find his way to the sink, and we said, we can't put them on the line outside, what the fuck else are we supposed to do.

I rolled over onto my back, away from Heba, and slipped a hand between my legs. My right hand; my left one still held the camera, its strap over my knuckles. What does a girl do if she can't sleep? I held the image of Jerome before me, above me, on top of me. He had a furry patch in the small of his back. I liked to grab hold of it when he was inside me; sometimes I'd pull out a hair. His ass clenching as he drove into me. I was making myself wet. Six weeks without sex; I'd hardly masturbated once, in my own room, my own bed, where it was my business. Heba would sense me; she'd smell me. How I longed to know what she would say, if we shared enough words to have such a conversation. If there are words. The things I always longed to know from her. Just the shape of her body, the curve of her uncovered neck. Have you ever felt, you know, *sexual*. Have you ever felt alone and safe enough to do what I'm doing, surrounded by twenty sleeping, or not sleeping, bodies. To do the old Molly Bloom. Does Qasim take his time with you. Do you ever like it. Was he really your first and only. Do you know what birth control is, have you ever seen a condom. Is this enough children, I asked you once, and you said, yes, enough, but maybe not, inshallah. Was it easy to give birth, I tried to ask once, and you gave me the strangest look and didn't answer.

Once you asked me, "Will I ever get to see the ocean?" and for some reason I thought, at that moment, of the line from the Book of Common Prayer—I think I learned it in high school? while studying *Moby-Dick*?—"The sea shall give up her dead." Which makes no sense, or maybe it does. "The sea shall give up her dead, and the corruptible bodies of those that sleep in her shall be changed, and be made like unto his glorious body, according to the mighty working whereby he is able to subdue all things unto himself." I must have learned it for a test, or I wouldn't be able to recall it so well. In the end (I should have put this into a poem), in the end you will see everything, god, I even wanted to say something like "in paradise." Thank god my Islamic vocabulary is terrible. How could you joke about something like that. You will see the ocean in paradise. Do the bombers believe that. What will I see in paradise. I've seen so much of the world as it is; I've never been forbidden anything at all. Who or what will I see when I get there, not that I believe in any such thing, and maybe, probably, neither do you.

I had my orgasm quietly, thinking for a moment about nothing at all.

And then dozed off. In fact I slept for nearly an hour, because Heba shook me awake, whispering, it's six fifteen. I rolled over and in the gray light both heard and saw at once the troop transport rumbling down from the road, the insistence of a diesel engine breaking into the morning, *erm, erm,* the roosters now and the wind in the grass and the trees, the muttering of voices among us, whiffs of cigarette. And I desperately needed to pee.

"Omar," I said, to whom I desperately did not want to say any such thing. Why could I not just whisper to Heba, *ana ath-hab ila al-hammam*? I knew the words. I had never spoken them, as such, to anyone. In her house I just went. I didn't refer to my own body and its needs. As if that was the only way I could be tolerated and not be a guest, who had to be attended to. This, I realized, just at that moment, was the psychodrama of my whole life, such as it was, in Wadi Aboud, a guest pretending not to be one, an observer constantly observed, a protector who needed protecting. It's the misery of the bladder and the colon that teaches us these things, that flattens our will, better to say our pretensions. In any case. "Omar," I whispered, more insistently, "I have to pee, I *really* have to pee."

He groaned. "Not now," he said, stating the obvious. "Pee in your pants if you have to."

Heba said something to him I couldn't catch, and he muttered back to her, and she raised her head and spoke to him more sharply.

"Fine, Heba will take you. Put your vest and helmet on."

"Of course my helmet is on."

"Leave the camera here."

Heba rose up first, in a crouch, and nearly toppled over. Her legs were asleep. She'd been lying with her long skirt tangled around her knees, probably cutting off circulation. Ya wele, yalla, she said, and took my hand, and giggled. As if to remind me that we were still girls. We crept in a little path through the prone bodies and no one spoke to us. The nearest trees were to our right, not fifteen feet away. Olive trees, the old ones, are so gnarled and knobby their trunks look like dark melted wax, the wax around a wine bottle, or maybe like lava, certain kinds of igneous rock, more than wood. Heba went first. I was keeping watch, as much as anyone could keep watch. We were out of sight of the troop transport. It was growing light now, actually light, but there was nothing to see from that perspective, only the grinding of diesel engines. The stream of her urine crept past my toes. That's how close we were.

Naomi

I always thought about my emotional life as a matter of triage. That's the truth. I could never accept, or assimilate, as many overlapping states of my mind as other people; it was too distracting. I could only ever be one person at a time, if that. And Sandy always knew that about me. He can't pretend he didn't. Or maybe he didn't; maybe he was more optimistic, the way Oberlin expected us to be.

I could not assimilate the fact of John Downs's existence. That he knew. I was never able to, say, work it into a conversation. Not ever. Not even when we lived in San Francisco and knew other mixed-race people. There's a reason I have to say this now: never, at any point in this continuum, have I been able to treat it as other than a fact. It was enough, at any point in my life, to be struggling to become what I already was: a girl, a woman, an atheist Jew. An atheist Jewish woman, a scientist. A lover. An atheist Jewish woman scientist/lover. A Zen student. A Zen priest. An atheist Jewish woman scientist Zen priest/lover. An atheist Jewish woman scientist again. A mother.

A mother A mother

A woman scientist mother. I shed all else.

Yoav

We were overnight in Forward Base 14, which is legendary for having the worst food of any base south of Hebron, maybe the worst in all of Judea. I never understood how it could be better or worse, frankly, since it all came from the same company, the same contractor, in Beersheva—it's pre-prepared food in plastic bags, how can you mess it up? The cook, if that's what you want to call him, was a Druse guy, Walid or Walif, and the soldiers would always yell at him to wash his hands again. Because that's what FB14 was really known for, not just bad-tasting food, but food that gave you the runs, the really bad, cramping, bloating diarrhea that made you not want to move the next day. It had happened to me already once, and my battalion commander, Natan, filed an official complaint, but nothing happened. It was the middle of the intifada and no one wanted to be stuck out in those miserable places.

I know you want to hear something profound, so I'm asking you to listen and not to judge. That impossible task, am I right? I'm no good at it either.

What I remember from that day, the thirteenth of May 2003? Excruciating pain. I woke up with a bellyful of gas and wished I had a needle to pop myself. Fucking hell, Natan, I groaned, I'm done, I'm a casualty. He wouldn't hear it. He handed me a roll of Tums. This was at four thirty in the morning and we were due to roll out at five. There's more trouble in Kiryat Arba, he said, Shlomo and Rivi were recalled, you're our one sniper, we can't move without you. Don't make me get in that transport, I begged him. I'll shit my pants, I'll stink up everything, I swear.

So shit, he said, what difference will it make to the way Wadi Aboud smells even on a good day.

I took a hot shower. That helped. Natan was banging on the door, bellowing at me, but did I care? Fuck him. I used up all the hot water, so Walid couldn't wash his dishes, not that he bothered in any case. But that only lasted about twenty minutes or so. I took Tums, I took Panadol, I took Imodium. I lay on the floor of the transport curled in a ball.

Sandy

I remember almost nothing from May of 2003 to New Year's. New Year's I remember almost accidentally because it was a party—I mean I allowed Naomi to drag me to a party, at Louis and Judy's, of course. They had, for our sake, kept the guest list small. Or maybe people hadn't wanted to come, once they knew the Wilcoxes would be there. We were Upper West Side personae non grata, of course, in many quarters, and a pair of Debbie Downers, I mean, who could possibly know what to say?

Louis was doing his best. It was one of his great performances, that evening. I wish I could remember his toast word for word. He read from a Hannah Arendt book, *Men in Dark Times*. He used the phrase, "the world is too much with us," and because it was Louis, I didn't want to smack him. The creases in his face! It was why people loved him, his Tevye-the-dairyman expressions. Of course I wanted to leave before midnight; I always do at New Year's parties, Naomi always objects, but this year I planned to put my foot down. There's nothing I hate more than those explosions of delight over the second hand passing twelve. I've asked people, earnestly, at these parties: which year, in our lifetimes, has been better than the last? Louis could see the look on my face, around eleven fifteen, and said, "Let's go out on the balcony."

Louis and Judy's balcony is hardly big enough for two people to stand elbow to elbow, it's decorative, that's how prewar buildings are, but we managed to wedge ourselves into the two obligatory wrought iron decorative chairs. It wasn't particularly cold. Blessedly, from their vantage point over the park, there was no evidence of New Year's, except for some random noises drifting up from midtown.

"I wonder," I said, after a few minutes of blessed silence, "whether anyone, even for a minute, considered canceling New Year's this year, I mean Times Square, the fireworks, the ball drop, because we're at war."

"You know the answer to that question."

"If we stop, the terrorists win. Of course. But I mean, in particular, because the visual effect, the image of explosions and flashes of light, loud noises from unexpected directions, might remind people of Baghdad, being not unlike tracer fire and Scud missiles."

"It's not even American to make that kind of comparison."

"I'm probably at the lowest ebb of feeling American, of Americanness, in my entire life, right at this moment."

"Hey, this is an election year. Hope springs eternal."

"You know that's not what I'm talking about."

There's a reason I'm recording this desultory chitchat. Don't tell me not to. He's gone, the one person on this Earth who loved me, on a good day, unreservedly. I have every reason to remember it in detail. I hang on to it.

"Tell me how the grief group is going," he said.

"I'm doing my best not to quit. I wrote my own obituary recently, that was helpful."

"That sounds like a bizarre exercise."

"In any case, it's a relief to go somewhere and feel like I don't have to make excuses. At work no one wants to talk about it. That's the mildest way of putting it. They've developed a way of looking right past me, ignoring the fact that I now have two heads. Of course, Mark and I have an understanding, and we do have to work that out, on the margins, every once in a while. Certain clients are still extremely sensitive about it."

"Understandably, from their point of view."

"I don't give a shit about their point of view, which is why it's useful to have Mark as a buffer. I do have to live in their world, or work in it, anyway, that's bad enough."

"Judy and I were having dinner with Jack and Irene Thomason a week ago, remember them? They used to live on the fourteenth floor. They moved to Seattle back in 1987 or '88. Their daughters were Rebecca and Katie."

"Vaguely."

"Well, they remembered you. Apparently Winter used to play with Rebecca and Katie all the time. They were full of questions. Having kept up with the news reports. Jack actually asked me, off to the side, whether you tried to stop Bering from going, if you considered having her extracted, you know, deprogrammed, like she was in a cult."

"That's a new one."

"I'm sorry to even bring it up. I just mean—I get it. All these questions floating around."

"In point of fact, she inherited a little bit from Herman and Phyllis's estate. Just a money-market distribution, I think it was thirty-five thousand dollars. All the kids did. That's what she spent when she traveled. She was over twenty-one, we didn't have any say over it."

"Jesus, Sandy, I'm not trying to make you feel defensive."

"Of course you aren't, but that's the historical record, it deserves to be out there."

"I wish you could have stopped her. I'll say that much."

I stopped and looked at Louis's face, his obnoxiously handsome, menschy, Mandy Patinkin face, which was not pointed my way; he was looking out over the park.

"That's the first time I've ever heard you make a positive statement, a statement on your own behalf, this whole time."

"You know I don't mean anything by it but pure love for her, for you."

"I'm still interested in the background, what prompted you to say such a thing. Having never heard you say anything, as far as I know, ever, about Israel."

"My opinion isn't important. In any case, it's not an opinion, more of an obligation. Between an obligation and a memory."

"Go on."

"You want me to go on? My parents bought Israel bonds. They were big believers. They considered emigrating themselves, in the fifties, after the Rosenbergs. They would have made great Zionists. Dad once said he would have had a better career there, there would have been more respect for his degree."

"Did they ever make the trip?"

"Once, close to the end. They didn't enjoy it so much. But on the other hand they loved it. Even with the food poisoning."

"Nothing is ever simple."

"Come on, Sandy. Say it like you mean it. Think about how Roosevelt treated the Jews trying to escape Europe, think about the *St. Louis* and how it was turned back. That generation learned an inarguable lesson about power. And, yes, violence. My position is, I have no right to contradict them."

"Did I ever give you any reason to believe, any, that my politics were Bering's politics?"

"I never heard you arguing with Naomi about it."

"Naomi's argument is with the universe, and God help anyone who gets in her way. She didn't want Bering to go any more than I did. God, I can't believe we're having this conversation."

"I think the occupation is a terrible mistake, for what it's worth. But a mistake Israel was forced to make. And I have no sympathy for Palestinians. I'm sorry to say that. They're human beings. I have a general humanistic regard for them, but no particular sympathy. Their whole culture, as far as I can tell, is based on antipathy and revenge. I followed events pretty closely in the seventies and eighties. I kept my mouth shut, because it wasn't the radical-chic thing to do to criticize the PLO, but I tell you, I've hated Arafat more than just about any human being alive."

"I get the picture."

"Don't be like that. Don't be cold. Admit it, it changes our relationship."

"It *changes our relationship*? Are you fucking kidding me?"

"I've been terrified about saying anything at all."

"You've been terrified about talking to me? Then that's the problem. You and Judy have literally saved our lives, these last eight months. It makes me respect you more, in the local sense. In the broader sense, it's the best explanation ever of the world we live in."

"I wouldn't take it that far."

"Opinion as obligation and memory that can't be disavowed, it just sticks to you, even when you know better. Add resentment, or undigested rage, or both, and it's the reason no one will ever have peace, ever, there's no starting over."

"Look at Northern Ireland."

"There's nothing to see. No comparison at all. You don't have half the world as a vested interest."

"At any rate, you can forgive me."

"That's not even the point. And no, I don't forgive you, particularly. I love you and I need you. That's different."

Yoav

Believe it or not, Bering Wilcox wasn't the only person I killed, in nearly nine months on the front lines. Of course she wasn't. Why aren't you talking to Aron, who was lying right next to me, who killed the Arab girl? I've forgotten her name. I killed a sniper outside Hebron the following week, in fact. Shot him out of a window. No one ever asks about him. I fired rapid-release grenades into buildings. I shot out the tires of a terrorist truck in Nablus and it rolled into a ditch and exploded. It was a war. Don't call it anything else. Just be glad it ended when it did and we haven't had another one, thanks to Bibi, basically. And don't tell me it's more complicated.

I shouldn't have to be the last one to speak. I'm no longer involved. I run a Sixt car-rental agency now, in Ashkelon. I have enough problems. Customers complain into my ear all day long. In my world, fifteen years is a lifetime. How was I to know what it was like to have two kids in diapers, carrying out the trash at three in the morning because I can't stand the smell of shit in the bedroom anymore? My life at nineteen was so precious, I was desperate to preserve it.

Naomi

Let's run down the cast of characters here, briefly. There's the Israeli government, chiefly and unimpeachably first, or rather all its post-1967 governments, but above all else Bibi Netanyahu, its brilliant three-decade champion, fluent and suave in the language of Model UN debating teams, the rationality of gates, seals, enclosures, fortresses, the aggrieved language of the child who has never wanted for anything, who would gladly make a logical argument for why everyone else should stop breathing if only he could have all the oxygen.

There's Shimon Peres. There's the relics of the Israeli peace movement.

There's the 60 or 70 percent of the Israeli public for whom Palestinians exist only as an inconvenience and an excuse, who have convinced themselves that they are legitimately terrified and at war.

There's the 60 to 70 percent of American Jews who were raised in a strange cult of irrationality called the Holocaust, which has next to nothing to do with the state-implemented murder of Jews in Europe from 1939 to 1945, about which they actually know very little. The Holocaust is a kind of logic outside logic, a peculiar grammar, in which every sentence carries a silent additional causative phrase, *because of the Holocaust*. I scratch my ass *because of the Holocaust*. I change my tires *because of the Holocaust*. Call it a cult of prosthetic victimhood, which it is, obviously, but that doesn't really explain anything at all: the world is full of perpetual victims. Better to say it's a cult of the periphery, because, of course, that's all Israel is to most American Jews. You say a prayer to it during Shabbat services. Maybe you went there once for ten days on a bus tour. It was hot. The people were rude but shockingly handsome and tan. You went to Masada and the Western Wall and tried to feel the things you were supposed to feel, and then you flew home with some new silver candlesticks with sharp edges. It doesn't change anything about your life, which could be any life at all. You could be a dentist or a reporter or a general contractor; you could be observant or not at all; but you're supposed to feel glad that Israel exists, your supposed homeland, and you do. Exists far away. Taking care of itself, apparently. *Because of the Holocaust.*

I'm just getting started. Can you feel me getting started? There are the Hashemites and the Ba'athists, the Salafis and the Wahhabis, the ruling classes of Jordan and Syria and Saudi and Egypt, the Ayatollah and the Revolutionary Guards, and Hezbollah and Hamas and the PFLP and Islamic Jihad and their Israeli funders, the secret agents from all sides (and yes, I include Mossad, of course, as involved as anyone) who keep them in place, but a special place has to reside in this story for Yasir Arafat, the rat-faced ersatz Father of his Country who couldn't be bothered to organize a government, who let his corrupt henchmen walk away with millions in foreign aid, who could have been a Mandela, or leaving that aside, even a Gerry Adams, or a Daw Aung San Suu Kyi, a Benazir Bhutto, but spectacularly failed to reach that low bar, and even more spectacularly killed or drove off any leader that could take his place or, god forbid, become a charismatic uniter of Fatah and Hamas and all the other factions, leaving only a UN-funded police state perched on high in Ramallah.

This is no way of apportioning blame equally. I learned from my own daughter, my murdered daughter, never to use the phrase "Israelis and Palestinians" as it is commonly used, at least in the English-speaking world, to indicate two implacable sides locked in an unsolvable and ancient conflict, because the conflict is not ancient, the conflict is not unsolvable, but most of all there are not two sides, there are a thousand sides and yet only one side, the side with the world's fifth-largest army, with nuclear weapons and riot-control machines they export to the rest of the world. Occupier and occupied, expeller and expelled, do not constitute "two sides," and it's the gift to the occupier the world has always given to construct the situation that way, likewise the use of indistinguishable "Arabs."

I'll tell you a secret: for a few months in the fall of 2003, outside of my normal therapy, outside of any of our family negotiations, I saw a specialized grief counselor. Josephine Cho was her name. Of all the shrinks' offices in New York City I've visited—and by now it's a lot—hers was the most purely and pitilessly decorated. It was so dark I felt I needed to grope around the first few times to find my chair. Josephine said I was constructing a theodicy of blame, that is, a causal field or universe defined by who did what to whom, which is a terrible idea for all kinds of obvious reasons. I told her that's exactly what I wanted. She quoted the Dalai Lama: that anger is like taking poison and expecting the other person to die. I told her I thrive on poison. What else was I supposed to say? Men have been telling women for centuries not to get angry, and wise women know it's never that simple. God knows Sensei held me to that line for years. God knows Sandy has never been able to accept it. And then Josephine asked the most obvious question of all: why are you in therapy, then, if you don't want to change? She said, I'm not here to be your sparring partner.

I told her I wanted a road map, a sense of how bad it was likely to get. She said, there's no road map, it's all about accepting your feelings and not getting stuck in habitual patterns. In other words, the problem with grief is that people are so accustomed to thinking of it in stages, everybody knows the language, but the stages aren't really temporal, they're not an algorithm. I told her that in my world an algorithm isn't really an algorithm, it's not necessarily linear. I told her that the thing about Bering's murder is because it's impossible to translate into simple heuristic terms, X leads to Y leads to Z, it seems precisely designed to activate my physicist's brain, the translation of the most complex physical processes into knowable equations, which is perverse, but also, in a way, loving, loving on her part, because it was her way of saying (as in fact in some ways she did say) that she died to illustrate a larger phenomenon, a systemic death, an algorithmic death, that she died as she lived, asking me to pay more attention, not to her necessarily but to what she stood for, her way of life, which was not to press all the buttons in the elevator but to press a sequence of buttons, for example to press all the numbers in our telephone number, to see if that would take the elevator directly to our apartment. She was a profoundly experimental child, but she wanted to *be* the experiment, and not be its observer, which is of course fatal in the sciences, you have to be aware of the interaction between the two and be able to work it into the equation, that's intrinsic to the General Theory, but what I only realized after her death was what Winnicott said, that there's no such thing as a baby, not really, there's no baby without a mother, in other words there's no Bering without Naomi observing Bering, every mother and child is a new experiment, and of course often the experiment takes the form of *If I do this will it lead to my death*. In fact that is the oldest and most basic parent-child experiment, you can observe it in ducks and lions. The experimental aspect in fact did not end with Bering's death, it only started there, because only then could I understand and identify and name the intrinsic force involved, which is, as I say, blame, the atemporal, asynchronic mode of refreshment which has, I'm sorry to say, made me feel more alive, made a second and more potent chapter in my career, the sparkling edge of the knife that cuts away the world's phallic satisfaction, its belief in its own goodness, that what it has created is good.

And what do you blame yourself for? Josephine finally asked, after she was convinced she couldn't deter me from this way of thinking. Where is your part in all of this?

Isn't it obvious? I ask the universe. Does it need to be repeated? It's Winnicott's answer, of course, which is the worst thing a mother can do, other than physical cruelty, is be absent, emotionally absent.

Bering was my youngest child. Why did we have three children? Why did we have two? Patrick was obvious and unavoidable, because we were happy utopians, and utopias always demand babies (or at least the seventies ones did—otherwise there would be no generations X and Y), but after we'd realized our mistake, why, how could we go on? I always forget that we were happy homeowners, happy rent-protected renters, that is, in the 1980s. We exchanged one utopia not for another one but for a happy compromise with so many sensual enhancements, and in that particular yuppie idyll you couldn't have just one child. All the books warned against it. You had to have an heir and a spare. That gave us Winter. But for god's sake, three! Who had three children in New York in 1982, on the salary of one assistant professor and one associate at a midrange law firm? Well, we did. Because, essentially, I was exhausted and waited a week longer than I should have to get an IUD. I forgot. I had been off birth control, at that point, for twelve months, at least, and I forgot, because Winter was four months old and Patrick was two and a half, and if you don't know what that means, ask someone who does. The shrieking hell of diapers and little balled-up fists, red faces and the-fork-always-almost-in-the-electric-socket. There is a Stockholm syndrome effect to having infant and very young children, and when we found out we honestly shrugged, thinking, *it can't get any worse.* We had already been through a winter with a baby above the Arctic Circle. We had run an honest-to-goodness farm in Vermont by the skin of our teeth.

But then look at the calendar of our lives and you'll see: Bering's young years, her little-girl years, were just when I was up for tenure and then denied tenure and then suing for tenure at Columbia. There are few photos of me during those years, because no one could bear to take my picture. I was running a Very Important Lab, and it had to continue to be Very Important because my career and income and life were on the line. She would say things, just as factual observations, like, "Mommy is always angry." "Mommy never comes home from work." We had Cordelia, our best nanny, during that time, '85–'89, thank god, and Cordelia effectively raised her, I'm not ashamed to say it, or I am ashamed, but not ashamed to say it, from about the age of four to seven and a half or so. Neither Winter nor Patrick had that kind of childhood. I'm not saying that Bering sensed the unfairness at the time, per se, but did she not feel, how could she not feel, that I was closer to the two of them? Because I emerged from the whole tenure experience a different person. Bering never got to know the mother who loved being a mother.

Which is also to say that part of this universe of blame, a substantial part of it, in fact, lies with my senior colleagues in Earth Sciences and above all with the Columbia University Promotion and Tenure Committee for 1987–88, Provost Ben Whittaker, and President Michael Sovern, all of whom were named in my lawsuit. Among the pitted and mottled and half-caved-in ghoulish faces of old men and their energetic lackeys who preside over this story, they are in some ways the most loathsome, because there is no arrogance on Earth like the arrogance of an Ivy League promotion and tenure committee, that vituperative priesthood whose MO is exclusion for its own sake, pure arbitrary selection, guided by no philosophy or system of value. Of course they would reject women, that was the point of the lawsuit; in an atmosphere of impunity men will always reject women. Bethanne, my lawyer, honestly believed we were going to trial. She wanted to take me to the Supreme Court. Her briefs were full of terms like "accountability metrics" and "mutually agreeable terms of assessment." The entire concept of an undefined hierarchy has to go, she said. When they settled after six months, she nearly lost her mind. Of course I was going to take their terms, their NDA, their clauses; I wanted to get back to work. "I'll never forgive myself if you take these terms," she actually said, and that made two of us.

Sandy

An image: The girls in the snow in Central Park, where the best sledding hills are. Around Seventy-Second Street. This was in 1990 or 1991. Winter was nine or ten. Already tall—she shot up like a bean around that time. She was pulling our real sled, an L.L.Bean toboggan Herman had given us years before. And Bering was trundling behind with the plastic discs. We were nearly there, in sight of the main hill, already crawling with kids in their puffy snowsuits, like confetti, when Winter put down the toboggan and said, "I'm too old to go sledding."

Naomi and I had been fighting the night before. We'd known it would be a snow day—Dinkins had announced it around seven, on the radio, while we were eating dinner, or is that just how I remember it?—and the fight was about, of course, which of us would take the day off. Patrick just wanted to be left alone; he was in eighth grade, in an intense computer phase. He and Paulie Simpson were spending the day in Paulie's apartment on the fifteenth floor, typing away in Usenet groups. But the girls needed closer supervision, of course, and I'd been in Cleveland for work the previous week, so Naomi thought it was my turn, and from my point of view I couldn't spend another waking hour away from the office with Mark breathing down my neck about billable hours. It was a classic case, as Brisman used to say. We hadn't resolved matters till nearly midnight. Winter's room was next to ours, and the walls in the Apthorp are thin. If we were up till midnight, she was up till midnight. We'd tried white noise machines. We'd given her earplugs.

"Of course you're not," I said.

"I'm tired. I want to go back."

What a well of misery is an unhappy family! It was as if we'd been cored out of life, drilled out in a cylinder of air, it was only us in the park that day. I wanted to raise my arms and say, I give up, I acknowledge I've failed. Bad parents salt the earth with their unhappy children. What job did I have on the earth, I thought, other than to make them marginally happy, happier rather than not, and look at what I've done instead.

"But I still want to go," Bering said.

"I'll go home by myself."

"You will not," I said. "Come on, I'll pull the sled."

"I don't want to be here," Winter said. She had started crying, which startled me. Winter never cried. Bering dropped the discs and tried to put her arms around her, as she would, and Winter butted her with an elbow, harder than she meant to, and Bering screamed and sat down in the snow. This was my life. I went down on my knees and pulled Bering to me. Other families were watching, of course, circling us, a wide berth. It happens to everyone, you could say, but no, it does not. We were overachievers. I couldn't drag everything home myself, and they refused to help, so we left the sleds there, all of them, and yes, as far as I remember, that was the end of sledding in Central Park for us.

This story has nothing to do with what happened to Bering, and everything; it's every moment of our lives as a family, and none of them; it's discrete and total. Everything matters and nothing matters. Fuck you, Borges. I wish I had the confidence to say you're right or wrong.

Yoav

All right. All right. You want the short version, the straight version? It went like this. There must have been an informant in the village. Wadi Aboud, that's what they call it, right? A trusted guy, someone who'd been working with our people for years. None of this came out in the official investigation, because the Shabak was desperate to keep his name a secret, of course. And they're allowed to do that. *I* certainly never knew his name, or anything about it. The only information I heard was that there was a cache of weapons in the village, and at least two people who were operatives for IJ, that's Islamic Jihad, of course. It was possible, it was plausible. It turned out not to be true. At least no weapons were ever discovered. But the rumor was that there were weapons, there were trained IJ fighters, and they were using the peace-keepers, the peace groups, as human shields.

That's why we were sent. Ordinarily if it's a confrontation between settlers and Arab civilians they don't deploy us, highly trained snipers. It's a waste of time and a recipe for trouble. We can all agree on that. They send the newest recruits. It's police work, essentially. You're evict-ing people, keeping the stone-throwers at bay, using rubber bullets and tear gas. Every soldier has to go through that period, but let's face it, these villagers, ordinarily, are soft targets. They have nothing of value. Now you see international reporters, cameras, witnesses, lining up to film these things. But during the intifada it was very different. The re-porters were in Hebron and Nablus and Ramallah. The real action was elsewhere. These peacekeepers, to be honest, were sitting it out. The ones with nerve were in the cities, or in Gaza.

But in any case, I have no opinions. As a soldier I was trained to have no opinions. That's what Natan always said. And as an ex-soldier I more or less stick to that policy. I have no theory or inspiration to share with you. It's basically just this: I live here, and what's mine is mine. Try to take it from me, and you'll have to kill me first. I'll tear out your hair and gouge out your eyes. I'll bite off your ears and chew them like gristle. In that way I have sympathy for the poor old Arab farmers and shepherds, who bite and kick as teenage soldiers carry them away. But it's them or us. They had their time to build a country, raise an army, and instead they sat back and let the Egyptians and the Saudis and the Iranians fight for them. No. It doesn't work like that. Enough said.

We got there just before dawn. Our position was an embankment right by the road, looking down into the wadi. Aron had the spotting scope, the night-vision scope, but there wasn't much to see. Nothing was moving. The olive grove was about a hectare to the south of the streambed. There was heavy brush cover between the olive trees and the stream, to a height of at least six or seven feet. The nearest buildings, where the village itself started, were a little higher and farther away from us, maybe three-quarters of a kilometer. We could see the path that led down into the wadi, or paths, at least two or three of them. But no one was moving.

Honestly I didn't think much of this operation. Look, as a sniper you're moved around from place to place, sometimes you're treated just as insurance, and the call never comes in, you never even put your eye to the scope once. We knew there were protestors and villagers asleep in the olive grove, they had stayed out all night as a vigil. Good for them. Not our business, particularly. In an hour the battalion trucks would come in and the commanders would commence a tricky cleanup before the bulldozers arrived. There would be screams and crying and cursing, and probably some chanting in English, the protestors filming themselves for their friends back home. You might have a military police detachment making some arrests. Occasionally, I heard, if things got too disruptive, they would arrest the foreign nationals, for their own safety, and drive them straight to Ben Gurion.

At the same time, anyone would say it was dangerous. Particularly with who-knows-what weapons hidden in the village. It would be easy, from a trained fighter's point of view, to use the protest as a smokescreen and move around to the other side of the wadi to attack the settlers. You could do some real damage before we had time to move positions. The call that came through to Aron—my radio was busted, as it turned out, but it didn't matter, we were joined at the hip all morning—said there was a chance they would burn some tires, or even burn the grove itself, rather than surrender it. There you have it: an actual smokescreen.

Remember that I was still in agony from the shits, from the terrible food. I had taken an Imodium or a Zofran or whatever Ad had on hand—Ad was the medic—but my insides were curdled milk, they were bubbling, my colon blowing up like a balloon with gas. You just want to take a needle and pop yourself at moments like that. I was actually rolling around in the dirt, trying to get comfortable, one hand on the rifle all the time, as we were trained, never let go of the rifle no matter what in combat. It didn't matter. I took some sightings just to get a sense of the terrain. I hadn't calibrated in a few days—calibrating a scope is sort of halfway between tuning a guitar and tuning a piano. You don't have to do it all the time, but you should. I was a mess. I wasn't ready. I was honestly, swear on my life, ready to tell Aron to radio in to Natan that I was too sick to fight, I was a casualty, it happens. If you don't have people calling themselves in no one will ever realize how bad the food is, how miserable we are. I wasn't exactly a new recruit, and I wasn't shy. Natan would have been surprised but he would have done it, ultimately. It wasn't as if the situation desperately called for two of us. I was just about to, I would have, too, if it didn't mean asking Aron to speak for me, that was the most embarrassing part of all. So if my radio weren't busted that day maybe I wouldn't be here today, maybe Aron would be in the hot seat, or, by the laws of chance, Bering Wilcox would be alive and back in the U.S., selling organic groceries or teaching autistic children or whatever peaceniks do when they go home and leave us alone.

It was just at that minute, of course, when the call came in. People were getting up, the protestors were converging, the troop transport came rumbling around to our right, heading down into the wadi on not so much a road as a pitiful dirt track. It got stuck three-quarters of the way down, and so Natan had everyone jump out of the back and race the rest of the way. That was a mistake as it caused a panic. Everyone acknowledges it was a bad move. The thing you want in a standoff, with clear sight lines, is to take it slow. I've said this a hundred times. If you move quickly, they move quickly, and people get shot. Protestors are like sheep. They spook easily. And wouldn't you, if you were facing down the guns, the grenade launchers, the tear gas? So the protestors spooked, they retreated at a run and hid among the olive trees. Leaving signs and equipment and bits of clothing and what have you. By this time Aron and I were watching and scanning. It was about seven thirty, hazy conditions, already warm. You could smell the countryside: the dust, the sweet herbal smell of the grasses, the bushes, the za'tar that was growing just down the slope from us, and I always think there's a smell of sheep, even though there were none in sight, that pungent smell of wool and drying dung. Just at that moment, too, swept over us the smell of smoke from a wood fire. I don't know where it actually came from, but the report said it was probably just a shift in the wind bringing it down the wadi from the village. We watched carefully. In those conditions someone could set a fire and you wouldn't see it right away, it would smolder in the grass.

Would I say I knew the exact moment I saw them? It was more a movement just out of the corner of my eye, and then I swept around and focused on them, two crouching men, they seemed obviously men, kaffiyehs wrapped around their heads, moving quickly and deliberately in a circular direction away from the protestors and toward the path to the settlement. It was a shot at 236 yards, that's what the report said. I'm telling you this, what I couldn't put in the report, I had my buttocks clenched together because I was going to shit myself at any moment, it's a miracle I hit anything in that condition. I didn't wait. I certainly didn't see any vest or any insignia. I saw an insurgent, a guerrilla. I knew how to recognize them. Aron and I fired at the same time, that's the procedure, because we were seeing the same thing. There were no words between us. That was our last moment of being soldiers, of course. And it's fitting that I spent it desperately needing to shit and not being able to, because, I think this is like a metaphor, isn't it true that the army is like the rectum, or whatever, the muscle that holds in all the shit, that prevents shit from spreading and covering the earth, the despised thing that is so much the better alternative only no one realizes it.

Bering

Is this all? I kept wondering. Is this it? Is this all? I tried to turn my head, to see if Heba was there, but I couldn't. And then, as I started to feel warm all over, Patrick said to me, in his ordinary teasing/accusing voice, of course this is *all*, this is what *all* means. I desperately wanted to ask him what the fuck he was talking about. This is what he was talking about. Me sitting here talking to you. Don't turn the page. This is what Borges meant. I read him in AP Spanish. I have called this symposium. Stay here, where I am not dead and you are not alive.

Did I become who you wanted me to be? Did I make you proud?

/1B

These waiting periods breed and erase each other, push each other out of the way and interact.

Elias Khoury, *Gate of the Sun*

AND THIS IS THE
OPPRESSOR'S LANGUAGE

I'm sorry for how weird this is

Don't be sorry. How could it not be weird?

Ive been meaning to write you a proper letter ever since I found
out your name.

When was that?

Actually its more complicated—I mean I didn't know FOR SURE.
Grandpa John told my mom that his other daughter's name was
Naomi. For years he said that's all he knew.

Then after he died Mom found the letters yr mom wrote him. They
must have had the address on the envelopes, but he just kept the
letters and threw the envelopes away.

In one of them she mentions something about her last name
being wilcox. so back when yr moms book came out she saw
her on tv and looked her up on wikipedia
and figured out it had to be her

But i was never convinced. Then one of my friends posted this video about yr sister, and i read some news stories about what happened, and it all kind of clucked

*clicked. Sorry for my typos

No worries. Take your time.

& then I found yr # on the New Americans website, so I'm not stalking you or anything.

Are you sure you don't want to talk on the phone instead?

☺ I know it seems obvious but my therapist says its really important to practice self care right now and I get really panicky when I talk to ppl I don't know on the phone

OK, texting is fine but just to warn you, I'm at the office, so I might have to take a client call at any time. I guess I should just say GTG when that happens.

what does that mean

"Got to go," I thought that was regular texting slang.

Oh maybe lol

Anyway please go on.

Nothing I just thought for some reason today was the day to get in touch with my cousin.

I'm glad you did.

Should i like tell you all about me?

Whatever you can say with your thumbs.

I live in Washington, Im in college at Howard but am transferring to Vassar next year. Im pretty tall but not athletic. I play the flute.

Right now Im a econ major but am switching to sociology when I
transfer. I grew up in Pasadena. Do you know where that is

Yes.

Grandpa John was a scientist, you know that right?

Yes. My mother told us that he was the first Black physicist to
get a PhD from Princeton.

Weird, I never knew that, I just knew he was an important scientist
at Salk, he did nanotechnology stuff. My parents are both drs.
Dad does reconstructive plastic surgery, Mom is a pediatrician.

Did your mom ever want to get in touch with my mom?

No. Shes pretty opposed to reaching out, just fyi. Hence the radio
silence all this time. Dad actually tried to talk her into it a couple of
times, he was the one who bought yr moms book. She said she
was happy to have the info. but didnt want any contact.

Why not?

Um, because racism lol

But she never even tried to find out what we were like, or how
we felt about what happened . . .

In yr moms book she says that discussing race is pointless bc
were on the brink of planetary destruction, she says race is a
meaningless non-biological category

Well, you have a point there.

But even before that, whenever we would try to talk to her about
it, she would just be like, we have enough problems trying to
keep one family together. referring to my dads family. He has six
brothers & 1 sister.

But that's not how I feel. I was always curious about you. Mom mentioned something about Bering Wilcox once and I immediately googled ☹ I was so upset when i saw the videos, i went down a rabbit hole & watched everything. I cried for 2 days & missed all my classes. I cant believe all that happnd to my own cousin and I didnt even know. I was so angry I actually threw up, no joke lol

I'm sorry. But I guess I'm glad you found out what happened to her. You deserve to know everything.

That made me mad bc I cd tell she was an amazing person & I never got to meet her.

She WAS amazing. You would have loved each other, I can tell already.

There was never any arrest or anything was there

No. That's a very long story I can tell you sometime. But the short version is, no one was ever prosecuted. The sniper is still out there, living his life. His name is Yoav Aronofsky.

It must really stress you to talk abt it im sorry

No it's OK, it's been years. I'm used to it I guess.

You never told me anything about you

Well, hmm. OK, I'm a lawyer. You figured that out already. I do immigration work for a nonprofit clinic here in Providence, defending people against deportations.

Where did you go to law school if i may ask

I went to Yale Law and Wesleyan as an undergrad.

How can you afford to work at a nonprofit & pay yr loans, does Yale have loan forgiveness

They do, but I was lucky not to take out loans, I inherited money from my grandparents that paid for law school. My parents paid for college.

ALL of it???

Yes. My dad, your uncle (?), is a pretty successful lawyer, I don't know if you know anything about him. Was a pretty successful lawyer. He just retired, kind of. Long story short, we grew up with enough money.

Well shit I grew up with "enough money" too but still have to take out loans

Yeah. "Enough" is a pretty relative term.

even among relatives lol

Ha ha ha. LOL.

its funny I can tell texting isnt yr thing

No, I do it when I have to but it doesn't come naturally to me, I'm too old.

Youre 37 right

That's like 100 in internet years.

Anyway, more about me: I'm actually getting married this summer. My fiancé's name is Zeno. He's from southern Mexico, from Chiapas.

VERY cool!!!! Congrats on that

You know that you would be totally welcome at the wedding.

Youre seriously inviting me to yr wedding??!?? You dont even know me

I do now. You're my first cousin.

Im totally questioning your judgment now

Don't. Anyway, it's just a thought. Any or all of your family is completely welcome. It's the weekend of August 16–17. Blue Hill, Maine.

Well mom wd never come & dad wont come without her, & Josephs still in high school so that pretty much leaves me. You are freaking me out

Don't freak out. Just think about it. If it's just you we can find a place for you to stay. You're transferring to Vassar? so that means you have to be in the northeast in Aug anyway. If you want to come, you can take a bus from NYC. It's easy.

I will think about it

I promise

GTG hahahahaha

/

From: "Winter Wilcox" <wwilcox@newamericansRI.org>
Date: May 2, 2018 at 10:23:41 AM EST
To: "Dad" <alexander.wilcox@feinlewinllp.com>
Subject: Mom & other news

Dad,
I've had this email in my drafts folder for a week. Since I gave up calling you.

I don't have time to be writing to you. I have clients coming in in five minutes. On the other hand, I don't really have a choice. Because there are things I have to communicate, believe it or not.

The world didn't stop on April 11th. This may come as a great surprise to you. In fact it had been moving, events had been accumulating, outside of your attention or imagination. Or, for that matter, mine.

I wonder if you even remember who Dr. Goyen was. You paid her bills, of course; I was in college, and the campus clinic didn't cover her. Do you remember? At some point you must have been paying five shrinks simultaneously. Goyen used to say, when I described the way you and Mom used to fight, that you had an emotional deficiency very common to men your age, a very specific lack, almost like a missing gene: you were incapable of grasping the effect of your actions on people close to you, and would always deny that your actions *had* any effect at all; or, if they did have an effect, it was always subject to interpretation. It was always "That's *your* opinion." Does this ring a bell?

So here's what I've been thinking: if I had a therapist now, she would ask me how I wanted to interpret your behavior, and I would say something, and then think, automatically, *that's just my opinion.*

In other words I've become habituated, over time, to your deniability.

Nevertheless, I want you to hear my interpretation. I want this on the record.

It isn't that we were in daily contact. And maybe that's my fault. Maybe I should have been more thoughtful about your being alone in the apartment. It's too easy to say that narcissists always live alone, no matter where they are.

When you chose to vanish, you were simulating death; you were saying, imagine me dead, imagine how much you'll miss me. When all our thoughts are addressed to a silent non-hearer.

And this is the point where an ordinary person would say, "Imagine how that feels."

Everyone feels neglected as an adult. I ask you to accept that I'm capable of imagining this of you. No one's contesting the fact that you felt abandoned in your marriage. But how characteristic of you, of our family dynamic writ large, to compound the pain rather than address it.

You have never been able to accept how aggressive your silences were, how much of the pain you caused us, and yes, I'm speaking of B and myself, was from the withdrawal of your attention and approval. This is just an extension of the same dynamic. You have never been able to decide what you want from having a family, and you make us pay, over and over, for your indecision. Maybe this goes back to never having had a family to speak of. But how much easier it would be to feel for you if I wasn't already constantly being asked to feel *for* you, to provide an emotional response for you to lash out against.

When you chose to vanish you were reenacting B's death. There, I said it. I'm just realizing it as I'm writing this. It's why I never should have started this letter. You should never start a thought you don't want to finish. You were/are reenacting for us (if not for yourself) the trauma of losing her, making us, me, feel again the loss of a voice I have always known, because that is what we are to one another in this family, not physical presences so much as voices speaking in a conversation that never really ends, and notice I didn't say *argument,* though of course it is often an argument. Not all families are unending conversations. But our kind of family is. We were all early talkers but of course B was the earliest of all. People would stare at her, chattering away in her stroller when she was eighteen months old. Remember?

What I'm saying is there's this element of self-congratulation in everything we do, even in our suffering. Especially in our suffering.

You know the Adrienne Rich poem. Or you did. Because I typed it up and sent it to you. "The Burning of Paper Instead of Children." You had Louise photocopy it and give it to all the first-year associates. I wonder what they thought of it.

"This is the oppressor's language yet I need it to talk to you."

"I cannot touch you and this is the oppressor's language."

(I looked it up online, my memory isn't quite this precise.)

Why am I quoting this at you? Well obviously because you and Mom taught me/us how to be, our argumentative ways, our endless

contestations on every subject, our warring interpretations, so when
I reach out to you that's the only way I can do it. Which is not repeat
NOT the same thing as saying, you are the oppressor. I'm not making a
political point here except to say that it's always a temptation to escape
and say nothing, as you have, but that it is possible, I believe it is
possible, to do something different, even with the fucked-up people we
are and the fucked-up relationships we have.

I assume that it will occur to you at some point that you have to
check your email. I've given up trying to call. The house number Mom
gave me rings and rings. I thought about driving up there but I don't have
time, I can't take a day off work to track down my father who can't be
bothered to return phone calls.

I was just remembering something you said at a party when I was
little—someone asked you what it was like growing up in Davenport and
you said, it was so boring we walked on the train tracks, waiting for the
trains to come, so we could jump off at the last possible moment and
roll down the hill, the embankment. We left pennies on the tracks so the
trains would roll them into slugs, then we used them to jam the cigarette
machines. That was entertainment in Davenport.

There should be some clever segue here but the truth is, I'm
pregnant and I'm too tired to write this letter properly. But in the interests
of time, Mom is a lesbian. She has a partner, Tilda, who works in her lab.
Tilda is probably in her late forties. They're basically living together.

Patrick knows, ICYMI.

You have allowed the world to go on without you but without actually
expecting it to *go on*. So don't be surprised. As if you needed more
solitude than was available to you in that apartment.

On the other hand: I'm not saying it's a bad thing. Someone had to
shake us out of these terminal doldrums.

Zeno and I are getting married in August in Blue Hill. August is
not that far away. These plans are not negotiable. Zeno's dad may
need a place to stay, and for various reasons, which I can't go into at

the moment, he may be coming to stay with you. You will bring him to Blue Hill. He hasn't been to the U.S. since 1979; Zeno says he's hardly left San Cristóbal in twenty years. You'll be his guide. (He's fluent in English, of course.) This isn't a request. It's not a favor. I'm making my expectations clear. Come. That's all there is to say. Don't think about it. Come.

THE RETURN

Recovered from: Drafts Folder (Unsent Message)

From: "Bering Wilcox" <carebear@hotmail.com>
Last saved: February 13, 2003 at 11:03 AM EST
To: "Winter Wilcox" <winter.wilcox@yale.edu>
Subject:

Hey. Hi.

Not sure how to start this. Or end it. Just that I can't wait to end it. It's an ouroboros email. Always starting, always finishing.

Don't read any more of this until you're alone. I'm sorry to be cryptic. Don't read it, for example, in the law school library, where you are probably reading it right now.

In fact, let's do this: consider this email a warning that you will receive a future email from me in the next day or so, also w/o a subject line, and THAT email will have confidential contents that should not be read or, say, printed out, in public. Don't open it until you're alone.

/

Recovered from: Drafts Folder (Unsent Message)

From: "Bering Wilcox" <carebear@hotmail.com>
Last saved: February 13, 2003 at 6:02 PM EST
To: "Winter Wilcox" <winter.wilcox@yale.edu>
Subject:

Okay. Second try.

I've never had to do anything like this in my life.

Do you remember that time we went to Six Flags? I mean the three of us. This would have been . . . Labor Day? Labor Day, 1998? (Or Memorial Day, somehow I'm sure it was one of those two.) And we got into that very strange argument about a French movie called *The Return*? Patrick and I had watched it with the parents the night before and you kept asking us what it was about and neither of us would answer.

Is this ringing any bells?

We were arguing about what it meant to be "weird." Patrick kept saying that any work of art that can be adequately summarized is a failure and that a great work of art has a genius that is so weird and particular it can't be expressed any other way, and that only a banal, conventional person likes summaries anyway, and you got into a screaming match with him about how he liked to flatter himself by calling himself a weird genius instead of a callous asshole, and that was fine, except that he was more concerned with the reverse, defining YOU as a boring, lame loser.

And I said nothing the whole time.

Well, there is something about my life and Patrick's life that can't be summarized.

The easiest way to say it is this: remember how I got into that habit of sleepwalking nearly every night when I was twelve? They tried everything, I tried everything. Locking the bathroom door so I wouldn't take a shower in my pajamas (that was messy). You know how it went. Everything except actually tying me to the bed.

I stopped sleepwalking, as you know, but on the other hand I didn't—I was thirteen by this time—I started sleepwalking in my dreams, and I swear, I sleepwalked, that is to say I found myself walking lucidly but not consciously, in the sense of agency, I could not control my motor movements—and I sleepwalked through some kind of door or threshold, I wasn't aware of having done so till I was on the other side, in a black-lit place, where objects gave off light only indirectly, so nothing could be seen except in silhouette. That's the best I can do by way of description. And I thought, I'm only going to be sad from now on. It was as simple as that.

I was so wildly depressed, but I knew I would keep functioning in my everyday life.

That was when I fell in love with Patrick, convinced that I was not a member of my own family. Or that none of us were actually members of one family. The rest of you appeared as a blur, washed out. Patrick was my friend, someone I happened to know. That was all I could be sure of.

I'm writing this to you at a sidewalk café table in Jerusalem. I didn't trust myself to be alone in my hotel room writing it; I thought I might start looking around for sharp objects. It was November when I started cutting myself, that would have been November of '95. I used the small blade on my Swiss army knife. The same one I still have today; it's in my bag back at the hotel. (Yes, the ones with our names on them; the ones Zayde got for us when we went to camp. Yours was blue, if I remember correctly.) Anyway the incisions I made were on my calf, the back of my calf, just below the soft skin of the back of the knee. It was November and no one was going to see my legs until May or longer if I could help it.

It bled a lot.

It's interesting being here and thus opening myself up to being a victim in a different way. I can say that dispassionately. Unlike Heba, for example, I can be vulnerable on both sides. That isn't quite right.

Maybe it's now, in this place that is also black-lit, that I feel capable of making a confession?

I am simultaneously in a hurry and deliberately not. There's only so long I can sit here. Every minute, statistically, of course, increases the risk. Also my butt is beginning to hurt.

Eventually, in some way, or maybe not, you can ask Patrick for his side of the story, because of course he is differently responsible, as the older child. I don't know what he'll say. I last spoke to him about this five years ago.

In another, better, life, we would have been found out, or would have had to out ourselves earlier, or something, and would have had family therapy, et cetera, it would be part of the family trauma and we would have been better off. I feel sure of that. But of course that can't happen now, in this life, nor could it have happened then. Post Mom's revelation about John Downs it would just be too much. I can't even connect them in my mind, sensibly, except to observe the obvious: secrets beget secrets, that's as banal an observation about families as it's possible to make.

I'm avoiding. Of course you can tell I'm avoiding, and you're skipping. You're probably not even reading this. Let me get to the body of the report. Patrick and I, had sex, I have to insert the comma as a way of taking a breath, on five occasions, January–February 1996, and then once again in August 1996, in Blue Hill.

I assume you've never seen *The Return,* and I don't recommend you see it, but I will say this: it's the sickest I've ever felt in a movie theater, the sick sense of recognition. I think the French understand something about incest that Americans (and frankly the rest of the world, maybe) do not. And it is absolutely related to a love of decay and "perversion," I know this all sounds horribly mawkish and obvious, but it's there, in Sade, in the cheese, in foie gras . . . okay avoiding again, here's the thing about *The Return*: the story involves a family whose son disappeared years ago and one day returns, inexplicably, the right age, the right appearance, claiming to be their long-lost child. He's twelve or thirteen and has a slightly younger sister, who hardly remembers the brother who disappeared. And they start a (maybe?) incestuous relationship. It's just the two of them, in the barn, or somewhere else on their rural property, and there's no sense of fear of being discovered. There's no sense of there being an outside world at all. They are finding each other as if there's no other person in the world.

Oh god, I'm just having a memory now of being at a party at Evergreen, freshman year, and some guy, who was much older, a super-senior, he had the blue-blackest dyed hair I've ever seen, was telling me about some French theorist (maybe Bataille?) who claimed that incest was the most natural form of sex, because in Genesis the first sex is all incest, all a product of one family; in other words incest is just a product of the idea of the family itself, since there can only be one Father and one God. Accept the concept of a family and you accept its secret violation, its violation of its own taboos or boundaries or markers as a prerequisite for being. Something like that. That sent me down such a spiral of depression, or can you even call it depression? It was the same thing with *The Return*: recognition. This is what happened to me, to us.

/

Recovered from: Drafts Folder (Unsent Message)

From: "Bering Wilcox" <carebear@hotmail.com>
Last saved: February 14, 2003 at 1:32 AM EST
To: "Winter Wilcox" <winter.wilcox@yale.edu>
Subject:

Third try.

I realized why I'm writing this: when I come home, which I will, and by writing these words I commit myself to it, I want to be able to look you in the eyes and know you understand me for the first time in our adult lives, which sounds melodramatic, but there it is.

Do you remember, but of course you can't remember the same way I do, how CEREBRAL our house was in 1995–96? Everyone so wrapped up in their projects. It was as if childhood was canceled and forgotten.

You and your Model UN and Amnesty and Dad with the Klaufelt case and Mom just being Mom, same as always, except it was right around then that she got her first laptop, which meant she was working in every room of the house. She worked right through dinner. This is not an autobiography or a species of blame, just a description.

And you can fill in the next line, ". . . and Trick was the only one who paid any attention to me." You remember that too. I am not blaming you. I am past blaming anyone for their particular expressions or intensities of love, for the purposes of this story in any case. I just need to get this out. P who always loved having a baby sister. P who teased but never hurt me, who always treated me as slightly more delicate. Who regarded himself as my tutor in all things. So he was the one who noticed, he literally said to me, what the hell is going on with your eyes, your eyes have changed. He took me into the bathroom and made me do that thing with the flashlight, rolling them around in their sockets, look at the floor, look at the ceiling. He made Dad look too. Of course there was nothing to see, but I said to him, in a low voice, at some point that same night, there IS something wrong with me, I'm always cold and I think I'm shrinking, and sometimes I can't taste anything either.

We were in my room at this point, I was lying in bed and he was fixing a Dinosaur Jr. poster that had fallen off the wall, because I'd only put it there with masking tape. I said to him, I think there's something the rest of you aren't telling me. No, he said, you're not dying, you don't have some mysterious condition, and the way he said it was so mocking, and I replied, I'm certain of one thing, and that is I don't belong to this family if it even is a family, I'm not related to any of you.

This is the last thing I'm going to say, and then I'm going to leave it, we're going to talk about it face-to-face, I promise you we will. I think ultimately what happened between me and Patrick has to be regarded not with disgust but with a feeling of strangeness and wonder. Because it's mythical, maybe biblical in nature. Not to say that it should have happened, obviously it was a catastrophic mistake. But there is something in here about the strangeness of life itself and how none of us want to admit it. This is obviously related to our family's other great secret, John Downs, although I can't say how. I don't know how to put it. It's ritualistic, it's ceremonial. It's so very dark. But the thing is: I'm no longer scared of talking about it, any of it. We have to burst this terrible vessel and actually FACE each other for once. I'm promising you I will have more to say, when I'm a little older, when I've finished whatever it is I'm doing here. My life project is to reconcile these things and if I believe in anything I believe it can be done.

GOOD MORNING, BUDDHAS

(SANDY IN A MOMENT OF SILENCE)

The image precedes its meaning.

Imagine a man who has left his life and still wakes in the dark every morning at six, listening to the rain. As if he has to get up and go to work. Imagine that, he says to the novel, the only one listening.

He's forgotten the size, the sheer size and weight, of the weather. Observed from a high meadow, a mountainside. Having not checked his phone he was ambushed by a storm the day after he arrived: two solid days of icy rain, sleet thudding on the roof at night, clouds like gigantic boulders rolling overhead.

It's late April. It's early May. He doesn't bother to check.

In the bookstore in Montpelier he bought three fancy notebooks with waxy red covers, ten dollars each, and a box of special recycled pens, each guaranteed to last three years.

/

His daily schedule, tacked with a Buffalo Mountain Food Co-op magnet to the fridge:

6 A.M.: Wake up, morning exercises

6:30: Breakfast

7:30: Cleaning/work period

10: Meditation with walking breaks

12: Lunch

1: Rest period

2: Long walk

4: Reading

6: Dinner. Listen to the news on the radio for 15 min.

7: Meditation

9: Reading, sleep

Errands on Saturdays

/

Before I arrived at Oberlin I'd never thought of masturbation as a serious hobby.

More of an urgent, occasional need, dispensed with quickly, in the basement toilet where Mother never went. But in East Hall, where he'd been given a private room, through some glitch in the system, he became a seasoned solo practitioner.

That's not quite right. Not quite honest. Not a solo practitioner so much as an accidental voyeur. It wasn't his doing that Rachel Glazer and Judy Shapiro's window faced his, over the narrow walkway between East and Halstead. They had taken down the standard-issue Venetians and hung a diaphanous white sheet in their place, which at night was all but transparent.

Maybe they thought, being on the top floor, at the back, that no one would be looking. Maybe they didn't care. It was 1970, after all. He kept his blinds down and flat, and then made a strategic crack with a piece of Scotch tape. And what was there to see? Voyeurs dwell in possibility. Most nights Judy was out with her a cappella singing group and Rachel was reading and smoking, exhaling into a wire-caged fan. They went braless, almost all the time, it seemed to him, and if he was up late he might catch a glimpse of a breast, a breath of a nipple.

That was his sexual revolution.

He had never before met a Jew, not in his conscious memory. In Davenport there were Jewish doctors and pawnshops and Finkel's, a dress store downtown, but he'd never been to any of those places. Never knew what a synagogue was, never heard of Hanukkah. In Honors English his teacher had made it through *The Merchant of Venice* without ever uttering the word *Jew*. It sounded dirty to him, wrong and insulting. He had been taught, without quite knowing why, to say *Jewish* or *of the Jewish persuasion*. And then Oberlin, where his next-door neighbor, tall and obscenely thin, with a shock of red curly hair, stuck out his hand the first day and said, "I'm Hyman. Hyman Gold. But most people just call me Hy."

At a table in the dining hall with Hy and Rachel and Judy and Irv Greenstreet and Dasi Lieberman and Debbie Landauer he ate silently, like a cow, ruminating, buffeted by waves of conversation. The girls talked with their mouths full. They fell collapsing with laughter into their food and could qualify a statement with three disclaimers without taking a second breath. He saw semicolons and colons popping in the air like fireworks. Their freckles and snapping eyes and angular faces, the many varieties and insistent shapes of their noses, the dark hair and warm brown eyes and full lips. The very swing of the way they walked. Unashamed of having breasts and hips. It made him dizzy. They were from places he'd never heard of, Mamaroneck, the Grand Concourse, Newton, Pikesville, they'd all been to the same camps, they all knew one another's cousins. They had their doubts about Oberlin; their friends at Penn and Columbia and Brandeis called it *Overland* because it was so damned far away. "My parents thought there would be cows wandering across campus," Hy told him. "That's all they know about the Midwest. Cows and corn." His father was an engineer at Bell Labs; they lived in a town in New Jersey he'd never heard of, Nutley. His parents still predicted he would last a semester and transfer to Rutgers. Or turn into a blimp eating nothing but processed cheese. "Check it out," Hy told Judy, pointing his pinky at Sandy. "Sandy came here from Iowa. Davenport, Iowa. That's only two hours away."

"More like four."

"Tell them the story of why you chose Oberlin."

"My high school history teacher went here. He recommended it. I applied."

"Sandy only applied to *one college*."

"Plus Iowa State." He made an elaborate bow from the waist. "I'm your resident hayseed. Ask me anything."

"Do you put mayonnaise and ketchup on everything?"

"Do you guys sit around in church and talk about how the Jews killed Jesus?"

"Do you listen to Perry Como?"

"Do you drive a pickup truck? Can I have a ride in it?"

"Have you ever seen the ocean?"

"Guys," Hy said. "Sandy's going to think we're a bunch of assholes."

"No," he said, "these are easy ones. No, no, no, no, and wait—no."

"That's okay," Debbie Landauer said. "I've never been to the beach either. And I live two hours away. Dad says sunbathing causes skin cancer."

Judy looked down the table at him, propped her chin on her hands—her elbows planted firmly on the table, inches away from coleslaw and a glass of lemonade—and said, reflectively, "I've always wanted to make it with a goy."

Hy snorted into his chocolate milk. The rest of the table dissolved in laughter.

"No, I'm serious," she said. "I mean, how would you ever know otherwise, right? We're liberated women. We deserve at least to *know what it feels like.*"

What does goy mean, he was about to ask, when a tray clattered next to him; a new girl sat down. She had a sweet face. That was his first and least original thought. Dark hair, chestnut hair, like they all did, long and loose, swept over one shoulder. Big, frank, long-lashed, curious eyes. Their knees were almost touching as she leaned over and said, "Hi, what'd I miss?"

It was after a dance, only two days later, an actual dance, a hootenanny, put on by the Earth Club, with a jug band and some painful attempts at do-si-dos and swing-your-partners; it was in his room, since he had a single, and a door that locked. They had done nothing but talk, more or less nonstop, pausing only for a few hours' sleep and to go to class, for forty-eight hours. Naomi leaned against the bed and rolled down her stockings. "I want to look at you," she said. "I want you to look at me." Candles guttered in Mason jars on the bookcase. He unbuttoned his shirt, lifted his belt buckle, let his jeans puddle around his ankles.

"Everything," she said, "everything off."

Her breasts were missile shaped; they pointed away from each other, at a forty-five-degree angle. With a mole right in the center, on the breastbone. Rounded hips, a little scoop of a belly.

"It's cold in here," he said.

"Oh, come on," she said. "I'll show you mine if you show me yours." She relit the tiny joint Hy had left them and held it out. "Courage," she said, with a French accent.

Pot made him feel like his lungs were full of burning hay, but he took it and sucked, desperately, while she let down her panties, stepped out of them, tossed them aside. Never in the presence of the thing before. The full luxuriance of it. "Don't just *stare*," she said. "You're creeping me out. Come here. Get on the bed. I don't bite."

/

To begin with, we hadn't just first met. I recognized her from a previous life. I have no doubt whatsoever about it. We recognized each other, that was all, and that's why it felt like starting a conversation that had just left off. Later when I read descriptions of karma in Intro to Eastern Religions I knew exactly what had happened.

I don't remember any of the words; I remember the sex. Maybe that's unforgivable of me? We told each other everything that happened in our lives up to the age of eighteen. As if catching up. I know that she told me, unashamedly, bluntly, in the midst of saying lots of other things, about what had happened with her mother, how the Great Secret had been revealed, and about what very little she knew about John Downs. It was the one thing I hadn't expected or ever imagined. But it was 1970 and the Loving case was only three years old and I suppose I believed, with great earnestness, that the future was already arranging itself in this direction. I didn't imagine what it meant. Of all the things about Naomi, I couldn't grasp actually what its implications were. I didn't even understand why she had to swear me to secrecy about it, why I was the only person who could know, alone among all our mutual friends. It wasn't until 1982—as far as I know, and I should know—that Naomi told anyone else, and it was Louis and Judy, of course.

But the sex—we had so much of it, to begin with. She was on the pill, had been since she turned seventeen, after a pregnancy scare related to a boy named Harvey at Ma-Ho-Wah Summer Camp. That's right: I wasn't her first, though she was mine. It mattered for about a minute; then we realized we were actually in love, it wasn't casual, it wasn't already about to end. We were (to use the term of the day) Lovers. Which involved endless ploys for sneaking into my room, because girls weren't allowed in East Hall after seven P.M. I wanted to move off campus (which wasn't allowed), I wanted to get married (which was ridiculous), I was infuriated, suddenly, at not being treated as an adult, when a month before I hadn't realized I wanted to be.

For obvious reasons Naomi waited a long time to tell Herman and Phyllis. A very long time (or so it seemed)—that is, until winter vacation. Hy had convinced me to drive home with him to Nutley, and he took me on the bus into Manhattan for the first time. That was a breathtaking day. And right in the middle of it I called her, long-distance, from a pay phone in Rockefeller Center. I'd come prepared with a roll of quarters and kept shoving them in. It was like a movie—it was, come to think of it, like Love Story. *In the background I could hear Phyllis crying and Herman shouting. "It's okay," she said. "I told them you're going to convert."*

"I will," I said. "If that's what it takes."

"We'll just type up a certificate," she whispered. "We'll make up a fake rabbi. They'll never know the difference."

Two days later she took the train in, saying she was going to see a matinee, and I took the bus from Nutley by myself, among all the stone-faced office men with their gray suits and briefcases, and we met in Central Park, by the Duck Pond. We strolled. We held hands. We looked up at the buildings—the Dakota! the El Dorado!—and imagined what it would be like to live up there. (Not imagining, of course, that we'd spend most holidays and many ordinary evenings in a CPW apartment.) We were still just eighteen. Someone should have taken a picture of us, the most photogenic we'd ever be in our lives. N was wearing a yellow leather coat—Phyllis had given it to her as a Hanukkah present.

Instead we got mugged. Two teenagers—one Black, one sallow skinned, Italian or Cuban or maybe Puerto Rican—came up out of the tunnel below the waterfall, behind us. One had a crowbar, the other a Bowie knife. They took my wallet and Naomi's purse, even when she shook it out and showed them a change purse, a return train ticket, a compact, and a packet of Kleenex. "Gotta take the purse," the sallow one said, apologetically, as if he weren't the one calling the shots.

/

Part two. Fast forward. I don't want to tell the story of our wedding, how we moved to San Francisco—it would take too long. And I hardly remember any of it. It happened. We left the sacred precincts of college, the scales fell from our eyes. The real world disappointed us. We became acutely interested in liberation, which at Oberlin everyone pretended had already happened. We tried drugs but they scared us. We weren't flexible enough for yoga. And then—what really matters is that we met Sensei in the spring of 1975. That was the start of the rest of our lives.

It happened very simply: a woman I worked with told us her friend Carl had just come back from Japan with his Zen master, and he was a trip. Anyone could go meet him and learn the secrets of the universe.

Carl's apartment was the top floor of a decaying mansion in the Western Addition; it had been a storeroom for a wool importer and underneath all the incense it still smelled of sheep, of lanolin, so strongly your eyes watered. He'd cleared out all the furniture in the living room, leaving only a Buddha on a stack of cinder blocks, and cushions of all shapes and sizes. We were supposed to come at eight but arrived early, and Sensei was alone, standing at the window, in his robe, eating Fritos out of a bag. He came over to us and shook our hands, bowing slightly, smiling. "Have some," he said. We could hardly understand his English. He poured Fritos into our cupped hands and we stood for a moment, looking into one another's faces, crunching loudly.

"You are all buddhas," Sensei said. "Time to act like it."

/

"Practice is not about patience," he told us. "Don't wait for enlightenment to find you. You are enlightenment. Straighten your back. Make your hands a perfect circle with nothing inside. That nothing is the nature of all existence and your hands are the life force that emerges out of nothing for a short time and then returns to it. Press the tips of your fingers together.

Not too hard, not too soft. Don't make white fingertips. Don't make droopy thumbs. By keeping that circle you are staying alive. You are on the tie rope walking between birth on one side and death on the other."

"Tightrope, Sensei."

"Tightrope. The point is you have only one moment to do the right thing. Otherwise you fall back asleep. Is that what you want?" he asked suddenly, loudly, as we were still arranging ourselves on cushions in front of him. "Do you want to live your life without understanding anything at all?"

"No, Sensei," we said.

Sensei looked me, me personally, in the eyes for the first time.

"You're fucking with me," he said. In his accent it sounded like fugging. "When you say it that way I don't believe you. Say it louder."

"No, Sensei."

"Louder."

"Louder."

"Louder."

/

Naomi and I immediately felt we had found a real spiritual teacher for the first time. I don't know how to express this in a way that gets beyond the clichés of the era and maybe it isn't necessary to get beyond those clichés, as we were no more self-aware or less desperate than anyone else. We were serious hardworking students; we had careers ahead of us; on top of law school I was volunteering nearly full-time with the farmworkers in the valley. What I mean is it seemed that new kinds of wisdom were opening up everywhere. I'm not afraid to use that word. We had friends who were doing Jungian therapy or gestalt therapy or very advanced yoga, or active in the feminist movement, studying Kate Millett and Angela Davis, or working in experimental schools, or absorbing Buckminster Fuller and trying to create a new architecture. Everyone had a thing. It all feels so ridiculous now, a series of caricatures. The great cultural work of a conservative age is to make everything that came before an object of ridicule.

We held a three-day sesshin only about a month or so after the Zendo was founded, and that was when Sensei gave us our first dokusan. Naomi and I had been sitting Zen at SF Zen Center for a while and we could sit zazen for multiple periods without much of a struggle—though my knees ached for days afterward—but we'd never had an interview, never studied koans. I was terrified Sensei would actually hit me when we were alone in the room together, sitting on our mats face-to-face.

Instead he didn't speak to me at all. He was drawn up in his robes like a boulder, completely impassive. I thought he was scowling. He handed me a wrinkled piece of paper with Joshu's mu koan. "Read," he said.

"Now show me the meaning of mu. What is this mu?"

I barked at him.

"Good dog," he said. "But I don't want a dog. Go away, dog."

I stood up and went to the door.

"No," he said. "Walking away isn't it, either."

Why am I writing about this? What's the point of recording all of this? I knew, or I thought I knew, right away that I would be a complete failure at Zen. Naomi came out of her first dokusan with a huge smile on her face and I was angry at her afterward, for days. We'd agreed never to talk about our interviews, that would be worse than talking about what happens in psychoanalysis—not that we knew anything about psychoanalysis, of course, not yet, we were just relying on our friends who did. All she said was, "Sensei actually understands me."

I always knew, from the first time we met, that Naomi was a genius. But it's one thing to meet a genius when she's eighteen and doesn't yet know it herself. In 1975 she was coming into her own. For the first time she was glimpsing the horizons open to her. Or whatever metaphor you want. And it was making her physically ill, just the tension of feeling her own powers. Zen did something to help that. I could never say exactly what it was. I didn't even care. She was happy, she was relaxed at home, she could stop working at times and even just go to a movie or cook dinner.

She was in love with him obviously right from the beginning.

/

A friend of mine from Oberlin, Erik Lindquist, moved to Greensboro, Vermont, to plant an organic apple orchard, and he typed one of his letters to me on the back of a listing from a real estate company. Picturesque New England Farm, it said, 60 Acres, Farmhouse, Barn, All Materials Included, A Price That Can't Be Beat. They wanted $15,000.

Sensei and Carl had already decided we needed a monastery. They were still, at that point, making all the plans for us—Sensei had taken Carl back with him to Japan that summer, so Carl could formally ordain as a monk and be the official abbot of the Zendo. After that we called him by his dharma name, Kodo. He was so terribly earnest, it was impossible not to love him at least a little, and of course respect him for giving up everything—he had dropped out of Cal in his junior year to go to Japan, and his parents, almond growers in Marin County, disinherited him completely, wrote him out of their will. But he had no head for business decisions. He could barely balance a checkbook. It was clear to me that the Zendo would never raise the money if the two of them were in charge.

None of us knew a thing about Vermont except Naomi, who had been to camp there a few summers as a kid. I think I'd seen Grand Hotel *once, so I knew it snowed. I showed Sensei some pictures I dug up in an encyclopedia, and he said, "Looks like mountains in Japan."*

In October, October 27, Mother died of a heart attack, just before her fifty-fifth birthday. I had talked to her on the phone the day before, coincidentally, after not speaking to her for more than a month. She'd had an undiagnosed heart defect from birth, the coroner said, after the autopsy.

It's hard for me to picture her in 1977. I hadn't been home since 1974, when we visited her on the way to California, just after graduation and the wedding. There was no money or time for us to visit her afterward. When we saw her in '74 it was clear she was lost in the 1970s. Hurlbert's, the store where she'd worked for twenty-five years, was getting ready to close, and she had no idea what she would do next. She complained she couldn't find any "decent music" to listen to on the radio. I don't think she ever had another job. She was drinking at midday when we visited and the house was already falling apart—the gutters were hanging off the roof, the basement had an inch of water in it. I tried to do a few things, but we could only stay three days.

So that October I flew to Chicago and rented a car and drove the two hours and went to the funeral and sold the house that same night to Bill Koerner from my high school class. He was buying up most of the houses on that block, hoping to build an apartment building, which never came to pass—but the next day I was on the plane back to San Francisco with a box of pictures and mementos and a cashier's check for $12,000.

My parents gave me nothing but life, I remember saying to Naomi at the time. Life, and a roof over my head, and a savings bond worth $400 when I cashed it in in 1970, to buy the car I could drive away in. Which is, in the greater scheme of things, a lot—everything except a sense of purpose, a way to live, or any attempt at self-understanding, not to mention the crucial deficit of love. Say you love me, I used to plead with Mother, when she stopped in my doorway at night to make sure I'd put down my book and turned off the light. Yeah I do, she said. Three equal stresses.

/

Naomi had a habit in those days of taping up her equations all around the house. There were several on the refrigerator door, always at least one on the bathroom mirror, and on the lampshade on her side of the bed. There was a stack of them on index cards at our little dining table by the window, and she would shuffle them in the morning while I made her scrambled eggs. I had no idea what they were, of course. I'd made it through a year of calculus in college and that was it—I was always very good in math, but just through dogged effort. I never looked beyond the horizon of a single problem. One day (this must have been in January or February—it was freezing in the apartment) she handed me three of the cards, as if we were playing poker, and said, "I want you to keep those somewhere safe in case anything happens to me."

I said, I have no idea what you're talking about.

"They're like my suicide note. Think of it that way. I mean, not that I'm going to commit suicide. But if I was, like a samurai, and if I was going to write a death poem, that would be it."

She was twenty-six years old, and she was bent over the table, smoking, of course, already on her second cup of coffee. Her skin was grayish-yellow, like putty. Her teeth were like old ivory. What part of that was the light from the window, what part was my own fear? What part is the filter of memory, with all its own stains? You, I, will never believe how much I loved her in 1978, and how afraid I was for her actual safety, even as I say at the same time that she was lovesick and whatever shreds of conscience she still possessed were simultaneously eating her alive and telling her to confess, or however you want to put it. She and Sensei went for walks around the city by themselves on Saturdays after zazen practice. Sometimes they were gone for two or three hours. Kodo was so jealous of her, it was sickening to see the expression on his face when they left together.

By that time everyone in the temple was referring to her as Suigen. We all had dharma names, of course—anyone who took the Five Wonderful Precepts had one. Sensei was doing precepts ceremonies nearly every week after his teisho. Mine was Ryumon, "Dragon Gate." Suigen meant, means, "Source of the Waters." Pronounced soo-ee-gen, but soon people began dropping the middle syllable. Sugen. It drove Sensei a little crazy. Different word, different meaning, he said. He would stop them and make them say it correctly. Because everyone was using it, even though the rest of us were still our ordinary selves. Trish was Trish, Frank was Frank, and I was always Sandy. Till the end I was Sandy.

And I, was I jealous? I was wholesome, to begin with, I believed in order in a way I can't explain to myself anymore, even though there was no evidence of order in my world. Maybe because I was never raised to imagine people being deceitful. In Davenport no one ever talked about or even imagined ambivalence or subterfuge or divided loyalties, which isn't to say they never existed, of course they did, but there was no language for such things, and if I had any concept of "cheating," it was on the level an eight-year-old might understand, like cheating at cards. There was a murder-suicide that happened when I was in junior high, three blocks north of us at DeWitt and Tapworth Place: Mr. Lemon found a stack of letters wrapped up with rubber bands in a shoebox, and shot Mrs. Lemon, the Avon lady, who was planning to run off to Chicago with her lover, then shot himself on the front porch, with the police watching. They had no kids, thank god. Mrs. Lemon who sat at our kitchen table and gave Mother a free makeover. I think Mother bought a single lipstick and that was it. The kitchen smelled like her gardenia perfume for days. This was the sum total of what I knew or thought about "adultery." We had every kind of open relationship happening around us, straight and gay, swinging, polyamory, but Nay and I were the straightest and narrowest, still having sex the way we did when we discovered it at eighteen. And I still thought it was more or less the greatest thing in the world.

I thought, without ever saying it to anyone, that Sensei had selected her as his dharma heir. That was a term I knew. I had read enough Zen books at that point to know how momentous it would be, for a Japanese Zen monk to give transmission to an American woman. In all those thousands of years, stretching back to the Blessed One, there were no women in the line of patriarchs. There were women who were nuns and enlightened crones, even enlightened prostitutes, but no official female Zen masters. Yet. And it didn't surprise me for a minute. She was a genius. Not only, maybe even not really, a genius scientist. She had the makings of a guru. You could see it, around Sensei, in the Zen Center, the way she hesitated before saying anything, and then said it perfectly, a single beautiful sentence. People who'd never met her, who'd just walked in the door, turned to her, if Sensei wasn't around, as the authority. There was that kind of electricity around her, to use a stupid expression. And so when she said, one

day, as if it had already been decided, which it clearly already had been—
"Once we set things up at the temple—"

/

There were ten of us who set out from San Francisco, in June 1978, to
found Mujo-ji in the remote mountains of northern Vermont, a place we'd
never been in person—Sensei, Naomi, myself, Kodo, Paul, Jerry, Trish,
Hildegarde, and the two Franks, Frank Lee and Frank Rosenmeyer, who
we called Frank R.

The farm was not in great shape, of course—that's why it was cheap.
We stripped the linoleum out of the kitchen and peeled back fifty years of
wallpaper. Thank god we had Paul, who'd worked construction to put
himself through school. Sensei designated him the housemaster, the temple
architect. I don't remember the word in Japanese. In the house we worked
entirely under his direction. I managed the accounts, Trish and Carl and
the Franks cooked and worried about the garden. And Hildegarde made
posters. Beautiful linoleum-block posters she printed herself, in the barn,
with materials she'd brought with her on the bus.

> HAYASHI MIRO SENSEI
>
> RINZAI ZEN MASTER
>
> DHARMA TEACHINGS
>
> EVERY MONDAY, 7 PM
>
> MUJO-JI ZEN TEMPLE
>
> 29 S. ALBANY ROAD
>
> CRAFTSBURY COMMON

She bought her own car, an old rusty Opel, so she could drive around
all over central Vermont putting up posters. She visited every food co-op,
every town hall, every cluster of yurts or puppet theater or feminist collec-
tive, not to mention all the other ashrams and temples popping up every-

where. The first week we had seven visitors on Monday night; the next week there were thirty. The floor in the dojo wasn't even dry. The house hadn't been painted. The kitchen had no sink. We conducted all our business out on the lawn. If it rained we crowded into the barn and Sensei sat on the seat of the old harvester to give teisho.

/

It goes without saying those were the happiest days of my life and our life, mine and Naomi's. We had the experience of purity, pureness of intention, working for the common good. We were so tired all the time and so exhilarated. I wish I could explain but never have been able to, least of all to my own children, what it felt like, mostly because I stopped believing in it myself for so long. I told myself it couldn't have possibly happened that way. We were all trying so hard to be just like Sensei and make every second and every word count.

"Wake up in the morning and tell yourself, good morning, buddhas!"

That was what he always used to say at the end of his teisho. It got a big laugh from the crowd.

And by the end of the summer we had five more people living at the temple. Darryl, Josh, Ben Lewis, Ben Roper (why did we always have these twin names?), and Suzanne. By then Jerry had built bunk beds in three of the four bedrooms. We could sleep eighteen, but not comfortably. That fall we partitioned the dining room and converted the parlor—that gave us some breathing room. Our buddha statue finally arrived, and we built a real altar. In October we had the Mountain Seat ceremony and formally installed Kodo as the housemaster and Sensei as the abbot and guiding teacher. Before then Hildegarde had bought a sewing machine and made us all formal robes, following Sensei's instructions. We were official.

And by that time Nay was almost ready to have Patrick.

Hildegarde left in January. She just drove off one day, in her little car, barely stopping to say goodbye. And we knew it was because of the baby. She'd been the first of the women to shave her head, the most severely modest. Sensei said many times that the baby was welcome, that Japanese Zen was not celibate, but Hildegarde wanted to be a nun in the Catholic sense, I guess.

God that first winter was hard. I mean I was from Iowa and used to cold weather, Naomi was from New York, and Paul was from Wisconsin, and of course Sensei viewed central heating itself as a luxury, he'd trained walking barefoot through snowdrifts, but everyone else was from California and had no idea what to expect. It's amazing, in retrospect, that they didn't all leave. We still had a steady stream of visitors, and that helped— new people in the kitchen, splitting wood, shoveling snow, filling the coal bin. The most recent arrival was the first one sent outside for whatever needed doing. Mostly, of course, we needed their donations. I was keeping the books and doing all the big purchases—coal deliveries, of course, and gas for the truck, plus the wholesale groceries we ordered through Buffalo Mountain Food Co-op and picked up once a week. No one was working an outside job. Hildegarde, before she left, wrote me a check for $100 every two weeks, as if she were paying rent. But then she was gone. So I would beg everyone coming in the door for money, telling them dana was expected at the rate of at least $5 a day. I didn't want to put the squeeze on our residents and start charging rent outright, and there was no way I was going to tell them to give all their assets to the temple, as if we were some cult. But most of them sat placidly at mealtimes and went to bed at night as if their sincere effort on the cushion was paying the bills.

Finally I stood up at announcements time after teisho on Monday— this was sometime in the middle of March—and said: We're running out of money and we're going to have to kick all of you out in a week. I said, we have a basic operating cost of seven hundred dollars a month while we're still in the cold months, and that lasts until May. We need to raise four hundred by next Monday and three hundred more by the following Monday. That's fifty dollars a person. And then I sat down.

And god, the arguing that erupted after that. The dharma should be free, Darryl or someone said, there shouldn't be a price of admission. We should be like monks in Thailand or Burma, someone said, and make the rounds of the local farms with begging bowls. We should all apply for food stamps. We should grow marijuana. We could make do with half as much food. We should only eat lentils and rice. We should stop using coal and heat the house with wood. Or go without heat altogether. We should find some rich patron, like temples do in Japan.

And someone said to me, with a twisted look, why do you and Suigen get to stay, just because you happened to have the cash to buy the place? Why should we recognize ownership at all?

Naomi just stared them down and said, I'm applying for a job as a science teacher in the fall, once the baby is born. And Sandy's going to work as a lawyer in Montpelier. He's taking the Vermont bar test this summer.

She was so pregnant at that point. Trish had sewed her a special robe with pleats in front, and she just stuck out, her sheer roundness, as she came in a room, her hands usually rested on the curve of her belly if she wasn't carrying anything. All pregnant women glow, they say, especially the first time, but I've never seen anyone with the aura she had. And the certainty. She was almost regal. Where did she get that kind of gravity, as a twenty-six-year-old? It's a stupid question. She got it from the practice, of course— she'd already had kensho, it happened very soon after she started sitting zazen, she told me, much later, and she only talked about it with Sensei. She said it was like being in a tunnel and seeing a train rushing toward her and just staring it down, letting it come, with no fear at all.

This was a time when she just told me how things were going to go between us. Never before, and obviously never since, have we had that kind of relationship, god knows, but from the fall of 1977 until April 12, 1980, Naomi was utterly and completely in charge, without having to ask for anything. We're going to have a baby, she told me, when she'd already known about Patrick for weeks. Of course we'd always agreed we wanted kids, but we hadn't discussed it for a year at least, at that point— always assuming that Naomi would wait until she'd finished her primary research, or even till she had her first job. I had no idea she thought it was possible to have a baby and live our lives at the temple, no idea she wanted to raise a child as a Buddhist nun, which she was, effectively. She'd quietly stopped taking her pills; that was all there was to it. She'd brought a six-month supply from San Francisco and never bothered to get more. All through the summer we'd been having sex only once in a long while, when we weren't just too tired. But in September she started zipping herself into my sleeping bag every night.

Of course she wasn't entirely serious about applying for a job, let alone my getting one. But it dispelled the whole argument, the starry-eyed fairyland hippie fantasy of those early Mujo-ji days, that all this was some kind of miracle. Money wasn't going to rain down from the sky. Darryl left in April, and then Jerry and Frank Lee—Frank's father had died and he had to return to Stockton and inherit the family business. Everyone else, in one way or another, began chipping in. Paul got a part-time carpentry job in Hardwick. Trish arranged to sell some old silver she'd inherited from her grandparents. We got serious about ordering seeds and reading up on farming, plotting out everything we planned to grow.

And then Patrick was born, on May 3. Nay had insisted on engaging a regular obstetrician, not a midwife. She was too much of a scientist to believe in anything but a hospital birth, she said, at least the first time. But she insisted she didn't need anesthetic, and they believed her, somehow— that was the force of will she had. It was a natural birth, though I wasn't in the room to see it. The nurses kept me waiting, even as I could hear her screaming, actually screaming, down the hall. That was obstetrics in the 1970s. I was convinced she was seriously injured, or had had an emergency C-section, or something, but then I was summoned back into her room and there she was, smiling, already toweled off, and Patrick was already nursing. Five minutes old, and already in the world like he knew perfectly well what he was doing.

For the first six weeks after Patrick was born we were exempt from morning practice and our work duties, though I still had to maintain the accounts—no one else could. Nay and the baby slept and ate, ate and slept.

A farmwife from the co-op gave us her whole supply of cloth diapers, and it was my job to wash them, nearly every day, and hang them out on the clothesline. It was the first thing you saw, walking up the driveway to the temple: a long line of white diapers fluttering from the corner of the roof, like prayer flags.

It was in that period—I don't remember which month—Tempest arrived.

We were down to twelve residents then. We sat in order of seniority in the dojo, and she was all the way at the end, in an old robe Trish had altered to fit her. She said almost nothing, but she learned fast. She'd arrived with long blond braids, but somewhere along the way had cut them off into a boy's bob, just above the ear. And she seemed, overall, extremely young—to have shown up on her own recognizance and been there for several months without ever receiving a letter or making a phone call. I wondered if she'd dropped out of college or simply run away from home. Privately I spoke to Trish and Frank and Paul and Kodo, and none of them had had a conversation with her longer than a few sentences, either.

It was on one of those dark mornings during fall sesshin—we were doing a full-week sesshin, in the beginning of October—I happened to pass as she was leaving dokusan, making her final bow with the door open, and heard her say something quickly to Sensei in Japanese. And he laughed.

She had a degree in Asian art history from Harvard. She'd lived in Tokyo with her family for five years as a child—her father was an attaché at the embassy, and her Japanese was all but fluent. She'd come deliberately, without telling anyone, in her own car (a two-door Volvo, which sat unused by the road), because she'd heard about Sensei from Eido Shimano in New York. It was her first time doing formal Zen practice, but she had been around Japanese Buddhists and their customs all her life. Why, I wanted to know, when all this came out, why hadn't she told us any of this, why keep it a secret, why would it have to matter one way or the other? She wouldn't answer me.

We were driving back from Morrisville on some errand—it was the first time we'd ever been alone together. I think it may have been the strangest conversation I'd ever had in my life. I wasn't used to this as part of a lawyer's everyday world, prying things out of people, assembling a time-line, demonstrating cause and intent. Moreover I wasn't yet used to dealing with rich people—I hardly knew any rich people. Tempest's last name was Chapman, I learned, and other than Tokyo she'd grown up on Eighty-First and Park Avenue. Her pedigree was Brearley and Choate, then Harvard, with a year abroad in Paris. Her mother served on boards and her father was a VP at Chase Manhattan. She—Tempest—had never been happy or well-adjusted, if anyone ever is in those families, but particularly so after her oldest brother hanged himself in the closet of his dorm room at Ando-ver. She was twelve at the time, still with her parents in Japan, and they waited nearly a month to tell her, having flown to the States and back for the funeral and left her in the care of a nanny without saying a word. Her nanny soon after gave her a Jizo statue and taught her to say namo Jizo Bosatsu, and that was the beginning of her Buddhist practice. At any rate, that's the story she told. It all came tumbling out. She was so carelessly open with me, for the run of a few sentences, and then she would fall back into silence and stare out the window and only answer with monosyllables.

She finally said, "Your relationship with Suigen is so inspiring to me, it's like a miracle."

I told her I didn't understand what she meant.

"Well, you're the only married couple here, and let's face it, you don't get to spend a lot of time together, for one thing. But also, I mean, let's be honest, you subordinate yourself to her. We all do."

"That's not the way I would describe it."

"It's a mystery to me. I think she's a bodhisattva, teaching us all detach-ment. I mean, you know Sensei is sleeping with her."

/

Something lifting, the weight of winter finally giving out. For four days it rained almost nonstop, and when he went out for his daily walk he could smell the earth for the first time. The last rinds of snow along the path melting away, and now, overnight, tiny green needles everywhere. It makes him dizzy, the sheer intensity of the seasonal change. In a cold climate, a seven-months-of-winter climate, the period of recovery and regrowth has to be that much more radical. Each season obliterates the last.

/

There was an older woman, Pearl Whitney, an occasional student of Sensei's, who had a vacation house in Stowe that was empty most of the winter. She'd given us permission to use it if we ever needed to—not that I could ever see the need. I made up an excuse about needing to stay overnight in Montpelier on temple business and drove down there the next morning.

I poured myself a little of Pearl's scotch and sat on her sofa and watched TV.

*This was 1979. I hadn't seen a TV in more than a year—we didn't have one at the temple, of course, and the one we'd had in our apartment in San Francisco was a tiny black-and-white, the kind with a handle on top, that barely worked and mostly sat in a corner collecting dust. Pearl's TV was enormous, state-of-the-art; it had a whole wall of the room to itself, in a gigantic walnut cabinet. I watched whatever was on—*Wheel of Fortune, Days of Our Lives, Wide World of Sports. *I must have watched two hundred commercials. There were shows I'd never heard of,* Three's Company *and* The Jeffersons. *I sat there in a Technicolor daze, hour after hour.*

For periods of the day I was in intense physical pain, concentrated in my chest and abdomen, like I've never had since, and I felt I might vomit, though I never did. It didn't occur to me to eat or drink anything else. There was a crocheted blanket over the back of the couch, and I wrapped that around myself. I hadn't thought to turn the heat on, and the house was freezing, but I was still wearing heavy work pants, wool socks, a thick sweater, and a down vest—the same thing I wore every day—so I hardly noticed it. Until I woke up in the middle of the night, the TV gone off the air, my breath making a cloud of frost, and realized I could freeze to death.

That was the first time I'd experienced such an intense, lucid wanting to die. It drew me out of sleep so that I was painfully aware of just how cold I was, which, of course, ironically, is what prevents death from hypothermia. I took a pillow from the couch and sat on the carpet in lotus position, with the TV still on, facing the screen full of snow and the sound of it like a waterfall. I felt myself crying—not sobbing, just tears dribbling down my cheeks.

I thought, How paltry a part of this story I am, how vestigial, how little I have to contribute. Isn't that, basically, the psychological effect of TV, a kind of negation of active life, or citizenship?

Or, to put it another way: what was being drawn out of my body, little by little, at that moment was an inner certainty I'd possessed (and who knows where it came from?) that things would turn and turn but finally come down right, like the song says. It was being leached out of my body. Which was a way of trusting the world but also trusting her. God I was sure that all this newness in the world, in the cosmos, all this revolutionary thinking, how my own mind had been altered (I thought, permanently), was going to result in something even if I had no idea what. Naomi had dared me to let her take the initiative, had dared me to trust her genius, that's what I thought was happening, when what it was was actually love.

I thought, for at least an hour, that what I would do was simply leave, leave Naomi and Sensei to raise Patrick, let their relationship take its course. I never doubted Patrick was mine—that came later—but he was still her baby, her body, sheltered by her.

Then I resolved to confront them publicly, institute divorce proceedings, and close down the temple and kick them out—I knew I could do it, I would be well within my rights.

I wanted so desperately for the TV to come back on.

When you marry someone in college you have no adult life to turn back to. *You have no foundation.* And of course I did that because I thought I had no foundation in the first place. My one certainty, in college, was that I wasn't ever going back to Davenport. God I wish someone had told me not to bind myself to another person so early in life, to wait, to discover, for lack of a better phrase, who I wanted to be. *Sensei said, Karma is like a clock that's always ticking, whether or not we ever look up to see what time it is.* And that's what it was, of course, what I was facing, the great catastrophic mistake of my life, which carried everything within it—my theoretically deep but experientially nebulous political commitments, and of course the fact of (guilt about) my own body, my tall, reasonably attractive, instantly recognizable white male body and its power, and the way I knew without knowing how people always responded to it, and of course my flickering visions of the future, how I'd always wanted to live in a nice house like some of my friends had, with beautiful framed pictures and deep bookcases and carpets and flowers in a vase at the dinner table, these openly bourgeois desires, which in my mind somehow fit in with everything else we were doing. All that had somehow adhered to Naomi in 1974, who even then had already told me everything I needed to know, everything that still applies, about herself. She was incorrigibly messy and had to be compelled to care about physical things around her, about hygiene, for lack of a better word. She had almost supernatural abilities in mathematics and quantitative thinking. She was the secret child of a Black man and had no idea what to do with that information. She was extremely moody and given to hyperbole and impatience and—though it wasn't as evident then as it became later—rage. She possessed a disarming kind of self-certainty that drew people to her and made her, simultaneously or later, very easy to hate.

And what was my relationship to her, exactly? This is what I'm trying to say: in my psychic state, when we met, when I was barely eighteen for god's sake, I was incapable of what could be called "love." This is why I'm using the word *binding*. Remember the line from the Song of Songs we read at the wedding, "Set me as a seal upon your heart . . ."? How terrifying a thought that is, to take another person as a seal on your heart, as if they hold the wires to your pacemaker.

And where was Patrick? Where was my infant child, in all these thoughts? We had been together in the same bed for the past three months, the three of us, as one person, bathing, feeding, changing, crying. I had had no other thoughts. It was like a dream; at times it was like it had never happened.

At that moment—I remember this sequence precisely—I began to wonder, seriously wonder, if he was mine. He had very dark hair, darker even than Naomi's. (It changed later, even a few months later, to the chocolate-brown color he's had ever since.) Did he have other Asian features? What about his eyes? I had never to my knowledge met a biracial half-Asian person. I had no idea what to look for. She had been having sex with both of us in July and August, presumably—and perhaps him more than me—what were the chances?

I was transfixed then. Mute horror.

I had to stand up, and I could barely move. Somehow I dragged myself to the bathroom and had dry heaves, then stretched out on the tile floor and fell asleep again.

Oh I want to be kind to myself, without excuses

I just wrote that sentence without knowing what it means.

I have to write this part as quickly as I can.

I came back into our room, it was midmorning, work period, she was stretched out on the futon nursing Patrick, and when I opened the door he detached and started crying, startled, and I took down my sleeping bag from the closet and said, "I'll be sleeping in the barn." "Why? Why?" she cried.

I can't I can't relive it

Then in a moment, as I stood there looking at her, as Patrick reattached and settled back, his eyes fluttering, about to fall asleep, she looked at me more calmly and said, "It's over."

"What's over?"

"You want me to say it out loud?"

"I want you to say it out loud."

I left then. I went and retched in the bathroom and then took my sleeping bag and spread it out in the hayloft, where we often kept overflow guests in the summer, if they could stand the heat. I went back to my office, which was (is) a little room, a former pantry off the kitchen, barely big enough for a desk and a chair. I made telephone calls. I went over our outstanding bills, cut some checks, stamped some envelopes, carried them out to the mailbox.

Everybody knew something was up. It was a very strange day. At midday meal—we'd given up on serving three formal meals a day by then, and only did oryoki at breakfast and dinner, so this was in the dining room at the long table, all twelve of us clustered close together on stools and benches—Kodo tipped over the soup pot and spilled hot miso all over the table. Sensei loved accidents usually and clapped loudly and laughed whenever anyone spilled or dropped something during oryoki, but this time no one said a word, just hurried to clean it up. I was sitting as far as I could from him and not making eye contact, and of course he knew what was happening, whether N told him or not (and I doubt she did).

That was the end of my relationship with him in the formal sense. I had stopped being his student. After that day, though we lived in the same not-large building on the same property for nearly eight more months, I never went to dokusan, never presented my koan, and barely attended teisho, always using the excuse that I was too busy in the office. I was still a Zen student. Just not his student. I sat zazen for the minimum requirement of three hours a day. I chanted and bowed and all the rest. My koan was very simple: How do I get through this day?

I never tried to confront him, even ask him the simple question: why? It never occurred to me. It should have. I deserved an answer. You deserve answers, Brisman said once, from all the men who betrayed and/or abandoned you. Starting with the father you never met, ending with Irwin Klaufelt. Yet you never asked for them. Their reasons remain opaque to you. Maybe you prefer it that way—and I finished his sentence, so I can remain opaque to myself.

1

I was in the barn, with a kerosene lamp, reading—I had picked up a novel for the first time in years, from a shelf of books in the upstairs hallway left behind by visitors. It was, of all things, Jaws. With the photo of the shark eating the naked woman swimming on the cover—and I heard footsteps on the floor of the barn, and the rasping sound of bare feet and hands on the ladder. I was preparing myself to see Naomi's face coming over the edge when I realized it couldn't be, she would never leave Patrick alone in our bedroom, and no one would be watching him at ten P.M., and then of course I knew who it would be, and I turned down the lamp and pretended to be asleep, I knew somehow that was what was required of me, and then I felt her hands, she unzipped the bag and cupped my face in her hands and kissed me, she was already naked, and it was absolutely dark. We fucked with her straddling me and when I came it was this great unbowing, you could almost hear the twang, the tension released, and then a pain all through my groin so intense I almost shrieked and she put her hand across my mouth. "Shut the fuck up, do you want to get caught," she whispered, Tempest whispered, and I knew exactly what I was doing—I was having sex with an adolescent, for all intents and purposes.

I went back to our room the next morning. Naomi and Patrick were asleep, stretched out on the bed, just as they had been when I left. Naomi opened one eye but Patrick stayed down. We huddled in the farthest corner of the room, so as not to wake him, and talked in the faintest whispers:

What do you want now? she said. What do you want me to do?

I don't want you alone with him.

I'm his senior student. I have to be alone with him.

No dokusan for a month. No private meetings. No walks. No trips.

She stared at me for a disconcertingly long time without closing her eyes.

Okay, she said finally. If that's what it takes.

And you have to tell him why.

Without seeing him privately?

Write him a letter.

She stared at me again, and I said: Otherwise we're leaving. We're leaving, or I'm leaving. And I will sue for custody. Don't fuck with me, Naomi.

Don't you ever talk to me that way.

Do you want me back or not?

Not if you're going to act like some abusive asshole. That's not the person I married.

Another long silence. She had strangely wide eyes and rose up from sitting on the floor into a kind of crouch.

I'm not sorry for falling in love with him, she whispered. I can't apologize for that. I can apologize for what it's done to you.

For what you've done to me.

For what I've done to you.

/

By the new year, the last of the 1970s—and we had a kind of party to celebrate, with cheese and crackers and even a little wine—the temple was down to just five of us, besides Sensei. Naomi and myself, Frank R, Suzanne, and Ben Roper. Paul and Kodo had left, and Trish—almost all of the original contingent. A lot of tearful goodbyes that fall, a lot of miserable quiet days. There were still crowds of fifteen or twenty or even thirty coming for Monday teisho, and people sometimes stayed around for a week or two, but they quickly sensed the vibe and departed.

Tempest, like Hildegarde, vanished without ever saying goodbye. We woke up one day and she was gone—she'd packed her bag, rolled up the sheets on her futon, and, we assumed, driven away in her car. We didn't think to inquire further. She wasn't the first person at the temple simply to disappear.

I met her once in New York, years later, at a party at the River Café. It was a benefit for the Fresh Air Fund. I hardly recognized her—she had her hair swept up in a chignon and was wearing a Chanel dress and pearls, like

*every other woman there. She'd married a guy she knew from Harvard,
the captain of the crew team. He shook my hand kind of aggressively, as if
he was used to meeting Tempest's exes.*

Nineteen eighty, the turn of the year.

/

*When I thought about the temple later—and I did think about it from
time to time, and dreamed about it even more often—I thought about
the kitchen counters, and the plastic tubs that held twenty pounds of rice,
and the upstairs bathroom with its little metal Buddha statue and incense
bowl on the windowsill, the brown toilet paper we bought in bulk from
the co-op that felt like sandpaper, but no one complained. What I dreamed
about was self-sufficiency. Of course this is part of Zen, and Zen brought
us to it, but the two are not necessarily intertwined. Later on I learned the
phrase "intentional living." That was what it was, and that was what was
happening everywhere in the 1970s, all those communes and collectives and
vegetarian restaurants and food co-ops and work exchanges and so on. That
was what we were, as a generation, required to abandon. Why? Sometimes
I think this is the great unanswered sociopolitical question of the age. It
wasn't Reagan, or it wasn't just Reagan—many of these projects continued
a few years into the 1980s, and dwindled or died on their own, of their
own volition. "We," meaning the committed, walked away from them.*

*It isn't enough to say Reagan, or to say, vaguely, "the culture changed,"
without saying why. I know on the West Coast things felt very different.
It felt for a time like the computer business and the running-shoe business
and the natural-foods business grew out of the same impulses. But in New
York by 1981 you would have thought the seventies had never happened.*

*You would have to do a kind of political archaeology of this vanished
civilization, or rather vanished outposts of a future civilization, to understand it.*

/

We lasted through January and February at a low ebb, sustained mostly by Patrick, who was seven and eight months old, learning to wiggle and sit up and fall down on a blanket on the kitchen floor. Naomi had taken over most of the cooking duties after Trish left, which meant we were operating mostly within arm's reach, me in my pantry office and her at the stove, handing the baby back and forth. Sensei was working in the barn, with Ben's help—they were building a large wooden frame, but Sensei wouldn't tell anyone what it was for. He gave the directions and Ben sawed and nailed and sanded, not quite seeing what they were making.

When the snow started to melt, at the end of March, Sensei announced at the end of teisho that he was building a hermitage for himself, a tiny cabin that would be at the other end of the property, in the woods near the creek. And after it was built, he was taking a vow of silence.

By this time I wasn't at all afraid of him, or avoiding him, though we hardly ever spoke. He had lost weight since the fall and didn't look well—in fact Suzanne had taken him to a doctor in Burlington and he'd been diagnosed with mild anemia. The treatment was iron supplements. Naomi had resumed seeing him in dokusan but she knew I was observing her every moment, and they never, as far as I knew, saw each other privately outside of the interview room. When he sat at the head of the dojo or gave teisho he was the same teacher, with the same laugh, the same loud, stretching voice, but in the house he was starting to walk with a shuffle, like a much older man.

He and Ben worked on the cabin every day, having built the frames already, of course, and by the middle of April it was finished. We had a small dedication ceremony and then he moved in. He came back to the temple for morning practice and breakfast, then stayed by himself all day, returning only for dinner and evening chanting. That lasted for a week.

Then he wrote on a piece of paper, I need someone to bring me my meals, I'm going into intensive retreat.

When he said "someone" he was standing in the kitchen, within earshot of both of us, and Suzanne, who was chopping vegetables at the counter. I can do it, Suzanne said, and Sensei said, No, Suigen will do it.

No, I said, not looking up from my desk, but raising my voice loudly enough to be heard. Suigen will not do it.

He stood still in the middle of the kitchen; it seemed to me he was even swaying slightly. I looked up at him but he cast his eyes down at the floor and sighed, and shuffled back toward the door.

That night Naomi was furious with me. It's my right to speak to him, not yours, she said. I'm not your property. And I insisted that she stick to our agreement. No private meetings.

The next day I had to take the truck into Hardwick to do our weekly shopping in the afternoon, and when I returned, pushing the wheelbarrow up the path filled with bags and boxes, it was lunchtime, everyone was eating in the dining room, Suzanne was feeding Patrick on her lap, and Naomi wasn't there.

I didn't say anything. I put my boots back on and ran down the hill, through the fields, through the mud, nearly slipping and falling, forgetting exactly where the cabin was and then sighting it through the trees. I came silently, stilling myself into short steps, waiting until my breaths had evened out. I came up to the cabin's one rear window, hearing nothing, and looked in.

The image precedes its meaning.
A man's ass, observed in the act of fucking.

There's nothing more to this story other than everything that comes after: the story opens wide and takes in the whole rest of our lives, including of course Bering and Winter, who weren't ever there, who were born in the horrendous agony and shitshow of the next three years.

Why, why, why, did we stay together? At first because there was just no alternative. We were directionless, and in the end, the dissolution of the temple happened so fast—in two days, from the moment I glimpsed Sensei and Naomi through the window to the afternoon we left. I simply announced, the next morning, that as of now Naomi and I were the owners of the property, everyone else was our tenant, and they all needed to leave within twenty-four hours, Sensei included. I drove to the bank in Hardwick and cashed out the temple account, a little more than $2,000, and divided it up in stacks of twenties on the dining table. Everyone got an equal share. Naomi was up in our room with Patrick and I was back to sleeping in the barn. I don't remember our conversations at all. I couldn't look at her. She'd just said, after coming out of Sensei's hut, pulling her robe back on over her bare breasts, "Take me away from here." So that's what I was doing. I drove to Morrisville that night and traded the truck for a Plymouth station wagon that stank of fish and cigars. That was our first family car. We drove through the night all the way from Craftsbury to Armonk, to Herman and Phyllis's house.

I feel such pain in writing these sentences. This material is inscribed on me—why do I need to put it down?

A few months later we got a letter from Suzanne—she sent it general delivery to the post office in Armonk. She stayed at the temple a few days after we left, sleeping in the barn, because I'd locked the house. Sensei, she said, remained in his hut the whole time. He didn't stir.

/

The image precedes its meaning.

Coming over the crest of the hill, Winter pauses and scuffs her feet in the mud. Trying to take in the moment.

A yellow farmhouse, in a hollow, a fold in the hillside, between two meadows. And its brown barn. In all its situatedness, its ordinary existence, in ordinary daylight, in an ordinary year. If we say it's picturesque, does that mean, essentially, that we've already seen it in a picture. It could be a hundred yellow farmhouses in a hundred meadows. It could be a hundred unreachable fathers.

She says to the house, I saw you in my dreams.

He stands up in the yard with a shovel in one hand.

"Son of a bitch," she says, loud enough for the house to hear it.

AN APPEAL

(OR, AN ATTEMPT AT AN INTERVENTION)

Winter was at the dining table, cutting out strips of blue and yellow construction paper and taping them into a paper chain. It was for someone's birthday; she loved decorations and wanted them for every possible occasion. Naomi had Bering in her lap, with the safety scissors, trying to show her how to cut a straight line, but Bering of course wanted to pick up Winter's chain and twirl it around. Winter, having none of this, held the chain over her head and pulled it across the living room, five or six feet of it, while Bering howled. It was such an ordinary moment, the kind of thing that happened nearly every day, why would anyone remember such a thing. Only because of the look Winter gave him, as he came into the room, a look of such concentrated disgust and determination, as if to say, I will carry my banner alone through this shrieking pit of a world.

In the kitchen, she picks up the phone and holds it to her ear to check the dial tone. Punches in her own number and listens to her own message, in English and Spanish.

"I brought you a letter," she says to Sandy. "It seems email doesn't get to you."

"You could have hired a process server."

"I was tempted to, believe me. But I wanted the satisfaction of seeing your face. It's a habeas corpus kind of thing."

"Well, you would know."

"What's that supposed to mean?"

"Didn't you say to me once that I'm the kind of lawyer who forgets the law is about bodies?"

"Dad," she says, loudly, swiveling actually to see his face, "I'm not here, I didn't drive seven hours—"

"What did you come in, a horse and buggy?"

"—to talk about traffic, or have a legal pissing contest."

"You've never been here before. Let me show you around."

"I don't have long."

"What do you mean, *don't have long*? You're staying the night, aren't you?"

"In Montpelier. We made a reservation."

"That was silly. You could have stayed here."

"Mom is a lesbian," she says lightly, the words falling where they may. "She's living with, or basically living with, a woman named Tilda. They've been together for several years. I'm guessing. Also, I'm pregnant. I'm going to go sit on the porch and pretend I'm smoking a cigarette. Make me some tea."

She smoked in high school; they all did, on and off. The girls' rooms always smelled like smoke no matter what Francine used to cover it: Febreze, Lysol, Endust. They smoked into those terrible window box fans and then never cleaned them, so they accumulated dust and grime, which in turn held the smoke. Years ago he finally threw the fans away, and all their old bedding, the mattresses, repainted the rooms, and when they were done it was as if no one had ever lived in them.

The kettle sings, finally. He's losing feeling in his toes. Something is opening in him, the widening of an aperture, perineal, a painful stretch that makes his eyes water. Fearful that everything in the margins, all his digits, for example, might not fit into the new picture. A horizon line, the thing that admits and expels, lined with cilia, with tiny fibers that glow.

"I have something to say," he says, clumping out onto the porch in his mud boots, the only shoes he could find by the door. Two mugs of tea in his shaky paws. "And I want you to listen without comment until I'm finished, which won't take long. We'll talk about you and Mom in a minute. I promise. Can you do that?"

She measures him.

"I can do that."

"What happened here," he says, "in 1980, around when Patrick was born, the part we never told you, is that your mom and Sensei were having an affair, sleeping together. It was briefly unclear whose child Patrick was. In fact, for several years we didn't know for sure. When I discovered what your mom and Sensei were doing, because I did discover it, that's when the temple broke up. And Sensei just disappeared. That's why we moved back to New York. Why it happened so quickly, why there was never any good explanation for it."

"Evidently this will come as a shock to you," she says, "but I already know that. We both know. *Have* known, for years."

His body sags. His brown paper sack of a body.

"Some friend of Patrick's came across it, ages ago. There was a web forum about sex scandals in American Buddhism, and someone posted a mention of Mujo-ji on a list of temples closed after the teacher was disgraced. And Mom's name came up in the comments. It wasn't pleasant reading. It must have been someone who was there, who was close to the action. This was in 2009 or 2010—before *Shiva*. Patrick got someone to bury it—some friend who does SEO. So you can't find it by googling her name. But it's still out there."

"I'll have to look for it."

"I don't see why you would."

"It matters how it's remembered," he says, a little more loudly than he intended. "I didn't think it did, but it does. That's what I've been doing up here."

"Remembering things?"

"Writing, actually. Writing a, a something, a book, maybe. An account, at least."

"I'd be interested to read it. Why are you talking that way?"

"What way?"

"Like you're having a stroke."

"I haven't had a conversation with anyone in six weeks. I'm not used to it. This is a bit of an ambush. I asked your mother to respect my privacy."

"I'm not Mom. You didn't ask *me* anything."

"Before I left New York," he says, with a throb in the glands, the jaw sockets, whatever those apertures behind the ears are called. Wondering if he really is having a stroke. "Before I left New York, actually the same day, I tried to kill myself. I was about to jump off the balcony."

"Which balcony?"

"Our balcony. In the apartment."

"I never thought of it as a balcony. There isn't even room for a chair."

"Are you mocking me or something?"

"I was trying to figure out if it was a figure of speech. I guess it wasn't."

"I'd been depressed for a very long time."

"Of course you had. We all knew that."

"And alone, of course, living alone, ever since your mother decamped. Very alone. I see that now. Gradually, you know, it happens, you lose contact with people—"

"Dad. Come on. You had one friend, and he died. One friend, and, frankly, no hobbies. And then Mom leaving."

"I made a plan. An excellent plan. I had a beautiful rationale. I did research. It was a one hundred percent thought-through, completely sensible, defensible suicide. It would have been, anyway. All my affairs were in order. Primo Levi was in complete agreement."

Her face is turned away from him, as if inspecting the yard; she sets the tea down on the chair's heavy arm, and her shoulders begin to shudder. She cries without looking at him. He should give her a hug. I haven't touched her, he's thinking, haven't touched either of my children, in how long? It would be an affront. How would she respond?

Back in the kitchen, he finds the paper towels under the sink.

Shuffles to her. Drops the roll in her lap.

"You ought to be hospitalized," she says, or croaks, wiping her face. "Someone who's attempted suicide shouldn't be alone for weeks in the middle of nowhere."

"I don't need that. I needed this."

"I can't take care of you right now. I'm pregnant, for god's sake."

"I don't need anyone to take care of me."

"Says the man who just tried to kill himself. You should come back to Providence with me. In fact, I insist on it. We've got two guest rooms. You're going to see a psychiatrist and go back on whatever meds and get stable."

"No."

"If I leave you here, that's tantamount to saying it's okay if I get a call in a week telling me you hung yourself in the barn."

"*Hanged* yourself in the barn."

"Thank you for being a tragic, pathetic figure, and also a gigantic fucking asshole, Dad."

"I'm serious," he says. "I'm fine. I'm not going to kill myself. I'm certainly a pathetic figure, but not a tragic one. I'm very happy you're pregnant. I don't hate Mom. Actually I'm not even that surprised."

"Seriously?"

"If I'd taken a minute to think about it," he says, with numbed lips, "I could have figured out that she was obviously in love with someone else, that there was someone in Woods Hole. I think she would have told me if I'd asked. Maybe she wanted me to ask. Maybe she was mad at me for not caring enough to ask. Anyway, it doesn't matter now."

"Because you're okay with it. Your marriage is over."

"Yes."

The novel has him by the hands. He opens his hands. Something is working in his life, some force, and he can't see it. He doesn't know where to look. But it has seized him by the hands and makes him move. One step back. One step to the side. The aperture, as he sees it, gets wider and wider. It doesn't make sense. It doesn't have to make sense. A lesbian, he wants to say to someone, to Louis, to Brisman, is someone who loves women. Naomi Wilcox does not love women. Never in her life has she loved women. She's never even had a passionate friendship, a crush, a woman who meaningfully disappointed her. Never the type to go out for a glass of wine. She loves *a* woman. This should be easier. She was seduced. She was lonely. Monogamy is a prison. She was initiated, she was offered a possibility. She's not a lesbian, she's not *gay*.

There was a lesbian student in her lab once, in the 1990s, Jacqueline, perfectly ordinary, he only met her once or twice when Naomi invited them all over for pizza. A pixie cut and a dimpled chin. Ugly jeans and a shapeless blue sweater. You should see her girlfriend, though, Naomi said, a real bull, leather from head to toe. He was shocked. People don't use that word anymore, he said, this isn't a fifties dime novel. No, she said, now it's a compliment.

She loves a woman. She should! The blunt force of the imperative. She should love someone. For reasons of symmetry, he should consider what it means to love a man. Dallas Goodyear. He would have been the one. There was something about him, some polymorphous quality, that suggested all the possibilities.

Winter is using the bathroom, the small one on the ground floor under the stairs, and the house is so quiet he can hear, without wanting to, the stream of urine, the sudden gush of the faucet. Whose body encloses another body. No wonder she had to come here. The house as an aperture through which the Wilcoxes flow, kept secret, or at least ignored, all this time. A dark fertility emblem. Why didn't Zeno come? He wants to say to the two of them, I give this house to you. As if that means anything. A house in place of citizenship. No, a way of saying, take it, take the land, no one else is here to claim it. Take this empty house, America.

"Tell me more about Mom," he says to her, though she's in the next room, the living room, adjusting the carpet with her toe, glancing at the headless Buddha.

"I don't know much. And I shouldn't be the one to fill you in."

"Well, you're here, so you don't have much choice."

"Her name is Tilda, and she's Mom's lab manager. I think? Anyway, she's a WHOI technician. She's worked there for a long time. And she has a background in social work. We talked about that briefly. She seems extremely nice. Very grounded. And no, I don't how long they've been together. At least a year. Probably longer. But they're definitely living at Mom's place. That part was clear. It doesn't seem like a casual thing at all. They're a couple. It didn't begin yesterday."

"It's the deception," he says, making a face, a clownish wry grin. "That's what everyone says about affairs. The lying, not the sex. I should know, of course."

"Have there been others? I mean, when we were kids?"

"No. Not that I know of. For a while I suspected she was having a thing with her collaborator. Jim. But she never admitted it, and it doesn't really matter. Once was enough."

"And you?"

"Faithful," he says, "doggedly faithful, as the driven snow, or the St. Bernard in the snow, or whatever the metaphor is. I know, it sounds incomprehensibly sad, given what things were like when you were young."

"I remember times when you were happy."

"I'm glad to hear you say that. But isn't it so sad, that you have to phrase it that way? *Times.*"

"I have a somewhat different perspective on my childhood," she says, after taking what seems to be a very long breath. "As you should know. I don't feel as wounded by it. Among the three of us, I was probably wounded the least. At least that's how it seems to me now. Given the people I work with, given the shit I have to wade through every day, I'm conscious of how wildly privileged I was, how stable everything was, actually, even if it didn't always feel that way."

"You were always furious with the rest of us because we wouldn't just *calm down*."

"And now I miss it. Even as bad as it was. I miss the five of us, being under one roof."

This is an unexpected thought. The kettle is hissing, about to whistle again. For some reason they're frantically in need of many cups of tea, to keep this thing going. He walks, half-hobbles, back into the kitchen. I have a child who actually misses her childhood, which, come to think of it, explains why she's chosen to reproduce. There's something there to build on, maybe. Winter's stubborn reasonableness.

"Come upstairs," he calls out to her. "I want you to see our room. Mom's and my room. Where Patrick slept when he was a baby."

They're on the landing now, cups of tea in hand.

"It's so small," Winter says, peeking in.

"Sensei had the master bedroom. Of course we didn't call it that. But he only slept on a futon in one corner; it was also the interview room. We had a screen set up."

"How did you fit so many people in this house? It's not so big."

"Six people slept in the other two bedrooms. Futons on the floor. Head to toe. Eventually we built bunk beds, too. That got us up to eight. That was the men's room, the women's was upstairs. Also we had people sleeping in the attic, when it wasn't the middle of the winter. And in the barn, in the loft. And camped out in tents, of course, in the summer."

"I can't believe I've never been here. You've owned this house for forty years."

"*You* can't believe it. I'm the one about to, apparently, become a grandfather."

"It's the whole stupid circle of life."

"How many more months? When are you due?"

"October. And no, I don't know the sex. It's too early."

What more is there to say? There must be something he's forgetting. Like, *I'm so happy for you.* Has he ever said such words, in his life, other than at work, for a client or a colleague? His mother never thanked or apologized to anyone in her life. She stripped him of the instinct. He had to acquire his own manners, painstakingly, awkwardly, by proxy. When they were babies, he would hold out his arms for a hug and say *squish squish*. Instead of *I love you*. His mind is making leaps. He wants to bind her to him, but to what? A man with no life, with nowhere to be.

"It's funny," she says, stepping back onto the stairs, "I was so sure I knew what had happened, I was coming here to condemn you—"

"Exactly what every parent always wants to hear."

"—but I'm sorry, I am, Dad, I should have been paying better and more attention, especially after Mom left. Not that it's ever been easy for anyone to pay attention to you, emotionally speaking."

"The one thing we are really terrible at," he says, "is taking care of each other."

They stand still for a moment, letting the statement reverberate, unanswerable, inarguable, not just through the waiting walls of the particular house but every house, a universe of houses, which is to say *beit*, he's thinking, the body and the universe as a house, some kind of Kabbalist theory he read once.

"I still think you should come back with me to Providence. Just for a couple of weeks."

"I have to stay here. I have to see this through."

"See *what* through, exactly?"

"Whatever it is I'm doing. It's just the choice I've made for myself, to be here, to write this book, or whatever it is, and I need you to respect that. I've been seized by something. Something is guiding me. And don't tell me that sounds like psychosis, because it's not. Not entirely *un*like it, either, but I'm healthy, healthier than I've been in decades, it feels like."

"The only reason I believe you is that you honestly don't sound like yourself at all."

"There's a form to life outside the form I thought I knew. That's the only way I can explain it. Whatever, it sounds mystical and woo-woo. I'm having a late midlife crisis. But it's real, it's actually embracing me, like I can feel whatever it is, physically, like a phantom limb or something, a phantom exoskeleton. This is my life now. I've retired from Fein Lewin, effectively. Mom and I are getting divorced. Apparently. I need to figure out my next steps, as they say."

"You need to actually *talk to her*, Dad."

"No, I don't feel ready for that. And I don't feel ready to go back to New York. I don't know if I'll ever want to live there again, after what's happened. We should have moved somewhere else after Bering died, honestly. I don't know why we never discussed it."

"Because you just don't give up an Apthorp apartment."

"That's the sick logic of New Yorkers, and I'm done with it. Little cocoons of habit and scar tissue, wasted, gnarled lives."

"I've never heard you talk this way. It's freaking me out a little."

"Well, look," he says, "look at the bomb you've just dropped in my lap. It's over, our forty-three-year experiment in married life. It really is. I thought I was the cause of it, but as it turns out, not really. And I don't feel angry or sad. I've spent basically my whole life feeling angry and sad and defenseless about Naomi Wilcox, at least since the ripe old age of twenty-seven, and now I've had this period of numbness, and I have to figure out what's next, after the numbness dissipates, if it ever does."

"None of that explains why you can't come down from this mountain to attend a wedding four hours away."

"I might. August is two months from now."

"But you won't commit."

"I commit to being alive. That's something."

"It's narcissistic and horrible, actually, to make me beg like this."

"I know it feels that way."

"But at least it's consistent."

She stands at the bottom of the stairs, looking up at him, her face divided into a triptych, as visible as ever: disappointment, satisfaction, and quiet rage.

"You should stay here," she says. "It's as if you've never lived anywhere else."

/

Winter has the car; it could be all day; it could be a couple of hours. There's no way of knowing. She has the car and is out of range. Cell phones don't work up in Craftsbury. Zeno marvels at it. The luxury of the poverty, or the other way around, or something. In Chiapas, people have phones. In Kinshasa. In Gaza. You have a phone but no house. You have a phone but no bank. No insurance, no mortgage note. No passport. A phone but no nation. Like the Cameroonians and the Afghans drowning in the Mediterranean: *they* have phones. They have good reception, they can call, and say, *I'm drowning,* and wait for someone to care. But here in Vermont, in the wealthiest country on Earth: no service. Whole towns, whole regions, still anchored to their copper wires. Luxurious hermits, with their sweaters and maple syrup.

It's a call he has to make, and here's the free time, marooned in this hotel. But it takes preparation. He tries some deep breaths. Before Winter, on his days off—few as they were—he watched movies, made carnitas or menudo or pozole, did his laundry, *then* called home. As often as not Zarita picked up and he talked to her, then asked her to put Papi on for just a minute. It required that kind of stillness of mind, just to have a five-minute conversation with his own father. He had to be rested or he would start screaming.

His thumb on the glass, its unreal smoothness, and the names that travel, if he flicks them, up and down the list, faster than he can see. *Papi* is the name he presses, or rather, as it seems, releases, and then the long number pops up on the screen. Chiapas is Central Time; it's nine thirty in the morning. "It's okay," Victor's voice rasps on the other end, "I'm awake, I never went to bed."

"Es Zeno," he says. "Papi, porque no duermes?"

"Speak English. You live in the United States of America."

"Papi," he says, and squints so hard he feels his eyeballs shrinking. "Por favor. Nada más quiero hablar. Una vez. Por favor."

"In the United States *of Trump*."

"Okay," he says. "You win. Why aren't you sleeping?"

"Because I watch the news and then I try to lie in bed, Zarita makes me, but I'm trembling all over, like I've had six cups of coffee."

"Nestor should never have bought you that satellite dish."

"On the contrary," Victor says. "You want me to die of boredom? I mean Zarita won't let me watch the worst of it. She won't let me watch the Fox News."

"You shouldn't be getting that crap anyway."

"Alberto, the neighbor boy, he fixed it up. I told him I wanted to watch the BBC. There's five hundred channels or something. Last week Zarita had the whole neighborhood in here watching *Doubting Abbey*."

"*Downton Abbey*."

"It's the twilight of the culture. Pure colonialism. The last days of the struggle. They say there's a Pizza Hut now, going up on the plaza, right by the university gates."

"It's your TV. Don't let them watch it."

"No hay ninguna imagen más triste," he says, in his reciting voice, "que un caballero viejo sin fuerzas, sin dinero."

"Quién escribío eso?"

"My friend Herman Díaz Contreras. You wouldn't remember him. He was a minor neo-Formalist, a protégé of Paz. He came to visit us all the time, in the seventies. What a drunk. A spectacular drunk. He once started a fight down in the plaza, it took three people to pull him off the other guy."

"Mamá odiaba a todos tus viejos amiguitos, papi."

"I still remember some of his lines, because they were so metrically perfect, after all."

"Papi," he says, "I'm calling with good news."

There's no noise on the line, and then a long, vibrating breath, an exhalation that could be bowed on a double bass.

"Are you there?"

"I'm not sure my heart is prepared for your good news, tortuguita."

"I'm calling to say, Winter is pregnant, we're having a baby, or babies, they're not totally sure. In October."

More breaths.

"Come on," he says, "say something, Papi. Wish me congratulations."

"Congratulations, hijo. We should observe the formalities."

"Say you're happy, you're happy to be a grandfather."

"Wait. Wait. Let me say it my own way. Will you listen? Are you listening? I want to tell you a story first."

"Okay, Papi. I'm waiting."

"You know I went to New York when I still working for my father's newspaper, in 1979."

"To see Castro when he visited the UN, right, I know."

"I told you how I loved New York. I loved being twenty-eight years old, and the thrill of being in the belly of the beast. I loved the infernal fumes. The glass skyscrapers and their godlike indifference, the mansions of the industrialists on Park Avenue. I loved the swarm of reporters everywhere Castro went, everyone stinking of sweat and cigarettes, holding out their tape recorders, hoping he would make a new pronouncement. They had come from all over the world, Sweden, Japan, Australia. I loved that, being elbow-to-elbow with the entire world. And Harlem, I loved hearing the music coming out of the windows when I walked on St. Nicholas Avenue. I loved the Black people I met. I loved their loud, insistent voices, even when you just asked for directions. But then I knew by the end if I stayed one second longer, or if I thought, *I want to go again,* I would turn into a pillar of salt."

"That's like something out of a Lorca poem."

"So I'm telling you, your mother made me promise never to let you migrate."

"Yes, I know, but it wasn't up to you."

"You say that so easily, but she was right, because she knew exactly this would happen."

"What? What would happen?"

"That you would love it and want to stay, you would become a tool and servant of empire, and fall in love with a Yanqui and make American babies, and I would never see you again, because, in her words, it's not a border, it's a war, and you have to choose this side or that side. It is irrevocable."

"Papi, listen to me," he says. Choosing not to enter into the argument, not to grant the premises of the argument, though it makes his eyes bulge in their sockets. "You have a Spanish passport."

"It's long expired, covered in dust in a drawer somewhere. It belongs in a museum. I couldn't find it if I wanted to."

"I called the consulate in Oaxaca, it's easy. Zarita will help you with the forms. You'll get a new passport, and fly to Mexico, and then Nestor will take you to the airport and put you on a plane to Boston, and we'll pick you up there. All you have to do is pack a suitcase."

"What are you talking about?".

"You're coming to our wedding, in August, in Maine."

"You never said anything about a wedding."

"It's not so important. It's a formality. The point is, you can come. You will see me, you will meet Winter, you will see it's possible just to get on a plane, it's not the end of the world, it's only six hours away, direct flight. You're an EU citizen, for god's sake, other people would kill to have what you have. You have power. You speak English. We'll pay for everything."

"In this brave new world, what marvelous things happen."

"Don't quote things at me, as a way of shielding your feelings."

"Those are my feelings. I depend on better thinkers to articulate them."

Wake up, he wants to say. Levante, papi. Ya basta, after all this time. From the window he watches cars make their way down the neat blocks, the ordered procession of the American imagination: gas

station, movie theater, hair salon. In the other direction the gold dome
of the state capitol rises against a dark hill. Even the wilderness placed
in proper order. There are advantages to imperialist order, he wants to
say, because here I can actually bear to remember things, the shout
from the street at two in the morning, the pickup grinding its gears as
it took you away, Nestor screaming because he was awake and no one
would bring him a glass of water. Twelve hours later you returned with
her, zipped into a stolen army body bag. I have actual memories, which
is a gift to life, it puts the rest of time in perspective.

Nineteen ninety-five was twenty-three years ago, he wants to say,
but that isn't even the point, it's more basic still. You who have never
uttered a sentence less than perfectly formed. You who have dressed
yourself in slacks and a button-down shirt and a matching sweater every morning, only to shuffle to your study in your slippers, as if await-
ing your students, your acolytes, your biographer. Why do I want so
badly to dislodge you, to make your teeth rattle? Because of the baby,
the sheer force of new life?

"I haven't even told you my own news," Victor says. "I'm planning
to write a book of my own. A novel. I'm finally going to take that story
of the slave rebellion, the manuscript, and make a novel out of it. I'm
calling it *The New Earth*. I haven't decided whether it's going to be in
English or Spanish. Or it could be in German. That would give it a
certain kind of heft. I've always wanted to write something in German.
But then my children and grandchildren wouldn't read it."

"You're willing to mention grandchildren, I see."

"Don't mock me. You know exactly who I am, Zeno Cuauhtémoc.
I want to move too, in my own fashion. I don't want to die here, having never left this chair in a quarter century. Having the same habits
of mind. Why do you think I let Nestor install that satellite dish, that
monstrosity on the roof."

"A satellite dish is nothing."

"No, it's something. I'm moving slowly. Tortuguita, you should
appreciate that. If you're a turtle, I'm a snail. Like the Zapatistas say."

"That's not funny."

"Never in my life have I thought of writing, only reading. I'm ready. I feel optimistic. Maybe it's making the recordings that did it, having someone to address, which is also no one, since I know you don't listen to all of them."

"I do listen to them, and this is what I'm saying, you can be optimistic, you can try new things, you can travel. Not everything has to be meaningful. It doesn't have to be a trip of continental significance. A family can just be that, epiphenomenal, not a political statement."

"How did you get to be so naïve?"

"Because you brought me up in the provinces without a proper education. Listen, life does not move at your snail speed. There will be a car coming to drive you to the airport in August."

"What I am asking is this," Victor says. "Do you know what it costs me to accept your story, the story of your success? Which is, whether you like it or not, the story of the empire's success. Do you know?"

"I can't answer that question. I don't agree with that question."

"Everybody wishes they had a different father, but you have this father, and this is the question he's asking."

"I'll give you an answer," he says, feeling like he's levitating, "the next time we see each other face-to-face. And maybe then you won't actually need the answer. When we meet again, Papi, which is this August, then you'll see."

"Time doesn't move that fast, time doesn't work that way. Maybe in Rhode Island it does, but not in Chiapas. You outpaced me, son, you left me behind."

"Lenin," he says, "said that there are decades where nothing happens, and weeks where decades happen."

"God forbid you should quote Lenin, you of all people, in Rhode Island."

"I'll be waiting for you. I'll see you. Until then."

/

Winter's crying so hard she has to pull over and let him drive.

Crying, then sleeping. He knows better than to say a word. White River Junction passes. The bunched-up mountains, like folds in a sheet, the massed clouds hovering everywhere. There's a kind of symmetry in the landscape he can't quite name. This is where white people come to have feelings, to be alone with their feelings but still have them. It's like a fucked-up fairy tale with no ending. It has excellent highways. This must be what Sweden is like, he's thinking, only smaller and less blond.

"Here's what I think," Winter says, suddenly awake. "Each generation decides they're going to do things differently. No previous assumptions. No transmitted values. You get married and your parents think, *this is a wedding?* That's what my mom and dad did. They literally got married barefoot in a field. A muddy field, in Ohio. Their friend played the oboe. My grandparents were so shocked they never talked about it afterward. No one took any pictures."

"My parents were married in Madrid," he says. "I think it was at a courthouse, or a notary's office. It took only twenty-five minutes, and my father said he was counting the minutes, because Michel Foucault was giving a lecture that afternoon. If you can believe that. They got married, went to see Foucault, and the next week they got on a plane and flew back to Mexico. Of course there's no pictures. But my aunt took a picture of them standing outside the airport, getting into a taxi, the day they arrived. They were so poor they couldn't even afford suitcases, just cardboard boxes held together with tape and twine. It's a great picture. They each have a portable typewriter in one hand, and they're holding hands with the other, and my mother is wearing these huge sunglasses. I never saw her wear sunglasses in my life."

"We're in the same position of doing it ourselves, no help, no guidance, and this is not what I wanted, I'm sick of making the world over and over. I want a wedding like anyone else's."

"That was never likely to happen."

"You don't have to be so fucking reasonable about it."

"I don't feel reasonable. I'm just as angry, I don't have to act it out in exactly the same way you do."

"Promise me, whoever our children are, we're just going to say yes to them, all the time. Not every time, but all the time. Our responses will average out to yes. Whatever they want, whatever they think of. Just yes. Yes."

"Yes."

"Yes."

"Yes."

/

From: "Winter Wilcox" <wwilcox@newamericansRI.org>
Date: May 15, 2018 at 06:34:21 PM EST
To: undisclosed-recipients
Subject: we're getting married!!!

Dear friends and family,
Sorry for the informality of this invitation, but in the spirit with which we are planning this event, Zeno and I are going to be married on August 25 (Saturday), at noon, in Blue Hill Town Park overlooking the bay in Blue Hill, Maine, and we would like you to be there. Directions: bit.ly/42x8y

We are not, in the orthodox sense, "planning a wedding." Blue Hill Town Park is public and picnics are allowed. We're planning to bring some food and drink and have a toast to ourselves. Kathy Wood, the town clerk, will be doing the official duties. If you'd like to contribute something to the celebration, we would love that. If not, just come. There are many hotels, Airbnbs, etc., in the vicinity.

You can let us know you're planning to come, or surprise us. Either way, please know that we will ask you to make all of your own arrangements. If you'd like to come in a group, organize one! We would love that.

There is no rain date. If it rains, bring an umbrella.

In lieu of gifts, please help us pay Zeno's legal bills by contributing at paypal.com/winterwilcox.

If Zeno is deported between now and August 25 we will be married at another time and place, as they say, TBA.

Thinking of you with love,
Winter and Zeno

SCENES FROM A MARRIAGE

(SANDY AND NAOMI IN NEW YORK, 1981–2001)

Coming back from the bathroom something long and sharp cut him across the forehead and he fell down. Sprawled on his back, his feet on the edge of the carpet, his shoulders on the cool parquet. Too surprised even to cry out. "Jesus Christ," he said after a moment. Sparks darting this way and that in the dark. Or in what he imagined was the dark. They were on his optic nerve, if not in the vitreous humor itself. The pain split out of its circle and made a wet band around his eyes. He imagined it for some reason like a slice of melon. But those were tears; he was crying. "Jesus Christ," he said again, and it came out as a groan.

"What, what is it?"

"I hit something. I fell down."

"Come back to bed."

"I said I *hit* something."

"The kids will be up soon."

The sock drawer, sticking out. The new wardrobe, with drawers that slid out, at odd heights, and opened sideways, so you wouldn't have to stoop and root. He could see it now, sticking out, she had left it there, that way, before going to bed.

"You left the wardrobe door open and it hit me. In the face."

"I'm sorry. Come back to bed."

"I'm sitting on the floor."

"Don't sit on the floor."

"I can't move."

"Don't be ridiculous."

"I don't *want* to move. I'm in pain. I'm hurt. Would you come see how I am, for once, would you ask, *are you okay?*"

"Come back to *bed,*" she said, her tongue thick with sleep. "It can't be that bad or you wouldn't be talking this much."

"I want a divorce," he said. He was speaking directly to the year. It was January of 1991. "We can't stay married, living this way. You're being *inhuman.*" He made a guttural sound, a glottal stop.

"All right, *all right,*" she said. Her ankles thrashed the bedclothes aside. "Let me get you some ice," she said. "I'll get you some ice, is that what you want?"

"Why don't you actually take a look at me first?"

"Shhh." She got down onto her knees and took his head in her hands. "It doesn't look that bad," she said. "Wait. No. Actually it does."

"I fucking told you."

"You should go to the hospital. I'm calling Dr. Chan's answering service."

"Now you're overreacting."

"I can already see the bruise."

"So it's a bruise. Just offer me some *sympathy,* for Christ's sake, I'm telling you, it'll go a long way."

"Shhh," she said again. She was wearing a black nightgown, with thin straps; he'd given it to her on Bering's first birthday. Still on her knees, she pulled his head against her. Her warm belly, her breasts loose, nearly flat against her rib cage. The silk tenting out against his face. "Shhh," she said. It was all she knew how to say. *I'm not Patrick,* he wanted to tell her.

"We can't go on living this way."

"Because you hit your head on a door."

"Because you're that thoughtless, yes. I could have been blinded, could have had a contusion—"

"No one's allowed to make mistakes in this house except you."

"A mistake is once. A pattern, a habit, a way of living, is contempt. Neglect."

"Go ahead and say it," she said. "*Abuse.* That's what everyone says now. Say you're an abused husband. I dare you."

"You'd have to care," he said, still pressed against her fleshy middle, "to abuse me, you'd have to have an agenda other than *not giving a shit,* other than *I'm going to sabotage my own happiness.*" He wanted to pull himself into a sitting position, to curl his head in a corner. Close up she still smelled like a mother, milky and yeasty.

"We're going to keep doing this," he said, "just like Bush is going to fucking invade Kuwait."

"Goddamn it," she said, "I just remembered, I have to buy another snack for Ber's class, Mattie Severenson's allergic to nuts."

/

Back when they were renting next door to Louis and Judy's place in Sagaponack—this would have been in the late eighties, when the kids were finally old enough to wander the beach on their own for part of the day, supervised by Hannah, who was already fourteen—Naomi would get up in the morning and say things like, *Judy's going antiquing and says we should tag along.* She would say those words. And he would be too tired to argue. To say, we are renting this place and in the apartment we don't exactly do that kind of thing, where the hell are we going to put antiques? To say, we are not antiques people.

It was in no way about the noun. She didn't want the noun. She wanted to *be* antiquing. Which was a way of saying, he thought, *I want to be with you.* It was a bid, a gesture. So they would go downtown first and have cappuccinos and scones, and get coffee to go in paper cups, which was exotic in those days, and drive, a little caravan of Volvos, from one circled entry in the newspaper to another. In the excitement of the moment he was even known to tie a sweater around his neck. He owned, he and Naomi both owned, Top-Siders to be worn without socks and Lacoste shirts in pastel shades. It was an altered state, the High Eighties. The shine of partnership was still on him; the Volvo, an '88 purchased in July '87, still had its new-car smell. And she was, as some women are, in their late thirties, at the peak of ripeness, of florescence. A mother of three, now with a wondrously curved behind, a little almond belly, high, proud, full breasts. While in any other circumstance navigating tiny lanes and high hedges with a newspaper and an old map would have driven them batshit and screaming at one another, here he went with the flow. He was smooth. They were a glowing couple. They were fucking yuppies. The four of them oohed and aahed over copper kettles and portholes, rusty farm tools, weathervanes, old postcards, lobster floats. He once found a harpoon, an actual whaling harpoon, eight feet long, and bought it on the spot for Louis and Judy as an anniversary present.

And then on the drive home, having purchased nothing for themselves, or worse, some tiny idiotic trinket, another random tchotchke that would float around the apartment for years (*who ever bought this blue china duck anyway?*), he could feel the rub, the friction, starting again, it was the feeling of bare legs against hot car seats, the place where the shorts started to pinch. It was like? It was not like. It was. It doesn't bear comparison. The metaphor collapses. The emptiness and exhaustion—not exhaustion, really more like enervation—at the end of a late capitalist ritual. Not that he would have used those exact words at the time. Naomi was still enjoying herself, with her hand dangling limply out the passenger window, sometimes even with her feet up on the dash, and she would inevitably say, "*This* is the summer we should really start looking for a place."

"We wouldn't use it enough to justify it."

"Then we would just make more money from renting."

"We don't have twenty-five thousand dollars lying around for a down payment."

"I could talk to Mom and Dad."

"We're not Louis and Judy," he would say, of course, at some point. "We don't have their life. I don't want the kids staying in the apartment all summer any more than you do. But we both work full time. Do you want to give up your lab for two months?"

"I'm basically out of the lab for all of August anyway."

"But we go to Maine in August."

"For a week, and if we had a place out here we wouldn't have to."

"It makes so much more sense, financially, for us to rent. There's just no reason to buy a vacation home we'll use maybe six weeks out of the year."

"Except that it would be *ours*," she would say, "and we could think about *retiring* there, and having *grandchildren* stay there, and—"

He hated that it made her so happy. How else to say it? He resented her not for being happy per se (although that too, of course, why not) but for being happy *here*, in this pantomime, this pretense of Waspy nautical seashore abandon, which had nothing to do with them, which was pure aspirational upward mobility, and her attitude. Why not? she seemed to say. Why not be happy here, since here is where we are? Where the fuck else in her life would she apply that standard? He hated her ability to suspend analysis, and the self-satisfaction that implied, weirdly, given that she was never ever satisfied the other fifty weeks of the year. She was not capable of becoming a different person at home, say, than in the lab, she was as tightly wound on the sidewalk as she was at her desk, but out here, out of reach of a computer—she didn't yet have a laptop to carry around with her everywhere, like a shield—she actually felt unburdened, the way you're supposed to feel on vacation, and he hated it.

"We have a house," he said, "an apartment, anyway, that *is* ours, the place where we'll most likely actually retire, and we don't feel that way about it. Although it's beautiful, or it could be, and we're incredibly fortunate to have it. We treat it like shit. It's a warren. It's a burrow. It's impossible to clean. It's impossible to *relate one room to any of the others*. And instead we're running around out here pretending to decorate a house we're pretending to have."

"Everybody needs a place to get away," she said, "except you. You're never away. You carry these resentments on your back, like a snail."

"Or a turtle. At least let me be a turtle."

/

He was not a builder, he was a sweeper, a vacuum, a Dispose-All. He threw away unsharpened nubby pencils or perfectly good sharp ones; pencils with worn-away or pulled-off or chewed-off erasers; crayons, broken and whole; markers with dry feathery tips or new wet pungent tips. He threw away anything escaped from its right place, if it was late enough, if he was bone-weary, if the day sucked, if a client complained, if Trick dented the wall again, if Naomi was having one of her everydays. Anything to make the house whole again. He was about to say *home* again. He threw away Gumbys twisted out of shape, Garbage Pail Kids, baseball cards, dog-eared or new; he threw away necklaces made of Froot Loops, macaroni spray-painted gold and glued to cardboard in the shape of a chai. He swept and vacuumed. He threw away report cards and art projects and book reports, loose pages from tax returns. If the day warranted it. Nothing to him worse than the sight of a coffee table or windowsill cluttered with undifferentiated *junk*, he could not and would not abide it, so he threw it all away. These kids who could not be bothered to remember to flush a toilet. This wife who could not find it within her to clean the hair out of the drain. This wife. This wife who did not find it within her to clean. Not that she didn't have *other responsibilities*. But to live in a house that did not dispose of its waste, a constipated house?

He asked Brisman about it once. Am I trapped for good in the anal stage, not anal retentive, obviously, but the opposite, whatever you call it? Or maybe just the converse of anal retentive? And Brisman looked at him sadly and said, the key word here is *trapped*. Which he thought was an obvious and unhelpful assessment.

Brisman also said, Obviously, the problem isn't that they're happy to live in shit, it's that they expect you to clean away shit for them. If you stopped, they would have to confront their own issues. Their issue is dependence, fundamentally, not lack of hygiene.

Because they are bound too closely to you. Does the novel bind or unbind them. Is it a new house or the same house. Does the novel put the family at its center, its logic unbroken. Is the novel on the side of the family, drowning in its excretions.

Instead of answering these questions, he thinks: I was looking for reasons to leave the house. I started the kids in Hebrew school because I needed a reason on Sunday mornings to leave the house. It was all about the calendar, the holidays, always looking forward. I wanted reassurance, I wanted to be bound to something other than her. Is that all Judaism was, of course not, but nothing is ever simple. It's a religion of days. Microscopically, macroscopically, apply whatever filter you want, it restarts every time you light a candle. It's so basic. Transcendence not required. Louis and Judy, whom they were just getting to know in those early days, first invited them to Tot Shabbat. Yes, he said. Yes, the children are Jews. How desperate he was for an excuse to leave that house. They went to one Saturday service, maybe it was just him and Patrick that time, and the usher handed him a kippah and a tallis. He was too embarrassed to hand the tallis back. Then, during the Amidah, Louis pulled the shawl up like a hood and he did too. Thinking it was the thing to do. There, under the cloth, something took him. Something touched him on the shoulders. Playing a patriarch, he reached out for Patrick's hair, that's how tiny Patrick was. And wriggly. God knows how he'd gotten him to stand still for the Amidah at all. His fingers searched for something in Patrick's hair.

Naomi would not go to synagogue. Then she would. But only because it was impossible, at that point, in 1986 and '87, for one person to handle all three children in public. You couldn't simultaneously hold Winter's hand, push Bering in a stroller, and keep Patrick from darting into traffic. She stood rigidly by the door, at first, refusing to take a seat, turning the corner into the lobby whenever Bering so much as burped. She would not sway. She would not cover her eyes. She would not hold a handout, let alone a siddur. When the Torah paraded up the aisles she crossed her arms and turned away, and bless her, her face retained a teenager's ability to project disgust, it would take the wind out of anyone's sails. "I'll give her full credit," Rabbi Art said to him once, in those early years. "I look at her and I see the very face of the unconvinced. It's a gift."

Talk to me, he said to her, a thousand times. Give me a story. Give me something to hold on to. Why you hate this thing you inarguably are, why you can't take it with a grain of salt, ceremonially, communally, half or a quarter seriously, why you want to deny your children any knowledge of it or the ability to see it for themselves. And she said, "The idea that in 1987 I should have to provide a rationale for *why children should not have a Jewish education* is so ridiculous it's almost funny."

"Then embrace atheism, or secular humanism, or Ethical Culture or what have you. Give them *something*. Find a group. Buy a book. Present a point of view."

"They'll understand my point of view when and if they make it to AP physics."

"Terrific. We'll take turns."

"Nope," she said, crossing her arms on the sidewalk as they passed Harry's Shoes. "There aren't turns. Because it isn't a comparison. It isn't a comparison and it isn't a conversation. One is objectively, provably correct according to a defined method, and the other is incoherent on its face, a series of Bronze Age fables mistaken for some kind of world-encompassing story about why one tribe in Canaan was better than all the other tribes three thousand years ago."

"As if Judaism was reducible just to that."

"When you say 'Judaism,' as if you know what you're talking about," she said, snatching Patrick's hand as he was wavering across the sidewalk toward a man on a ten-speed bicycle, "I can't decide whether I want to cry or punch you in the face."

"So tell me. Give me your definition."

"I prefer silence. I would have thought you could have understood that. Given where we come from and who we were. Were, and maybe still are."

"You still consider yourself a Buddhist."

"I consider the teachings to be accurate, even if the circumstances are unbearable."

"I have no idea what that means."

They were waiting at the light; Bering started to cry. Naomi unbuckled her and hoisted her up to her hip. "Easy," she said. That was their special word together. "Easy, Bear Bear," she said. "I'll make you peas and carrots."

"I hate peas and carrots," Patrick said.

"I wasn't talking to you."

"I actually want to live in a community," he said. "So shoot me." As if talking to himself, which, for all intents and purposes, he was. "These kids need a context, a symbolic system, a history. They need texture. They need *songs,* for Christ's sake. *Something* to chew on. Something to fight with. You can't just say *you'll understand when you're older.* You don't really get to choose these things. They'll *be* Jewish in any case. They'll know themselves to be Jewish, whether or not they have a clue what it means. Is that what you want?"

"*You* want to be Jewish," she said, as Bering took a mouthful of her cardigan, as they crossed the street, "because, what can I say, you're a fetishist, it's always given you a thrill. Your former Judeophilia, I mean. And because of whatever sick camaraderie you have down there at the office. It's good for business. It gives you a certain warm self-righteousness. Look, you've always been the guy who needs something to define himself. The habitual joiner."

"All that may be true," he said, blindly ignoring her, "but the fact remains. You have three children. You have to choose for them. They can't choose for themselves. If you withhold Judaism now, they'll eventually go looking for it somewhere. What is withheld looms large. Believe me. You could wind up with three fanatics. Give them a taste of it, a few gestures, it could wind up seeming like *no big deal*. Just like any kid on the Upper West Side. Think of it strategically."

She burst out laughing and all three kids stared at her. They were passing into the driveway, into the Apthorp courtyard, and her baleful laugh carried up to the putti, the crenellations. "That," she said, "may be the most Jewish thing you've ever said."

"You're such a self-hating cliché."

"No, I mean it," she said, and looked almost like she wanted to give him a hug. "You're right. I haven't been admitting it to myself."

"What?"

"*This*," she said, waving vaguely up, toward the cloudy November sky, framed by the Apthorp's four sides, and down, at the stroller, at Patrick's tiny Stride Rites and the gum-spotted pavement. "This thing we're doing. You can't resist it. You have children and they pop out and start asking *What am I. What am I.* Greedy little grubs. You have to tell them something. Because god forbid they should not know themselves, they should have no category."

"All I'm saying is let them know the truth. Truths."

She gave him a fierce look.

"You've forgotten the very first thing," she said, "the most basic thing, the twelve-linked chain of existence that begins with ignorance. Ignorance before birth. Ignorance as the condition of coming-into-being."

"I haven't forgotten."

"You know I actually studied it," she said. "Not just my stupid To-rah portion. The whole thing. The tradition, writ large. In high school. I got obsessed, for a good six months. I thought I might become a rabbi, until Grandpa Sy said, *a woman rabbi,* and actually spit on the floor, on my mother's carpet."

You're making up that story, he wanted to say.

"Try to let them grow up in a bearable world," she said. "Go ahead. Be my guest. Take them to synagogue, see what happens."

/

Couples therapy, the first time, started in September of 1986 and lasted till New Year's. The second round was in 1991, and turned into family therapy, briefly. Family therapy again in 1993. Couples therapy, the last time, in 1998, the year of Monica Lewinsky, a painful and ridicu-lous time for anyone to have a serious conversation about anything.

"At this point," Dr. Bergner said—he was a friend of Brisman's, an all-but-retired psychiatrist, giving them a huge discount—"The ques-tion is not about litigating the past but about mapping out a way for-ward. Don't bother trying to answer the question of *why are we here.* Talk about *what now.*"

/

Why these scenes? Why scenes at all? A novel is supposed to proceed by way of scenes, isn't that what Henry James meant, a procession of narrated events instead of mere narration. Authority placed in the evi-dence of events over their interpretation. Characters mean nothing but themselves, speaking. Scenes are proof, the way, in 2018, footage from body cameras attached to police bodies are proof. If only they could see it happening in real time, the jury would be forced to. Who is the jury, in the case of the novel. Is the reader (singular) the jury. Are the readers (plural) the jury. In which case who is their spokesperson, their foreman. Whose body is the camera attached to. I cannot narrate these scenes, he's thinking, I can remember them, I remember a thousand of them, too vividly, I remember them by their distinct smells. That is not a way of placing them in order. The point is the binding, and the novel by telling them is unwrapping the binding and rewrapping it so none of us can leave. That is what is meant by love. He would never apologize for loving the infants who, when startled, stuck their arms straight out, frantically grabbing for the nearest thing that would catch them, never apologize for not believing in divorce, biologically speaking, the long juvenility of the human child requiring the father to stay close by, in case heavy objects need lifting.

/

The summer of 1995. Or 1994? When Patrick was going into his junior year. On their way to Sagaponack again. There was a tote bag, a blue-and-white striped Lands' End tote bag, with a PSAT review book sticking out: that was the last thing packed and pounded into the Volvo's trunk. Blueberry lip gloss and spilled coffee. The sheer mustiness of an unused car, a car that sits far underground, 70 percent of its life, tombed in concrete. And the tang of adolescent sweat in its sweet and sourest concentrations. Three long bodies in that backseat, prematurely stretched, a collection of limbs he couldn't quite bear to look at. Trick, scooch *over*, Bering murmured, not looking up from *The Education of Little Tree*. And Patrick rolled down the window, right there on the Triboro, and stuck his elbow out, the wind raking back his hair. In the glare of the June sun his acne actually didn't look so bad. The Retin-A might be working after all.

"Arms in the car," Naomi ordered.

"Are you kidding? There's no room."

"Not in traffic, Trick," he said. "That's crazy. Go on, roll it up. We'll put on the AC. Once we get off the LIE, stick your arms out all you like."

"I said," Naomi said, squeezing the wheel, not quite clenching her teeth, but getting there, "*Patrick, arms in the car.* Or I stop. Right here."

"All right, all right, *Mother*."

That was Patrick's new thing, calling her *Mother*. After watching too many Merchant Ivory movies and all the episodes of *Brideshead Revisited* and *Upstairs, Downstairs,* which you could check out of the library now, apparently, on VHS. A dose of odd and possibly ironic Anglophilia. He'd played Professor Higgins in the school production of *Pygmalion* the previous fall, and in a manic fit of preparation read a whole stack of Shaw plays, *Man and Superman, Major Barbara,* and wrote a paper for AP English on Shaw's campaign against the orthography of the letter E. After that it was Wilde for a solid month. Then a detour, not surprisingly, to read Nietzsche. And Goethe. *The Sorrows of Young Werther,* somehow, carried him right into the arms of Forster, *Maurice* and *Where Angels Fear to Tread.* Whence the Merchant Ivory. You have to give him credit, Sandy thought, for the ability to exhaust a subject.

"We'd be arrested," Winter said. "Wouldn't we, Dad?"

"For what, honey?"

"Stopping a car in the middle of the Triboro. For no reason."

He cast a look over at Naomi, who just at that moment had taken off her sunglasses, stuck one of the temples between her teeth, and left the whole assemblage hanging there, beneath her chin, like a Calder sculpture. "You want a toothpick?" he asked. "I think we have some in the glove compartment. From last year's party at Nelson's."

"If I had a toothpick," she said, removing the sunglasses for a moment, "I'd be liable to poke someone's eye out with it."

"*Dad,*" Winter said. "Earth to Dad."

"Stopping a vehicle in traffic, that's a class-three misdemeanor. On the other hand, hazardous behavior in a moving vehicle is *also* a class-three misdemeanor. Interestingly, though, projection of an adolescent through the window of a moving vehicle is *not* a criminal offense at all. So pull your socks up."

"What about assault with a toothpick?"

"Felony assault with intent to commit grievous injury. That's ten to fifteen in Sing Sing."

They were on the Grand Central now, sliding through Astoria. Traffic not bad at all for a Friday at four. The blessed first weekend in June, when the accidents and unforced errors of the outer-borough skyline looked as if they were planned that way. The soot caked on the road signs, the spindly trees with their fresh leaves—*look, Ma! I'm salad!*—the beetle-browed brick row houses hard up against the freeway. He hated Queens—does anyone *like* Queens?—in his own particular way, because it remined him of Davenport. Fortunately in good traffic it was a feeling he only considered for fifteen minutes.

Here was the family in neutral weather. He'd wrapped up the Witkowskis before Memorial Day, an inheritance lawsuit dating back to the Iran-Contra hearings: nobody won, the settlement was mutually disliked, the check cleared. He never wanted to hear another word about the wholesale carton-and-packaging business. Naomi had received a five-year extension of her NSF grant in April, $1.5 million. She had to leave in a week for a UN conference in the Maldives.

"We should take a vacation in August," he said, "an actual vacation. There's still time to plan it. Let's go to Italy. Venice, Florence, Rome. Two weeks."

"I have to prep a new class."

"You can do that before we leave."

"I'm all for it," Patrick said. "Let's rent a Tuscan villa."

"As long as Mom and Dad promise not to fight the whole time," Bering said, barely audible, "I'm all for it too."

Patrick and Winter snorted at the same time. "Jinx," Patrick said. "Bering, the good thing about renting a villa is we can just wander off and do what we want and ignore them."

"Nobody said anything about renting a villa."

"It's cheaper than three hotel rooms."

"Why three?"

"I get my own. We're all teenagers now, Dad, for chrissakes."

"You're not getting your own room, you can change in the bathroom."

"Patrick is disgusting," Winter said. "I'm not sharing a hotel room with him."

"It's not happening," Naomi said. "This isn't the year."

"Give me one decent reason why we can't. I have vacation time. Everybody's out of the office in August anyway. You're a college professor, for god's sake, this is supposed to be one of the perks of your profession. We have the money."

"You have no idea what my summer schedule is like, you haven't asked."

"Okay. Tell me about your summer schedule."

"I have everything written down in my planner, it's in the trunk."

"You can't keep your schedule for the next three months in your head? Roughly?"

"Dad," Bering said, "she's saying she *doesn't want to go*. Take the hint."

"I would, if that were an acceptable answer."

"Why isn't it?" Patrick asked. "She's saying she doesn't like us enough to spend two uninterrupted weeks with us. Isn't that her prerogative?"

"You know that's not what I'm saying. We go to Maine every year. I like Maine. We have a standing reservation at the inn."

"We'll go at the beginning of August," he said, "and still go up for half a week. We can fly and rent a car."

"Because all of a sudden we're made of money."

"You know that's not the issue. We're fine for money, at the moment. But you know what, forget it. Forget I brought it up."

"Oh, Jesus, now you're going to make this into a whole thing."

If this were an E. M. Forster novel his feelings would turn into a noun. The half-wakened hope in his chest, uncurling its wings. A vague disappointment, muddy footprints in the foyer, tracked in from the garden. He cracked open his briefcase, for something to do, and took out the minutes of the May partners' meeting. It's extraordinary, Brisman often said, how long you've been together, and yet you appear to have no language of gestures between you, you refuse to recognize one another's appeals. Which are not the same thing, of course, you can have a language but refuse to speak it. Funny that Brisman didn't see that distinction. If it isn't a noun, what is it. Is this why the novel became a proper noun. He had nothing else, so it hugged him, he could smell its fur, as if to say, there is more to this story, or, there is more to this misery. Is that the good news or the bad.

/

Christmas Day of 2001. They watched *A Beautiful Mind* at Lincoln Plaza, all five of them, of course, a ritual observance, but skipped Shun Lee and went to Empire Szechuan on Columbus instead. Shun Lee is a relic, Bering said, it's cadaverous and depressing in there, and nobody disagreed. Nobody was talking much. Politest Christmas ever in the Wilcox household. Some pall over everything, and not just the obvious. Winter and Bering both had extensions on term papers and had been holed up in their rooms working. Patrick of course was down on the Lower East Side, a fresh college graduate, in his own place, largely incommunicado: things were happening in his life, no one knew what, except maybe Bering—her new cell phone often beeped, on its slide-in charger in the kitchen, with his unread messages. Unbeknownst to the world, those two were always in touch.

"So listen," Naomi said, over the spare ribs, scallion pancakes, veggie dumplings. Everyone ignored her. She drew up to the table. "I have something to say."

How exactly did the speech go? He's numb to the details. She hadn't told him, hadn't given the faintest indication, that this was the moment. They hadn't discussed it in months. He'd seen the letters from John Downs, that was all. A long-overdue reckoning, in his mind, but a private one. He halfway assumed she would take the fact of John Downs's existence with her to the grave. If he pressed that thought a little harder, which he never did, he would say, maybe when we have grandchildren. If we have grandchildren. Or at least when the kids are firmly, irrevocably grown. When, or if, we've made sure they've survived their childhoods. Who knew that instead she would carry those facts like a suicide vest into a Chinese restaurant on Amsterdam and Sixty-Ninth? On Christmas Day, no less, the year's strangest day for Jews, no less for him, a former celebrant. Nothing ever feels right that day. You're like a traveler in a strange country who showed up without reading the guidebook. He often felt on the verge of tears those awkward Christmases.

Bering started to sob. That was unexpected. The waiters approached, alarmed. Their main dishes hadn't even been delivered. She pushed back her chair and walked outside, they watched her, not wearing her coat. And he thought, oh, if only there were more than one of me. Every third-person narrator feels this way. Or they should. Break me open and start again. If I had known my children, if I had known them as they deserved to be known, at the time. He couldn't follow Bering, though he wanted to; there was violence in the air. Somebody might throw a spring roll, or a fork.

"Mom," Winter said, "I have something to say that you're not going to want to hear."

She was wearing a thin gray cardigan with silvery threads over a black tank top, and, for once in her life, she'd put on makeup; Patrick was supposed to be taking both of them, both girls, downtown afterward to a bar co-owned by some Harvard friends. This was a stopping point in the trajectory of their evening. She looked fearsomely grown-up.

"I just don't understand," Naomi said, almost plaintively, "why anyone would be so upset at this news."

"There are two sets of facts here," Winter said. "One, who our real grandfather is. John Dow, that's the name?"

"Downs."

"Believe me, I am so very, very happy and relieved that you finally have been able to let this secret go. I'm blown away. I'm taking it in. It's so much better to know than not to know. We have a new family now. Fine. Great. I hope I get to meet them."

"We'll have to take that one step at a time."

"Listen to me. I haven't gotten to part two yet. There are five of us, five separate people, in this conversation, three of them completely left out until this moment. You said you wanted to wait until we were ready. What made you think Bering was ready?"

"Someone needs to go get her so she can speak for herself."

"Leave her alone for a minute and just listen. What I'm not hearing from you is whether you've thought about what it means to keep this a secret from us, from the world—"

"That isn't true. Louis and Judy have always known. Our shrinks knew."

"—the implication being that you were ashamed. You've passed your entire life, and that's why, that's the secret. Just to be clear. So you just left this gaping hole in our, whatever you want to call it, *self-knowledge,* because you preferred to live as a white woman. Just say it. It's understandable. It's okay. For your own sake, say it, and then we can learn to live with it."

"I didn't *prefer* anything. I am a white woman. And you're acting as if that was the easy option." Naomi's voice cracked, if that's the word for it. She looked bleak and old, but only in the way, he wanted to tell someone, she's looked old since the age of twenty-six. "Let me know when you've given up the better part of two years of your life to suing your company for the right to keep your job. I'm a civil rights pioneer. I do not have to fucking apologize. It's because of *me* that you two can ignore me, and everything I did, and pretend that my allegedly being Black is what really matters."

"Nobody's ignoring you," Winter said, "and you *are* Black, whether or not you want to be, as far as I'm concerned. And so are we. You should never have withheld that from us, as if it was a stigma. That's why I'm angry. I'll live, but I'm still angry. Patrick? What about you?"

"Three-pepper chicken," the waiter announced, setting down an unfamiliar dish. Patrick had insisted on ordering two items from the list of specials; no one ever did that at Empire Szechuan. It wasn't a place you went looking for new experiences.

"You want me to answer that question, Win?" Patrick asked. He had peeled the label off his Tsingtao and set the green bottle on the lazy Susan like an exhibit. He was sweating; he looked ghastly. Clearly he hadn't seen much sun lately. "While Bear just stands out in the cold?"

"We'll get her in a minute. It's probably better if she doesn't hear this."

"I have no idea why you would say that. But okay. I guess it's your show. Are you ready for this? Mom? Dad? You really want to know what I think?"

"Go ahead," he said. "Yes. You might as well."

"I was born on a farm in Vermont, a place I've never seen. You, Dad, are from Davenport, Iowa. Or so you say. I've never been there either. I could spend my whole life asking questions about my parentage. I guess I've never had the curiosity gene. If you're telling me Zayde isn't my biological grandfather? I'll live. I have a Black grandfather? I wish I'd known that a long time ago. But this family has never had a coherent story to tell about itself. Dig as deep as you want, you'll just come back to that point. Whatever centrifugal force bound us together originally, you know, the accidents of time and genetics, it's pretty weak, if you ask me."

"Which is why I really don't think this ought to change anything," Naomi actually said. "He isn't *your* father. *Your* parents are exactly who they've always been. It's prehistory. It's an asterisk. I think we can all agree that race isn't something we should be preoccupied with, in this theoretical way. None of you have ever been mistaken for Black. You all had Black friends, growing up. You know the difference. We're forward-facing people. It's a new century."

"But Winter isn't wrong," Patrick said, picking up his chopsticks. "What you're not seeing, or at least not saying, Mom, is that we *are* Black, and so are you. According to what you've just told us. According to how America works. You are biracial. In a slightly different universe, you would be the Black daughter of a Black father in a Black family, and only by the barest of accidents were you able to construct the fantasy world we're living in now, where we think we're a quote-unquote white family." He dipped a corner of scallion pancake, chewed, wiped his mouth. "Someone *really* needs to go see how Bering is doing."

"You're not going to defend me?" Naomi said, rounding on Sandy. "They're accusing me of being a liar, a fraud."

He gave her the blandest look he could manage, as if to say, of all the times I could help you, and now you ask.

"I won't have it," Naomi said. "This is not who we are. All these nonsense orthodoxies, this is what my entire life has been trying to get away from, and the rest of you can't pretend you don't know better. I taught you better than this."

The manager, a tall woman he remembered, she'd been running the place for at least a decade, set down the kung pao shrimp, the dry-fried green beans. Orange chicken, Bering's favorite.

"I'm going to get her," he said. "Enough is enough."

He walked like a man who'd just climbed out of a freezing lake, like he couldn't stand the touch of his own clothes; a stiff march out into the night and the air, the cabs streaming by. Thank god Bering hadn't left. She'd probably forgotten her keys. Just then, as he turned to look, a Black woman in a gold puffy coat and oversized hoop earrings was lighting her a cigarette, holding one tip to another. "Thanks,"

Bering said, and the woman side-eyed him. Her eyelashes were frosted gold to match her coat. She was a famous singer or rapper, he knew her face from magazine covers. "It's okay, girl," she said, "everyone has bad nights sometimes."

Strange things happen to families having tragedies in public, but he didn't know that yet. He had not yet had a camera flash go off in his eyes.

"Ber," he said, "please come inside and eat something, we've agreed, we're taking a five-minute break so everyone can gather their strength."

"Dad, why are you still married?"

"There's no answer that could possibly satisfy you right now."

"It must feel terrible knowing that you couldn't do anything to protect us from this, this—I don't even know what to call it. Biographical fraud. Familial schizophrenia."

"I didn't know she was going to bring John Downs up tonight."

"But it was going to happen *some night*. You were an accomplice to this lie, you too were holding this over us—"

"Please," he said, groping, reaching for a shard of long-ago couples therapy, "besides just being angry, Bear, tell me what you're feeling right now. How this affects *you*. You're going to wake up tomorrow morning and feel—what? This is an honest question."

"I have beetles crawling up my spine," she said, drawing on the cigarette and looking downtown, past the Barnes and Noble, the line of fancy cosmetics stores he'd never noticed, the sclerotic richness of these turn-of-the-millennium streets. "There's something covering my face, it's like the sleeve of a thick sweater. I keep hearing something hissing, like a bike tire deflating, only I can't find the hole and it just keeps going, more air, more air."

"What the hell are you talking about?"

"You asked how it affects me, and I'm telling you, there's actually nothing new about this feeling, I've had it for years."

"I don't get it. You mean you always knew you were Black?"

/

There's a ship sailing through this conversation.

He has to go outside to think about it. Without thinking, he walks down the front steps in his socks. The dusting of snow overnight melted, the ground is like walking on a cold sponge. Let that soak in.

Oh god, he wants to say, through every American life, there is somewhere a ship of bodies crossing from east to west. Not corpses, living bodies. Living death in life. A ship of chained humans-as-bodies. It doesn't matter exactly what words you use because everyone knows.

When you marry someone so young, he said to Brisman once, part of you, emotionally, remains frozen at that age forever. Whoever you were. Whatever you were afraid of. All the things you didn't see, things you dismissed. Or could be cavalier about. Part of me is still eighteen, only a few months removed from my disastrous childhood. Astonished that anyone would think to love me. When Naomi told me about John Downs she used the word *Negro*. That's how long ago it was. I had never had a conversation with a Black person longer than a few minutes. I hardly knew how to look a Black person in the eyes, at age eighteen in 1970. And here people think it's possible for ~~their emotional lives~~ novels to have nothing to do with politics.

That last sentence he did not say or think, he only lived it. His life was only crushed by it.

Bodies in the hold! he wants to scream, at the uninnocent, un-listening fields, the maples and firs lining the creek at the bottom of the hill. What is it about Americans that they think they can pretend, no bodies in the hold? And then, on the other hand, if you keep insisting—Bering, keeping insisting—you become ridiculous.

Bering knew she would become ridiculous.

Ships that only sail in one direction.

How? he asks the maples and the firs. How could I think, could I imagine, our lives would not be crushed by Naomi's announcement?

/

"I always knew someone was lying," Bering said. "I thought maybe I was adopted. I thought, *I don't belong here.* And then I told myself, *that's just daydreaming, we all look alike.* Mom is weirdly darker than Bubbe and Zayde, but not *that* much darker. Everybody thinks they're adopted when they're little. But still, and this is not just about skin color, please believe that, Dad, I knew someone wasn't being totally honest about our family, something was left out, somebody was *making something up.*"

"You are exactly the same Bering you were an hour ago, in every way that matters."

"There's no way you can actually believe that."

"Just with something added, added information. Maybe, who knows, new family members. It's not cancer, it's not the BRCA gene. Winter and Patrick seem to be taking it in stride, and here you are acting like it's a death sentence. One would think you didn't *want* to, you know, have *African American heritage.*"

"That is so sick and perverse, Dad, even for you. Only a white man would ever say such a thing."

Who are you to tell me, he was about to say, and stopped. Those words, the way her lips moved, the puckering it takes to say *white.* She wasn't angry; it wasn't funny. She was unmoved and descriptive.

"If Mom had told us when we were kids. If we had grown up understanding it, if we had had a chance to internalize it, figure it out, work out our own relationship to it, we, or at least I, would have been incomparably better off. It is actually not so unusual. As you know. We had plenty of biracial friends."

"Which is why I'm so baffled."

"Because it sucks to be lied to, Dad, and it sucks not to know who you are and where you came from. I know this doesn't compute for you, since you've spent your whole life pretending Davenport doesn't exist. But New Yorkers are never allowed to be that anonymous. You are a particular thing and not some other thing. I'm a depressed white Jewish girl from Seventy-Ninth and Broadway. Or I was until about twenty minutes ago. The sickening thing, in fact the thing that has been making me sick for years, is the shame, the pretense, and Mom refusing to admit there *was* shame and pretense, and you defending her, as if this is all our problem and you're doing us a favor."

"How was that conversation supposed to go? 'Kids, your actual grandfather is a Black man I've never met'?"

"Yes. Just like that. That would have been a thousand times better."

"We didn't know how to answer the questions a kid would ask."

"So then you're saying you discussed, you considered it."

"As a matter of fact, no. I never brought it up. It was your mother's business, her story to tell. I had other things to worry about. Obviously," he said, hating the words, hating himself for saying them, "I should have been more concerned."

"I'll just ask you again, Dad: why are you still married?"

And still he wanted to insist to her: why is this night different from all other nights? Of all the unforgivable things, hurts, insults: why this one?

Because with any mother, even Naomi Wilcox, you take certain things for granted. Whose loins, whose seed. Why else would you be bound together, other than by these nonnegotiable conditions? You don't *know* your mother; you're possessed by her. He had never had that problem with Naomi. He knew that with her every condition was negotiable, but he'd never managed to tell them that. He'd abandoned them to her whims.

I ask the very sidewalks to be my witness, he might have said, the novel wants him to say, casting a glance up at the ash-black sky, the equinoctial sky, I ask the concrete and the asphalt to be my witness, and the shop windows, the cornices and pointed bricks of this Upper West Side, where I have raised a family, god help me and them, all is lost. What is the Bat Signal, what is the SOS, all is lost.

"Well, there you have it," she said. "You, Sandy Wilcox, don't get it. You are a bystander to your own life. You could have helped in only one way, by leaving, by breaking the shell of this rotten egg so that the rest of us could get out, too."

Bering had never, not once, addressed him by name. She'd never, not even at thirteen, fourteen, had that kind of cockiness. To square off and regard him, full in the face, while flicking her ashes at the restaurant's basement hatch. Not a trace of her quiet wounded teenage self, her wet folded wings. They'd installed a locked cabinet for pills when she was fifteen; he'd thrown away all his razors and switched to a Norelco; every night for years he counted the knives in their block in the kitchen. She refused therapy; she wouldn't go on antidepressants. Bering, get out of bed. Bering, go for a walk. This is what he was holding in his mouth, like a coin, a metal lozenge, while she addressed him and put him in his place, in the third person. As if on the stage. In her production of *Antigone* the director had insisted every actor walk onstage wearing a mask and then take it off. That was how it felt, under the lights, her face revealed.

A great spasm came over him, a rupture. Maybe, he thought, maybe it isn't too late to protect her, if you leave now.

Oh, Sandy, we cry out to him, as the chorus, leave now, and dissolve this novel. Be fully crushed. We the readers, we the first-person plural. We should have a say.

"Give me a cigarette," he said.

"I had to bum this one. And since when have you ever smoked?"

"I have the feeling I'm about to start. Come on, let's go to the newsstand. I can't be much of a father, apparently, but at least I can buy you cigarettes."

"That's very funny. And I appreciate what you're trying to do. It's too late for that kind of courage."

"At least let me give you my keys. You don't have to come back in. Go home, get warm. You can take a cab and meet Patrick and Winter later. I'll pay for it."

"I'm not going out. I don't feel like it."

"Promise me you're not going to be sad your entire life."

"I wish you knew what you were saying when you say things like that, Dad," she said, already turning away from him, "but I can't be the one to tell you."

MEN, FEELINGS

Like an egg cracked over a pan, the story spreads until it stops. It finds its boundaries by exhausting its materials. They are not quite exhausted. Sandy is in the kitchen, holding his phone. The windows are open. It's just past lunchtime. He had his fifth turkey sandwich of the week. A dry sunny day, high and dry, they used to say, hoping for rain, when they had a garden to manage. Patrick is the name and the number. He's forgotten the country code for Germany. Or does Patrick still have a phone registered in India. He talked to him last at Hanukkah, it worked then. Having traveled overseas very little in the cellular age, he has no idea how it works. Or when his passport expires. If he were compelled to leave. He would never be compelled to leave.

Faint clicks and the throb of a voice. No, his son says to someone, his secretary, presumably, get Heinz to look at it before you send it. A mumble of other words. His son in an office, with a secretary, in East Berlin, speaking German.

"How the hell *are* you?" Patrick says. "How's Vermont? It's good to hear your voice, Dad."

"I'm fine. Better."

"I thought you were keeping a vow of silence for three months."

"Winter came to see me," he says, "so I figured, if I can talk to her, I can talk to you."

"Have you talked to Mom?"

"No. I'm not ready to take that step."

Two blackbirds fighting in the big maple on the far side of the yard. Blackbirds or grackles. He's not close enough to tell. A blur of wings, skittering in the branches. The leaves, this early in May, are no wider than two fingers.

"You know Mom apparently has a new partner. I don't know how you feel about that."

"I'm in favor of happiness and fulfillment. That's my general policy. But how do *you* feel about it?"

"I would say I'm withholding judgment until she tells me herself. She has to take some accountability in this."

"I've told her the same thing. Frankly I'm surprised she hasn't reached out."

"You know, we all have things we haven't disclosed," Patrick says in a creaky voice. "You and I. In fifteen years, a lot of scar tissue, a lot of defenses. I have a five-year-old son, for instance. His name is Mathias."

"That's not funny."

"No, he's very real. He doesn't speak English hardly at all, but he knows how to say *grandfather.*"

"Hold on," he says. "You're breaking up." He puts down the phone.

Without putting shoes on, he opens the door and steps out into the grass. Again the aperture that is his life, his apparent life, has opened suddenly and crazily, a corona around the sun. He should stare directly into the sun. It's the novel, of course, knocking on his rib cage, its indifference to order. Crazy registers, a hum outside the range of the human ear. Is there such a thing as referred sound, as there is referred pain? It was a question Naomi was obsessed with, somehow, when they were in Alaska. She filled notebooks with equations. The liquid sea, which is everywhere, mathematically, at the same time. How long was it, how many weeks, before they told Herman and Phyllis? He remembers a shouting argument Naomi had with them about a bris, on the kitchen phone, everyone pretending not to notice. Patrick had been circumcised in the hospital in Morrisville. It was standard practice in 1979; no one gave it much of a thought. Apparently this was a mortal sin. After that Naomi didn't speak to them for nearly a year.

"You should have told me to sit down or something," he says, picking up the phone again. "I'm old. I'm fucking old."

"Men your age run marathons and start second families. Sometimes third families. You need to get some wheatgrass juice, some Rolfing. Fortunately you're in the right place."

"Were you planning to tell us, ever?"

"I'm telling you now. His mother is Katerina. You remember Katerina?"

"You wouldn't introduce us to her, remember?"

"We're not a couple, Mathias lives with her, but I have established rights of paternity. I might bring him to the wedding, in fact."

"You're coming to the wedding?"

"I'm thinking about it."

"What's stopping you?"

"What's stopping *you*?"

"I asked first."

"I'm worried about my health. I haven't been on a plane in several years. And I kind of depend on a fixed schedule, basically an eating schedule, because, you know, I have anorexia."

"I had no idea it was quite that serious."

"I mean, why would you. I'm not trying to be mean. Just that you haven't seen me in ages, you wouldn't know the way I've sort of set up my life around it, really."

A Bilson Oil truck rumbles up South Albany Road.

"I think you and Mathias should come. I wish you would come."

"Because you're coming, too?"

"You haven't asked about my situation. Give me time to explain."

"I've closed my door. I've told my assistant to hold my calls. Go ahead, Dad, as you always used to say, I'll give you half a billable hour."

"I attempted suicide, back in New York, right before I left. That was why I left. I tried to jump off the balcony in the apartment. I didn't quite make it. But I knew I couldn't go on, you know, go back to work the next day. So I fled, I went into hiding, up here, so to speak."

"Jesus, Dad."

For lack of anything better to do, and not wanting to speak, he turns to the last page in his notebook and writes, *Mathias, Age 5. (last name?) Born in 2013 (?)*

"I'm not sure what to say."

"There isn't anything *to* say."

"Don't be ridiculous. I want to know the details—what stopped you?"

"I'm not sure. A random thing, a momentary distraction. It broke the spell. I don't know what else to say. It doesn't really matter. I'm here now, I'm not trying that again. But it's sort of as if I had succeeded, in the sense that I've removed myself from life. I have no purpose, at the moment."

"You had no purpose before."

"That's nice of you."

"Isn't that the fucking truth? The last time I talked to you, at Hanukkah, you sounded like a zombie. You and Mom both did. I'm not surprised any of this has happened, and I doubt Winter is, either. You had already removed yourself from life. Certainly from parenthood. But more generally—I don't know, maybe you were still engaged at work. Or somewhere. But the person I talked to six months ago had no pulse, as far as I could tell. Clinically depressed, for sure, not that there's anything new about that. Are you still seeing Brisman?"

"Brisman died in 2012."

"I had no idea."

"It was pretty sudden. I had every intention of finding someone new but never did."

"Medications?"

"Oh, I take Cymbalta. Have for years. Leonard writes the prescriptions. I get them in three-month packages, in the mail. Automatic refills."

"It seems to be working."

"Don't be glib. You can be on antidepressants and still have every reason to commit suicide. They're two different orders of magnitude. But look, it's over now. No more impulses, no ideation. My mind cleared, you could say. I came up here and now I feel like I'm on a different planet."

"You told Winter about this?"

"I asked her to give me time. She thought I should be hospitalized."

"You should be. You had a slow-moving nervous breakdown, or whatever the term is. We used to see it in the monastery. Usually it happened about six months in, with the new monks, the novices. They'd start shuffling their feet, avoiding eye contact. Like prisoners. Not eating. We called it the zombie monk look. That was our signal to put them on the bus back to Delhi."

"You're not coming to the wedding, is that it? If I don't apologize for the choices I made, arguably good or bad, pointless or necessary, under the most extreme stress of my life, in another country, fifteen years ago?"

"I never said anything about the wedding."

"It sounds like that's what this comes down to."

"Then think of it this way. If there was ever going to be a basis for a future relationship, one in which Mathias gets to know his grandparents, you know, a détente, I think that's where it would have to start."

"More blackmail."

"You can call it that, but it's just life. People have their limits."

"I wish," he says, gritting his teeth, "that there was one person in my life who didn't treat me as a kind of insurmountable heap of limits and caveats and shoulds and coulds and if-onlys, who believed me when I said sincerely, I'm trying to start fresh, in my own way, please give me the benefit of the doubt."

"Seriously, Dad, though, did you think you could do that without apologizing? With no amends?"

"And have *you* ever stopped to wonder what you're actually blaming me for?"

"I don't know what the fuck you're talking about."

"Who drove her away? Who made her feel she could never come home, that she had to find herself in a fucking mud hut in the West Bank with a fucking target on her head?"

"It sounds like you have an answer in mind."

"I'm just saying that's the real issue."

"Bering," Patrick says quietly, "was not a child. No one made her do anything. She was an activist. She had more courage than the rest of her family, her community, her friends and relations, her entire *social demographic,* put together. The issue is your inability to see her, to grasp her actual significance in the world, her memory and what it means. You treated her like a wisp of smoke, a puff of dust."

"You could have carried on yourself."

"Not with a public family disagreement. Come on."

"There are any number of ways you could have made it a public issue."

"And maybe I will. But then, in the moment, I lost heart. We all lost heart. We needed you and you weren't there."

"This is becoming very melodramatic."

"As it should be. It should be a play, a drama, a fucking Antigonic demonstrata or whatever you call it, with a chanting chorus in the background, it has those dimensions. You left her corpse on the battlefield and cursed your family. How does that feel, to hear it that way?"

"It feels like you're talking to me. I prefer that to the alternative."

"Oh, Dad, for fuck's sake."

THE HAMMOCK

They go on with their lives. It's June. The babies are coming. It was an ambiguity on the first ultrasound, but now the heartbeats are separate, detectable. Did you know, the technician asked her, did you sense it, and Winter guesses she did. It could explain, generally, the size of her feelings since April. The absolutely necessity of getting certain things straight. She has a bump now; her body is reshaped, it moves according to a new and stubborn logic. She places her hands there. Anywhere else just feels incorrect. Much is happening inside her, not kicking, yet, but throbbing. General movement. Expansion.

They've chosen which of the two extra bedrooms will be the nursery—the smaller one, closer to them, only six steps across the hall. Zeno's friend Miguel, a painting foreman, arrives one Saturday afternoon and finishes the job in three hours. Spruce Mist, the color's called. She spreads decals of birds in flight all around the ceiling. A shower's planned, at the office, for the third week in July. Earlier than usual, but considering the wedding. Zeno gets a deal on a high-end noiseless ceiling fan, just in time: she's been sleeping with the sheets off, unbearably hot, but not wanting to turn on the A/C and catch a cold. She turns it up all the way and they lie in the dark, facing into the wind, eyes watering.

"Nestor says we should leave," Zeno says. "He's found a perfect place for us and the babies. A new apartment, in Mixcoac. His friend just remodeled it."

"I emailed that woman Lourdes knows at Human Rights Watch, the Mexico City office, she never wrote me back."

"You'll find work. Maybe not right away. But so what, you'll have twins, you'll be busy."

"My work is here," she says. "My clients are here. In Mexico I'll be advising millionaires, getting their kids student visas off the books."

"You can volunteer at the border, fly back and forth."

"Not forever. You'll be starting a company, we'll have no cash flow, we have to buy a house."

"You talk like a person with no assets, no capital."

"Okay, yes. I have savings. I have an inheritance. It's not nothing but it's not enough to live on, not really, especially because I don't make any money now. It's supposed to be our nest egg, our retirement."

"In Mexico," he says, "I promise you, where I can own a business, not just be a day laborer, I will make actual money. You won't have to support me."

"You don't have to be macho about it."

"No es una pregunta de machismo, es la verdad. I'm not saying I don't want you to work. I would never say that. We can be equal partners there, that's what I mean."

And he thinks, maybe she's the tiniest bit threatened by that. Which would be understandable.

"This was never the plan," she says into the wind. "I'm not trying to argue with you. We both know you're at least half right. But you came here. You love it here. You love it more than I do."

"Eventually all this madness is going to end," he says. "In twenty years half of Trump's voters will be dead. There won't be so many new ones. We'll come back. We'll retire here. In any case the kids will be citizens, go back and forth."

"That's wildly optimistic."

"You have to think historically," he says. "In terms of the grand cycles. The wave that goes one way and then the other. White people are dying. They're drying up. They're destroying the Earth and taking it with them. But it won't work, in the end, because the Earth is greater than they are. That's how all the prophecies go, you know, the Popol Vuh, the Lakotas, the Ghost Dance, the Kalachakra."

"I had no idea you were such an expert."

"I'm not an expert, just charming as fuck."

Cuauhtémoc Solar Imports. He shows her the full-color PDF Nestor emailed him, a legit business plan, forty pages of charts and statistics. Suppliers in Ningbo and Xiamen. Another friend helped him pull it together, the rich husband of a woman he works with, a party planner. DJs meet these people. He has potential investors; he just needs a head of sales, a customer liaison, someone with experience in the business.

Now it's late on a Wednesday at the office, the doors mercifully shut. Her phone rings and it's an international number, a country code she doesn't recognize. A robocall. Her phone almost never gets them. It could be Nestor; he's used spoofing apps before, when he's too lazy even to pay for minutes on Skype. "Winter," a woman's voice says, with a German accent. "I'm sorry to call you like this, you probably don't remember who I am. I'm Katerina Wilgehoff."

"Patrick's friend. You're the one who used to be a nun in India."

"Oh good. You remember that much. And Patrick's fine," she says. "It's not an emergency."

"Okay."

"No, I'm actually calling for a much stranger reason. I would have sent you an email, but it's the kind of thing that would sound very odd over email. I have to give permission for Patrick to travel with my son, to your wedding."

"And why would he want to do that?"

"This is the awkward part. I'm not exactly sure what to say. It's really for Patrick to explain. His name is Mathias, by the way. He turns six next month. He barely speaks English. I hope there will be other children for him to play with. The wedding is happening as planned, isn't it? I have to verify that, for the form."

It strikes her what this is really about just as she's reaching for her coffee cup, and for a moment she holds the coffee up in midair, like a salute.

"The wedding is happening," she says. "Patrick hadn't told me he was coming."

"I think he changed his mind only recently. I don't know the details."

"You know," she says, suddenly desperate to keep the conversation going, "you're the only person I've met, or spoken with, who's known Patrick for the last—well, almost twenty years."

"He doesn't have enough friends. He doesn't put enough time into relationships, I tell him that often."

"That's not what I mean. I mean I don't know anything about *you*, Katerina, and you're a big presence in his life, clearly."

She raises her hand in a supplicating gesture, a why-don't-you-get-it gesture. There is so clearly, she wants to say, not time for this kind of thing anymore. When, in the twenty-first century, did the rest of you miss this message. For Christ's sake, state your family ties. Make your allegiances clear. There is no time left for this kind of pussyfooting, she wants to say, or coyness, expressions that don't translate well into international telephonic English, you, Katerina Wilgehoff, my nephew's mother. My new nephew, invented on the wires, out of the air. "I wish you would come to the wedding too," she says. "I have a feeling you should be there. You're invited."

"Thank you, that's very kind. But maybe it would be a little too dramatic."

She starts to laugh, or cough, often it's impossible to tell the difference. Sometimes when she laughs she thinks she feels the babies move, tiny as they are. "I have to go," she says. "Thank you for calling. And seriously, think about it. Don't worry about drama. No one will even notice you, I guarantee it. In a good way."

/

Jorge is sick in bed again, a lot of coughing and wheezing and a low fever. Zeno was supposed to finish installing a set of rooftop panels with him in Woonsocket; now it's pushed back a week. And his wife, Marisol, needs someone to look at her car; it's developed a rattle underneath, a *clack-clack-clack* loud enough to draw attention. Actually it's Samantha's, their eldest daughter's, registered and insured in her name, but Marisol uses it to get to work. A blue Toyota Celica, at least fifteen years old, probably passed down through three or four owners, none of whom paid it very close attention. You have to think about rust, consciously keep it in mind, especially if you grew up in a hot climate and never heard of a salted road before you came to New England. The bands that keep the catalytic converter in place have rotted away and the whole exhaust assemblage is hanging down at an angle, at least an inch away from the chassis; he's been underneath the car for an hour, *Moby-Dick* in his earphones, scraping off the flaking brown layers and letting them fall on his coveralls, trying to find a nub of metal worth soldering back in place.

"Tio Zeno," Luís says. His Nikes scuff the asphalt. He's eight. "Mom says you should come inside and take a break."

"Just give me a minute."

"She says there's something she needs to tell you."

"Okay. One sec."

In San Cristóbal no one ever washed a car. Not that he can remember. The rain washed the cars, or they got dusty. Taxi drivers must have, or drivers for rich families. Of course they didn't always own a car, so how would he know for sure, one way or another? For a time his parents shared a motorbike, a Honda; then later there was a Nissan pickup truck his mother drove, though it wasn't always parked outside the house. More likely it was shared; it belonged to the Movement. Circumscribed as it was by a tightly packed little city, walkable from one side to another in an hour, his life hardly ever included rides in a car, unless it was packed in the back of a pickup to go to a party or a picnic ten minutes away. Only very rarely did they travel as far as Margaritas, or even Tuxtla. He only very dimly remembers the days when she brought him with her out into the Lacandón, doing her fieldwork, learning Tzotzil, becoming an organizer. There are pictures, Papi has them, of him and Nestor running barefoot in the forest with the other kids, the kids of the village, presumably. He always asked to go back. He wanted a bow and arrow, he wanted to learn to use a snare, to see a jaguar. I want to see the Indians, he remembers saying to Papi once, in English, and he said, tú eres igualmente indio, with a laugh.

"Oye, Zeno," Marisol says. "Ven acá." She's wearing pink flip-flops; he didn't notice before, her toenails painted bright blue. "*Ven*, por dios, come on."

"Que pasa?"

"Agentes."

"Dónde están?" Pushing himself out, he catches his finger on a sharp edge somewhere; a few drops of dark blood against the grease. "Dame un Band-Aid," he says, gingerly tugging out his earbuds, and his phone buzzes in his shirt pocket.

"Ya metete, muchacho, come *on*, Zeno."

He follows her up the steps, making a fist to stop the bleeding. "Cierra la puerta," he says. "Tienes el flyer, lo que te di, con las instrucciones?"

"Luís, ve a despertar a tu papi. Now."

"No, déjalo." His phone buzzes three times in a row. "I have to wash my hands," he says. "Call Samantha. Where's Roxana?"

"At a sleepover. Ya llamé a los padres."

"Take my phone out of my pocket and call Winter. Put her on

speaker." The water runs too hot; it nearly scalds him. He scrubs frantically with Lava soap, kept in a plastic yogurt cup by the sink, just as he has it at home. A strange detail. The kitchen smells of tomato soup in a saucepan. Crusts of a grilled cheese on a plastic Elmo plate. Swings, the boat swings in the waves, and nearly capsizes. Marisol speaks to Winter and Winter answers in her professional Spanish. He doesn't want to speak to anyone or go anywhere. He wishes his face would go numb, his face freeze into a mask. Who is the superhero who whirled himself into a cone of silence, where has he heard that phrase before. The Wilcox Cone of Silence.

"Don't go outside," Winter is saying over the speaker. Marisol hands him back the phone. "I'm here," he says, switching it back to normal mode and holding it to his ear. "I'm fine. We're all fine. Have you heard anything?"

"There was a raid at Chalkstone and Fallon."

He puts the phone to his chest and listens. As if they use sirens, as if they announce themselves. Chalkstone and Fallon: he counts the blocks. Five.

"Just whatever you do, don't get in your truck. I'm coming over."

"You shouldn't do that."

"I know what to do. I can document everything."

"If it happens, it happens. I'll talk to you."

"Don't be a fucking hero, Zeno. Whatever happens. Don't resist arrest. You're a father, for fuck's sake. I have my purse, I'll be there in ten."

I am asleep in a hammock at sea. Swings, the boat swings in the waves, the roar of water against water, the boards creaking. I am my own center of gravity. Holding the flashlight while Mami uncovers the well. A rope with a hook attached goes down, and the cords of her neck straining as the long box comes up. Murmuring to herself as she assembles the parts of the rifle. The cold creeps under the folds of his blanket. Hold the light still, she says. It takes a moment for him to recover the words. She murmurs to herself in Spanish, repeating the instructions given to her in Spanish, but speaks to him only in Nahuatl. Did she ever speak a word to him otherwise, other than to explain a school assignment, and even then her voice sounded so odd, so unlike itself, como una profesora. He has to translate his memories, he lost the cadence of the language, except when it comes back to him in dreams. Why shouldn't I be the one assembling a rifle. He has never held one in his life, except when she passed hers to him to hold while she lowered the wooden box back down into the well for safekeeping. She could have trained him and did not. Papi once said she told him that if she had had a daughter she would have trained her, they would have fought shoulder to shoulder. She would not train her sons. Maybe she thought you would know it intuitively, he said, all you ever did was play with toy soldiers and make guns out of broomsticks. I don't know. I never intervened, one way or the other.

Papi, he said, you would have allowed her to take us? To La Realidad?

Yes. I wouldn't have stopped her. Although the Zapatistas themselves had strict regulations and never used child soldiers. But if she had wanted to teach you, herself, inculcate that way of life. That was the way it was between us. She embodied something, she was struggling to embody something, and I wanted you to share that, or you would share nothing of her at all. That's how I felt, for better or worse. No one imagined her life would be so truncated.

Did that conversation ever even happen?

Swings, the boat swings.

Luís has the TV on in the other room. It's a video game, *Halo* or *Call of Duty*, he's played it with him before. Bursts of gunfire, muffled explosions. He ducks his head in. Marisol has closed the curtains; the boy's face is lit up with shifting screen light. "You okay?"

"I'm fine."

"Que pasó con papi?"

"He's still asleep."

Has the moment passed? Marisol comes out of the bathroom, wiping her hands on her jeans. "Ay, estoy tan ansiosa," she says, almost apologetically. "Tengo ganas de un cigarro."

"Yo tambíen."

If he had a cigarette right now he would have to smoke it, share it with her. He stopped when he first arrived in Providence, because they were so expensive; he could barely afford to eat. Now he keeps a pack in the glove compartment and smokes once or twice a week. Winter hates the smell, and mostly he's lost the urge. He associates smoking with the urgency of high school, the piles of books he'd never read, the girls he kissed and rolled around with on his mattress on the floor, under the David Bowie and Morrissey posters he'd stolen from Nestor. He was so sophisticated, for a chiapaneco. Being with Marisol always reminds him of those days. A girl with a nursing degree and a skeptical eye, as likely as not to slap him across the face, even if she barely comes up to his chin.

To live in a concrete building, indifferently built, with cracks in the walls, tiny lizards peeping in and out of sight, in the unnoticed heat, the heat anyone in the lowlands simply treats as air, as oxygen. That was his life in college, such as it was. It holds him still. A kettle, a hot plate, and Maruchan noodles. To have never seen a wood-frame house, a white-painted window frame, single-pane, with the paint flaking off in his hands. To have never pressed a hand against a window, the cold burning through, the webs of frost. Why one and not the other. What does a building have in common with a body. What does a building fear. Someone is knocking at the door. Not the back door, where Winter would come in. Someone is knocking at the front door.

THE BOOK OF NAOMI

She knew the word *schvartze* before she knew the word *Black*. Knew it because it always seemed to be in the air around her, though never directed at her, not in her conscious memory. Halb schvartze, halb Yid. Spoken with a thick-tongued laugh at the absurdity of it all. It was one of those jokes that no one ever bothered to translate, that clung to the lips of her grandparents like crumbs of coffee cake. Not *her* grandparents, who were all dead, but the people she thought of as like her grandparents, the tantes and uncles who clustered around the picnic tables at Fechner's, in the shade and out of the sun, god forbid they would get any sun, who never wore the right clothes for the season and who spoke English in varying degrees of indecipherability. Her father's parents had been from Budapest—they spoke Hungarian, not Yiddish—and her mother had lost both parents before the age of ten; though they both understood it vaguely they never spoke Yiddish in the home, not a word, not even as a joke. It wasn't until she was in junior high school and began having serious conversations of her own, conversations after Current Events class, this was in 1967, conversations about Israel and the United Nations and the Holocaust and Martin Luther King and Abraham Joshua Heschel (whom some of her classmates' parents knew personally), that she first heard the word *schvartze* in another context, a context other than simply floating in the summer haze above the grass, and she asked Leo Rosenfeld, whose grandmother still babysat for him every day after school, what *halb schvartze halb Yid* meant, and he looked at her with serenely troubled eyes, and said, it means something that doesn't exist, someone who's half Black and half Jewish.

Did anyone ever talk to her about the sun? Barbara Halevi, in the class below her in junior high, was the dark one; her father was the other kind of Jew. He was born in maybe-Egypt, maybe-Lebanon; she once heard someone say he was Babylonian. Barbara was what people called olive-skinned, so she always thought that applied to her too. Dusky, another girl said once, when they were scanning their faces in the bathroom mirror at school, dusky and glamorous. Probably she'd read it out of a magazine.

It just never mattered, she told Sandy, years later, and then Pritchard, in their first or second session. Because my hair was always back in a ponytail, and anyway, no one noticed a Jewish girl's kinky hair. My face always turned away, toward the page, toward the blackboard. I was so unworldly. I lived in the same house, went to the same schools, all through childhood; the same predictable friends. Inside that world, I was a known quantity and you'd be amazed what people take for granted.

And outside that world? Look at that kike, the blond boy in Pennsylvania said. Leaning out of the window of a station wagon, the next pump over at the gas station. The boy was pointing for the benefit of his little sister; he was fourteen or fifteen, she looked about ten. A real kike, he repeated, louder. Her parents were inside, using the facilities. She stared at him. He had a buzz cut, a child's haircut. Everything about him seemed too big or too small. What are you looking at, dirty Jew? Shut your mouth, Barney, his father said, and slammed the door and drove off, just as her parents reappeared, smiling, holding hands. Thrilled to be on the road in America, their daughter off to college, the breeze from the Poconos in their faces.

/

The Prius is fixed. It sits in the driveway with a self-satisfied glow, look-ing, for all intents and purposes, brand-new. "You can't see the damage at all," she tells Mohammed, the body shop owner. "It's as if it never happened."

"Please," he says, taking back the clipboard and tearing off the yel-low copy of the receipt, "like us on Yelp. Tell your friends."

"Okay," she says, because that's what you say. She doesn't feel up to driving a new car. The loaner they gave her, a white CRV, was bad enough. In New York, she wants to tell him, you take your car to the mechanic, they don't wash it for you. They don't vacuum. It comes back looking like shit because that's what cars are supposed to look like, if you don't want them stolen.

Is this her new life? Sandy still hasn't called. It's nearly the end of June. Two and a half months. Winter sends her brief updates. The babies are fine. She's experiencing more dizziness but less nausea. They haven't made another plan to meet. She should call her. The email con-fused her; she didn't write back. Does she still want them to come to the wedding? Now it sounds more like a casual party with friends. Is this how millennials do things? Is Winter even a millennial? She's lost track. Of course we're going, Tilda says. That is, of course we *should* go. She made an effort. It's not perfect. We should tell her yes, we should ask what we can contribute.

And then there's something else, a dim reminder: Winter texted her something, weeks ago. You can press a button and see someone else's contact information, that's called *sharing a contact*. Winter texted her the button for Tonya and wrote, Just in case you want to reach out to her. I want you to have the option.

There's a telephone number with a 310 area code but no email. She thought Tonya would have an email. Though they don't use email, these youngest ones, except for school. If you sent an email she might not see it for weeks. You have to text her, or, of course, make an actual phone call.

/

Hello Tonya, this is your aunt Naomi.

Winter gave me your number.

Is it really you?

Yes. It's very strange to be first contacting you this way.

You can call me if you want

I can't at the moment. Actually I'm in a meeting.

Lol

No I really am. I just felt the need to reach out to you and it couldn't wait. I don't know why.

That's cool, Im ok with talking like this

it's weird though, I definitely have a lot of questions

I feel terrible that I was never able to meet your grandfather and you and your mom while he was still alive.

Yes, I would have like that

*liked

but my mom, you know, is kind of a different story

Winter mentioned that she's not eager for there to be contact . . .

honestly I think she's mostly mad at Grandpa for keeping it secret for like 50 years. They were still mad at each other when he died. But yes, the bottom line for now is that this is my deal and she doesn't know anything about it, neither does my dad.

But tbh your book has been a major issue for me

as I think Winter might have told you

> She didn't but that's ok. Lot's of people have "issues" with my book.

> I'm happy to answer your questions. Let's talk about it. I really want to.

> Can you come meet me in Woods Hole? That's on Cape Cod. You can take the train from Poughkeepsie to Boston. You're welcome to stay with me. Or I can get you a hotel.

> Or I can meet you somewhere. I can meet you in New York.

. . .

. . .

. . .

would it be weird if we met at the wedding

> What wedding?

Lol winter and zenos wedding

> You're going? Winter invited you?

She didn't tell you?

If this is family drama I realllly I want to come

> I'm just not sure if

> Sorry, I'm having trouble finishing the thought

tbh youre freaking me out a little

> It's fine. I'll be there. I will meet you there!

Are you sure

                                        I am. I'm sure.

Ok I have to go now bye

nice talking to you

Another buzz.

                                Call Winter. It's an emergency.

/

"We held the wedding the day after graduation," she says to Tilda, "so everyone we knew would still be there. There were no invitations. If you wanted to come, you could come. That's what happens when you have a wedding in a pasture: there's no limitation on seats. The only rule was that you had to bring a dish that could feed twenty people. Roy Archimbault's band played afterward—he went straight from college to tour with Frank Zappa. They were called Roy and the Pain. They drove up in a flatbed truck."

This time Tilda's driving. Naomi's given it up, driving long distances. Driving in states of agitation, as if her life offers road trips any other way. Driving in unfamiliar traffic if she doesn't have to. Why should she? If Sandy was in the car, he drove. In all those years she never felt comfortable driving in Manhattan, and now the world has turned into Manhattan, car-wise: crowded, remorseless, eager to cut you off at every turn. You could get shot just for pulling up on the wrong side of the pump. That's an outsized response, Pritchard would say, when you feel helpless. How else is there to feel. Winter thought it was a miscarriage; false alarm. They've cleared that hurdle. Tilda all but ordered her to stay in bed. Lourdes is on her way. We are rushing to her bedside, to my daughter's bedside.

"Originally we planned to get married under this enormous oak tree, very romantic, but there were so many people who wanted to see that the band dragged us up on the stage and we did it there. The rabbi came in from Cleveland; he looked absolutely terrified. And then there was Steve Chapman, the Oberlin chaplain, everyone called him Chap. It was an interfaith wedding. Nobody even knew what that meant. They took turns, standing on either side. The rabbi wouldn't look Chap in the eye. Our friends had made a chuppah out of an Indian tapestry with a picture of Krishna on it; they held it up with four bamboo fishing poles. Roy had rehearsed the traditional wedding march with the band, but actually it wasn't the wedding march, it was 'God Save the Queen.' Then he did a version of 'Sweet Jane,' with my friend Jane Mays accompanying him on the oboe."

"That sounds about right for Oberlin in 1974," Tilda says.

"When you get married so young, that's what happens. It's not about you. It's more like the old way of getting married, where the bride and groom are guests. The village marries you. That's how it was. We wanted so badly to affirm everything and say yes to life. Thank god that impulse didn't last very long."

"Go on with the story. I'm enjoying it."

"My parents were there. Mom couldn't really move: I'd told her not to wear heels and hose. Dad took off his shoes and rolled up his pants. He kept saying, 'I feel like I'm at Woodstock.' They'd brought us a bottle of champagne, that was their wedding present, and somehow Roy got hold of it and sprayed us with it after Sandy broke the glass. Which wasn't actually a wineglass at all; it was a water glass someone had stolen from the dining hall. Then the band played 'Hava Nagila.' There were no chairs, so Dad carried me around on his shoulders, and Sandy lay flat and people held him up, right off the stage."

"He crowd-surfed at his own wedding, to 'Hava Nagila,' in 1974."

"It was a carnival. It was medieval. There were men wearing jester's hats. Someone had brought barrels, actual barrels, of homemade wine. After dark, we just wandered from one bonfire to another, and finally we wound up sleeping on a blanket on the ground, under that same goddamned oak tree. We were leaving for California the next day, and we didn't have a hotel room. None of this makes you the least uncomfortable, does it?"

"I'm the one telling you to keep going."

"You wouldn't be bothered, for example, if I told you about the sex we had on our wedding night."

"But you're not telling me that. Are you."

"I could, if I wanted to."

"We're talking about forty years ago. I think I can handle it."

"Who am I kidding," she says. "I was too freaked out. On a blanket, with people all around us. There was another couple doing it, not far away; he was whooping like a cowboy. People yelled at them to keep it down. We tried. But it hurt too much. I was sensitive. In those days I would still seize up like that sometimes. And it was cold."

"I had a similar experience at a Dead show. In a van. In the parking lot. I was—sixteen? Fifteen. In that brief period where I was trying to convince myself I liked boys."

"It's nearly six thirty," she says, watching a sign for a strip mall slip past. Panera, Subway, Starbucks, Chipotle. "Shouldn't we stop? I'm hungry enough to eat something unrecognizable."

"We'll be there by seven fifteen. I told Lourdes to order takeout and we'll pay for it."

"I'm still not sure, exactly, what we're supposed to *do*."

"You're going to sit and hold your daughter's hand and tell her it's all going to be okay."

"I'm not sure anyone will find that reassuring."

"You're a loving person," Tilda says. "I wouldn't be with you if you weren't. You were once a loving person with Winter. This is the biggest crisis of her life. It's a nightmare. You may not be able to do much, but anything right now is better than staying away."

"The woman at her office I spoke to said they're going to argue for an immediate stay of deportation, based on the assumption that Zeno was targeted for being engaged to a New Americans lawyer."

"Was he?"

"Who the hell knows? He might have been. He's got no arrest record, no priors. Just an expired visa. That's all she told me. It might work with the judge. They're trying."

"It's madness."

"It's not. It's state terrorism. It's a Nazi-style campaign, starting with the most vulnerable, and then they'll start tearing green cards, and then naturalized citizens. It's a white supremacist strategy, beginning to end."

After such a declaration, what then? I know from Nazis, she feels like saying, but doesn't. She settles back in the seat, less comfortable than the driver's, somehow. Wads her fleece into a pillow and leans against the window. Fixes the vent so it blows spring evening air on her face.

"Keep telling me the story. It's helping me concentrate."

"For real," she says, "the next thing I knew, I woke up in the car, rolled up in a blanket. With the seat belt buckled over me. We were already past Cleveland on I-80. Sandy picked me up like that, first thing in the morning, put me in, and drove off, without saying goodbye to anyone. All our things were already packed in the trunk. The bride and groom are supposed to do that, he said, it's romantic, they're supposed to disappear. I wanted to fucking kill him."

"That was a strange choice to make."

"He'll surprise you like that. Big asshole gestures that come out of nowhere. We're living through one right now, of course. But that was part of what drew me to him, you could say: his unpredictability? I wanted a *man*. I can't tell you how badly I wanted a *man*. How many years, in therapy, it took to work this through. Or not. Maybe I never did. I believed in the word made flesh. In those days every loser out there was trying to look like Jesus, but Sandy was the real deal. He looked *noble* to me. I sound like a fucking asshole even saying it. Bering called it phallo-transcendentalism; she wrote a paper about it in college. Why girls are still looking for that magic mixture of Thoreau,

Heathcliff, and Kurt Cobain. I had a bad case of it. But so did the seventies. When we got to San Francisco the whole place had guru fever."

"The part you've never told me about is what happened next. About your teacher, your Sensei."

She takes a breath and blows it out.

"About 1994," she says, "I decided, with Pritchard's help, that I would no longer think of myself as an object, or a victim, or a survivor, that I would narrate the choices I myself made, and no longer describe myself, for example, as *seduced*. Or *mentally abused*. I created a counternarrative. This was psychologically essential at the time. I had a colleague at Columbia, an older man, a man I couldn't avoid, who I found was doing exactly the same things Sensei did. I was falling into each and every one of his traps."

"And what happened?"

"I adjusted the algorithm. This is the most banal way of putting it. We're having a banal conversation here. This might as well be management consulting. But it's true. On a constructive level, it worked. He left me the fuck alone. It closed off an entire branch of my career. I might never have worked on global fluid mass, except that Tom was standing in my way on so many other things. And then he retired, only a few years later, when it was too late. He'd done all the damage he could do. Most academics wait that long to pull the plug. Now he's dead, and this was twenty years ago, and that should be an illustration of the pointlessness of the whole exercise."

"You're losing me, love. To be honest. I'm confused."

"Well, look. This is the way Pritchard would say it. I was so smart, and so conflicted about being smart, and about all the things I *understood* and recognized before other people did. This was the way it was at Oberlin, when I was doing math, and then physics, and then at Berkeley, when it was geophysics. I had these amazing feelings of power, and I was afraid of them. And I was looking for a man to tell me how I could stop worrying, stop waiting for the conditions of the universe to be perfect before I could go on to do my work, to *see* me and appreciate me, you know, fully understand what I was capable of. And look, Sandy was the first person in that category, but Sandy is no genius. He doesn't have that kind of brain. He has great argumentative capacities, he's good at what he does, but he never had much of a concept of what I was working on. He was afraid of it, honestly."

"And Sensei wasn't."

"Sensei—I mean, he always wanted me to call him Miro. When we were alone. Miro was actually extremely good at following my explanations. And he was curious. He wouldn't stop asking me questions. Why do waves wash up on the beach in this way and not that way. He was testing me, at first, to see what I *couldn't* explain. And then finally one day, this was early on, he asked me to work on this question. *Why* is the motion of water so complicated? *Why* are fluids so hard to calculate? I got so frustrated I actually threw a cup of tea in his face once. What does that mean, *why*? Scientists don't deal with *why*, that's what I kept telling him, they deal with *how* and *that*."

"Why *are* fluids so hard to calculate? I've always wondered."

"I can't tell you."

"You know the answer, and you can't tell me."

"I don't know the answer, I *am* the answer. That's how koans work. They're not formulas. For you to understand, you'd have to go through the whole process yourself."

"You are the answer, in other words, you embody the answer, the answer is your life. That sort of makes sense to me."

"If it does, I'm not explaining it correctly."

Tilda laughs, the way she does, a full-body, shaking laugh, and slaps her on the thigh. "You've still got it," she says. "May the Force be with you."

She draws her knees up to her chest, which takes an effort. Grapples her hands around them. When did her joints become so lazy, so prone to complaint? She walks every single day. She takes pills. Things Tilda gives her. Bone broth, a.k.a. soup. Supposed to build collagen. But when the organism wants to roll into a ball, it can't. What the hell?

"What are you doing, exactly?"

"I don't know. I just had an impulse to, I don't know, hug myself."

"Never a bad idea."

It hurts to put her face against her knees. Making her spine into a C. Painfully aware of each vertebra, of being a spinal creature, when one doesn't normally think of oneself as one. Humans, given enough freedom and space, think of themselves as permeable, polymorphous. Wasn't that what Freud said, in a way.

"Was I guilty, is the obvious question. Did I feel guilty. Did I feel *bad*. No. Not exactly. For a long time I convinced myself that he knew and wasn't saying anything. Or that it wasn't happening, period. It was incidental. I had all the feelings one could have, basically, because it went on for so long. Sensei used to write me love poems in Japanese, and then translate them out loud, in dokusan. I kept them, and everyone was so impressed that he would give me these bits of calligraphy, because no one else in the group spoke Japanese. Until the end, when this girl showed up—she'd lived in Japan and was fluent but didn't tell anyone. *She* knew what was happening immediately. In one way or another she told Sandy; I never heard the details. Or wanted to. That's really how it all blew up. The truth is that Sandy never knew, he never suspected anything. That's the hideous part. It just devolved into scandal and ruin."

"But you stayed married."

"It was like a bubble bursting! Once we stepped back out into the real world it was almost as if it had never happened. At least that was how I felt. We had Patrick. We had our careers. Weirdly, what happened was that we were too upwardly mobile, our lives had too much of a trajectory, even if we'd just spent the better part of three years as monks on a farm. We tried to drop out, half-heartedly, and then dropped right back in. I suppose that's a common boomer experience. What am I saying, I *know* it's a common boomer experience, though no one would have described it that way at the time. And then what happened was, for the next twenty years or so, in the midst of everything else that was happening, I would sort of come to and realize that Sandy never forgave me, and part of him still hated me. We tried couples therapy, three times. Well, once it was family therapy–cum–couples therapy, or something. And obviously we had our own shrinks, Pritchard and Brisman. We had the full armature, the apparatus of analysis, to keep us from actually seeing each other whole."

Seekonk, the signs say. East Providence. The city, such as it is, coming into view, at sunset. Sunspots on the skyscrapers, the tiny assemblage of a downtown. Red brick glows when the light hits it. A gauzy summer evening, almost seven o'clock. The harbor an unconscionable blue. The New England coast flaunts itself obnoxiously on summer evenings, but what's pure kitsch in Woods Hole reads differently here; it seems almost noble. There's probably a word for it in Japanese. In fact, climatologically, Providence *is* quite Japanese. Four stark seasons and winter hovering over everything, and the unpredictability of the sea.

"I'm so afraid of doing this," she says. "Because I actually think I'm a different person around you. I don't want to just slip back into my old self, but I always do."

/

Four women at the kitchen table, eating pizza and salad, drinking wine. Lourdes, Yolanda, Tilda, Naomi. The novel assembles itself around them. A radial, a radius. Facing inward, facing outward. A knot. A fist. A clot. Nine at night, the windows open, the ceiling fan whirling unnoticed. Fans installed by Zeno in every room downstairs, because the ceilings are so high, ten feet, it's a heat trap in wintertime. Run the fans on low and dial down the thermostat three degrees. She eats like she hasn't tasted food in months. The singed crust, the briny wave of clams and garlic. Lourdes and Yolanda keep checking their phones, standing up to talk to someone in the dining room, in the hall. Eleven people detained in one day, the biggest ICE raid in Providence anyone can remember. Since before it was ICE. How long has it been ICE, she tries to remember, it all changed with the Patriot Act, before that it was the INS, wasn't it. She doesn't want to sound like an idiot. Her contributions are irrelevant.

Winter is asleep, she's been asleep since the late afternoon, after staying awake more than twenty-four hours. Let her sleep, Yolanda said, she needs her energy, we all have to be in court tomorrow. To file the preliminary injunction. That's as much as she understands. They're talking about judges, the merits of various judges and immigration courts in different states. Lourdes does some other kind of law, but she's been volunteering on immigration cases since 2017, since she went to help out at the airports after Trump announced the Muslim ban. Yolanda is catching her up on the details. Tilda can follow it all, she's making notes on her phone, or something, and asking intelligent questions. Where is rage in this conversation, she wonders. She's always wondered. How can you do this work and not be possessed by it. She'd like to ask that question but now's not the time. She thinks about Zeno, who is physically slight, at least by some standards, he can't be more than five foot seven or eight, but maybe that's tall for a man from Chiapas. The ICE detention centers, as she understands it, are in prisons, they essentially *are* prisons. Does Zeno know how to defend himself in prison. Will he be raped in prison. She can't help it, she's thinking, this is where her mind goes. A man in prison in America is tested by his, no that's not the word, is symbolized by, is substituted with, the image of his anus. Not to be crude. Brutal, but not crude. It's the nature of the system, where *prison* equals *prison rape,* doesn't it. A woman thinking of her son-in-law's anus and its violation, its rupture. The anus, which is, in its way, a border. A valve, a disc of muscle that holds in and allows out, an engine of control and limitation, which is why the violation of the male anus is so frightening and aversive, because the male anus is the state. It's basic Freud, even if he never observed it as such (or did he? Whenever she took her copy of *The Freud Reader* off the shelf she felt vaguely guilty, as if Pritchard was looking over her shoulder, and soon put it back). To complete the metaphor: Zeno is an anus within an anus, or rather an anus within a colon, the colon of the state, deciding whether or not to shit him out. The citizen remains sovereign over his own anus only within his own state, where he can shit where he likes.

"Naomi," Lourdes says, "come talk to me for a second, okay?"

She gives Tilda a baffled look and follows her into the darkened dining room, dark and pristine, a glass-topped table, a line of pillar candles down the center, a new set of chairs. Clean in the way only a young childless couple's house is clean. In a mode of anticipation. Soon everything will be dented and stained and scarred, every piece of hard furniture a trail of old enmities, bangs and baggies of ice.

"Sit, Naomi, please."

She likes Lourdes. Winter and Lourdes have been best friends for years now, since first semester of law school, and in those days things were substantially better, more ordinarily communicative—because Winter was a student and they were paying for everything, because she still needed help, at least initially, cosigning her apartment lease and buying a couch and so on. They saw a lot of Lourdes, especially after she and Winter moved in together and stayed roommates till the end, in that place on Orange Street, the fourth floor of a very large house, with a rotating cast of others taking up the third bedroom. The same scent trails after her. Lourdes is so physically robust: tall and curvy and poised, if that's still an acceptable word, or just erect, with an adorable button nose and close-cropped curly black hair. She had bad acne when she was younger, and late-in-life braces, but now she's the image of a kind of professional womanhood, a Dominican Prep for Prep graduate who's put up with every kind of impossible shit to get where she is— her father murdered her mother when she was still a baby, or maybe the other way around. It seems unforgivable not to remember which. In any case she was brought up by her grandmother and aunts in Mott Haven. A survivor. She commands respect.

"So Winter filled me a little in about your separation," Lourdes says now. "I understand that Sandy has been out of reach for a while."

"I haven't spoken to him in more than two months."

"And he doesn't know about what's happened?"

"I don't know how he could possibly have heard. Does Patrick know?"

"Not unless you've told him, I think. But I need you to call Sandy now. Or very soon. Tonight."

"Why, exactly?"

"For professional reasons. We could use his help."

"Winter can't call him?"

"We're trying to put as little of a burden on Winter as possible."

"I'm afraid," she says, "that if the message comes from me, there'll be other things we'll have to discuss first. It's not quite as easy as just dialing a number."

Lourdes puts out a hand, a little more than halfway across the table, palm down. A hand to say, I would touch you if I could. Only then does she realize she's been sitting with her arms crossed, and uncrosses them, but keeps her hands safe in her lap.

"Maybe you can put that to the side for the moment, just keep it brief, and tell him, please, to call me ASAP. It's more important that he talk to me, but I don't want to be the one to cold-call him out of the blue."

"There's always the question of whether he'll even pick up."

"Text him first and tell him it's an emergency."

"My phone's in the car."

"So go call him in the car. That'll give you some privacy."

"Now?"

"Yes. Now."

There's a smell settling over the world. She recognizes it, on the front steps. Scorched rubber, bad brakes. Their second Volvo, the wagon they bought in '94, smelled like that all the time, and the mechanics could never explain it. Finally they just got used to it. Jerusalem smelled like it, of course, and she attributed it to all the terrible drivers. The smell of emergency. Not *an* emergency. Emergency, something that emerges.

/

"So this is it," she says, when Sandy picks up. "The long awaited."

"I suppose it is."

Her eyes run up and down the windshield. The sheer totality of the present, which is to say, his voice is the same, unbearably the same. The world is not the same, his voice is the same, sameness in a tangled net of differences.

"What changed?" he asks. "Why call me today, after, what is it, nine weeks? I thought you would stick it out longer. You're not sick, are you?"

"What would make you think that?"

"People our age get sick."

"For Christ's sake, Sandy."

"You're a lesbian," he says. "Winter filled me in. You've been together with her for some undefined period, longer than six months, maybe even a year? Have I got that right?"

"I wouldn't say *lesbian* quite yet," she says, "I'm with a woman, yes, who has a name, which I'm sure Winter told you. Her name is Tilda."

"And I'm assuming this means—"

"Why assume anything, at this late date?" She wants to laugh but has to settle for an inner feeling of hilarity; her voice isn't cooperating. "Why not just *ask,* Sandy?"

"Okay. Do you want a divorce?"

"Yes."

"How should we split things up?"

"Fifty-fifty."

"Requiring sale of all assets?"

"Nope. We can work it out somehow. I'm flexible."

"And the apartment?"

"I don't want to talk about the apartment. Get a lawyer. Not a local one. Call Diana Taub; her brother's a lawyer in Boston, he can find you somebody good. Send me a proposal. I want this to be as quick and easy as it can be."

"There's more to it than that. We should probably meet."

"Not at the wedding, I'm guessing."

"Can we save that conversation for another time?"

"It's all one conversation. You haven't yet figured out why I'm calling, so I'm going to tell you. Zeno's been detained. He's in the Wyatt Detention Facility. It happened yesterday afternoon. Winter nearly had a miscarriage. She saw the OB, she's okay, but there was some bleeding. She's still at risk. I'm at her place. With Tilda. Also Lourdes is here, remember her? She wants you to call her. That's it. I'm an intermediary, frankly, if you can believe that."

"What's Winter's address?"

"What's that got to do with anything?"

"I just need half an hour to pack some things. I'll be there a little after midnight."

"You can't stay here," she says. "There's nowhere for you to sleep. It's a small house."

"Then book me a hotel. And call Patrick. Also, do me a favor and email Mark, tell him I'll be calling first thing in the morning. Cc me and Lourdes."

"I'm not your secretary."

"Do you remember what it's like, Naomi, to help people? Actually help people, and not stand in the way? Granted, it was never your strong suit. But we did a lot of it, once upon a time. Right here where I'm standing. We *collaborated*. In very close quarters. Amid all the other terrible things, we actually worked together, and being here, I remember it quite vividly."

"I'm sorry I never told you," she says. "I shouldn't have kept it from you. You shouldn't have had to find out from Winter. I shouldn't have kept it from her, or Patrick. There was no reason for it to be a secret, other than that I was a fucking coward, in my old life.

"But things are different now," she says. "I'm ready to come out.

Being a lesbian is banal these days. I could write another memoir, about being a closeted lesbian woman of color in the sciences, or however you say it."

"It depends on what you're trying to say."

"I'll call Patrick. We should get off the phone. You're right, I'm terrible in emergencies. Tilda always says so."

"Fine, we can figure everything out, I'll call you when I'm on the road."

/

The assignment was simple; it was called "The Story of My Name." Mrs. Lowell handed out the mimeographed sheets with a sample in webby cursive. My name, Irene Thomas Jenkins, is the story of two families and also the story of my own life. It begins with my great-great grandfather, Willoughby Jenkins, who arrived on the frigate . . .

She was fifteen. She did all her homework in the workroom over the garage. She had a Remington manual typewriter, left over from Herman's old office, and two drafting tables the Puchners across the street gave her for free, with a roll of surveyor's graph paper Mr. Puchner had used once in a mechanical drawing class. And a space heater; the workroom wasn't insulated. It had a single glowing orange coil and smelled like old sweaters catching fire.

My name, like many names chosen by Americans of Judaic heritage, comes from several sources and refers to our heritage.

"Naomi" is a Hebrew word, referring to an important personage in the Hebrew Bible, specifically the Book of Ruth, or תור תליגמ. In the Book of Ruth, Naomi is the mother-in-law of the main character. She is an Israelite (a Jew) whose husband and both sons have died. Ruth is her daughter-in-law, who is a Moabite (not Jewish). The only way for them to survive is for Ruth to convince one of her dead husband's relatives, named Boaz, to marry her and support her, even though she isn't Jewish. Naomi tells Ruth how to make Boaz fall in love with her by sneaking up on him and seducing him at night. It doesn't seem like this plan will ever work, but strangely enough, it does. Ruth is determined to please God even though she isn't Jewish. Not only does she become Jewish, in the end, but we learn that the son she has with Boaz is the grandfather of King David.

I don't believe my parents had any special reason for choosing Naomi. It is a fairly common Jewish name for females. I have always liked the sound of it.

Schifrin is another fairly common Jewish surname. It comes from the German or Yiddish word "Schiff." According to The World Book Encyclopedia, "Most European surnames, other than names of aristocratic families, originated as names of occupations, like Miller, Potter, or Weaver, or the German Metzger (butcher) . . .

She walked across the yard in her sandals, skidding on the matted leaves. The light was already on in the kitchen window; it was nearly five. Ranger bounded across the room when she opened the door, but she pushed him away. Bunched clouds like a burst of steely cauliflower over the Tribkes' tennis court.

"I have to know why you named me Naomi," she informed her mother, bent over the sink, scouring a Pyrex dish. The kitchen smelled like peas and aspirin. "It's for school. Mrs. Lowell's class. The assignment is 'The Story of My Name' and I don't have one."

"Neither do most people."

"Do you want me to get a C? Is that what you want? Again?"

"It's an unfair assignment. Or else it's supposed to be fiction. The *story* of your name. Did she say it has to be true? Then you should just make something up. Anything. The story from the Bible."

"I did that already. It's boring."

"With that attitude, anything you write will be boring."

"It doesn't have anything to do with me."

"Actually it does," her father said, from the dining room. He was bent over an old radio, taken apart in bits, spread out on the table on newspaper. With a jeweler's loupe in one eye. The gooseneck reading lamp from his study lighting his hands, a solid golden cone, in the dimness.

"Ignore him," her mother said. "That part is a fantasy."

"It's not at all a fantasy," Herman said. "You know, Naysle, that your mother and I were second cousins. *Are* second cousins. Great-Aunt Estelle and Great-Grandpa Milton were sister and brother. So, it's fair to say, there were a few objections when we got married. There were some busybodies on the Grand Concourse who whispered about us. They said it was indecent. They said it was hasty. The rabbi got involved, briefly. And as I heard the story, the rabbi pointed out that these kinds of marriages, in the Torah, are not only not forbidden but even occasionally commanded. Something like that. And one of his references of course was Megillat Ruth. So I actually wanted Ruth, believe it or not. Your mother thought that was too much of a stick in the eye. At that time Milton and Estelle were both still alive. It was a sensitive subject. So we compromised and went with Naomi, which anyway is a much prettier name. So we went ahead and got a shayna maydel who fits her name perfectly, and you can put that in Mrs. Lowell's paper. Quote me on the record."

After that she let the screen door slam behind her. A cold wind was blowing, insistently now, north-northwest, a slipstream, breaking around the house, humming in the gutters. She turned her face to it, the way she was taught in sailing class. Sliced it with her hand. It smelled almost like snow, but she could still stand it. Once she'd pretended to be sick and stayed home the entire first week of school in January after Christmas vacation. *Naomi is abnormally sensitive to the cold,* was the note her mother sent to school every primary year. *Please do not require her to go outside for recess.*

I hate the cold, she'd written in a letter to Sarah Steinfelder, her best camp friend; it wasn't finished, it was still sitting on her desk. *This is something you'd never know about me. I mean not the way other people complain about winter. It's much more than that, it's something violent in me. It's like I'm terrified by the power of the weather. That's what I told the head-shrinker Mother dragged me off to. It's like a phobia. I get it in waves too, swimming in the ocean. It's like I think the world is trying to kill me. I could tell he had no idea what to do with me. He had a consultation with Mother afterward; I wanted to stand and listen at the door but there was another patient in the waiting room, so I just pretended to read a magazine and strained my ears. The only word I heard was (gag) "menstruation." She never said a thing about it afterward. That was last February.*

I hate the weather but I'm fascinated by it. I can't leave it alone. It's like picking a scab with me. The thing I hate draws me like a magnet.

Now she faces the wind, which is, she knows without knowing, a liquid thing. It flows, pools, surrounds. In the liquidity of her life, the amniotic feeling, inside but just outside the house which is also the womb, she knows, she says to Sarah, if only the letter would dictate itself, *I know I'm not actually their child, and don't tell me how I know, but it has something to do with this, it has to do with the weather.*

It's November of 1966, but it could almost be April of 1968, the evening of April 4, all the TVs and radios on full blast, and she could almost be bursting through that door again, now a full-time resident of the garage, to say to Phyllis, tell me the story of my name again, Dad's still at the office, he won't know I know.

DISCOURSE ON LOSS

March 23, 2003
A DOCUMENT TO BE RELEASED TO NAOMI
WILCOX AFTER MY DEATH

I met Phyllis Wexler in the game room, where I was on duty behind the desk, checking out billiard cues and bowling shoes and Ping-Pong paddles.

It was a slow day and I was catching up on my reading for a tutorial I had begun the previous spring semester. It was an independent study called Revolutionary Minds of the Nineteenth Century, where we read Marx, Nietzsche, Freud, and Darwin. I had *Introductory Lectures on Psycho-Analysis* propped up under the desk where my supervisor couldn't see it if he popped in, and Phyllis, without a word, leaned over the counter (wearing a low-cut blouse for 1951) and picked up the book to read the spine. I thought she was going to make some sarcastic remark, but all she said was: "That's a book I need to be reading." I told her I didn't know what she meant and she said: "I have the strangest dreams, all the time. I'm up half the night."

I don't know why I said anything at all to her. I should have kept my mouth as absolutely shut as my parents had always warned me, around a girl like that. But I said: "When I can't sleep I always have to go for a walk."

I had never in my life been so forward with any girl, Negro or otherwise, and I was terrified. It was as if I was in a movie—and I was besotted with movies in those days, so maybe that accounts for it. The movies and the Freud. I tell you my heart absolutely froze. But she just nodded, and in my mind, skipped away, although of course she didn't actually skip. It was just the lightness of the way she walked, which said something about how bored she was at Kutscher's Resort, how desperately bored anyone under forty was in that awful place with its stultifying rituals, awkward jokes, and disgusting food—which we ate just as the guests ate, in the little alleyway behind the back door of the kitchen, on picnic tables. Everything in that kitchen that could come out of a can did—even potato salad, and I had no idea there was such a thing as canned potato salad. Even now I can barely believe it.

This was 1951, which I suppose is what they now call the height of the Catskills era. The one bit of knowledge I carried in my breast all that summer was just how many of the guests had come out of the camps—you saw those numbers displayed on so many forearms, short hairy men in polo shirts who spoke only Yiddish or English with thick accents, and their wives, who moved in groups and whom I could barely see at all, never wanting to make eye contact. They were rude, generally speaking, when they noticed me at all, and I heard the word *schvartze* every day, behind my back or even in the vicinity of my face, not really understanding that it carried the force of *nigger*. Of course, there were other guests who were polite or even solicitous, and who, if they saw me reading, asked if I was in college and what I was studying. But not many. Kutscher's

Resort was (as I understood these things) solidly middle-class, not *upper*-middle-class, which meant (I think someone explained this to me) that you'd see the women by the pool reading *Life* or *Time* or the *Saturday Evening Post* or *Reader's Digest,* whereas at other resorts it would be *The New Yorker* or *Partisan Review.*

I doubted I'd ever see her again, and hoped not, in a way, because clearly I couldn't control what came out of my mouth. On the other hand, I was so bored, and it was so hot. I didn't have the patience for customer service or the charm to get big tips. Rudy Baker, my one and only friend on the staff, because I knew him from home—he also grew up on V Street—had people eating out of his hand. He was one funny guy. He could do imitations, and he had a gigantic, blinding smile. And he made three times his hourly salary in tips. He'd talked me into coming, and I was so miserable. I was at the desk again, same place, three or four days later, and in she came, carrying of all things a copy of *Black Boy.* "Do you mind?" she asked, and actually pulled up a stool to the desk. I hadn't noticed there were stools. "I haven't read that book," I said, and she looked surprised. I had assumed she was going to use it as an excuse to talk to me. "I haven't either," she said, "it's assigned reading for a course I'm taking in the fall. I start college in the fall. SUNY-Binghamton."

I said: "You're going to think I'm extremely rude, but if you stay sitting there, I'm going to get fired." "I don't see why," she said, "I'm a guest." "But I'm not." "Well, then I propose"—and she leaned over the desk and whispered—"Meet me at seven by the back tennis courts, I know you're allowed to walk there, I practice all the time at night and I see staff on that road, that's where the deliveries go, isn't it."

I said okay just to get her off my desk.

I was so bored, and lonely, I hadn't really made friends

other than Rudy among the staff, and when you're in that state
of mind you're not just in ONE state of mind but in several;
you feel like you're a different person at different hours of the
day, and what might seem illogical and dangerous at eight A.M.
became not only acceptable but sensible and necessary at
nine P.M. There was just a surplus of hours in which I had
nothing to think or feel, and nobody to be, and I was learning
something important, how menial jobs are essentially payment
for not being yourself eight or ten hours a day. This isn't true
everywhere in the world; in France, for example, waiters and
taxi drivers and repairmen have autonomy and self-respect,
they have a métier, but that's not the American system, where
every attendant at the gas station is required to have the same
smile and say, "Have a nice day." Which is why I required my
children to work those kinds of jobs as teenagers, so they would
never want to have to depend on them later in life. I would
call myself dehumanized, which is not an excuse, simply a
self-assessment. Others have coped with much worse in better
ways. I went to meet your mother. I didn't tell anyone about
it, though others talked about their little assignations and
rendezvous all the time. Rudy had a wicker picnic basket under
his bed, which contained two glasses, a half-full bottle of wine,
and a cheap plaid blanket. I borrowed it without asking; he
was nowhere to be found. I was guided by some force outside
myself. Or at least that's how I justified it, psychologically, in
the months and years afterward.

It was lust. That may be painful for you to hear. I never
wanted to retell this story; I'm doing it because you asked me
to. I've chosen to do it now, after refusing, because of Bering.
Now it's ten days after her death, her murder. I've been sitting
in silent agony all this time, Naomi. I can't unburden myself
to anyone. My sponsor is dead. I can't even go to a meeting
without arousing Vi's suspicions that I'm drinking again, and

I'm not. Yet. So I'm taking off this burden and giving it to you. It was lust, I was young and desperate, without even a good place to, yes, masturbate, not a word I thought I would ever type on this typewriter. I suffered from congestion of the humors, from a buildup of certain fluids. And, yes, there was curiosity, there were fantasies. I was ashamed then; now it's too late to be ashamed. Doesn't everyone fantasize, especially when young, about different bodies, about the conjoining of different shades and skin tones? The sum total of my sexual experience, in 1952, consisted of a few "sessions" with my second cousin Louisa, who was two years older, and often visited my family in the summers, and three weekends with my one actual girlfriend, Iz, Isadora, that previous spring. Iz and I had done everything that wasn't likely to result in pregnancy, and then later, when she received counseling and supplies from a sympathetic doctor in Virginia, everything else. But we'd already broken up; she had gotten engaged to one of *her* second cousins, Jimmy England, as it turns out. Left over from those weekends, I had a single item, what we called in those days a French letter. I carried it in my pocket when I went to meet your mother at the tennis courts.

What else is there to tell? I spread out the blanket behind some bushes that screened us from the road, the courts, the lawn, the nearest buildings. The gardeners at Kutscher's had created this particular horseshoe-shaped cul-de-sac, it seemed, away from prying eyes. We both felt horribly awkward, I think. We finished that bottle of wine in what seemed like a few minutes, talking about college, what it was like, about sororities and football games and her roommate. They'd already begun exchanging letters. We talked about Joe McCarthy and the HUAC hearings, about the Hollywood blacklist. Her parents were ardently anticommunist, and she argued with them bitterly. She told me how she kept a stack of Paul Robeson

records in her room and listened to them late at night, and
how Robeson's baritone vibrated through the whole house.
It was 1951. I told her to listen to modern music instead,
like Billie Holiday and Lester Young. She said she couldn't
follow jazz, it just went around and around in a circle and
every song sounded the same. In those days there was a station
broadcasting out of Port Jervis that could be heard all across the
Catskills, and the jockey played jazz all night. I often listened
to it while reading *Das Kapital* by flashlight. I told her all these
things, and she put her hand on my arm. We both looked at
that hand for quite a while, and thank goodness, we both had
the sense not to say anything. Then I kissed her. The rest went
pretty much as could be predicted.

I removed the condom in the dark; I didn't know it had
broken. Or if it had broken. I threw it into the bushes. The
mosquitoes had descended and we were swatting them away
furiously. We got dressed quickly. I wanted to offer her my
flashlight, but I only had the one, and no way of buying
another. "It's all right," she said, "I can make it back, no one's
going to see me. I see really well in the dark."

Those were the last words I heard from your mother's
mouth, and that was the last time I ever looked at her directly.
We avoided each other the rest of the summer, or rather she
avoided me; I had no choice in the matter. That next morning
I had a hard time convincing myself it hadn't been a dream.
I had returned Rudy's basket, knowing he'd miss the wine,
and see the stains on the blanket, but what would he do, take
fingerprints? I hadn't been myself, it was a temporary lapse
of reason and judgment, I could have been killed. I thought
about it purely in moral terms, that is, until I received a letter
from Phyllis seven months later, in January. It was waiting
for me in my post office box when I returned to Rutgers after
Christmas vacation. She had had a friend find my name in the

college directory. The letter, which I tore up and threw away immediately afterward, said just that she was expecting, she hadn't enrolled at SUNY-Binghamton after all, in fact she was already married. She didn't mention her husband's name. It was a handwritten letter, of course, just a few sentences, on flowered notepaper, the kind girls in high school often used in those days. At the top of the page it said "Phyllis Wexler." The last line was: "No one else agrees with me but you deserve to know."

The only two people I've ever shared this story with besides you are Lenora and the girlfriend I had immediately before Lenora, Sandra, who I met when I first moved out to California and started working at Salk in 1968. Sandra was tough. She was an industrial chemist at Union Carbide, the first Black woman to get a PhD in chemistry—certainly at UCLA, maybe in the whole country. Old-fashioned people in my family might have called her "mannish." She wore a green leather jacket and wore her hair natural, but cut short, nearly as short as mine. When we fought (which was often) she would accuse me of sentimentalism, which to her was the worst offense a Black man could commit. She accused me of mourning my "white daughter" and "white family." I've never met a person in my life more committed to the concept of racial purity. Many, many years later, when I got sober, and actually met with a psychiatrist (this was after I retired), I was able to admit a) that Sandra was right and b) that she made me so ashamed of myself, and my feelings, that I bottled them, literally, in the bottle, for decades. I wish I could have told Sandra all of this, not by way of confrontation but by way of clarification, because I was never fair to her either; I left her for Lenora because I couldn't stand to be so threatened by a woman, so eclipsed by her ambition. But she died of breast cancer in the late 1970s, as a result of chemical exposure during her research. I was one of six people at her funeral. Everything I'm saying here matters; I hope you can understand that. All these events are really one event, or one fact, the fact that we have never met and probably at this point never will. There are many stories about broken love affairs or keen romances cut off by the racial divide, and this isn't one of them, but I did, from time to time, think about you. In my long years of loneliness, my student years that seemed to go on forever, those years at Princeton when I was twenty-five or twenty-six, and hardly less awkward than a teenager, I would think about you and wonder how you were, and what your name was. If I had known your name I might have tried to find you. I say that now, guilty as ever of sentimentality at the wrong times, guilty of uselessness. I am so angry at myself, at the end of writing this, but for what reason exactly I can't say. I have always had good reasons for my decisions, except once, and I wouldn't undo that one either, or only to the extent that I would undo the night I myself was conceived. That's what we do in AA, we choose life. I choose life for both of us. I wish it actually made any kind of difference.

PALESTINE: ON THE POVERTY OF METAPHOR

[Published in the *Guardian*, March 20, 2003: "The Poverty of Metaphor: An Unfinished Essay by Bering Wilcox, Peace Activist Killed by the Israel Defense Forces"]

From: "Bering Wilcox" <carebear@hotmail.com>
Date: February 22, 2003 at 09:20:35 PM EST
To: "Patrick Hakuin Wilcox" <dharmaboy@yahoo.com>
Subject: essay draft

PALESTINE: ON THE POVERTY OF METAPHOR
I am writing this from the village of Wadi Aboud in Occupied Palestine (otherwise known as the West Bank or the Occupied Territories) in February 2003, the third year of the Al-Aqsa Intifada or Second Intifada. I have come here as an international peace activist with the group Warriors for Peace. I am 21 years old and on leave from Evergreen State College in Washington State, USA, although I am a native New Yorker at heart.

I was raised in a liberal Jewish family in a largely Jewish

community—or at least the Upper West Side often felt that way—and so I heard and read about Israel from a very young age. Although my parents, both ambivalent in different ways about Judaism (my mother was born Jewish but does not practice; my father was raised as a Christian and is something of a Judeophile but never converted), never supported mainstream Zionist thought, the existence and righteousness and importance of Israel was never in question among my peers, either at Hebrew school or among my friends, many of whom were more conventionally American Jewish than I was (Reform or Conservative or in a few cases Modern Orthodox shuls, Jewish summer camps, elaborate bar/bat mitzvahs, Birthright Israel trips, etc.). I was a young child when the First Intifada started and a teenager during Oslo and the developments that followed, but most of what I heard about was the suicide bombings carried out by Hamas and Islamic Jihad and Fatah and the PFLP. With a very few exceptions there was no question among my friends that Arabs (who were always called Arabs, not Palestinians) were the enemy, who had fought against the state of Israel from the beginning and would never be content until every Jew was driven out of Israel and the whole country destroyed. No one considered this a racist view or even a "view" at all; it was just a fact. Israel was a tiny, fragile democracy, a triumph rising from the ashes of the Shoah, where everyone, including Arabs, had the right to vote, where science and technology were creating an ideal country of the future, and "the Arabs" were a monolith that controlled the rest of the Middle East as one big dictatorship and didn't want to share even the tiniest bit of the region with Jews, because they had always hated and resented Jews and kept them away from their rightful homeland for 1,500 years. I heard, not often, but often enough, my peers, my ostensible friends, and their parents, or echoing their parents, say things like, "The problem isn't that Israel has the bomb, it's that they haven't used it yet." Or, "The Arabs should consider themselves lucky that any of them got to stay in Israel, I don't know why we can't just drive them all out, period."

It wasn't really until I left New York that I was able to see how

every aspect of this viewpoint, every single assumption within it—
not the genocidal-fantasy aspect of it, the more rational, politically
normative, high-school-debate-stage, Benjamin Netanyahu–on–CNN
aspect of it—is complete nonsense. It's not even worth debating.
Israelis themselves, nearly all of them, know perfectly well that the
vision of Israel sold to American Jews is propaganda; it's not that they
don't believe in their heart of hearts that they have a right to be there
and Palestinians don't, but they argue from an entirely different set of
facts, they have a coherent politics that comes from seeing Israel as
a complex, multilayered, internally divided, and contradictory society
with its own fucked-up history. It's just different to argue from the point
of view of lived existence. And it's not even unforgivable that they
fully endorse the Potemkin Village show given to American Jews; it's
that American Jews are willingly naïve and obtuse enough to fall for it,
time after time. Israelis appreciate the political value of the metaphor.
American Jews don't even see it AS a metaphor. That's what I want to
write about here.

Because until I left New York and went to college, although I was
surrounded by "intellectuals" my whole life, I had never met anyone
who actually studied the history of the Middle East. I know now that
I could have gone to Columbia and studied with Said etc. but in high
school no one mentioned that. I had never gone to Israel, but even if
I had gone in high school it would have been on one of those package
tours where Americans are bused from Yad Vashem to the Western
Wall to Masada to the beach in Tel Aviv and fed dry falafel and hummus
out of a can. Thank god instead I walked into Professor Walker's class
(Introduction to Middle East Studies) my first semester at Evergreen
and was handed a stack of actual books to read. I have never worked
as hard in any class in my admittedly short life. We read Tom Segev
and Benny Morris and of course Said and the Shahak Report and
David Grossman and Mahmoud Darwish and Ghassan Kanafani and
Elias Khoury, people no one in New York seems to know about, the
actual authorities on the subject.

Here I was in Olympia, Washington, on the edge of the Pacific, among the firs and spruces and cedars, going to parties in mountain meadows, biking everywhere in the gentle rain that seemed to float over campus nine days out of ten, always a little colder than I should have been, because my East Coast body refused to adjust, and while I was missing home tremendously, in every way I was so horrified at my own emotional and intellectual and political laziness, and that of my parents and literally the entire world that raised me, a world that refused to see Palestinians or talk about them or what happened to them. I had never heard, in my life, the word *Naqba*. I had heard, a hundred million times, the words *Holocaust* and *Shoah*. I thought as a historically literate person and left-wing person I could rattle off the last century's greatest atrocities in my sleep, but I had never heard the word *Naqba*. I visited Professor Walker's office hours every week, always shivering. He handed me stacks of books from his own shelves to take home. You should study Arabic, he said. You're working as hard as a PhD student.

He said: It's always the Jewish students who have the hardest time in my class. Either they drop in the first weeks or they come out radicalized. One woman, he said, looking out the window at the rain, and pulling on his beard, absently, one woman I got to know later on, who took my class like you, as a first-year—she compared it to being scalded. The way you scald tomatoes or beets, to take the skin off. I'm not endorsing that analogy. Just relaying it.

I wound up taking his advice, of course. I enrolled in an Arabic study abroad program as soon as I could find one, and that's how I wound up in Cairo last year. That's how my skin came off, but of course, not like a tomato, not like a beet, like an onion, or an artichoke: in layers, in scales or scabs, and there's no end to it.

I want to tell you about the thesis I tried to write in Professor Walker's class but couldn't. Which is why officially I still have an Incomplete. I think that's symbolic and I'm hoping I can hold on to it, but of course if I ever want to graduate ("graduate," such a relative concept at Evergreen) it will turn into a fail and I'll have to work out something, I'm sure he'll give me credit for independent study in the field or whatever they call it. The thesis was called, of course, "Palestine: On the Poverty of Metaphor." And the idea was this: the Israel/Palestine conflict, since the end of the Cold War, has become not only an index for global conflict, a kind of fulcrum for all the tensions between "The West" and "The Arab World" or "The Muslim World"; it's become the ultimate metaphor for unsolvable conflict between entrenched ethnic/tribal/family opponents (I used as one of my comparisons Robert Kaplan's book *Balkan Ghosts,* which supposedly convinced Clinton not to intervene in the Yugoslav wars until it was almost too late). Basically what I was trying to argue was that most people (including most diasporic Jews) have no actual understanding of the conflict at all, only a metaphorical understanding, and the same was completely true of me, in one particular way. People (and when I say "people" I mean so many of the responsible adults in my life, therapists, teachers, friends of my parents, the works) kept saying to me, or within my earshot, that my parents' marriage was "like the Israelis and Palestinians."

Just as a tiny bit of background. My parents, who are still married, are very much an odd couple. My father, a corporate lawyer, is fastidious in his personal habits, sort of emotionally withdrawn, judgmental, and depressive (or actually depressed, it's hard to tell). My mother, who is a geophysicist and expert on oceans and global warming (she's a professor at Columbia, the first female professor in her department), is a total mess. In every way. Her office and her closet, everywhere she goes, are a mess. She's loud, chronically late, drinks too much coffee, and is a workaholic, often staying late at her lab, whereas Dad gets home every day exactly at six forty-five and has my entire life. We live in a very beautiful, fancy building (it's sort of run-down on the inside, though) and have a large apartment for New York, and we're comparatively rich. Compared to the rest of the world, and obviously the rest of New York, if not our particular precinct between 59th and 96th, Riverside and CPW.

It didn't feel that way when we were growing up. All of us (my older brother and sister and myself) went to private schools at one point. We rented summer homes on Long Island but never bought. It's true that some of our friends had more money (fancier apartments, mansions in the Hamptons, vacations all around the world) but we were very much in the middle of the pack. We never lacked for anything, though of course it didn't seem that way at the time.

Here are some things they fought about:

- whether or not to buy a house on Long Island
- whether Mom would ever put away her laundry
- how to load the dishwasher
- whose fault it was that we, the kids, fought so much, so brutally, said such hurtful things to one another
- whether we would ever put away our laundry
- whose responsibility it was that the bills always were paid late, the taxes unfiled, school forms lost
- why leftovers rotted at the back of the fridge
- why we had to go to Hebrew school (Dad insisted, Mom opposed)
- whose fault it was that they fought so much
- whose fault it was that all three kids needed therapy
- who was the more destructive and abusive (yes, that word was bandied around, all the time) parent

Underlying conditions, the kind all couples have, just maybe a tad exaggerated in this case:

- My mom concealed from us the fact that her biological father was African American. Her mother had an affair (probably not, probably just a hookup!) with him at a Catskills hotel in 1951. Her parents (my great-grandparents, both died in the 1970s) concealed it and my grandfather consented to marry her anyway (they had been engaged at the time). She revealed this to us, the kids, only two years ago. My dad has always known.

- They lived in a commune/Zen temple in the late 1970s. I don't know many details about it. It's impossible for me to imagine them as Buddhists, chanting and bowing and sitting silently for hours. But they did, there are pictures to prove it, and, well, what changed? What turned them from communards into such predictable, bourgeois UWS types, seemingly overnight? They're obviously hugely disillusioned, though why and about what I can't say.

- Obviously they got married way too young. They met as freshmen at Oberlin and got married as seniors, when they were my age. I strongly suspect neither of them had had sex beforehand (or since? Who knows? No evidence of affairs, but I could be wrong). Emotionally, they're so deeply stunted, but not in an interesting way; they're too successful, too used to getting what they want. Over time they become more and more like caricatures, embarrassing to be around.

I don't have to go on with the ridiculousness of the analogy on its face; what matters is the irresistibility of the comparison. Why? Why does Israel/Palestine draw this kind of farcical metaphorization, this use of the intimate/the domestic as pessimism, you could say?

Maybe it would help to imagine the I/P conflict as if it HAD happened to a family, as if it could be diminished to that scale. Take a family that lives in a pretty, ordinary suburban house, like my grandparents' house in Armonk. The family, the Mortons, is several generations under one roof, just for the sake of argument, so it's ten people total. They've lived there for, say, forty years. A very long time, as U.S. houses go. One day another family, the Pattersons, shows up and says: Hey, this is our house! Because our great-grandparents lived here a century ago! Look at these old documents to prove it! They don't ask permission, they just move into the hallway, with all their belongings. And guns. The Mortons can't help noticing how many guns they have stacked up in the hallway.

So the Mortons go to the courts to try to get help. They go to the police. No one wants to help. The judge says, "Look, while you were just living your lives, the entire system of jurisprudence changed, and now the government that granted your deed of ownership no longer exists. Plus, your marriage licenses and birth certificates and college degrees have no meaning either." "But wait," the Mortons say, "the government may have changed, but how can THEIR documents, which are so ancient that they're past the point of historical authentication, hold more sway than ours, which were legally enforceable, like, a week ago?" "Because the Pattersons have suffered incredible harm and were nearly wiped out not long ago, in a way that was mostly our fault," the judge says, "and we feel so guilty about it that we need to solve their problem by giving them a place to live, and they really want your house. It's just one house, after all! One house, out of all of Armonk!" The judge doesn't care that the Mortons, if forced out, will have no place to go. "There are lots of other sympathetic families that will take you in," he says. "Whoever you are, since we have no proof you're really a family called Morton at all."

So one night the Pattersons wake up the whole house at two A.M., turn on all the lights, and say, "that's it, time to go." They have their guns at the ready. The Mortons have prepared as best they can. The dad and the uncle manage to snatch pistols away from the Pattersons and fire a few random shots, killing the family dog. But at the end of an ugly day of pushing and screaming and shots fired, plaster dust everywhere, and hiding in closets, the Pattersons have thrown the Mortons and all their belongings out. The police stand by and watch. By sundown the next day, the Mortons have arranged their couches and tables and bedspreads into temporary huts in the yard, and the police have convinced the Pattersons to stop shooting.

You get the idea. The Pattersons keep the house; the Mortons keep the yard. They refuse to leave. After all, it's their yard, too! Every day, they bang on the windows until the Pattersons appear with their guns and threaten to shoot. They try to block the steps to the front door and the driveway and the garage entrance, but the Pattersons deploy their sons—they have so many sons!—as armed guards. And every day, the Mortons send lawyers to the courthouse, filing motions and demanding to be heard, demanding to speak to the chief of police. Conditions are deteriorating. They have no proper latrine. They have no running water. Their shanties are not insulated. The children defecate in plastic bags and throw the bags at the armed Patterson guards. The guards turn to the media photographers—because the house is surrounded by reporters from all the major networks—and say, "Look what we have to deal with, look at these dog-killing, shit-throwing animals."

Do I have to spell out how these two things have nothing to do with one another? If you actually try to explain Israel and Palestine in a nuclear family context, you have to resort to something fantastic, out of Kafka. This, to me, is the beauty of what I'm doing: it actually has nothing to do with my family at all, it has nothing to do with the husband-wife dyad, the family romance, Oedipus, displacement, Electra, any of it. How refreshing it is to say that! As if for the first time in my life I'm not crushed by the logic of the nuclear family, warped by the closeness of relationships within the home and the "choices" they force on us, not choices at all. Yes, of course it's true that "Israelis" and "Palestinians" are more closely related than anyone wants to admit, from a genetic, archaeological point of view, but this conflict is not about that. It's a colonial war over land and resources with a religious/ideological/racial overlay, not the other way around. It's South Africa in a thimble. How much more awake and alive, I feel, typing these words! I've come to the point in my life where I can finally say IT ISN'T ABOUT ME. And this is also why I believe that no, it isn't about loving thy neighbor, it isn't about "share the land, harvest the peace," it isn't about "hands across the barricades," it's about the UN once and for all imposing a final determination about who goes where and who gets what. And if that means emptying the settlements by force, so be it. If that means imposing hundreds of billions of indemnity on Israel, so be it. Or incorporating all of it into a multiethnic state with a non-Jewish majority. As I keep telling people, I'm a strategic peace activist but not a pacifist. In a different situation, at a different moment in history, I would sign up to fight in a heartbeat. And although out loud, when reporters show up (there's been a trickle of them, even here) I have to loudly condemn "the violence on both sides," I don't. I don't condemn Hamas or IJ. I don't even condemn the bombers. I oppose the tactic of suicide bombing because, as a tactic, it's a huge mistake. It magnifies the world's hatred of Palestinians exponentially. But I don't condemn the bombers. People who talk about "the culture of death and martyrdom" in Palestine are full of shit. They don't know what it's like to be the second or third or fourth generation with no passports, no enforceable rights, no jobs, under constant threat of attack. The occupation produces death, not the culture.

But I'm getting off track. What I wanted to say, what I'm still trying to find the words to say (obviously, failed again!), is that the world WANTS to see the Is and the Ps as a binary, as the Hatfields and the McCoys, the "warring ethnic hatreds" interpretation, because the world, meaning the int'l community, wants to disclaim its own responsibility in allowing Israel to be established as an artificial colonial state by forced expulsion and ethnic cleansing, but more than that: a binary proposes symmetry. I have a thesis lingering in the back of my brain about how the mind craves symmetry in its explanations, it's the most elegant equation, it's Newtonian, and of course nature seems observably symmetrical on the surface, although as I understand it actually even that assumption is very naïve, there are so many natural phenomena where symmetry doesn't apply, like hyperbolic space curves (?), but in any case, maybe what distinguishes the human from nature is that human relations and societies and even families are just NOT symmetrical or balanced, they don't correct or find homeostasis, and this is why we perceive time the way we do, because the imbalances of one relationship spill over into the next. In other words, humans find asymmetry unbearable, which is why they have to invent a future. Does that make sense? And the horrible thing is that the future doesn't actually solve anyone's problems, it's just an excuse for not doing what needs to be done today. "Kicking the can down the road," etc.

The Palestinians are obviously the can.

WYATT

"Say West Africa is like this," Joseph says, and traces a finger along the curve of the bottom of his palm. "Here are the countries of the southern coast. Cameroon. Nigeria. Benin. Togo. Côte d'Ivoire. Liberia and Sierra Leone. Guinea. Guinea-Bissau. Senegal. And finally us, the Gambia. So small you can hardly see it, even on a map of Africa. Nearly swallowed up by Senegal. It looks like an accident. About as big as Massachusetts, I think. You can drive across it, from end to end, in a day, if you're lucky. Though no one would. You would take a boat."

Joseph has a gauze ring taped over one eye; the ends of the tape are dry and fraying. It needs to be changed. And a split lip, still purple and scabbed. He drinks coffee from his plastic cup with great care, as if it's liable to burn him, though it's twenty minutes cold.

"The Gambia," Zeno says, to prompt him. "I remember learning about it in geography class."

"The river, that's why the country exists, of course. Because the British needed to keep possession of it away from the French. As for me, I grew up on the coast, in Banjul. In the middle of the city. I attended the best school in the country. My father was a senior civil servant, he was the minister of agriculture under President Jawara. He had a degree in agronomy, he'd done groundnut research all over Africa, working with the World Food Programme."

"My parents were professors. In Mexico, in Chiapas. Literature and linguistics."

"Chiapas, where the Zapatista uprising occurred, in the 1990s."

"Of course, yes."

"In any case, I will make this sad story short. My father had eighteen children. You could say, officially and unofficially. I was one of the oldest. My mother was his first wife. He was an honorable man, in his way. He wanted to provide for them all. But he died very young, only fifty-three. He had tertiary syphilis and couldn't work for the last few years. So I left, as soon as I could. I was nineteen. I hitchhiked and rode buses to Tunisia. Then I paid to stow away in a cargo ship, a tanker, full of olive oil, going to Palermo. Then a ferry to the mainland, and more hitchhiking to Rome. In Rome I sold CDs and DVDs on the street for three years. I worked my way up and became a distributor, a wholesaler. Then my aunt, who lived here, offered to sponsor me for a visa. She had a convenience store and a fried chicken place in Warwick. I came. I got married. That was in 2004. My wife, Adzi, is Nigerian. She has a green card. We have three kids. My aunt died last year; I inherited the business from her.

"One of my youngest brothers, Paul—so young when I left, I hardly knew him—he works in the tourism business, doing slavery tours. For African Americans, mostly. Of course the Gambia was a major center of the slave trade. But most of that back-to-Africa business still goes to Ghana, where they have the slave castle and so forth. In the Gambia it's just beginning. I could do that. My English sounds pretty American now. That's what Adzi says. Though the kids disagree. I could be a tour guide, an interpreter. I know the history well enough. Whatever I don't know I can get online."

"If you lose your case."

"Oh, I've given up hope. I've told Adzi I'm ready to go," Joseph says, and takes a sip. "Let me tell you the story. One of Adzi's cousins used to work in the back of our store, selling calling cards. Separate business, separate books. But it turns out he was doing credit card fraud as well. It was almost too easy, dealing with the people he dealt with, all these immigrants who'd never even had a bank account in Africa, and all of a sudden they get credit card offers in the mail, they bring them to him, thinking he can explain—and he signs them up, only he keeps all the info and uses the card himself. It was a grand jury case, and I was indicted as a co-conspirator. The prosecutor argued that I managed the store, I worked only a few feet away from him, he paid me rent—how are they supposed to know what it's like? He could have been buying nuclear weapons and I would have had no idea. I don't speak Yoruba. I don't speak Igbo. Sometimes I don't understand Nigerians when they speak English. I was given five years' probation, no prison time, none-theless that makes me a felon and a visa overstayer. So here I am. Now tell me your story."

/

Put your hand to a wall and see what it tells you. Plaster, drywall, matchboard: whether it's insulated, where there are cavities, the studs, the frame. In an ordinary house the walls are soft and porous, relatively speaking; Jorge says he can even feel how many layers of paint, a use-ful skill before you have to start stripping them away. A cinder block wall, on the other hand, tells you nothing. You can't negotiate with it. Poured concrete, even less. It has nonnegotiable properties. Of course he worked on concrete buildings, steel buildings, when he first came to Providence, but that was only work, there was no footing in it. A house is something a man could build alone. He wants to write that down somewhere. His own philosophy. Wood first. Not wood, native materials. Obvious materials. Pliable materials. A concrete building is immovable, a future ruin.

To wake every morning to the smell of Lysol and hinges, the clang of doors opening and closing. Here no one mutes the ordinary sounds a concrete-and-steel building makes, though it would be easy enough.

"Qué es eso," he murmured to the next guy in line, as they were led in the first night, shifting uncomfortably in the jumpsuit. He looked familiar, like a chiapaneco, very dark, very short, very Mayan.

"Wyatt," the guy murmured back. "No has escuchado de Wyatt? De dónde eres?"

"Providencia."

"No, coño, de que país."

"Mexicano de Chiapas, San Cristóbal. Y tú?"

"Yo soy de Guatemala. Sayaxché."

That was all. He disappeared, when they were given cell assignments; he hasn't shown up at the tables, even at meals. Did the conversation even happen? Maybe he's sick already. After three days. He didn't get a name. People, in general, seem reluctant to give their names, or to socialize, for that matter. Were they speaking English or Spanish?

On the intake form he checked *No significant medical conditions* but then, as an afterthought, wrote *Allergy to honey.* The woman behind the desk looked at him skeptically. "Never heard of anyone being allergic to honey. You mean bees. Ain't no bees in here."

"No. It's bees *and* honey. Believe me, I know. I've had it all my life. Checked out by doctors and everything."

"Trish," she called out to a CO waiting by the door to bring the next one in. "They put honey in the food in here?"

"Honey, like real honey? Hell no."

"Maybe in the commissary, though, in packets."

"Maybe."

It is sold in the commissary, as it turns out. He asked, his first time at the window. Fifty cents for one packet. No, I don't want any. Who would buy such a thing. The solution is simple, then: don't take food from anyone else, don't accept anything offered. He hardly ever eats desserts, anyway, out of habit, sweet foods of any kind. Other than Jell-O.

He inherited his father's pathological love of Jell-O. And even better, those one-shot gummies they sell at Chen's, lychee and strawberry and mango flavored. He could eat a bag of those, watching TV. But no cakes, pastries, homemade breads, unless he can check the label. In his ordinary life honey is relatively easy to avoid. Bees are a much bigger deal. Jorge always goes up into attics first, when they're checking out a new project, in case there's a hive. He carries netting, an EpiPen, and a bee helmet folded up in the back of the truck. Twice, that he can remember, he's been stung. The second time, in college, he wound up in the hospital. Thank god, they were already in a car, in Chava's tiny Volkswagen pickup, when he felt the burning in his wrist and the immediate sensation of a thumb gently pressing his windpipe, and Chava whipped around and drove straight there, he knew where to go, his mother was a nurse, in fact. After that the doctors gave him an epinephrine kit, but he lost it long before he moved to the States and had no insurance to get another one. Winter insisted, and a doctor friend wrote her the prescription. Even that one is probably years out of date.

It's not prison, or it is prison. Depending on how you look at it. Joseph says there are guys who have been here over a year, year and a half. The worst cases, the ones with no friends or family, their cases get snagged somewhere in the system and they just wait. Or they could be gone tomorrow. Blown like leaves, you know how it is. On the other hand, even if you're lucky, you have money in your commissary, money for calls, it's a project, keeping up with everything. Joseph has three kids to speak to. Has to keep their spirits up. Can't decide whether he worries most about the youngest, a boy, or the oldest, a boy. Eight and fourteen. His daughter, twelve, she's fine. Keeping the family together. An excellent cook, knows how to shop with coupons. The boys are so angry at him they don't even want to talk on the phone.

"My mother used to make us promise, no matter what, we'd never go to the U.S.," he tells Joseph. "If we had to migrate, she said, if things got that bad, we were supposed to go to Spain. To her, politically, the U.S. was absolutely anathema, the worst of the worst, the imperialist power behind every misery and outrage in Latin American history. It wasn't just us—she used to get into fights with people all the time who were leaving, or had returned, who had family in California and Arizona and Texas and Florida. It wasn't nearly as common then as it is now, of course. But she knew what was coming. The real migrant economy, the remittance economy, the brain drain. Stay and fight, she always said. Quédate y lucha! Stay and organize. People from El Salvador, Honduras—she'd meet them on the roads, at truck stops, and tell them to go back."

"But you went anyway."

"I felt guilty. And then I felt stupid for feeling guilty. What did she know, anyway? She was a linguist, not an economist. I tried to read all the Zapatista books, I did, in college I had a whole stack of them by my bed. Mostly to impress girls. People would come visit us, her comrades, and say, you're welcome anytime. Nestor, that's my brother, he got really into it. He spent a year teaching in Oventic, that's one of the caracoles, the Zapatista villages. It wasn't for me. I tried. My dad insisted I learn the basics of Marxism, so I took a class on it in college. Marx and liberation theology. You could say I agree with it in theory but I don't practice. I'm too selfish and impatient, I like to do things my own way, I don't like organizing. All the bullshit and the drama. My whole childhood was discussion groups and meetings."

Joseph has taken to chewing his nails. He quit smoking years ago, he says, but now he desperately wants one. He'd give anything for one. You can get Nicorette and patches at the commissary but they're always sold out. His cuticles are raw and shiny; it hurts to look at them.

"When I first met you," Joseph says finally, "I would have thought you were from India or maybe one of those funny small countries, Belize or Malta or Mauritius. But not Mexico. Your English has no Spanish accent."

"Yes, that was my father's strangeness, his insistence on speaking it at home. He said, you could be a diplomat or spy, that's all you'll be good for, if not a scholar, no one will ever recognize you for what you really are."

"No one recognizes anyone else here anyway. People you talk to, they think Africa is one country, or like Trump, you know, they say, everyone lives in huts there, it's a shithole."

"Look, it's almost six. You should get in line."

"You too."

"But go ahead of me, you need more minutes."

/

Every time on the phone Winter sounds a little better, more like herself. "We have a date for a hearing," she says happily. "I'm not sure how it happened. Yolanda made a lot of calls. Everyone she didn't talk to, I talked to. It's been kind of a firestorm. Your name went out on all the activist networks, Congress calls, everything."

"And Jorge?"

"Still in the hospital, we're working on compassionate release."

"Otherwise he ends up here."

"Worst-case scenario, yes, though probably not for a while. He's in bad shape, amor, I won't lie. I don't know all the details."

"What else is going on."

"*I'm* feeling a lot better, thanks for asking."

"I'm sorry."

"Don't worry. I'm just giving you a hard time. I'm fine, Tilda is handling a lot of stuff around the house, feeding people, getting things delivered. I'm starting to really like her."

"Me too."

"My mom and dad are able to sit in the same room, that's an accomplishment."

"Tell me more about them."

"There's nothing to tell. I don't know the details, I don't have the energy. I've just left them to work it out between themselves. Mom's staying here in the house, she and Tilda are in the upstairs guest room. She sits around on her laptop most of the day. Running her lab, or whatever it is. Working on papers. She takes a lot of walks. Dad's in the Homewood Suites. He's been going into the New Americans office, using my desk to make calls. We've been all together for dinner every night. It's fucking bizarre is what it is. They're not even legally separated, as far as I know. But what the hell, here's Mom's new wife, pass the salad."

"Listen," he says, "there's one thing you have to do. I never picked up the new exhaust fan for the attic from Home Depot. Right now it's just a hole up there, covered with a piece of plywood."

"It's not an emergency, is it?"

"It's July. You could spend an extra hundred dollars a month. The AC has to work that much harder."

"I don't know anyone qualified. Jorge can't do it."

"Anyone can do it. You just have to go pick it up. It has eight screws. You'll need a crowbar or a hammer to take off the plywood. My tools are in the pantry where they always are. It takes two people to lift it up the attic stairs, that's the only thing."

"I'm not making any promises."

"I'll feel better, knowing it's done. You have to vent an attic in the summer. It's a fire hazard. Those are asphalt shingles."

/

"Listen," Joseph says, "there's a story people tell, or at least my father told it, and he said his grandfather told it to him, and so on. A very, very old story, where I'm from. My friends all knew it too. It has to do with a slave revolt centuries ago, probably in the 1700s. The way I've heard it is this. A very large group of Wolof captives were sold to a certain English trader at James Island. James Island was the trading post at the mouth of the Gambia. It was a private transaction, not officially agreed to by the Royal African Company. But very large. Over five hundred men, all sent at once, on six ships, bound to be sold to the Spanish in Mexico. What the trader didn't know was that several dozen of these Wolof were seafarers, pirates, who had been captured on a raid far inland, but who in fact lived on the coast and were intimately familiar with oceangoing ships. They had previously captured slave ships, in fact, returned them to land, and resold the cargo for their own profit. Some of them even spoke English and had negotiated with English agents face-to-face.

"So these Wolof pirates were all shackled and chained in the hold of the same ship. They could freely converse with one another. None of the crew aboard understood Wolof. It took them at least a week to organize a plan, by which time they were in the middle of the Atlantic, maybe two-thirds of the way to landfall in the Caribbean. Somehow, they were able to break out of their shackles, gather together in the hold, and attack the crew by surprise. No one knows how they did it. But they were pirates; they were used to fighting on ships. They killed the crew and threw them overboard, and then flayed the captain alive. They peeled off his skin and lashed him to the bowsprit to be eaten in bits by seabirds. Then they freed the rest of the people on board, and one by one, they set out to board the other ships traveling together as a squadron. By the time they were done, there was a dark column of birds in the middle of the ocean, diving down to eat the bodies of the murdered crews of six ships, dozens of seamen, before they sank.

"But then they faced a reckoning: they couldn't easily turn around and return to Africa. The trade winds were against them, and worse, they didn't have nearly enough food or water to recross the Atlantic. They had to continue on or die of thirst, you get me? The problem was that in those days there were hundreds of British Navy ships crisscrossing the Atlantic. This was a very large shipment of slaves, and it was scheduled and expected. There was no way for them to hide. So they split into three pairs of ships, with one captain and expert navigator leading each pair. The idea was for them to sail separately, find remote harbors, gather whatever supplies they could without attracting attention, and rendezvous off Abaco—that's in the Bahamas.

"Long story short, two of the ships were captured quickly, one foundered and sank off Barbados, and one disappeared entirely, never to be heard from again. The two that were left were commanded by a Captain Jaco. That was the name the English gave him. Jaco, sometimes Jacob. He was famous because of his absolutely black skin, even among Africans, black like a burned stick. They said he ate the pancreas and kidneys of men he killed, he had a taste for human organs. How he was put into irons in the first place is a great mystery. In any case, after raiding several small settlements near Nassau, he and his crew happened upon an English frigate sitting at anchor, raided it at night. The crew were impressed men, some from as far away as India and Ceylon, some Portuguese and Brazilians. Once the captain and first mate were captured, they refused to fight and surrendered immediately.

"So there they were, in two large trading ships, and a frigate, fully stocked with gunpowder and real arms—muskets and bayonets, cutlasses and pistols. That was when Jaco had the idea not of returning to Africa, but of doing something much more daring: taking the ships back to England and exchanging them for a king's ransom. Who knows what he really had in mind? Was he thinking just about striking a deal, or was he wanting to strike a blow for revenge? In any case, he did it. The three ships sailed for England.

"And think of it! I know, we can't think of it. We don't know enough of the details. I heard this story so many times when I was little and could never get enough. Jaco's story. How he sailed for England with that motley crew, of course that's where the word comes from. My father used to tell me that a freak storm came up in the middle of the Atlantic, what they call now the Bermuda Triangle, and the three ships disappeared, and that's why there's no record of the voyage in the history books, just a rumor passed between slaves in the Caribbean, what they used to call the Antilles, of ships offshore waiting to take them on a suicide mission. Except I've asked every Caribbean person

I've ever met and no one ever heard that story. So how it got back to Gambia I'll never know. But there's another version of the story, at least one, that says Jaco's ships made it all the way to England. They attacked and boarded a fourth ship, this one a ship carrying missionaries, Church of England prelates and seminarians, and impressed those men of God, and forced them to negotiate once they reached Portsmouth, on pain of death. Jaco received a good ransom for those ships, and was able to buy a ship of his own, in Bristol; he was set to sail for Africa again, but at midnight the authorities tried to arrest him, and rather than be captured, with his men, he filled the ship with buckets of pitch and set it ablaze. The burned wreck of his ship lies at the bottom of Bristol Harbour."

Joseph drains his cold coffee all at once and crumples the styrofoam cup with both hands, dropping the pieces on the table.

"I used to say I wanted to be a pirate, or at least a fisherman, I wanted to go out onto the open sea. Instead I never even learned to swim."

"I tried to learn," Zeno says. "I can hold my head underwater now."

"I never even got that far. My kids make fun of me."

"There's still time."

"No, I had my chance. I had so many possibilities. Instead I just worked all the time, that was my life, a typical immigrant, and now I return to Africa, the way Jaco wanted to. Only three centuries too late."

"You can never stop people moving," Zeno says, trying to pin down the thought, "unless you kill them. They move like tides move, like the wind moves. You can never predict where they'll end up. That's what I get from your story. Your life is never just a matter of moving in one direction."

"I'm tired, though. I deserve to rest."

/

He has a sore throat, a bit of a cough. He buys packets of Lemon Lift tea from the commissary and sits nursing one tea bag for hours. The water in the dispenser is never hot enough; they don't boil it, someone said, so you can't scald people with it. It hardly tastes like anything. Joseph has it even worse; he spiked a fever overnight and is in the infirmary. The world, the cyclorama of the prison, rotates around him, shifting, a snatch of talk and then another, languages he barely recognizes. Normally the rec tables divide into quadrants, two Spanish-speaking, one Chinese, one everybody else, but now there seems to be unease everywhere, people standing, looking, watching the clock. As if something is likely to happen.

"I'll be fine," he tells Winter.

"I don't want you to be fine. I want you to be home."

"I'm worried about Joseph, I'm supposed to call his son."

"Give me the number, I'll do it. I'll find out about their lawyer, too."

"You've got too much to handle already."

"It's just a professional courtesy, I don't have the bandwidth to get involved."

When he gets back to the table where he was sitting, there are three cups in a row. Which one was mine, he asks Hidalgo, the guy from Baja California, who once was a professional luchador, earlier he was telling a story about fighting Perro Aguayo. Hidalgo points. It wasn't the right one, he can tell immediately, it's black tea, it's sweet. He spits it out, right there on the floor, on Hidalgo's shoes. It's sweet, his throat's closing. Someone is holding him up by the shoulder. How could anything be that sweet.

THE BOOK OF ANTECEDENTS

It began on an ordinary February day in 1992—sheer contrast, bright light and terrible winter shadows. Sandy was making dinner, preparing a roast of some kind, with an apron on, the phone rang in the kitchen. A rasping voice on the other end, an old man with a slight but discernable Central European accent, said, this is Irwin Klaufelt calling from Cleveland for Alexander Wilcox. I heard you're a good lawyer.

He flew to Cleveland first-class; a tall Black man—a chauffeur, he guessed, though in an ordinary suit and overcoat—met him at the baggage claim, holding a card: *Alexander Wilcox, Esq.* He was expecting a moldering old mansion in the woods, a home for Miss Havisham, but they drove up the circular drive of a six-story Mies building, the Sheffield Arms. A maid, an actual uniformed maid, took his coat. His feet sank into the carpet. The living room had a corner view: a forested hillside, bare and snowy, the purring interstate, more woods, the slate curve of a river. Above the white-brick fireplace there was a small bright painting in a battered gold-leaf frame. He would have called it expressionist, if he had to guess: three elongated figures in purple and green reaching for an orb that would have to be the sun.

"Are you wondering if it's real?" Klaufelt asked him. He was an elf;

not more than five-three or five-four. He reached out a liver-spotted hand and shook with a probing grip. An ivory turtleneck and a tweed jacket, his hair obviously and badly dyed black. "Mary's making us fresh coffee. Sit. Please. I read about Fein Lewin in the paper last year, the Braunstein settlement. You seem like an up-and-comer. Normally of course I have my usual personal attorney, but this issue is a little beyond his scope."

He was used to these kinds of clients. Fein Lewin was a go-anywhere do-anything firm. He'd made house calls. A few times in Scarsdale; once in Miami Beach. Mostly Mark and Simon and Mort handled that end of things. Comes with the territory, Mark told him, once you're at the level where you get invited to the bar mitzvahs, you also make the shiva calls. You show up in the hospital. An amazing amount of paperwork gets done that way, once the breathing tube is in.

"I'm assuming you know something about art," Klaufelt said. "Art and estate issues, obviously. Your eyes went right to the painting. That's the kind of person I need."

"A little. Should I take a guess?"

"Go ahead and guess."

"If it's not a Chagall, it's from someone quite similar. German or Austrian, Weimar period. Or maybe a little earlier. Obviously it's valuable. I hope it's properly insured."

"It's a Chagall," Klaufelt said. "It belonged to my grandfather Jonas Klaufelt, of the Klaufelt Galleries, in Vienna and Munich."

A silence falls over them. He holds the memory like you would in a Jim Croce song, in a snow globe, swirling with bits of white plastic, in the gelatinous liquid air. Which is to say the hush of a fiction being created, a fiction within a fiction within a fiction.

"His galleries were closed in 1938. You know the story. The paintings were widely distributed. Museums, some, but mostly private hands, in my case. They come up at auctions. In Germany, Austria, obviously; also France, the Netherlands, Luxembourg, Monaco. By now, probably also Russia and China and Dubai. I've tried to keep track of them all, but I can't."

"And this is the only one you still own."

"Define *still*," Klaufelt said. "I bought it myself. At Christie's. In 1976. For twenty-two thousand dollars. It has my grandfather's stamp on the back. He bought it from Chagall personally. I bought it so I could sue Christie's for selling without provenance. But that was before I knew anything about anything." He shook out his hands, as if he'd lost feeling in them just in the last few seconds. "I have a specific place to start," he said. "It's a good story for the press, too. Jonas Klaufelt, strangely enough, was a descendant of a rabbi in Amsterdam, Manasseh ben Israel, who once sat for a portrait by Rembrandt. An etching. Around 1919, Jonas was able to buy that very etching. He sold it, under duress, in the thirties, and then it wound up in the National Gallery in London. It's unrecoverable. But at the same time Jonas *also* bought a set of four etchings Mannaseh ben Israel commissioned from Rembrandt for a book, *Piedra Gloriosa*. That's what I'm after. Owned by an anonymous collector based in Davos."

"And you're sure of the provenance? How many copies of the book exist?"

"Nine are known to exist. And yes, it's the one. The stamp is there. It was auctioned in Paris in 1982. I have the catalog. There's no doubt in my mind, this is the one."

They paused while Sandy wrote dutiful notes.

"So look. That's me. I'm a widower. My kids are grown and gone. Obviously I want for nothing," Klaufelt said. "And I can't stand golf. I wouldn't play bridge if you put a gun to my head. My place in Boca is just like my place here: books as far as the eye can see. And a few more paintings. I've hired detectives, I've worked with independent researchers, a few PhD students. I've got files and files of documentation. Basically a list of everything Klaufelt owned before the lights went out. Now I need a lawyer who can tolerate my eccentricities and who wants to get things done. A burning sense of justice is required here. I want to see ten works back before I'm dead. Tell me that's an unrealistic goal."

"Holocaust restitution cases can take decades, Mr. Klaufelt, and you're just one plaintiff, not a foundation or museum. The expenses are huge. Focus on one case, that's my advice. The Davos collector, the one you just mentioned. Tell me about him."

He opened his briefcase and balanced a pad on his knees, clicked a pen.

"Just one more thing before we get down to business," Klaufelt said. "To clear the air. I met your father-in-law once. At a conference. We were in the same business, briefly. Look, I don't support intermarriage in theory. My daughter, Mandy, she lives in California, Palm Springs." He gestured at the piano across the room, rows of frames, faces, backdrops. "She dated a guy at Penn, Chris, nicest person you could ever hope to meet. But he was a blond fullback from Edina, Minnesota. I mean he could have been an altar boy or something. It was hopeless. That was the worst fight we ever had. But she ended it. Look, what I'm saying is that this isn't the same. In every generation there are a few. The righteous gentiles. I know the story. I can see it in your face. Herman told me you insisted on putting the kids in Hebrew school. You know he told me, he said, if I believed in reincarnation, which I don't, I'd swear he was a Jew in a past life."

"I appreciate that, coming from him."

"Yeah, normally the father-in-law is a tough sell. He told me also that you had a lousy childhood, if you don't mind me mentioning it. Pulled your way up and never looked back. I mean I know you lead a sophisticated life now, good schools for the kids, partner in the firm, but I admire those basic qualities. And I don't believe there's any such thing as a monopoly on suffering. I'm not exactly the rend-your-garments type. I believe in action. But look, Sandy, I just have to ask you one question. Before we go forward. Why lead a Jewish life, for all intents and purposes, and not be Jewish? I mean, you're sitting here, you can pick out a Chagall, you've worked on Holocaust cases—it's uncanny. It upsets me a little. I don't like people I can't explain."

"It's a fair question," he said. "I'm not religious. You could say religion, per se, is still a mystery to me."

"But Jewishness isn't."

"My mother wasn't Christian, we didn't even go to church on Christmas. We had no sense of belonging to anything. We just *were*. She was a sad drunk who fell asleep watching TV on the couch almost every night, and it was my job to cover her with a blanket and turn off the set."

"And you were the smart kid who checked every book out of the library and just waited, waited, till it was your turn to leave."

"More or less, but that doesn't answer your question. Until I met Naomi and her friends in college I had never had a conversation to speak of. No one I knew in Davenport put any effort into talking. There was no warmth, no heat. No one had opinions. You have no idea what that's like. The sheer weight of all that silence."

"You needed a mishpocheh."

"Exactly."

"And you got one. How does it feel?"

/

That next September was Yom Kippur; he and Patrick and Winter were fasting. Louis and Judy were hosting the break-fast. Naomi was at work, as she always was on the high holidays, unless it was the weekend; then she spent the whole day swimming or playing tennis. He was sitting with Patrick in the living room; Patrick was reading *Slaughterhouse-Five* and he was reading Abraham Joshua Heschel's book *The Sabbath*, a gift from Louis. It was five o'clock, the home stretch, the worst hour for fasting; he was allowing himself a cup of chamomile tea. The phone rang.

It was Carl. Sandy hardly recognized his voice. I manage a natural foods store in Seattle, he said, sorry, I have to keep this short. Long-distance's so expensive. Listen, he said, Sensei's dead. He had stomach cancer. I got a letter, an official announcement in Japanese. Thought you and Naomi would want to know.

He stood there in the kitchen, holding the counter, out of an indistinguishable dizziness. Winter and Bering were arguing over whether their dolls could climb a mountain; he needed to poke his head in and lightly intervene. They needed a periodic reminder someone was listening. "Girls," he said instead, loudly enough for the whole house to hear, "we're leaving for Louis and Judy's in half an hour."

"I want to have dinner here," Bering called back.

"It's Yom Kippur. It's a holiday. Judy's making babka."

"Her babka is gross," Winter said. "Last time she put wheat germ in it."

"We'll stop and get rugelach on the way."

He needed to call her now, he couldn't take this news alone. He needed to spill it out, tilt and let it slide into her lap. Into her new and separate life. She would pick up the phone in her office if she was there, but the phone in the lab, she had reported recently, was broken. You're still the mother of three kids under thirteen, you need to be reachable. She'd shrugged.

He dialed both numbers, they rang and rang.

He ought to say Kaddish. It was Yom Kippur, the Book of Life still open. A time to acknowledge one's ancestors. He went to the French doors and opened them; it was September, the sweet fall air came pouring in. Open the windows when you chant, Sensei said, often, more energy, better air. "Yitgadal v'yitkadash sh'mei raba," he started, not thinking, then put his hands together. "Namu amida butsu." They had no incense in the house. Candles, yes. A picture, maybe, somewhere. "Shema," he said, dropping a comma between every word, to close things off, "Yisrael, Adonai, Eloheinu, Adonai, Echad." That was enough. You only need one prayer for these occasions.

A man's ass, observed in the act of fucking.

"I'm bored," Patrick said, standing in the kitchen. "I can't sit still."

"We have to leave in a minute anyway."

"That doesn't help. I'm *starving*."

"Go ahead and eat something, then."

"No way. I can do it. April bet me I couldn't."

"That's not the point of fasting," he started to say, and then laughed. Laughed and laughed. He sat down at the dining table, weakly, still laughing, tears starting in his eyes.

"There's something wrong with you, Dad."

"I'll be better in a minute."

/

I'm thinking about converting, he told Rabbi Art. The novel refuses to put quotation marks around these words, to mark them as spoken. It came out more like a whisper; then he cleared his throat. "Refuse me now," he said, "so I can go back and think about it and remember why it's a bad idea."

"We don't do those theatrics," Art said. They were leaning against the wall outside Winter's Hebrew school classroom, which was also Ayelet's, Art's oldest daughter. Against a bulletin board labeled *Radical Jewish Women*. Rosa Luxemburg, Emma Goldman, Anne Frank, Susan Sontag, Grace Paley, Bella Abzug, Ethel Rosenberg. The women of the Warsaw Uprising. "We have a class," he said. "You sign up for the class. The next one starts in October, after Sukkot."

"You don't sound thrilled about it."

"I'm waiting to hear more."

"I thought that, with three kids in Hebrew school, and one non-participating Jewish parent, my converting would be a good idea."

Art shrugged.

"Your kids are Jewish," he said. "By law, by custom, and, thanks to you, in practice as well. That's great news. We've been over this. We've talked about your status. That's not a reason for *you* to be Jewish.

You've never mentioned it before. No one should become Jewish out of obligation. You can't feel coerced. That's the whole point. Conversion is out of the ordinary. It has to feel wrong."

"And yet you offer classes in it."

"What can I say," Art said. "There's nothing unusual about feeling wrong. In case you haven't noticed. These conversion classes, they're like AA meetings. There's a lot of unburdening. You start talking about the meaning of righteousness and tikkun olam, sacred space, tzedakah, and all of a sudden people have a lot to say. They start to feel ill. They remember the people they used to be, the values they used to have. I could start a pretty efficient cult in there if I wanted to."

"It must feel depressing, starting from square one, with people who ought to know better."

"We all know better," Art said. "But forget that. What about you, Sandy? Why now?"

"It's a long story."

"Yet you brought it up. Five minutes before class gets out."

"Because my eyes start to water when I pray," he said. "With the kids, I mean. When we say Shema before bed. Et cetera. It may be a tear-duct issue. You know how it is with these apartments, with the dry air."

"Don't bullshit. Admit it. If you want to get closer to God, at least say the words."

"I want to get closer to God."

"You know that's not what I meant."

"I have to write an application essay, and yet you say you don't do theatrics."

"In your case, to be totally honest, to spell it out, Sandy, the reason I'm concerned, I hesitate, is for the sake of your marriage. I tell people all the time that they shouldn't convert for the sake of a marriage, and here in your case I'm saying the opposite, you shouldn't convert, as it were, *against* a marriage, i.e. against the wishes of your partner. There is a serious issue of shalom beit here."

"You've got to be kidding."

"Why would I be kidding? Look, if you want, let's do this privately. I'm a rabbi and I say you're Jewish. You're as Jewish as I am. You're as Jewish as you want to be. Just don't tell Naomi. Go on living your life, don't use the C word. Everyone here assumes you converted a long time ago anyway."

/

The years he worked for the Klaufelt estate—what years? How can you bear to count them all, individually?—also the years his children turned from rolling-on-the-floor, elementary-school, runny-nosed larvae to arch commentators in complicated shoes, with their feet on the table, reading the Sunday *Times,* who required staggering bills to be paid, whose idea of a concession to his viewpoint was to stop smoking unfiltered cigarettes. He was working all that time. *Klaufelt v.* was a filing cabinet in his office; then it was another office, all to itself, staffed by two associates at a time. They won judgments. He was in the news. He gave interviews to reporters in far-flung places. He appeared on TV in Germany, Belgium, Holland, and the UK, and once on *The MacNeil/Lehrer NewsHour.* No one counts those things. The triumphs of his career.

The Davos collector eventually had a name, Max Lundgren. He was the black sheep of a Norwegian shipping family who worked in offshore banking and shuttled between Davos, Panama, and the Canary Islands, but they were able to serve him with papers at his girlfriend's condo in Miami. He forgets all the details, it was a byzantine case, but the conclusion was relatively simple: the etchings weren't in Davos at all, they were stored in a secure warehouse in Normandy, the rent was hundreds of thousands of euros a year, and when the storage company sued Lundgren for nonpayment—he had gone bankrupt without telling anyone—the contents wound up seized by the police, Fein Lewin hired publicists who took it to the French press, and in 1996, he flew with Klaufelt to a press conference in Paris with the Justice Minister, handshakes and kisses all around. It was the first time the etchings had been displayed publicly in centuries. They negotiated a long-term loan with the Cleveland Museum of Art. Klaufelt won an award from the AJC and attended a conference in his honor in Jerusalem.

And afterward? Klaufelt seemed to have lost all his energy. He flew in faithfully for the yearly meeting of the Commission for Art Recovery at the Sherry-Netherland, set up by Ronald Lauder and some of the other prime movers in the field; that was the only time they saw each other face-to-face. Other families, other estates, wanted to hire him; he took meetings with them, got them in the door, introduced them to Mark, relayed them to other partners. You're like fricking Santa Claus, someone said. He went through a box of business cards every month. In 1995 he got the firm's biggest bonus and blew it renting a villa outside Nice for six weeks. Because that's what you did with money in 1995. Louis and Judy came to visit, that was the good part, but the kids were miserable, it was always too hot and the beaches were full of wrinkled topless dowagers; they were supposed to be practicing their French but everyone spoke English; Winter fell off her bike and broke her wrist, and then couldn't swim anyway, unless Naomi painstakingly wrapped her arm in plastic wrap and rubber bands. Patrick had a habit of walking into the village, by himself, in the late afternoon, in the stunning sun, while everyone else was drowsily reading or napping. He was buying Thai sticks under the counter at the local tabac, which he smoked on the patio when everyone was asleep, after midnight; Naomi caught him. Smoking Thai sticks and reading Rimbaud and Verlaine. Well, he's learning, he said. It takes a lot of money to be this dissolute. There was a girl, too, a woman; he never knew who she was, but the first week of school Patrick had a fever and they got a call from Dr. Ling, who said, he asked me do a full-panel test and I'm glad I did, because I don't see a lot of sixteen-year-olds with syphilis. Not on West Seventy-Second Street.

Patrick wrote a paper about it, too: "Ibsen's *Ghosts:* A Personal Reflection on the Unspeakable Disease," and submitted it with his Harvard application the following year.

That was the time, September of 1995, that Naomi smashed Patrick's laptop, using Bering's field hockey stick, and then threw it down the garbage chute. The Donaldsons, who had just moved in upstairs, actually called the police on them, domestic disturbance, but Federico, beloved Federico, best in the pantheon of best Apthorp doormen, convinced the cops it was a mistake, a misunderstanding, and managed to get them to leave without going upstairs. The worst of all the Wilcox family fights? Maybe. It was up there. You *should* have gotten HIV, Naomi screamed at him, you *deserve* to get AIDS and die, if you have so little regard for yourself, for us, and meanwhile Bering was in the bathroom, cutting herself. Not for the first time. She'd taken some award of Naomi's, a glass trophy in the shape of a prism—from the Geophysical Union—and bashed it till it came apart in shards. There was blood on the floor, in the sink, soaked into the bath mat, in handprints on the shower curtain. The cops should have come, the ambulance should have come, they should have put Bering on a mandatory psych hold or just committed her right then. Instead Louis came and helped him clean up. Bering was asleep, bandaged; he'd given her half a Valium, not knowing what else to do. Patrick was gone, sleeping at a friend's. Winter was doing her homework at the dining table. Naomi had barricaded herself in the bedroom with a bottle of Burgundy from one of the cases they'd shipped home. Mopped the floors, swept the glass, rinsed the curtain in the shower. It occurred to him later that they should both have been wearing gloves. Not that he would have worn gloves to touch his own daughter's blood in his own house. The world smelled like burning hair.

Louis said nothing at all. It was after eleven on a Tuesday. They worked until he couldn't feel his arms. There was nothing he could say—can I offer you a drink. Would you like some ice cream. As if they were midwives cleaning up after a birth, was the terrible analogy that came to mind. It was violent and bloody and tribal, the scene they cleaned up without speaking. They were the gangsters in the Tarantino movie, the one that had come out the previous year. Harvey Keitel in a tuxedo. He was too tired to remember the name.

Did they know then, in 1995, that they would be burying her? They probably did. Come to think of it. I'll walk you downstairs, he said to Louis, I need some fresh air, and they rode the elevator down in silence. Then on the sidewalk, under the awning, Louis turned and gave him a look that frightened him more than anything else that had happened. Something like, Where the fuck is this going, my friend. What the hell have you got yourselves into up there. Less than nothing was what he knew to say. Less than nothing. Less than no answer.

/

When the call came, in December of 2000, after the Bush election, that first catastrophe of the millennium barely begun, it was astonishingly simple. He heard it on his voicemail. "My name is Yael," the man's voice said, with a strong accent, but somehow reassuring; it turned out he was a psychiatrist in Haifa. "Yael Rubenstein. I read an article about you in *Haaretz,* you and this Irwin Klaufelt, who says he's a grandson of Jonas Klaufelt, the famous art dealer from Vienna. He isn't. Jonas Klaufelt was my grandfather. I knew him. He lived two floors above me, growing up, in Beersheva. I know everyone related to him. I have the genealogical records. Mr. Wilcox, I hope you don't know anything about this, and I'm not going to have to go to court to prove it, somehow, but just out of courtesy, not because of the money, which is outrageous in itself, but just in case you might be curious: This Irwin Klaufelt is some kind of sick man. An impostor."

The judge, Irene Chang, looked away from him, at her BlackBerry, which buzzed every few seconds against the desk blotter. He had never seen a judge's chambers quite so sparsely decorated. Not even a diploma on the wall. "I've never seen a case of malfeasance quite like this," she said, turning back to him. He didn't know the name for the hair treatment that made the ends turn in, so that her silver hair framed her face like the idea of an enclosure, not a helmet but a kind of bubble. "To give you credit, Mr. Wilcox," she said, "Mr. Klaufelt was pretty sophisticated. But the lack of due diligence is astounding. We're talking about eight years of representation, here and overseas. I don't know what the bar is going to do with you, counselor, I sort of hope they'll be sympathetic. In all other ways you've been a model of excellent legal behavior. I'm guessing you've heard phrases floating around like *your career is over,* but I'm here to tell you, your services would be more than welcome in Legal Aid, although with kids in college, that's not likely to be much use. I think the humiliation, the sheer pointlessness, of this case is surely the worst punishment. I'm going to take you at your word, obviously, or else we'd be having a very different meeting. But I'll say this: you're not the only person to devote eight years to a case that just crumbles into dust. Not the first, not the last. At least you got paid for it."

/

"So listen," Louis said. In La Caridad, drinking Presidentes and eating black bean chicken, arroz moro, maduros, and ropa vieja. The years run together and then they run into walls. It has to be in winter, this memory, the windows steamed up. "I just want to say this, and then I'm finished with the topic, but it's good to see you eating again."

"Naomi says I'm gaining weight. How would she know."

"Don't talk like that."

"I'm just reporting the obvious. She hasn't looked at me, like actually *looked,* in months." This is how we locate ourselves in the 2000s: between outrages. The TV in the corner, set to CNN, streams pictures from Abu Ghraib, the man in the hospital gown and pointed hood. "Sorry to be such poor company," Sandy said, "the radiator froze again in our bedroom, I woke up in rigor mortis. I took three Advil but everything still hurts."

"Take it easy," Louis said. "Seriously, don't get worked up, it's no good with this food. You have to eat it on a settled stomach. Even then, heartburn chances an easy fifty-fifty."

"We should start playing poker again."

"Now you're talking. I thought you'd never ask. We consider you on sabbatical from the game, you know."

"That's a long sabbatical. Three years."

"You were never exactly laying down the huge bids, or the great hands, so people are willing to go with the flow."

"What year is this, anyway?"

"Sometime in the second Bush administration." Louis watched a waitress bending over to pick up a high chair. It was the early evening, whenever it was; the booths were full of families, piled high with tiny puffy coats. Young fathers, hunched over and shoveling in. You eat between crying fits and diaper changes. You learn to eat with your left hand and bounce a baby on your right knee. Sandy was having a hard time having thoughts. Maintaining an interior monologue. He said to Brisman, *I no longer notice things. I no longer feel myself to be present.* So we will not consider him, here, fully present.

"I want to lose big," he said, "and that girl you're looking at is about nineteen years old."

"Now *you're* looking at her. What do you mean, 'lose big'?"

"I don't really know what I mean. But I think I mean Atlantic City, or Vegas. One of those thousand-dollar-ante games. I mean lose my shirt, like *really* lose. Lose so that it hurts. So that you have to report it on your taxes. I would like to know what that feels like."

Louis watched the traffic sympathetically.

"What you're really saying," he said, "is you want to have new feelings."

"Sort of."

"Because you lack the old feelings. You're numb."

"What exactly is wrong with being numb? We talked about it in grief group, and I got so upset I went home and looked it up. It's a beautiful word. The root is the same as *number,* it literally means 'unable to differentiate.' It describes so much of what the twentieth century was all about. It came into popular use after World War I, because of shell shock, at the same time as *trauma.* But *numb,* in my view, is far superior, in English, because it points to a physical-affective experience. We all know how it feels to be numb. To have your foot fall asleep when you're squatting to change a tire."

"You're making that up."

"The etymology part, yeah. It's an educated guess."

"And there you have the problem. You'd rather argue than admit you've been walking around in a daze for a full year, waiting to get hit by a car. As if you're the only person any of this has ever happened to. Your emotions are your own but they also follow a pattern and they partake in the atmosphere of the world. You are also a victim of history."

"Now you sound like Patrick."

"In that case, Patrick is correct."

"I find it hard to speak about him in the present tense. I feel, sometimes, like I've lost two children, but only one voluntarily."

"I hope you shared that with him before he left."

"Louis," he said in a striated voice, "let's say you're not my therapist, and not my life coach."

"I'm the person who happens to be buying the drinks. Also, I walked seventeen blocks in the rain."

"As if you ever complained about walking seventeen blocks before."

"You're not the only one with symptoms. My foot's giving me problems. I don't know what's going on with it. Remember when we were coaching soccer, and the kid kicked me with his cleats? I still get twinges from that."

"That was easily eighteen years ago."

"The scars of parenthood last a lifetime, was what the doctor said to me. I remember him telling me this insane story, where a guy is driving on the Taconic, one of his patients, and his daughter, right behind him, somehow gets out of her car seat, puts her hands over his eyes, and says, 'Guess who, Daddy?' And he drives off the side of the road. Almost dies of a ruptured spleen."

"What happened to the little girl?"

"I don't remember."

"How can you not remember? Isn't that the point of the story?"

"It's not the point of the story. Presumably she was fine. What are you going to do, give her a time-out for nearly killing the family? Also there's another thing I should tell you. I'm scheduled for a biopsy."

"Way to bury the lede. Where?"

"At Mount Sinai."

"Be serious, you moron."

"It's nothing, a benign polyp, it came up during my prostate exam. Dr. Morgan said I have to do it, just to be safe. Judy's all worked up. We're getting into that dreaded phase for old men, the Rectal Phase. I feel like I'll never hear the end of it."

"From rigor mortis to the rectum. This is a stellar conversation."

"I'd rather be doing this than anything else."

That was unexpected. Louis swigged his beer emphatically, signaled to the waiter for another. Eyes bouncing around the room, settling nowhere. This is what it means to begin a slow death. He wanted to reach out and grab Louis's arm, alarming everyone. Or push him mercifully in front of a cab. I am bound to you, this is one life. It only makes sense held together as it is. These scars in this order.

/

He was in Detroit supervising a deposition when Judy called and said, This is it, it could be eight more hours, or none; he had to fly first-class, surrounded by lumbering Chrysler-Plymouth dealers stinking of aftershave and their Hermès-swathed wives chattering about Del Posto and *The Book of Mormon*. *You couldn't even get a good joke out of it,* he wanted to tell him; the hospice nurse had just left and Louis was sitting up in his Eames chair, wrapped in a blanket because he was always cold, his face a rictus of agony; no position was comfortable, he kept moving from the chair to the hospital bed they'd wheeled into the den; Judy moved with him, terrified his stent would fall out; to stay awake he had to go low on the morphine but then his eyes would start to rotate, frantically, when the pain returned, and Judy would say, *press the button already,* and he would gobble something that sounded like I don't want to miss it. Or I don't want to miss him. His voice was mostly wasted by the second tumor in his throat. He held him by the hand, he held him by the shoulders, his thin rail of a form through the pilling flannel of his old pajamas. I could have at least gotten him nicer pajamas, Judy said, and instinctively he looked into Louis's face to wait for the next line. He thought, or might have said out loud, Louis Zoldofsky, I will bury you a bloody mess, the way you helped me bury Bering, but then who will bury me?

The elevator opened and he threw himself into Naomi's arms.

AN ACT OF SHEER MANIPULATION

Patrick is trying to install the latest update of MATLAB and the system keeps glitching, refusing the admin password even after he's changed it three times. Govinder, the head of IT, is taking up his chair, hunched over his laptop, and so he's sitting on the edge of his desk, drinking tea, watching a bread delivery van unload crates of rolls for the Vietnamese sandwich shop at the end of the block, Autobahn. When Winter comes up on his phone he's momentarily confused; it's three in the morning in Providence, and he knows a Wynter, one of Mathias's old babysitters; did he enter the names incorrectly? Zeno's dead, his sister's voice is saying. I know he's dead. They said anaphylaxis, they administered CPR, they didn't have epinephrine on-site, that's what they're claiming, I know he's dead.

"The prison didn't even call, ICE didn't call, a friend of his called. Joseph. At six. It took us two hours to get through to someone."

"Where are you now?"

"At the hospital. Parked outside. Mom and Dad are in the waiting room. They won't let anyone in. I'm supposed to be home, in bed. Everyone thinks I could miscarry at any moment."

"So he's been treated, they haven't actually informed you of anything. The doctors don't work for ICE. They're not obligated to lie."

"I know how these cases go, Patrick, I do this for a living."

"You can't get a court order to see him?"

"Not overnight. Probably not at all."

"But certainly not Mom and Dad, as they're not blood relatives. You should be inside."

"I don't need you to be rational, Trick. Just listen and don't give directions."

"Okay, okay. I'm here."

Govinder unplugs his laptop and tucks it under his arm. Treffen sie mich im konferenzraum, he murmurs, closes the door.

"This can't happen twice in my life," she says. "It cannot happen. I cannot be on the phone with you for the second time in fifteen years having the same conversation."

He wants to say something like, believe me, this *can* happen, because he's the asshole in the family, but there's more to it than that. He wants to say something about the shadow of vulnerability. A.k.a. the shadow of history. To live, as ostensibly white Americans, outside that shadow. Naomi would say, outside of that shadow but within the larger shadow, the death of the planet as we know it. But are you really, on any scale, are you immune from the violence of the state and its formations, its manipulations, its supremacist cancers. You are not. And not just because you happen to have a hyperactive conscience. Is it a form of bad faith not to admit that as a result of your upbringing you often feel you live outside any shadow at all, and you deserve to live that way. Or is it just unattractive, uncool, to keep on admitting it, to hedge everything you say with caveats that sound like apologies. Now the term for it is *virtue signaling*. This is the crux of their lives, apparently. It explains everything and everyone they've become, what they've survived and not survived. A politics of in/vulnerability. It seems so nineties to put it that way, with the slash. So what. I'm a child of the nineties. What thou lovest remains.

To say, this can't happen. This is not acceptable. Acceptable to whom.

Instead he says the only thing he can think of, which is, "Zeno is tough. He's young. He's not sick. Probably they're just monitoring him, that's normal, with anaphylaxis, they have to make sure it doesn't rebound. Look, in three weeks I'm coming to your wedding. I expect you both to be there."

"You're not coming."

"I am. I'm bringing Mathias. He needs to meet his aunt and grand-parents."

"I would say the chances of my wedding happening are zero to five percent."

"I bought the tickets already," he says, lying. "Unless you want me to come right now. Should I come now? I can be at the airport in an hour."

"Yes. Come now." She swallows, loudly. How can he hear her swallow. "No, forget it. Come to the wedding. For Christ's sake. Whatever it is. A wedding or a funeral. Bring your son. *Your son,* for fuck's sake. I want to see him in the flesh. Otherwise I'll never believe he exists."

JERUSALEM

Is there one moment that matters more than the others. In this moment that matters more than all the others. Is this the moment that matters more than all the others.

The central question that governs how novels are written: how to choose. The novel sits, dividing time. Sifting time. The novel has to become more than its source matter, its raw material. But why, on the other hand, *more than*. Wouldn't it be better to say, This is the material, let it close over your head, like a warm pool.

Can't the novel just say: At this moment of all moments in the story, there is no need for tears or explaining. Aeneas looks at a mural of the Trojan War and says, Sunt lacrimae rerum et mentem mortalia tangunt. Here are things to cry over, our minds are touched by mortality. Lacrimae rerum, tears over things. But is the mural even necessary. Why not just the things themselves. Or does the mural become another thing. Is it all material in the end. If a woman happened to be in the temple when it collapsed, did the mural become the dust that choked her.

Tell a story of a mind and does the mind become paper or tears. In what way does it become useful. In what way does it become warm.

Which part is separable from the others. The novel opens its arms and says, come at me any way you can, in any case I will be here I will not be here.

/

Their rooms were on the twelfth floor, facing away from the street. Facing north, over rooftops, toward the walls of the Old City: Winter recognized that much. The walls of a fortress in full sunlight. She pounded on the window clamp till it gave way and swung open. Birds squawking, unfamiliar birds. The air tasted dry and slightly sweet. Ambulance sirens, or some kind of sirens, were sounding in the distance; she couldn't tell what direction.

The headache was like fingers pinching her temples; her vision was turning hourglass shaped. She drank what was left of the Evian bottle from the plane and took three Advils. The next step, the responsible step, would be to turn on the TV, turn on CNN. In New Haven, in her apartment, CNN had been on continuously since the night of the first attack on Baghdad, usually with the sound off. Lourdes kept it on while she studied. She needed to call Lourdes from her new Israeli number, tell her she'd landed safely. Gal, the woman from Soldiers for Peace who'd met them at the airport, had handed the phone to her, in a Ziploc, wrapped up in its charging cord. This is how we'll reach you, she said. I'm giving it to you, not your parents. So they can rest. You're on call. Don't lose it.

Patrick hadn't gone to bed, as far as she could tell. He was still sitting on the floor, legs drawn up into lotus position, the hood of his maroon sweatshirt shielding his face from view.

"I'm ordering room service," she said. "It's seven thirty. The lawyers get here at nine. You should take a shower or something."

She remembered getting out of bed, sometime in the night, hearing the lock turn in the door, not conscious of herself in a T-shirt and underwear, and embracing him in the dark. He let his backpack fall. That's all he had, all the way from India. A book bag. A single change of clothes. He gripped her with his enormous arms. When was the last time she had hugged her own brother. He was not the hugging kind. She was not conscious of herself crying, she was wrung-out, dissolved. Go back to sleep, he'd said, we'll talk in the morning. Whenever that is.

She paged through the menu, looking for the simplest option. Israeli Breakfast. Shakshuka. Sliced melon. What's NIS to the dollar, she would normally have asked him. He had a way of knowing these things.

"Two continental breakfasts," she told the woman who answered the phone, "room 1209, one coffee, one Earl Grey."

Orient me, she wanted to say to him. Give me a map, at least. There wasn't one in the room, and she didn't have a guidebook. She could open her laptop, she'd brought that, and maybe the hotel had a Wi-Fi signal or an ethernet cable. Israel is a connected country, they say. Lots of software businesses. I know nothing about Israel. Fleeting headlines. A jumble of worksheets in colored pencil. Vaguely, a map. It's the size of New Jersey. New Jersey, plus a desert large enough to test atomic weapons. Lebanon to the north, Egypt to the south. Where is Syria? Where is Jordan? How far is, say, Saudi Arabia? How far is the Wailing Wall? What about Masada? Becky Tarkovsky, the cheerfulest girl in her class, always a little heavy, broad, cruelly chastised as such, called Tankovsky, gave a slide show about climbing Masada in the fifth grade. A fortress. A mountain. The Hellenized Jews, the Romans, the resistance, which also included the Maccabees. How many Bs in *Maccabee*. You climb it, it's a rite of passage. Sweaty brown boy soldiers with their shirts unbuttoned, handing you bottles of water. How many of you have been to Israel, Mrs. Cortland asked, and about half the class raised hands. How many of you would like to go? Becky gave her a puzzled and hurt look, so she raised her hand.

She had feelings about being Jewish. She did! Just not Israel-sized feelings. She thought challah tasted like marshmallows, in her view a good thing. When they went to Bubbe and Zayde's for Passover the coffee table was laid with a million strange sweets, the whole Manischewitz selection, gummy fruit slices and seven different kinds of macaroons and chocolate-covered matzo. She would have liked playing find the afikomen with a different, less competitive brother. She was in favor of Hanukkah over Christmas, even if Christmas had been an option. She liked eight days of presents, the attenuated feeling of surprise after surprise, not gorging on them all at once.

It's embarrassing, to be reduced to these feelings. To have had no reckoning. I need a crash course, she wanted to tell someone, I'm bewildered.

"There's a disease called Jerusalem syndrome," Patrick said. He was standing up now, doing yoga, with a kind of cloth wrapped around his waist. Warrior pose. His legs were so pale, milky, it made the hair on them even blacker. A lifelong aversion to shorts. She couldn't remember the last time she'd spent significant time with his legs. What was the source of his lifelong, no-matter-what confidence? Slash arrogance? "People come to Jerusalem for the first time and have a psychic breakdown, convinced they're Elijah or Moshiach or Christ or the Virgin Mary. The hospitals get hundreds of cases a year. They get expelled from the country, put on a permanent blacklist. It's the last thing they need here. More messiahs."

"What's your point?"

"No point. Just trying to say something, clear the air."

The phone rang. It was plugged in on the floor, on the other side of the bed. After a moment she recognized the melody: ". . . Baby, One More Time." "Jesus, that scared me," she said, and flipped it open.

"Hello," the voice said in a British accent. "To whom am I speaking?"

"Winter Wilcox. I'm Bering's sister. We're not speaking to reporters at the moment."

"Miss Wilcox, I'm not a reporter. I'm Mohammed Shirwan, calling from Chairman Arafat's office at the Palestinian Authority in Ramallah."

"Yes. Okay. Go ahead."

"Chairman Arafat has instructed me to release a statement to the media regarding the death of your sister, Bering Wilcox. I'm calling to share it with your family. May I read, please? The statement is, 'The Palestinian Authority expresses its grief and outrage at the unprovoked murders of Heba Ta'qim and Bering Wilcox, an American citizen, who were unarmed peaceful protestors attacked by the Zionist occupiers on March 13 in Wadi Aboud. The Chairman expresses his personal condolences to the Wilcox family and would like to say to them: Bering Wilcox has become not just your daughter, but the daughter of the Palestinian people.'"

"Thank you," she said. The line went dead. She cupped the phone in both hands, still warm from the charge. "That was Yasir Arafat," she said to Patrick. "Sending his condolences." Someone was knocking at the door of the room; he stood up to answer it. Shalom, she heard him say, boker tov, boker tov. So infuriating, so correct. He came back carrying a tray in each hand. "Did you hear what I said?"

"I always kind of imagined hearing from world leaders about Bering."

"We have no resources for this," she said. "We're not prepared."

"How could any Jew in the world be prepared for a call from Yasir Arafat. It's like we're in a bad spy movie."

"What I mean is, we're not prepared to, you know, *communicate about our feelings.*"

He didn't answer for an indeterminate interval.

The vacuum, she wanted to say, pouring milk into her tea, not sure what other word could explain it. When she'd opened her eyes the morning after hearing the news, yesterday morning, that is, she'd known with absolute certainty that a space in the world had closed. Now I only have one sibling, one other, there are four of us now and an emptiness where the fifth was. How can this be, how can a given increment of space seal itself and disappear. It felt obscene; she felt it like rising bile in the back of the throat. She had a flight to catch in a few hours, and so forced herself out of bed. That was the beginning of the indeterminate hours that ended here. In the hours that are lost when a plane crosses time zones faster than time elapses, there is also a vacuum. Another life, a substitute life, into which no news can intrude. Her thinking was all very sloppy, but it mattered. Something had to be said about who Bering was the moment before she was not.

"Sorry," he said finally. "I'm saying mantras in my head."

"Say them out loud, then." She swallowed the tea rather than sipped it, and scalded her tongue.

"Okay. I will, maybe, a little later. What were you saying, about feelings?"

"I mean," she said wildly, grasping at the thought, "I know you've been talking to Bering, emailing back and forth, and I've been emailing with her, some, and presumably Mom and Dad have, at least occasionally, but when was the last time we spoke, the five of us, as a family?"

"I don't know."

"Okay, I'll tell you. As far as I remember, the last meaningful conversation was when Mom told us about John Downs. And that wasn't even a conversation, because she stormed out. We never got to finish that thought. We moved straight on to why Bering should or shouldn't go to Palestine. Listen to me, Patrick, I'm afraid we're going to be frozen, as a family, in midargument for the rest of our lives."

"You're probably right."

"That's all you have to say, *you're probably right?*"

"No, it's not all I have to say. I have a great deal more to say, but I don't know when I'll find the vocabulary, or when the rest of you will be ready to hear it."

He looked sick, suddenly. Put down his coffee cup abruptly, pushed the plate away. His face puffy and deflated.

"Try me, then."

"No, it's not that simple. I'm out of practice being a Wilcox right now. I was in the middle of a retreat forty-eight hours ago. I was trying to do five hundred prostrations a day. Look at these bruises on my knees."

"I don't know what any of that means."

"You're not supposed to. I'm not supposed to be here. I was trying to start a new life, not be dragged back into this one."

That, she wanted to tell him, is the first honest and unironic sentence I've heard you say since you were eleven years old. He picked his laptop off a chair and sat on the bed, crossing his legs again. The effect of the shaved head was to make his prominent caterpillar eyebrows even bigger, and highlight the tiny veins in his temples. A narrow, squared-off head, when you looked at it from the front. Most of the time she saw him, as she had seen him since babyhood, as Bert. Exasperated, rigid Bert, drawn up in frustration. You who have been forging ahead my entire life, she wanted to say, where has it gotten you? She felt terribly, unfamiliarly sorry for him, melodramatically sorry. To put her arms around him again.

"We have no choice," she said, momentarily not recognizing her own voice, "we have to be there for each other, right now. You know we've never had the best relationship. It doesn't matter. We need to be radically honest. No more secrets. Look, just look at what secrets did to us."

He started laughing but it came out as a groan; he rolled over on the bed and pulled his knees up, a pale and grotesque baby. "Oh god, Winter," he said, "I love you, but you have no idea what you're talking about. You're not wrong. You're absolutely right, in fact. It's just absolutely not that simple."

"I don't get what you're saying."

"For one thing, Bering doesn't belong to us anymore. If she ever did. It's a question of scale. The last thing she would ever have wanted is to be remembered in some fucking family drama."

"But we *are* her family, it *is* our drama."

"We have a choice," he said, still lying on the bed, still a fetus, "we deserve to have a goddamned choice about that. There shouldn't be only one means of exit."

The bile was rising up again, she wanted to spit it out. She was seeing something with every part of her other than the brain. There was a question she was supposed to ask, but something stopped her. Who was Bering before she was not. Patrick knew and she didn't and didn't want to. A lawyer never asks a question she doesn't want the answer to. She swallowed the bubble, the pocket of air that was her sister's life, and went into the bathroom to throw up.

/

In the Istanbul airport everyone was clustered around the TVs, watching the war

I was convinced everyone knew who we were I kept waiting for her face to come on almost angry that it didn't appear

This was one day afterward, only about fifteen hours afterward

I watched the accordion folds of the movable walkway, when my eyes closed I saw a piece of gray paper folded like the children's game, what's it called?

With a pulpy heart in the middle the size of a fingernail

On the flight from Kennedy Naomi fell asleep crying her head on my shoulder we had been in the air three or four hours

A sound arose from her I had never heard before it seemed to come directly from her chest or shoulders, an animal wail

People around us looked alarmed gradually they spoke to the flight attendants and were relocated the flight was only about half full

So we were alone in the middle section, it was a 747 we were in coach, three banks of seats in each row, we were DEF

She wailed like an animal, driving her head into my shoulder

Winter was delayed her credit card was declined it was too late had to get on the next flight but it was El Al, she said no I'll be detained

I couldn't sleep I took a Xanax

In the Istanbul airport, I left Naomi at the gate, we still had an hour and a half till boarding, I needed coffee, desperately

Everywhere soldiers with heavy weapons, submachine pistols, grenade launchers, bullet belts—I had to show my passport and boarding pass twice, they passed it back without comment

But then a voice called out to me Wilcox, Wilcox

And a soldier who was very short, barely up to my chin, said her name, said something in Turkish, said Allah something something, put his hand over his heart, over the strap of his rifle

I was suddenly hungry I pointed and ordered various breads with the coffee, but when I tried to chew gagged and had to spit my mouthful into a trash can

Here I am writing this without looking down at the page

How am I writing this at all as if this is the point

What happened to me

I had always wanted to go to Istanbul

It was one duty-free counter after another, duty-free and soldiers, and then, out of nowhere, a Popeyes fried chicken

I rounded a corner, unprepared, and there was a large screen showing CNN, and her face was there, a photograph I had never seen, her head covered in a scarf, her arms around two other girls, her face and her name, her very tanned face, shades darker than the girls on either side, women, I should say

She would always come back from camp so dark, the darkest of all of us by far

And then in a few weeks it would fade

Oh I wanted to say I want to bury you, here in the airport, here on TV, why should another minute go by

What would it even mean a burial a ceremony in an airport, by the Chanel counter, by the Guerlain counter, the Macallan counter, bury the television itself, not the image

Stone Age tribes in Africa when shown television believe the image to be inside the screen, there is no disidentification, every image must take a material form

How and where is that private burial where the image and the material are the same, how can you bury the news

In the Istanbul airport it made sense to me, we had all the materials, duty-free counters sell all the materials for a funeral—perfumes for the body, drink to be spilled on the ground, food for the offering, tobacco to be burned, another offering, Popeyes fried chicken for the wake

In the Istanbul airport it wasn't funny

I made my way back to the gate and Naomi wasn't there, she was at one of the credit-card pay phones they still had in those days, in 2003, speaking to Winter, making sure her flight was scheduled

I needed desperately to call the office I wouldn't call the office

Where the hell were you, she said, don't leave me alone like that

Don't leave me alone like that

I record this for posterity those were the words she said

/

"I just am trying to get a grasp of the situation," Mark said. "I'm sorry to have to ask. But tell me. As a friend. Just so I know. What the hell was she doing there, what was her intention. I have to be able to explain this to people."

"She was an international observer, a peace activist, working with other peace activists."

"That doesn't help. Everybody says they're a peace activist. I'm seeing stuff on the news, on emails, saying she was basically like a human shield, standing in front of IDF tanks. I want to be able to say they're full of shit. I really, really do. For everyone's sake, Sandy. I don't mean to be cavalier."

"I'm not accusing you of being cavalier."

"You're my friend. I can't imagine how this could have happened. I'm in shock. Margaret's in shock. We were crying at dinner. I was up at two in the morning, couldn't get back to sleep."

"That means a lot. Thank you. Thank you, Mark, as a friend."

"There's an emergency partners' meeting tomorrow. When you have the details, anything we can do, shiva, services, whatever, you tell me. But in the meantime. We have people lighting up the switchboards, clients, reporters, Senator Clinton's office, Schumer's people, of course, and I have to know what to tell them."

"Tell them she was an international observer, which basically means she took videos of everything that was happening. She was carrying a video camera. She was clearly identified as an observer, a volunteer, and they shot her in the heart in cold blood."

"Clarify who you mean by 'they.'"

"An IDF sniper, a soldier."

"It could have been an accident."

"Her friend, who lived in the village, who was also observing the protest, was also shot and killed. Next to her. Not five feet away."

"An Arab, you mean."

"The woman whose house she was staying in, who rented an apartment to the group, Soldiers for Peace. Heba. Twenty-nine years old, a mother of three. Who happened to be there also to witness the protest, the destruction of the olive trees."

"You know Jason Silver, from the ADL. Murray Silver's kid. He's the legislative subdirector or whatever they call him. I've introduced you."

"Right, I remember."

"I want to put you in touch with him right away. It's important to get out ahead of this thing, people calling her a sympathizer, that kind of nonsense."

"I don't know what that means."

"I think you do know what that means."

"Maybe this will come as a surprise to you, Mark, but there's a spectrum of opinions on the Israeli-Arab question, even among Jews, and Bering's position was to the left of you or me. That shouldn't have gotten her killed. If you're calling her a terrorist, if you're saying the ADL wants to call her a terrorist, just come out and fucking say it, so I can resign now and consider my legal options."

"Sandy. Sandy. Hold your fucking horses. No one's saying anything, at the moment. That's what I'm trying to get you to recognize."

"I'm going to be in touch with Clinton and Schumer myself, of course. And Carolyn Maloney. Or Jerry Nadler. I'm surprised Nadler hasn't reached out already. I was expecting a statement."

"I can tell you why. He's waiting. Everyone is waiting. This is an unprecedented situation. A U.S. citizen. A Jew. A New Yorker. In this predicament. It's like something out of another era, like the Weathermen bombing, the town house in the Village, or Lori Berenson, the girl in the Shining Path. Like that novel you gave me, *American Pastoral.*"

"She was holding a *video camera*, Mark."

"You don't have to tell me. You've told me. This is my line. I'm telling people, from now on, it's a tragedy that happened to a well-intentioned young lady, a personal friend, who thought she was committed to peace."

"I need you to back me up."

"I will back you up."

"We're going to ask, as a family, for a House resolution demanding a full investigation into the killing of an American citizen, a civilian noncombatant, an international observer."

/

Naomi stayed in bed, staring at the ceiling, while he showered and shaved, ironed his shirt, ironed his jacket. The room service breakfast came with an *International Herald Tribune* and a *Jerusalem Post*. Bering's picture, the same picture. Above the fold, on the right. Below the fold, on the left. Her head covered, wrapped in a kaffiyeh.

He opened the curtains. It seemed necessary to do things in order. After great pain, a formal feeling comes. He unscrewed the thermal pitcher and poured the coffee. He drank coffee. He drank juice. He wondered what kind of juice it was. He picked up the sugar packet and read the Hebrew word for sugar.

"I had a dream where I was lying on my back at the bottom of a well," she said.

"Floating on the water?"

"No. It must have been a dry well. I wasn't wet. That's the whole dream. I was lying on my back, looking up out of the well, and then I was looking down at myself lying in the well, and saying, to myself, Don't you want to get out of the well, and I answered myself, No I don't, I'm just fine, right here, I'm not going anywhere."

"There's the *Haaretz* columnist, Gideon somebody, coming at seven tomorrow. In his car. He's set up a meeting at Oz Lieberman's house."

"What meeting?"

"Peace and human rights people. And refuseniks, IDF conscientious objectors. Writers. Concerned Israelis. Knesset members. That's what his email said."

"You can go."

"What if I don't want to go alone."

"You and Winter and Patrick, I meant."

"What if I said I needed your moral support."

"You've never in your life needed my moral support."

"I've never been in a situation like this."

"But look at you," she said, "look at how prepared you are to handle it. I keep waiting for you to say, *I expect you to rise to the occasion,* or something, and you never do, you just keep on coping, that's your special talent. So you can go, in other words, you don't have to be obnoxious about it."

"I don't think it's good for anyone to lie in bed all day."

"I'm going to get up and go for a walk. Don't worry about me."

"You need someone with you."

"I do not. No one's going to recognize me. Just another American Jew, another tourist, getting lost. I fit in. This is my homeland, so they say. I'm supposed to fit in. You, who've never been called a kike once in your life, how would you know."

"You have no idea how much worse things could get."

"That's hilarious, Sandy."

"Just for my information, when have you ever been called a kike? Has that ever actually happened?"

"The word *kike* is a state of mind, a facial expression, my love. It doesn't need to be spoken out loud. Jason, god love him, he works in my lab, he's terrific, I love his flannel shirts—he's from West Virginia, he went to Ohio State, he's got a jaw that goes out to here, every time I open my mouth, he looks at me and thinks, *kike*."

"You've never said anything about it before."

"I don't make a habit of feeling aggrieved. In my everyday life. Here, on the other hand. What the hell else is there to do. Every block, every stone, that's a finger pointed at somebody."

"Very poetic, considering you haven't moved an inch."

"In Jerusalem Jews don't need a walking tour. Jerusalem is a state of mind."

1

1:1 The words of Naomi daughter of Herman, of Armonk in the land of Westchester. 1:2 To whom the word of the LORD came in the days of George W., president of America, in the third year of his reign, and to Ariel, prime minister of Israel, in the second year of his reign.

1:3 Then the word of the LORD came unto me, saying, 1:4 Before I formed your daughter in the belly I knew you, and before she came forth out of the womb I sanctified you; I ordained her to be a wayward child, servant of the LORD, and I ordained you a servant of the LORD, prophet unto the nations.

1:5 Then I said, I think you are mistaken and have switched our places, Lord GOD, because she's the loudmouth in the family, and has the gift of prophecy, though we usually just call it *bellyaching* or *Bering the Unbearable*—and 1:6 the LORD said unto me, I have ordained her to suffer the world directly and you indirectly, through her. This is my command.

1:7 And I replied to the LORD, and said, really our worldviews are just extremely different, and I have no business prophesying, at least on any subject you're interested in, because I don't believe in you, to begin with, and you don't understand basic climate dynamics.

1:8 Then the LORD put forth his hand, and touched my mouth. And the LORD said to me, Behold, I have put my words in your mouth.

1:9 See, I have this day set you over the nations and over the kingdoms, to root out, and to pull down, and to destroy, and to throw down, to build, and to plant.

1:10 And I was stricken with grief so that I no longer knew my own body or my living children's bodies. 1:11 In the city of Jerusalem I was stricken, and I wandered the streets, past the kosher pizza restaurants and the kosher outdoor cafés, the stores selling tchotchkes to Brazilian and Italian and Filipino and American tourists, past the beautiful parks and soccer fields, the trees dripping with water from a thousand sprinklers.

1:12 I looked everywhere, in the alleys and the parking lots, in the Old City, passing from one world to the next, passing all the checkpoints unnoticed, though I wasn't carrying my passport, 1:13 I am so clearly Naomi Schifrin from Armonk, and this city is so clearly open to me and made and maintained for me. I walked over all the stones made glossy by millions of footsteps, and I looked everywhere for my daughter and did not find her.

1:14 Until I could look no more, and then I bought a large bottle of mineral water and sat at a plastic table on Shadad Street. I must have looked flushed and exhausted, for the man who served me spoke in Arabic, then Hebrew, then English, asking me, Are you all right. He brought me wet paper towels for my forehead. I closed my eyes and rested.

1:15 And in my rest I dreamed I walked out of the gates of Jerusalem, and wandered through the land, taking giant steps, though I did not know where to. And in no time I reached the shores of the sea, the blue-red sea, the color of blood inside the body. I looked at the sea, and said, I know you. I know your temperature and salinity, I know your thermal densities and benthic layers, you are not mysterious to me as you are to these thong-wearing girls from Tel Aviv, who shield their eyes from your glitter at midday.

1:16 Come, sea, and swallow the land, I prayed to the LORD. I mean it. Let the sea swallow the land so no one can have it. Collapse the land under the waves, all of it, from the Dome of the Rock to Yad Vashem, from Nablus to Beersheva, clear to the banks of the Jordan, from the Golan to Gaza. Better that it disappear. Make it a flood without end, I said to the LORD, or rather, prepare yourself, the flood is coming, this is a courtesy notice.

1:17 I, who have been a prophet my entire working life. I, who have known it was coming. I, who said to my daughter more than once, When you're my age, the icebergs will have largely melted, the Arctic will have hot beaches in the summer, millions will be dying of famine every year, New York will flood every decade.

1:18 She will never be my age, and I sow your fields with salt, Israel, I drive your flocks into the ocean, I explode your arms factories and infect your websites with malware and viruses. 1:19 Israelis and Palestinians, yoga instructors and microbiologists, ice-cream dispensers and mobile phone salesmen, cellists and taxi drivers, as well as/who may also be murderers of children, I sweep you together into the sea, to die in one another's arms.

1:20 I spoke to the LORD directly, from my plastic chair in the shadow of a rack of T-shirts, in the shadow of the Church of the Flagellation, around the corner from the Via Dolorosa. I said, Here I am, in the center of your world. Here I am, a pilgrim. Do something to me. Do something with me. Give me a sign.

1:21 Then the LORD put forth his hand, and touched my mouth. And the LORD said to me, Be silent, you have cried out to Jerusalem.

1:22 I said, I have not even begun crying, no one has heard me.

1:23 The LORD said, The world is old, no one listens.

1:24 The LORD said, I belonged to the land, but not this land. I was an ancestral deity. I am tired. Mourn your dead, bury your dead alone, I will not be there.

1:25 I believed him, I walked back to my hotel. It didn't take long.

1:26 In the streets of Jerusalem, I felt my footsteps echoing, through time you are supposed to hear them echoing, the span of centuries, it's what everyone says, only no one is listening. No one is listening. As if you were never there.

/

Oz Lieberman's large apartment had high ceilings, teak furniture, and tropical plants. Balinese hand puppets, Rajasthani miniatures, kachina dolls. You could close your eyes and forget you were in Jerusalem. You could be in Berkeley, or Ann Arbor. Or the Upper West Side. Oz was a Sanskritist who taught at Hebrew University, Patrick knew his name. The peacenik of peaceniks, one of the founders of Soldiers for Peace. He'd been shot twice by settlers and walked with a cane.

Gideon, who'd picked them up and driven them, such a short distance they could have walked, was tall and had a full black beard. He was born in Milwaukee, he told them, his father was a surgical resident there, they'd only returned to Israel when he was a teenager. Hence the nasal accent, full of shiny consonants. The living room was full. Oz and Gideon led them from face-to-face, quick introductions, handshakes, a few embraces. The sense of recognition was overwhelming. These are the people I grew up with, Winter kept thinking, only in slightly darker shades and looser-fitting clothing. We could be in Miami, or Tucson. That observation must itself be a cliché. This is a transplanted room. This is another life. I could have had this life, they could have had my life. When we shake hands, that knowledge passes through our hands. She had changed clothes: her job-interview jacket, her best DVF blouse, suit pants, low heels. She felt more like herself, her current self, her new self. She was handling it. Yale Law, she actually said, a few times, my second year. She had her leather portfolio, a pad and a pen. She took notes. Patrick stared at her, no comment. Sandy didn't notice. "We're here to honor the Wilcoxes," Lieberman began, in a formal Oxford-English voice. "To share their grief."

Current political situation, shift conversation to IDF HR violations
    Likud strategy, de facto control of West Bank
    Settlers as proxy, paramilitary violence—chronic instability, consistent control & intervention
    (Gideon speaking) World's conscience, younger generation finds Pal oppression unacceptable
    B as symbol, no choice but to accept
    Wilcox fam will be embraced by Israeli activists & Pal partners
    Foundation, scholarship, funding opportunities
    Shift US-Israeli relationship toward HR

"Patrick and Winter and Sandy," Gideon finally said, turning to address them, "I don't know if there's anything you want to say. We certainly didn't expect you to come with a prepared speech. This meeting comes at an impossible time for you, but we know you won't be in Israel long. And who knows when or if you'll be able to return. It's very awkward, but that's the way it is here. Things happen on a very compressed schedule. Opportunities present themselves very seldom, if ever."

Patrick took a sip from his coffee cup, shaking the beaded necklace wrapped around his wrist. Sandy nodded, thin-lipped, and, Winter thought, was about to stand up—but no. He looked at her, unreadable.

She put down her own cup and wiped her hands on her pants.

"On behalf of all of us," she said, "thank you all for coming. It means so much to have your support."

"Speak louder," a woman said in the back of the room.

"I said *it means so much to have your support,*" she said. "We haven't had time to think about any of these issues, obviously, but I assure you that we want to honor Bering's memory in a way she would have intended. Our first priority is pursuing the legal case and securing justice for her. This comes next."

She looked at Sandy fiercely, as if commanding him to nod, and he did.

"Say something about who Bering Wilcox was," another woman said. "If you don't mind." She had a French accent. "We had never heard of her, of course. She was so young, there are many volunteers. The newspapers are saying, over and over, she was Jewish. Was she Jewish?"

"She was Jewish. She had a bat mitzvah. Our synagogue in New York is Beth Shalom, it's Reconstructionist. Dad isn't Jewish, and we have his last name. My mother's name is Schifrin."

A few mumbles, even a suppressed tittering. "Beit shalom," someone said, "what an irony."

"I think what Winter is trying to say," Gideon interposed, "is that the Wilcox family is Jewish but not religious, not keeping kosher or Shabbat." He said something else in Hebrew, a longer explanation, clearly, with a pained expression.

"She was a very passionate activist," Winter said. "She felt very close to the family she was living with in Wadi Aboud. She was learning Arabic, she was studying Middle East history in college. She felt a, a profound sense of responsibility."

"And why Israel in particular," an older man in a beret asked. "She felt responsible for Israel, as an American Jew?"

"Yes. But more than anything she wanted to understand it, to see it up close, I think."

"You're saying . . . ," the old man said. He mopped his forehead with a napkin. His face was mottled with liver spots, his syllables were German. He could have been in his seventies, eighties. Winter avoided the math. "And I don't mean this as an insult, I just want to understand you, she was still in college, she was studying, this was like a study-abroad program. Like an exchange student. I'm just trying to understand."

Patrick raised his hand. "I can answer that," he said. "Bering was interested in how people live with themselves."

"Go on, please. I'm listening."

He stood up. Close up, she could smell him: he'd been wearing the same hoodie for three days.

"She would have been fascinated by all of you, in this room," he said. "Which is so much like the rooms we grew up in in New York. Probably some of you are from New York, you know what I'm talking about. She would have wanted to ask you the same questions she always asked: how can people live comfortably, how can they enjoy their many creature comforts, and let's face it, there are so many of them, in a world like this? Particularly so very close to the face of the other. Pressed up close to the fence. That's what she said to me about Jerusalem: pressed up close to the fence, pretending it isn't there. She found it fascinating."

"People often do, young man," the man said, "when they visit for the first time, but that isn't the same as living here, living through the wars, the sirens, the bombs."

"Exactly as she would have said. But that's the double bind, isn't it. To come from elsewhere and be told you have no right to speak, but also you have no right to learn."

Shut the fuck up, Trick, she wanted to say.

"No one said she had no right to learn."

"I'm not criticizing you. I'm posing this as a philosophical problem, an existential problem, how people live intelligent, perceptive, acceptable lives, in situations of horror, terrible suffering, for which they are responsible just by existing, whether close or distantly. That's what Bering would have wanted. If you want a foundation, a scholarship fund, it has to address that question."

"Better to endow a university department of philosophy," the man said, or tried to say, but Gideon cut him off. The event was over. Expressions of gratitude, sympathy, apologies. Patrick remained standing but no one approached him; Winter shook all the hands, accepted business cards and pamphlets, an inscribed book. Sandy was speaking to Oz, who gripped him by the arm, hard. They were whispering urgently in one another's faces.

"I have to apologize for Moishe," Gideon said, driving them home. "For the tone of his questions."

"Those were perfectly valid questions," Sandy said. "I was glad he asked them."

She looked at him over her shoulder. He was folded uncomfortably next to Patrick in the backseat, the car was a Nissan compact. Inspecting his hands.

"Moishe is a throwback. He's done everything. Chaired the Communist Party, sat in the Knesset. He was imprisoned in the 1970s, accused of collaborating with the PFLP. He was close with Ghassan Kanafani, the great writer, who was killed by Mossad in Lebanon. Why he comes to these meetings I don't know. Everyone he knows is dead. His cause is dead, his Israel is dead. Unrecognizable. I think he just wants us to know we're all as hopeless as he ever was."

"But you don't believe him," Patrick said.

"If I believed him, I'd be sitting next to you on your plane back to New York."

"I'm not going back to New York," Patrick said, but they were already pulling up to the hotel entrance, Sandy reaching over his long knees.

/

Patrick had a friend from Stuyvesant, Matt Weiss. A sometime friend. Part of the same circle. Matt played bass in a ska band, Skanking Heads, and sometimes they asked Patrick to play keyboards; he brought his Korg to parties and filled in weird riffs, like Bernie Worrell in *Stop Making Sense*. He hadn't seen him since graduation, though he popped up every now and then in the Class Notes. And now Matthew Weiss was a reporter for NPR, based in Tel Aviv. He found a Hotmail address attached to some long group thread from back in college.

Hi Matt,
    It's Patrick Wilcox, I assume you've seen the news about my sister Bering, I'm in Jerusalem, the David Citadel Hotel, just wanted to reach out.

A minute later, he'd barely lifted his hands from the keyboard, the room phone rang. "I'm on my way," Matt said. "I'm in my car. Are you free in an hour? Meet me in the lobby."

"I can't give an interview," he said. "We're not speaking to the press officially. You may be wasting your time."

"I'm not here as a journalist," Matt said. "Tell me what I can do. Assume I can get you a meeting with just about anyone. What questions can I answer."

"I want to see where it happened. That's probably out of the question."

"Be in the lobby at five. Bring your passport and a big bottle of water."

"Why water?"

"It's a desert. People tend to forget that. Your skin dries out, you get thirstier than normal. Trust me."

He pulled up with a friend, Nasir, in the backseat. It all happens quickly, the novel takes quick breaths, no time to spare. Nasir was also a journalist, for *Kul al-Arab,* the Arab-Israeli newspaper. He'd volunteered to come, to help with translation. They handed him a styrofoam take-out container of fries and a shawarma rolled in foil. "We won't be able to stop and eat on the way," Matt said. "I don't want to get there in the dark."

"Thanks. I haven't been very hungry."

"Eat a few fries at least," Nasir said. "There's nothing worse than cold fries."

They stopped at a red light to let a stream of pedestrians pass. Old women with wire shopping carts; young Orthodox mothers in long skirts and head coverings pushing double strollers. Soldiers in full battle gear, both corners. A knot of teenage boys with skateboards in flannel shirts, their fringes peeking out underneath. Another mother in an abaya with three little boys in matching blue tracksuits.

"You've never been here before, right?" Matt pointed. "That's Zion Gate. The Western Wall, right behind it. This is Mount Zion. We go right around it. Beyond that, Abu Tor. Arab East Jerusalem. Beyond that, settlements. We'll be at the checkpoint in about fifteen minutes."

"It's too much to take in," Nasir said. "That's what I always feel, being in the middle of Jerusalem. Everywhere you look, you see a different world, a different century. It freaks me out."

"You couldn't pay me to live here," Matt said. "Of course NPR wants me to. I'm supposed to. I tried it, for six months. A Haredi guy threw a rock through my windshield because I was driving on Shabbos."

He was supposed to say something, and didn't. Something funny. Or a question. To buoy the conversation. Three guys in their twenties, a car smelling of cigarettes and fast food. So desperately did he want the world to return to that scale. I had opinions, he thought, I had views. Regardless of never having been here. It never stopped me before.

"Nasir," he said finally, "won't it be a problem with you, at the border. Are you allowed to pass."

"I'm an Israeli citizen, and I have a press card. Sometimes I get hassled a little. We'll see. Everyone knows *Kul al-Arab*, we're pretty moderate, politically, no one wants to fuck with us. I go back and forth often. My mother's family lives in Beit Jala, right over there, just on the other side of the line."

"But you grew up in Israel."

"In Akko, on the coast. It's a Palestinian city, almost entirely. Now I live near Tel Aviv. I'm a cultural reporter, mostly, I cover music and nightlife and food, not politics. I hate politics."

"Nasir went to college in Ottawa," Matt says. "He loves hockey. He loves the Tragically Hip. He's too good for this world. That's how we met, indirectly, because he was out in Tel Aviv watching a hockey game."

"What he means is, I was only a block away, two years ago, when the nightclub was bombed in Tel Aviv," Nasir said. "The one story like that I've ever covered. Because I was in the wrong place at the wrong time. It was the Dolphinarium, you must have heard of it, it was maybe the worst of the suicide bombings. Twenty people were killed. Teenage girls, waiting in line. I was there five minutes after the bomb went off. Matt thought I was a bystander, not a reporter, he started to interview me with his microphone. I have nightmares about that night, even now."

"You never told me that," Matt said.

"Maybe now isn't the time."

"Matt," he said, unable to keep silent a second longer. "Can I bum a cigarette."

He rolled down the window all the way as soon as it was lit. That first drag, the smell of dry grasses, something turned and curled in the sun. Rooftops and wires. Thin snaking streets, up and down the hills. Houses spilling over one another. High fences on either side of the road. Masses of construction equipment to their left, graders, backhoes, bulldozers.

"For the border wall," Nasir said. "They're building it right now. Big sections are already done. You'll see it, here and there. It still has that new-wall smell. That's a joke. I had to go interview some rappers in Dehesheh, the refugee camp in Bethlehem, they were already doing graffiti on it. You can see where it's burned by Molotovs. Guard towers, razor wire everywhere. It's a good backdrop. We took lots of pictures, you can see them online. Listen, Patrick, if you want me to shut up, just say so."

"No. Not at all. I'm just not going to keep up my end of the conversation."

Here, he was thinking, his thinking clarified suddenly by nicotine. Here is a problem with description slash representation. As in, how am I going to represent this in my mind. This journey. This journey in the bardo to where Bering died. To this place I will never return.

All of which is to say, unwilling to take up the task of comprehension, assimilation, at the speed of ordinary life, and then having it forced upon oneself in a state of trauma, of psychic overload, spiraling, grief, confusion, no signal-to-noise ratio, not even a gauge, like having to learn all of quantum entanglement in a single night, one of those nightmares where you have to take an exam but never took the class. There is no question of its being necessary, necessary alone, to go to the place where it happened, but not to remember it, necessarily, let alone represent it, not to act as a camera eye or an eye, that is not to act as a central consciousness or any consciousness, but to do the thing that cannot be represented or indeed be done in any logical sense, to embody something without knowing what something is. Borne along in my helplessness to do everything wrong correctly.

As they came to the bardo/checkpoint the wall appeared on the left side of the car, a cleared dirt field, a parking area, high fences closest to them and then the wall beyond it, made of concrete slabs joined together, each one maybe six feet wide, unmistakably a prefab structure, meant to move easily up and down hillsides. It made no difference at all what anyone thought of it. Like an Ikea bookcase. This, he thought, this is my great contribution to the discourse on borders and state sovereignty. An Ikea bookcase works fine as long as you put it up, fill it with books, stand it against a wall, and never try to move it, adjust it, or disassemble it. It has exactly one mode of usefulness. It's both disposable and, potentially, permanent. No one wants it, exactly, but for a certain period you can't live without it. And who can calculate, exactly, how long that period might be. It inspires no great feelings of loyalty. It's a placeholder, a marker of an intention to do better. At least not worse.

"I've been living in India," he said, and took a long swig from his water bottle, the taste of the cigarettes making him suddenly thirsty. "Up in the Himalayas. In a Buddhist monastery. Actually, I'm becoming a monk. I was. I am. But right now it's ninety-nine percent just studying, taking classes. Learning Tibetan, mostly."

"Now *that's* unexpected."

"I know. I haven't exactly been moving in a straight line."

"In a way, though, it makes perfect sense. I always figured you'd be running a hedge fund or living in a basement in Brooklyn learning the sitar."

"Those might still be valid options."

"I'm sorry if we seem a little casual," Matt said, lighting another cigarette with his free hand. "I can't imagine how horrible this is. As my friend. As an outsider, an American. I really mean that. I mean, if it were my brother, someone in my immediate family. *That* I've never experienced. But here I talk to people every day who've lost family members, who've seen people shot, blown up, tortured."

"Of course. I get it."

"I wish I could explain it, the feeling. You just really do feel insensitive, insensate, to the carnage after a while. It's like background noise, it's a kind of boredom, but guilty boredom. Because, after all, it's not me. I can still go around the corner and get a pizza with Nasir. I can still look at porn online. We're in year three, of course I haven't been here myself the whole time—"

"But he acts like an Israeli, he really does. His Hebrew is actually pretty good. He curses at stoplights like an Israeli. I predict he'll meet some nice girl and settle down, maybe get an apartment in Yafo, near the beach."

"God for-fucking-bid, Nasir, that's not even funny."

"You know what Israelis do when they get too stressed out? They go to India and learn yoga. You should go hang out with Patrick, take a vacation."

"That sounds more like it."

"That's the thing about living here, Patrick," Nasir says. "You should understand that much. So many people like the idea of living in Israel, or Palestine, for that matter, but when you press them, they're not willing to stay full-time. They want that passport, that residence card, whatever, they're willing to buy a condo, but they're keeping that other citizenship just in case, and if they're born here, they always reserve the right to leave. If they have the right to leave."

"But then," Matt says, "there are those that would give anything, have given anything, for the right to stay, permanently."

"Of course. Obviously. So what you've got are the part-timers and the full-timers, the escaping-to and escaping-from, the exiles and the expats, the importers-exporters, the theoretical citizens, the wishful thinkers, the open-air prisoners, in Gaza, in the refugee camps, still in Lebanon and Jordan, too, and then the zealots, who will set up a camper on a hilltop and act like they're Abraham, Joshua, and Moses. But where we're going, Wadi Aboud, it's an even more special case. The fellaheen. The villagers, the farmers. Those very few who have stayed on the land. In some places, you know, they still have olive trees that go back to Roman times, those trees essentially live forever. When I was a kid, visiting my mother's parents in Beit Jala, we used to drive out here and buy fresh olive oil, just pressed, in plastic Coke bottles. And za'atar, that's thyme. And sheep's-milk cheese, I don't know how to call it in English."

"Feta."

"No, it's not feta. Anyway. The fellaheen. The workers of the land. Not dispossessed. Not thrown out of anywhere. What the fuck do they know about Zionism, or the Holocaust, or for that matter the PLO, or these idiots who insist on calling it Samaria and saying King Solomon conquered this part and the Bible says the boundary's over here, it goes all the way to the Jordan. As if nothing else happened between 72 AD and 1949. These people, they're different, they still practice a lot of the old customs, they're like First Nations people in Canada. Indigenous. It's easy to get romantic about them, but their lives are hard. Even at the best of times."

"Right," he says, feeling he has to say something, at last.

"I read your sister's essay on metaphors, the one that was published in the *Guardian* yesterday? I was impressed. For an outsider, not speaking much Arabic, she really understood some things."

So then what is a human being? he asked Rinpoche once. In New York or at the monastery. In the assembly room or the tutoring room. Shortly after he started practicing. I'm still trying to get a handle on it, he said. The Heart Sutra says: Form is emptiness, emptiness is form. I understand this about matter. I understand it as an obvious principle of physics. I don't understand it about life. How am I simultaneously something and nothing. It seems to me, you either give credence to the illusion that a human being is a being, something that exists, has needs, is worthwhile, or you don't. Why should I care? Why should I care if there's nothing to care about, if there's no actual substance, no substrate, no continuum. This is an emotional black hole for me. I'm losing interest.

He doesn't remember exactly what Rinpoche said in reply. One of the standard responses, one he would, in a few years, give to students himself. A human being is made of five heaps, we say. Form. Feelings. Perceptions. Impulses. Consciousness. And how they cling together, like drops running down a window. The Buddhist theory of mind. Rinpoche took his time explaining it, politely, but imagine trying to explain psychoanalysis to someone who's never heard of Freud. *I'm losing interest,* he actually said, to a monk who'd been memorizing complex texts since the age of six.

When what he really wanted to know was: what will happen to everyone I know, including myself, when I actually tell the truth for once about my life. Will they decompose. What does a shattered person look like. Is it a return to constituent fragments, in other words, is it actually therapeutic to be shocked and have to recompose your illusion.

Bashir, his analyst in New York, had said absolutely not. He said, you have no idea how traumatic it would be for your parents to know, for Bering to know that they know, for Winter to know, even as a by-

stander, she failed to protect her sister. Or for her to deal with uncon-
scious feelings of envy. Or whatever it is, I won't speculate. The point
is, it's not your secret to tell.

This made no sense to him. Whose secret would it be to tell, he
asked Bashir, if not mine, mine and hers? What if I asked Bering for
permission, what if we came to an agreement to tell them together?
That would never happen. How do you know? Trust me. Trust me, the
psychoanalyst said. Full stop.

He said, this information is just information, it's relatively
inconsequential—and Bashir said, look at your family history, look at
what your mother withheld, and tell me information is inconsequential.

Let's zoom out a little. Here we are, ordinary human beings, ordinary human animals. Let's de-specialize. Let's not make a fetish of our
precious sensibilities. Incest is pretty ordinary. So is mistaken paternity.
If we were guinea pigs, or sheep, or goldfish—

This is beyond absurd, Bashir said, you know it's absurd—

Why can't we just get over ourselves and our preoccupations, that's
what I wonder. I mean, do we really have to cling to our little lives. Isn't
that the source of all our problems, fundamentally. Can't we just stop
clinging to these armatures, these dead cells.

Maybe you can, but you can't ask them to do that. You can't force
them to do that without permission.

"You should take a look at the map," Matt said. "It's in the glove
compartment. I use it every time I'm out here. B'Tselem, the human
rights group, makes it. They have to produce a new one every couple of
years. It's the only accurate map of the West Bank, the only one that
shows the true extent of the settlements, the area lines. Study the code
carefully, if you're not familiar with Areas A, B, and C."

"If it was an X-ray," Nasir said, "it would be a cancerous lung, or
a liver."

"You see how the blue areas are the settlements and military posts.
Talk to any old Israeli left-winger, the Peace Now people, and they'll

explain how the IDF seeded its own outposts all along the borders on the West Bank in '67. That was Shimon Peres's doing. The supposed peacemaker. He wanted to make it strategically impossible for Israel to ever give up the land. They'll tell you that there never was an occupation, just a future annexation. The whole discourse is wrong. According to that logic, there never was an ideological split between the military and the settlers; the settlers are just the inexorable flood that makes the military presence logical and necessary. Think about it that way, and all of the past six decades of Israeli-Palestinian history basically goes up in smoke. It's pure diversion, arguing about the wrong thing."

"Then what is the right thing?"

"The single state," Nasir said. "Full citizenship for Palestinians. Jews become a statistical minority protected by the constitution. Like South Africa after 1994."

"What Nasir means to say is, the single state is a pipe dream, no majority or even large minority of Israeli Jews would ever agree to it. If you want to know why Israel and Palestine are fucked, that's why, it's because the one thing they actually should be negotiating, no one wants to talk about, and the stuff they actually are 'negotiating,' in scare quotes, doesn't mean anything anyway. That's the very long story short. In other news, you can find Wadi Aboud on that map, it's not even marked on the official Israeli ones. It took me a second, when I heard the news, to remember where Wadi Aboud was."

"I'd never heard of it," Nasir said. "But I've only been south of Hebron twice in my life, both times with this guy. It's not someplace you go casually, unless you have family. The fellaheen tend to be private and suspicious of outsiders. And they should be. Israeli intelligence is everywhere. Frankly, it's easier to show up as an outsider. Though there are spies everywhere—among the journalists, in the peace groups, the visiting politicians. Israeli spies, Hamas, Iranians, Hezbollah, Saudis, Egyptians. That's who they were looking for, supposedly, according to the reports. I'm sure you saw that. Infiltrators using the protestors as shields."

A map is not a body, but then a body is not a body. You can't look at yourself whole. Think about metonymy, substitution. What is a map, after all. What is geography. The inscription of natural features. High places. Bodies of water. Areas of fertile soil. Deep or protected harbors. River valleys. Rift valleys. Tectonic activity. Fault lines. It's not an X-ray. A map is not history. A map is not the word *land,* as in, "The land of Canaan." No one used GPS. There was no surveying.

A sick map is not a sick country is not a sick body. The country is not a body, but then a body is not a body. First I went to psychoanalysis, he wanted to say, now I've gone to Buddhism, to answer the question of what it would mean if I actually told the truth. What would it mean for the two of us, for the five of us, for the *n* of us. It was an urgent question, but apparently not urgent enough, because I didn't answer it in time. If you read the second and eighth chapters of Nagarjuna's *Treatise on the Middle Way* and meditate for a long time, Rinpoche had told him, not two weeks ago, you will understand that actions are unfindable. Eventually you will also find that the person acting also does not exist. What appears to have inherent existence proves itself to be just the opposite: a product of causes and conditions. Okay, he said, but when you say, *meditate for a long time,* how long is a long time? Rinpoche just laughed. Do your three-year retreat, he said. Then you'll know what it means, a long time.

Israel, he wanted to say, holding the map, is an illusory entity, a transient collection, a product of causes and conditions. Was there ever a better way of putting it. You feel the precariousness of all definitions, all ways of fixing an object in view. When no one even agrees on the name of the thing. No wonder everyone reaches for it as a metaphor. We chose impossible questions that could never be answered, let alone answered in time. The novel does not let us answer questions, even the ones we ourselves have asked. I came too late. Do I feel validated, as a Buddhist? I get it now, as a Buddhist. I am invalidated. All my efforts are in vain. Care Bear, I should have come for you and told you it was okay, no matter what, it was still going to be okay. Am I allowed to think of you as my first lover, she asked him once, and he said, You can think whatever you want, just know that I still love you, no matter how you answer that question.

He opened his eyes when they turned off the bardo/highway into the bardo/village.

Concrete-block houses, stone houses. Ruined walls, empty lots. A half-finished foundation, the rebar still sticking out. Flowerpots ghostly under a single white streetlight. Posters, graffiti in Arabic and English. *This Is Free Palestine.* A long line of cars and trucks on one side of the street. Doors opening, light flaring. He rolls down the window to try to see the stars. "Wait here," Nasir said when the car stopped. "Don't get out until I tell you."

After a few minutes a door opened and a man leaned in and embraced him. His sweater smelling of sweat and cigarettes. "This is Omar," Nasir said. They staggered out of the car together, Omar never quite letting go of him. "Omar is Heba's husband." "Hello," Omar said, wiping his face. "Hello. Thank you. You are welcome." He put his arm around Patrick's shoulders and led him into the house.

He ate whatever was offered to him. Barely aware of the taste, at first. Reminding himself to chew. Rice and stewed vegetables, he couldn't say what they were, and lamb in a slightly sour sauce. Sumac. This was a lamb slaughtered for the funeral, Nasir said, it's a local tradition, I think. Shukran, shukran, he said. An older woman, her face very round under the abaya, touched his wrist and smiled, showing her gold molars.

Heba's children. He sat on the low couch and was introduced to them, one by one. Salaam, he said. Hello. Hello. Hello. Nasir sat next to him, knees touching, and did his best. There were at least twenty people in the room. Chattering and crying. Trays of tiny coffee cups passed around. The coffee doesn't have sugar in times of mourning, Nasir whispered, that's the custom. He sucked the grit between his teeth. Hello. Salaam. The kids were smiling, giggling, hiding behind their older sister. Nasir said, "They're saying you don't look very much like your sister, she was very pretty." Matt sat near the door, speaking earnestly in Hebrew with a young man in a Puma tracksuit and slicked-back hair.

"Heba's funeral was the day before yesterday," Nasir said, translating for Omar. "It was covered by Al Jazeera."

"Tell him I watched some of it online."

"He wants to take a picture with you."

"Of course, that's fine."

"Think about it. Make sure you're okay with it. It'll wind up online, in the newspapers. It's up to you. This visit can be completely off the record, you know, it's your choice."

"He's probably taking just as much of a risk as I am. If he thinks it's fine, I think it's fine. I can't believe this is even a question we have to ask."

After an hour—he checked his watch, as discreetly as he could, thinking about how long it would take them to get back, having no other awareness of time—an old man was introduced to him as El-Hajj, who gripped him by the hand, and it took a moment for him to realize it wasn't a handshake, it was an invitation to rise. "Now we're going to walk down to the fields," Nasir said, "the olive trees. If you're ready." They walked down the stony streets of the village, Matt offering cigarettes all around. Dogs padded softly after them. A quarter moon. The stars throbbed over them. Down a hillside, a faint path. "This is the way they take the sheep," Nasir said. This is where the sheep go. Have the sheep changed. Are they the same sheep. Has anyone done genetic studies of Palestinian sheep. Do the sheep go back as far as Abraham. El-Hajj said something to Nasir, and they both laughed. El-Hajj, wearing a long robe, he wished he knew the name, and the head covering, he wished he knew the name. You should at least know one name, the name of one object. He could hear a winding bass line, it took him a moment to place it. "Straight to Hell." It ain't Coca-Cola, it's rice. He wanted to mention that to Matt, knowing he would understand. Though he didn't understand.

I was here, following El-Hajj by the light of the stars to my sister's death.

"You have to be careful," Nasir said to him, translating, "there are settlers living just on the other side of the valley, they patrol at night."

Go straight to hell, boy.

El-Hajj had a flashlight dangling from a cord around his neck, a powerful spotting lamp, given to him by Soldiers for Peace. Blinding at a hundred yards. He switched it on and aimed it into the olive grove, the spindly branches and knotted trunks. "There," Nasir said. "They were right there. He's showing us. You can walk down, he'll stay here, pointing the lamp. Do you want me to come with you? Or Matt?"

"No, I'll go."

He counted his steps, for some reason. Thirty-four steps. A dog, which had followed them from the village, ducked in and out of the light beam. He couldn't turn back to face them, the light was too bright, it burned the back of his neck. "Am I in the right place?"

"That's it."

"Ask El-Hajj to turn the lamp off, please."

There was nothing to see. He closed his eyes, to let the retinas cool. He kneeled. He knelt. What is the verb. He put his face to the ground and sniffed. The absence of an object, the disintegratedness of the last moment. I am smelling time, he thought, I am inhaling pure time. This soil bears no analysis, it disintegrates. He didn't have anything that would hold it. So fine, feathering through his fingers. He scooped a handful and put it in his jeans pocket. I would give anything to be other than who I am. He stretched his arms out. What would she want me to say. Because her consciousness is still here, of course, that's why I feel calm. I could be so happy here, low to the ground.

"When the journey of my life has reached its end," he recited, the part he'd memorized on the plane. "And since no relatives go with me from this world, I wander in the bardo state alone, may the peaceful and wrathful buddhas send out the power of their compassion . . ."

That's it. That's all he remembers. He fell asleep in the back of the car and woke up at the hotel gates, face smeared with spit. Matt argued with the guards, two African-Israeli soldiers, Ethiopian Jews, that is, shining their lights in at him. Dangling grenades from their vests. Action figures, GI Joes. He shielded his eyes and held up his passport, just like he did at the checkpoint. Yehudi, he said, too loudly. He stumbled in under the lights, a drunk tourist getting out of a cab. No one in the lobby looked up.

/

On the fifth day they had breakfast in the hotel's inner courtyard, under a grape trellis. Able to manage, maybe, sort of, for the first time, the sideways looks, the discreet pointing, faces turned their way. Bering's picture wasn't on the front page of any of the papers, Patrick had checked that before coming down, though there were articles in *Haaretz* and the *Times of Israel,* plus the *Guardian* and the *New York Post:* "Wilcox Used as Human Shield for Killers, Spies Say."

He had 337 unread emails. Entreaties from reporters, mostly. Forwarded articles from friends. Random condolences, people he hadn't heard from in years.

"I got a call yesterday from Roger Waters," Winter said. "From Pink Floyd. He was very nice. He said to let him know if we need anything. I wanted to tell him how we used to dance around in our pajamas to 'Another Brick in the Wall,' it just didn't seem to be the moment."

In the center of her plate, Naomi had arranged a pyramid of melon balls. Cantaloupe, two or three unidentified yellow melons, watermelon, honeydew. With sprigs of mint and lemon slices. You couldn't help looking at it. Knowing a woman who rarely noticed what she put in her mouth. A waiter, a young woman who seemed to Patrick startlingly familiar, like so many faces in Jerusalem, set down a cappuccino in front of her and retreated.

"We have to issue a follow-up statement," Winter said. She and Patrick had collaborated on this language, with input from Matt. "It needs to say that Bering's death was a war crime and we intend to pursue justice in Israeli courts and by demanding an international investigation."

"Your father," Naomi said, forking a ball and squeezing lemon on it, "has decided that the Wilcox family is taking no further action."

Patrick turned toward Sandy; he wanted to fix Sandy in view. Starting from the top: his hair, now entirely silver, neatly parted. His widow's peak. A family trait. He would have one too, if he ever grew hair again. His forehead, with its light freckles, now becoming liver spots. His glasses. His knobby, too-long ears. No one had inherited those, thank god. His *complexion*. A word no one uses anymore. Euphemism, what is beautiful to hear. How did you manage to turn the world, he wanted to know, so that you are still the center of it.

"Listen," Sandy said. "I want to explain myself. I don't think Bering was really here as a political person. If we turn her into a cause, that's all she'll be, a symbol, a football. Her whole interest in being here transcends that. I, for one, am not ready to get ensnared in Palestinian politics. I don't have a handle on it. And those will be our allies, like it or not. Not the Israeli human rights people, who we can understand, who will listen to us, but the Palestinians, who are already making her into a martyr."

Winter took an orange from the centerpiece, maybe an orange not designed to be eaten, like the lulav and etrog during Sukkot, who knows, and peeled it. There has to be a word for predictability in human personalities, that mirror that makes a family portrait, a fixed resemblance. This is a family portrait, you could stumble on it in the Met, in the long European galleries where all the paintings blur together, how boring Europe was, in the sixteenth to eighteenth centuries, how dreary, all those fleshy aristocrats, obscure nymphs, milkmaids lit by tapers. In this portrait the father presides, the son glances his way, a look of muted fury, the mother holds a fork up to the light, the daughter peels an orange. Did they have oranges? She could be doing needlepoint instead. In the portrait the absent child is represented by a locket or cloisonné brooch, even a lock of hair preserved under glass.

"Dad," she said, "we literally cannot do that, we cannot withdraw from the scene, having come here. Everyone is waiting for us to make a statement. We have a role to play. Bering didn't die alone. We have leverage, Heba Ta'qim's family does not. They didn't do anything wrong. They're farmers and herders, they just want their land, they want to be left alone."

"Which is another way of saying we don't really belong here at all, we're interlopers, and we won't suffer the consequences of whatever comes next. We can't protect Heba's family. But we can and must consider the *other* consequences, American consequences, since that's who we are, starting with me resigning from Fein Lewin. I've already drafted the letter."

"That's absurd. No one would expect that."

"Either that or I'm tied up in ten years of litigation after they fire me. You have no idea what a liability I am, just sitting here."

"I think," Naomi said, "the children have a right to know why you would describe yourself as 'a liability,' with Bering not even buried yet. A liability because you can't side with Palestinians, even by implication."

Whose point of view does the story rest on now? Naomi is thinking about the well. The muddy bottom of the well, the mud in her hair. I will shave my head, she's thinking. A grieving mother shaves her head, it happens in Italian postwar films all the time, she took a class on it in college. Or was it the Vichy collaborators who had their heads shaved, that could be what she's thinking of. They had extraordinary dark circles under their eyes, accentuated by the cinematography, of course. You couldn't achieve that effect ordinarily, no matter how little you slept.

An Oxford shirt. An Oxford collar. Has Sandy ever worn, in public, a collarless shirt. Even in Maine, even at the beach, button-downs and polos. She opens her mouth. "Consider the fact," she said to her children, "you have a handsome father. He's so tall, he's like a ladder, like a ladder-back chair. He has great posture. He has a great forehead. He's so quiet, he has authority. You can tell he doesn't give a shit what anyone thinks."

"Fuck you, Naomi."

"It's not that you're wrong," she said, "exactly not that, I'm not questioning your assessment of the trouble we'll be in, the places we'll be expelled from, the friends who will stop talking to us, no doubt this is all true, it's the absolute certainty with which you express yourself, that has us all questioning your right to call yourself human."

"This is exactly why we can't, all of a sudden, pivot, as a family," he says, "and turn into activists, and sail the seas of outrage for the rest of our lives. We don't have it in us."

"Speak for yourself," Winter says.

"That is exactly the problem. I can't. I'm not able to take part in this, this festival of rage."

Rage, she wants to say, you know nothing about rage, just like you know nothing about chemistry, or the physical properties of materials. There is a crucible in the mind. Pour the rage out, let it cool, under the right circumstances, and it stretches, becomes ductile, becomes thread, I will sew my clothes with that thread.

"And you? Mom?" Winter asks. "Any more thoughts?"

"I can't override him. He's the lawyer."

"You've got to be fucking kidding me."

"None of you want to hear this," Sandy said, "but here's how I want to put it in our statement. 'Bering's life was singular. We want to preserve the memory of how she lived, not how she died.'"

"It's inexcusable," Winter said. "Count me out. I'll make my own case. I'll move here, if I have to."

"Then the story is going to become about a schism in the family, it's going to magnify everything you don't want to talk about, and make you a target twice over."

"Forget it, Win," Patrick said. "You have to go back to law school."

"I know that perfectly well."

"Don't be an overachiever. He's won. Go on with your life."

"It's not about winning," Sandy said.

"You've convinced yourself of that, yes."

He fixed Sandy in view. He fixed Naomi in view. These wrathful entities, beasts of Mara. He would keep them in his field of vision until they reached their perfected forms. This was also a question of scale. What does Bering deserve: to be larger than this small world. She has passed through this bardo. In this sense Sandy was entirely right. He wished he could tell him that, without giving him any satisfaction. The transformation had to be on a different scale. I will never see any of you again, he wished he could say, and that's fine, that's how she would have wanted it, but he didn't want to give himself the satisfaction.

"We're supposed to be shattered," Winter said, speaking only to Patrick. "We're not supposed to *go on*. What, we come to Jerusalem, quietly collect our sister's body, and fucking leave?"

It should have been possible to see the other diners, at other tables, but on the periphery she could see only white: the hotel staff, the waiters, had clustered around the table, she would not look up at their faces, they were listening. Or they were shielding them, a protective cordon. For whose benefit. The manager had told them to. She still thinks of it often. Murmurs of Russian, Amharic, Azeri. Migrant voices. Here too. This is a different kind of picture. "I have to go to the bathroom," she said. Not a lie. She had to pee and she might vomit again. Their faces looked at her, finally, these others, their faces made way.

\

From: "Patrick Wilcox" <dharmaboy@yahoo.com>
Date: March 22 2003 at 06:08 IST [GMT+3]
To: "Naomi Schifrin Wilcox" < nwilcox4@columbia.edu>, "Sandy Wilcox"
<alexander.wilcox@feinlewinllp.com>, "Winter Wilcox" <winter.wilcox@yale.
edu>
Subject: contact info

There is free Wi-Fi here at the airport so I'm writing before I get on the
plane.

I wasn't able to explain my future plans to you, and I don't know
when I'll have another opportunity.

I will be entering the traditional three-year retreat in July. This means
I will be in meditation and study intensively at Dawa Ling in Nepal, with
no outside contact, no breaks or time off, until July 2006. I will not be
answering emails and will probably deactivate this account.

The policy of the monastery (and my teacher, Karma Tsedrup
Rinpoche, I've told you his name but I'm sure you've forgotten it) is that if
there is a family emergency, i.e. the death of another family member, you
can send an email to info@dawamonastery.org and they will notify me.
Likewise, if I get sick or die while on retreat, they have your emails.

If this is the last email you ever receive from me, I'm sorry. Or am I?
I wish I had the energy to say more. I don't have the time to draw up an
official will, so, Dad, I'll just say please give my Bubbe/Zayde trust, and
whatever other inheritance there is, to B'Tselem, the human rights NGO
in Israel. Winter, make sure he does it.

This was my plan before Bering died. She knew about it and
encouraged me to go. It has nothing to do with the timing or nature of
her death. Only in the sense that I'm not changing it. Don't think I have
nothing more to say to you. I'm saying it. Every day, for the next three
years, I'll still be saying it.

ARRIVALS

"I went to Maine once," Shannon tells Tonya. She's holding up her phone to take a picture as they pass over the bridge into Ellsworth. "To Acadia. I think I was eight. Maybe nine. We drove all the way from Wilkes-Barre. I don't remember it very well. Mountains, cliffs, ocean. That was the coldest water I'd ever swum in. I didn't understand that Maine wasn't the same as the Jersey shore. I just plunged all the way in, not testing it with my toe. It was like fire."

"Duly noted."

"And I remember my parents couldn't figure out what the big deal was with Maine lobsters. I mean, they serve lobster in the restaurant every day, in season. With black bean sauce. Sichuan style. Ginger and scallion. We went in and ordered at one of those places, and when they just brought it out, boiled whole in the shell, with a little cup of melted butter, my dad looked so horrified. That I remember."

"I've never had lobster. It's not a thing in California."

"I think it's a thing everywhere."

"Not like this, though."

"Well, you should try it. You should try everything once."

"That's why I'm here."

"White people: a trial run. Before Vassar. It's not a bad idea, honestly. I mean, I'm from Wilkes-Barre, I had my whole life to prepare."

"When I met you," Tonya says, "remember? In Bunk Two? Remember what you asked me?"

"What size tampons you'd brought."

"After that. You asked how many Chinese kids went to my school."

"And when you said, at least a third of my school is Chinese, my next door neighbor is Chinese, my best friend is Chinese, I almost started crying."

"No, you *did* start crying. And you said, you're probably more Chinese than me. I thought that was the weirdest thing anyone had ever said to me."

"I was just so happy to have a friend, that's all."

A tall, gaunt man with a shaved head, holding the hand of a tiny blond boy in a green raincoat. His eyes follow the bus as it pulls up. *Ellsworth City Hall,* the sign says. No one else is waiting. Three short brown men, the only other passengers, disembark from the rear door, carrying lunch bags and yellow construction helmets. "Hey there," he says, climbing the steps, ducking instinctively, as if he's used to banging his head on things. "You must be Tonya. I'm your cousin Patrick. Let me help you, hand me a bag."

Make a lump of pie dough, wrap it in plastic, leave it in the fridge for a week, and it turns gray. You pick it up and wonder what it is. Is it cheese, maybe. Play-Doh or clay. An unhealthy color. A color of neglect. Have I ever, she's wondering, seen a human being the color of clay. A pure product of the earth. In Introduction to Fairy Tales Professor Fleischner assigned them Sholem Aleichem and Isaac Bashevis Singer, but now she can't remember the difference between a golem and a dybbuk. Which one is it, the one the rabbi makes out of clay, sort of like a cross between God and Dr. Frankenstein. It would be impressive if she could refer to the right one, in a family of Jews. But not worth the risk of getting it wrong. Shannon, it turns out, took two semesters of German in high school; she's sending Mathias into peals of laughter in the backseat, making him name all the parts of the body.

"Patrick," she asks, "how long have you lived in Berlin?"

"Since 2013."

"Naomi said something about how you were a Buddhist monk in India."

"I was a monk, a Tibetan Buddhist monk, for ten years. In that time I moved around quite a bit, different monasteries and colleges. Have you been to India?"

"I've always wanted to go. My parents went when I was little, separate trips, as medical volunteers, but they weren't allowed to take family."

"They're both doctors, Winter told me that."

"Mom's a pediatrician, she practices near our house in Pasadena. Dad's a dermatologist, he works at USC."

She doesn't know where to put her hands. Unused to riding in the passenger seat with a stranger. Ordinarily, at home, she would kick off her sandals and sit cross-legged, even put her feet on the dashboard. The prerogative of short people everywhere. Shotgun is where you make yourself comfortable, take up space. Do the hands go folded in the lap, crossed over the seat belt.

"This must feel unbelievably awkward, coming as the sole representative of the family," he says. "I'm very glad you're here."

"It sounds like there's a 'but' in there somewhere."

"The one thing I would say, I guess, the thing to keep in mind, is we haven't seen each other, we haven't been together as a family ourselves, in the same place, in years. More than a decade. So the whole thing is awkward. Which has nothing to do with you. I'm entirely in favor of your being here. I wish Mom hadn't kept it a secret all these years. I was extremely upset, to put it mildly, when she told us. Just don't be surprised if the whole thing feels as if we're all meeting for the first time, sort of."

"I can't," she says, "I just can't imagine what it would be like to be you, walking into a party at our house. It would be horrible and funny. So I'm prepared, I guess, at least in theory. That's why I brought a friend."

"I'm just here for the lobster," Shannon says. "And to find out what the deal is with Maine."

"What do you mean?"

"Why do people like it here? It rains all the time, the beaches are rocky, the water's too cold. There's mayo in everything. Even the blue-berries are the wrong size."

"We've been coming to Blue Hill every August since I was younger than Mathias," he says. "It's just in our family DNA, it's our happy place, I guess. So to speak. I assume that's why Winter wanted to schlep all the way up here. We always assumed that we would get married here. We talked about it, as kids. Which I know is the whitest possible answer: *we've always done it this way.*"

"Well," Tonya says, weirdly feeling like she's being asked to take some kind of bait, enter into a meta-discourse she doesn't want, "every-one has to go on vacation somewhere."

"Oh come on, Tonya," Shannon says. "Maine is where whiteness goes to die. It's one cliché after another. I feel like it's like a secret club; you only get it if you belong, if you have, like, a sailboat, and a private island."

"I'm from California," she says. "I don't have any of this baggage. I've never owned anything from L.L.Bean in my entire life. So I'm keeping an open mind, thank you very much."

"My personal favorite thing?" Patrick says. "Go out to Schoodic Point at dawn. It's about an hour's drive from Blue Hill, so you have to get up at about four. At least four. It's the easternmost point in North America. Or at least the U.S. Go out on the rocks and watch the sun breaking over the Western Hemisphere."

His phone makes a *ding ding ding* alert sound. He takes it out of his pocket, glances at it, puts it away.

"Someone trying to reach you?"

"No, it's a reminder I have set up. I have a condition where I have to eat at certain times. Like diabetes."

"Oh."

There's a home video she's seen, in digitized form, of Grandpa John teaching Mom to play catch in their driveway, sometime in the mid-1970s. Side by side, could there be a resemblance between them. Would anyone ever say, looking at Patrick, that man has a Black grandfather. Nature or nurture. Why even ask the question.

Her freshman writing class was called Black Genealogies. This was everything they talked about: what does it mean for a Black family to be called a family. When the whole point of chattel slavery was to turn babies into commodities and Black couples into breeding machines. Children stripped from their mothers like calves or chicks or lambs. No names, no languages, no paternal lines. They talked about *Roots* and *Beloved* and the Moynihan Report, Hortense Spillers and Alice Walker and Randall Kennedy. The final paper was a family history. She wrote, *I locate my family's shame over our "unknown relatives," the Wilcoxes, in the fact that my grandfather didn't (he himself admitted) fall in love with a white woman. He just had sex with her once. It was what is now called a hookup. This is a common occurrence and always has been, but because it evokes the stereotypes of the Black man's desire for sexual conquest of the white woman he punished himself by feeling guilty and passing on that guilt to the rest of us. According to Merton (2003), "Denied or unstated paternity is a form of inherited trauma, both for children who cannot locate their parents, and for children who grow up not knowing their siblings, or even knowing that they have siblings."*

"Winter told me you're transferring from Howard to Vassar. That's got to be a huge change."

"I went to Howard because my dad went there," she says. "Simple as that. To him, Howard is college. I knew the minute I got there it wasn't for me. Too cliquey. Too many clubs, too many sororities. Too *upwardly mobile*. Too in love with itself. I'm kind of an introvert. I like watching movies and folding laundry. It takes me hours to write an essay, I'm a perfectionist. I had a bio professor who kept getting mad at me because I spent way too much time in lab, doing every experiment three times. I just got absorbed in every problem. And she finally hauled me into her office and said, you don't belong here. You should transfer, you should find a SLAC. I said, what the hell is a slack. A small liberal arts college. So that was it. She gave me a list of twenty places, I applied to almost all of them, and financial aid–wise it came down to either Vassar or Pomona. There was no way I was going to Pomona, it's fifteen minutes from my house. Priority number one for me in college is getting the hell away from southern California."

"You strike me as more of an East Coast person."

"Thank you for saying that. I never want to leave. Even with the crappy weather. That's why I'm curious about Maine. East Coast people seem to love it here."

"It even says so on the license plates," Shannon says. *"Maine: Better Than the Alternative."*

"We managed to rent two houses next to each other," he says. "It turned out to be a big group. Unexpectedly. You and Shannon. Me and Mathias. Sandy, that's my dad. Winter and Zeno. Naomi, my mom, and her new partner, Tilda. Lourdes, that's Winter's maid of honor, and her husband, Sami. Zeno's dad, Victor. He came all the way from Chiapas."

"And here I was thinking the wedding might not happen at all."

"When you're not even sure if the groom is going to make it alive, you've got an unstable situation, that's for sure. At least it encourages people to show up."

"I had no idea your mother had a partner, that your parents were separated."

"Another very recent development."

"I hope they're registered somewhere. I had no idea what to bring."

"No gifts. Just donations to Zeno's defense fund."

"That seems just sad, though, doesn't it? A wedding should be happy. One hundred percent happy."

"I like your thinking. You should absolutely buy them something. But I can't imagine what. I'm not much of a housewares guy."

"You could get them, like, a set of towels with lobsters on them," Shannon says. "Or a scented candle."

"I said happy," she says, "not tacky as hell. Patrick, are they into cooking?"

"Zeno is. Winter used to make a lot of watery soups with tofu and carrots, back when we were all vegetarians. I don't think she's progressed much beyond that stage."

"I'll get them an omelet pan."

"O-kay," Shannon says slowly. "That's random."

"My grandfather was kind of obsessed with omelets. It was basically the only thing he knew how to make really well. We would go over to his house on Sundays and he would make us omelets for lunch. I should give them his pan, actually. We never use it."

"A fifty-year-old pan."

"Heirlooms make the best gifts."

"Someday," Patrick says, "not today, not this weekend, I wish you could tell me a little bit about him."

Here it comes, and still she isn't ready. How can that be. Persona non grata, she said to Mom, I'm not there to represent him, I don't even want his name to come up, that's so not the point. I'm not in a position to explain his choices. I'm going to make that clear right off the bat. It's not about the past, I think we all understand that. On the other hand, in towns like this, everything smells like history. It's just all there. In New York City, she read somewhere, there's a place you can go, a city park, where there are still mounds of oyster shells left by the Lenape. All these deep ancestral textures. Mottled, marbled skies, a sky like a plinth, an obelisk. You see these gaunt old men with cheekbones that probably go back to the *Speedwell*. And the long names, like Obawonkiplonk. Wiscasset. Kennebunkport. Agawam. You just want to say something about the past, otherwise what is there to talk about. What's the connection. California people, she wants to say, irrelevantly, go back to the Spanish, the missions. We're basically essentially Spanish. That's our reference point for *old* in the landscape. Flyover people, Midwesterners, Westerners, go back to the pioneers in their log cabins. Only here do people really go back to England, to the thirteen colonies. You feel the Pilgrims coming straight up on the shore, their buckled boots in the sand.

But she has to say something, so she says, "God, I'm not sure what I could really say. Other than I miss him. I mean, he had a position, he had his reasons for hanging back when your mom contacted him. But only he could explain it. I definitely couldn't. Have you ever seen a picture of Grandpa John?"

"Never."

"I'll text you a bunch of pictures. That's a good place to start. You can see a lot just from looking at his face. When I was little, I asked him if he was a million years old, and he said, yes, basically. His hands always smelled like chemicals, and I thought he was a mad scientist, inventing crazy things in his lab. Then I learned it was just the soap he used at home. See, there I am, free-associating. I can't come up with a single useful sentence."

"I guess if you start from absolute zero, everything has to help."

"I'll tell you something else and then we have to move on to another subject or I'm going to start crying. He couldn't tell jokes. My mom says the same thing. He just could never come up with anything that would make people laugh. Not that he had no sense of humor; he liked *my* jokes. He just never told any. One time, he said, the problem is, I just don't think anything is really that funny. And I think I actually agree with him."

"You do."

"I'm a lighthearted person, maybe you've noticed. But that's different. Comedy is tragedy plus time, right? It's like I fall on one side of the spectrum and he was on the other side, but it's still a spectrum. If you have a good memory, nothing is ever all that funny."

/

Victor's right there, at the curb, under the sign that says *NO STOP-PING NO STANDING:* short and painfully thin, face shadowed by a Panama hat, reaching up to wave with an old's man hand, a hand like a claw. In a green linen blazer and white linen trousers. A plasticky red suitcase from about 1983, and a leather satchel, an actual satchel. And a bag from duty-free. They shake hands, in front of the Audi's open trunk, Sandy wondering if they should embrace instead. "Pleased to make your acquaintance," Victor says. He enunciates very precisely. Like a minor diplomat, a European functionary, in a movie from the fifties.

"You didn't have any trouble at customs?"

"I was fingerprinted," he says. "With lasers. That was all. And a couple of questions. I told them I've come to visit my sister. That's the treatment an EU passport buys you. I'm assumed to be neither a migrant nor a terrorist."

"You must be exhausted."

"I thought I would be. I was visiting Zeno's brother Nestor in Mexico City these past few days. Sleeping on a couch. But then I fell asleep on the airplane, and now I feel almost refreshed."

"Zeno was telling me it's been a long time since you traveled outside Mexico."

"A very long time. Decades."

With bent fingers, making an effort, Victor adjusts the A/C vent, tilts the seat slightly, crosses his legs. They're making their way smoothly away from Logan, exit after exit, the traffic murmuring. The flat glassy Boston summer light.

"If you're hungry, we can stop anytime."

"Thank you. I'm almost never hungry. But if you'd like to stop, by all means. It's very kind of you, to come all the way to pick me up."

He wants to ask, where did you learn English. How did you learn to speak it that way. The most obvious, patronizing question. But there must be a history behind it. The way he passed it down to Zeno. Victor sits folded in the seat with his hat in his lap, drawn up into himself, perfectly contained. A black-and-chrome pickup barrels past them from the right, coming off an exit ramp, with a sticker covering the back window:

TRUMP
HE'S GOT BALLS

There are, yes, a pair of red plastic balls dangling from the trailer hitch. Sandy wants to point, laugh, shake his head, say anything at all, like *Welcome to America*, but there's no way to know how that would sound. They've just met; their conversation hasn't found its level, if there is a level. And then the truck is gone; it dissipates, like a fart, before he can be sure Victor even noticed it.

"What is there to talk about," Victor says. "Two old men, in a car, hurtling through New England on a summer evening. Though I should warn you, I suffer from narcolepsy. I could fall asleep at any moment. Don't take it personally."

"Zeno told me you've only been to the U.S. once, in 1979, when Castro visited New York."

"In the flesh, only once. But I've read American books all my life. Zane Grey. Theodore Dreiser. Willa Cather. Faulkner, of course. Kerouac. Allen Ginsberg. He was very popular in Mexico City when I was young. 'America, go fuck yourself with your atom bomb.'"

Up the ramp onto 95, the great artery. Clots of traffic, eighteen-wheelers in the left lane, minivans bearing thickets of bikes on their rear bumpers. To Portsmouth. To Portland. He checks the time on his phone, now attached to a bracket on the dashboard. Four hours and fifteen minutes. A rain of texts, one every few seconds, none of which he can follow. He's been added to all the groups but doesn't recognize any of the numbers.

He looks across at Victor, who has indeed fallen asleep, tilted against the headrest. And for some reason thinks of Dallas Goodyear. What's the connection? A person who falls into your life from some other galaxy, someone who ought not to be real. Which is not a judgment on the real so much as a testament to how boring you've let your life become. This was true in the seventies and it's true now. How turgid and boring, how narrow the grooves of my mind. And I could feel it happening, and did nothing. The thickness of my tongue, the grooves of my mind. The thickness of my tongue. And I could feel it happening, and did nothing.

"The night before last," Victor says, waking up with a heavy sigh, "I had dinner with a woman, while in Mexico City. Pilar. Pilar Castañeda Contreras. I was in love with her when I was seventeen."

"You hadn't seen her since then?"

"I saw her at her husband's funeral, twenty years ago. They were good friends of mine in university. Then when I went to Spain for my doctorate we fell out of touch. I called her, on a whim. I was curious. For all I knew she was dead too."

"They're always strange, these encounters at our age. I've had plenty of them. You see how old you've become."

"Pilar looks just like her mother did forty years ago. She wears all her jewelry, as if concerned the maids will steal it when she leaves the house. Whereas when I knew her, fifty years ago, she was a Trotskyite and an excellent poet. And Bernardo was a Maoist. I was neither, I was a skeptic. They used to get into the most violent arguments, that's how they fell in love. I asked her if I she still wrote poetry, and she looked at me as if I had asked her if she still makes porn movies."

"I remember the Trotskyites and the Maoists. We had them both at Oberlin."

"And what were you?"

"I think I claimed I was a Christian pacifist."

"That isn't a political position."

"It was in Ohio in 1971."

"Ohio is where the Kent State massacre happened, isn't it?"

"I was there, actually," he says. "Or nearly there. With a whole contingent from Oberlin. It was all chaos, roadblocks, ambulances, soldiers and police—they forced us to turn our car around, we couldn't get anywhere near the campus. So we just sat there, pulled over next to a cornfield, and listened to the news on the radio."

"I have it now," Victor says. "I have a picture in my mind. And now I want to put a picture in your mind. I don't know if it's possible, since you've never been to Mexico City. Just imagine a big city street, honking buses, taxis, motorbikes, dust everywhere, and gunfire, a totally chaotic scene, young students, teenagers, protestors, running straight through the traffic, pursued by cops and paramilitaries. They shot straight through the cars and the buses, so there was glass everywhere. Glass and smoke. I hid in a Chinese antiques store. The owners had barricaded themselves in the basement, but the doors of the store were still open, so I got underneath a fountain, or a fish tank, all the way at the back of the store, and lay there. The explosions outside were so loud the fountain splashed me, I was soaking wet. El Halconazo, or the Corpus Christi massacre, I think it's sometimes called. In 1971. I experienced it for all of five minutes. Hiding in the shop, I was so terrified I fell asleep. I lay there for hours, and then finally when I woke up everyone was gone. It was the middle of the night, all the windows of the shop had been broken, but I was unharmed. So I walked home, soaked with the water from the fountain. My parents were convinced I was dead. They'd sent their driver to search the city morgue and the hospitals."

Sandy's eyes are tearing up; it's the dry refrigerated air, the vents blowing in his face. Normally he has to keep them that way, so he won't fall asleep, lulled by a German engine. Dry air, dry thoughts. What a ridiculous conversation for us to be having, he wants to say. Given our actual lives, our actual losses. As if we have to prove our bona fides, documentary voice-overs. On the other hand, what other conversation should we have, since we're trying to be neutral. Father of the groom, father of the bride. We who have lived long enough to be bystanders. Should we talk about ICE detention, the relative merits of forced or voluntary deportation. He wants to say something about history, and repetition, and Dallas Goodyear, but he doesn't have the language. He asks the novel for help, but nothing helps him.

This is what he wants to say, as stupidly as a man waking from a forty-year dream. Are you a white man. Victor. Are there white Mexicans. Do you recognize me. Can you help.

What role was I supposed to play?

"I have a theory that we're the last generation who can say certain words seriously, unironically," Victor says. "Like *Trotskyite*. Or *poetry*. We're space oddities, like the David Bowie song. Those of us who prefer to remember. I asked Pilar about that day, she was there too, of course, and Bernardo was arrested not long after, and tortured. She said, it's ancient history, it's like talking about who killed who in the Conquest. She took out her phone and wanted to show me pictures of a new summer house she's building with her son in Amalfi. I don't begrudge her any of it. She really was brilliant, though. It occurred to me later that she and Bernardo probably did a lot of cocaine in the eighties; maybe that burned all her memories away. I had the advantage of living in a sleepy provincial town where no one could afford it; cocaine just passed by us, quite literally."

"You sound like you're writing a book."

"As a matter of fact I am, but not about that. The book I'm writing is a based on a manuscript I once read. It's a historical myth that may be true. There was once a slave revolt in the Caribbean, in the early eighteenth century, that was so widespread and well organized it actually reached England, where it was defeated. It was a counterattack from the Western hemisphere. I'm calling it *The New Earth*."

"I've never read about that."

"That's because it's a very closely guarded secret. Or, more likely, as I say, a myth. It's a tribute to Esperanza, of course. My late wife, Zeno's mother, I'm sure you've heard a little about her."

And with that Victor falls asleep again.

I will come back here, to the place where I've swallowed all the poisons and survived. That was nothing, that was a bad trip. What is survival, at any rate? A sour taste in his mouth, like bile, but less bitter, more subtle and generalized. A sub-taste. A sensory field you first pick up with your taste buds. You could carry it around for weeks and not notice it. And it's been months of intense forgetting, psychic redirection, so forgive him if it takes a minute to recognize it, the taste of death, correction, the taste of wanting to die, the sureness of life sliding toward its limit, I had a plan, I had a date and time, I had an appointment. Oh, happy death. He can hardly feel his hands on the steering wheel. I had it and I threw it away. It hurts. Oh God, he says to the air, why am I here, in this life after life. The novel tries to hold him but he's learned not to leave his hands by his sides. All those mornings, the weeks of counting down, waking up with one thought, it was as if death was a glowing orb, warm and reaching out for him. I want you and you only, I want to be dissolved, unreversed, out of time, I want nothing, nothing, nothing but union.

"The striking thing to me now," Victor says, waking up again, "is this: we were together for eighteen years, and now it's twenty-three years since she was murdered. My life without her has been significantly longer than my life with her."

"We have that in common. Almost. In six more years, Bering will have been dead longer than she was alive."

"She very rarely wanted to talk about herself. She was incredibly voluble and conversant when it came to issues of the present, organizing, strategy, the movement, Marxist theory, linguistics, Noam Chomsky. But with me, in private, she said almost nothing. Our best conversations were in letters, actually; for a few years, before it became too dangerous, we sent letters back and forth while she was in the field. At home, she cooked and wrote, wrote and cooked. And held secret meetings, meetings I wasn't invited to, after midnight. She talked with the boys in Nahuatl only, to make sure they'd learn. We didn't have money to travel, and she desperately wanted to take them back to Chicontepec, in Veracruz, where she was born. We only managed to go twice, while she was alive."

"She sounds like an extraordinary person."

"She stood halfway between two worlds. Two metaphysical systems, two value systems. To have left Chicontepec and gone to the university at age seventeen, and leave everyone at home thinking you had rejected them. And then when she went back, years later, as this idealistic young linguist who believed she was importing indigenous revolutionary thinking into the academic world, they wouldn't talk to her. That's why we went to Chiapas. She couldn't do her field research at home, she could only study Nahuatl from a distance, comparatively. It's why she started working on Mayan languages in the first place. That was the great sacrifice of her life, and I think that's what turned her into a revolutionary. But I never had time to ask her, to force her to write some of these things down. She refused to write, or be interviewed. But eventually she would have let me in. I'm sorry, I've said enough. I could ramble on on this subject for hours."

"What other subject is there?"

"Well, the concerns of the present."

"We still have two and a half more hours to Blue Hill. Let the rest of them worry about the present. Go on, this is helpful to me. Keep talking."

"I really only have one more thing to say, in this train of thought. There is the person I knew, and then there's the photograph of her on January first, up on the balcony at the Palacio with her rifle. Subcomandante Milagros. Which one is the real one. This is problematic, because of the nature of memory itself, just the fact that, like it or not, we forget things. We say we don't, but we do. A person fades into memory, it's a synecdochic process, certain elements of them come to stand for the whole, and then you forget the rest. With a person like her, of course, it seems almost impossible to resist the synecdoche and allow her to be remembered with a mask on. But that's what I try to do, for my own sake, for the sake of the boys, I try to say, Esperanza was not just Subcomandante Milagros."

Keep talking, he wants to say. Stay awake. I could keep talking to you for the rest of my life, whatever rest there is. Isn't there, in every life, a voice you never get tired of hearing? That was Louis. Louis made him want to stay alive, so they could have another conversation. Whatever incidental thing happened on a given day, it was worth talking about. When I lost him, he wants to say, I lost the ability to track my days. How did this only occur to me now? Everyone needs a friend, an interlocutor. Only the universe doesn't replace them when they disappear.

"You should come to New York now, on this trip," he says. "Why not? I have to go back there after the wedding. I've been away for months. You'd be welcome to stay in the apartment."

"Not this time, I'm afraid. I have a doctor's appointment when I get back to Mexico City, Nestor made sure of it."

"Surely that can be rescheduled by a week or so. Come on, I can show you around. Seriously, I have nothing to do. I'm newly retired. Do it as a favor to me. Help me figure out what to do with the rest of my life."

"It's extremely painful for me to be here. I wonder if you can appreciate that. I don't think United States citizens generally understand how despised they are by the rest of the world. The educated world, the observant world. I wonder if any of you are capable of hemispheric thinking, any kind of global awareness at all. And I don't count myself as a person who hates easily. I've been fascinated with Americans my whole life. Of course, Jews can be fascinated by Germany, too, and never want to visit. Do you have any idea what I'm saying?"

"It may surprise you, but yes, I do, absolutely."

"Tell me more, then."

"I once had to fly halfway around the world, to a country about which I had at best profoundly mixed feelings, to retrieve my daughter's body."

It sounds like a practiced sentence. It isn't. It isn't even the right sentence. I was so consumed with self-hatred, he should say, so cynical, because how else can you survive as a lawyer, a professional dodger of unpleasant truths, I was convinced I could never be transformed, I had no ground to stand on and say *Bering Wilcox deserves justice*. Because I deserved nothing, she deserved nothing. No one could convince me there was another language. And yet, here he is, that no one, only fifteen years late, saying *hemispheric thinking*. He feels something lifting. A sense of departure of the senses. "I've never been to Mexico City," he says. "I've only ever been to Acapulco, once, in the 1980s. For a legal conference. I remember they served us beer with tomato sauce, chilies, and shrimp in it, with salt on the rim, like a margarita. That's all I remember about Mexico, to be honest."

"A michelada, that's called, but in the DF we call it a chelada, with just the lime juice and salt, no chilies. In Chiapas they put Maggi seasoning in your michelada, I can't drink that. Too thick, almost soupy."

"I don't know anything about Mexico at all, is what I'm saying. I need to learn about Mexico."

"I wouldn't, if I were you. At your age. You'd just be exchanging one darkness for another. Still, if you have nothing better to do, it could turn out to be interesting. Come to Chiapas, I'll hire a van, show you a few things."

I'm coming, he wants to say. This is hemispheric thinking. I'm not leaving. I'm coming but not leaving. It can't be so far. I'm not leaving I'm leaving I'm not leaving.

AMERICA IS DEAD

Under a string of paper lanterns, close enough to hear the slosh of the waves at high tide, Zeno grills long rolls of skirt steak, salt and pepper on each side. Breathes up the smoke. Drinks from a can of some local beer, he's never had it before. Lourdes and Sami stocked the house, they came a day early. Snacks laid out everywhere. Coolers of ice. A volleyball net. Papi behind him, in a lawn chair, drinking some kind of fancy mezcal de pechuga on ice. Never in his life, as far as he can remember, has the man drunk mezcal before. Not his thing. He drinks brandy, sherry, Calvados. The habits of a graduate student in Madrid in 1977. He had to come to Maine to taste mezcal. "Ya te lo prometî," Nestor says, over FaceTime, the phone in Papi's hand. "Ya lo se, el viernes a las nueve." Winter and Naomi are setting the tables he moved outside. It's a decent-sized group. A rehearsal dinner, that's a new concept to him. You're supposed to rehearse a wedding and then have a big party for the out-of-town guests. Everyone is from out of town. No one has a town.

"I'm trying to get him to go to New York, while he's here," Winter says. "Sandy's offered to take him. We'll change the return ticket, it's no big deal. He hasn't seen New York since the Carter administration. He could go to the Metropolitan Museum, the Morgan Library."

"Another time."

"There won't be another time."

"I haven't made any preparations," Victor says. "One doesn't make a casual visit to New York City. I have friends, colleagues, I should have contacted them."

"Food's ready," Zeno calls out, putting the platter on the table.

"Victor," Winter says, stepping out onto the deck, "sit here, at the head, I put a pillow down on the chair for you."

"Mija," he says, "call me something else. It feels sacrilegious. Not my Christian name. Papi, Papa, Dad, anything. Call me 'comrade.'"

"Bueno, camarada, ven, siéntate."

"When you speak Spanish, I can't help feeling you're subtly mocking me."

"She can't help it," Zeno says. "You're very mockable."

"*Mockable* isn't a word in English. Or Spanish. You mean, a figure of ridicule, an absurdity, a pompous fool out of Molière. Whereas I picture myself as an ignored prophet, a Tiresias."

Winter says nothing. It's not his fault. Dinner is ready, actually ready, there's the corn, the salad, the slightly overripe avocados that had to be dissected, the meat, the other salad. Tilda, Tonya, and Shannon should have come in from kayaking by now. *Antigone* doesn't belong to the Wilcoxes, but something ought to be said. Something ought to be done. She likes the force of the repetition. Families like ours don't mourn in public. Isn't that the root of the problem, fundamentally. Did someone say that, or was it just on the subliminal wavelength she sensed all along. She needs Sandy to witness this, but he's inside, it's not his fault, someone sent him to the liquor store and he's still unpacking a case of rosé. "Dad," she calls, "leave it, the food's getting cold."

/

At first Tonya tried keeping up with Tilda's strokes, but Tilda said it wasn't necessary, tandem kayaks are a pain, and the harbor is flat, calm, a burgeoning high tide, they skim across it even with her paddle propped across her knees. Shannon, in a single kayak, has fallen far behind.

"So you and Shannon met at camp."

"Right. Quaker camp. My grandfather was Quaker. Sort of. I don't know all the details. But he paid for it."

"Your grandfather who was Naomi's real father, you mean, or the other one."

"Naomi's father. John Downs. Grandpa John. I don't really know what the right term is. I hate the word *biological.*"

"As if any of this was about biology."

"Exactly. And you and Naomi, if you don't mind my asking, how long have you been together?"

"Officially, since April. Unofficially, we moved in together in— when was it. November. My lease ended December first."

"Sorry. That was rude."

"It wasn't anybody's proudest moment. Naomi has a strange way of convincing people to do things."

"Seriously."

"It took a lot of courage for you to come. I'm not sure I would ever have done something like that."

"I did a lot of reading about Bering," Tonya says. "Watched all the videos on YouTube. I got totally sucked in. I couldn't believe someone like that was my cousin. I don't know exactly how to explain it. It really changed my whole way of thinking. That's why I decided to find Winter, first off, and then when Naomi texted me, I was like, fuck it, I'm Bering Wilcox's cousin, I'll never have a tenth of her courage, but I can do this, at least."

"Have you said that to Naomi?"

"I mentioned it to Winter. Kind of in passing. I don't want to, you know, force them to talk about it."

"I think they need to hear what you just said. Naomi, especially."

"Why?"

"I don't know. It's just an instinct. Naomi thinks no one remembers Bering, that she's been completely forgotten."

"Has she ever googled her?"

"Let me rephrase that. She *tells herself* Bering's been forgotten, that's the story she's landed on. As far as I can figure it out. We've hardly ever discussed her. Like you, I did all my research independently. I've seen grief do fucked-up things to people, but the Wilcoxes are a special case. It was the one thing that made me question my feelings for her. Even more than reading *The Shiva Hypothesis*."

"I just read the first few chapters online. It scared the shit out of me."

"It's a very troubling book. I think it came from a very dark place. Obviously. Not that I want to argue with her intellectual conclusions. I can't do that. But it's not so much a book about conclusions, it's about how you frame them, it's the tone she uses. I don't think she really means everything she said, basically."

"Maybe not, but the damage is done."

"But you came anyway."

"I went through some boxes of Grandpa John's letters last summer. He never used email; everything's on carbon paper. In my grandmother's attic. Including some letters to Naomi. He was straight-up mean to her. So bitter. Condescending. She wanted to meet face-to-face, but he was too angry."

"I don't think anyone can undo that kind of pain."

"Right. I just bring it up to say, maybe she had her reasons, in a fucked-up way. She felt rejected, clearly. Whatever she wanted to claim, or even see, in him, he wasn't having it. I'm not trying to give her an out. A reason is not an excuse. My dad always used to say that."

"I'm impressed," Tilda says. "At your capacity to withhold judgment. I guess that's the right way to put it."

"I'm just curious as fuck, basically," Tonya says. "Probably this is all going into a book someday."

"Not you too. Not more writers in the family."

"We don't have any in ours."

/

Someone asked a question about happiness. The novel wants to know. Is it possible to describe happiness. Is it possible to describe one's way into happiness. Given the right conditions. Is there a version of happiness that does not contain, or imply, a state of terror. If the state is a terrorist state, one that sucks foreign nationals into its vast maw of low-wage labor and preserves them in limbo, invisible yet omnipresent stateless persons, as useful symbolically as actually, the unstated marginal factor sustaining the illusion of the health of the settler state. This is a sentence fragment; it's missing its predicate. What then. Should we celebrate. What is there to celebrate. We're not talking about parades or festivals, vast feasts, acts of thanksgiving; we're talking about the celebrations appropriate to bourgeois life, quiet gestures of continuity, the passage of good genes, invisible capital. Welcome to the family. The elaborate machinations of disinterested taste.

The novel goes to sit in another room where fewer people are talking all at once. This is not its kind of disinterest. The novel goes over to the record player and watches the record revolve. Brian Eno, *My Life in the Bush of Ghosts*. In this setting it appears very much like an animal. But also like a disappointed, abandoned project, not all of its fur glued on properly. There is so little time. There's just so little time. If you say authentic life is not possible under the capitalist terror-state, you are charting such a long curve, maybe not even a curve, another way of saying, Melinda Roberts didn't mean what she said to me in tenth grade, after school in the parking lot. I will drop the curtain of mediation over all my memories.

Look, the novel says. Look. When I grasped you the first time you didn't wonder if it was real fur. You were surprised to still be alive. That's the point we're trying to get to. In a prison somewhere there is always a person whose back is stiff, in agony from sitting hours on a concrete floor, saying to another person, Hold me, I am afraid. That's the point we're trying to get to. Not because one is the same as the other. Nothing is the same as anything else, and yet a five-year-old still wants cake for her birthday. That's the point we're trying to get to.

/

There are two ways up Blue Hill, Winter explained to Zeno before he left, the steep direct route, in the sun, the classic berry-picking route in *Blueberries for Sal,* and the shady, winding route through the woods on the far side. Wilcoxes always go up the one and down the other. Zeno, Patrick, Sandy, Mathias. Three fathers, two sons. The wedding is tomorrow. They have plastic yogurt tubs, sunscreen, water. Faint clouds, tacky air, highs in the low eighties. Sandy read Mathias the book last night and Mathias said excitedly, ich möchte den Bären sehen. No bears, Sandy said. Mathias turned red and threw the book across the room.

No, Patrick said, Grandpa's wrong, there might be bears, we just have to look very carefully.

Now Patrick's trying to remember the first time he climbed Blue Hill. He was tiny. Bubbe and Zayde were there, he was clutching Zayde's hand. 1983 or '84. That's it, just holding Zayde's hand, and the trail going up into the sun, the smell of pines baking, the thin sap sticking your fingers together. Mathias ran ahead, clutching his old Nalgene bottle. Hurricane Island Outward Bound. His chubby calves already turning pink. Katerina is no fan of the sun; she doesn't like beaches. Correction: she likes Nordic beaches, where the sun shines once or twice a year.

"There was one case about a catering company," he says to Sandy, over his shoulder, trying to stir up a conversation. "I remember that one. The daughter suing the mother, or the mother suing the daughter."

"Cakes Manhattan."

"Right, the one where the daughter had a detective follow the mother around to prove she was actually working for another baker, and then the mother put Ex-Lax in the daughter's salmon puffs, to put her out of business. Wasn't that it? Was it ever resolved?"

"I have no idea. There was a motion to dismiss, that's the last I heard."

"It must be strange, leaving all this work in midstream."

"I don't think about it. It hasn't crossed my mind, literally, not once. Mark finally did get me to do a Skype call, a few weeks ago, a kind of debriefing. Little that it mattered, months after the fact. It's a decent-sized firm, partners get sick or die or have to take emergency leave, it happens. I was on the way out, everybody knew it. I was so depressed I could hardly string three sentences together in a meeting."

"At least you know that now."

"I knew it then. I just didn't plan to be standing here describing it, five months after the fact."

"You don't have to get testy about it."

"Do I sound testy? I don't mean to be. Just accurate. I thought, since our last conversation, we'd basically given up euphemisms for the time being."

"Fair enough."

Zeno, ahead of Mathias, has already squatted down at the first berry bushes. They grow so agonizingly low to the ground, Patrick wants to tell someone who cares, wild Maine blueberries, on a hillside facing the ocean, blasted by the north Atlantic all winter. People who don't pick fruit for a living, even as a habit, can be romantic about it for a week in August. Life that grows out of cracks, the lichen of the fruit world. That special tang of a pie baked out of hostility. Saltwater taffy and the taste of all those who have gone down in ships. All my ancestors, shackled or not. Cramped in holds.

"Since you're the one of us still employed," Sandy says, "give me an update. Do quantum computers exist yet?"

"Yes and no."

"That's clever."

"Okay, let me put it this way. We can imagine what a quantum computer can do, even simulate what it can do, to a certain degree, but that's entirely different from actually doing it. Right now things are incredibly messy. You've got the big players, Apple, Google, Intel, throwing millions and millions at cooling systems and superconductors and microwaves that spin a single electron. The hardware research is all backed up. That's not what Avansys does. We develop software for hardware that doesn't exist. It will, though. The last three years have demonstrated that. Thus the money getting kicked our way."

"You don't sound thrilled."

"There are too many state-surveillance-type applications, remote targeting, alleged crime detection, satellite image crunching, that kind of thing. If I had the energy to care, I'd be trying to ban this stuff, not develop it."

"Tell me about your energy, then."

"Fuck off, Dad."

"I'm not allowed to ask about your mental state."

"At the moment, no. Ask me when I'm back home, when I've gotten over the stress, the disruption, of traveling. Trust me when I say: you don't know what it's like."

"For a moment I thought you were going to use the word *trauma*."

"Would there be something wrong with that?"

"I dislike its casual overuse, its general application, that's all."

"For fuck's sake, Dad, you tried to commit suicide five months ago."

"I wouldn't call myself traumatized, then or now. That would be ridiculous. Primo Levi was traumatized. Paul Celan was traumatized. People who were raped, locked in underground pits, people who survived the Khmer Rouge or the Cultural Revolution get to call themselves traumatized. Torture victims. Victims of attempted lynchings."

"I get it, you can stop now."

"Zeno is a victim of trauma. Winter isn't. As terrifying as her experience was. You have to draw a line somewhere."

"I'm glad that we have you to be our gatekeeper."

"I have no idea what that means, but yes, there have to be rules, if you believe in justice, people actually pursuing claims and facing

consequences. This counts, not that. Otherwise you never get Milo-
sevic captured and standing trial, you never get to charge people with
war crimes. Et cetera."

"Now, there is a system that has worked out exceedingly well for
the world's victims of state terrorism. It's inspiring, honestly, after the
particular life you've had, that your belief in the power of systems and
structures remains intact."

"I never said it did. Failure isn't trauma, either. Failure is just failure. It doesn't migrate. My depression is the result of my choices, my
reasoning, my personal weaknesses. You can want to give up, frankly
I'm astonished more people *don't* want to give up, but that isn't because
the world has damaged you. I am my own fault, in other words."

"I really hesitate to disagree with you there," Patrick says, "but
that's actually bullshit. Not the part about having responsibility. Everyone has that, to a degree. But the idea that you remain an invulnerable
bystander, completely in control, a rational perceiving agent, because
you haven't personally experienced the violence that killed your daughter, nearly killed your almost-son-in-law—how can you seriously say
that, Dad? Are you that callous, or clueless?"

Zeno turns on his heel and looks at them, shading his eyes. Mathias,
head-down among the bushes, hasn't heard. They've stopped in the
faint shade of an overgrown sumac, as if that means those in the sunlight, twenty feet away, won't hear them. Shade as cloaking device.
He rubs his forehead, already coated with dust, and drinks water. His
alarm is about to go off. He should eat one of his energy bars. All this
without looking once at Sandy, who appears to be inspecting a sumac
blossom, off camera, as if he's never seen one before.

"There's lots of berries," Zeno calls out. "Come help us, guys."

"In a minute. I'm just catching my breath."

"The point I'm trying to make," Sandy says to the sumac, "is that
saying everyone is equally oppressed is like saying no one is. Violence
is real. Its consequences are real. I haven't suffered them. I can only
help ameliorate them, or make them worse. If it's B and not A, I'm of

no good to anyone, I should exit the scene. I'm not saying this is a fun way to live. I just don't see anyone making a valid argument to the contrary."

"I wonder if it ever occurred to you, even once, in your forty-plus years with Mom and the three or two of us, that you were actually the only white person in the family."

"Not that I think that's true, exactly, but let's provisionally say that yes, I thought about it often."

"There's this thing called secondary trauma—"

"I know all about it. Brisman talked about it. It doesn't apply to me; it applies to ER doctors, social workers, aid workers in Africa."

"It applies to me."

"Whatever you say."

"No, I insist, this is my life we're talking about, not yours. When I got sick, I let it get worse and worse because I wanted to die. Period. And I almost got my wish. I'm still recovering from that. Actually I'll always be recovering from it, the way things look now. This condition isn't going away. It'll probably result in an early death. That's what the research says, anyway."

"And?"

"And?"

This time Mathias looks up, bewildered. Zeno stands up, as if propelled, and beckons him, as if to say, leave the crazy people alone, but Mathias isn't having it, of course. He pulls his hand away and rubs his eyes in the sun. This is a test of the world. The child is about to cry. Do you go to the child, do you leave the child crying in the dust. You, Patrick wants to say to Sandy, how many times did you shoo us away on this actual hill so you could finish the argument. How children beg their parents to stop fighting. Is this the real drama of the gifted child: not being able to make the fighting stop. He wants to say to Sandy, something inside me is wilting or shrinking. My shell is wrinkling. My emotional intelligence. You have cut me to the quick. What is the expression. The best expression would be to never have come at all.

There's a speeded-up feeling, as if they've been engaged in a lifelong game of chicken, driving parallel toward the edge. Was it Sandy and Naomi, once? Now it's Sandy and Patrick. Has it ever not been.

"Thank you for answering the question I wasn't prepared to ask," he says to Sandy, this time regarding him straight on. The old man has bloodshot eyes. Or are they always that way. His legs, in shorts, are terrifying. A color that shouldn't appear in nature. As if they've been encased in casts all winter, the little dark hairs here and there as feeble as dead capillaries. "Now I know why I came."

"This conversation isn't over. What I meant to say was—"

He cuts him off clean. Moving straight ahead with long legs, picking up his son's hand, moving farther up the hill. "We were worried there might be bears," he says to Mathias. "We were arguing over whether to keep going. I told him he was being a foolish old man."

"Gibt es also Bären oder nicht?"

"You and I are stronger than any bear."

/

Winter has to sleep on her side now, it's a fixed position, one direction or the other, and shifting is itself a project, moving and rearranging the body pillow, throwing one arm up and over or around. Three bodies, all of whom by now wish they could move independently. The babies are well aware of each other, they seem to be constantly pushing and readjusting themselves in relation to the other, you can see their elbows and knees protruding when they're most active. Five to six thirty in the morning is playtime, evidently. "I think we have to buy a king bed," she says. "Just for you to have a place to go."

"You definitely see why people buy them. I never understood it before."

"They do sell them in Mexico, right?"

"I don't know. I've never shopped for a bed in my life."

"I've never given this much thought to sleeping in my entire life."

"You've never had to grow an animal, let alone two animals, inside you."

They talk a lot about animals. It's a constant point of reference. How do lions, or elephants, know how to give birth. Chimpanzees. The most intelligent, communicative, higher-order species. How is it that they never wonder. What does it feel like to depend entirely on inner logic, the body's logic. How birth is the most biological, animalistic, moment in human life. There is literally nothing, she observed at one point, to distinguish a human mother giving birth from, say, a gorilla giving birth. Primates are essentially identical in this way, according to the documentaries. Only one happens with millions of dollars of equipment and personnel involved. Not that they're naturalizing the process themselves. Winter's OB had to suggest they hire a doula and make a birth plan. My mother, Zeno said at one point, at least according to Dad, witnessed dozens of births in her life, at home in Veracruz, at La Realidad, and elsewhere in the mountains, she saw hemorrhages and stillbirths, the whole works, and she wanted a nurse if not a doctor attending every birth in Mexico, the way they do it in Cuba. She didn't put a lot of stock in home remedies. She was an indigenous communist, not a naturopath. It's easy to theorize about these things, but then you have to face the maternal mortality rates. If women are going to be soldiers, *and* have babies, they need doctors.

But still, knowing that there's an ER within reach, you can speculate about lions. And how they sleep all day.

"I don't know how to feel," she says. "It's our wedding day. I don't know what I feel, I'm too goddamned tired. It's still dark."

"We are the sacrificial objects in this ritual."

"Very funny."

"No, I was talking to the rabbi, Rabbi Art. You know he came by to say hello last night."

"I saw him. We hardly got to talk."

"He said, however you feel is how you're supposed to feel."

"That's typical."

"I appreciate it. I thought he was very understanding."

"Hearing you say that," she says, barely able to form the words, "I wish we could do it all over again. I wish we could move back to New York, and go back to Beth Shalom, raise our kids there, as sweet liberal Jews, maybe even take over Mom and Dad's apartment, since they don't seem to want it—"

"We could try that."

"Very funny."

"You could change your attitude about the case, and say, I have the right to live here with whoever I want to marry, dig in your toes."

"Dig in your heels. I'm too tired to have this conversation. It's making me sad. Fiction always makes me sad. I don't want to go along with it, after a while. Even when I know I have to."

"Don't worry, soon enough it'll be too late."

"It's already too late. We've made our decision."

"You should never say that the morning of your wedding."

"I was married to you years ago, Zeno Alfonso Cuauhtémoc Rodriguez. I was probably married to you in a past life."

"In a past life, we were both Aztecs. Or maybe Egyptians, or ancient Hebrews. Or Chinese. Anyway, we were the same thing. That's why we recognize each other. That's why people who are very different find themselves attracted. Just a cosmic lottery machine, that spits out those little balls."

"That's lovely. I'm going back to sleep."

/

"Look at you," Naomi says. "You're already dressed. And here I am still drinking coffee. I should get upstairs."

"Shannon's still in the shower," Tonya says. She came out on the porch barefoot, holding her heels, uselessly; she should have left them by the door. "Then Tilda's next in line. You have about fifteen minutes."

"Is that called a head wrap?"

"Sure. You can call it that."

"Gorgeous. Very regal."

"I got this outfit for my sister's wedding, last summer. My mom FedExed it to me. She insisted. I thought maybe it would be a little too formal."

"It's an art, wearing high heels on grass. I've never mastered it. All my heels are in New York anyway. Probably growing mold. There's no use for them on Cape Cod."

"So what are you wearing, then."

"Oh, it's a blue pantsuit-type thing. Tilda helped pick it out. Very mother-of-the-bride. She's doing something with my hair, too. It's not my strong suit. I've never known what to do with it, other than keep it cut short. Otherwise it's a frizzy mess."

Tonya sits carefully, eyeing the wood slats of the deck chair. You can't get water spots out of a dress like this. Facing Naomi, she feels aware, as she hasn't been in years, of feeling, well, big. She isn't big. She just isn't skinny. She has hips. Everything is exactly where it's supposed to be on you, her aunt Linda said approvingly, giving her a once-over when they had brunch during Christmas break. And then tried to get her to go out with her friend's son, a chef in Silver Lake. But then there was that time at Ennie Chang's house, a very odd group hanging for some reason the weekend before the start of senior year, and she asked Ennie if she could borrow a bathing suit. They were the same height, and Ennie was on the swim team, super fit, broad shoulders, busty, she had that All-American Girl Jock physique, but two of her teammates, Madison and Skylar, whispered something about *does it really stretch that far* and Ennie turned extremely red and said she didn't have an extra. It's not about measurements, you could say, it's about scale. She wanted to ask, Ennie, just curious, what's your cup size. But why make it her problem? Madison and Skylar saw her death stare and for some reason started talking about Adele. How much they loved her. How she was a queen who didn't take anyone's shit. That voice. Hello, hello from the other side.

"I want to say this, and don't take it the wrong way," Naomi says. "No. Forget it. I've already thought better of it. Forget it."

"Go ahead. You might as well say it now."

"All my life I've been mystified by Black women's hair. How it grows. How you style it, shape it. The products. How you keep it in place. You know, like everyone else I know. The one rule is that you don't touch it. And don't comment on it, if you don't want to come across as an asshole. Not that I've known many Black women that well. Our department assistants, at Columbia. I had one postdoc, too, Kimberly, years ago, she's a professor now at Vanderbilt. The kids' teachers. Anyway, my point is, all these years, my entire adult life, it never occurred to me until very recently that I have a Black woman's hair. That's how obtuse I am about these things. I could have dreadlocks if I wanted to. Salt-and-pepper locs. I could, you know, reclaim my heritage."

"But do you want to?"

"No. I'd feel ridiculous."

"Then I don't get what the problem is."

"My point is, I spend a lot of time—no, rather, I *don't* spend a lot of time, but probably I should, reflecting on how different my life would have been. If John Downs actually had been my father. And also how similar. I'm sure I would have still wound up a scientist. But I would have been a Black woman scientist, a trailblazer."

"You *were* a Black woman scientist."

"It doesn't count, does it? If nobody knows?"

"Naomi," she says, "look, I don't know quite how to say this—"

"I should stop. I know. You didn't come here for me to dump all this in your lap. You're not my sounding board."

"Just curious, though. I don't mean to pry."

"Don't apologize. Just ask."

"You have had therapists, in your life, I think you mentioned you have, and it's like you've never processed any of this, I don't know, *material* before."

"My first therapist didn't even know the story."

"You're kidding."

"I didn't think it was relevant. This was back in Berkeley, in 1975. I mean, we were living in San Francisco, but I was a student at Berkeley. He was provided free by Cal's health department. I was referred because my advisor was worried about me. And he had every right to be worried. I wasn't eating. I smoked more than I ate. Sandy didn't know what to do with me. With that particular shrink, I just lay on his couch, closed my eyes, and talked about math. I'm not sure he understood anything I was saying. But I seriously believed, at that moment, that math controlled the structure of the entire universe, and nothing else mattered. It was very complex stuff, fluid dynamics, and we didn't have good software, we were still doing a lot of calculations with pen and paper. I could feel it eating my mind. I needed so much help, my god. He actually said very little. Also, *he* was Black."

"Jesus. Way to bury the lede there, Naomi."

"His name was Gregory. I must have known his last name, but I've forgotten it. God, he was always so beautifully dressed. Not that I noticed or cared at the time, but in retrospect, wow. Beautifully tailored suits. Shades of brown, tan, dark green. Listen, Tonya, you have to understand, in Berkeley, in the midseventies, being Black was nonnegotiable. You were or you weren't. No one was interested in my little story. I was Naomi Schifrin from Armonk, a sweet Jewish girl with glasses and a big brain."

"And later on?"

"I don't know. It was always one factor among many."

"I don't even understand what that means."

"In New York, when I was in actual analysis—look, Freud didn't think about race, as such. The idea of being racially different from birth, or the trauma of a withheld racial secret, in my case, the idea of withheld Blackness, or whatever you want to call it—that just doesn't compute. My analyst was somewhat interested in my late realization that my father wasn't actually my father, that my mother had had sex with another man, how that changed my relationship with Herman. My dad of record. My adoptive dad, technically. It was a sexual trauma, not a racial trauma, according to him. He actually said, at one point, that before I'd told him the details, he assumed my mother was raped by a Black man."

"I don't know what to say to that either."

"And now I'm doing exactly what I said I wouldn't do. Your job is not to absorb all this crap from me. If anything, you should be spending more time with Winter and Patrick. They've done much more with their feelings than I have. I'm such an infant, honestly, when it comes to these things. I should go back into therapy, but I've lost the patience. And try finding a sophisticated therapist in Falmouth. It's too late for me, honestly, to do anything about it that won't cause more problems than it would solve."

"You reached out to me. That's not nothing."

"And you're being extremely patient, and I don't totally understand why."

"I want to tell you something," Tonya says, "but for the time being, let's keep it between us, okay? I've actually been to your apartment."

"You have?"

"Not actually inside. I looked up the address, it's easy to find. I got into the building. I dressed up, I borrowed a briefcase from my friend's mom, and I told the doorman I was there to see Mr. Wilcox in 14L. He just waved me in. I got up to the door, and knocked on it, and then I completely lost my shit and ran back to the elevator. I don't even know if Sandy was there. He was probably at work. It was just a weird impulse, I can't explain it."

"When was this?"

"In April. I was staying with my friend Alicia, at NYU."

"Sandy had probably already left for Vermont by then."

"I really like graveyards," she says. "I think it comes from living in southern California, where there's no history to speak of, right? I always wanted to go to one of the missions, or just any place that was historical, and my brother said I was creepy and obsessed with graveyards. Mission Dolores, in San Francisco—that's one of my favorite places in the world. I liked gothic novels, you know, Edgar Allan Poe, ghost stories. It's just a feeling, I don't know. Not so much an interest in history, although I love history, it's that feeling of the physical space of the dead. So I got a little obsessed with you guys, and don't take this the wrong way, but as if you were all dead. I don't know how I would have responded if Sandy had actually opened the door. Of course it started with Bering, and I don't want to insult her memory, but I did research on her, I just couldn't believe what happened to her, and that she was my cousin. But it's not just that. It must be why people get obsessed with genealogy and take DNA tests. I just had a craving to know more, but honestly, I don't know if this is the right word, but I was looking at you guys as objects, curiosities, not actual living people."

Naomi turns toward her, but that's not the word, turns into her, bends her body around her to say what she's going to say. And she recoils a little bit. Not wanting, at this moment, to be touched. "Listen," Naomi says. Her face is doing something odd and awkward. Earnestness. "This may sound very strange, but that, what do you call it, that impulse, that *attitude,* is how I know we're actually related. You are your grandfather's granddaughter. I think you're going to be a scientist."

"Oh hell no."

"No, okay, what I mean is, a scholar. A researcher. God help us. An academic. I can just tell."

"How can you tell, though?"

"Because"—she fumbles, making a shrug with her hands, *what more do you want from me?*—"You have a mind that wants to be left alone."

/

They walk arm in arm from the car to the chuppah. Priyanka's brother, Arjun, a classmate of Bering's in second grade, now a member of the New

York Guitar Quartet, brought his friend Tom from Berklee, a mandolinist; together they play "You Are the Everything." There aren't enough chairs; half the people are standing, clustered at the back and around the edges. At least a hundred people, their cars parked all along the road. At the last moment Lourdes stands up and takes Winter's other elbow. She's swaying, her smile seems a little lopsided. The sun beats down. It's hard for an eight-months-pregnant woman not to feel lopsided. There's a microphone, courtesy of Sami; at least she won't have to yell.

/

Patrick has put on his burgundy vest and robe and freshly shaved his head. Mathias sits on the cushion next to him, his legs pulled up.

He taps the bell, which came with him on the plane, wrapped in a blanket, in its own suitcase. Three times.

"The metta prayer," he says into the mic. "I wish happiness, and the causes of happiness, to myself, to all of you assembled here, and to all beings in the universe. I wish myself to be free from injury, and the causes of injury, and I wish the same for all of you, and all beings in the universe. I wish myself to be free from anger, fear, anxiety, and all afflictions of the mind, and the causes of these afflictions, and I wish the same for you, and all beings in the universe."

/

Who is assembled at this event? Nearly a hundred guests. Members of three families. Seated in rows, on folding chairs. Where are the others seated, in their shining bodies? To the left of the low stage, under the billowing branches of the red maple. Esperanza is there, John Downs is there. Their residue floats and fails to settle. It's August, it's humid. I am there. You are there. The novel is there. Patrick closes his eyes and wills the mandala into being. Trick, she says; her curtain of hair falls over the sun. She takes a seat so the ceremony can begin.

/

"I apologize for the lack of planning, even though it was deliberate," Winter says. "I wish we had programs. We didn't know there would be quite so many of you. This wedding is going to be very simple. We've asked all the members of our family present to give a blessing. Just whatever they want to say. Then Rabbi Art will say the sheva brachot and the justice of the peace will do the honors. I just have one more thing I would like to add.

"It was so tremendously important to me to get married here, in Blue Hill, and I apologize for making you come here, all this way, but thanks all the same. This may sound melodramatic, but it was important to me to get to see it one last time, before Zeno and I and our babies, god willing, move to Mexico. That's our plan. We're moving to Mexico City in October. For reasons, I can't actually renounce my American citizenship, at least not yet, but emotionally, I've already renounced it. In solidarity with Zeno, I don't ever plan to come back, until he can come back. It sucks, because a wedding isn't supposed to be a farewell, but in this case it has to serve as both."

No one moves. The trees move, lightly, in the light breeze. A truck rumbles along the road toward the library, grinding its brakes. Lourdes wipes the corner of one eye. Victor looks away, toward the harbor, as if he hasn't heard her, or is thinking of something else.

/

America is dead. That isn't the right way to say it. The United States of America is dead. If I say it's dead to me, is it dead. If I say, mother country, I have no other, you are dead. The way the sunlight glows in the leaves of the red maple on the lawn: dead. The blue hill over the blue waters of the bay: dead. What thou lovest remains: dead. It was always a projection, that's the problem, no one can see it from end to end, thus the familiar phrases, sea to shining sea. Sucking on a chili dog outside the Tastee Freez. No one can contain it, therefore it seeps away but remains as a residue.

/

"I remember my mother," Zeno says. "She would say that a wedding can't start unless you thank the Earth and the sun, which gives us life, and the water, which gives us life, and the four directions. I don't know the precise words. But I want to start by saying thank you, thank you to the Earth for this beautiful day. Everyone, please, I want to draw your attention to the sky. Look up at the sky. Just look up.

"You have no idea how lucky you are, I think, most of you, to have such a beautiful sky to look at. This is what I love about New England. Maybe it's because I install solar panels for a living. So many days of the year, there's a clear, unpolluted sky. You can see the weather. It almost hurts your eyes. Please, appreciate it by looking up sometimes. Don't take it for granted. I never did, as a visitor. Think of yourselves as visitors.

"I say this for myself and my father, Victor, who would prefer not to speak, and my brother, Nestor, who couldn't be here but is listening over the phone. One day, we will all be reunited."

/

"I have very little to say," Sandy says. "I didn't prepare any remarks. Or at least not on paper. I wasn't sure of what would be appropriate."

Alone, a figure on a stage, he sways. He's lost weight, Naomi is thinking. Not that he had so much to start with. His wrists seem thinner. His suit, he bought a new suit in Providence, hangs excessively. It should have been taken in.

"I brought a glass for you to break," he says. "That's the tradition. To remember the broken walls of Jerusalem. I'm sure we can all associate other meanings with that act of breaking. You could even say that broken is all we are. Why even break the glass, it's redundant. The Wilcox family couldn't even get it together to mail invitations. What you see here are the remnants of a family. Et cetera.

"But you know what? To hell with all of that. I refuse to be broken because *they* refuse to be broken. Winter and Zeno, you've inspired me. I refuse to wail, today. Don't even break the glass. Pour something into it and drink it down. We don't have any time to waste. Or usable materials. Winter and Zeno, your marriage is a small boat in a huge ocean. Sorry, it's a terrible metaphor. You're sailing against the current, or the tide. Hold on tight. Hold fast."

/

"My children," Naomi says, her hand grazing the mic stand, "have all gone to live in camps. They're drawn to camps. The places on the far edge of the world where the dispossessed are just holding on. The Tibetans, the Palestinians, and the immigration offices. They left the security, the enchanted metropolis, the putative home of their kind, they rejected it, the comfortable lives their friends all seem to be living, the logical consequence of their expensive elite educations, to live out what Lenin described as the rejection of their own class status in favor of that of the dispossessed, the act of solidarity which those of us who remember, say, 1972, all realized would be the only true ground of a revolutionary movement in the United States, for about fifteen minutes.

"And you know what? They were right. In the historical sense. The camps have come closer and closer. You might say we, by which I mean people like me, rich white or approximately-white people, people in nice apartments with nice cars, didn't realize we were living in them the whole time. I should have known, if anyone had known, because I did the same thing in my time. I went to Alaska, I took my babies to Alaska, and lived there through an entire winter, to discover what's essentially the same thing. The world is actually ending. The planet is actually dying. And whoever's left will be reduced to camps. It's coming closer and closer. I have lived my whole life trying to mimic the fenced-in world I grew up in, without knowing it.

"So I offer the only blessing I can think of. Winter and Zeno and your children to come, oh my god, I am so sorry, to begin with, to have left you this Earth, and I am so sorry for my life, which has been one long mistake. Your lives will be worse than mine. It's a long tailing-off, a long diminishment from this point. But at least you know that. You know yourselves so much better than I ever knew myself. We are witnessing such a shift in the scale of self-knowledge on this planet. God knows what's going to happen because of it.

"But I can say, as a blessing, that your lives will not be like our lives. I think, wholeheartedly, that's a good thing. To put it very very simply, you won't waste decades wondering what it's like to be happy. You are happy. Winter and Zeno, you're so happy together I even forget to feel envious, I forget all of my regrets. I forget the smell of death, the smell of this dying planet. I forget all the mistakes I've made. For once in my entire life, I feel glad to be a mother."

/

They have to leave the park at seven, so the party moves back to the house. Everyone comes. Sami sits by the laptop, FaceTiming with Nestor, who dictates tracks. Everyone dances, even Sandy. Even Patrick. Lourdes pulls them out onto the floor. Lying on a couch in Roma Norte, Nestor can tell exactly what kind of party it is. You need lots of classic soul, Aretha, James Brown, the Ohio Players. Eighties hits. Recognizable songs. Then you can pull in different directions: a little salsa, a little Fela, some basic house. Something that pulls generations together, like the Fugees' "No Woman, No Cry." He's done parties in Cancún, Zihuatanejo, Tulum, on yachts; you have to build up to anything interesting.

Just on a whim, he puts on Caetano Veloso singing "Soy loco por ti, America."

Winter takes the phone from Sami so that Nestor can see her giving him the finger. He sticks out his tongue and laughs.

No one wants to leave. No one has to leave. But Naomi's flagging, and her room with Tilda is in the house next door.

"Hold on a second," Sandy says. "Take a walk with me."

"A walk."

"Yeah, I don't know. On the beach. It's low tide. There's a flashlight in the house."

"That's very romantic, but no."

"Oh, come on. It's our kid's wedding."

Who dictates these scenes? The novel feels very close, closed in. Gathered. Folded. She has the feeling he's about to make one of his big gestures, and she doesn't want to be there. But has to be there. No one else would make an adequate witness. When married, she wants to say, you become the chief witness of your partner's life. You are the only source, reliable or definitely not. This is a problem, but also not. People want to be witnessed. They want, and don't want, someone to remember, to count, not necessarily the same as accountability. And that contract, disturbingly, doesn't end when the marriage ends, not if you've been together as long as we have. You feel the pull of duty in that regard. Fuck me, she wants to say, I will want to be there at his deathbed too, and Tilda will say I have to, she'll drive me to the door. The novel is a bad pattern, a defective liturgy. For people who have given up actual ceremonies and just make it up as they go along.

She has to go back to her house anyway, to find the appropriate shoes. Then they walk. They descend the rickety stairs and pick their way through the rubble, the sheets of slippery sea grape, shells, cracked and discarded floats. Maine doesn't make it easy. It's resistant and prickly. The kids complained, at least Bering and Winter complained, in their first-bikini years, they preferred the Hamptons, even the Jersey shore. Or, if it had to be Maine, why couldn't we buy a boat. There were the years where every other question seemed to be, why can't we act more like our rich friends. She says, "I'm remembering when

Winter and Bering used to complain about coming here, when they just wanted to sunbathe and have boys admire them."

"I don't remember that."

"Oh come on. Several years running, when Winter was thirteen, fourteen. Nineteen ninety-five-ish. They sulked in the car all the way up here."

"There was so much sulking, in general, I've probably lost track."

"Around the same time Louis and Judy wanted us to buy the place next to theirs in Sagaponack."

"We should have, we'd have made a killing. Imagine what it would be worth now."

"I honestly don't remember what stopped us."

"Other than the general atmosphere of sulking and not being able to agree on anything, you mean."

"Other couples," she says, "were able to channel their unhappiness into major purchases, furnishing houses, investing in art, et cetera, and we never had the knack. Or having affairs. Or, whatever, having competing hobbies. We just sat there and stewed."

"That's your narrative?"

"Isn't it just an observation?"

"I'm not disagreeing with you. I just want to know your side of the story."

"You're looking for an itemized list of faults?"

"I actually think we could be friends. That's what I'm saying."

"Based on what evidence?"

"The fact that we're here, to begin with. We dealt with a family crisis and didn't end up wanting to murder each other."

"In case you haven't been paying attention, the family crisis isn't over."

"Why can't you just admit it, Nay? You can live with me as an ex-husband better than you ever lived with me otherwise."

"It's too easy. You're asking events to do the emotional work you can't do, could never do."

"Says the person who shacked up with a new partner, like literally moved in, without telling her husband. In the annals of marital cowardice, that's a new one, at least for me."

"If you want to be right about everything, I'm happy to go back to the house."

"No," he says, "actually, this is the point, and I think you can tell just as well as I can: neither of us has to be right, because it doesn't matter. It's a moot point, and that's what makes it easier for us to actually have a conversation. The major decisions have all been made, and this is just the aftermath. All the heat has gone out of the dialogue, because we don't have to hide anything from each other."

This point buys them a minute of silent walking.

"You're going to be a miserable single divorcé," she says.

"No one uses that word anymore. I think it just became too widely applicable, and no one could remember whether or not it took an accent."

"I don't want to be flooded with guilt for leaving a suicidal man."

"That's a totally separate question."

"I don't see why."

"Being miserable and being suicidal are two unrelated states," he says, feeling extremely calm. Calm and elated, all at once. "At least in my case. I've been miserable, in one way or another, my entire adult life. I was suicidal only for a short window of time. Was it a way of addressing my misery? Of course, but that's a reductive view. Being suicidal elevated me. It forced me to put things into perspective. It was the one thing I've ever done, maybe in my entire life, with complete autonomy, in silence."

"See, when you put it that way, I think you really ought to be institutionalized, at least for a while."

"I think that window has passed. Which is not to say I don't need to find a new therapist, a better therapist than Brisman. But first I have to have a place to land."

"Vermont isn't holding you."

"It would have been better if the house had burned, in 1980, along with the hermitage. I think our lives would have been so much easier."

"Or we could have just sold it, like normal hippies, ex-communards."

"You can't burn away karma, that's the thing, it's the same as the prohibition against suicide. It's as stupid to think so as it is to ask binary questions, like *was it my fault* or *was it your fault*."

"Was what my fault?"

"Well, anything. Take your pick."

"Okay, but what comes to mind?"

"Well, there's always the big one, the perennial one."

"Enlighten me."

"Oh come on."

"No, we're different people, we can see the same four decades differently, that's already been established."

"Was it our fault that Bering died, is what I mean. Was it?"

"Yes. Definitely yes."

There ought to be a pictorial frame for some relief. The novel wants to relieve them of the responsibility of speaking. But for the moment the air closes in and he can't see anything.

"You're serious."

"But also absolutely not. I thought that's the point you were making."

"You began with yes, though, that was your first response."

"We drove them away, Sandy. For Christ's sake. I just made my first-ever public statement on the subject, I thought you'd be listening. Our children fled us, us and New York. I don't blame them, which is not to say they're blameless. They have agency. God, I'm so tired, can we go back?"

"You could be proud of them, and say they have a strong sense of vocation, a mission, you could—"

"*You're* free to think whatever you like. I take accountability for the fact that I was a shitty mother, preoccupied with the fact that the planet is dying."

"I'm not talking about your mothering skills writ large. About Bering, specifically."

"About Bering, specifically, yes, I take full responsibility."

"Okay, so tell me what that means."

"It means I've lived my life, the past fifteen years, in an unforgiven state, an unforgivable state. I stopped trying to reassure myself that I was a good person. Or that you were. Or whatever. I would never have written *Shiva* otherwise. Forget that—I would never have conceived of the *argument* of it, the basic premise. Remember what Sensei used to say about how the garbage person becomes a monk, the garbage monk becomes a Zen monk, the garbage Zen monk becomes Buddha? When he said that I imagined falling through one trapdoor, then another, then another. What if all our worst instincts, our worst flaws, I mean as a species, are all true? That's what the book is about. If we accept that conclusion, what then?"

"And you no longer believe that?"

"I don't know. I'm agnostic, to be honest, though you are never to say that publicly. Thoughts occur in time like everything else. They degrade, they drift. Maybe that book is just a useful exercise. Letting the abyss look into you, et cetera. It helped me. I hit bottom, and then I found Tilda. I'm just being completely honest now. Tilda asked me to have different thoughts."

"You found *her*."

"No, absolutely not, not in the sense you mean. She asked me out on the first date. I kissed her. But I suggested she move in. She took months to say yes. It was mutual, all along the way. This must be very painful for you to hear."

"At the moment I'm too distracted by the details of our lives to process it, but it will be, eventually."

"You do realize, by the way, that when I say I take full responsibility for Bering's death, I also mean full responsibility for marrying you, that I haven't forgiven you, either. Separately."

"Of course I understand that."

"I could say something harsh, and binary, like, I stopped loving you in Jerusalem, really stopped, once and for all, and I should have left you then, of course I should have. Judy told me to."

"I never knew that."

"You never respected her enough to think her capable of such a thing. But yes, she did. We had coffee at Café Amadeus, I'll never forget it. She said she'd lost all respect for you, she couldn't believe the Sandy she knew would be such a coward. But then, when I'd made my decision, she never said another word. Just kept on as my friend. I swear to god, I don't know what we would ever have done without those two."

"They were always our alibi."

"It's so ridiculous, and old, and pathetic, to be having this conversation in the past tense, but here we are, of course. Seriously, we have to turn back now. The tide is coming in, we'll be walking back through the water."

"That sounds like a metaphor."

"It's not a metaphor, and that's the whole problem, isn't it, lazy metaphorical thinking instead of seeing what's in front of your face."

"Speaking of which, I had quite the argument with Patrick yesterday."

"I heard. From Winter, via Zeno. Just that you two looked very upset, he politely kept his distance, also for his own sanity."

"He insists on using the word *trauma* for everything. He's traumatized, Bering was traumatized too, I suppose."

"Sandy," she says, "I'll try to put this in the nicest possible way. But if your self-reflective phase means anything at all, you need to learn to stop having semantic arguments. For fuck's sake."

"He presents himself as passive, as a victim, as unrecoverable, and I'm sorry, that's absolute BS, he's made his own choices. No one told him to live in a monastery with primitive toilets in Nepal for three years."

"Then let him feel that way. He's nearly forty. You haven't seen him in years. The last thing he needs from you, or you from him, is more opinions."

"I actually would like to help him."

"But you can't. Unless he asks. I don't see him asking."

"Who made you so fucking wise."

"Tilda was a social worker for years, you know. The vocabulary does creep in. All those years of analysis and just throwing up our hands, and now this, I'm partnered with someone who's an extremely subtle thinker *and* doesn't tolerate excuses."

"Lucky you."

"I can't tell how you mean that, and I don't care. I'll take it as genuine. It could happen to you too, you know, though I'll admit it's a little hard to imagine. Just don't marry someone Winter's age, or I'll have you killed."

"And on that happy note—"

He turns around, abruptly, hands on hips, to judge the distance, and is instantly blinded: the harbor has turned into something else, a glowing field. The water throbs, a skyline in reverse.

"There's no bioluminescence here," Naomi says. "This isn't happening. Those bays are farther down the peninsula. They don't move. This isn't happening. Do you have your phone?"

"Want to take a picture?"

"I want to see if there are any NOAA updates, anything new in the literature."

"Well, no. I forgot it. Didn't think we'd need it."

"The whole point is that you never think you'll need them and then you do. We are pathetically old."

"I wish you'd stop using that word."

"I could call someone who would know. Though it's a little late."

He's taking his shoes off. He's gingerly putting a foot down, on the shells, the rhombic stones, picking his way forward. There's a shift, a slide, a decline in the register. Oh, come forward, other world. It isn't water, it's viscous. It isn't viscous, it's solid. It glows around his feet.

Only when he's recovered his balance, enough to look up, does he see the golden ships, three of them. Tall-masted eighteenth-century ships, their foresails open, moving from his left to right, toward the mouth of the bay, toward the open ocean. There are people aboard, human figures, hoisting ropes, adjusting the rigging. Without knowing, he knows who they are. Victor told him. It happened, he wants to say, it's still happening. They're headed east. He raises both hands and waves frantically. Recognize me, but the ships show no sign. Take me aboard. Bless me. Do something, show me what to do. They're picking up speed; they'll be out of sight. Show me the way to turn time back. They won't help him. They are not there for him. But he's seen them; that has to mean something. There is another register in which this could be told. Oh, open, window. Oh, open, mercy.

Naomi calls out behind him; he's walked too far ahead of her. She didn't see the ships: he knows that, without having to ask. It's his vision. There's nothing wrong with that. "Come toward me," he says. "It's a solid surface. It holds my weight. We're going to walk home this way."

"Give me a fucking break, Sandy. Someone slipped you an edible at the party. Was it Tilda? She came fully supplied, but I told her not to give them out. It's not the right crowd."

"Not that I know of, but maybe it was in the food. Come on, try it. You have to take off your shoes, though. I'm pretty sure it only works that way."

"You've mistaken me for someone who does alien visitations, fire-walking, auras, and Reiki. Stop that. Come back here, you idiot."

"We never had a proper processional. At the wedding, I mean. It was too muddy. Come on, walk with me."

He's at least ten feet from shore, looking over his shoulder, at Naomi's face, lit up by the shifting non-waves, the simulated water, which feels warm and rubbery underfoot, not unlike a mat at the gym. Finally she removes her shoes, slowly, looking at him. That look. When did I first see you, when did I first look openly at your face. I have come to the place where I have eaten all the poisons and survived.

"Actually hold my hand," he says, when she's close enough.

"In case I fall through."

"Well, who knows what happens next?"

"And you're telling me you know where the house is, in the dark."

"It's not dark."

They take tentative steps, trying to be brave. What are we, he wants to say, other than children at the end of the world. He has his shoes in one hand, and wants to throw them away, they feel so superfluous. We could come to anything. The shore has all but disappeared; if he had a free hand he would shade his eyes and try to see it.

/

It's freezing, Patrick's wearing his thickest sweater, his purple yak-wool sweater from Nepal, the one he bought in a market in Kathmandu the day before taking the bus to Dawa. He brought it, remembering what Maine nights are like, even in August. The car windows keep fogging.

He left Mathias sleeping in a bed with Abby and Clothilde, Lourdes's kids. It's no problem, Lourdes said. We're all in the same house. Mathias, so sober and steady, it's what happens when you have the soberest and steadiest parent possible. They FaceTimed with Katerina the night before and he chattered away happily, switching between German and English.

The Blue Hill fairgrounds, a chain-link fence under a yellow street-light. Tire Discounters. The Surry Store. Racing the light, racing the dawn. It's at least an hour to the national park gates at Schoodic, fifteen more minutes to the point, on the coast road that skirts Mount Desert Island, Acadia, Bar Harbor. He wrote a paper on it in AP American History, the settlement history of northern Maine. The Wabanaki and the Mi'kmaq. The gist was that all the land still belonging to the U.S. government actually was unceded Wabanaki confederacy territory.

His teacher, Mr. Lewes—remember him?—wrote, You seem determined not exactly to contradict the facts, but replace them. History doesn't work that way. It's not an exercise in hypotheticals. Justice for the Indians isn't served by ahistorical fantasizing. But he still got an A.

Two other cars in the parking lot. Hard to tell when they arrived. No one in sight, but the rocks at the point are a jumble of crevasses and overhangs, and everyone has their own spot. Clouds piled like whipped cream, like mashed potatoes, on the horizon. Decadent clouds, lit up in pink and peach like a Liberace concert. Such great words from that era: *scalloped, ambrosia. Fantasia.* They saw *Fantasia* once at the old theater on Broadway across from Lincoln Plaza, the one with the gigantic seventy-millimeter screen. He sat with Bering in his lap most of the way through, she hiding her head in his sweatshirt. The dancing brooms, Mickey conducting the orchestra. Poison as comfort food. She was young enough to still be revulsed by it.

It was around that time that he became convinced he could see in the dark. Not only that. In a dark movie theater he would look down at his ankle, say, and see it glowing, faintly. Rinpoche once told him that even completely naïve people, with no knowledge of tantra, can perceive the sambhogakaya in glimpses. The radiant body sometimes just appears. He liked to walk around the apartment in the dark, late at night, at ten or eleven, and sense the locations of walls and doors. A strange object brushes against you. They had these lamps with woven shades, coarse as burlap, it was like brushing up against a body.

There are no special instructions for extinguishing consciousness, it doesn't happen, Geshe Rabten said once, when he asked directly. That's why suicide doesn't work. It doesn't solve anything. Karma doesn't have an escape clause. Suicide results in an unhappy rebirth, and that's it. Not even the most accomplished yogi can just cause their own light to go out. If so, they would all do it, of course. No one would choose to live this way if they didn't have to.

He fills the backpack with fist-sized rocks, they're littered everywhere between crevasses, and tests its weight. Twenty pounds. Thirty? The point is to defeat all the reflexes and make swimming impossible. Those were the online instructions. It was disconcerting how specific they were, how authoritative. Search for suicide chats on the dark-web and you'll never scroll to the end. Jump from the highest possible point, obvious. Determine the depth of the water, obvious. Drowning is the object, not waking up paralyzed. This is the challenge with Schoodic, obvious. Tides. Inaccessibility. Fuck it all, just breathe and go, breathe and go. No one's around; he does a visual check, standing atop a boulder. Carry the backpack, yes, heavy as the massive one he once hiked up Katahdin, intending to do the entire Maine section of the AT, though he only lasted four days. The waist and sternum straps buckled. He leaps from rock to rock, across ten-foot fissures; that's the pleasure of coming to Schoodic, the childish joy. Mathias should have seen this. They loved coming here and getting out of sight of Mom and Dad, causing them terror. When they were four and five and seven. They were once four and five and seven. The surf vibrates when you get close enough, the crests of spray flying up over the last rocks, the outcrops, the cliffs. The farthest east, world's end, the continent juts into the Atlantic, but settlers avoided Maine, too jagged, cold, and inhospitable; they went to Newfoundland and Nova Scotia or Massachusetts and Virginia. Neither Vikings nor Englishmen. Maine was a fishery and the Dawn Land. The mind floods with analysis, sedimented knowledge. He can feel it flowing out and away. At the last minute, he sent Katerina an email with all his passwords. Mathias is already his named beneficiary. He feels it flowing out, a striation of data and capital. He already exists in more than one place. Now the very lip of the rock is here, a place he's never been. A ten-foot plane, at least, and a clean, level walk to the end, and the boiling surface of the water, dusty blue, tourmaline or some other shade, he can't remember, it boils against the rocks and recedes and boils up again. His face is already covered with salt. He licks it off his lips. Breathe and go. It already happened. He's not surprised. He remembers to point his feet as he goes, and lift his arms to the sky.

/2

Why is there only a Wailing Wall, why hasn't anyone ever built a Wall of Joy?

Ingeborg Bachmann, *Malina*

THE WORLD

From: "Sandy Wilcox" <alexanderwilcox4@gmail.com>
Date: January 2, 2019 at 11:48:35 PM CST
To: "Naomi Schifrin Wilcox" < nwilcox4@columbia.edu>
Subject: Mexico City update

Dear N—

Winter says I should provide you with more updates and not waste time emailing pictures b/c they're all uploaded to her Google Drive anyway. So here goes:

Happy new year. Feliz año nuevo.

It turns out the leak we were all afraid of wasn't such a big deal— Guillermo came in over the holiday and covered the stains with new plaster, which obviously has to be painted, but there's not much more to it than that. I think it's going to turn out to be a solid apartment. It turns out I don't mind living at street level, at least not this street. We face the park, as I told you, and it's very quiet most of the time. Condesa is a beautiful neighborhood, with trees everywhere, and outdoor cafés. I don't know how you and Tilda will feel about it. (Not that you're going to be living here, of course.)

I think Winter and Zeno should be down here, just for the sake of not carrying so much stuff up and down the stairs, but they want the babies on the third floor so they'll sleep. Zeno's been breaking his back installing the solar panels on the roof.

I don't have to tell you anything about Bering and Heba; I'm sure you're seeing Winter's Instagram every day. They're pretty happy now that abuelo has his own cuarto, I think. Rafaela has been keeping them inside much of the day because the smog is the worst this month, and I tell her to come let them roll around in the living room down here, because there's much more space to move around. As a result "working at home" hasn't resulted in much work for me.

But what am I supposed to be doing? I haven't figured out that question. You could say I have the luxury of not having to figure it out, but that won't work for me. I have to be busy with something. I reread the pages I wrote in April and May and I don't know if there's really enough there to make a book. Not that it isn't a story worth telling. It just needs MORE, and I don't know if I have the energy and courage to write more. I do have a title, though: *Ghost Cave in the Mountain of Darkness*.

We FaceTimed with Victor on New Year's, and he extended his offer again. So I think I really am going to visit San Cristóbal de las Casas. I said I would drive, because why go to the expense of owning a car here and locking it up in a fortified garage if you can't use it, but Zeno absolutely forbade me to travel by myself overnight, and it's at least a two-day trip. I suppose I'm still in tourist mode, wanting to see every possible thing. So I'll fly, the flights are cheap, and if Zeno can get the time off we might all go. Of course he's very excited to bring Bering and Heba there. All his friends on Instagram keep asking when he's bringing the babies home.

I hope you don't mind that I told Tonya she can stay in the apartment over spring break. She's looking for internships in the city over the summer, and I think she should definitely stay there again if she gets something. It's better all around if the apt. isn't vacant. And she's a family member, so the board can't object. She asked about paying rent and I said absolutely not.

On less pleasant subjects: in answer to what we talked about last week, I think you're right, one of us should reach out to Katerina. Even if it's true that Patrick is permanently out of their lives. I assume you haven't heard from him either. Winter talks to him about once a week, but he's asked her not to share details. All I know is he's out of the hospital, he's finished physical therapy, he's medicated, he has a therapist. No idea whether he's back at work. Or if he will be.

(I did get a letter from the EU citizenship lawyer saying she needs to confirm the members of his immediate family and his birth date and birth certificate. So when you're back in the city, please get his birth certificate out of the files, scan it, and email it to me.)

But back to Katerina: we are Mathias's grandparents, we've met him, he knows our names and faces, I think we ought to be allowed to see him again. We should go to Berlin and see him. Just as an expression of love. I have no idea what she'll say. Maybe Winter can speak to her instead. I told her she should go see Patrick, but she can't leave the girls. She's exhausted, obviously, even with help, the nursing is more or less nonstop, and they ought to be sleeping more than they are. I offered to go up and sleep on the couch to take a shift, but she won't do it. And she wants to start working, she's already had an offer from Human Rights Watch, and three US firms with CDMX offices have gotten in touch, though it's mostly corporate work, she says, and she won't touch it. In any case it's not realistic, and may not be for a year. I try to get her to see that.

The question hovering over all of this is: what am I doing here? Am I trying to soften the violence of Zeno's expulsion (what else can we call it?) or to soothe my own ego, my late-in-life regrets? I feel my presence here is unacceptable in some ways. (But honestly, what else is new?)

This is going on much too long. Just one another thing: as promised, I started with Dr. Gomez. This week will be my fourth. Wednesdays and Fridays. He's very classical, he won't say a thing about Victor, how and where they met. All I know is they attended the same high school, a famous one, downtown near the Zócalo. He informed me on the first day that he does psychoanalysis in four languages, Spanish, English, French, and Catalan. He wears brown suits and a rotating cast of shirt colors, never the same twice, never matching his tie. He has an Eames chair and a lot of potted palms. Like 1983 all over again! What else can I tell you? Also on the first day, he said, don't bother thinking you need to explain everything. When you're in your sixties, that's not how analysis works. He even quoted a line from Beckett: Human beings, you will see how similar they are. I said, doesn't that undercut the whole point of your profession? He just smiled and said, first you have to see it, then you'll know.

Write back when you get a chance.

Yours, S

From: "Naomi Schifrin Wilcox" < nwilcox4@columbia.edu>
Date: January 4, 2019 at 11:23:02 AM EST
To: "Sandy Wilcox" <alexanderwilcox4@gmail.com>
Subject: Re: Mexico City update

Hello Sandy,
Thanks for your long letter. I read it in the checkout line and got so absorbed the cashier yelled at me. Tilda says she's going to delete the email app from my phone because I'm a hazard. Actually I think I'm going to ditch my iPhone altogether and get one of those senior citizen phones with huge buttons where you can only make calls. Because I AM a hazard, truly.

Unlike you, I don't have much to report. There was a big rainstorm on New Year's Eve and T and I spent the next few days picking up branches in the yard. It seems like everyone we know went away somewhere over the holidays. Which I don't mind so much, but it makes her irritable. She's finally trying to teach me to knit, a terrible idea. If a woman scientist hasn't started knitting by age 60, there's a good reason, I keep telling her.

But maybe I should try knitting, because it'll keep me from compulsively reading the news. I don't know if I've told you, but since August I've changed in that way. It's no longer fifteen minutes in the morning and maybe a distracted hour with the radio on at night. Now I'm actually absorbing it, mentally taking notes.

Of course I stayed away from politics when writing *Shiva,* except to describe in a general way how political inaction about climate change is a symptom of the overwhelming anthropogenic urge to self-destruction. But now I'm thinking I got it wrong, or backward. In other words, maybe the urge toward self-destruction manifests in all political systems, or projects, over time. Or all institutions, I don't know. But this is clearly what we're seeing in the U.S. right now, on every level. This is the age of willed, willful self-destruction.

T was saying the other night that I should write a sequel to *Shiva,* only this time more like a memoir, where I talk about my grief as a scientist and a mother and how since the book came out I've had this, ahem, journey of self-discovery that changed my perspective . . . and after I stopped making pretend retching sounds, I started thinking about it. I don't know that it could be a book, but it could be a decent paragraph.

What really happened? I became small. I became a body again, thinking about simple bodily needs. A capital-W Woman. That's how Tilda makes me feel. Also a capital-J Jew, in my own perverse way. And while I haven't found any way to feel capital-B Black, who the hell knows. In any case, I feel unapologetic and I'm done lying.

That sounds so simple, but what could be more profound, in a country so committed to not knowing itself? I'm so very glad Winter and Zeno did what they did. I am done with these tight-assed Northeastern liberals and their migrant peons, acting like it's a representative democracy and living like it's Dubai. I feel profoundly relieved Bering and Heba don't live here. I'm glad they escaped, that's the word, and you went with them. Glad in all my capital-letter senses. In fact I am the only remaining Wilcox on American soil. And maybe not for long, not forever.

Talk about sentences I never thought I would write.

In any case. More to come.

N.

ARRIVALS

"The place is all yours," Judy says. "I've just been making coffee while I waited for you. The cleaners were here yesterday, or else I'd be dead from allergies. Winter's room seems like the most livable, in terms of sleeping, from what I've seen. It's the one with the Stop sign on the door. Naomi should be here later today, she said."

"It's weird," Tonya says. Parking her rolling suitcase, for now, at the dining table. "It's her apartment and I'm staying here, not her."

"She said she prefers just to visit for the time being. While she figures out what to do, the next steps. My place is only a few blocks away, at any rate."

Not so much an apartment as an old house. The floors creak. Old wood, dusty wool carpet. Bookshelves everywhere. She went through a Woody Allen phase a few years ago, wanting to see what all the fuss was about. *Hannah and Her Sisters. Husbands and Wives.* It was funny to sit in the Howard student center with her earbuds on, watching Mia Farrow rock shoulder pads in outfit after outfit. But it turns out you don't really appreciate apartments like that until you stand inside one. It wraps around you. The museum posters in the dining room: Matisse, Degas, Giacometti. Tanglewood. Some framed amateur prints of

Maine, probably one of the kids' high school projects. She recognizes the Blue Hill swimming rock.

And then, in the hall, Bering. Bering in a toga. She recognizes her from a hundred Internet photos. In a toga and heavy stage makeup, on her knees, onstage, looking up into the floodlights. At about age fourteen.

"They've kept her room more or less closed for fifteen years," Judy says. "If you think it smells dusty in here, you haven't seen anything. There's a lot of junk, it's all disordered, of course she didn't live there for the last two years anyway. Naomi told me she'd go through it with me, but she keeps putting it off. You can have a look if you like."

"Thanks, I'd rather not."

"It must be bizarre for you, being here. Your sort-of-aunt's house."

"That's one way of putting it."

"And you'll be here until you go back to school, the rest of January, basically."

"Yeah. I came back from California a little early. Naomi said I should have a chance to see this place, at least once, before they give it up. If they give it up."

"You're at Vassar."

"Right, I'm a junior, as of this semester, technically."

They're still moving within a few feet of one another, because it's better to stay that way. The apartment doesn't fully want them there, clearly. Judy moves back into the living room and taps something out on her phone. Tonya looks at one bookcase, floor-to-ceiling, which appears to be arranged newest to oldest, bottom to top. Mostly political hardbacks, recently, probably gifts—Rachel Maddow, Paul Krugman, Al Franken—glossy and uncracked. Novels she recognizes from her mother's book club, each with a bookmark, or MetroCard, or stray receipt, about a third of the way through. *Sea of Poppies. Paradise. The Corrections. Madame Bovary: A New Translation. The Savage Detectives. Gilead.* Then an entire row of books about Hinduism, Hindu mythology. Impenetrable. Above that the spines get darker. *Playing and Real-*

ity. A Good Enough Parent. Living a Jewish Life. A Big Jewish Book. The Sabbath. Parenting Teenagers. I'm OK—You're OK. Up at the top they blur together; the room gathers shadows at the ceiling, but she can make out *Be Here Now* and *Chop Wood Carry Water* and *The New Whole Earth Catalog.* It gives her vertigo. Looked at in a certain way, it's an entire life. She pinches her eyes shut. There's something missing. What is the key, what is the trick, to seeing these people whole? The air itself conspires against her, it's too thick, it's warping her vision. Someone else is in the room. She can smell hair. And incense. Almost like the braiding shop on Figueroa she went to in high school, the one time she'd saved up to buy her own extensions. Someone else is in this room, who wants to be embraced.

"I can open the windows or the French doors, depending on how much fresh air you want."

"Open the doors," Tonya says. "Here, I'll help you."

Did you want to be held for so long. Did any of us expect to be, who have shared this embrace. The lights come on. Get up from the chair, get up from the bed. Stretch. Yawn. Get a drink of water. Something else is happening. Put the book on the shelf. The book is the embrace, I see that now, holding it like this. The novel says I. I came to life, put on this strange garment. I held you, gave warmth to you. It's what animals do when they're afraid. I held you as long as I could and then let go, not knowing what happens next. A little life, a little death. You can carry it with you but you don't have to. You can go on to the next thing. There is an imprint on your skin that will wear off soon. You are released.

TIMELINE OF THE WILCOX AND DOWNS FAMILIES

1951: Phyllis Rosenwald meets John Downs at Kutscher's Resort; Phyllis becomes pregnant. Phyllis is already engaged to Herman Schifrin; the Rosenwalds and Schifrins agree to move up the date of the wedding and to keep John Downs a secret.

1952: Alexander (Sandy) Wilcox is born to Mabel and Thomas Wilcox in Davenport, Iowa; Naomi Schifrin is born to Phyllis and Herman Schifrin in the Bronx (Grand Concourse and 146th Street). The Schifrins move to Armonk, New York, later the same year.

1955: Thomas Wilcox dies in a drunk-driving accident. John Downs receives his PhD in physics from Princeton and moves to Los Angeles for a teaching job at Occidental College.

1960: John Downs's son, Jonas, is born.

1966: John Downs's daughter Vivian is born.

1969: Phyllis reveals to Naomi that her real father is John Downs.

1970: Sandy and Naomi meet in December of their freshman year at Oberlin.

1974: Sandy and Naomi graduate from Oberlin and are married the same month. Naomi begins graduate school in oceanography at Berkeley and meets Hayashi Miro Sensei, begins practicing Zen daily. Sandy is working as an organizer of farmworkers in the Central Valley.

1975: Sandy enrolls at Boalt Hall School of Law.

1977: Sandy's mother dies.

1978: With his inheritance, Sandy and Naomi buy Albany Hill Farm in Craftsbury, Vermont, and create Mujo-ji.

1979: Patrick Hakuin Wilcox is born at Morrisville Hospital in Vermont.

1980: Sandy discovers Naomi's affair with Sensei; Sensei leaves for Japan. Mujo-ji is closed, and Naomi accepts a one-year research position in Barrow, Alaska.

1981: Winter Mabel Wilcox is born in Anchorage, Alaska.

1982: Bering Schifrin Wilcox is born in New York City. Sandy has a one-year federal clerkship in Brooklyn and then begins working for Fein Lewin. Naomi begins teaching at Columbia. After a year living in Columbia faculty housing, they move into the apartment in the Apthorp.

1988: Sandy first meets Irwin Klaufelt, the (fraudulent) heir to a fortune in Holocaust art.

1989: After being denied tenure at Columbia, Naomi sues and is reinstated.

1997: Patrick graduates from Stuyvesant and enters Harvard. Vivian (Vivi) Downs marries Jayson Marshall, while both are residents at UCLA.

1999: Winter graduates from Dalton and enters Wesleyan. Tonya Marshall is born to Vivi Downs and Jayson Marshall.

2000: Bering graduates from UNIS and enters Evergreen State College. Empty nest. Naomi hires a private detective and makes contact with John Downs for the first time. Irwin Klaufelt is revealed to be a fraud; Sandy narrowly avoids being disbarred for malpractice and manages to save Fein Lewin from massive damages.

2001: Patrick graduates from Harvard. On Christmas Day, Naomi reveals John Downs's identity to her children for the first time.

2002: Patrick meets Rinpoche at a talk in New York City, quits job, ends analysis. Winter graduates from Wesleyan and starts Yale Law. Bering takes a leave from Evergreen and moves to Cairo to study Arabic. Patrick takes preliminary monastic vows, moves to India, and begins intensive study of Tibetan. At the end of her year in Cairo, Bering hears about the Soldiers for Peace movement and decides to volunteer as an observer in the West Bank.

2003: Bering is killed by an IDF sniper during a protest against the destruction of olive trees in Wadi Aboud on the West Bank. Naomi, Sandy, Patrick, and Winter travel to Jerusalem immediately afterward. Following Bering's death, Patrick enters a three-year silent retreat at Dawa Ling Monastery in Nepal, cuts off all contact with his family. John Downs dies at age seventy-five, without ever having met Naomi.

2006: Winter meets Zeno while working at a summer immigration law clinic in Providence. Winter graduates from Yale Law (she took a year of leave after Bering's death) and moves to Providence. During his retreat, Patrick becomes seriously ill and has to be hospitalized in Delhi.

2008: Patrick finishes the retreat, is formally ordained as a lama, and takes a teaching job in an American college exchange program in McLeod Ganj, while remaining close to Rinpoche.

2010: Patrick and Katerina (both monastics) meet and become romantically involved.

2011: Naomi publishes *The Shiva Hypothesis*.

2012: Naomi's parents die within six months. With her inheritance, she buys a house in Woods Hole. Katerina disrobes (gives up her status as a nun) and moves back to Berlin, where she takes up a job in software management.

2013: Katerina gives birth to Mathias, Patrick's son, in Berlin. Patrick moves to Berlin to work for Avansys.

2017: Naomi goes on extended research leave from Columbia and moves to Woods Hole full time.

2018: April: Sandy leaves New York and moves to Vermont.

ACKNOWLEDGMENTS

My father, Clark Row (1934–2013), a forestry economist and member of the Intergovernmental Panel on Climate Change, and my father-in-law, Eric Posmentier (1943–2020), a geophysicist, both did early research on global warming (as it was then called) in the 1980s and 1990s. Although my father died before I'd written more than a few pages of this book, his lifelong concern about the future of the Earth's environment shaped my understanding of the subject. Eric was able to answer some of my naïve questions about measurements of sea level in the Arctic and the mathematics of ocean science. Eric and his wife, Xiahong Feng (both professors in the Department of Earth Science at Dartmouth), pointed me toward Di Jin, who took days out of his schedule at the Woods Hole Oceanographic Institution to give me a tour, introduce me to other scientists, and tell me about working and living in Woods Hole and Falmouth.

Eric and Loveleen Posmentier, my in-laws, were married for thirty-seven years and raised a family on the Upper West Side in the 1980s and 1990s, and although *The New Earth* isn't about them, the way they rebuilt their friendship and mutual trust after their divorce inspired my thinking about Sandy and Naomi. Thank you also to Rob and Miriam Foshay, my uncle and aunt, for sharing their memories of student life at Oberlin in the late 1960s and early 1970s.

I was first drawn to write about Palestine by accounts of the deaths of Rachel Corrie and Tom Hurndall, international volunteers killed by the Israel Defense Forces during the Second Intifada. I learned about Rachel Corrie's life from her posthumously published journals, *Let Me Stand Alone*. I'm grateful to Eden Coughlin for sending me her first-hand account of volunteering with the International Solidarity Movement in 2002–2003. Most of all, I'm grateful to Hari Kunzru, Betty Shamieh, Moriel Rothman-Zecker, Isaac Kates Rose, Yehuda Shaul, Fida Touma, Aboud Qasyami, José Tavdylogo, Hanoch Piven, Barbara Barham, the staff of Area D Hostel in Ramallah, and the volunteers of Taa'yush and the All That's Left collective, who helped during my research in Palestine and Israel.

In studying the history of Chiapas and the Zapatista movement, I was guided by Gloria Muñoz Ramírez's *The Fire and the Word*, Hilary Klein's *Compañeras: Zapatista Women's Stories*, Dylan Fitzwater's *Autonomy Is in Our Hearts*, Rosario Castellanos's *The Book of Lamentations*, and *Professionals of Hope: The Selected Writings of Subcomandante Marcos*. I'm grateful to Hugo Herrera and his staff at Kukulik Travel for their help during my research in Chiapas.

Professor Guy Newland of Central Michigan University patiently answered my questions about Tibetan Buddhist theories of time and conventional causation. I also learned a great deal from Daniel Cozort's *Unique Tenets of the Middle Way Consequence School* and *Highest Yoga Tantra*; Anne Klein's *Knowledge and Liberation: Tibetan Buddhist Epistemology in Support of Transformative Religious Experience*; Jeffrey Hopkins's *Meditation on Emptiness* and *Emptiness Yoga*; and Georges Dreyfus's *The Sound of Two Hands Clapping*. Bering's poem "The Upper West Side Book of the Dead" was inspired by one of the concluding prayers in *The Tibetan Book of the Dead*, as translated by Chögyam Trungpa and Francesca Fremantle.

Richard Bonneau, Professor of Biology and Computer Science at

NYU, first described quantum computing to me during a chaotic family dinner many years ago, and I borrowed some of his descriptions on Patrick's behalf, although any mistakes or misrepresentations are entirely my own.

Rabbi Zach Fredman's expansive view of Judaism and Jewishness has inspired me throughout the writing of *The New Earth*. I'm indebted to him in more ways than I can say.

Sonya Posmentier, Mousa Jiryis, Mary Guerrero, Yehuda Shaul, Celia Mattison, Melissa Vera, and Jonathan Lethem read earlier drafts (or parts of drafts) of *The New Earth* with painstaking care, and I'm very grateful to them for their suggestions and support.

Megan Lynch first acquired *The New Earth* for Ecco Books in 2014, and I'm indebted to her for believing in this book in its infancy. In 2019, Sara Birmingham stepped in as my editor, and has been the best and most patient guide and source of encouragement I could have hoped for. Denise Shannon, my agent, has been at my side through the many years it took to finish this project. I'm also grateful to my current and former nonfiction editors at Graywolf Press: Fiona McRae, Steve Woodward, and Ethan Nosowsky. And most of all, I'm grateful to my mother, Constance Row, for believing in my writing fiercely and unreservedly, even when it's not easy for her to read.

Additional support for time I spent writing *The New Earth* came from the Guggenheim Memorial Foundation, the Whiting Foundation, the College of New Jersey, and NYU.

I finished the first draft of *The New Earth* during the first six months of the COVID pandemic in the spring and summer of 2020, while my family was in lockdown in Vermont. Sonya, Mina, and Asa gave me the space and time to write in that strange moment when it seemed the world had stopped breathing. They are my first and foremost champions and I owe them everything.

ABOUT THE AUTHOR

JESS ROW is the author of the novel *Your Face in Mine,* the essay collection *White Flights: Race, Fiction, and the American Imagination,* and two collections of short stories, *The Train to Lo Wu* and *Nobody Ever Gets Lost.* He's received Guggenheim and NEA fellowships, a Whiting Writers Award, and an O. Henry Award, among other honors. His writing has appeared in the *New Yorker, The Atlantic, Granta, The Best American Short Stories,* and many other venues. He teaches at NYU and lives in New York City and Plainfield, Vermont.